Jeanne Whitmee began After her marriage and of speech and drama, she achieved a lifelong ambition to become a professional writer. She worked for some years as a freelance writer for popular women's magazines, writing short stories, serials and, at one time, a weekly column. To date she has published more than thirty novels under various pseudonyms.

Jeanne Whitmee has two married daughters and four grandchildren and now lives with her husband in Cambridgeshire.

By Jeanne Whitmee

JEANNE WHITMEE OMNIBUS

The Lost Daughters
Thursday's Child

JEANNE WHITMEE

WARNER BOOKS

A *Warner* Book

This omnibus edition first published in Great Britain by Warner Books in 2001

Jeanne Whitmee Omnibus Copyright © Jeanne Whitmee 2001

Previously published separately:

The Lost Daughters
First published in Great Britain by Judy Piatkus in 1996
Published by Warner Books in 1997

Copyright © Jeanne Whitmee 1996

Thursday's Child
First published in Great Britain by Judy Piatkus in 1997
Published by Warner Books in 1998

Copyright © Jeanne Whitmee 1997

The moral right of the author has been asserted.

A CIP catalogue record for this book
is available from the British Library.

ISBN 0 7515 3172 3

Printed and bound in Great Britain by
Mackays of Chatham plc, Chatham, Kent

Warner Books
A Division of
Little, Brown and Company (UK)
Brettenham House
Lancaster Place
London WC2E 7EN

www.littlebrown.co.uk

The Lost Daughters

Chapter One

The Four Daughters

Fairway, Virginia 1955

Chapter One

For as long as Cathy could remember she had lived in the house in Laburnum Close with Daddy and Johnny, which was her name for the motherly war widow who came in each day to look after them. Mary Johnson was the only maternal figure in Cathy's life. She had no memories of her real mother at all. There were photographs of her of course: a large one on the mantelpiece in the front room and another beside Daddy's bed. Cathy knew that her name had been Jenny and that she had curly auburn hair and green eyes just like her own. She knew too that her mother had loved her very much, but only because Daddy told her so. Sometimes when she was in bed at night she would close her eyes and try very hard to remember, but however hard she tried the memories refused to come.

Number thirteen Laburnum Close was the semi-detached Victorian villa where Daniel Oldham had taken his young bride when they married in 1943. It had been his parents' house then and Cathy had been born here while Daniel was still in the RAF. Soon after that Cathy's grandparents had both died, leaving number thirteen to the three of them. But their family life had been sadly curtailed when Jenny Oldham died too, leaving Daniel and his baby daughter alone. All this Cathy had learned from her father. All she remembered was being here with Daddy – and Johnny of course.

All the houses in Laburnum Close had been built in the nineteenth century. They had high corniced ceilings,

1

panelled doors and a long narrow hall that led right through from front door to kitchen. It had a floor of blue, red and black mosaic tiles. Cathy had used this to devise complicated hopping games that she played on wet days when she couldn't go out to play. Upstairs there were three bedrooms and a bathroom and above them an attic reached by a steep staircase. The attic had sloping ceilings and one small dormer window. It was stiflingly hot in summer and icy cold in winter, so it was used mainly for storing junk and unwanted items of furniture. Cathy loved to play up there on rainy days, dressing up in the old discarded clothes packed away years before by her grandmother, and acting out the fantasies that fill the minds of all lonely children; fuelled by an over-developed imagination and derived from all the many stories she had read.

Downstairs there was a big living room and a cosy kitchen with a big cooking range. But the front room was Daniel's. His grand piano stood in the bay window – in almost solitary splendour because there was very little space in the room for anything else. It was where his pupils came in the daytime; an endless stream of people with musical aspirations. They came in all shapes and sizes, all ages and both sexes, and filled the house for hours each day with the sound of the scales and arpeggios which they pounded out with varying degrees of skill and proficiency.

In the evenings Daniel would put on what he called his 'penguin suit' and go off to work, playing with a dance band at various venues all over London, leaving his young daughter with Johnny or an obliging neighbour. Cathy was used to the arrangement. She would watch television and do her homework, then go to bed dutifully at the appointed time.

Through her early years when Cathy knew of no other way of life it had all seemed quite normal and acceptable. She loved her father, and although she often wished she could share more of his time, she was always happy enough

2

to be with Johnny. It was only when she started school that she began to see other girls led quite different kinds of lives. They had mothers as well as fathers; fathers who went to work in the daytime in offices or factories and came back to spend their evenings and weekends at home with the family. Some, like Carla Maybridge, had brothers and sisters too.

Carla was the most popular girl in the class and Cathy could hardly believe her luck when the pretty, outgoing girl befriended her. The first time she was invited round to the Maybridges' house for tea she got a glimpse of what real family life could be; a glimpse so attractive and seductive that she longed to be part of a big, noisy family herself.

The Maybridges lived two streets away in a house very similar to her own home. But the similarity ended with the bricks and mortar. The moment you stepped inside it was all so different. Carla's family filled the house to bursting point. Every room, including the attic, was lived in with a delightful carefree abandon that would have had Johnny shaking her head in horror.

Carla had four elder brothers and a sister, and the six of them plus their parents filled the three-bedroomed house to bursting point. Toys, sports equipment and school books littered every available space. No one ever seemed to put their clothes away or hang up their coats or school bags. Cathy loved it, and when she returned to Laburnum Close after one of these visits, her own house seemed silent and empty by comparison.

Mrs Maybridge was a plump lady who always wore an apron and seemed to live permanently in the kitchen. She was totally unconcerned by the chaos all around her; never shouted or got cross. Mr Maybridge was a cashier at the local bank. He had thinning hair and horn-rimmed glasses and seemed to spend most of his spare time digging in the back garden which was full to bursting with every kind of vegetable and fruit.

On Sunday mornings the family went to Mass at the little

3

Catholic church near the park but once they were home the rest of the day was spent pursuing whatever activity they wished. They were all allowed to have friends round to the house – as many as they liked. The more the merrier, Carla said with a nonchalant wave of her hand.

Sitting in the large untidy living room Cathy would watch as Mrs Maybridge opened up the big round gate-leg table and began to set it for tea. Surreptitiously Cathy would count the cups to work out whether she was expected to stay. Usually she was. Mrs Maybridge didn't stand on ceremony. She didn't issue formal invitations. If there were ten children in the house she provided tea for them all. It just meant making one tin of salmon do the work of two.

When Cathy was eleven and the time came to move schools Carla announced that she was going to St Margaret's, which was a Catholic school. Cathy begged her father to let her go too.

'But you already have a scholarship to the high school,' Daniel argued. 'St Margaret's is private for non-Catholics. It would be very expensive. I don't think we can afford it.'

Cathy pouted. 'Carla says that if you're clever enough you can get in cheaper. You have to take an entrance exam.' She watched her father's face for signs of the vulnerable chink in his armour that she almost always managed to penetrate. 'Everyone says what a good school it is and all the people I like best are going there,' she said wistfully. 'If I have to go to Mitchell Street High I shan't know a soul. I'll be lonely and miserable.'

Daniel gave in in the end. Cathy was interviewed by the headmistress of St Margaret's. She sat and easily passed the entrance examination, and Johnny took her along to be kitted out with the smart blue and gold uniform.

Cathy loved her new school, but at St Margaret's the differences between her own home life and that of her friends soon became even more apparent. Now elder brothers and sisters were bringing home their teenage friends. There

4

were parties, and the passing down of trendy clothes and the latest records. Christmas that year was preceded by weeks of secret preparations, noise and surprises. A time charged with excited anticipation. At thirteen Laburnum Close, although Daniel did his usual best, life seemed tame and lonelier than ever before.

'Why haven't I got any brothers and sisters, Johnny?' asked Cathy one afternoon towards the end of term, as she sat watching the housekeeper preparing the evening meal.

Johnny turned to look at her and realised for the first time that the child was growing up. 'Your mother died before she had time to have any for you,' she said softly. 'I'm sure if she'd lived you would have had some, duckie.'

'But you've only got Matthew and you're not dead,' Cathy pointed out.

'Ah, but Matthew's father died in the war. It takes a mother *and* a daddy to make babies.' Johnny would have thought that Cathy would already know this and made a mental note to have a word with Daniel about telling his daughter the facts of life. It really was time someone prepared her for womanhood. Daniel Oldham was a good man and a conscientious father, but there were times when she wondered if he realised that Cathy wouldn't always be a little girl.

When his housekeeper tactfully pointed out to Daniel that he was neglecting his parental duty, he was dismayed. Somehow he hadn't given a thought to his daughter's growing up and all that it entailed. He shook his head.

'I don't think I know where to start, Johnny.' He looked hopefully at the housekeeper. 'I suppose you wouldn't . . .'

She frowned. 'Well – I will if you really want me to, but I must say that I think it would come better from you.'

Daniel raked a hand through his thinning fair hair. 'What did you do – about Matthew, I mean? It must have been difficult for you too, as a widow with a young son.'

5

'Luckily they have sex education classes at his school,' she said. 'And somehow it doesn't seem so important with boys. There aren't so many – well, physical complications.'

Daniel smiled and kept his opinions on that to himself.

'I have explained to him that girls and women should be treated with consideration and respect,' Johnny went on. 'But he's a sensible boy. Kind and sensitive too. I haven't any real worries about him.'

Daniel nodded. 'I must admit that I'd find it less awkward if Cathy were a boy,' he said. 'But I suppose I'll just have to do the best I can.'

On Saturday afternoons she always had her music lesson. It was a special time for both father and daughter, one of the rare times they spent together. Cathy played the piano well for her age and Daniel was proud of the way she always practised without being reminded, as soon as she came home from school each afternoon.

After her lesson they would have tea together and Daniel would hear what had been happening at school and try to sort out any problems that Cathy might have. So it seemed natural to choose this time to make his first fumbling attempt at acquainting his daughter with the facts of life.

'Cathy – you're twelve now. You're growing up,' he began awkwardly. 'Soon certain – things will be happening – changes in your life and your – body. Maybe you will have noticed that – er . . .' He slipped a finger inside his collar and it was only then that he noticed that Cathy was smiling. It was a wise, sympathetic, womanly little smile and all at once he had the odd feeling that their roles had been reversed; that he was now the child, Cathy the parent.

'It's all right, don't worry, Daddy, we've done all that growing up stuff at school,' she told him reassuringly. 'Carla told me some too. She's got an elder sister and lots of brothers too, you see.'

Daniel was taken aback. 'Oh – well, that's all right then. I just wanted you to know that if there's anything you don't understand – anything that worries you – you can ask me. I'd rather you came to me than anyone else.'

She smiled at him. Thanks, Dad.'

He looked at her anxiously. He had the distinct feeling that he was getting away with this just a little bit too easily. Did she really know, or did she just *think* she did? And how did he find out for sure? 'So – is there anything you're not sure of? Anything you want to ask me now?'

Cathy considered for a moment, her head on one side. 'Well, there is one thing,' she said thoughtfully.

'Yes?'

'How old do I have to be before I can . . .?'

Daniel's mouth dried. 'Yes – before you can what?'

'Wear high heels? I've seen this lovely pair in Mason's in the High Street and I wondered . . .'

Daniel laughed, relief making him light-hearted. She was still his little girl after all. At least for a while yet. 'I should think you'd need to be at least sixteen for that kind of thing,' he said, ruffling her hair. 'But I'm no expert. We'll ask Johnny, shall we?' He took an envelope out of his pocket and placed it on the table. 'Now young lady, when you've finished your tea there's a surprise in there for you.'

Her eyes lit up. 'Tell me. Look I've almost finished anyway.'

He nodded towards the envelope. 'Open it for yourself.'

Shaking with excitement, she tore open the envelope and stared at the two slips of paper inside. 'Tickets for a concert. At the Royal Festival Hall. *Tonight*. Oh, Daddy!'

'Have you seen who the soloist is?'

She looked again at the tickets. Gerald Cavelle. *Uncle Gerald!*

Jumping up from the table, she threw her arms round Daniel's neck.

'Thank you, Daddy. Oh, I can't wait.'

* * *

7

Cathy cherished the Saturday afternoon music lessons. Daniel's life was so busy all week. When he wasn't teaching or playing with the band he was working away in the front room on what he called his 'composition'. Playing a few bars, making alterations and playing again, his glasses low on his nose and his brow furrowed in concentration as he filled in the notes on the manuscript paper. Cathy knew that composing meant writing music and she wasn't to disturb him when he was doing it. She resented it a little. There was so little time for them to share. Surely there was already enough music for people to play and listen to without him writing any more? But when she confided her resentment to Johnny the housekeeper explained patiently that it was his hobby and important to him.

'Leave him to it, Cathy, love,' she would say kindly. 'It helps him relax.'

Because of his preoccupation with his music, having him all to herself was a special treat, which was partly why Cathy took so much trouble over her practice. She was afraid that if she gave up the piano maybe they would have no time together at all.

There was nothing she liked better than to get him into a reminiscent mood. She never tired of hearing about his youthful days at music college and the things he and his best friend, Gerald Cavelle, used to get up to.

When the war broke out Daniel had to give up his studies and go into the RAF. And by the time it was over he had married Jenny and Cathy had been born, so that returning to his music studies had been out of the question.

His friend, Gerald, had been luckier. He was a year younger than Daniel and had gone into ENSA when he was called up, where he could continue with his music. After the war he had returned to college and now he was a well-known concert pianist.

In spite of the fact that he was her father's best friend and her own godfather, 'Uncle' Gerald Cavelle had been no more than an exalted name to Cathy for years. She listened to his records of course. Daniel had them all. And she had occasionally heard him on the radio, so the idea of seeing and hearing him in the flesh was so exciting she could hardly contain herself.

Cathy had seen the Festival Hall from the outside when Daniel had taken her to the South Bank Exhibition four years ago in 1951. She sat enthralled, stunned by the atmosphere of the beautiful concert hall and thrilled by the music she was hearing live for the first time in her life. When it was time for the piano concerto and the conductor led Gerald on to the platform to a storm of enthusiastic applause, she stared hard at the tall handsome man dressed immaculately in tails and white tie. Nudging her father she whispered: 'Is that really *him*, Dad? Is that Uncle Gerald?'

Daniel squeezed her hand. 'That's him,' he said proudly. 'How would you like to meet him after the concert?'

She looked at him, her eyes round. 'Oh – could I?'

'Of course. He knows we're here and has invited us to go round afterwards.' He squeezed her hand and lowered his voice. 'Shhh now, they're about to begin.'

When they tapped on the door and stood waiting in the corridor Cathy looked up at her father and reached for his hand. She was suddenly overcome with shyness and her heart was beating fast. Gerald Cavelle's playing had been magnificent, better than anything she had ever heard, and now she felt very much in awe of the famous godfather she had never met.

But the voice that called 'Come in' sounded normal enough. A pleasant deep voice that sounded much like anyone else's. Daniel smiled reassuringly at her as he turned the door handle.

Gerald sat at a dressing table, his back to them. He had taken off the black tail coat and white tie and now he wore a dressing gown over his shirt and trousers. Catching sight

9

of Daniel in the mirror he jumped up, turning to greet them, his face beaming with pleasure.

'Daniel, you old so and so!' He grasped Daniel's hand and shook it vigorously. 'So glad you could make it. It's wonderful to see you. It must be years.' He stopped short at the sight of Cathy standing behind her father. 'And who is this little lady? Not my goddaughter surely?'

'Certainly is,' Daniel said proudly. 'Quite the young lady, isn't she?' He gently pushed his daughter forward. 'Say good evening, Cathy,' he prompted.

Tongue-tied and pink-cheeked, she mumbled a polite greeting. Gerald sat down and reached forward to take her hands and draw her towards him, looking intently into her face.

'The last time I saw you, you were about the size of sixpence and yelling your head off at the font,' he said. 'And now look at you.' He smiled. 'Now tell me, what did you think of my playing this evening?'

'It was – very nice.'

He laughed. 'Very nice? Is that all?'

She wanted to tell him that it was the most wonderful, magical music she had ever heard. That she had loved every minute of it and would remember it for ever. But she was far too shy. Acutely aware of the pressure of his cool hands and the dark eyes searching her face, she blushed crimson and stared at her feet. Daniel came to her rescue.

'Cathy enjoyed the concert very much,' he said. 'Especially your playing.'

Gerald smiled and gave her hands a final squeeze before releasing them. Turning back to the mirror again he said: 'I'm only teasing. I wouldn't expect a child of your age to enjoy anything that went on for so long.' He took up a silver-backed hairbrush and began to brush back his smooth dark hair. 'Poor baby, you must have thought it would never end.' His eyes smiled at her reflection in the mirror. 'I wouldn't blame you if you were bored stiff.'

'I *wasn't* bored,' Cathy said, stung out of her shyness. 'I listen to your records all the time at home. And the Grieg Concerto is one of my favourites. And anyway, I'm not a *baby*. I'm twelve.'

'Cathy!' Daniel stared at his daughter in dismay, but Gerald threw back his head and roared with laughter.

'I can see I've underestimated your daughter, Dan,' he said. 'Of course you're not a baby, Cathy. And to make up for insulting you I shall insist that you let me take you and your dad out to supper.'

Cathy was too excited to sleep that night. Long after she was in bed she was still thinking about the wonderful evening she and Daddy had spent with Gerald Cavelle. He was a very special, magical kind of person, like no one she had ever met before. Closing her eyes she pictured his tall, slim figure and the handsome face with its high forehead and dark eyes. Tanned skin was drawn tautly over high prominent cheekbones, and the faint shadow on his jaw gave him an exciting, slightly foreign look. Best of all she liked the smooth dark hair with its slight frosting of silver.

Over supper he had been very courteous to her, treating her as an adult in a way that she found quite intoxicating. The restaurant where he had taken them was sumptuous and plushy with crystal chandeliers and soft red carpets. The head waiter had greeted Gerald like royalty, ushering him and his little party to the best table and pulling out the chair for Cathy with a flourish that was fit for a queen. They had eaten exotic, delicious food and Gerald had insisted on pouring her a glass of wine.

'Only half a glass, Dan,' he said to Daddy with a twinkle in his eyes. 'It can't hurt her. After all, it is a special occasion.'

Afterwards, as they said goodnight, Gerald had insisted that they must certainly meet again.

11

'It's so sad to lose touch with old friends,' he said. 'We mustn't go for so long again without making contact. It's been marvellous seeing you both.' He shook Daniel's hand warmly.

'Thanks for the tickets,' he said. 'And for the supper. It's meant a lot to Cathy.' He lowered his voice. 'And so will the other. You'll never know how much.'

Gerald smiled. 'I'm glad I was able to help. Do let me know if there's anything else I can do for you, Dan. You and I go back a long way. Don't forget, I'm only a telephone call away.' He bent to tilt up Cathy's chin with one long finger. 'As for this little lady – well, she really is quite something. I shall certainly look forward to seeing more of her.'

Cathy cherished fond hopes of developing a regular relationship with Uncle Gerald. She boasted about him quite shamelessly at school after that special night. But although he had sounded utterly sincere at the time he made no attempt to get in touch again. Cathy talked about him incessantly in the weeks following the concert. She often asked Daniel why they didn't go again to see him play, or why they didn't telephone to invite him to come and see them. Daniel always shook his head, saying that Gerald was busy with an overseas tour or that he wouldn't be able to find time for them in his busy schedule.

'Maybe Uncle Gerald could help you get a better job,' she suggested. 'I heard him say he'd help you if you asked him. When I'm sixteen I could leave school,' she urged, her face serious. 'I could get a job and then you can get Uncle Gerald to fix up some concerts for you.' Her face lit up as she visualised a golden future. 'It would be lovely to have your picture on all those record sleeves like his and to go abroad, wouldn't it? I could come with you. We'd have a lovely time.'

Daniel shook his head. 'It's not as simple as that, love.'

'You work so hard though, Dad,' she added anxiously. 'And you get so tired. You know you do.'

12

But Daniel only smiled and gave her a hug. 'Concert pianists begin when they're very young. I used to dream about it when I was younger, but I'm too old a dog to learn new tricks now.' His expression was wistful. 'Maybe I never really had that kind of talent anyway. Perhaps I've only ever been good enough to be a useful jobbing pianist anyway.'

'You're not to say that,' she told him, vehemently. 'I bet you could have been as good as Uncle Gerald if you'd had the chances he's had – *better* even.'

Sometimes Cathy wondered if it was her fault that her father hadn't had the chances he deserved. If she hadn't been born, who knew what heights he might have reached? But she kept these thoughts to herself, a little too afraid that they might be true to voice them.

Cathy had just had her sixteenth birthday when Daniel knew for certain that he was seriously ill. For weeks he wondered what to do, who he could confide in. At last it was his housekeeper he turned to.

He chose a Monday morning after Cathy had left for school, an hour before the arrival of his first pupil. They sat at the kitchen table as they often did at this time of day, sharing a pot of coffee.

'Johnny, I've got something rather shocking to tell you,' he said suddenly.

Mary Johnson looked up. She had known Daniel Oldham for fourteen years and she liked and respected him. Although she was only a few years his senior she always felt that he was much younger. She mothered him much as she did her son, Matthew. He had never shocked her and she didn't believe him capable of doing so now. She smiled.

'Shock away. My mind is as broad as my back.'

He looked up into her eyes with a look she was never to forget. 'I'm afraid I'm going to die, Johnny.'

13

She put down her cup very carefully on its saucer and stared at him. 'Oh please don't say things like that.'

'I'm sorry if that was rather abrupt, Johnny. I'm afraid it's true though. I didn't know how else to tell you. I've got this wretched tumour thing, you see. Oh, I'm all right at the moment and apparently I will be for a while. But it will get worse.'

Swallowing hard at the lump in her throat, she asked: 'But surely – an operation . . .?'

He shook his head. 'No. Apparently not. Eventually I'll have to go into hospital of course and I'm worried sick about what will become of Cathy.'

'Well, you can stop worrying about her at once,' she said firmly. 'I've looked after her all these years. She's like my own child. I'll not see her without a home and someone to care for her.'

'But you've got your son to bring up on your own, and your mother living with you too. I couldn't expect you to take on my daughter. Especially as you'll be out of a job with me gone.'

'I'll get another job all right,' she told him. 'And my mother's a great help. Why shouldn't I take Cathy? She's a good girl and no trouble.'

'But she's growing up, Johnny. And, to be truthful, I haven't much money to leave, to provide for her. There's the house, of course, but it's her home. The only home she's ever known. I wanted her to stay on at school – maybe go on to university. I believe she's capable of it. She deserves the best I can give her. I might just have managed if I'd kept going.' He sighed and rubbed a hand across his jaw. 'Somehow I must find a way to provide the means.'

Johnny reached across the table to cover his hand with her own. 'You shouldn't be fretting like this,' she said. 'Cathy's got a good head on her. She'll make her own way in the world. She wouldn't want you to worry about her future.'

14

'But I do. What shall I do, Johnny?' He looked up at her with haunted, despairing eyes.

'What you should do is to make these last months with her as happy and memorable as you can,' she told him. 'You're not without friends. And you can be assured that I won't see Cathy alone in the world.'

'Do you think I should tell her – prepare her?' he asked.

Her heart went out to him. 'No. At least, not yet. She's too young to cope with news like that. Just enjoy the time you have together. Make these coming months ones she'll remember with happiness.'

'You're right, Johnny.' His face brightened. 'I know, I'll take her on holiday. We haven't had a proper holiday together for years. She's grown up so much these past couple of years – right under my nose without my noticing. It's time I got to know my daughter properly while there's still time.'

They went to Bournemouth during the Easter holidays. It was early April and quiet. The holiday season hadn't really started, but neither of them minded that. The weather was pleasantly warm and as they walked along the almost deserted sea-front they talked as they had never talked before. In the evenings they went to concerts or to the pictures, but one afternoon when it was raining Daniel took his daughter to a tea dance at The Pavilion.

She'd never been to a proper grown-up dance before and at first she was a little nervous. Daniel danced the first dance with her himself, but after that she didn't lack partners. As he watched her circle the floor in the arms of a series of young men he realised for the first time that his little girl really was a woman now. And so like her mother that at times it hurt him to look at her. For a moment he was angry that he wouldn't see her grown to full maturity, know the joy of giving her away in church to the man she loved on her

15

wedding day; never hold her children in his arms. Surely to God he might have been granted that one small thing in return for the disappointments life had dealt him – all the years he had spent alone. Was it really so much to ask? But his anger soon faded. His main concern was for Cathy. Had he really done all he could to prepare her for life? It was at that moment, watching her enjoying herself, that he decided the time had come for him to tell her the secret he had kept from her since childhood. There might not be another chance.

When they emerged into the late-afternoon the rain had stopped and the air was fragrant with the earth-rich scents of spring. They walked back to their hotel through the pleasure gardens, enjoying the freshness of the air after the rain, the spring flowers and the tangy scent of the pines.

Cathy was in a happy mood. Her step was so light that her feet hardly touched the ground as she danced along at his side. She was humming one of the tunes the band had played: *All I Have To Do Is Dream*. Her sweet, light voice tore at his heart.

'Let's sit down a minute,' he said. 'There's something I want to tell you, Cathy.'

She stopped singing and looked at him. 'What is it, Dad?'

'Nothing to worry about. Just something I think you should know.'

They sat down together on one of the benches and Cathy looked at him anxiously. 'You look very serious. Is it something I've done?'

He shook his head. 'No, of course not. Look, Cathy, it's about your mother. There's something I really should have told you a long time ago.' He paused for a moment, looking apprehensively at her expectant, upturned face. He'd started now. There was no going back. He was no good at beating about the bush, there was only one way to say it. He cleared his throat. 'The truth is – she didn't die.'

16

Her eyes widened. 'You mean – she's still alive?'

'Oh, no. She was killed in a car accident about eight years ago. The fact is – she left us, Cathy. When you were a baby.'

'*Left us?* But why, Dad? Didn't she love us? Didn't we make her happy?'

'I thought we did. I *believed* we did. I'm still convinced that she was happy – until . . .'

'Until what?'

'Until she met someone else, Cathy. Someone who captivated – obsessed her, heart, body and soul. She had to be with him – said she couldn't help herself.'

Cathy was shaking her head. 'I don't understand. Didn't you try to stop her?'

He bent forward on the seat, elbows on his knees, hands clasped. How did you explain the heartbreak, the stark, gut-wrenching misery of rejection to a sixteen year old? 'You can't make people love you, Cathy,' he said sadly. 'Not once they've really stopped. Of course I tried. I pleaded with her to stay with us, if only for your sake. Looking back now, I suppose it was emotional blackmail. I wanted her to stay so much I didn't care what I did or said to make her. But in the end I could see that it was no use. It was tearing her apart not being with him. In the end I had to let her go.'

Cathy bit her lip. 'So she wouldn't even stay for her own child – not even for – me? And you've always said she loved me, Dad.'

'She did love you. Nothing surer than that. It broke her heart to leave you. I know it did.'

'But she left just the same.' She felt the hurt of betrayal bite deep into her heart, and when she looked at her father she saw her own pain reflected in his eyes. 'Why didn't you tell me this before?' she asked, her voice thick with tears.

He shrugged his shoulders. 'At first you were too young to understand. It was easier to let you believe she was dead.

17

After all, she wasn't coming back and you didn't remember her. Then, when she was killed ... It didn't seem right somehow to betray her memory. I suppose if I'm honest I didn't want you to know I'd lied to you all those years.'

'Who was he, this man?' she asked angrily. 'Did you go and see him?'

'She never told me.'

'Didn't you ask her? Didn't you try to find out?'

'She said it was better I didn't know. And I suppose I was cowardly enough to prefer to remain ignorant.'

'Did they get married?'

'No.'

'How do you know?'

'They couldn't. We were never divorced. All I know is that she went abroad to live. I never saw or heard from her again – except through a solicitor of course, after the accident.'

They sat for a moment in silence, then Cathy said: 'So – so why are you telling me now, Dad?'

He looked into her eyes, saw the deep hurt his revelation had inflicted and decided that he couldn't tell her the real reason. 'You're a woman now,' he said. 'I saw you this afternoon how grown up you are. I thought it was time I levelled with you. Can you forgive me, Cathy?'

For a moment she searched his eyes, then she threw her arms around his neck and hugged him hard. 'Of course I can. Poor Dad. How unhappy you must have been. I'm so *glad* it was you who brought me up. You've done a terrific job – been both mother and father to me. I couldn't have had a better childhood.' She kissed his cheek. 'I love you so much, Dad. I'll always love you.'

'I love you too, sweetheart.' Daniel cleared his throat and made himself laugh as he disentangled her arms from his neck. 'Hey, come on, just look at the pair of us. We're getting all soppy.' He stood up and pulled her to her feet, tucking her hand through his arm. 'Come on now, time we

18

were getting back to the hotel. I'm starving, aren't you? What are we going to do this evening? Shall we go to the Winter Gardens again? Or do you fancy that film at the Westover?'

It was late in October 1960 when the leaves from the sooty plane trees in Laburnum Close carpeted the ground, that Daniel died. He had kept his illness from Cathy almost to the end, hiding his pain and putting his weariness down to hard work until his final collapse. He had been in hospital only a few days when the end came. For Cathy it was a devastating blow. For days she went around in a daze, unable to take it in.

Johnny took her home to stay with her. At first the girl was stunned and disorientated, asking repeatedly why he hadn't told her and why no one had done anything to help him?

'There was no more they could do, love,' Johnny told her gently. 'He knew that. He just wanted to keep going till the end, for your sake. And the doctors were able to help him with that. It was all he asked.'

But to Cathy it made no sense. She felt angry and cheated, terribly alone and afraid. There was so much she wished she had done and said. Now she would never have the chance. Why hadn't he treated her as a grown up – trusted her?

When the solicitor wrote, asking her to see him at his office, Johnny decided that she must go along with her. No doubt the question of whether to sell the house would arise and goodness only knew what else there was to be sorted out. How could a girl of barely seventeen be expected to make such monumental decisions about her own future?

Sitting side by side on the other side of Mr MacAlister's enormous oak desk they looked at him expectantly. He was a tall man with sparse grey hair and heavy horn-rimmed spectacles which made his pale eyes look large and impersonal. 'Your legal guardian will be joining us shortly,' he said,

19

pulling out his watch impatiently and peering at it. 'I do hope he isn't going to be late. I really can't begin until he arrives.'

Cathy and Johnny exchanged a puzzled look. 'I'm sorry, but there must be some mistake,' Cathy ventured. 'I haven't got a legal guardian.'

Mr MacAlister looked at the copy of Daniel's will which lay on the desk before him. 'Oh, but you have. Did your father not acquaint you with the fact?'

'I didn't actually know he was dying,' Cathy said wryly. How much more was there that he hadn't told her? 'Do you think you could tell me who this guardian person is, please?'

The solicitor looked at her incredulously for a moment, then . . . 'The name I have here, the person I've been in contact with on behalf of your father's estate, is Mr Gerald Cavelle, of Albany Place, Mayfair. He is also your father's executor.' He cleared his throat and frowned at them over his spectacles. 'I'm told he's a – *ahem* – a musician. A concert pianist in fact.'

Cathy was staring at him. '*Uncle Gerald?*'

The solicitor looked relieved. 'Ah – so you do know who I'm talking about?'

'Of course. He's my godfather.'

Mr MacAlister nodded. 'I see. Very suitable. He would be the obvious choice.' At that moment the door opened and his secretary ushered Gerald in. Cathy sprang to her feet and went to meet him.

'Uncle Gerald!'

He took both her hands. 'My dear child. I'm so desperately sorry about your father. I was abroad at the time or I would have been at the funeral. I only got back two days ago.'

The solicitor cleared his throat pointedly. 'Hrrrmph. If we might get down to business? I have another appointment in twenty minutes.'

* * *

As soon as the details of Daniel's will had been gone through Gerald took charge. First he put Cathy and Johnny into a taxi and took them to tea at Fortnum's.

'Now – what's to be done with you, young lady?' he asked, smiling at Cathy across the teacups. 'How much longer do you have at school?'

'I can leave now,' Cathy told him eagerly. 'Right after I've taken my O levels.'

Johnny glanced at her and leaned forward. 'I know it's really none of my business, sir, but I do know that Mr Oldham wanted Cathy to take her A levels and go on to university.'

Cathy looked at her in dismay. 'I'd never get to university, Johnny,' she said. 'I'm not clever enough. I'll be lucky to get any O's. I don't even *want* to stay on. Besides, by the time I've done another two years at school all the money will have run out, won't it?'

Gerald leaned across the table. 'You needn't let that worry you, Cathy. If university is what you want, I'll see you through.'

She blushed. 'I couldn't let you. Dad wouldn't have wanted that,' she muttered. 'Besides, I really don't want to go – *honestly*.'

He glanced at Johnny. 'I'll arrange for the sale of the house. There will be a lot to do. Maybe Cathy and I could go along together some day soon and sort things out there. The place will have to be cleared before the sale. I'll invest the money for her. No need to worry about that. I have a very good financial adviser.' He looked at Cathy. 'Maybe you'll change your mind about university by the time you get your exam results. In the meantime, where are you to live? It would hardly be proper for you to move into my bachelor flat. Besides, I'm hardly ever there.'

'She can stay on with me indefinitely,' Johnny put in quickly. 'She's perfectly happy with Mother and Matthew and me, aren't you, love?' Cathy nodded reluctantly. 'And I don't live far away from Laburnum Close,' Johnny said conclusively. 'So it's handy for her school.'

Gerald nodded. 'That sounds like an ideal arrangement. I'll see that you're appropriately recompensed, Mrs Johnson. And I'll open a bank account for you, Cathy, and see that an allowance is paid in monthly.' He looked at Johnny. 'I haven't much of an idea about what young girls need, so perhaps you'd better work something out on a monthly basis and let me know the amount.'

Johnny blushed. 'Well – if you say so, sir, though I'd like you to know that she's as close to me as my own child and I'd gladly have looked after her without an allowance.'

'I'm sure you would, Mrs Johnson, and I'm very grateful to you for all you've done, but I'm sure you'll agree that it is better to have things on a proper businesslike footing. After all, I am Cathy's legal guardian.' Gerald smiled at Cathy. 'Meantime, young lady, maybe you and I should start getting to know one another better. I'll make sure we keep in touch.'

Cathy wondered if he would remember or just fade into obscurity again as he had before. But he was as good as his word, telephoning regularly every week to ask how she was and if there was anything she needed.

The house in Laburnum Close sold quickly. The price was right and the young couple who bought it saw potential in the spacious, elegantly proportioned rooms. Gerald rang Cathy as soon as the offer was accepted to let her know.

'You realise what this means, of course,' he said.

Cathy bit her lip. 'I'll have to go and sort Dad's things out, you mean?'

'No, *we* will. I told you I'd go with you. It's not the kind of thing you should have to tackle alone. When do you want to go? What about next weekend? I think the sooner the better, don't you?'

22

The following Sunday was decided upon. Gerald suggested they should make an early start, offering to take Cathy out to lunch afterwards. He called for her soon after breakfast in his smart little sports car. Creating quite a stir in Chestnut Grove as he unfolded his long legs from the driving seat and walked up to the front door. He wore casual clothes: jeans and a sweater. Cathy thought he looked terribly handsome and as she settled into the car beside him she felt very proud and grown-up.

The late-November day was grey and cloudy and the moment she opened the front door of number thirteen with her key, the sad loneliness of the abandoned house hit her. Standing in the hall, she was aware for the first time of how old and shabby everything was. Johnny's little semi-detached house in Chestnut Grove wasn't luxurious, but it had a woman's touch. There were flowers and pretty ornaments in the living room, scented soap and talcum in the bathroom, and sparkling white net curtains at all the windows. Standing in the hall she wished she could have made this house more homelike for Dad. If she'd been older maybe she would have learned how to do it – how to keep house and make him more comfortable. She looked up at Gerald apologetically.

'I wish you could have come here before,' she said. 'When Dad was alive it didn't feel so – so sad and empty.'

He slipped a comforting arm around her shoulders. 'Come on, let's make a start, shall we? I suggest we make a tour of the rooms first and pick out the things you want to keep. I've brought some labels with me. The sooner we begin the sooner we'll be finished.'

'I don't see how I can keep anything,' she told him wistfully. 'Not furniture anyway. I've nowhere to keep it.'

'Is there anything you particularly want?' he asked her.

'I would have liked to keep the piano, but . . .'

'If you want to keep it, then you shall,' he told her

23

firmly. 'It can stay at my flat. And you can come and play it whenever you want to.'

Her eyes lit up. 'Can I? Oh, Uncle Gerald, thank you!'

He winced. 'When I say you can have it, I'm making one condition.'

'What's that?'

'That you stop calling me *Uncle*, for God's sake. It makes me feel as though I ought to have a long white beard. Just plain Gerald will do, thanks very much.'

She laughed. 'I'll try to remember.'

They worked hard all morning. Gerald took charge, organising everything with brisk efficiency, and to Cathy's relief it turned out to be much easier than she had imagined. Together they packed the china and saucepans; sorted through Daniel's clothes, setting aside the best for the Salvation Army to collect. They labelled the furniture ready for the saleroom and made the decision to leave carpets and curtains in situ in the house. When the time came for the attic to be investigated Cathy asked if she might have a little time to herself there. She wanted to look through the boxes full of old letters and photographs she knew were there. Maybe there was something of her mother's she could keep as a souvenir. Gerald nodded understandingly.

'Take as long as you need. I'll go and root around in the garden shed,' he told her.

It was cold and dark in the attic. The one small window was festooned with cobwebs and dust lay thick on everything. Cathy found that many of the old boxes full of letters and photographs that she knew were there had gone. Johnny had told her that Dad had known he was ill for some time. He must have come up here and destroyed everything personal before he died. Disappointment overwhelmed her. She'd hoped to find some relics of happier days; some of her mother's clothes. Maybe even her parents' wedding photograph, which she didn't remember ever seeing. She searched through the boxes that remained. They contained nothing but rubbish. There were some of her old toys, most of them broken now and useless. The old clothes she used to dress up in, that had belonged to her grandmother, were moth-eaten and ragged now, fit only for the dustbin.

She sat on the floor and looked around her dejectedly. Was this really all there was to show of the life she and Dad had shared? It was as though her whole childhood lay here in the dark little room under the eaves, dusty and disintegrating. This time next week it would all have been carried away by the dustman – over and forgotten. Tears began to trickle down her cheeks. Suddenly the stark, final reality of her father's death hit her like a hammer blow.

'Oh, Daddy,' she choked back the tears. 'Daddy, *Daddy*, I miss you so much.'

She didn't hear the footsteps on the stairs and when the attic door creaked open she started violently, her head twisting round as she looked up at the dark figure blotting out the light.

'Cathy, I'm sorry I startled you.' Gerald crouched beside her. 'What is it, darling? What have you found?'

'Nothing. That's just it, *nothing*. I thought there might be some old letters – snapshots – but there's no trace of anything. It's as though we – Dad, my mother and I – never existed. I feel like – like a *ghost*.'

He put his arm round her shoulders and drew her close. 'Have a good cry. Don't bottle it all up. It's not good for you.' He tipped up her chin to look into her brimming eyes. 'I wouldn't mind betting you haven't had a proper cry since Dan died, have you? Go on, let it all out. There's no one to see but me.'

Totally overwhelmed by his gentleness, she gave vent to the emotion that welled up inside her. It was such sheer luxury to drop her head on to his shoulder and sob out her grief, gasping and hiccuping with the abandon of a five year old.

Gerald had been right about the tight rein she'd kept on her emotions since Daniel had died. She'd been afraid to weep in front of Johnny; afraid that the kindly meant sympathy and the fussing that would inevitably result would be interpreted by the other two members of the household as monopolising her. Cathy was acutely aware that they had first call on Johnny's time and attention. They were her family. She, Cathy, was the outsider. There was Matthew, Johnny's nineteen-year-old son, tall and serious seeming to show with his silent, unsmiling forbearance just how much he resented the presence of this female interloper. She would have died rather than weep in front of him. Then there was Johnny's mother, old Mrs Bains, whose sharp eyes seemed always to be watching her, waiting to seize on the first sign that she was taking advantage.

But Gerald was impartial. He quietly stroked the auburn head that rested on his shoulder and let her cry, saying nothing.

After a while the sobs ceased and she began to feel much better. Without a word, Gerald pulled out a large clean handkerchief and pressed it into her hand. She sat up, mopped her face and blew her nose, then she looked up at him.

'Sorry.'

'Don't apologise for doing what you should have let yourself do long ago.'

She managed a smile. 'Thanks, Gerald.' Suddenly to her surprise she saw him quite differently. Until now she had held him in awe, but now they had shared this small intimate moment she felt they were closer – almost equal.

He glanced around. 'Is there anything up here that you want?'

She shrugged helplessly. 'No. It can all go out for the dustman.'

'Right. Give me a hand to stack the boxes at the top of the stairs then. Oh, and Cathy . . .'

'Yes?' She paused in the act of lifting a box.

'Don't ever let me hear you say you feel like a ghost again.' He took the box from her and put it on the floor. Then he took both of her hands in his. 'You're young and full of vitality. One day quite soon you're going to be a beautiful young woman. Your whole life is in front of you and from now on you have to look forward, not back. That's how your father would have wanted it. And that's the way it's going to be.' He bent and brushed her forehead with his lips. 'That's a promise. Now, come on, let's get these boxes downstairs. I don't know about you but if I don't get something to eat soon I shall fade away.'

Cathy had dreaded Christmas that year; her first without Dad and in the house of people who, however hard they tried, were not her family. The little house was crowded with the four of them. There were only three bedrooms and Johnny had doubled up with her mother in order to accommodate Cathy. She was acutely aware of the sacrifices that were being made on her account, and so afraid she would feel like an intruder at Christmas. But as it happened it was better than she had thought.

Johnny loved Christmas. She was a wonderful cook and made sure that she involved Cathy in all the preparations. She set Cathy and Matthew the task of decorating the house whilst she and her mother went out to buy last-minute food and presents on the Saturday afternoon before the holiday.

It was the first time that Cathy had been alone with Matthew and she felt rather shy. She knew that he worked as a junior clerk in a solicitor's office, but they had never talked about it so she hadn't the slightest idea what his work involved. When he came home from work each evening he disappeared upstairs to his room as soon as he had eaten. She had always assumed it was because of her. But today, dressed in jeans and a sweater instead of the formal clothes

27

he wore to work, and whistling a popular tune as he worked, he seemed more human somehow – more approachable.

For the first ten minutes they worked together in silence, she handing up the brightly coloured paper chains and he pinning them.

'Do you like your job?' she asked at last, remembering Mr MacAlister's forbidding office and the baffling legal language used in all his correspondence. 'Isn't it boring, trying to work out what it's all supposed to be about?'

He looked down at her with a slightly surprised expression. 'Not really. Not when you get used to it. And going to court is really interesting. The law is a fascinating subject, you know.'

'I suppose it is, but you only work in the office, don't you?'

'At the moment, yes, but I don't intend to be a clerk for the rest of my life.'

'Oh? What are you going to do then?'

He came down the ladder and began to bunch some sprigs of holly together. 'Didn't Mum tell you? I'm studying for my law exams in my spare time. Some day I'm going to be a fully qualified solicitor.'

Cathy looked at him with a new respect. So that's what he did upstairs in his room all evening. He wasn't keeping out of her way at all.

'Won't that take ages?' she asked him. 'I thought you had to go to university for that.'

'You can do it this way too. It does take longer, but I don't care as long as I can be earning while I study,' he said stoically. 'Mum had a real struggle to bring me up. My dad was killed at Dunkirk, you know. She had to work hard to keep me on at grammar school. And now she's got Gran to look after too. I mean to pay her back one day.'

'I know what you mean.' Cathy was thoughtful. 'My father made sacrifices for me too,' she said, remembering how she'd selfishly insisted on going to St Margaret's

28

without a thought of what it might mean to him. 'I'd have liked the chance to pay him back. Now I never will.'

He looked at her a little apprehensively, hoping she wasn't about to cry. The fact that she didn't sent her up in his estimation. He smiled at her for the first time ever. 'I'm sorry about your dad, Cathy,' he said awkwardly. 'It was rotten luck. I was only a baby when mine died so I don't remember him.' He touched her shoulder awkwardly. 'But I don't suppose your father would have wanted paying back anyhow. I expect he was happy to do it for you.' He gave the bunch of holly a final twist. 'Will you hold the step ladder for me while I fix this over the mirror?'

They smiled at each other and Cathy knew that any resentment, real or imaginary, that had been between them in the past had vanished once and for all.

On New Year's Eve Gerald rang to say he was taking her to a concert. Cathy wore her best dress, the one that Dad had bought her the time they went to Bournemouth, and sat proudly in the front row at the Wigmore Hall. She longed to tell the people on either side of her that the soloist was her guardian. He played Rachmaninov's Second Piano Concerto and as she listened wraptly Cathy was convinced that it had never been played with more style and brilliance. After the concert an attendant came to escort her round to Gerald's dressing room where he was waiting to take her out for dinner. They went to Quaglino's and Gerald encouraged her to order all the things she liked best.

It wasn't until they reached the coffee stage of the meal that she discovered why.

'I'm afraid this is by way of au revoir, Cathy,' he told her. 'I'm going on a concert tour in two days' time: the United States and Canada. I'll be away for about eight months. No need to worry about anything though. I've arranged for your allowance and Mrs Johnson's to be paid into the bank and if there are any problems just ring my agent. Here's his address and phone number.' He passed her a card across the table.

The news came as a blow. Although she had known of course that he spent much of his time out of the country, she hadn't been prepared for him to go away this soon – or for so long. She slipped the card into her handbag without looking at it, her cheeks pink and her eyes downcast. 'I see. Thanks, Gerald.'

He laughed gently at her crestfallen face. 'Don't look like that. I'm not deserting you. You've got a very busy few months ahead of you at school, haven't you? It'll go very quickly, and I'll be back in this country in time to hear your exam results. Then we can celebrate.'

She pulled a face. 'If there's anything *to* celebrate.'

'I'm sure there will be. And we'll need to talk about your future by then, won't we? Whatever happens.'

'I know all that. It's just – just . . .'

'Just what?'

'Just that you're – the only family I've got now and I'll – miss you.'

She felt foolish the moment she'd said it and to her dismay found her eyes filling with helpless tears. She fumbled miserably in her bag for a handkerchief, fighting off the embarrassing display of emotion. Now she'd ruined the whole evening. How *could* she be so stupid?

Gerald hurriedly asked for the bill and, when he had paid, took her arm firmly and escorted her out of the restaurant. When they were seated in the car she looked at him apprehensively.

'I'm sorry.'

'What for?'

'For being such an idiot – for embarrassing you.'

He smiled wryly. 'Don't give it another thought. I've been in much more embarrassing situations and lived to tell the tale,' he told her. 'Actually it's rather flattering. Most of the women in my life are glad to see the back of me.'

She wondered a little at this remark. So he saw her as a woman? *Most of the women*, he said. How many were there in his life? As far as she knew he had never been married, but a man as good-looking, as famous and talented as Gerald, was bound to have had dozens of glamorous girlfriends.

'Tell you what,' he was saying, 'when I come back we'll have a grand reunion celebration – anything you like. You can choose. And look – any time you want to visit the flat, just go along. I'll tell the caretaker to let you in. You can play the piano or just be by yourself if you feel the need. I know it's a bit of a squash at Mrs Johnson's. How does that appeal?'

She sniffed, nodding into the darkness. He was placating her. He didn't think of her as a woman after all. He still saw her as a child. But she *wasn't* a child any more. She was seventeen now. She hadn't felt like a child for ages; not since Dad died.

But in spite of everything Gerald had been right about the time flying. Once the holidays were over and she was back at school there was so much to do. She hadn't forgotten Matthew's words about paying his mother back for her sacrifices. Perhaps it was too late to pay Dad back, but he had wanted her to do well so she would do it for him anyway. Now Cathy too disappeared to her room with her books each evening. Johnny complained that she and Matthew were like lodgers.

'Ships that pass in the night,' she said, half joking, half serious. 'I'm sure all that bookwork can't be good for you. You'll ruin your eyesight, the pair of you.' But secretly she was proud of her hard-working son, and of Cathy too, for the industry she knew came hard to the girl. In spite of what she had said, it seemed that she meant to pass those exams and stay on at school after all. There had been a time soon after Daniel Oldham's death when Johnny had worried that the child didn't care any more. But it seemed her fears were unfounded.

With Cathy's new desire to succeed came other changes. In her friends for instance. Carla made no secret of the fact that she disapproved.

'I don't know what's got into you,' she complained. 'You're no fun any more. This is the fourth week you've refused to go dancing or to the pictures on Saturday. You have to have some time off. Don't you want to meet any boys?'

'I've got a lot of time to catch up,' Cathy said. 'I've let things slide.'

Carla sniffed disdainfully. 'You've changed,' she said. 'Ever since you've been living with the Johnsons you've turned into a swot. Don't tell me it's that awful Matthew? You don't fancy him, do you – spots and all?'

Cathy denied the accusation hotly. 'Of course I don't! Why does everything have to be because of some boy? If you must know, I want to repay Dad for all he did for me, that's all.'

'What for? He won't *know*, will he?' Carla said insensitively.

'Well, I'm doing it anyway. Gerald expects me to do well. I don't want to let him down.'

'Ah. Now we're getting to the truth.' Carla smiled triumphantly. 'Gorgeous Gerald the famous pianist. It's *him* you fancy, isn't it? I might have known. It's been nothing but Gerald this and Gerald that ever since last autumn.' She tossed her blonde curls disdainfully. 'You've turned into the most awful little name-dropping show-off since he came on the scene, and now you're a swot too – just like Rosalind Blair.'

'I'm not!'

Carla ignored her protest. 'It isn't as though you *have* to do it either. I mean, everyone knows that a girl as plain as Rosalind has to work hard. Can you imagine any man asking *her* to marry him?'

They were in the cloakroom and Rosalind was close

enough to overhear. Cathy blushed and whispered: 'Shut up, she'll hear you.'

Carla glanced round haughtily. 'I don't suppose I've said anything she doesn't already know,' she said, unabashed, and looked challengingly at Cathy. 'Right then, are you coming dancing with me on Saturday or do I ask someone else?'

'I think you'd better ask someone else,' Cathy said firmly.

'All right, I will. If you want to turn into a cabbage you'd better get on with it and the best of British luck!'

Cathy watched as Carla shook her head and walked away. She was beginning to see her friend for what she was: shallow and selfish. All the same, she missed their weekly outings and Sunday tea at the Maybridges' gloriously chaotic house. Working for her exams was hard going but she was determined to do the best she could so that Gerald would be proud of her. Whenever her spirits flagged she got out the postcards he had sent her from each of the places where he'd played: New York; Los Angeles; Boston. She imagined the hectic, glamorous life he must be having; the concerts and the parties; the beautiful women he must be meeting every day, all of them falling over each other to get close to him. And she wondered at the thought that he could actually find the time to write to her. He must be just a *little* bit fond of her. Then she would imagine the scene where she would tell him of her success, and picture the look on his face. It was all the incentive she needed.

She put on her coat and heaved the heavy satchel on to her back. She'd have to hurry or she'd miss the half-past four bus. She reached the door at the same time as Rosalind and when she saw the other girl blush and look away Cathy decided to try to apologise for Carla's cruel and thoughtless remarks.

'Look, Rosalind, I'm sorry about those things that Carla said. She can be very catty at times. Take no notice of her.

She was cross with me because I wouldn't go dancing with her on Saturday.'

Rosalind's colour deepened. 'It's all right,' she said, tugging at the strap of her satchel. 'There's no need for you to feel sorry for me. I'm used to being called plain.'

'She thinks I'm a bore because I'm working hard for my exams,' Cathy went on. 'She was getting at me really. She knows how embarrassed I get when she makes loud remarks about people.'

'She was accusing you of being like me. How awful for you!'

Cathy looked at the other girl's hurt expression. 'Oh, no. I take it as a compliment. If I can do as well as you always do in exams, I'll be very pleased.'

'I work hard because I have a plan. Besides, there's nothing much else to do.' Rosalind looked up with a smile and suddenly Cathy saw to her surprise that she wasn't plain at all. The brown eyes behind the spectacles were large and lustrous and she had small, regular features and nice teeth. If she had her straight dark hair cut differently . . . Someone had once said that Rosalind's mother had been an actress before she married, though Carla had scoffed at that rumour.

'No actress would let her daughter walk around dressed like that,' she said. And Cathy was reluctantly inclined to agree. Rosalind came to school in a sad assortment of shapeless skirts and blouses that Carla insisted were rejects from a jumble sale.

The two girls had fallen into step but suddenly Rosalind stopped.

'Don't feel you have to walk with me, Cathy,' she said. 'I told you, I'm used to catty remarks – and to being on my own. You don't need to apologise for Carla either. I know you're not like her.'

'I don't feel I've *got* to walk with you, I want to. After all, we catch the same bus so why shouldn't we walk together?'

Cathy glanced at the other girl, hoping she hadn't sounded patronising. 'That's if you don't mind?' she added.

Rosalind hesitated for a moment, then smiled again, blushing, this time with pleasure. 'No. I don't mind,' she said. 'I don't mind at all.'

Chapter Two

Rosalind had a longer journey home than Cathy. It took her half an hour to get to the street in Burnt Oak where she and her mother occupied a flat. After she got off the bus there was a lengthy walk and by the time she arrived at Courtney Avenue the strap of her satchel was biting into her shoulder and her back ached. As usual she let herself into the rundown Edwardian house with her own key and trudged up the uncarpeted stairs to the first-floor flat.

Rosalind didn't mind coming home to an empty flat each afternoon. She was used to it. It meant she would have an hour's peace and quiet to get on with her homework before her mother got home from work. That hour was essential. Once she had her O levels behind her she was determined to go on and take her A's. Her whole future depended on how well she could do.

In the cramped little kitchen with its window overlooking the dusty back garden she put the kettle on for coffee and took down the biscuit tin, then went through into the living room and began to unload her books on to the table. She had set her sights on passing at least two subjects with good grades. She'd been told that she wasn't university material but already knew what she wanted to do so it wasn't a problem. She was determined to go to a business college, the best one she could find, and take a diploma course in hotel management. The careers mistress at St Margaret's had tried to talk her out of it, feeling that the quiet, somewhat withdrawn girl had none of the right attributes for hotel work. But it was all Rosalind had wanted to do ever since she could remember and she refused to be discouraged from her goal.

As she waited for the kettle to boil she thought about her brief and unexpected talk with Cathy Oldham. Ever since her first year at St Margaret's she'd admired the tall, striking girl with her auburn hair and green eyes. It was strange – people often talked of green eyes when they really meant grey, or blue-green, but Cathy's were a true, clear green, like emeralds. When you looked into them it was hard to look away; they were quite mesmerising. Yet Cathy wasn't at all the type one associated with green eyes. Rosalind had always felt that, and today it had been confirmed. Cathy was thoughtful and kind, just as Rosalind had always known she would be. She felt a sense of satisfaction in having her instinct proved right. She'd never really understood why Cathy and Carla Maybridge were such friends. They were so different.

Rosalind took a biscuit from the tin and munched thoughtfully. She wished in some ways that she could be more like Carla, who seemed to attract people like a magnet. But she was only too aware of the power she had and used it in all the wrong ways. She was self-centred and thoughtless, often to the point of cruelty to those less fortunate than herself; though goodness only knew she had no need to be. Everything seemed to fall effortlessly into her lap. She was pretty and popular with both girls and teachers alike, and although she only ever managed to scrape by academically she was always at the centre of things. Cathy on the other hand seemed quite unaware of her own attractiveness. She was a more serious, introspective kind of girl. Rosalind had heard about her father dying. She knew Cathy had no mother and that she'd had to leave the home where she'd grown up. Watching her at school she'd recognised the suffering in the other girl's face and manner and, herself the only child of divorced parents, had longed to reach out to her; to sympathise. But she hadn't known how, or where

37

to begin. In the end, afraid of receiving a snub, or some scathing remark from Carla, she hadn't even tried. Today as they'd walked to the bus stop together she had searched her mind for some words to express her understanding and regret, but to her frustration, they'd refused to come.

Rosalind had been almost eight when her parents had divorced. Until then her life had been divided between Aunt Flora who kept a boarding house in Cleethorpes and the hotels and 'digs' up and down the country where her parents, Una and Ben Blair, stayed as they toured with their singing act. Flora Mawson wasn't a real aunt. She was Una's late mother's oldest friend and the nearest she had to a blood relative now that her parents were dead.

Rosalind had been born while her parents were touring with ENSA during the war. Una, furious to discover that she was pregnant and forced to take time off, had deposited her new baby with Aunt Flora in Cleethorpes as soon as she could, and rejoined Ben who was touring at the time with a production of *The Desert Song*. She was soon to discover that during her absence he had become more than friendly with a dancer in the same company. It was the beginning of a long string of infidelities and eventually the end of the marriage.

By the time Rosalind had reached school age she was spending term time with Aunt Flora in Cleethorpes and the holidays with her parents wherever they happened to be working. Aunt Flora had pointed out to Una somewhat tersely that the boarding house was her bread and butter. Heaven only knew, the summer season was short enough and fond as she was of Rosalind, she really couldn't have the child taking up one of her rooms while her parents 'gadded about' all over the country. So as soon as school broke up for the long summer holidays Rosalind would pack her suitcase and join the mother and father who were little more than strangers to her.

Sometimes they would be booked for a resident summer

show at the seaside, which was nice. Ben did his best to act the role of father, taking her on the beach and playing with her when he wasn't rehearsing. Una, on the other hand, needed all her free time for having her hair done and making sure she looked good off-stage as well as on. Less enjoyable summers would be spent touring, which meant long dreary Sunday train journeys and a succession of dingy digs and lodging houses where Rosalind would be required to keep quiet and not play on the stairs. In the evenings while Una and Ben were at the theatre she would stay in her room with the radio or a book. Later, she would lie awake, rigid with misery and unnamed fears as the sound of quarrelling initiated by her mother's emotional tantrums reached her through the thin partition walls.

It had been around that time that her ambition had been born. When she grew up she was going to stay in one place all the time. She would have the kind of life where she would feel safe; one which would certainly have nothing to do with the theatre. She hated the musty, cheerless backstage environment; the faces made bewilderingly unfamiliar with orange make-up; and the tense, highly-charged atmosphere that seemed to exclude everyone not associated with it. Stage people weren't like anyone else, she decided. It was as though they were split into two: one person on the stage and another off it. They seemed to keep all the best bits of themselves jealously guarded and stored up for the audience, so that there was nothing left over for those, like herself, who stood on the fringe of it all. Standing in the wings or occasionally seated 'out front' she found it difficult to believe that the two glamorous people on the stage, smiling so adoringly into each other's eyes as they sang their romantic love songs, were the angry, morose parents who came home every evening to quarrel and shout at each other until the other occupants of the house banged on the walls in fury.

But quite apart from her dislike of the theatre, Rosalind

recognised that she had no aptitude or talent for the life. She had not inherited her mother's lustrous violet eyes and mane of raven hair. Her own hair was an indeterminate brown and poker straight, and from the age of four she had had to wear glasses. Neither had she Una's vivacious, mercurial personality. The years of being pushed into the background and passed around had set their seal on her character. She was much too shy and lacking in confidence to make a performer even if she had wanted to be one.

By the time she was seven she had decided that when she grew up she would have a hotel of her own; one where people – especially children – were made welcome. It wouldn't be like Aunt Flora's boarding house with its porch full of rusting buckets and spades and wet mackintoshes. And it certainly wouldn't be like the cabbage-smelling, brown-wallpapered digs and theatrical lodgings where she spent her summer holidays. During the long hours she spent alone she planned it all. *Her* hotel would be warm and comfortable with cosy fires and bright lights in all the rooms. There would be delicious food to eat, pretty curtains and warm, soft beds. The bathroom wouldn't be cold and draughty and there wouldn't be any of those horrid hissing gas heaters where the hot water was always running out. Best of all, there would be a garden where children could play and go where they pleased. It would feel like a *home*, she told herself. It would *be* a home.

Soon after her parents' traumatic split-up Aunt Flora decided to retire. Her announcement spiked Una's guns on the awful weekend when she and Rosalind had arrived in Cleethorpes to throw themselves on her mercy.

'I'm going to sell Sea View and go down to Devon to live with my sister Gladys now that she's widowed,' she told a tearful Una as they sat facing each other across the kitchen table. 'So it's no use you expecting me to take the child on permanent like.'

It was evening and Rosalind was upstairs in bed,

supposedly asleep. But the sound of voices floated up the stairs to reach her through the open bedroom door. The mention of her own name brought her instantly alert. Throwing back the bedclothes, she tiptoed out on to the landing. Creeping down to the bend in the staircase, she crouched by the banisters and listened to the voices of the two women as they discussed her future.

'She's a nice little thing and no trouble, I grant you,' Aunt Flora was saying. 'But she's getting older all the time and she's coming to the age when she needs a parent's guidance. I'm sorry, Una but I'll be frank with you. I feel it's high time you were a proper mother to the child.'

'And how do you think I'm going to do that with no job and nowhere to live?' Una's voice was shrill with resentment. 'She's Ben's kid too. But does he want to know about her? Does he *hell*! Shouldn't think he gives a damn whether he sees her again. Off with his fancy bit of stuff, he is, and no thought for anyone but himself.' She gave a bitter little laugh. 'Groping the chorus girls – that's all he's ever been good for!'

'Maybe you should have thought of that before you married him,' Aunt Flora said dryly. 'After all, if I remember rightly, you took him off someone else in the first place. Quite cocky about it, you were too, at the time. Stands to reason if you could turn his head, then there'd be others who could do the same.'

'That's not getting my problem solved though, is it?' Una snapped. 'What the hell do I do with a kid? How can I work with her round my neck?'

'Get a day job,' Aunt Flora suggested. 'In a shop or something. She's at school in the daytime.'

Una gave an indignant little squeal. '*Me?* A shop girl? I'm an artiste, Flora. A *soubrette*.'

'That's as may be, but whatever fancy name you like to call yourself, the fact remains, you're that child's mother, and beggars can't be choosers.'

41

'You've hit the nail on the head there. That's what I'll be all right. A *beggar*. I should never have had her. I never wanted a kid. It's all his fault, the careless swine. Not taking proper care. Now I'm lumbered and off he goes, scot-bloody free.'

Una was working herself up into one of her 'states'. Rosalind knew all the signs. She'd heard her enough times through the walls late at night. But this time it was all about her. This time she was the cause of Una's anger. Aunt Flora always said, '*Eavesdroppers never heard any good of themselves*' and now she knew that was true. The words: *I should never have had her, I never wanted a kid* and *I'm lumbered* brought a big lump to her throat and made her eyes sting with tears. Getting up from the stairs she scuttled back to bed and pulled the bedclothes up over her head, pushing a fist into her mouth so that they wouldn't hear her sobs. No one wanted her. Not even Aunt Flora. But why? What had she done? She'd tried hard to be good and keep out of the way. She didn't make a noise or ask for things. She missed her father too. Happy-go-lucky Ben with his sparkling brown eyes and his big laugh. She'd always thought he loved her and the shock of her mother's revelation that he didn't want to know about her any more hurt intolerably. Suddenly she felt very scared. Would they put her in an orphanage? That's what happened to children that nobody wanted, wasn't it? To seven-year-old Rosalind the future looked bleak and frightening.

It hadn't turned out like that, though there had been times when she had almost wished it had. It was 1951 and variety theatres in provincial towns up and down the country were closing for want of support. Television was what people were interested in now. All the top-name artistes right there in your own living room. When you could see them all without getting out of your armchair, why should anyone pay to see number four touring shows with tatty costumes at the local Hippodrome? Especially with the price of admission going up the way it had since the war.

All through the school holidays Una dragged Rosalind up and down Charing Cross Road, trying one agent after another. They climbed endless narrow dusty staircases, drawing one blank after another. Una had walked out on the agent who had represented her and Ben in a fit of pique when he told her with brutal frankness that her voice was thin and didn't stand up without the backing of Ben's strong tenor. That had been a bad day; one of the worst. Back home in the bed-sitting room they shared Una had raged and wept by turn, calling Ben by every bad name she could put her tongue to. But there were bigger fish in the sea, she told Rosalind, her cheeks pink and her eyes glittering. She would find a better agent. She would be a big star and show them all. The trouble was – she hadn't. *Soubrettes* weren't in demand any more, except at Christmas time for panto. Una was offered the role of Fairy Bluebell in *Jack and the Beanstalk* at a converted cinema in Peterborough, but she had heard that Ben and his new partner were playing Birmingham that year, with no less than three well-known television personalities topping the bill. If he heard – and he certainly would hear – that she was playing a number three date in a *cinema*, she'd die of shame and humiliation. There were more emotional tears and tantrums, which Rosalind had to soothe and placate. By now she was getting used to it.

The divorce finally came through and Una was awarded custody of Rosalind. Ben's maintenance cheques came regularly, which should have pleased her. It meant that they could afford the rent of a better flat, and eat properly. But it also meant that if Ben could afford the maintenance, he was working, while she was not. The thought that he was doing better than ever without her tore her apart. Snippets of news of him reached them via the grapevine and his name appeared in *The Stage*, the theatrical paper which

Una still bought and read avidly from cover to cover. His new singing partner was an outstanding success. 'Ben and the lovely Benita', they were billed as. Her real name was Freda Morton. She was blonde, and, at a mere nineteen, much younger than Una, a fact that wounded her deeply. They were booked for a world cruise on a new P & O luxury liner. After that there was television and radio work. When Rosalind spotted a photograph of them in the *Radio Times* one week she had to tear out the page and pretend it contained something she needed for school. To have let her mother see it would have been to trigger off at least a week of black depression.

For Una, things went from bad to worse. She had a handful of cabaret engagements; two disastrous club bookings where she was booed off the stage for being inaudible above the chatter of drinkers; then the jobs dried up altogether. She began to go to pieces alarmingly. Slowly the roles of mother and daughter were exchanged. It was ten-year-old Rosalind who wheedled Una out of her abysmal depressions; coaxed her to get up and put on her make-up – have something to eat. It was Rosalind who cleaned the flat, did the shopping and most of the cooking while Una lay in bed and sulked, mourning her lost career and her broken marriage; bitterly blaming her errant husband for it all. Her moods would swing from frenetic optimism to bleakest misery. It was nerve-racking, but to her resigned daughter it became no more than the normal daily routine.

The only good thing to come out of it all for Rosalind was that she was able to get a place at St Margaret's School. Una's deceased Irish parents had brought her up in the Catholic faith and when Rosalind came home from school distraught over failing her eleven-plus through the tension and overwork of her home life, Una's conscience jerked her sharply out of her apathy. In many ways it had been her saving grace. Dressing in her most sober outfit, she had taken Rosalind along to St Margaret's and demanded to see the headmistress. Una could be very persuasive when she put her mind to it. She claimed indignantly that her daughter's ability had been shamefully underestimated and that, as a Catholic, she was entitled to a place at St Margaret's.

The kettle boiled and Rosalind made her mug of coffee and carried it through to the living room where she had laid out her books. She had an English essay to write and she'd better get on with it, she told herself, looking at the clock. When her mother came home she would expect the evening meal to be ready.

The achievement of getting Rosalind into St Margaret's had been a turning point for Una. It had proved to her that she could get things moving if she made the effort. That autumn she had finally pulled herself together and taken charge of her life. Admitting to herself that her stage career was over, she took a job in the gown department of a West End department store. She hadn't found it easy. At first she had arrived home each evening tired and dispirited. Kicking off her shoes, she would declare herself exhausted and unable to do the job one day longer. But as the time went by and the lure of the footlights gradually faded she seemed to grow resigned to her new role as a single working mother. More than that, the job began to grow on her. She was promoted to second sales, then first, which meant a rise in salary and status. She had been in the job for five years now and she and Rosalind had settled down at last to something approaching a normal life.

Occasionally Una had been invited out by a man, but it never lasted very long. She had little interest in men who worked in shops or offices. They failed to excite her. She found them dull and boring. Sometimes, Rosalind wondered if she still loved Ben, but she never dared to ask. The mere mention of his name was enough to throw Una into a rage for the rest of the day.

It was almost an hour later when Rosalind looked up from her finished essay. She had worked longer than she'd intended. Hastily stuffing her books back into her satchel she laid the table for the evening meal and went into the kitchen. It was only then that she noticed the letter. It must have come after she had left for school. Una had thrown it on to the kitchen table along with the newspaper and a couple of circulars. It was addressed to Rosalind in her father's handwriting. Intrigued, she turned it over in her hand, wondering what he could be writing to her about. She had seen her father only a handful of times in the last nine years. Ben made contact with her only occasionally, usually by way of postcards from the more exotic places he played. Una always said that they were really meant to show *her* how well he was doing and not because he gave a tuppenny damn about his daughter. He sent her birthday cards too, and always a present at Christmas, but she saw him very rarely and this was the first time she had ever received a letter from him. Curious, she slipped her finger under the flap of the envelope and drew out the sheet of paper inside.

My dear Rosalind,
This is to invite you to come and stay with us for a few days in the Easter Holidays. Freda and I have bought a nice little place of our own in a village in Northamptonshire. Now that they've built the new M1 it's easy for us to get to at weekends. We've got a week out at Easter before we start rehearsing for a summer show in Brighton and we'd both love you to come and spend it with us. Now that you're older I want you and Freda to get to know each other as I'm sure you and she would get along well. Please try to come, Rosalind. Maybe you don't realise it, but you are the only blood relative I've got and in spite of what you might think, I've missed you all these years.
Give my best regards to your mother.
Hoping to see you soon,
Your loving father

Slowly and thoughtfully Rosalind folded the letter and pushed it into her skirt pocket. She was filled with mixed feelings. It was flattering to think that her father wanted to see her. Una had always been at great pains to point out that he cared less than nothing for her. Sometimes she could be so convincing that Rosalind had almost believed her, but by the sound of this letter he *did* still care about her. She found herself moved by what he had written and keen to accept the invitation. She had to admit that she was intrigued to meet Freda too, and to see this home they had bought for themselves. But the thought of her mother's reaction filled her with apprehension.

Una arrived home that evening in a good mood. She breezed into the kitchen where Rosalind was peeling potatoes and did not seem to notice that the meal was hardly started.

'Guess what?' she challenged as she took off her coat. 'I've been offered a new job. I was called into the general manager's office this afternoon. *Shaking* with nerves, I was. I thought I was going to get the sack. Then – right out of the blue – Mr Blake said he wanted me to organise a series of fashion shows the store is about to promote. He thought I'd do well because of my stage experience and – get this, Rossie – because of my *flair for fashion*. Can you believe that?' She threw herself into a chair and kicked off her shoes. 'He said he'd noticed how well turned out and attractive I always am!' She rolled her eyes and stretched out one shapely leg, hitching up her skirt to peer at it critically. 'Maybe your mum isn't over the hill yet, eh? Of course I'd noticed him giving me the once-over when he came up to the department, but I thought he was just – well, older men are like that. So you see, Rossie, – your mum isn't as useless as you thought she was.'

'I never thought you were,' Rosalind said.

Una leaned back in her chair and stretched her arms

luxuriously. 'Oh, I've got *so* many ideas. Bring a bit of life to the place, that's what I intend to do. Drag the department into the twentieth century.' Rummaging in her handbag for her cigarettes, she lit one and blew out a cloud of smoke. '*Just think*, I'm told I'll be attending the managers' meetings – having my say. Imagine, Rossie, your mum, *fashion show organiser*. Next thing you know we'll be moving to a better flat – nearer to the West End perhaps – or even a house. How'd you like that?'

Rosalind went on peeling potatoes, making no comment. Una always over-reacted to everything. She liked to dramatise what happened to her, good things as well as bad. There had been promises of better flats, ships coming in and dreams coming true many times before, alternating with dire prophecies of poverty and destitution. Still, it was good that she had something to be excited about this evening, Rosalind told herself. It would make it easier to break Ben's news.

The meal was easy, cold meat and chips, with tinned plums and custard to follow. When they had eaten Rosalind fingered the letter in her skirt pocket and wondered if it was the right time to tell her mother what was in it.

'I had a letter today,' she said tentatively

'Oh, yes, who from?'

'Dad, actually.'

Immediately she had her mother's attention. 'Ben! What did he want?'

Rosalind took out the letter and spread it out on the table for her mother to read, watching her face anxiously as she did so. Una scanned the few lines briefly, then frowned and read it through again. Finally she threw back her head with a derisive snort.

'A little place of our own, eh? How *sweet*! He must be feeling his age if he wants to settle down in some dump at the back of beyond, that's all I can say. Perhaps he's scared of losing *her*, so he's planning to bury her in the country out of harm's way.'

Rosalind bit her lip. 'He says he'd like me to go and stay in the Easter Holidays.'

'I can see that!' Una snapped. 'I suppose it suits him to admit he's got a daughter now that she's grown up. What about all those years you and me struggled on our own? Did he want his beloved *only blood relative* to go and visit him then? Like hell he did! Dead scared he might have to do something for you!'

'He never forgot to send us the money though, did he?'

'He did no more than he had to,' Una said bitterly. 'He could easily have afforded to send a bit more with what he was earning. Anyway, I'd have had him in court so fast his feet wouldn't have touched the ground if he'd stopped my maintenance. He knew that all right. That'd have looked bloody good in *The Stage*, wouldn't it?'

Rosalind's heart sank. Clearly Una would see her acceptance of her father's invitation as blatant betrayal. She got up and began to clear the table. Una lit a cigarette, watching her daughter through narrow eyes.

'You want to go, don't you?' she challenged.

'No.'

'Don't lie to me. You're disappointed because you think I don't want you to.'

Rosalind turned and looked at her. 'Well, you don't, do you?'

Una shrugged exaggeratedly. 'Why should I care? Go if you want to. Actually I was planning to take a week of my holiday at Easter. It was going to be a surprise. I thought we could go off somewhere and have a little holiday. But if you'd rather spend it with your father and his *tart* . . .'

'It's all right. I never intended to go anyway.'

'No? Then why did you show me the letter?'

'I thought you'd want to see it. I've never kept secrets from you, have I?'

Una looked away. 'No, you haven't. You've been a good girl; a better daughter than I deserve.' She ground out her cigarette and looked at Rosalind, her dark eyes brimming with the sudden tears that were so typical of her. 'It's just that I couldn't bear the thought of losing you, Rossie. That's really what upset me. Ben's all right. He's successful and he's got *her*. You're all I've got. I don't know what I'd do if I lost you now.' Reaching out for her daughter, she hugged her close.

Rosalind gently disentangled herself from her mother's suffocating embrace. 'Don't be silly, Mum. Even if I did go and visit Dad, you know I'd come back.'

'But you won't go, pet, will you? We'll book up somewhere nice for the holiday. I've got a bit of money saved. We'll go to Southend if you like, or Hastings. You've always liked the seaside. We can celebrate my new job. Just the two of us.'

'Yes, Mum,' Rosalind said resignedly. 'That'd be lovely.'

She didn't know what to do about her father's letter. For the two weeks that followed it burned a hole in her pocket and tortured her conscience. Again and again she got it out and read it, knowing she must reply and wondering what excuse she could make. Una's comments had made her curious. What lay behind the sudden invitation? Just why did he want her to visit when he had made so little attempt to keep up their relationship before? Finally, knowing that she could put off writing her letter of refusal no longer, she made up her mind to do it that very evening as soon as she had finished her homework. But before she had the chance to begin something happened to decide the matter once and for all.

Una was always unpredictable. Her reactions were never what one expected and Rosalind was used to her erratic changes of mood. But when she arrived home that evening and announced that she had decided that Rosalind should accept her father's invitation, she took her daughter completely off guard.

'But – I thought you didn't want me to go?'

Una turned to look into the mirror over the fireplace, unable to meet her daughter's candid brown eyes. 'I know, darling, and it's true, I didn't. Not at first.' She fiddled with her hair, lifting it away from her neck and viewing herself sideways. 'I know what I said, but I've been thinking. You're not a child any longer. You're a young woman now, and I know I can trust you. Maybe I'm being mean to both of you. After all, Ben is still your father, whatever he's done to me.'

A thought struck Rosalind. Suppose her father were ill, as Cathy Oldham's father had been ill? Perhaps there was some special reason for his wanting to see her; one that perhaps her mother knew about. Her manner certainly suggested that she wasn't being completely honest about this sudden change of heart.

'Well, if you really don't mind, I would quite like to go,' she said.

'Then you go, darling.' Una turned to her with a smile. 'Write him a nice letter straight away.'

'And you really don't mind – about our holiday and everything – about being alone for Easter?'

'Not a bit,' Una assured her brightly. 'I shall spring clean the flat or something. I'll find plenty to occupy me, don't you worry about me.'

Ben replied by return, saying how delighted he was to receive his daughter's acceptance and how much he was looking forward to seeing her. Arrangements were made that she should travel to Northampton by train on Good Friday where he would meet her with the car.

When she first stepped down from the train and looked around her she thought he wasn't there. Peering into the faces of the milling strangers on the platform she saw no one

51

whom she could recognise. Then she saw the man standing close to the ticket barrier looking anxiously around him and her heart contracted sharply. She had been expecting him to look the same as when she last saw him, but this man looked so much older. She reminded herself that it had been several years – six in fact – since they had last met. Her mother was now thirty-seven and she knew that Ben was six years older. That made him forty-three. He had put on weight. And his hair, once thick and wavy, was thinner and touched with grey. To Rosalind's dismay he looked old and she felt a lump gather in her throat.

As she stood watching he turned his head and saw her. For a moment he hesitated. He took a step towards her, then another. Then he was almost running. She put down her case and held out her arms.

'Dad.'

Unable to speak, he drew her to him and hugged her for a moment, then he held her at arm's length. As his eyes searched her face the familiar smile lit his eyes and to her relief he looked young again; more like the father she remembered.

'You're so grown up,' he said, shaking his head. 'I can hardly believe it. My little Rosalind. I'd begun to think you wouldn't come until I got your letter. Oh, it's so *good* to see you, baby.' He drew her arm through his and lifted her case. 'Come on, the car's waiting and Freda's got the tea on at home. She can't wait to meet you, but she wouldn't come to the station – said it was our private moment; yours and mine. She's very sensitive, Freda. I know you're going to like her.'

Sherwood Magna was enchanting. Rosalind had never seen a real village before. She thought they only existed in the pages of picture books, but this one was everything she had ever dreamed of. It had a village green with a duck pond, a thatched pub and an ancient church complete with tall elm trees. As well as an abundance of pretty cottages there was a manor house and a Georgian vicarage standing slightly aloof on the edge of the village. Rosalind turned to her father as they drove through.

'Where is your cottage?' she asked excitedly.

'Right here.' Ben turned in through an open white gate and along a short gravelled drive. As the cottage came into view Rosalind gasped with delight. Built of honey-coloured stone, it was small and square, had latticed windows and a thatched roof through which protruded a stout red brick chimney. Surrounding it was half an acre of garden consisting mainly of old apple trees, frothy with pink and white blossom. Under them, growing among the grass, was a wild profusion of bluebells and daffodils.

'Oh – it's *lovely*!' Rosalind breathed.

Ben brought the car to a halt and switched off the ignition. 'It's not so bad, is it?' he said proudly. 'When we first saw it it was almost derelict and there's still a lot to be done. We want to build a new kitchen on at the back, but we got a grant towards installing the bathroom and having the mains water and electricity laid on. When we found the cottage the only water came from a well out at the back.'

'A well? I didn't know there were any left. Can I see it? Is it still there?'

Ben laughed as he got out of the car. 'It certainly is. I wanted to have it filled in but Freda wouldn't hear of it. She's planning to make some kind of feature of it.' He opened the boot and swung her case out. 'Come on then. Come and see the inside of the place and meet Freda.'

The front door was painted white and Ben swung it open and stood back for Rosalind to enter. He had to bend his own head to pass under the low lintel as he followed her into the dim, stone-flagged hallway. To their left an open door gave on to a square living kitchen that ran from front to back of the cottage with a window at either end. Rosalind could see an Aga standing in a tiled recess and a dresser, its shelves edged with red and white gingham frills.

The floor was of red quarry tiles and in the centre of the room a table was already laid for tea with a gingham cloth and willow-patterned china. The back door was open and through it Rosalind glimpsed a paved yard and the well that her father had told her about.

Ben looked around. 'Well, this is it. Freda must be around somewhere . . .'

As he spoke a woman appeared in the open doorway. At once Rosalind was struck by her youth. Then she remembered that Freda was still only twenty-six, less than ten years her senior. Standing there framed in the doorway, the sunlight turned her fair hair to spun gold. She was slender, with the kind of figure Una had once had but now had to struggle to retain. She smiled and took a tentative step towards them.

'So this is Rosalind,' she said, holding out her hands. 'I've wanted to meet Ben's daughter for so long. This is a special occasion.'

Rosalind took the hands held out to her and felt her own squeezed warmly. 'How do you do?' she said shyly.

Freda smiled, her blue eyes sparkling. 'I'm fine. And I can't tell you how much your father and I have looked forward to having you to stay. I'll show you your room. I'm sure you must want to freshen up. Then we'll have tea, it's all ready.'

She slipped an arm around Rosalind's shoulders and guided her back into the hallway and up the narrow staircase. 'We've only got two bedrooms so it was easy to decide where to put you,' she joked. 'We had to turn the third into a bathroom. Before that there was just a loo out in the yard.' She giggled. 'Not very cosy in the middle of winter.'

The room was tiny. The walls were painted white and the ceiling sloped. On the bed was a rose-patterned bedspread that matched the curtains. Rosalind looked out of the tiny dormer window into the garden below with its tumble of apple blossom, daffodils and bluebells. Turning to Freda, she said: 'It's lovely. The whole place is lovely. Thank you for asking me.'

'Not at all. I only wish you could have come the other times we asked you.' She was busy turning down the bed to reveal frilled pillow slips. 'Ben was so disappointed. He's worried a lot about you, you know. He felt you were growing up without knowing him.' She turned with a smile. 'You're very like him. Well, I'll leave you to unpack. Come down when you're ready. I'll put the kettle on.'

When she'd gone Rosalind sat on the bed. What had Freda meant about the other times they had asked her? She knew nothing about them. Had her father written before – telephoned perhaps? Had Una turned down the invitations on her behalf without telling her? Slowly and thoughtfully she began to unpack and put away her things. Somehow, without betraying her mother, she must find out.

The week went by all too quickly. The village and the cottage were a delight to Rosalind. Freda and she got along well right from the start, and getting to know her father again was much easier than she had thought. The weather was fine, warmer than normal for the time of year. They had picnics and drives out into the beautiful undulating countryside, fresh and green with burgeoning spring.

One evening Ben and Freda treated Rosalind to a première of the songs they'd been rehearsing for their latest repertoire. She sat enthralled in the pretty drawing room of the cottage as Ben played the little upright piano and the two of them sang. From the first it was clear to her that Freda's lovely bell-like soprano voice was better than Una's had ever been. It blended beautifully with Ben's melodious tenor. One of their new songs was particularly moving. Rosalind hadn't heard it before. It was from the new musical version of *Oliver Twist* and was called, *As Long As He Needs Me*. Something in the way Freda looked – the depth of emotion she put into the song's lyrics – seemed to

Rosalind to encapsulate her feelings for her father. Later, that night as she lay in bed, she reflected that, unpalatable as the fact might be to Una, it was undoubtedly Freda who was responsible for Ben's leap to success.

It was on her last day but one that Ben had a telephone call from his agent and had to go up to London. After they'd waved him off together at the gate Freda turned to Rosalind.

'Well, we've got the day to ourselves. What shall we do with it?'

Rosalind shrugged. 'I don't mind. We don't have to do anything. I just like being here.'

'Do you? Do you really?' Freda blushed with pleasure as she looked at her. 'Ben worried so much about whether you'd like it here – whether you'd like *us*. He thought you might be bored.'

Rosalind laughed. 'Bored? In a place like this. After Burnt Oak it's like a little corner of heaven.'

Linking her arm through Rosalind's Freda began to walk back to the cottage. 'He felt he didn't really know you, you see – the grown-up you, I mean. He had all sorts of notions about how you might have changed. It was almost like inviting a stranger. He was so apprehensive; nervous as a kitten on the day you arrived.'

'Nervous – at meeting me?' Rosalind guessed that what he had been afraid of was that she might have allowed Una to poison her mind against him. She looked at Freda. 'On the day I first came you said something about the other times he'd invited me?'

'That's right. We only had the flat in town then, of course, but we'd both have liked you to come. Ben was so pleased that you'd been able to get a scholarship to St Margaret's at a reduced fee and he wanted so much to keep track of your progress.'

Rosalind frowned. 'No. You've got it wrong. I got into St Margaret's free – on a scholarship.'

56

'Of course. How silly of me.' Freda turned away quickly but not before Rosalind had seen her flushed cheeks. Clearly there was more to all this than she realised and she was determined to get to the bottom of it.

'Tell me,' she demanded. 'Tell me the truth. I didn't get in for nothing, did I? Dad pays.'

They were inside the cottage now and Freda sat down at the kitchen table, her face troubled. 'Oh, dear. I've put my foot in it. I shouldn't have said anything. Forget it. Ben would be so cross if he knew.'

'I won't say anything,' Rosalind promised. 'Just tell me. I have a right to know.'

Freda sighed unhappily. 'Your mother wrote. It seems you passed the entrance exam all right, but when they knew Una had lapsed – that you hadn't actually been brought up in the Catholic faith – they weren't so sure. In the end, when your mother persisted, they agreed to a compromise and offered you a place at a reduced fee.'

'And Mum wrote to Dad and asked him to pay?'

Freda nodded. 'Oh, he was happy to do it, believe me. More than happy. He felt it was the least he could do for you. And it was your mother who stuck to her guns and insisted on a place for you.' She paused. 'All the same, Ben would have liked to see you more.'

'And she wouldn't let me come?'

'She thought it would unsettle you. She pointed out that you'd suffered enough over the break-up. And of course we were never in the same place for more than a few days at a time.' She reached out to take Rosalind's hand. 'Look, I know how you feel, believe me, I do. My parents were divorced too. They never stopped arguing, even after they split up, and most of their rows were about me. I know how guilty and wretched it makes you feel, but you shouldn't. It's not your fault, Rossie. Please try to remember that.'

Rosalind swallowed hard. Freda was trying hard to be fair, to make excuses, but they both knew that keeping her

57

from her father had been Una's way of paying him back for taking a new and younger partner, and for being a success. 'Yes, I suppose all they both want really is what is best for me,' she said. 'Thank you for telling me.'

'It's between ourselves, mind?' Freda said anxiously.

Rosalind frowned. 'Of course. I promise. After all, I asked you to tell me.' She longed to go away by herself, creep upstairs to the privacy of her room to think it all through; to try to justify her mother's cruel deception. But Freda was changing the subject, obviously anxious to lighten the mood.

'Right. Now, have you ever thought of trying your hair in a different style?' she said brightly. 'And what about wearing something a little more frivolous – maybe a bright colour? Red would suit you. Let's go upstairs and see what we can find for you.'

When Ben came back that evening he looked in through the kitchen window and saw the two of them busy preparing supper; laughing together over the stove as relaxed and friendly as sisters or school friends. He could see that Freda had been doing Rosalind's hair. She'd washed and set it so that it fell in soft curls, framing her small face. She wore a little make-up too, and a red blouse that he recognised as one of Freda's. It warmed his heart to see them getting along so well. He'd had so many fears and misgivings about this visit; been so afraid that his daughter might be lost to him for ever.

It had been a good day. He'd just signed a new recording contract and heard that there was a strong possibility of a spot for them on a television Christmas Special to begin filming in the autumn. He had stopped off on his way home to buy a bottle of champagne with which to celebrate. He couldn't wait to see Freda's face light up when he told her. What a wonderful week it had been. Golden spring days in their new home; the prospect of well-paid work; but perhaps best of all, having his daughter back after the long parting.

On the day that Rosalind travelled back to London the weather broke. Ben drove her to the station and stood with her on the dripping platform as they waited for the train.

'Thank you for giving me such a marvellous time,' Rosalind said. 'I've enjoyed it all so much.'

'I'm glad. It's been wonderful having you with us.' Ben smiled down at her. 'Now that you've been once, I hope you'll make regular visits to the cottage.'

'I'd love to.' She looked up at him. 'Dad – are you and Freda going to get married?'

He smiled. 'I was wondering when you were going to ask me that.' He cocked an eyebrow at her. 'Did you ask her?'

She shook her head. 'No, I didn't like to. But I can see how much she loves you.'

Ben sighed. 'I love her too. And I know it's what she'd like, but I feel it isn't fair. She's so much younger than me, Rossie. All of seventeen years. I'm old enough to be her father. It's too big a gap.' He laughed. 'Do you really think a lovely girl like Freda deserves to be tied to an old man? It wouldn't be fair.'

'But you're not an old man. And if you love each other, surely . . .?'

Ben bent to kiss his daughter's forehead. 'It's not quite as simple as that, baby, as you'll find out for yourself one day. Sometimes love can be a selfish thing. And it's hardly ever enough on its own. Ask your mother,' he added with a wry smile. 'Sometimes there are . . .' The end of his sentence was drowned by the crackling of the public address system as the station announcer began to speak.

Rosalind wondered fleetingly if her father still had a weakness for other women; if that was why he didn't want to marry again. But she was sure he was wrong about

Freda. She wouldn't care about the age difference. She loved him unreservedly; anyone could see that. Rosalind hated the thought of sweet, gentle Freda being hurt or feeling rejected. She hadn't turned out to be at all like Una had led her to believe. She wasn't a tart at all.

The London train pulled in alongside the platform and Ben handed her case up to her and slammed the door securely.

'Bye-bye, baby. Write to us if you have a minute off from all that studying.'

Rosalind leaned as far out of the window as she dared. 'Dad,' she said urgently as the train began to move. 'Dad . . .' She reached for his hand and he took it, walking down the platform with the train. 'Take care of Freda.'

He laughed. 'I will.'

'And, Dad – I never thanked you.'

'Of course you did.'

'No. I mean for the – for my . . .' The train was beginning to gather speed now and Ben was forced to let go of her hand. '*For my school fees,*' she called. 'It was good of you to pay them. It's a nice school. I – I love it there.' The distance between them was lengthening, but she could still see his face clearly. His eyes were slightly puzzled as he looked at her, his hand half raised.

'I'll do well, Dad,' she called, her throat thick with tears. 'I'll work hard and make you glad. I promise.'

When she arrived home the flat was empty. She looked for a note but there was none. Una must have slipped out to the shop for something. Looking round she saw that her mother hadn't fulfilled her promise to spring clean the flat. There was dust everywhere and unwashed dishes in the kitchen. She went to her room and began to unpack, putting her things carefully away in the wardrobe and drawers. She was still wearing the red blouse that Freda had given her. It fitted perfectly and the colour made her feel light-hearted. Freda had shown her how to put the rollers in to her hair too, to give its straightness a lift. And as she was helping her to pack she'd popped the coral lipstick Rosalind liked into a corner of her case.

'I've never used it. It isn't really my colour,' she said. 'But it suits you beautifully so you might as well have it.'

Rosalind found it at the bottom of the case and put some on, peering into the dressing-table mirror as she pressed her lips together. It did make a difference. So did the blouse and the hair. They made her feel quite a different person. Perhaps she wasn't quite so desperately plain after all. Freda had told her she had nice eyes and that maybe next time they needed testing she could ask the optician about trying the new contact lenses. It would be lovely not to have to wear the glasses any more. She heard the sound of a key in the door and went out to meet her mother.

Una stood with her back to her in the small hallway, taking her key out of the lock. She wore her best suit and her highest heels with sheer black stockings, and there was a suitcase on the floor beside her. When she turned and saw Rosalind she gave a small cry of alarm.

'*Oh!*' She clutched at her throat with one gloved hand. 'Oh, my God, you scared the living daylights out of me. I wasn't expecting you home till later this evening.'

Rosalind was looking at the case. 'You've been away after all then?'

Una was instantly defensive. 'Yes. Anything wrong with that?'

'No, of course not. I just thought you said . . .'

'What on earth have you done to yourself?' Una interrupted, peering at her with narrowed eyes. 'Where did you get that awful blouse and what *do* you think your hair looks like?'

Rosalind put a hand up to her hair uncertainly. 'I set it – put some rollers in. Freda showed me how, and she gave me the blouse. She said the colour suited me.'

Una gave a disapproving grunt as she lifted her suitcase and headed for her bedroom. 'Huh! I might have known *she'd* had a hand in it. You look an absolute fright. The woman obviously has no taste at all.' She dumped her case on the bed and turned to look at Rosalind standing in the doorway. 'Well, don't just stand there. Come and give me a hand to unpack. Or better still, go and put the kettle on, I'm gasping for a cup of tea.'

Ten minutes later Una appeared in the kitchen doorway in her dressing gown and slippers.

'Tea's made,' Rosalind said. 'There aren't any biscuits though.'

Una sat down at the table. 'I know. I haven't had time to go shopping.' She glanced at her watch. 'The shops will still be open. When you've had your tea you'd better pop down to the corner and get a few things.'

Rosalind's heart sank. 'All right.'

'Well, don't sound so enthusiastic about it! I expect you've been spoiled rotten down in Little Piddling or whatever it's called, but you're home now. Time to come down to earth again.' She looked at her daughter speculatively. 'I take it you had a good time?'

'Yes, thanks.'

Una sipped her tea. 'Well – aren't you going to ask me if I did then?'

'I – thought you'd tell me if you wanted me to know.'

Una looked at her sharply. 'What's that supposed to mean? Being sarky, are we?' Before Rosalind had time to reply she hurried on: 'Well, as it happens I *did* have a good time. I stayed in a hotel in the West End and saw the latest shows. I had some wonderful meals too. We ate at the Savoy Grill on Friday, and last night . . .'

'We?' Rosalind looked at her mother enquiringly. 'Who did you go with?'

'I was coming to that.' Una put down her cup. 'I've been seeing Don – Mr Blake – ever since I started my new job,'

62

she said. 'I never said anything before because he's been in the throes of divorce, poor love. His wife is a vindictive bitch by all accounts, so we've had to be very discreet. It's all over now though and this week has been a real tonic for Don after what he's been through. And for me too, of course.'

'I see.'

Una looked at her daughter sharply. 'No, you don't! It wasn't a dirty weekend or anything like that. Don has asked me to marry him.' She sat back, smiling with satisfaction. 'And you might as well know that I've said yes.'

Rosalind was already wondering just how much her mother's forthcoming marriage would change their lives. 'Does he – does he know about me?' she asked.

'My God!' Una raised to the ceiling. 'If that isn't typical. No – *Congratulations, Mum.* No – *I hope you'll be happy.* Just, *What's going to happen to me?*' She lit a cigarette and blew the smoke explosively at the ceiling. 'You're your father's daughter all right.'

'Of course I'm glad for you if it's what you want,' Rosalind said painfully. 'But I do need to know where I stand too.'

'You *stand* wherever you want to. Of course Don knows about you. How could I keep you from him? He's quite looking forward to meeting you if you want to know. He's perfectly happy for you to live with us when we're married.' She tapped ash thoughtfully into her saucer. 'Or perhaps after this week you'd prefer to go and live with your father?'

Rosalind coloured. 'I haven't been asked,' she said quietly.

Una laughed. 'No? And it's my guess that you won't be, so you'd better make the best of what's on offer, hadn't you?' She stubbed out her half-smoked cigarette and reached across the table to give Rosalind's shoulder a push. 'Oh, for God's sake, stop looking like a wet weekend and cheer up! Don's got a good job and plenty of money. We'll be living like lords when he and I get hitched. You'll be quids in.'

Rosalind washed up the cups while her mother went off to have a bath. The flat was no palace, but she hated the thought of moving into a new home with a man she'd never met. What was he like, this Don Blake? And would he really take kindly to sharing a house with her? She thought fondly of the cottage and dreamed of living there. But it was only a weekend home – not even that during the summer when 'Ben and Benita' would be sharing top billing in Brighton. She couldn't see any way she could live with them while she was still at school, even if they wanted her to. She dried the cups and put them away carefully. It boiled down to the same old thing really. Everyone else had their own lives. She was in the way again. An embarrassing liability.

Chapter Three

As the last notes of the concerto died and the audience
broke into enthusiastic applause, Gerald rose to his feet
with relief. His palms were sticky and his head was buzzing
with tension. As Carl Kramer led him forward to take his
ovation Gerald thought he caught a fleeting look of concern
in the conductor's eyes. Those mishandled phrases in the
slow movement, the faltering fingering. He had recovered
in seconds. It would have taken a seasoned musician to
spot them. But Carl Kramer *was* a seasoned musician. One
of the finest conductors in the world. They had worked
together many times and they respected each other. Carl
would certainly have noticed. But it was clear from the
audience's reaction that for them Gerald's performance
had been as brilliant and faultless as ever. He took a final
bow and walked off the platform.

In his dressing room he removed his tail coat and white
tie and slipped into his comfortable dressing gown, then he
poured himself a large Scotch: the treat he always allowed
himself after the performance – never before. Sitting down
at the dressing table he regarded himself critically in the
mirror. The signs of fatigue were there in the lines of
tiredness and the dark smudges around the eyes, the slight
hollowing beneath the cheekbones. But surely it was only
natural? The tour had been the longest he had ever made,
the schedule heavy and exhausting. He flexed his fingers,
trying to ignore the painful stiffness in the joints. What was
worse than the stiffness was their sudden and unpredictable
refusal to obey his commands; those inexplicable memory
lapses. Works he had performed a hundred times would

be momentarily wiped out as though he had never played them before, often frighteningly, like tonight, in the middle of a performance. But surely even that was understandable at the end of such a punishing schedule? He tried to assure himself. It could all be put down to tension – nervous exhaustion – though he was forced to admit that he had never experienced it before.

As he sipped his whisky and felt the warmth seeping through his veins and relaxing him, he heard the first bars of the Beethoven symphony through the dressing room intercom. The concert was continuing. Music and the show, like life, went on. However talented, however acclaimed and celebrated a concert artist might be, there was always a new someone, more talented, more brilliant than ever before, waiting to thrill and inspire the fickle and voracious fans. Had his time come already at the age of forty-one? Was his career tottering on the edge of oblivion just when he should be in his prime?

He swallowed the last of his whisky and hurriedly changed into his outdoor clothes. The fans wouldn't gather until after the concert was over. He would get back to his hotel and have an early night. He didn't feel like seeing anyone. If Carl wanted an explanation then he should have one. He was entitled to that. But he must first think it out – make it a good and a plausible one. It wouldn't do to have rumours starting. And at the moment he didn't feel up to it. His mind didn't seem to be functioning properly.

Leaving his hire car in the car park he took a taxi back to the hotel. He couldn't face the mad jostle of the New York streets tonight. Once in his room he rang down to room service for sandwiches and coffee. He ate, then undressed and showered. He was just about to get into bed when there was a soft knock on the door. With a sigh he drew on his dressing gown and went to open it. Kay Goolden stood on the threshold. She wore a pastel mink jacket over her black Givenchy evening gown and the expression on

66

her exquisitely made-up face was a mixture of anxiety and annoyance.

'So *here* you are! I went round to your dressing room after the concert and you'd gone. I've been worried sick.'

His heart sank as he turned back into the room, leaving her to follow. 'I'm sorry. I wasn't feeling too good. I thought an early night would . . .'

'But you didn't even leave me a message,' she interrupted indignantly. 'Surely you hadn't forgotten that we were having dinner together?'

Gerald sat down on the bed. He had forgotten. The worry over the mess he had made of the slow movement had rattled and upset him. The last thing he wanted at this moment was Kay whining about a forgotten dinner date.

Kay Goolden worked in the PR department of his recording company. They'd met when she was doing the publicity for his last but one album and they'd been lovers for the past year. Kay was good at her job, but he'd wished more than once since the tour began that he had never suggested her accompanying him. She could be protective to the point of claustrophobia. Sometimes she treated him like a retarded five year old, leaping in to speak for him as though he was incapable of speaking or thinking for himself.

He rubbed a hand across his brow. 'I'm sorry, Kay. I told you, I wasn't feeling too good.'

'What is it?' She crossed the room and placed a hand on his forehead. 'A touch of flu maybe. Shall I get you some Paracetamol?'

'No, thanks.'

'It's no trouble. I've got some in my room. Maybe I'd better move in here with you tonight, then I can keep an eye on you.' She crossed the room to the telephone. 'I'll ring down to room service and get them to . . .'

'Leave it!' He felt the familiar irritation twang his nerves.

'For God's sake, Kay, I told you, I'm all right. Just tired, that's all.'

'All right, there's no need to snap my head off.' She slipped off her jacket and moved closer to him, slipping her arms around his waist and rubbing herself against him provocatively. 'I think I know what you need to relax you,' she said softly.

He pushed her away. 'No, you don't. Not this time.'

Kay stiffened, her seductive smile changing to a pout of resentment. 'What's the matter, Gerry? You can tell me. Didn't the concert go as well as you wanted it to?'

He looked at her intently. 'What do you mean by that? Who's been talking to you?'

'No one.' She backed away from him. 'For heaven's sake, Gerry, why are you so damned touchy? What on earth is the matter with you?'

'I told you, I'm tired. It's the tour. Thank God there's only one more week to go.'

'It's not just that. You haven't been yourself since we left London. Are you tired of me – is that it?'

He sighed. 'Look, Kay, I don't need this just now. Leave me to get a decent night's rest, will you? I'll be fine in the morning.'

Her face darkened. 'You've found someone else, haven't you? It's so obvious. There was a time when you couldn't get enough of me, but ever since we came on this tour you've showed a marked lack of interest to say the least.'

'There's no one else, Kay. Why must you always assume that what ever is wrong with me is down to you?'

'What else am I supposed to think? It's not very flattering, lying in bed next to someone who turns his back on you night after night. I'm not so thick that I can't take a hint, you know. I don't have to be hit over the head with a sledge hammer!'

Gerald winced. Her voice was like a steel saw, grinding into his already aching head. 'For Christ's sake, Kay, surely you of all people can understand that the tension of two concerts a day for weeks on end . . .'

She gave an explosive little snort. '*Tension!* There was a time when all that adrenalin made you as randy as hell. Now you're saying it just claps you out, are you? Well, I don't believe you, Gerry. I wouldn't put it past you to be two-timing me with one of those giggling little groupies who hang around after you. But then I suppose at your age flattery and reassurance are pretty important, especially when your playing is on the skids!'

'What the hell do you mean?' His head was pounding as he reached out to grab her wrist.

'Let go of me!' She shook him off angrily. 'Who the hell do you think you are?' Tears of humiliation stood in her eyes as she faced him. 'I've had about enough of your temper tantrums on this trip, Gerry. You've really shown yourself in your true colours. I've worked damned hard ever since we met to build a good image for you and to shield you from the public. If this is all the thanks I get I might as well let your precious fans find out what you're really like!' She flounced to the door. 'Tonight is the last straw as far as I'm concerned. I'll be taking the first plane home in the morning. If you want another publicist you'd better get on to Zenith and get them to send you someone!'

He groaned as the door slammed behind her. A scene with Kay was the last thing he needed tonight. But truth to tell, all he really felt about her leaving was relief. Women could be so demanding. They wanted all of you. At first it was enough just to be seen with a celebrity – to bask in the reflected glory. Then they wanted more of your time – or your money, or both. Finally they wanted to own you, body and soul. To eat you up and swallow you whole. He'd first discovered this fact when he'd married Sara at twenty. She was a fellow music student and together they planned to take Europe by storm with their talent. The marriage had lasted just eighteen months. When it failed Sara had blamed him for wrecking her career; accusing him of doing it deliberately because she had more talent than he had. Was there, anywhere in the world, he asked himself, an undemanding woman capable of thinking of someone other than herself?

Remembering Sara's wild accusations reminded him of Kay's remark about letting the fans see him as he really was. Was it a veiled threat? Would she really be vindictive enough to rat on him to the press? He decided not. It would cost her her job with Zenith Records and she'd never let that happen. Then he recalled something else she'd said; something even more disturbing. *Especially when your playing is on the skids*. Kay was hardly a music buff. If she'd noticed . . . His heart sank. It was even worse than he'd thought.

Gerald woke feeling much better. He had been worrying for nothing, he told himself. Last night's little lapse was due to nothing worse than fatigue. As for Kay – she had lashed out wildly, knowing that any remark about his playing would hurt. All the same, he hoped she'd meant it when she said she was catching the first plane home. She'd been getting far too possessive for comfort lately.

He got up and showered, planning the day ahead. The sooner he talked to Carl, the better, he decided. He was dressed and looking up the conductor's number when the telephone rang. It was Reception. Mr Kramer was here to see him. Could they send him up?

Carl Kramer was a handsome man in his late-fifties. His Jewish parents had arrived in America from Poland at the turn of the century and proceeded to bring up their large family. Parents and children were all musical and Carl had been involved with music since childhood. Since the end of the war he had risen to the heights, first as a concert violinist, then as conductor. During his career Carl had seen many concert soloists come and go. He and Gerald Cavelle had worked together on many occasions and he liked and respected the pianist enough to be concerned about him.

Gerald went out to the lift to greet the maestro with a feeling of apprehension. For Carl to be coming to him was ominous to say the least. But as the lift doors opened he put on his brightest smile and held out his hands in welcome.

'Carl! This is an unexpected pleasure. I hope you'll join me for breakfast.'

'Thank you, but I've already breakfasted.'

Almost as tall as Gerald, the conductor had a shock of silver hair and piercing eyes that were so dark as to appear almost black. Gerald met their searching look now with some trepidation.

'Coffee then? You'll have some coffee?'

The conductor smiled and bowed his head. 'That would be very pleasant.'

In the suite Carl took the seat Gerald offered him at the breakfast table, which had been laid out on the covered balcony that overlooked Manhattan. He watched as Gerald poured coffee, noticing the slight tremor of his hand as he passed him the cup.

'You must be wondering why I am here,' he said. 'I went to your dressing room after the concert last night and found you'd left.'

Gerald shook his head. 'As a matter of fact I was about to ring you – to apologise for last night.'

'There is no need. You covered the mishap extremely well. I doubt whether the audience was even aware that anything was amiss. I am concerned however – for you, my friend. I think you are not yourself. Are you ill?'

'No!' Gerald took a deep draught of his coffee. 'At least I don't think so. I don't really know. I put it down to tiredness. I certainly feel much better this morning.'

'I'm glad, but – forgive me, Gerald – there have been other occasions during this tour.'

71

He looked at the conductor sharply. 'You've heard . . . someone has said . . .?'

Carl lifted his shoulders. 'These things soon get around. Bad news travels fast, as they say.' He put down his cup and leaned towards Gerald. 'I'm here this morning to give you some advice as a friend and fellow musician, Gerald. Cancel the rest of your tour. There can't be many more concerts to go. See a doctor. Treat yourself to a good rest.'

Gerald's heartbeat quickened. 'What are you saying, Carl? You think I'm – finished?'

'No, *no*! It could be nothing worse than tiredness, as you say. But I have to be frank with you; the way you are playing at the moment is doing nothing for your reputation.' He reached across the table to touch Gerald's sleeve. 'Check on your health, my friend. Eliminate the worst possibilities and deal with what is left. It could be that your concentration is suffering through overwork and that all you need is a prolonged holiday.'

Gerald swallowed hard. Inside he felt the cold hand of fear clutch at his guts. He'd been fooling himself into believing that it was all in his mind. Now he knew otherwise. Others had noticed. It was true. He had a problem. A real problem. One that he was going to have to meet and cope with – alone. He forced himself to smile.

'Maybe I'll do as you say, Carl. Though I don't know about cancelling the rest of the tour. There'd be one hell of a stink if I cried off now. We're due to fly to Boston the day after tomorrow and it's a heavy programme. Twelve concerts during next week.'

'Then see a doctor today,' Carl advised. 'Face it, Gerald. You're not up to one more concert. Let alone twelve. If you go ahead you'll risk damaging your career, perhaps permanently. Cancel. They can hardly argue with a doctor's opinion.' He pulled out one of his cards and began to write on the back. 'This is the name of my own physician. He's

72

the best there is. Tell him I sent you and he'll fit you in this morning.'

Gerald tried to control the trembling of his fingers as he took the card. 'You make it sound – so serious,' he said with a shaky laugh.

'It is,' Carl said candidly. 'What could be more serious than your health, Gerald? Especially when it is threatening to affect your career? Please, take my advice and see him.'

On his way out of the hotel Gerald enquired about Kay at the desk and learned that she had checked out at nine-thirty that morning – booked herself on the eleven-thirty flight for London. He looked at his watch. She'd be boarding about now. He'd been glad when she'd said their affair was over, but now he wasn't so sure. It might have been comforting to have had someone along with him when he saw this Doctor Brewster. As he crossed the hall he took out his dark glasses and put them on, then he asked the doorman to call him a cab.

Gerald came out of the Curie Medical Building and stood for a moment on the pavement watching the people and traffic rush by. People – scores of them – all going their own way, their minds intent on their own worries. Odd, but he'd never given them a thought before. Until now people had been divided into two groups. Music lovers and others. If they didn't go to his concerts, if they weren't fans, they simply didn't exist. Now, in his stunned state, he suddenly saw that to some extent they all had something in common. They were all basically insecure when it came to their own mortality; all afraid, not only of death but of facing the future alone.

Doctor Brewster had been chillingly positive in his diagnosis, but he had advised Gerald to seek a second opinion for his own peace of mind.

'When you get back to London you should see your own

doctor,' he had advised. 'There are tests you could undergo and it would be wise to do so, so as to be perfectly sure, you understand?'

'And the treatment?' Gerald had asked. 'How long does it take to be cured? I'm a concert pianist. I need to be able to work.'

His heart was leaden as he remembered the look on the doctor's face and the way he had shaken his head.

'I have to be perfectly frank with you, Mr Cavelle. Parkinson's Disease is manageable. Nowadays, thanks to research it can be controlled. As for a cure, that is something that so far has eluded medical science.' He looked thoughtful. 'I have a colleague who is working on a research project at Edinburgh University. I'm sure he would be interested in your case. I'll write to him if you like.'

'Are you okay, sir? Can I get you a cab?' The doorman was used to seeing people come out of the Curie Building looking dazed and he prided himself on his sympathetic and helpful manner. He put a tentative hand under Gerald's elbow but he shrugged the man off impatiently.

'I'm quite all right, thank you. It's only a couple of blocks. I'll walk.'

I've got to get home, he thought. There has to be an answer. It couldn't be possible in 1961 that there was no known cure. Even this morning the papers were full of the latest space shot. The Russians had already put a man out there and now the Americans were planning to do it too. Why were they so bloody keen to get to other planets when there were people dying of incurable illnesses on this one? It was ridiculous. There must be a doctor somewhere with the answer. He'd pin all his hopes on this doctor in Edinburgh. Being a guinea pig was better than nothing! He'd ring his agent – tell him to call off the rest of the tour. Then he'd get the hotel receptionist to book him on the next flight to London.

Home. He pictured the flat, its spacious rooms echoing with emptiness. His piano standing silently in the window. Then the thought of that other piano, Dan Oldham's baby grand that he was storing for Cathy. He wondered whether she had been to play it during his absence and found himself hoping that she had. It was comforting to think of her there. Suddenly, and with startling clarity, he remembered her eyes, green as the springtime sea, and that extraordinary amber-gold hair. *Cathy*. He said the name to himself, remembering how sweetly she had clung to him that afternoon in the attic of that hideous little house in Edgware. 'I'm coming home, Cathy,' he said aloud, and somehow found solace in the thought that there was at least one person who would be happy to see him.

Chapter Four

The envelope was waiting beside Cathy's plate when she came down to breakfast. Three pairs of eyes watched her as she nervously slid her finger under the flap. She glanced at Johnny.

'I can't look,' she said, passing the envelope across the table. 'You open it.'

Johnny shook her head. 'Oh, no. I think you should see it first, love,' she said. 'Go on. Take a deep breath and look. We're all waiting.'

But still Cathy stared at the folded sheet of paper. 'Oh dear. I wish . . .' Suddenly the letter was snatched from her hand by Matthew whose long arm shot across the table without warning.

'Oh, for heaven's sake, give it here.' He unfolded the letter and scanned it quickly, then gave her a rueful look across the table. 'Oh, well,' he said with a sympathetic look. 'Better luck next time, eh?' He tossed the letter back to her and rose from the table to pull on his jacket. 'Time I was going, I suppose.'

Cathy snatched up the letter, her cheeks very pink, and read it hurriedly, then she too was on her feet, half crying, half laughing. 'Matthew Johnson – you absolute *pig*!' She punched him on the shoulder.

Old Mrs Bains clicked her tongue disapprovingly. 'Oh dear, oh dear. What a way to talk. Young people nowadays.' She wagged an admonishing finger at Cathy. 'You may have failed your exams, young lady, but there's no need to . . .'

'But I *haven't*,' Cathy said, swinging round, her eyes shining. 'Look.' She held out the letter. 'Two grade ones, three twos, a three and a four. And that was only RE so as I'm not planning to be a nun it isn't important.' She laughed delightedly. 'Oh, I can't wait to tell Gerald.'

Matthew grinned at her. 'Took a good shock to make you look though, didn't it, chicken?' He looked at his watch. 'Have to go or I'll miss the bus. I'll have my champagne and cake when I get home, okay?'

After he'd gone Cathy helped Johnny to clear the table and wash up, her head still spinning with euphoria.

'I want to leave school now that I've got my O's, Johnny,' she said. 'I don't think I could face another two years of slogging away.'

'Your father had his heart set on your going to university,' Johnny told her as she put away the dishes. 'I think he felt you were capable of it.'

'Fathers always think their daughters are cleverer than they really are,' Cathy said. 'I want to get a job and start earning my living. Then I can pay you for my keep out of my earnings. It isn't really right that Gerald should keep paying.'

'I don't think he is, yet. There must still be money left from the house,' Johnny reminded her. 'I don't think you need worry yet awhile.' She looked anxiously at the girl who was like a daughter to her. 'It's a mistake to rush into some dead end job just for the sake of leaving school, love,' she said kindly. 'I dare say everyone feels as you do at this stage. If you really don't want to go to university how about training for something at college?'

Cathy stood staring out of the kitchen window dreamily. 'I can't really think of anything I'd like to study,' she said. 'My music isn't good enough and I hate the thought of shorthand and typing, or anything else that means being stuck in some office all day. I had thought about nursing. I like looking after people.' She turned with a smile. 'And I really enjoy helping you in the house – cooking and sewing and making things nice.

77

You've taught me such a lot about that since I've been here.'

'What about domestic science then?' Johnny said triumphantly. 'You could take a course in that. And maybe when you're qualified you could teach it in some nice school. It'd certainly stand you in good stead for when you have a home of your own.'

Cathy took the letter out of her pocket and looked at it again. 'It says we have to go to school tomorrow afternoon,' she said. 'There's a meeting with the head and the careers mistress so that we can make up our minds what we're going to do next term.'

'Right, then you can get it all fixed up.' Johnny wiped her hands and took off her apron. 'I dare say they'll be able to give you a list of colleges. Would you like me to come along with you?'

Cathy shook her head. 'I'd better go alone. I'm going to have to get used to doing things for myself from now on, aren't I?'

Upstairs in her room she made her bed and then sat down to look at her letter again. The grades were better than she'd dared to hope for. But then she had worked hard. Now all she wanted was to have the pleasure of telling Gerald and seeing his face. He'd be home very soon now. The last postcard she'd had from him was of Times Square, New York. *Only one more week*, he'd written. And that was a fortnight ago. She would be hearing from him any day now.

Would he be surprised that she hadn't taken up his invitation to go to his flat? she wondered. There had been lots of times when she had wanted to. She still missed Dad. On some days it was so bad that she just wanted to be by herself. Johnny always knew when she felt like that and left her alone, but playing his piano – even just touching it – would have helped so much. One Saturday afternoon she had even taken the tube up to the West End and walked right up to the building. But it had looked so grand and so formidable that she had walked straight past. She hadn't had the nerve to go in and ask the caretaker for a key as Gerald had suggested.

She wondered how all her friends had fared in the exams. Carla had hardly done any revision at all. She'd been much keener on going to the pictures or dancing. Rosalind Blair would have done well though. She always did. She had known exactly what subjects to take because she had no doubts about her future career. It must be nice to have no doubts about what you really wanted to do, Cathy thought.

When she arrived at St Margaret's the following afternoon the hall was full of excited chatter as the girls exchanged news and exam results. To Cathy's surprise Carla had scraped through four of the five subjects she had taken and seemed not to mind at all having low grades.

'I've decided to go to teacher training college,' she announced.

Cathy stared at her incredulously. 'Is that really what you want?'

Carla pulled a face. 'Dad's idea. He reckons it's a safe, secure job. His alternative was the bank. Teaching's the lesser of two evils, I reckon, and you do get lovely long holidays.'

'But it means you'll have to stay on and take some A's.'

Carla shrugged. 'I suppose so. Still, who knows what might happen in the meantime?' she said. 'I might meet some handsome millionaire and get married.'

Miss Hanley, Cathy's form mistress, was doubtful about the domestic science idea. 'I think you should go away and give it some more thought, Catherine,' she said. 'I really feel that you're capable of something a little more academic. Domestic science is fine, but you have a good enquiring mind and I'm afraid DS wouldn't stretch you enough.'

'I did think about nursing,' Cathy said.

Miss Hanley smiled. 'Well, I think that might suit you better, but you couldn't begin training until you are eighteen. You don't want to hang around doing nothing for almost a year, do you? So why not stay on for your A levels?'

All the way home Cathy's mind was full of what Miss Hanley had said. So much so that she walked right past the car that stood at the gate without looking at it. It was only as she was letting herself in at the front door that she heard his voice and stopped dead in her tracks. *Gerald!* He was back – and *here*!

She stood in the hall uncertainly, suddenly overcome with shyness. It was eight whole months since she had seen him. Had she changed? she wondered. She peered into the hall mirror and saw two shining green eyes and the mass of fly-away auburn hair that would never stay in place. Why do I have to be so *ordinary*? she asked herself despairingly. Not only that but she had a spot coming on her chin. Carla wore make-up all the time now, even for school. Maybe Cathy should start using it more. Slipping silently up the stairs, she combed her hair and applied a dash of the pink lipstick Carla had persuaded her to buy when they were in Woolworth's last Saturday. Standing back she regarded herself. Better, she supposed. Hardly the height of sophistication, but better.

He stood up when she came into the room and her heart gave a dizzying little jerk when he smiled at her.

She affected surprise. 'Gerald! I didn't know you were back.'

'I got in some days ago, but I had a few things to clear up,' he told her. 'There's always such a lot to do when you've been away.' Bending towards her he said teasingly, 'Well – does your old guardian rate a kiss after his long absence?'

Cathy blushed crimson and pecked his cheek.

'Mrs Johnson has been telling me your good news,' he

said with a smile. 'Congratulations. I think you deserve that special dinner I promised you. In fact, I think I should take you all out.' He looked at Johnny who shook her head.

'No, we couldn't let you do that, Mr Cavelle. Besides, it's Cathy's success. I'm sure you'll have a lot to discuss with her too.'

Gerald looked doubtful. 'I'd love to take you all out to dinner, Mrs Johnson. I owe you a lot for looking after Cathy so well.'

Johnny blushed. 'You don't owe me anything, Mr Cavelle,' she said. 'Cathy is like one of my own. I'd have taken her in anyway after her father passed on. Even if I'd had to keep her myself.'

Gerald felt chastened. 'Of course. I only meant . . .'

Mrs Bains, who was sitting in her chair by the window, a shawl over her arthritic knees, broke into his sentence with a sound that was half cough, half grunt.

'Besides, I like to be in bed by nine,' she put in. 'My days for gadding about to restaurants are over and done with.'

'That's right,' Johnny said with an apologetic smile. 'I couldn't really leave Mother anyway.'

Johnny treated Cathy to a shampoo and set at *Fleur Coiffeur* in the High Street on the day designated for the dinner date with Gerald. When she got home she went up to her room and studied her appearance in the dressing-table mirror. The hairdresser had backcombed and teased her auburn hair into the new bouffant style that was becoming so popular. She wasn't altogether sure that it suited her finely drawn features, but it certainly had the effect of making her look more grown-up. She took out her newest dress, made of pale lilac voile, and sat on the bed to shorten the skirt. Everyone was wearing them much shorter now and she was determined to look fashionable. With her pocket money she'd bought a pair of tights in a matching shade and she planned to wear her little black patent shoes with the flared heels. As she

81

stitched she wondered whether she'd pass for twenty. With some mascara and eye shadow she felt fairly sure that she would. This afternoon she'd have a trial run with it.

When Gerald called for her she'd been ready for more than half an hour. Standing just out of sight behind the front room curtains, she watched patiently for the car. When she saw the long sleek bonnet of his new silver E-type Jaguar turn into the road and draw up outside she ran through to the living room where the family sat at their evening meal.

'Gerald's here,' she said breathlessly. 'See you later.'

'All right, love. Have a nice time,' Johnny smiled.

As the door closed Mrs Bains looked up, chewing on her steak and kidney pie ruminatively. 'Mark my words, there'll be no good come out of that,' she muttered darkly. 'I don't like the looks of that chap. Too conceited for his own good if you ask me.'

Johnny shook her head reprovingly at her mother. 'Mr Cavelle is Cathy's legal guardian, Mother,' she said. 'He's a famous concert pianist and he was Mr Oldham's best friend. Besides,' she added for good measure, 'I think he's rather handsome.'

Mrs Bains gave her characteristic grunt. 'Huh! Handsome is as handsome does,' she said predictably.

Matthew grinned across the table at his mother. 'You walked right into that, didn't you, Mum?'

The restaurant Gerald had chosen was quiet. There was a small dance floor and a band that played quietly and discreetly as they dined. Cathy thought Gerald looked a little thinner; tired too, but that was understandable after the heavy schedule of his recent tour. She asked him to tell her about the places he'd visited.

'You won't believe me when I tell you that the little I saw of any of the cities I visited was seen through cab windows,' he said with a wry smile. 'All I really saw was concert halls, hotel rooms and airport departure lounges.'

'I always hoped Dad would go on tour sometime and take me with him,' Cathy confessed. 'But he said he wasn't good enough to be a concert pianist. I'm sure that wasn't true, was it?'

She looked at him so appealingly that he couldn't meet her eyes as he answered. 'Your father wasn't as lucky as me. I had a wealthy grandfather who paid for me to study and kept me going until I was established.'

'Did you? I didn't know that.' She stirred her coffee thoughtfully. 'Did you know that Dad used to compose?'

'No, did he?'

'Yes. I used to think he might be successful with that someday. When we cleared the house I was hoping to find some of his manuscripts up in the attic.' She shook her head. 'He must have destroyed them all when he knew he was ill. He never had any confidence in himself, you know.'

'You still miss him, don't you?'

She looked up at him. 'I always will,' she said. 'I don't think I'll ever want to stop missing him, however much it hurts. Because if I ever did it would mean I'd started to forget and that's the last thing I want.'

He looked at her for a long moment. 'It must feel very special to be loved as much as that,' he said wistfully. He took a deep breath and smiled at her. 'Now, I suppose this is where I should ask you what you're planning to do next. What's it to be? A levels . . . University . . .?'

'Neither. I want to leave school,' she told him. 'There were two things I fancied doing: one was nursing and the other was domestic science. But you can't start training to be a nurse till you're eighteen. That would mean hanging around for another four months. So it's going to be domestic science, or rather Home Economics. There's a technical college quite near where I can go so I'll be able to stay on at Johnny's.'

He was laughing. 'You're a young lady in a hurry, aren't you?'

She shrugged. 'I've made up my mind. That's all.'

'Why Home Economics? I'd have thought with all those academic subjects, good grades . . .'

She sighed. 'Why do people always think that domestic science is for idiots? There are a lot of good careers to be had with an HE diploma. And anyway, it's what I want. Why should I do something I don't like just because I got good grades?'

He held up his hands in mock surrender. 'All right. I bow to your superior knowledge of the subject.' He reached across the table to pat her cheek. 'You'll make some lucky man a wonderful and accomplished wife some day,' he said.

She blushed and looked away. Did he really mean that, or was he just patronising her?

Cathy began her Home Economics course at the local technical college at the end of September. She enjoyed it and made some new friends. Occasionally she ran into some of the girls from St Margaret's. Carla envied her. She admitted that she was finding her A level studies a bore and complained about the mass of homework she took home every evening.

'And to think I've let myself in for two years of it,' she wailed.

Rosalind, on the other hand, seemed to be enjoying herself. When they met one rainy November evening at the bus stop she told Cathy she was taking Geography, Sociology, English and Maths. Hotel management was still her aim, she explained. She was interested in Cathy's course.

'Maybe some time in the future we'll find ourselves working together,' she said. 'After all, your subject and mine aren't entirely unrelated, are they?'

84

Cathy told her about the Saturday job she had just taken at the restaurant of the Queen's Head.

'It's a small place and you have to be willing to do a bit of everything,' she said. 'I help in the kitchen and occasionally wait on tables when they are busy or short-staffed. I think they're looking for another weekend girl. If you're interested I could ask for you.' She smiled. 'We could be working together sooner than you think.'

During the autumn Gerald was away again. Cathy received postcards from Switzerland and Edinburgh, but he was back in England again at the beginning of November and one Sunday he took Cathy out to lunch. He asked her what she planned to do at Christmas.

'Nothing special, just spending it at home as usual,' she said. 'Johnny loves Christmas and we always have a nice time. Why, what are you going to do?'

'I thought I might go abroad somewhere,' he told her. 'I have this favourite little place in Switzerland. It's high in the mountains and quite breathtaking in winter. I wondered if you might like to come with me?'

For a moment she was speechless with surprise. 'Why me?' She blushed. 'I mean – it's nice of you to ask me, but there must be someone who's longing for you to ask them.'

He smiled at her. 'I rather thought that someone might be you.'

She laughed. 'You're teasing me. You must have a friend – a girlfriend?'

'Actually no. At least, not one who likes me enough to spend a whole Christmas with me.'

'Oh.' She bit her lip, wondering just what that might mean. 'It's not that I wouldn't like to go, Gerald,' she said. 'It's just that I think it's only fair to help Johnny. There's always such a lot to do.' She looked at him. 'I know. Why don't I ask if you can join us?'

He shook his head. 'I don't want to impose. Besides, I have the distinct feeling that old Mrs Bains disapproves of me. I find that baleful look of hers and those snide remarks rather off-putting.'

'You shouldn't take any notice of that. She's the same with all of us. It doesn't mean anything.'

He slipped an arm round her shoulders. 'Don't worry about me. It was just an idea. I'll be fine.'

She frowned. 'But what will you do? Where will you go?'

'Probably nowhere. I'll stay at the flat and watch all the old films and Christmas Specials on the box.'

'Oh, Gerald.' Cathy chewed her lip, then suddenly she brightened. 'I know, I'll come and cook your Christmas dinner for you.' She pulled a comic face at him. 'If you think you're brave enough to risk it.'

He laughed. 'That sounds wonderful. But what about Mrs Johnson?'

'All the hard work will be over by then and she won't mind if it's just for Christmas Day,' she said. 'She'll probably invite you back for Boxing Day. Well, what do you say?'

He smiled. 'If you really want to do it, I'd love it.'

Cathy shopped for all the ingredients of the Christmas dinner, leaving Gerald to buy the wine only.

'I haven't learned enough about that yet,' she confessed to him. 'I'd probably choose something awful and poison you.'

He collected her and all the bags laden with Christmas fare early on Christmas morning and drove back to the West End. She found the flat looking much as she remembered it; almost clinically tidy and unlived-in. To Cathy it seemed unnaturally so.

Gerald had been surprised when he learned that she hadn't taken him up on his offer to use the place in his absence. Seeing her gazing longingly at Daniel's piano, he invited her to play it.

'I had it tuned when I got back from the tour,' he said,

'along with my own. They get so neglected and the central heating is bad for them.' He saw her hesitating. 'What's the matter – out of practice?'

She nodded. 'Afraid so.'

'What does it matter? There's no one here but us.'

She went over to the piano and ran her fingers lightly over the keyboard. The familiar smooth feel of the ivory brought back nostalgic memories of those Saturday afternoons; the precious times she and her father spent together. Sliding on to the stool she flexed her fingers and began to play a little Chopin nocturne. When the last note had died away she felt Gerald's hand on her shoulder.

'You play very nicely,' he said.

She looked up at him with a wry smile. 'Exactly. That's why I didn't even try to take it up seriously.'

He looked dismayed. 'Oh, but I didn't mean . . .'

'It's okay, Gerald,' she said. 'You don't have to flatter me. The only reason I kept on with my lessons was that it was the one time I could count on getting Dad to myself for a while. I know I haven't inherited his talent.' She swivelled round on the stool. 'Now, I'd better get that turkey into the oven.' She looked up at him. 'Are you going to help?'

He laughed. 'You bet. That's half the fun, isn't it? You'll have to tell me what to do though.'

The kitchen at the flat was equipped with every modern convenience. There was even a dishwasher and an electric tin opener, which intrigued Cathy. Gerald submitted to having an apron tied around his waist and, under Cathy's supervision, set about preparing the vegetables. When everything was under control he opened a bottle of wine and poured her a glass.

'I think we've earned this,' he said. 'And I must say I'm impressed. You've learned a lot during your first term at college.'

She laughed. 'I learned most of this years ago,' she

87

told him. 'Dad and I had been on our own a long time, remember?'

'Of course.'

'And Johnny taught me how to cook.'

'It's as I said. Some day you're going to . . .'

She stopped him with a look. 'Don't laugh at me, Gerald!'

His face dropped. 'My dear girl, I wasn't.'

'That's all right then. You can't go around pretending that a girl's only ambition is to walk down the aisle in white satin nowadays, you know.'

He looked suitably chastened. 'I stand corrected.'

She grinned disarmingly. 'That's okay then. You can set the table if you want to be really useful.'

After her admonishing remark Gerald was careful about what he said. Therefore when he complimented her on her cooking his tone was guarded. Her gracious response to his compliment filled him with relief.

'Cooking can be as much of an art as music,' she told him gravely. 'And as creative.'

'So you've just proved,' he said diplomatically.

After they'd eaten he gave her his present: a beautiful pair of earrings in pearl and jade that he'd bought in New York. They'd originally been chosen for Kay, whose birthday was in October, but he hadn't seen or heard from her since she'd flounced out of the hotel on what had proved to be the last day of his tour. And the green of the jade went so well with Cathy's colouring that it was easy to pretend they'd been bought especially for her.

When she opened them she was overwhelmed. 'Oh, *Gerald*! I've never seen anything so lovely. I'll cherish them always.' She passed his neatly wrapped gift across the table to him. 'I'm afraid this makes mine look so cheap.'

'Nonsense. I'm sure I shall love it.' He unwrapped the tie she had chosen so carefully and exclaimed with pleasure.

'Exactly what I wanted. It will go perfectly with my new jacket.'

'You're just saying that.'

'No, really.' He got up and held out his hand. 'Let's have our coffee by the fire. I've got something to tell you.'

He poured a cup of the coffee he had insisted on making himself and handed it to her. 'My one culinary accomplishment,' he told her as he sat down opposite her.

She sniffed at her cup. 'It smells delicious.'

'I always bring a supply back from Switzerland when I go.'

She sipped appreciatively, looking at him over the rim of her cup. 'You said you had something to tell me.'

'Yes. I've made a rather momentous decision, Cathy. I'm retiring from the concert platform – giving up my playing.'

She stared at him, lost for words. 'Giving up? But surely . . .?'

'Perhaps it would be more accurate to say that playing is giving *me* up,' he went on. 'I've developed a slight – health problem.'

Putting down her cup, she stared at him, her eyes filled with concern. 'Gerald, what is it? Please tell me.'

He shook his head, smiling. 'Nothing for you to worry about. It's a – a kind of arthritis, I suppose you could call it; a stiffening of the joints. I had a lot of trouble with it on the tour.'

'But – but that's terrible. Your music – you're at the height of your career. Surely you can't just throw it all away?'

He smiled ruefully. 'I don't seem to have much choice in the matter. I've still got some time to run on my recording contract. I'll be able to fulfil that. Mistakes can always be edited out. But I'm afraid live concerts are out from now on.'

She moved across to him and took his hands in hers, looking down at them. They looked as strong and powerful

89

as ever. It was hard to believe that they were not. She looked up into his eyes. 'Isn't there something they can do?'

'Nothing, I'm afraid.'

'But – don't you mind terribly?'

He sighed. 'Oh, I don't know. At first it was a blow, but I've had time to think since and I've got a few plans chasing round inside my head.'

'Like what?'

'Ah, that'd be telling.' He bent towards her and kissed her forehead. 'I promise you this though. As soon as one of them begins to take shape, you'll be the first to hear about it.'

They stacked the dishwasher together and sat down to watch the Christmas afternoon movie on television. But Cathy couldn't concentrate on it. All she could think of was the devastating sacrifice that Gerald was having to make. What could she do to make it up to him? Looking across the room in the fading winter afternoon light she watched his profile. The firelight accentuated the hollows under his cheekbones and deepened the eye sockets so that she couldn't see his eyes at all – couldn't even begin to guess what he was feeling. Her heart stirred and she got up quietly and went to sit on the floor at his feet, laying her head on his knee. She felt his hand stroking her hair and presently she raised her head to look up at him.

'Oh, Gerald. Are you dreadfully unhappy?'

He shook his head. 'No. And I'll tell you why. I've found that when you lose something in life there's always a compensation – something to take its place.'

'Or some*one*,' she said. 'Like you came along for me when Dad died.'

'That's a very sweet thing to say.'

'But it's true. You helped me so much. I hope I can help you now that you need someone, Gerald. You will let me, won't you?'

He didn't speak for a moment, then he said quietly,

'You learn who your friends are on occasions like this, you know.'

She turned, kneeling to look at him better. 'Are you saying that your friends have deserted you?'

'I have to confess that it does feel a bit like that.' He sighed. 'But there again, I'm a firm believer that you get what you deserve. Maybe I haven't been a very good friend to others in the past.'

'I can't believe that.'

'Oh, but you should. My kind of life leaves very little room for loyal friendships.'

'Well, you've got mine and you always will have,' she said firmly.

He leaned forward and took her face between his hands. 'Thank you, Cathy. I can't tell you how much I appreciate that. Will you do something for me?'

'Of course. Anything.'

'Will you please let what I've told you be between ourselves for the present? It isn't common knowledge and I'm not sure that I want it to be. There's a lot for me to sort out before I make it generally known that I'm retiring too, so keep that under your hat too, will you?'

'Of course. I won't say anything, I promise.'

Still cupping her face in his hands he drew her towards him and kissed her very gently on the lips. As she felt his mouth, warm and firm on hers, she caught her breath, closing her eyes as she felt the room spin around her. Reaching up, she wound her arms about his neck, but after a moment he took them away and kissed her hands, holding them close to his chest.

'Dear little Cathy,' he whispered. 'You've grown up, haven't you? You're very sweet, just as I always knew you'd be, and we've had a wonderful Christmas Day together. But I'm going to take you home now, before – well, before it's too late.'

91

'But you're coming tomorrow, aren't you – to spend the day with us?'

'No, darling.' He smiled at her gently. 'I'm planning to go away for a few weeks.'

She shook her head. 'Again? You never said. But not yet surely? Not until after Christmas?'

'Maybe not immediately but very soon. I think it's best this way.'

Sitting beside him in the car she was silent. She had the distinct impression that when he had said *before it's too late* he hadn't been talking about the time. And yet he clearly didn't intend to see her again; at least not for a while. Her mind was in a spin. The devastating news he had imparted about retiring from the concert platform, their closeness. The kiss; intimate and more disturbing than anything she had ever experienced before. Finally the unsettling feeling that the fact that he was going out of her life again was somehow because of something she had unwittingly done. All of these things swirled bewilderingly in her head. She needed time and solitude in which to work them all out.

He stopped the car a few doors along the road, switched off the engine and turned in his seat to look at her.

'You're upset.'

'No. Well, yes, but . . .'

'Because of what I told you?'

'Because – yes, partly.'

'My poor Cathy. I never meant to burden you. It was only that . . .'

'You could never burden me, Gerald. It's got nothing to do with that.' She looked down at her hands. 'Will you tell me something?'

'Of course, if I can.'

'Are you going away because of me?'

'No. Whatever makes you think that?'

'Oh, nothing really. Anyway, I'm glad.' On a sudden bold impulse she reached out and drew his head down to hers, kissing him firmly on the mouth. Then, before he could speak, she jumped out of the car and ran down the road to the gate. When she got there she turned briefly and half raised her hand, then slipped out of sight behind the hedge.

Gerald sat for a long time at the wheel of the car thinking about what he had done – what he had started. She was so sweet; so uncomplicated. For a moment a sudden thought tantalised him. How good it would be to have her with him permanently. The word *sacrificial* came mockingly into his mind and he cast it out angrily. It wasn't like that. She was attracted to him, he'd always known that. She was too young and naive to know how to hide the fact. There would be no sacrifice involved if it was what she wanted. There was so much that he could give her – so much they could give each other.

Chapter Five

Una had been a little dismayed at first to learn that after the wedding Don intended them to occupy the house he had shared with his first wife. But on the Sunday afternoon when he had taken her and Rosalind along to see the house in Jay's Lane, Stanmore she had changed her mind.

Blake's Folly was a detached house, built just before the war in suburban Tudor. It occupied a corner position on a pleasant tree-lined avenue of the kind that Una had always admired and the moment they drew up at the gate Rosalind saw her expression brighten. The double oak gates flanked by two monkey puzzle trees were, to her, the epitome of respectability.

Don opened the car door with a flourish and escorted Una proudly up the curved driveway. Following them, Rosalind heard her mother's squeak of approval at the impressive entrance porch which was hung with reproduction lanterns.

But Rosalind's first impression of the house differed from her mother's. Less eager than Una to go into the house she had noted the front garden, with its clipped velvet lawn and shrubs mercilessly manicured into shape. Her heart sank. It was more like a municipal park than a garden and she thought longingly of the glorious profusion of blossom in the cottage garden at Sherwood Magna. Even the rigid and precise rows of bedding plants in the front garden at Blake's Folly looked regimented, as though they wouldn't dare to flag or drop untidy petals on the weedless soil. When she learned later that the gardener who came in twice a week to discipline the garden was an ex-sergeant major in the Royal Artillery she wasn't in the least surprised.

As the three of them stood waiting for Don to find his key and unlock the front door Rosalind peered surreptitiously through the windows. Even from the little she could see it was possible to get an idea of what was in store inside. Through the pristine net curtains she caught the glint of gilt-framed mirrors and the crystal and silver adorning mantelpiece and sideboard. But once Don had opened the door and they had crossed the threshold, vulgar opulence seemed to sneer at her from every corner. In the lounge a large squashy three-piece suite, its sides held in place by silken ropes, thick enough to moor the *Queen Mary*, squatted formidably, daring the visitor to offend its dignity by sitting on the striped plum and peacock upholstery.

In the dining room a reproduction Jacobean dining table, realistically distressed with dents and gashes, gleamed with an artificially induced patina, and everywhere one's feet sank into thick carpets in rich shades of antique red and gold.

The kitchen units were white, ranged around the walls like icebergs lying in wait for the *Titanic*. Una stood in the middle of the floor, exclaiming with pleasure as Don gleefully opened doors and demonstrated every gadget the Ideal Home Exhibition had ever dreamed of. Rosalind stood in the doorway, wistfully remembering the warm kitchen at Ivy Cottage with its pine and gingham homeliness.

But if Rosalind found the place ostentatious and unwelcoming, it was clear that Una did not share her view. As they walked round she could feel her mother growing more and more excited by the minute. Encouraged by her delighted smiles and enthusiastic remarks, Don led them proudly up the dog-leg staircase with its richly carved oak banister. At the top a square landing led to the four bedrooms and a lavish bathroom with a rose pink suite which he displayed with his characteristic flourish. He was an effusive, dapper little man with a pencil moustache and horn-rimmed glasses. Eager to encourage her approval, he looked at his intended enquiringly.

'Well, dearest, what do you think? Can you see yourself living here with me?'

Una sighed ecstatically. 'Oh, Don, of course I can. It's lovely! I'd no idea.'

He smiled with relief. 'Good. It would be such a waste to sell up and start all over again, I'm sure you agree, and anything that isn't to your taste can easily be changed.'

'Oh, I don't want to change anything,' Una said. 'Except perhaps the bedroom,' she said, peering once more into her predecessor's boudoir. 'I think I'd like to have my own choice in there – in the room you and I will share.'

'Naturally, poppet. Buy whatever you like.'

'Thank you, darling. You're so good to me.' To Rosalind's embarrassment Una gave a coy little giggle and pressed close to her future husband's side. Don slipped an arm around her waist and squeezed her affectionately.

'Our room must be just as you would want it. Just pop along to the furniture department at the shop and choose whatever takes your fancy.'

Una was just planting a grateful kiss on his cheek when she noticed Rosalind standing awkwardly by the stairhead, unsure of what she should do. 'You can choose your bedroom if you want,' she said. 'Go on, have a look round.'

Rosalind shook her head. 'It's all right. I don't mind which one I have.'

'But you haven't even looked at them yet,' Una said irritably.

Don looked round at her. 'Yes, do choose, Rosalind,' he said. 'Any one – oh, except this.' He planted himself protectively in front of the door of one of the back bedrooms. 'This one was Mother's. Have either of the other two though. And of course the same applies to you. If you want to change anything in it, please feel free.'

'I really don't mind which I have,' she said awkwardly. 'And I'm sure it'll be fine as it is.'

Later, after Don had taken them back to the flat and was parking the car, Una admonished her.

'Why do you always have to be so sullen with Don?' she said sharply.

'I wasn't.'

'Yes, you were. He's bent over backwards to please you. A lot of men wouldn't want a teenage girl cluttering the place up, you know. He's even willing to keep you while you're still getting your education, remember. You might at least try to show a bit of gratitude and interest in your new home. I just hope you realise how lucky you are.'

Rosalind muttered an apology. The truth was, she had the uncomfortable feeling that Don merely tolerated her for her mother's sake. He was pleasant enough to her it was true, but it wouldn't be easy learning to share a house with a man after so long. The next two years while she was studying for her A levels would clearly be difficult. The thought of them made her even more determined to work hard and get into business college. If nothing else had motivated her, moving away from the prophetically named Blake's Folly and the newly wed Una and Don would have been enough incentive to keep her striving for independence.

The wedding took place on the second Saturday in August. The ceremony was conducted at the register office and was followed by lunch at a local hotel, attended by a few friends and colleagues of Don's. Una had remarked more than once to Rosalind that her own colleagues in model gowns had behaved in a nasty jealous manner since her engagement to Don and that none of them deserved to be invited. Besides, she wouldn't be working at the shop any more after the wedding. There would be enough to occupy her at home, she added with satisfaction.

After lunch the happy couple left for a honeymoon in Majorca, leaving Rosalind to go home alone to the flat in Burnt Oak and prepare to pack up their belongings ready for the move to Stanmore on her mother's return. She was still alone when her O level results came through. Her only celebration was the meeting at school when she shared her success with her classmates, including Cathy Oldham who, she discovered to her disappointment, was leaving school to go to the technical college. She'd cherished a fond hope that they might become friends when they were both in the sixth form and it had been a blow to find that Cathy was leaving, whilst the sharp-tongued Carla was to stay on.

During the two weeks that Una and Don were away she received a postcard from them. It showed a picture of the hotel and, in the background an impossibly blue sea and cloudless sky. Her mother had written: *Having a wonderful time. Wish you were here*, on the reverse side, which made Rosalind smile wryly.

By the same post there was a letter from Ben. He and Freda were appearing in their summer show, *Knights and Belles*, in Brighton, and he wrote inviting her to go and spend a week of her summer holiday with them. She wrote straight back accepting. It would give her mother and Don more time to themselves. She was sure they would be pleased.

But when she told Una on her return she was anything but pleased. 'I must say I think it's very selfish of you,' she said. 'You know how much there is to do with shifting all our stuff over to Stanmore and everything. Now I'll have most of it to do on my own.'

'But I've already packed most of it up,' Rosalind said. 'And it isn't as if the place isn't already furnished. Surely all you have to do is unpack your own things. I'll see to mine when I get back.'

'If you think all I have to do is unpack you're *very* much

98

mistaken,' Una said with a determined look. 'I've got no intention of living with that woman's stuff in the house.' She wrinkled her nose. 'All those tassels and standard lamps and ruched cushions. Ugh! Pure thirties. No, I intend to bring the whole place up to date and that takes time.'

'But you said you didn't want to change anything but the bedroom,' Rosalind said. 'I thought you liked it.'

Una snorted. '*Like it?* You've got to be joking. I'll do it gradually, of course, bit by bit so that Don doesn't notice, but that stuff of *hers*, it's all got to go. It's too old-fashioned for words. That silver will have to be put away too. I'm not making a slave of myself cleaning that lot!' She looked at her daughter with unconcealed resentment. 'Still, if you've already said you'll go to Brighton to Ben and that floosie of his, then you'd better go, I suppose. I don't want them thinking I'm stopping you. Though I must say you might have had the consideration to ask if it was convenient first.'

Brighton was a joy. Rosalind had never been there before, even when she'd joined her parents on summer shows in the past. They'd never aspired to more than number three dates in their days together, which, Rosalind accurately guessed was the real source of her mother's present resentment.

Ben had booked her a room at the hotel where he and Freda were staying. It had an air of subdued luxury and was a far cry from the dingy back street lodgings of the past. In the daytime they took her exploring the town, showing her the little lanes with their intriguing antique and curio shops. One morning she went along with Freda to the hairdresser and had her hair cut in a short gamine style that accentuated her large expressive eyes and delicate bones. Afterwards Freda treated her to a new skirt and blouse.

'I expect you'll be allowed to wear your own clothes in the sixth form,' she said. 'I daresay you'll be glad to ditch your school uniform.'

99

Rosalind was grateful. She had very few clothes apart from her uniform and wild horses wouldn't have forced her to ask Don for money to spend on clothes. When she confided this to Freda she looked thoughtful.

'Don't you like him, Rossie?'

Rosalind shrugged. 'He's all right, I suppose. I just hate feeling – you know – beholden to him.'

Freda slipped her arm through hers. 'I know what you mean, love. Why don't you try to get a Saturday job? You could put the money by for your clothes then and be independent.'

Rosalind thought this a very good idea and over coffee they discussed what she might do.

In the evenings she went to the theatre with her father and Freda. Instead of the cheerless, cramped dressing rooms Ben had shared with Una when they were together, 'Ben and Benita' now occupied one of the star dressing rooms, adjacent to the stage. It boasted hot and cold running water and two comfortable chairs as well as the twin dressing table and wardrobes. Ben proudly introduced her to the backstage staff and the other artists as his 'clever grown-up daughter', and with the permission of the stage manager, Rosalind watched the show from the wings and thought Ben and Freda very good, even better than when she'd heard them rehearsing at Easter. Their voices seemed to blend together more effectively every time she heard them, and their obviously happy relationship put across a warmth and sincerity that made them popular with the audience.

It was towards the end of the week that Ben took her out on her own one morning. Freda remained behind on the pretext of having sewing to do, but it was clear to Rosalind that Ben meant to have a heart to heart talk with her. They had coffee in a small café near the hotel, then walked for a while in the late-summer sunshine, admiring the smooth green of the promenade lawns and inhaling the fresh sea breeze. Then, just when Rosalind thought she must have been wrong about the heart-to-heart, Ben bought them an ice-cream cornet each and invited her to sit down.

'Tell me, are you happy about this new marriage of your mother's?' he asked.

She paused for a moment before answering. 'It's up to her really, isn't it?' she said non-committally.

'That's not what I asked you. This chap – what's his name – Don Blake? Do you get on all right with him?'

Rosalind wondered if Freda had said something. 'He's all right,' she said. 'I suppose it's just that Una and I have been on our own a long time.'

'Exactly. It's bound to make a big difference to your life. So, how do you feel about the changes it will bring?'

'It won't be that different. Stanmore isn't far from St Margaret's. It's a nice place. And the house is better – well, *heaps* better than we've ever had before.'

'Yes, but what about *you*?' he asked impatiently. 'Look, you don't have to pretend to me, Rossie. There's something you're not happy about, isn't there? Tell me.'

She squirmed inwardly, wishing she hadn't said anything to Freda. 'No, there's nothing really. It's just that it's going to be a bit strange at first, and I don't like the idea of having him pay for things for me. But I'll get used to it. I'll have to, won't I?'

'Not necessarily.' He looked at her for a moment. 'Look Rossie, the reason I'm asking you these questions is because there's something you should know. Freda and I have had an offer – to go to Australia. As you know, we're recording a TV series when we've finished here at the end of next month. After that we're off to Oz.'

She looked at him. 'Sounds wonderful. How long for?'

There was a long pause before he replied. 'That's just it, baby. Probably for a long – a *very* long time.' He took her hand. 'Our kind of act is going out of fashion over here, you see, but in Australia it's still quite popular.' He laughed. 'And heaven knows, the country's big enough to tour for

101

yonks. TV is getting off the ground in a big way over there too. Our agent has had an offer for us from someone who caught our act here. He thinks we could make a real hit over there.'

'Oh, good. Congratulations.' Rosalind gave him her brightest smile to hide the sinking feeling inside her chest. Just when she was beginning to rebuild her relationship with her father he was about to go out of her life again. 'If it's what you want, that is.'

He looked into her eyes. 'It is, of course. It's a wonderful opportunity and we're both thrilled. The thing is, baby . . . Look, Free and I have talked this over and we both agree. We'd like you to come with us.'

She stared at him. '*Me* – come to Australia?'

'Yes. What do you say?'

Just for a moment her heart leapt with excitement. Dad and Freda actually *wanted* her with them – sharing a new life in an exciting new country. Then she thought of her own plans for the future and the snags and impracticalities came crowding in. 'I don't see how I can, Dad,' she said, shaking her head.

'Why not, love? You'd enjoy it out there.'

She sighed. 'But it wouldn't work, would it? There's my A levels for a start.'

'Oh – well, I daresay you can do them over there – or the equivalent.'

'Not if you're going to be touring. Then afterwards I want to go to business college. Study hotel management.' She looked at him. 'I really want that, Dad. It's all I've worked for.'

His face dropped. 'Yes, I know you do, love. But they must have those courses over there too. You could get into a college somewhere, surely. We'd see each other as often as we could.'

She shook her head. 'I don't think so, Dad. It wouldn't be any different than it was before, would it – when you and Una were together and I was at Aunt Flora's? And I think I'd feel lonely – even lonelier on my own in a strange country. You'd feel you had to keep coming to see me too. No. Better for you and Freda to be free to concentrate on your work.'

He was silent for a moment. 'I can't see what's so special about the hotel business. Isn't there anything else you'd like to do?'

'Not really.' She shook her head. 'Anyway if I toured with you I wouldn't be able to study for anything anyway, would I?' She wanted to add: *I'd just be another piece of luggage you'd have to carry around. A dead weight,* but she knew that would hurt him so she didn't say it, even though she knew it to be true.

Almost as though he read her thoughts, Ben was silent for a moment. 'You could come over for a holiday though,' he said at length without conviction. 'You could come over every year if you wanted.'

It was so typical of Ben. Una had always said that one of his biggest faults was his inability to face up to the realities of life. 'Yes, of course I could,' Rosalind said, forcing a brightness she didn't feel into her voice. 'I'll have to start saving up right away, won't I?' She smiled at him reassuringly. 'It was lovely of you both to ask me, Dad, and I do appreciate it, but it wouldn't work, really it wouldn't. I want to study and make a career for myself. I want to be independent.' His depressed silence showed that he had reluctantly accepted the fact and Rosalind felt close to tears. Once again she was odd man out. It seemed that she didn't really fit in anywhere. She was a millstone round everyone's necks. Una's reproachful words echoed in her mind. *I hope you realise how lucky you are.* How bitter it felt to know you were a nuisance and a liability; that the best emotion you merited was guilt. She looked at Ben's anguished face and reached for his hand.

'Dad, don't feel bad about it. It's my choice. I want you

103

to go and be a big success, honestly. We'll write to each other, and as soon as I can I'll come and see you.'

He squeezed her hand. 'I want you to know that you can come any time you like, baby,' he said earnestly. 'If you change your mind and want to come out, just wire and I'll send you your fare. Promise me you'll do that?'

She smiled at him. 'Okay, if you say so.' A thought suddenly struck her. 'What will you do about Ivy Cottage?'

'We're letting it on a short lease,' he told her. 'Maybe one of these days we'll come back and retire there.'

'So you're not selling it?'

'No fear. Not after all the work we've put in. Anyway, even if we don't come back it'll be a little nest egg for Free and me in our old age.'

When Rosalind went home from Brighton it was to Blake's Folly – except that it didn't feel much like home. Una met her at the station and complained at once about the new hairstyle.

'I see you've been letting that woman influence you again,' she said scathingly.

Rosalind lifted a hand to her hair. 'Don't you like it?'

'No, I do *not*. It makes you look as if it's been cut with a knife and fork.'

'It's called the Italian cut,' Rosalind said hopefully. 'It's all the rage in Brighton.'

Una snorted derisively. 'Whoever told you that was having you on.'

Rosalind felt rebellion welling up inside her. 'No, they weren't,' she said warmly. 'I had a lot of nice compliments from the artists at the theatre.'

Una shrugged her shoulders. 'Rosalind, you really will have to learn to tell a real compliment from people just having a laugh at your expense,' she said. 'I'm sure you don't want to go around looking silly. Grow it out as quickly as you can, there's a good girl.'

She had chosen the room over the garage for Rosalind. It had two windows, one facing the front garden and another looking on to the side entrance. It was a darkish little room, shaded by the evergreen trees at the front and the wall of the next house at the side, but there was enough space for the few things Rosalind had. Una had added a desk and an armchair to the existing furniture, making it clear that she expected her daughter to spend most of her spare time here.

Rosalind saw at once that while she had been in Brighton her mother had lost no time in making changes. In spite of her decision to replace the first Mrs Blake's furniture gradually she had refurnished most of the ground floor in one fell swoop, replacing the heavy oak reproduction pieces with contemporary furniture in light woods. The heavy velvet curtains with their braided swags and tails had been replaced with plain pelmets and curtains made of brightly coloured fabrics in jazzy designs. From what Rosalind could gather it had already caused a disagreement between her mother and Don, who was of the opinion that the spindly style of furniture Una favoured did not go with the style of the house.

'I told him – we'll just have to change the style of the house then, won't we?' Una recounted to Rosalind. 'After all, I have agreed to save him money by living in the house his ex-wife chose. How many women would do that? And he did say I could change anything I liked, didn't he? You were witness to that.'

Rosalind said nothing. She hoped she wouldn't be expected to take sides in any arguments.

'Oh, yes. He said change anything you like and that's what I intend to do.' They were standing on the oak-panelled landing and Una suddenly swept her arm around impatiently. 'I hate all this dark, gloomy wood. I'm working on having it all done out in cream emulsion. And do you know, he keeps that room locked?' She pointed to one of the back bedrooms. 'It was his mother's and he keeps all her things in there, would you believe? Even her clothes! Creepy if you ask me, not to mention the waste of space. Still I had to give in on something, I suppose,' she added grudgingly. 'But I'll get that cleared out too in time, don't you worry.'

Rosalind made a non-committal reply. Her mother looked at her enquiringly.

'Well? I haven't heard anything about your holiday yet. Still climbing the ladder to success, those two, are they?'

'The show was very good,' Rosalind said as she started to unpack her case. Her back to her mother she added: 'They've had a very good offer. They're going to Australia.'

'Oh, yes? How long for?'

Rosalind could feel her mother's envy and resentment boring into her back as she put away her things. 'It's an extended tour. They might even stay there, I think. Settle down for good.'

'Huh!' Una tugged viciously at a corner of the bedspread. 'I suppose they want us to think they've hit the big time. I'll believe that when I see their names in lights.' She straightened up and looked at Rosalind, her eyes flashing like chips of ice. 'They didn't ask you to go with them though, did they? Oh, no. It only pleases Mister Bigtime to own he's got a daughter when it suits him. He won't want you hanging round his neck. Once he's left the country you won't hear from him again. Just you mark my words.'

When she'd left, slamming the door behind her, Rosalind sat down on the bed and swallowed hard at the lump in her throat. Every instinct that was in her had wanted to scream at her mother: *But he did want me. He did ask me to go too.* The only reason she had held back was that Una might have insisted on her accepting the invitation.

When the new term began she went back to St Margaret's eagerly. The sooner she could pass her A levels and move on to college, the better.

*   *   *

106

It was one wet afternoon in November that she met Cathy Oldham at the bus stop on her way home and heard again about the position of Saturday girl that was vacant at the Queen's Head. Her spirits rose. It was just what she was looking for. If she could only get it, it would be good experience for her as well as extra pocket money. Cathy promised to put in a word for her and two days later she telephoned to say that Rosalind could go along and see Mrs Gresham, the manageress, that afternoon after school.

The interview was a success. Mrs Gresham engaged Rosalind to work every Saturday from nine till two and then from six till ten in the evenings. The money wasn't exactly generous, but she was promised that there would be tips. It was a temporary job to last until the New Year, after which they would review the situation. Rosalind was thrilled. She had a job that would bring her extra money, get her out of the house at weekends and gain her some valuable experience too. And a bonus was that Cathy would be there too, so she wouldn't be entirely among strangers.

It was in the spring of the following year that Una had the first indication of the truth about Blake's Folly. Although she no longer worked at Hallard's with Don she had agreed to go in for a few weeks at the beginning of each new season to organise the fashion shows. Don was away for three days in March, attending a management conference in Eastbourne, and she was spending a day in the office, making out her VIP invitation list. She was deep in the list of account holders when one of the girls popped her head round the door. Una looked up irritably.

'Yes? What is it, Peggy?'

'There's someone in the showroom to see you.'

Una frowned. 'Didn't you say I was busy? Who is it anyway?'

'It's Mrs Blake.'

'What do you mean, Mrs Blake? Which Mrs Blake?'

The girl stifled a giggle. 'It's *her*,' she hissed in a stage whisper. 'You know – Mr Blake's ex.'

'Didn't you tell her that Mr Blake is out of town?'

'Yes, I did. It's you she wants to see.'

Una felt her face colouring. 'What does she . . .?' She bit off the end of the question and took a deep breath. 'I suppose you'd better send her in then, Peggy.' As the girl turned she added, 'Oh, and send down to the restaurant for a tray of tea – Earl Grey – and some chocolate biscuits.' Might as well let the woman see that she was civilised.

'Yes, Mrs Blake.' The girl withdrew, a smirk of gleeful excitement on her face. Just wait till she told the other girls about this. What she'd give to be a fly on the wall!

As soon as the girl had gone Una reached for her handbag and took out her compact, powdering her nose and tweaking at her hair. If only she'd known she would have put on something smarter. Truth to tell her knees were knocking with nervousness. Her best frock would have given her confidence. She uncapped her lipstick and applied it generously, pressing her lips together. She had just slipped it back into her bag when the door opened and Peggy ushered the first Mrs Blake in.

At first glance Una was surprised at how ordinary she was. Aged about forty-five, she had greying hair drawn back into a chignon and wore no make-up apart from a little pale pink lipstick. But there was a certain classiness about her that made Una feel over made-up and common. To compensate she smiled widely.

'Please – won't you have a chair? I've just sent down for some tea. I hope you'll join me?'

'How kind.' The other woman looked perfectly relaxed as she sat in the chair opposite and crossed one leg over the other. Una's sweeping glance of appraisal registered that she had good legs and that the charcoal grey suit she wore, although plain, was expertly

108

cut. The white blouse was obviously pure silk and her accessories were expensive-looking. 'Actually I've come to ask a favour of you,' she said, accepting a cigarette from the box that Una pushed across the desk towards her.

Una was relieved. That meant that she was in the position of being able to grant or refuse. 'Of course,' she said sweetly. 'Anything at all that I can do, Mrs – er . . .'

'Monica.' The woman smiled. 'Call me Monica. After all, it's rather embarrassing to keep calling each other Mrs Blake, isn't it?'

Taken aback by the woman's cool composure Una nodded agreement. 'Oh – er, yes. My name is Una.'

At that point Peggy came in with the tray of tea. She searched the faces of both women for signs of battle and withdrew, disappointed.

Una poured the tea, glad to have something to do with her hands. 'So, what is this favour, Monica?'

'It's just the little desk in the dining room. It's Regency – an antique; the only genuine antique in the place as it happens. And the one piece that is actually mine. I bought it at a sale two years ago with my own money. I wondered if you and Donald would agree to my having it?'

Una was shaken. 'Did you say it was the only piece that was actually yours?'

Monica nodded. 'Yes. Everything else was Donald's mother's. We always lived with her, you know, right from the first. It was Mrs Blake senior's home. Not mine.'

Una felt as though all the breath had been knocked out of her body. 'So Don never bought the house?'

'Good heavens, no. He wouldn't leave his mother. She was widowed quite young, so I believe. And he was her only child. They were very close. Almost unhealthily so,' she added under her breath. She gave an ironic little laugh. 'Strange that she died just after I left him.'

Una crumbled a biscuit as she allowed the information to sink in. 'He still keeps her room just as it was,' she said. 'All her clothes are in the wardrobe and everything.'

Monica nodded. 'A shrine. I can well imagine.'

'What was she like?' Una asked.

Monica sighed. 'I suppose there's no harm now in saying what I think,' she said. 'And anyway, she's dead.' She looked at Una. 'She was a monster. An absolute monster. She wrecked our marriage and made my life a living hell. And she had Donald utterly under her thumb. It was always what his mother wanted. No one else mattered to him.' She smiled. 'But that's something you'll never have to put up with. The house and Donald are all yours now.'

Una had the uncomfortable impression that she would have liked to add: *And you're welcome to them.* She cleared her throat. 'Well – of course you must take the desk.' Privately she thought the thing ugly and old-fashioned. It had been next on her list for the auction room anyway. 'Just ring and let me know when you're having it collected.'

'I will. Thank you so much, Una.' Monica stood up and began to pull on her gloves, smoothing the soft kid over her fingers. 'It's been so nice to meet you. I've been trying to pluck up the courage to write, but I was passing this afternoon and, knowing that you work here, I thought I'd just pop in.'

Work here indeed! Una bridled indignantly. 'I only come in occasionally, to do a little administrative work.' She stood up and held out her hand. 'You were quite lucky to catch me actually. Goodbye. And if there's ever anything else I can do, just let me know.'

Monica looked at her curiously. 'The same goes for me, Una. I can assure you I bear no grudges. I hope you feel the same about me. And if ever you want someone to talk to . . . believe me, no one understands Donald Blake and his little idiosyncrasies like I do.'

When she'd gone Una sat for a long time deep in thought, her invitation list quite forgotten. The woman had a bloody cheek with her patronising offers of help and advice. All the same, a lot of things were clear now. Don's inhibitions in the bedroom; his strange prudish habits. The way he always undressed in the dark and refused to look at her until she'd put on her nightdress. He'd been unreasonably reluctant to dispose of that awful old furniture too and he was adamant about that room of his mother's. She felt a chill run through her veins. It was creepy – almost as though the old woman still occupied the house. As though she were still watching everything they did. Well, she'd soon put a stop to all that, Una told herself firmly. When Don got home from Eastbourne he'd find a few changes. And he'd be getting an ultimatum.

It was two days later that the row erupted. Rosalind arrived home to hear the raised voices of her mother and step-father. She stood just inside the door, her stomach quaking in the old familiar way, reminded of those far-off days when she had wakened in the night to the terrifying sound of her parents' quarrelling. In the hall tea chests were stacked ready for collection. On closer inspection she saw that they contained clothing, books and ornaments. There were several framed photographs and on top of one a rose-embellished chamber pot was precariously perched. From the landing Una's shrill voice could be heard. Rosalind could tell from experience that she was well on the way to working up one of her 'states'.

'All that stuff has got to go,' she was shouting. 'Either *it goes* or *I* do. And that's only the beginning. I want this house put on the market straight away. I want a nice little bungalow on the new estate – with picture windows, central heating and a patio. And if you don't get it for me, Don Blake, you can live in this mausoleum by your bloody self!'

Chapter Six

Lying in bed in his hotel room Gerald stared at the moonlit ceiling. Although he had drunk almost half a bottle of whisky before falling into bed, sleep still eluded him and he felt depressingly sober. He turned his head and watched the curtains gently moving at the window. He hated the Swiss way of folding the shutters over the windows at night. It made the room so inky dark; made him feel so alone.

For a while he watched the floating pattern, made by the moonlight on the ceiling, then he tested his memory by picturing the scene outside the window, trying to recall every little detail. It wasn't difficult. He knew this place so well. It was here that he'd spent his ecstatic honeymoon, in those far-off, long-gone days when life was uncomplicated and love was new and exciting. In recent years this was where he always came when there was some crisis in his life, a decision to make or something to think through. It had never failed to soothe and heal him. Till now.

Far below his hotel window was the street, asleep now and grubby with the day's traffic. But it would be washed clean by morning before anyone was up. What bliss if one's life could be washed clean of cares and guilt each morning.

The pavement was bordered by shops, neat and clean, their windows tempting with artistically displayed wares. Above the little town the mountains rose in a majestic, snow-capped sweep, proud and protective. In the quiet of the night he could hear the sound of water as it flowed from the springs high in the mountains to feed the lake below. He imagined it, chuckling over smooth stones as it rippled along the channels carved out over the centuries; falling in sparkling cascades over rocky crags to run finally, tamed and subdued, gurgling under the roads through the little man-made culverts on its way to the lake. When the springs froze in winter, the lake gradually dried up and became a snow-filled hole in the ground bereft of its lifeblood until the warmth of spring released it and the little town laughed with the sound of living water once again.

Gerald felt his own lifeblood freeze as the words of Doctor Gruber echoed inside his head. Gruber was the consultant he had seen that morning at the clinic in Zurich. He had undergone all the tests and now had the initial diagnosis confirmed by two consultants, the finest in their field in the world. One in Edinburgh and one in Switzerland both recommended to him in New York by Dr Brewster. Could he really turn his back on the truth any longer? He was still comparatively young. In his prime some might say, certainly at the height of his career. Everything in him railed against the prospect of winding down, as he had been advised. To bow out now, just when he was getting rave notices; just when he knew the exhilaration of being considered the cream of his profession. It was unthinkable. But every time he rebelled against it he was pulled up sharply by the memory of that concert in New York. The terrifying night when his memory had failed him and his fingers had turned into useless lumps of dead flesh. That must never happen again. He dare not risk the shame, the humiliation. But what to do?

Still reeling from the shock in the clinic this morning he had vaguely heard Doctor Gruber telling him that with the proper drugs and treatments, a healthy diet and sensible lifestyle, he could still lead a full and useful life. He had wanted to shout, asking what a full and useful life meant when the whole purpose of one's existence had gone. Now he remembered the man's voice as he made his calm pronouncement. Soothing, placatory. His eyes all compassion as he handed out what to Gerald amounted

114

to a death sentence. Oh yes, the man had a good bedside manner, he'd give him that, Gerald told himself bitterly. No doubt he could turn it on and off at will, like a tap. Well, so he should. God knew he was paid enough for it.

He sighed. Drugs. The proper treatment. A sensible lifestyle. What did all that add up to? A regimen of pill-taking or injections that would reduce his brain to a senile pulp? A boring diet of lettuce leaves, lentil casseroles and non-alcohol wine? No parties or late nights? No cigarettes? No driving? What was the point? He might as well be dead, he decided hopelessly, blinking back the bitter tears that scalded his eyes. He pictured his friends' shocked faces. Oh, they would show compassion. Some of them might even be sincere – to begin with. They would certainly feel sorry for him, but in spite of their pity they would eventually drop him. *Poor old Gerald. He's finished, you know. Can't play any more. Can't do anything really. So sad at his age, isn't it?* It was difficult and embarrassing, being around sick people. He should know. He'd avoided them himself in the past.

There were other things in his past that he wasn't proud of. Was this illness some kind of retribution? he asked himself. His past misdeeds catching up with him? What was it the mystics called it – Karma? He thought of Daniel Oldham, the person who had been his best friend in their student days. He had treated him badly all those years ago, yet the man had come to him for help when he needed it. Perhaps this was his chance to redeem himself.

This morning after his consultation he had left the clinic like a man in a dream. All he had wanted was to get away from the bustle of the city and be alone to think. He had taken the little mountain train and come here to the only place where he could relax in familiar surroundings. Now he must make himself think about the future. Face up to what was left of his life and decide what to do with it.

Tomorrow. He smiled wryly as a hackneyed phrase leapt into his mind. *Tomorrow is the first day of the rest of your life*. Well, it would be that all right. Whatever happened, whatever he decided, he had things to do and people to see. What was the term they used? *Putting one's affairs in order*. His heart felt like lead in his chest. It wasn't exactly something to look forward to.

At last he slept. And when he wakened the sun was rising over the mountain tops. It was the way he loved to begin the day, which was why when he came here he always slept with the shutters open. Slipping out of bed, he pulled on his dressing gown and went out on to the balcony. The air was sharp and pure, clear as crystal as it hit the back of his throat. He breathed it deeply into his lungs and felt it strengthen him and lift his spirit. He watched as the sun outlined the mountain-tops in silver. The craggy peaks turned from grey through violet and rose to palest lemon, then to burning gold as the sun rose triumphantly above them into an azure sky. It was a sight he never tired of and his heart soared. He felt so well. He *couldn't* be ill. It wasn't possible.

Sitting on the balcony in the quiet of dawn he made himself think. He'd let his agent go ahead with the coming season's bookings. There were three Promenade Concerts booked; the tail end of his recording contract still to fulfil and a tour of cathedral cities with the LSO. He'd manage the recording but, as for the concerts, he would have to cancel them all. There was nothing else for it. He dared not risk another live performance. And the sooner he spoke to his agent about it, the better. This must be his priority. He took a leisurely bath and shaved, then rang down to room service for breakfast.

Over hot coffee and croissants with his favourite black cherry jam he laid his plans carefully. So far no one knew about the diagnosis except of course the three doctors he had consulted. Only Carl Kramer had witnessed his lapse at the New York concert. He would write to him and thank him for his concern and for recommending the doctor, tell

116

him it was caused by exhaustion and that he was fine now. No one need know the real reason for his retirement. No one at all apart from his doctors. He was damned if he would submit himself to the humiliation of their pity. He would find a place to live – a permanent home. That was the one thing he had never had. No more travelling. He found that the idea appealed to him. The moment he got back to England he would contact the estate agents and start searching. Somewhere in the Cotswolds perhaps – or Dorset; peaceful and serene. It would be something to look forward to.

As soon as he knew that his agent, James Kendrick, would be in the office he rang down to Reception and asked them to put through a call to London for him.

When the telephone rang James himself was at the other end. 'Hi there, Gerry. What can I do for you?'

When he made his announcement there was a silence at the other end of the line. Then James said incredulously: '*Retiring?* Are you mad? What the hell are you talking about, Gerry?'

'What I say. I'm giving up.'

'But – but for how long?'

'For *good*. I'm taking an early retirement.'

James spluttered incoherently at the other end. 'Look, what's happened to make you decide a thing like that? Has something upset you? Anyway, what the bloody hell are you doing in Switzerland? I think you'd better come home pretty damned quick and talk about this, don't you? I mean, in case you've forgotten, you've got commitments.'

'I know. I'll do the album for Zenith, but I want you to cancel the rest – the concerts.'

'*Cancel?* You're out of your tiny mind! Look, what's going on?'

'Okay, okay. I'll come home. I'll see you tomorrow, but I won't change my mind, James. So you'd better get on and cancel those concert dates right away. We don't want anyone

117

suing us, do we?' An irate James was still demanding to know what was happening when Gerald hung up. It was going to be a damned sight harder than he'd envisaged. He might even have to confide in James after all, but he'd swear him to secrecy. He began to pack. There was a train for Zurich at midday. He could catch a late-afternoon flight and be back in London this evening.

Chapter Seven

It was summer before Cathy saw Gerald again. He kept in touch, of course. From time to time she would receive a postcard, a brief message scribbled on the back. Her allowance was paid into the bank regularly on the first of every month too. But then Gerald had nothing to do with that. It was arranged at the bank on a standing order.

She thought about him a lot during the early months of the year, remembering the way he had confided in her on Christmas Day. She wondered why he didn't telephone or come to see her. Even if he was away he must come back to London occasionally. She wondered about his decision to retire too. Perhaps he had changed his mind by now. He had seemed a little depressed at Christmas. People often made hasty decisions when they were depressed. Maybe he had found a doctor who could cure this rare stiffness of the joints thing he had. By the look of the cards he sent he had been travelling again: Switzerland, Edinburgh, but she had no idea whether he was working or not. If he wasn't playing Cathy could only guess at the reason for his absence, if reason there was.

She'd said nothing to anyone about her conversation with Gerald on Christmas Day. Johnny had been surprised and slightly put out when she had discovered that he wasn't taking up her invitation to spend Boxing Day with them. She'd remarked rather tartly to Cathy that she would have thought he had better manners than to wait until the last minute and then send a message with her.

'He could have telephoned me,' she said resentfully. 'I daresay he's got a better invitation from one of his famous friends. I suppose the likes of us aren't exciting enough.'

In her chair by the window Mrs Bains gave a meaningful sniff that said more than mere words ever could.

Cathy burned to tell them that they were sadly misjudging him, but she had promised. Her lips were sealed.

Her course in Home Economics was almost through its first year. In the initial few months it had all been new and interesting, but lately Cathy had found it becoming tedious. Long warm summer days spent learning how to apply physics and chemistry to household skills seemed endless when everything outside the window hummed with the glorious promise of summer. Environmental studies were more interesting, entailing visits to housing estates, both urban and rural, but while they stood grouped around their tutor, hearing about modern drainage methods and the horrors of Victorian sanitation, Cathy longed to be by the sea or in the countryside. Back in college there were lectures on the basics of architecture and the structure of the domestic house. A lot of it was very interesting but somehow it failed to absorb Cathy. Before long she began to feel that Miss Hanley had been right and she might have chosen unwisely. The course didn't stimulate her imagination – didn't stretch her enough.

Her weekend job was pleasant enough. The Queen's Head was a small hotel and Mrs Gresham, the manageress, and the rest of her staff were kind and friendly, patiently helping Cathy over her first fumbling attempts at waitressing and her ineptitude in the kitchen. It was a far cry from helping Johnny at home, but she enjoyed the work once she'd become accustomed to the routine. She even eventually grew used to Raymond, the frighteningly volatile chef, whose explosive and unpredictable bark, she soon learned, was much worse than his bite. But she couldn't envisage herself choosing hotel work as a future career, unlike Rosalind Blair whose burning ambition seemed to be to run a hotel of her own.

She and Rosalind had become quite friendly since they had started working together at the hotel. Rosalind was grateful to Cathy for tipping her off about the weekend job at the Queen's Head and, more recently, she had been delighted when her temporary job was extended to a permanent one. She was so keen and eager to learn, which made her popular with the rest of the staff. She certainly seemed to have an aptitude for the work. She seemed a shy girl, hesitant and diffident, but her natural reserve seemed to disappear magically when she was dealing with people. It was almost as though she became a different person. Cathy grew to like her more and more as the months went by.

Gradually coming out of her shell, Rosalind confided to Cathy that she was desperately anxious to earn some money. She explained that her divorced mother had recently remarried and she didn't want to be a burden on her and the new step-father for any longer than was absolutely necessary.

Hearing about Rosalind's circumstances made Cathy wonder how she would have felt if her father had ever decided to marry again, and she decided that it would have been quite hard to accept, especially if she had resented the woman as much as Rosalind appeared to resent her new step-father. Since Daniel's death she had thought about her mother a great deal, wondering at her father's acceptance of her betrayal. She was convinced that if someone she loved let her down like that she would never get over it. She was sure she had not inherited Daniel's sweet, forgiving nature.

It had been early in the spring when Matthew had begun to invite Cathy out. Neither of them had much spare time and because of this neither of them had many friends, but they found they shared similar tastes in music and films. When *West Side Story* came to the Roxy, Matthew asked her to go with him. The beautiful, sad story made a deep impression on Cathy and the strong vibrant music of Leonard Bernstein reminded her sharply of the bitter-sweet melodies that used to echo through the house in Laburnum Close when her father was shut away on one of his creative sessions. She saved up and bought the album, playing it upstairs in her room on the record player Daniel had bought her on her fifteenth birthday. Somehow it reminded her of her father. If only he'd had more confidence in his musical abilities, she felt sure that he too could have been a famous composer.

Since seeing *West Side Story* together, Cathy and Matthew had been to the cinema several times and once or twice to dances. He was good company. Quiet and thoughtful by nature, his reactions were comfortably predictable. But although the other young people they knew began to link their names together, looking upon them as a couple, Cathy never thought of him as anything but a friend.

By the end of June she had decided that Gerald had slipped out of her life for good. She resigned herself to the fact that the novelty of having a ward had worn off for him. Sometimes she asked herself if he could have dropped her because of something she had said or done. When she remembered the brazen way she had kissed him at Christmas she went hot all over with shame. At the time it had seemed all right; a perfectly natural thing to do. Now she saw that she had revealed herself as naive and childish. It was just as well he had decided not to see her, she told herself. Remembering that occasion she would have been too embarrassed to look him in the eye.

It was just two weeks before the end of term when she swung into the house one afternoon, calling out to Johnny, as she always did, to tell her she was home. She was hanging her jacket on the hallstand when the door of the front room opened and there he stood – Gerald, a wide smile on his face.

'Cathy!'

She felt the hot blood creeping up her neck and into her face, '*Oh!* Oh, hello,' she said weakly.

He laughed. 'You look shocked.'

'I'm surprised. I didn't see the car.'

'I parked it in the next street. I wanted to surprise you. Well?' He took a step towards her. 'You don't seem very pleased to see me.'

She blushed. 'I thought I never would any more,' she said stiffly. 'I thought maybe you'd gone abroad – or forgotten about me, or something.'

'If I'd known you were missing me that much I'd have come sooner.' His eyes teased her. 'Come on, admit it. You've been much too busy enjoying college to give your poor old guardian a thought.'

She stared at him. How could he be so wrong about the way she felt? And how dare he walk in as though he had seen her only yesterday?

Seeing the flush that coloured her cheeks and the expression in her eyes his smile vanished and he reached out to take her hand and draw her towards him. 'You really *are* upset, aren't you? I'm sorry, Cathy. If I'd known . . .'

'It's all right. Of course I'm not upset,' she said, panic sharpening her voice. 'And you're right. I have been busy. Time's absolutely flown. So – what brings you here now? Were you just passing or do you have time to stay for a few minutes?'

'Mrs Johnson has very kindly invited me to tea.' He was looking at her oddly. 'But actually I've told her I can't stay.'

'No? Oh, well, it can't be helped. It was nice seeing you anyway.' Her heart beating fast, she began to push past him towards the stairs, reaching for the newel post, but he stopped her with a hand on her shoulder.

'Cathy!' He looked seriously concerned and her anger faded a little. 'Look, the reason I can't stay for tea is because I've booked a table for two – for dinner.'

'I see. Then we mustn't keep you.'

'For *us*, silly. For you and me. I want to talk to you.'

'To me? What about?'

He raised an eyebrow at her. 'Why not come along and see?' He looked into her eyes. 'I'm serious. I really do need your opinion on something. Something very important.'

He was humouring her. Just as though she were ten years old. A truculent child who had to be indulgently coaxed out of a bad mood. Tears of angry frustration pricked at her eyelids. Did he really think he could ignore her for months and then come back and expect her to behave as though he'd never been away? Avoiding his eyes she said, 'I don't think I can make it this evening, Gerald. I've got some work to do. I'm afraid it won't wait.'

He sighed. 'Oh, dear. It's worse than I thought. I really am in the dog house, aren't I?'

Johnny had come out into the hall and he turned to her. 'Mrs Johnson, will you please tell this young lady that I badly need her to come out to dinner with me?'

Johnny looked unsmilingly from one to the other. 'Off you go and change, Cathy. I'm sure you don't want to keep Mr Cavelle waiting, do you?'

Gerald looked at her, his head on one side. 'Surely your essay or whatever it is will wait for a couple of hours, won't it?'

The two of them stood looking at her. She was outnumbered. She couldn't keep up her pretence of being too busy without looking ridiculous. Without a word she turned and climbed the stairs. When she had gone Gerald turned to Johnny.

'Any idea why she's upset, Mrs Johnson?'

'She isn't a child any longer, Mr Cavelle,' Johnny told him frankly. 'She's a young woman. You can't fob her off with treats and promises. And she's still very insecure. She needs to know where she is.' And without another word she turned and went back into the kitchen.

* * *

He took her to a Chinese restaurant. Cathy had never eaten Chinese food before and she was intrigued by all the little dishes and the delicious delicate flavours. Gerald watched with an indulgent smile as she tried first one thing, then another, struggling manfully with the chopsticks. She had changed so much in the few months since he last saw her. She was taller and her slender figure had developed softly rounded curves. Her face had lost its blurred childishness. The delicate bones were more defined now, with gentle shadows that accentuated her green eyes. Mrs Johnson had been right. Since he had seen her last Cathy had grown from a schoolgirl into an attractive young woman with the tantalising promise of real beauty yet to come. Yet through it all she hadn't lost that quality of untouched innocence he found so piquant. Compared to the sophisticated women he knew she was as refreshing as a spring morning.

'Tell me what you've been doing with yourself since Christmas?' he invited.

'Nothing very much. I've been too busy working.' She went on to tell him a little about her course and about the films that she and Matthew had seen – the dances they'd been to.

He listened politely for a while, then said suddenly, 'Cathy, there's something I want you to see. I've found a house. It's in Suffolk, near the sea. Will you come and look at it with me?'

She looked up at him, the prawn she had been trying to convey to her mouth dropping back onto her plate. 'You're leaving London?'

'Yes. At least, I'm thinking seriously about it.' He dabbed at his lips with his napkin and pushed his plate away. 'That's what I wanted to talk to you about. I've been thinking of buying a house in the country. I've never had a real home, you know. I seem to have spent my entire life in transit.'

'What about when you were a child?' she asked.

'My grandfather brought me up,' he told her. 'At least he paid other people to do it. He lived alone in a large house in Manchester where he owned a cotton mill. My mother was his only daughter and he hadn't approved of her marriage to my father, apparently. They were both killed in a train crash in 1923 when I was two years old.' He smiled wryly. 'I daresay he saw it as divine retribution. I don't remember either of them at all.'

Cathy's heart was stirred at the thought of Gerald losing his parents as a baby. 'So your grandfather adopted you?'

He nodded. 'Out of a sense of duty more than anything else, I think. There was no one else to take me you see. He certainly never showed me any affection. I was raised by a series of kindly young women who had a disconcerting habit of going off and getting married just when I was beginning to depend on them.'

Cathy was silent for a moment. 'I thought I was unlucky, losing my mother when I was little,' she said. 'But at least I had Dad. But your grandfather paid for your musical education though?'

'Yes.' Gerald picked up his glass and regarded the clear red colour of his wine. 'I think he felt that as it was the only talent I had he'd better foster it,' he said with a hint of bitterness. 'Couldn't have his only grandchild turning out a total failure and disgracing him.' He grinned wryly at her. 'Besides, I daresay he was relieved to get me out of the house.'

Cathy watched thoughtfully as he took a long drink of his wine. She pictured the lonely little boy in the big old house with no one to read him a bedtime story or play with him. How sad it must have been never to have known a parent's love. It had obviously affected Gerald deeply. 'So now you're going to have a home of your own at last. Tell me about the house you've found,' she invited.

'I didn't have a very clear idea of what I wanted when I set out,' he admitted. 'Thatched roof and roses round the door, I suppose. Everyone's dream of an idyllic country home. Then I found this one. It's nothing like what I had in mind and it's far larger than I need. But it's so beautiful, Cathy. I fell in love with it the moment I set eyes on it and I just couldn't get it out of my mind. Then I had an idea. I'd already thought I might teach, so why not buy the house and turn it into a kind of music school? I could coach especially talented young pianists for the concert platform as I'd planned, but if I buy this house I could make it into a kind of musical retreat; organise weekend seminars – concerts and master classes – that kind of thing.'

'It sounds interesting, but I don't quite see where I come in.'

He looked at her thoughtfully. 'You are the closest to a family I've got. That's important to me and I'd like your opinion. Before I can even begin to think about this project there will be an enormous amount of work to be done. I thought you might be interested – have some ideas. You know, the woman's angle.' He laughed, looking at her plate of cooling food. 'And I think you'd better abandon those chopsticks and eat up your dinner. Mrs Johnson will be wanting you home. I think I'm already in her black books as it is.'

'Oh, but I want to hear more about the house. I can't wait to see it!'

'Then you'll come with me – this weekend – Sunday?'

She laughed as she obediently resorted to a fork and began to finish her food. 'I can see that if I want my curiosity satisfied I'm going to have to.'

As she finished her meal she reflected that tonight she had learned something else about Gerald. The more she was with him, the more she understood him. He was so easy to be with. She had missed him – blamed him for staying away so long. Yet now she saw that he had been busy trying to build a new life for himself. It must take courage to do that alone. To start again when your name

127

had been famous. How selfish she had been to think only of herself. She thought excitedly of the house he planned to buy and the fact that he actually valued *her* opinion. And she couldn't wait till Sunday.

The day dawned dull and cloudy, but the low cloud thinned to a fine mist which soon melted away to reveal a clear blue sky. As the sun rose higher a fine heat haze danced on the road ahead as Gerald drove the Jaguar eastwards. As they drove he told her more about the house and the village.

'It's called Melfordleigh. Only a few houses, a church and a pub. It's the kind of place that sailors, fishermen and artists like. It's a pretty village. Two long winding streets dip down towards the sea and there are lots of little lanes running off, with surprising glimpses of little gardens and courtyards full of colour.'

'And the sea? Is there a beach?'

'Not as such. There are little creeks that run out to the sea – perfect for mooring boats. And there's a long finger of land that curves out to sea for about half a mile. It makes a wonderful walk. But the best part is that it's quite unspoilt. The tourists haven't filled it with amusement arcades and whelk stalls, thank God. Luckily it's far too quiet and tucked away for the day trippers' tastes too.'

'And your house – the one you hope to buy?' Cathy found his enthusiasm infectious.

'It stands in about two acres of grounds, at the top of the village. There's a stream running through – what used to be the millstream actually. The watermill used to be downstream and at one time Cuckoo Lodge was the miller's house.'

'Cuckoo Lodge? I like the name.'

He pulled a face. 'Do you? I thought I might change it. I'm afraid my friends might think *I'm* cuckoo, burying myself in the country.'

'But you're sure it's what you want?' Cathy asked.

'I'm sure. For me it seems the perfect answer. This way I can still be involved in music and have the peace and quiet of the country too.' He smiled at her wryly. 'I don't doubt that the very friends who'll laugh the loudest will be only too happy to come and stay once I've restored the place and moved in.'

'Weekend house parties? Sounds like fun.'

'Not unless they're willing to work,' he told her. 'This project is going to be my living, remember. If they come they'll have to be willing to take a class or give a lecture.'

.'So – tell me some more about the house. How old is it?'

'The main part is Tudor, but there's an extra wing that was built on in Queen Anne's reign.'

'As old as that? And how big?'

'About six bedrooms upstairs. Downstairs it's difficult to say. Some walls may have to be taken out. There seems to have been a lot of alteration over the years. Goodness knows what might be lurking behind the hideous modern fireplaces. I'm hoping for some inglenooks.'

Cathy found herself looking forward to seeing it all for herself. She smiled at him. 'You make it all sound so exciting,' she said. 'I can't wait.'

When Gerald announced that they had arrived and drove in through broken gates that hung drunkenly on rusting hinges, Cathy felt a stab of disappointment. They stopped next to a tumbledown corrugated iron shed and Gerald switched off the engine and turned to her.

'That's what is laughingly termed the garage. At the moment it's blocking the view, but once it's down you'll be able to see the house from the gate. Come on.' He got out of the car, looking as excited as a child.

Cathy followed him hesitantly along a path of trodden grass, wondering what he could possibly see in a place as rundown as this. She'd had such high expectations and now that they'd actually arrived the place was such a let down. Then, as they turned the corner of the disintegrating garage, she stopped short and caught her breath. In front of her, its brickwork glowing rose red in the summer sunshine, was Cuckoo Lodge. Long and low, its two storeys were topped by a russet-tiled roof. Two rows of windows glinted at them like welcoming eyes.

'Like it?' Gerald was studying her face carefully.

She nodded, the house's magic spell rendering her speechless. It seemed to take on an almost tangible magnetism, reaching out to her invitingly as she stood there staring. 'Oh – I see what you mean,' she breathed. 'It's lovely.'

He was fishing the keys out of an inside pocket. 'Right, come on then, let's go in and see what you think of the inside.'

The heavy front door creaked back on its hinges, opening immediately on to a long, low-ceilinged room. At first they could hardly see anything, but when Gerald folded back the shutters on the windows the sun streamed in. Their footsteps raised dust which danced in motes along the beams of golden light. Now that she could see, Cathy saw that at one end of the room a huge Victorian fireplace almost filled one wall, while at the other a door stood open on to a square hall out of which rose a staircase.

'How odd that the front door leads straight into the living room,' she remarked.

Gerald nodded. 'I mentioned that to the agent. It seems there have been many alterations over the years and at one time the place was actually used as a pub.'

Cathy looked into all the rooms. There were two others downstairs besides the large living room; both of them looking on to the back of the house. Their windows had views of the tangled garden, rank with couch grass and weeds that reached halfway up the window frames. The kitchen was a built-on lean-to affair. It was a nightmare, with only the basic facilities – a stone sink, equipped with

130

a hand pump, a massive iron mangle and a rotting pine dresser. 'Does it have mains water and drainage?' she asked. 'And what about gas and electricity?' Dropping to her knees, she inspected a damp patch near the skirting board. 'Looks like rising damp,' she said. 'You'll be lucky if there isn't dry rot in these boards. The place has probably never had a dampcourse.'

Gerald's eyebrows rose. 'I'd no idea you were so knowledgeable,' he said. 'I'm impressed. I knew I was right to bring you.'

Standing up, Cathy dusted off her hands and gave him a long, level look. 'All this is part of my course at college. If you're going to patronise me, Gerald, I'll go and wait for you in the car.'

Suitably chastened, he reached out to touch her shoulder. 'I'm sorry.'

She stepped aside, dislodging his hand with the merest flick of her shoulder. Walking into the hall, she asked: 'Shall we look upstairs?'

There were six rooms on the floor above. Gerald remarked that two would need to be converted to bathrooms, but Cathy disagreed.

'If you want to keep all six rooms you could easily have two with en suite bathrooms,' she said. 'They're certainly big enough to be able to spare a little space. And that massive cupboard on the landing would make another for general use. You'd need to put in central heating too,' she mused. 'And the windows would probably need replacing. A house of this age is probably listed, which means you'd have to apply for permission and abide by their rules.' She looked at him, her head on one side. 'Have you checked the roof timbers for woodworm and beetle?'

Gerald began to laugh. 'Forgive me, Cathy, but I can't get over you. I shan't need a surveyor at this rate. On the other hand, I'm only just beginning to realise how much all this is going to cost me.' He pulled her to him and kissed

131

the top of her head. 'Let's go and find some lunch. I can't face any more of this on an empty stomach.'

Cathy had quite surprised herself. She was only just realising how much information from the lectures on architecture she had actually absorbed. And putting it into practical use was much more enjoyable than she could ever have imagined. Already she was picturing Cuckoo Lodge as it could be and the prospect of having a hand in its restoration filled her with excited anticipation.

They left the car where it was and walked down through the village. Cathy adored it. Off the steep, winding main street, little alleyways led to pretty cottages, their gardens and little courtyards filled with flowers. There were surprises everywhere. When they reached the bottom of the hill the air was fresh and invigorating with the salt smell of the sea. Facing them, a forest of masts lined the quayside where dozens of boats were moored. Creeks separated by banks of glistening wet sand wound like silver threads out to the sea.

Facing the quay was the Admiral Nelson, the most amazing building that Cathy had ever seen. The first-floor frontage was a replica of a ship's fo'c'sle, its dark timber decorated with brightly painted mermaids and dolphins. And the front entrance of the hostelry was guarded by a voluptuous figurehead with flowing blonde locks and an impossibly large bosom with nipples the size of oranges.

'The landlord tells me they were all that was salvaged from a ship that was wrecked off the coast here in 1811,' Gerald told her. 'If we're lucky we might get a table in the window with a view of the quay.'

They were lucky. The landlord remembered Gerald from earlier visits. Being a classical music lover he had also recognised him as a celebrity, but, guessing that he was off-duty, tactfully kept the recognition to himself.

The food was excellent. Sitting in the fo'c'sle window was

like being at sea and Cathy enjoyed it very much as she told Gerald enthusiastically.

He enjoyed her pleasure, appreciative of the fact that she was still young enough to behave so openly. 'And the house?' He looked at her enquiringly. 'Tell me the truth. Do you think I'm a fool even to consider it?'

She looked at him carefully before deciding that he really did want her opinion. 'Well – there *is* an awful lot that needs doing,' she said guardedly. 'It's going to cost you a lot of money.'

'Yes, I'd already worked that out for myself. What I want to know is – will it be worth it?'

She smiled. 'I think so. There's a certain something about the place. It's as though it wants you to save its life. *You*, I mean. Not just anyone. Standing there, looking at it, you can almost feel it *begging* you.' She glanced up at him. 'I expect you think I'm being silly?'

'Not at all. I knew I was right to bring you. I felt that the first time I saw it.'

'Of course you'll need to get experts in to advise you,' she went on practically. 'I mean, it would be silly to run yourself into unnecessary expense. It's a sad thought, but the place might have gone beyond help.'

He nodded decisively. 'I'll get on to someone tomorrow. I've got the name of a reliable firm of architects and surveyors. I just wanted you to confirm the hunch I had about the place. You've done that. Thanks, Cathy.'

'I don't know why I'm encouraging you to buy Cuckoo Lodge,' she said. 'If you do, I don't suppose I'll see much of you.'

He looked up at her sharply. 'Why do you say that?'

She shrugged. 'You'll want to supervise the restoration to begin with. Then when you move in you'll be busy arranging your new life – your music students and weekend seminars.'

'I won't lose touch with you though.'

'Won't you?' she said wistfully. 'You did before. I've hardly seen you since last Christmas.'

He averted his eyes from her direct green gaze. 'That was different. I was out of the country for much of that time.'

'Of course. Sorry.' She spooned sugar into her coffee and stirred. It was none of her business what he did with his free time, of course. And yet he had said she was the nearest he had to family. In that respect they were both in the same boat. Suddenly she looked up and said, 'Gerald, you must have known my mother.'

He looked up in surprise. 'Yes.'

'So – what was she like?'

He shrugged. 'She was beautiful. Stunning auburn hair like yours and green eyes.'

She shook her head. 'I know all that from her photographs. I meant, what was she like – as a person?'

'Well – what can I say? It was a long time ago. She was Dan's wife – your mother.'

She twisted the spoon between her fingers. 'You know of course that she left us – Dad and me? When I was a baby. Went off with some lover.'

'I did hear something, yes.'

She bit her lip. 'Dad was so forgiving. I don't see how he could be. I know I could never forgive someone who let me down like that. He only told me what really happened a few months before he died, you know. Until then I'd always thought she died when I was little. He didn't want me to think ill of her, especially after she was killed.' She looked at Gerald. 'You did know she was killed – in a car accident?'

'Yes. And he never told you.' He smiled gently. 'That sounds like Dan.'

'I've tried not to, and I know he wouldn't want me to, but I *do* think badly of her,' she admitted. 'Dad didn't deserve to be treated like that and I don't see how anyone can leave their baby.'

'We none of us know what we'd do, faced with the same dilemma,' he said softly.

'I keep thinking that maybe if she'd stayed – if Dad had been happier . . .'

He reached out to touch her hand. 'Cathy, don't torture yourself, wondering what might have been. I've learned that it's no use raking over the past. What's done is done. We can never know what might have happened if things had been different. Look at me. I'm losing so much through this – this wretched ailment of mine. But it's no use wishing for something we can't have. Things happen. We have to accept, adapt, and make the best of it.'

'You said something like that once before.'

'I'm not a wise man but at least I've learned that much.'

'You've got so much courage, Gerald. I wish I had half as much.'

They walked back up through the winding street to Cuckoo Lodge to stand staring at the house again. Gerald looked at Cathy. 'You still haven't seen the rest of it,' he said. 'There's lots more.' He took her hand. 'Come on, I'll show you.'

At the back of the house was a huddle of tumbledown outbuildings: a decaying wash house, its brickwork green with moss, an unspeakable corrugated iron privy, apparently occupied by several hundred spiders, a fuel store, and a rather imposing barn built of stone and timber.

'Once these are down you'd be able to see the garden from the back windows,' Gerald said with a sweep of his arm. 'Thought the barn might make rather a good studio. It was once used as a grain store for the mill and the agent seems to think it's structurally solid.'

They skirted the buildings, wading through the waist-high grass to what had once been a beautiful garden. Cathy recognised a group of lilacs, and there were fruit trees cordoned against a sun-warmed wall of pale pink brick. Foxgloves, ox-eye daisies and roses, long since gone to rampant briar, struggled for supremacy with invading nettles and rosebay willow herb. There was a huge gnarled apple tree with the remains of a swing hanging from one of its springy branches. Cathy was enthralled. 'Oh, Gerald, this could be lovely!'

A rusty iron gate at the bottom took them on to the bank of the stream where willows dipped their graceful fronds into the glassy green water. Among the reeds yellow flag iris grew in profusion, throwing their bright reflection into the stream. Looking into the dark water Cathy glimpsed a large brown speckled fish moving sluggishly among the weeds. Then suddenly she was startled as a family of mallards emerged from the curtain of willow, stirring the water into a thousand spreading ripples. The big fish vanished as the mother duck fussed noisily with her flotilla of ducklings, sending them scudding through the creamy water lilies. Cathy laughed delightedly.

'Oh, Gerald, look. Aren't they sweet? I wish I'd brought some bread so that we could feed them.'

He watched her enjoying it all. It made him ache deep inside to see her spontaneous pleasure. She was so young – so easily pleased by simple things. She reminded him so much of . . . He turned away abruptly. 'Time's getting on. I think we should make tracks for home.'

She followed him reluctantly back to the car. As he settled himself in the driving seat he said, 'I'll get that firm of architects on to it tomorrow. I wonder how long it would take them to make the place habitable? Always supposing it's possible.'

'I'll keep my fingers crossed.' Cathy sighed. 'Oh, Gerald, I do envy you. It'll be so *exciting*, watching the house come back to life again.'

He'd already started backing the car out into the lane, but now he stopped and switched off the engine, turning in his seat to look at her. 'How would you like to be part of it?' he asked. 'How would you like to come and live here with me when it's done?'

Cathy felt the warm blood creep up her neck and into her cheeks. 'What – what do you mean?'

'What I say. After all, I am your guardian – and your godfather.'

'But – I have my course to finish.'

He studied her face for a moment and then turned away. 'Of course. You have your own life – all your own friends. And then there's Matthew, isn't there?'

She frowned. 'Matthew? What does he have to do with it?'

'He's your – what do you call it? – steady boyfriend, isn't he?'

'No.'

He started the engine again. 'You talk an awful lot about him, or perhaps you hadn't realised that.' He was out on the road now and began to press his foot down on the accelerator. 'Forget that I asked you, Cathy. Silly of me to imagine that a girl of your age would want to bury herself alive in a hole like this – and with a sick old man.'

Shocked, she turned troubled eyes on him and laid a hand lightly on his wrist. 'Gerald, you're not sick. And you're not an old man. You know you're not.'

He glanced at her. 'I must seem like one, to you.'

'But you don't. And there's nothing I'd like more than to live at Cuckoo Lodge and be part of all the exciting things you're planning.'

'It's all right. You don't have to be kind or feel sorry for me, you know.'

For the next few miles they drove in silence, Cathy puzzling over what she could have done or said to upset him. She wasn't aware of having talked a lot about Matthew. And going to live at Cuckoo Lodge with Gerald would be like some kind of wonderful dream come true. But how could she make him see this without making a fool of herself again?

137

They drove for most of the way in silence, each occupied with their own thoughts. The countryside gave way to buildings. They were almost home and Cathy had begun to despair, fearing that they would part on a sour note when Gerald suddenly turned to her.

'Would you like a drink before you go home? I think perhaps we should talk.'

She nodded silently, wondering apprehensively what they would talk about.

She'd been expecting him to pull up at a coffee bar or café and when he drew the car on to the forecourt of the Dog and Feathers she was a little surprised. Apart from the Queen's Head she had never been inside a pub before, but she didn't want him to know, so she tried to look as though it was something she did everyday.

It was a typical suburban pub, with folksy decor: mock beams and chintzes, horse brasses, and a log fire that was powered by electricity. But it was comfortable enough. As it was early in the evening there were few customers and plenty of seats. Cathy settled herself at a table by the window and Gerald asked her what she would like to drink. She said the first thing that came into her head.

'A dry martini, please.' The heroines in films always drank dry martinis and it had a sophisticated, feminine sound to it.

If Gerald was surprised he didn't show it. He came back to the table with the drinks and sat down beside her. 'Cathy – first I must ask your forgiveness. I'm sorry if I embarrassed you.'

'You didn't. It's all right.' She couldn't look at him. Raising the glass to her lips she took a mouthful of the pale liquid and almost choked on the bitterness that coursed down her throat like liquid fire.

'Are you all right?' he asked, seeing her eyes water.

She nodded. 'Yes . . . it's . . .' She pulled a face. 'I've

never actually had one of these before. I'm sorry but I'm afraid I don't like it very much.'

Smiling gently he took the glass from her hand and put it on the table. It was the proof that he'd been pushing her too hard. She'd probably much rather have had a lemonade or Coca-Cola. She was trying so hard to please him. 'You don't have to drink it.' He leaned closer. 'You don't have to do anything you don't want to, Cathy. It was mean of me to pressure you like that. Selfish. It's just that sometimes the thought of starting again – of being alone – scares me.'

She squeezed his hand and looked earnestly into his eyes. 'But I *would* like to live at Cuckoo Lodge with you,' she said. 'When I've finished my course.' She smiled at him. 'Anyway, it's going to take ages for the place to be ready, isn't it? There's plenty of time.'

He sighed, his heart heavy. Plenty of time was something she took for granted – whereas he . . . 'Of course,' he said. 'Plenty of time.'

'And you will take me again – to see the work, won't you?' she asked. 'To see the house taking shape? I've had such a lovely day, Gerald.' She glanced at him. 'Oh, and by the way . . .'

'Yes?'

'I don't see you as an old man. And I don't feel in the least sorry for you. So there!'

He laughed, leaning across to kiss her forehead. 'I'm delighted to hear it!'

Chapter Eight

The row over Mrs Blake senior's room marked the end of the honeymoon for Una and Don. For days afterwards Rosalind had to endure mealtimes frigid with animosity when neither her mother nor Don spoke one word; embarrassingly making whatever requests were necessary through her. Once, when Una addressed a scathing remark to no one in particular about living in the past, Don looked up from his *Daily Telegraph*, his face dark with anger.

'For Christ's sake, woman! Here we are on the brink of nuclear war and all you can think of is your damned bungalow.' He pushed the newspaper under her nose. 'Here – read about it.' He jabbed a finger at the headline that read: **CUBAN CRISIS. Kennedy Calls Up 150,000 Reservists.** 'If something isn't done soon about Castro none of us will have any *need* to worry about living in the past. We won't ever see 1963!' He strode out of the room.

But even thoughts of being blown to Kingdom Come didn't prevent Una from complaining. At night, through the walls of her room, Rosalind could hear the angry hum of their voices, spiked with the odd distinguishable word or phrase – *selfish* – *obsession* – *living in the past*. Her heart sank as she buried her head among the pillows, reminded miserably of her anguished childhood. At times she almost wished she had given up her cherished career dreams and accepted Ben and Freda's invitation to go with them to Australia. Rows, even those she was not directly involved in, made her feel physically sick. Voices raised in anger made her stomach churn and her heart thump uncomfortably and all the fears and insecurities of her

140

childhood crowded in on her till she felt suffocated and wretched.

As Una and Don quarrelled behind their closed door she would shut her eyes and force herself to picture the lovely home she would have one day. A home that would be her livelihood too. Once she had achieved that no one could ever take it away from her.

Even when Don wasn't home there was little peace. Una constantly carped about him, tacitly urging Rosalind to take her side. She began to dread coming home from school each afternoon to hear a catalogue of Don's shortcomings. The weeks went by and the Cuban crisis was resolved, but at Blake's Folly things grew worse instead of better. Don stubbornly refused to move from Jay's Lane, paying no heed to Una's threats to leave him. She began to realise that he wasn't as easygoing or as eager to please as she had been led to believe. Without referring to the fact, both of them knew that with no money of her own, no job or home, she had little choice but to stay. His calm complacency infuriated Una, who felt trapped and cheated.

'If you ask me he's some kind of pervert,' she said waspishly for the hundredth time one day in early-November as she and Rosalind were having tea. 'Keeping all his mother's things locked up in that room like some kind of holy sanctum. I couldn't put up with that, could I? I mean, it was like something out of a horror film. When he came home and found I'd turfed them all out that afternoon he went white with rage – *white!*' she repeated with lurid satisfaction. 'I tell you, Rossie, I thought he was going to hit me.' She puffed out her breath explosively. 'Not that he wouldn't be sorry if he tried anything like that, I can tell you. Even your pig of a father knew better than to lay a finger on me. Don might think he's got the upper hand, but just you wait. I'll think of something, never you fear.'

Rosalind ate up her tea quickly, wanting desperately to take herself off to her room and get on with her homework.

She hated hearing her father spoken of in those terms. And she found the atmosphere of hostility in the house oppressive and nerve-racking. She didn't really blame Don for being angry. On that awful afternoon Una had not only forced the lock on the bedroom door but thrown all Don's mother's clothes and possessions into boxes and telephoned the Salvation Army to come and collect them. All without an ounce of respect for his feelings on the matter.

Rosalind had once made the mistake of trying to make Una see his point of view. 'She was his mother, Mum,' she ventured. 'He must have been deeply hurt to see you throwing all her things out as though they were rubbish.'

Una bridled. 'They *were* rubbish,' she said unrepentantly. 'There was stuff there that must have come out of the ark. Anyway, she's dead. It's unhealthy, hoarding dead people's things.' She glared at Rosalind. 'Anyway, who asked for your opinion? It's *me* he's married to. I'm his wife and mistress of this house now. I should be able to have some say in what happens in it.'

Privately, Rosalind thought Una had got away with plenty of say so far. She had already thrown out most of the furniture without too many reproaches from Don. But she knew better than to express the opinion.

'What that poor Monica went through God only knows,' Una muttered darkly, rolling her eyes ceilingward. 'Thank heaven I wasn't here when his old cow of a mother was alive. Mind you, if I had been things would have been different.'

'Who's Monica?' Rosalind asked mildly.

'Don's first wife, of course. I told you. She came to see me when he was at that conference. Not a bit like he said she was. Really nice and ladylike. She told me a thing or two about Don and his precious mother!'

Rosalind was of the opinion that 'poor Monica' had visited Una simply to make mischief, but again, she kept that thought to herself, knowing better than to antagonise Una still further.

Since the big row, Don had taken to staying out till quite late each night on the pretext of working late at the office. And with Rosalind alone in her room, busy with her homework, Una soon found time hanging heavily on her hands. As week followed week her belligerent mood changed to one of wounded martyrdom. One evening when Rosalind went downstairs to make herself a bedtime drink she found her mother poring over her photograph album. There was a glass in her hand, and beside her on the table was a half-empty bottle of gin.

'Look, Rossie,' she said, pointing to the album. 'This one was when we were in *Here We Are Again* on Clacton Pier, summer of '39, it was. Just before the war started. See, all dressed as pierrots for the opening chorus. Those were the days. I was just fifteen. It was my first job.' She shook her head and dabbed at a tear on her cheek. 'Your father was twenty-two and so handsome. I fell for him the moment I set eyes on him. They were happy days. It was before we were married of course – long before you were born.'

Trying to ignore the implication, Rosalind pushed a mug of cocoa towards her mother. 'Come on, have your cocoa, Mum. You've drunk too much of that stuff. It always makes you depressed.'

Una raised mascara-smudged eyes towards her daughter. 'Depressed? Bloody devastated more like! Oh, Rossie, I thought all our worries were going to be over when I married Don. I really thought he loved me and wanted me to be happy. But he doesn't want a wife. He wants a replacement for his damned mother. He's *useless* as a husband. He's living in the past when he was a kid and he and his mother were living here together.'

She snuffled into her handkerchief. 'He told me he admired me – said I was attractive and smart. He said he liked *strong* women. But he still wants all his own way.

143

Sometimes I get the feeling that what he really meant was that he'd like me to take a hairbrush to his backside!' She looked at Rosalind's shocked face, her eyes slightly unfocused. 'There – didn't know there were men around like him, did you? Well, you do now. Creepy, isn't it?'

She closed the photograph album with a slap and sighed despairingly. 'I tell you, Rossie, if I had any money I'd be out of this morgue tomorrow. I've been thinking lately. I've a good mind to go back to the stage. I believe my voice is as good as ever it was. I practise every morning when I've got the house to myself. I've a damned good mind to look for an agent and see what I can get.'

Rosalind's heart sank. She remembered only too vividly the tempers and depressions; the fruitless trips up and down Charing Cross Road; the dingy back street bed-sits and always being hungry. Suppose they had to move away – some place where it was too far for her to get to school? She bit her lip, ashamed at the selfishness of the thought, then reminded herself that if no one else was prepared to consider her future, she would have to take care of it herself.

'Don't be silly, Mum,' she said firmly. 'You know you don't want to start on that kind of life all over again. I'm sure Don thinks the world of you really. Why don't you say you're sorry – make up your quarrel and forget all about it?'

Although Una shrugged her shoulders dismissively, she must have taken Rosalind's advice to heart in some measure because after that evening things improved slightly. Una and Don began to speak to each other again and, to Rosalind's relief, the atmosphere in the house relaxed a little.

At Hallard's store there was to be a grand Christmas fashion show and as usual Una was organising it; travelling up to Regent Street with Don each morning and returning with him in the evenings. Rosalind was glad. At least her mother had something other than Don's intransigence over the house with which to occupy her mind. And one of the benefits was that Rosalind came home after school each day to an empty, blessedly peaceful house in which to get on with her homework.

As well as sending out the usual invitations the fashion show had been widely advertised and was to take place on 5 December. Anticipating a good attendance, it was to take place in the restaurant on the top floor of the Regent Street store. Una had been given *carte blanche* to engage any outside help she needed and had used an old contact from her theatrical days to find a professional scenic designer – a young man called Stuart Hamilton who, according to Una, had some really new and innovative ideas.

Once end of term exams were over at St Margaret's the sixth form were free to take the odd day off and Una suggested that Rosalind might like to go along and help with the show preparations. At first she was reluctant.

'I don't know the first thing about fashion shows, Mum,' she said. 'I'll only get in the way.'

'No, you won't. There's heaps to do. Holding it in the restaurant means we have just a few hours to get everything ready. Every pair of hands is needed and you're not doing anything else, are you?'

Rosalind had little choice in the matter. But when she arrived on the morning of the show she felt awkward and in the way. Everyone else seemed to know exactly what they were doing. There were florists, busy with their arrangements; hairdressers, snipping and teasing, buyers from the various fashion departments scurrying in and out of the lift pulling rails of garments behind them. Electricians balanced on top of ladders and carpenters hammered away. Even the lowliest junior assistant from the model gown department fetched and carried purposefully while Rosalind simply stood around, feeling inadequate and useless.

She was just wondering if anyone would miss her if she

crept away when a voice startled her: 'Hello. You're looking a bit lost. Anything I can do?'

She turned to see a tall young man in jeans and an open-necked shirt looking at her. He had fair hair that flopped over his forehead and his grey eyes held a hint of indulgent amusement as he looked her over appraisingly.

She blushed and lifted her shoulders in a helpless gesture. 'My mother – Mrs Blake – asked me to come along and help, but I just feel in the way.'

'Hell let loose, isn't it?' he said sympathetically. His voice was soft with the merest hint of a Scottish accent. 'It might all look chaotic but I can assure you that everyone knows what they're doing. It'll all come together beautifully by this afternoon.'

'I'm sure it will. That's why I feel in the way. It's all so organised. I'm sure if I touch anything it will fall apart in my hands and ruin everything.'

'Of course it wouldn't. But I do know how you must feel.' He smiled warmly and offered his hand. 'I'm Stuart Hamilton. I designed the set.' He pointed to the stage where sequin-scattered gauze was draped against a dark blue velvet backdrop.

'It's designed to resemble a moonlit frozen waterfall,' he explained. 'I'm just about to check and see if it works, so cross your fingers.' He cupped his hands to his mouth and shouted above the hubbub to the electrician who was waiting somewhere out of sight to turn on the lights.

As the sharp blue and white beams flooded the stage the set came instantly and magically to life, so that it shimmered and sparkled like living frost.

Rosalind gasped with delight. 'Oh! It's *lovely!*'

'I thought it was a good idea to keep it simple,' Stuart said modestly. 'Icicles and frost are so pretty aren't they? No colours to clash with the clothes.'

'No. You're very clever.'

'Not really. It's just my job.' He smiled into her eyes.

'You know there is something you can do. It'd save my life right at this moment.'

'Really? What's that?'

'Rustle up some coffee. I wouldn't mind betting there are a few dry throats around gasping for a cup.'

Glad to have something to do, Rosalind turned towards the kitchen. 'Of course. I should have thought. I'll get something organised.'

When she came back from the kitchen with a borrowed trolley and coffee, tea and biscuits for everyone she found herself on the receiving end of smiles of gratitude. She found Una at the back of the restaurant, in earnest conversation with Stuart. She was using the voice she reserved for people she wanted to impress.

'Rosalind, I'd like you to meet my friend, Stuart Hamilton,' she said sweetly, simpering up at the young man. 'You're not going to believe it, Stuart, but this is my daughter.'

'We've already met.' He took a cup from the trolley. 'What a thoughtful idea to lay on coffee for us all. I'm sure we're all dying for a cup.'

Rosalind blushed, grateful to him for pretending the idea had been hers.

Una looked from one to the other. 'Stuart is a freelance scenic designer,' she said.

He laughed. 'The term "freelance" is a bit of a euphemism. It's just another way of saying I'm out of work.'

Una swept his modesty aside. 'Not for long, I'm sure. Hasn't he done a wonderful job for us, Rossie?'

'Super. When the lights were on just now it looked like something out of a fairytale.'

'I know. None of those garish reds and greens usually associated with Christmas events,' Una said with satisfaction. 'I hope Stuart will be able to do this again for us. Though I'm sure some West End producer will have snapped him up by then.'

'Much as I'd like to work for you again, Mrs Blake, I hope you're right.' Stuart looked at his watch. 'Well, I think I've done about all I can for the moment. What about a spot of lunch?'

Una shook her head. 'Not for me. Lunch is out of the question, I'm afraid. As soon as I'm satisfied that everything is done here, I've got to find time to change and get my face and hair done. I shall be busy right up until we open the doors.'

He looked at Rosalind. 'What about you then? Will you join me?'

'*Me?*' Rosalind was taken aback. 'Oh, well . . .'

'Come on, I hate eating alone,' he said persuasively. 'You have to eat something and with your mother so busy . . .' He smiled. 'Nothing fancy. A glass of wine and a sandwich is what I usually have.'

Sitting in the small pub that Stuart took her to, at the back of the store in Argyle Street, Rosalind felt tongue-tied and awkward. She'd never been out with a member of the opposite sex before. At least not alone like this. At the bar, she'd tried to pay for her own lunch and been overcome with embarrassment when he'd insisted on paying. Now she sat listening to him telling her about the flat in Earls Court he shared with an old school friend called Julian Travers; his art school training and the way his career had been disrupted when he was called up for his National Service.

'Didn't you like being in the army?' she asked, feeling stupid.

He raised an eyebrow at her. 'It was a terrible waste of time, frustrating too.' He leaned towards her. 'I actually missed getting a marvellous job because of it – to do the costumes and sets for a production of *Romeo and Juliet* at Stratford.'

'Stratford on Avon?' Rosalind asked, impressed.

He cleared his throat. 'Ah – well, no. Stratford East as a matter of fact. But it would have been a marvellous shop

148

window for me.' He put the last of his beef sandwich into his mouth and chewed thoughtfully. 'Still, maybe the big break will come eventually.'

Rosalind sipped at her glass of red wine. She found it rather acid, but would have died rather than admit it. 'What does your flat-mate – er – Julian do?' she asked. 'Is he a designer too?'

He shook his head. 'No. He's a playwright, though he works for a firm of solicitors in the daytime. He's enormously talented. As a matter of fact he's writing a musical play, with the help of a musician chum of ours. The three of us are hoping to work on it together.'

'Did you know that my mother was in the theatre before she worked at Hallard's?' she asked him.

'Una?' He looked at her over the rim of his wine glass, his eyes widening with surprise. 'No *kidding*? She never mentioned that.'

'She gave it all up some time ago.'

'Why did she do that?'

'To bring me up basically,' Rosalind said. 'She and my father had a singing act, you see. They separated – divorced. Una got custody of me. I was quite small at the time.'

'So she gave up her career? What a sacrifice. She must be a very devoted mother.'

'Mmm.' Rosalind looked into her glass and said nothing.

'And then she married Mr Blake. The general manager at Hallard's?'

'That's right.'

'And your father – do you still see him?'

'I used to. But he and his new singing partner have gone to Australia. He writes though. I had an airmail letter last week to say they've arrived safely and have their first booking.'

'You must miss him.'

'I do. He did ask me to go with him, but I decided not to.'

149

'I can't blame you, with a wonderful mother like yours. I'm sure she would have been devastated to lose you. Does she miss being on the stage?'

'I think so – now and again. Sometimes she talks about going back to it. That's why she loves doing these shows. It's the closest she gets to working in the theatre nowadays.'

'You know, now that you mention it, a lot of things fit about Una,' he said thoughtfully. 'She's obviously been a very beautiful woman in her time. And that voice of hers . . . so musical. It's the voice of a singer.' He leaned towards her and looked at her with eyes that seemed to melt into hers. 'But what about you, Rosalind? You haven't mentioned yourself. What do you do?'

Suddenly her mouth dried and her hands became clammy. She put down her glass, afraid that it might slip through her fingers. 'I'm still – studying,' she said, feeling her cheeks burn. Saying that she was still at school sounded so silly. Odd, she had never been ashamed of the fact before.

'Studying? You're a student then?'

'Yes. Well – no, not exactly. Not at college.' She lowered her eyes. 'I'm taking my A levels actually. I want to go on and study hotel management.'

'Hotel management. Really?' He was looking at her as though she were the most fascinating person he had ever met and she was acutely conscious of the fact that her hair needed trimming and there was a hateful spot coming on her chin. Even at this moment she could feel it shining like a beacon. 'What made you choose a career like that with your background?'

'I don't know really. It's something I've wanted ever since I can remember. When I was little and my parents were touring I used to join them in the school holidays. The hotels and boarding houses where we stayed were always so dreary.' She laughed self-consciously. 'I suppose I've always believed I could do better.' She pushed nervously at the bridge of her glasses, wishing she'd taken Freda's advice and seen the optician about having a pair of the new contact lenses fitted.

He was nodding understandingly. '*Believing*. That's the key word, isn't it? If you think positively you can make anything come true. I used to feel like you when my parents took me to the pantomime at Christmas. In the little border town where we lived, up near Berwick, we only got small touring companies and the sets were no more than tatty backdrops and curtains. I used to go home and draw designs for the sets as I'd like to have seen them: enchanted forests, castles and majestic ballrooms. I'd actually build them in miniature out of old shoe boxes, and work out how to light them to make them look real.'

'You must have had a natural talent,' Rosalind said shyly.

He smiled ruefully. 'I only wish there was some kind producer who'd share your confidence in my ability.' He looked at his watch. 'Heavens, look at the time. We'd better be getting back to Hallard's if we want to be there for the opening.'

The restaurant was almost full when they arrived. As there was nothing more for Stuart to do he sat with Rosalind at the back and watched with her as the gilt chairs gradually filled up and the assembly of elegant women filled the rows set out in a horseshoe around the catwalk. The atmosphere heightened as the excited, high-pitched chatter of the audience mingled with the soft music of the hired string quartet. On the stroke of two-thirty the curtains parted to reveal Stuart's setting and Una herself stepped out into the spotlight to open the show. She had changed out of her slacks and sweater into an elegant black velvet suit trimmed with sequins and jet beads that picked up the light glamorously as she moved. The senior stylist from the hairdressing salon on the fourth floor had swept her hair up and secured it to one side with a diamante clip. When she had made the opening introduction Stuart nudged Rosalind.

'Your mother's really terrific, isn't she? It's easy to see that this is her line of work,' he said. 'That voice of hers reaches every corner of the room effortlessly. And she looks an absolute knock-out.'

'Yes.' Rosalind felt plain and clumsy as she watched her mother step gracefully aside to make way for the first model to step on to the catwalk. Listening to her rich, resonant voice and seeing her move in that stylish and elegant way made Rosalind feel hopelessly inadequate. She'd never be as attractive as Una if she lived to be a hundred. Physically, she took after her father, whose handsome features seemed to her to sit uneasily on a feminine countenance.

Almost as though he could read her thoughts, Stuart reached for her hand and gave it a small comforting squeeze. 'I don't know when you're free, but I'd like to see you again some time, Rosalind,' he whispered.

She turned to stare at him in astonishment. Had she heard him right? Surely he hadn't said he wanted to see her again? Not *her*. 'Sorry. What – er . . .' She cleared her throat. 'What did you say?'

He laughed gently. 'I said, I'd like to see you again. You look shocked. Is it such an appalling prospect?'

She was grateful for the subdued lighting as she felt hot colour suffuse her face. '*No!* I mean, no, it isn't appalling – not at all.'

'So – you'd like to? To see me, I mean?'

'Yes.' She swallowed hard. 'When?'

He shrugged. 'What about tomorrow evening? I'm not doing anything. Are you?'

'No. That would be lov – er – very nice. Thank you.'

He slipped out of his chair and bent to whisper in her ear. 'I've got to go now. I'll come and pick you up tomorrow around seven, all right?'

'Yes – fine.' As he began to walk away she suddenly remembered that she hadn't given him her address. She half rose from her seat, then sat down again, biting her lip. It would look as though she were running after him. Besides, he could always get it from the phone book if he really intended to come. She couldn't believe that he would actually turn up. She sank low in her chair, her cheeks burning and her heart beating fast. She was shaken by the way he had made her feel. What could a young man as stunningly attractive as Stuart possibly see in her?

When she told her mother that he had asked her for a date, Una stared at her incredulously. 'He asked you *out*? I do hope you didn't push yourself at him,' she said unflatteringly. 'Young men don't like girls who make the first move, you know.'

'I didn't,' Rosalind said. 'He's picking me up at home tomorrow evening.'

'Where's he taking you?'

'I don't know. He didn't say.'

'Well, if he suggests going back to his flat you say no, do you hear me?' In Una's book there was only one feasible reason for a boy like Stuart to ask a girl like Rosalind out. After all, what could possibly attract him to a plain girl with whom he had nothing in common? She looked at her daughter curiously. 'What did you talk about when he took you to lunch?'

Rosalind shrugged. 'He told me about his training and his National Service. He said that his flat-mate, Julian, is writing a musical play and he's hoping to design the sets and costumes for it.'

Una's eyes sharpened with interest. 'Did he now? Any chance of having it put on?'

'I don't think they've got that far,' Rosalind said.

Stuart arrived on time, having driven out to Stanmore in his flatmate's car, borrowed specially for the occasion. Rosalind saw him from behind the curtains of her bedroom window where she'd been watching and was inordinately relieved that he had, after all, known where she lived. She had been ready for three-quarters of an hour; wearing a new dress she'd bought that morning with some of her weekend job money. She'd washed her hair and applied a little make-up. The effect was hardly dramatic, but it was the best she could do. When she saw Stuart getting out of the smart little red Mini car her heart began to drum with excitement. She'd been so afraid that even if he knew the address he might not turn up. She'd even mentioned her fear to her mother that morning. Una had laughed dismissively.

'Oh, he'll turn up all right,' she said. 'He'll be wanting to work with Hallard's again. I don't think he'd have the bare-faced cheek to come back and ask me for work if he'd stood you up.'

Rosalind reached the top of the stairs just in time to see Una already opening the front door. She too seemed to have dressed for the occasion. She wore tight-fitting black slacks and a white angora sweater. Her wrists jangled with chunky bracelets and Rosalind could see even from this distance that she was wearing her false eyelashes. As she watched, her mother embraced Stuart warmly.

'*Stuart!* Do come in, darling. How handsome you look. You know, I can't tell you how pleased I am that you've offered to take poor Rossie out. So kind of you. She doesn't have much fun, poor love. She hasn't any friends – spends most of her time tucked away upstairs with her books.' She took his coat almost forcibly from him, then smiled up at him coquettishly. 'Now, you will have a drink while you're waiting, won't you? After all, it is almost Christmas.'

Stuart smiled. 'Thank you. A drink would be very nice.'

Rosalind walked slowly down the stairs. They were in the drawing room, now furnished in a bizarre blend of peacock blue and jade which went together surprisingly well. Una stood at the new cocktail cabinet where she'd already made up a shaker full of martinis. When she caught sight of Rosalind, standing hesitantly in the doorway she said, 'Ah, there you are, darling. Why don't you put some music on? That new record *Stranger on the Shore*. Or perhaps Stuart is more of a classical fan?' She looked enquiringly at him as she pressed a glass into his hand.

He shook his head. 'I like most kinds of music, thanks.' He looked at Rosalind. 'Aren't you having a drink with us?'

Una wagged an admonishing finger at him. 'Orange juice for Rossie. She's still a schoolgirl, remember. Can't have you leading my little girl into naughty ways, can we?' She sat down, crossing her legs and hitching up one velvet trouser leg to display a shapely ankle adorned with a fine gold chain. 'Now – where are you off to, you two?'

'I thought we'd go to the pictures,' he said.

'Very nice. Well, don't be late home, will you, Rossie?'

She walked with them to the front door and while Rosalind was putting on her coat, said, 'Oh, by the way, we're having a party on New Year's Eve. Would you like to come, Stuart? There'll probably be some theatrical celebrities there. You never know, you might meet someone who could be useful to you. Bring your flat-mate too if you like. Julian, isn't it? The more the merrier.'

Hot with shame and humiliation Rosalind followed Stuart silently to the car. It was the first she'd heard about a party. And as far as she was aware, Una didn't know any theatrical celebrities. If Stuart and his friend came with high expectations they were likely to be disappointed.

As he settled into the driving seat he looked at her. 'You're very quiet. Are you all right?'

She nodded. 'My mother treats me like a child. I'm eighteen.'

He laughed. 'Parents are hell, aren't they? Don't worry. My mother used to be just the same when I lived at home.' He drove in silence for a moment then he said: 'Of course, your mother is incredibly young to have a grown-up daughter.

I daresay seeing her child growing up makes her want to hang onto her youth.'

'Maybe.' Rosalind began to feel better. Stuart was so kind and understanding. She still couldn't believe that he actually wanted to take her out.

After the film they went to a coffee bar close to the cinema. During the film Stuart had held her hand. It had felt so warm and comforting in the dark, but now, as they faced each other across the small table, Rosalind found herself embarrassed and tongue-tied once again. She thought of Carla Maybridge, who was always boasting about her numerous conquests and the older men she had dated. '*You have to show them you're in control, that's the trick,*' Rosalind had heard her boasting to an eager audience. If only she could be more like her, self-assured and confident.

'Thank you for taking me out,' she said shyly. 'I enjoyed the film very much.'

'So did I.' He smiled. 'I enjoyed being with you too.'

She shook her head. 'I can't think why.'

He looked concerned. 'Why do you say that?'

Her throat constricted as she stared hopelessly into her coffee. He wasn't going to see her again so she might as well be honest. 'Because I'm not pretty. I can't think of a single interesting thing to say. And I haven't a clue when it comes to knowing how to dress.'

'I don't agree. You're much too hard on yourself.' He reached across to take her hand. 'But *if* any of those things were true I'm sure there's plenty you could do about it.'

She looked up at him. 'Such as?'

He smiled. 'Well, for a start, you have all Hallard's fashion departments at your disposal.'

'I can't afford to buy clothes from Hallard's.'

'Then there's your hair.'

'It's poker straight.'

'It's a lovely colour, like a ripe chestnut, and it's thick and shiny. Have it well cut or even permed.'

Her hand went automatically to her head. 'I did have it cut last summer when I went to visit my father in Brighton. Lots of people said it looked nice, but Mum didn't like it so I grew it again. I was thinking of getting some contact lenses too.'

'No need. Glasses suit you – though you could get more flattering frames. You have beautiful eyes, Rosalind. Hasn't anyone ever told you that?'

'No.' He was looking at her with such sincerity that she blushed crimson and fumbled in her handbag to hide her embarrassment.

He looked at his watch and sighed. 'Oh, dear. I suppose I'd better get you home. I don't want to get into your mother's black books.'

He stopped the car two doors away from Blake's Folly, saying that the corner wasn't a safe place to park. Turning towards her, he cupped her face in his hands and looked at her. 'You should try to have more confidence in yourself, Rosalind.' Very gently he removed her glasses and lifted the heavy fringe away from her forehead. 'You have beautiful bones. A face like something from an Egyptian frieze. You shouldn't hide it.' He drew her towards him and kissed her, his lips holding hers firmly as they trembled like a captive butterfly under his touch.

'My poor frightened little Rosalind,' he whispered, stroking her hair. 'Relax, darling. Keep telling yourself that someone thinks you're beautiful. It's true.'

When he pulled her gently into his arms she allowed herself to melt against him and when his lips sought hers again she responded as everything in her cried out to do. Closing her eyes she gave herself up to the warmth of his kiss and even when he gently parted her lips with his tongue she resisted only for a moment. It was like a miracle. Someone actually *wanted* her. Not just someone – Stuart. Handsome, talented Stuart. And because he had said she was beautiful she believed it. She actually *felt* beautiful.

157

When he released her she was trembling. He looked at her for a moment. 'Are you all right?'

'Yes. I'm fine.'

'I think you'd better go in now or your mother will be worrying.'

'Yes, of course.' She took her glasses from the dashboard where he had put them and slipped them on again. As she was getting out of the car she turned and asked him: 'When – when will I see you again?'

He laughed and she saw the gleam of his eyes and his teeth, shining white in the dimness. 'At the party of course. On New Year's Eve.'

'Oh, yes. I forgot.' She licked her lips. 'What about Christmas?'

'Off home to Berwick.'

'Of course. Well – thank you for a lovely evening, Stuart. See you on New Year's Eve then.'

'You bet.' As she got out on to the pavement he started the car. 'Happy Christmas, Rosalind,' he called out. 'Take care of yourself. And remember what I said.'

'I will. Happy Christmas.'

She stood watching until the red tail lights of the car rounded the corner and he was gone. Then she hurried indoors, hoping that Una wouldn't be waiting to quiz her about the evening. All she wanted was to snuggle down in bed, put out the light and re-live every detail of the whole magical evening, hugging his words and the warmth of his kisses to herself like some wonderful gift.

Chapter Nine

Gerald was walking across the reception hall of Zenith's offices in Marble Arch when he bumped into Kay Goolden. If he'd seen her in time he would probably have avoided her but she'd already spotted him stepping out of the lift and it was too late. As she made her way determinedly towards him, her high heels tapping on the marble floor and her face alight with determination, his heart sank.

'Gerry darling! Long time no see. What are you doing here? Have you decided to renew your contract after all?'

'No.'

'You're going to record for another company?' She shrugged. 'Well it's a shame after all these years, but I can't say I'm surprised. If it's a question of money . . .'

'It isn't. I'm retiring from music. At least from public performing.' He allowed himself a small ironic grin. 'As I'm quite sure you've heard.'

'Well, one hears so much on the grapevine,' she said with a dismissive lift of her shoulders. 'One learns to take most of it with a large pinch of salt. I must say, though, that I'd hoped it wasn't true.'

'Well, it is, so you can consider the rumour officially confirmed.'

She looked at him thoughtfully. 'That can't have been an easy decision, Gerry. I know you, remember? We go back a long way. Music has always been your whole life. What happened to bring about this change of heart?'

'Sometimes life takes a twist that makes us take stock and realise that there are other things besides work.'

She raised a cynical eyebrow. 'The road to Damascus

syndrome, eh? Very philosophical. I also heard that you'd inherited a young ward – the daughter of a deceased friend?'

'Well, you heard correctly on that count too.'

She took a step towards him and laid a hand on his arm. He caught a whiff of *Arpège*, the perfume that would always be exclusively Kay to him. She was looking marvellous; slender as ever in her dark tailored suit. She'd changed her hairstyle too. Now she wore it longer, high in front and with the ends flicked up. He was slightly dismayed at the discovery that he still found her attractive.

'Gerry . . .' She was looking almost imploringly into his eyes. 'What's the matter, love? There's something wrong, isn't there? Surely you can tell me.'

'Tell you what? Why is everyone making such a mystery of my retirement? It's just that I'm sick of concert halls – of temperamental conductors – of living out of suitcases. I want a different, a more peaceful life, that's all. Call it old age creeping on if you like.'

'Nonsense!' She laughed. 'You're in your prime and you know it.'

'Well, I don't know about that. All I know is that I want out of it. God knows I've made enough money to see me comfortably through the rest of my life. It's time I enjoyed the benefits a little.'

'And that's really all it is?' Clearly she didn't believe a word of it.

'Yes. That's all it is.'

'And you're not going to touch a piano for the rest of your days? What a diabolical waste!'

'I didn't say that.'

'No, you didn't, did you?' She paused, looking at him speculatively. 'Come and have lunch.'

He hesitated. 'If you're hoping to pump me, forget it. You won't get anything else out of me, Kay. There *is* nothing else.'

'What a hurtful suggestion. As if I would!' She laughed and slipped her arm through his. 'Come anyway – for old times' sake.'

They took a cab and Kay told the driver to go to *L'Escargot Bienvenu* in Greek Street. It had once been their special place, their favourite restaurant.

Seated at a secluded corner table upstairs, she took off her jacket. Under it was a plain white silk shirt and he noticed that she was wearing the gold chain necklace he had bought her in New York. When they'd ordered she rested her elbows on the table and leaned forward to study his face. 'You've lost weight.'

'Thanks.'

'No. It suits you, that lean, hungry look.' She smiled and reached for his hand. 'I'm sorry I was such a bitch in New York, darling.'

'It doesn't matter. Maybe it was the pressure. Our relationship had been under a strain for some time if we're honest.'

'I agree that we both needed some space. I think I've had mine. At least enough to clear my mind.' She raised an eyebrow at him. 'How about you?'

He nodded. 'Yes. Me too.'

'I'm forgiven then?'

'Nothing to forgive.'

Their food arrived and when the waiter had withdrawn she looked searchingly at him again. 'So – what have you been doing? What are your plans?'

'I've bought a beautiful old house in the country and I'm going to open it as a rather exclusive school of music.'

Her eyes widened in surprise. 'Good heavens! I don't think I quite see you as the professor type.'

'No?'

She ate in silence for a while, glancing up at him occasionally.

161

'What about this child? Is she going to be expensive – boarding schools and so on?'

'No. She's well provided for, living with the woman who brought her up. Not a problem.'

'Just as well, eh? I can't really see you as a father figure.' Kay chuckled to herself as she sipped her wine. 'So you're going to live like a recluse, out there in the sticks? Well, I give you six months at the outside. After that you'll be climbing the walls with boredom, a man like you, used to parties and masses of people around you.'

'Not a bit. I'll have my students. I'm planning to invite friends and colleagues to come at weekends and give master classes. I shall have plenty of company and a busy life.'

'And what about feminine company? Planning to live like a monk, are you?' She raised her eyebrows suggestively at him. 'I'm sorry, darling, but I'm not convinced. It doesn't sound like you at all. Not like the Gerry Cavelle I used to know and love.'

'Well, maybe I'm *not* the Gerry Cavelle you used to know and love.' Fighting down his mounting irritation, he made himself smile at her. 'Come on, that's enough about me. Tell me what you've been doing?'

'I'm leaving Zenith at the end of this month,' she told him gleefully.

'No, really?'

'Yes. I had a wonderful offer from Summit Films, almost twice what Zenith is paying me. And they approached me. I didn't even have to apply.'

'Well, why wouldn't they? You're a damned good publicist.'

'I've taken the lease on a gorgeous flat in Chelsea too.'

'Congratulations!' He raised his glass to her. 'You're obviously on the up and up. Here's to your success.'

She touched her glass to his and drank, appraising him over the rim. 'I'll be giving a flat-warming, of course. I'll see that you get an invitation. All your old chums will be there.'

'Ah . . .' He looked guarded. 'Thanks all the same, but I'm expecting to be away a lot after Christmas, supervising the work on the house.'

'Oh, surely you can spare one evening!' She put down her glass and regarded him speculatively for a moment. 'It really is lovely to see you again, Gerry.'

He smiled. 'Yes. Good to see you too.'

'Quite like old times, eh?' She put down her glass and leaned across the table, lowering her voice. 'Look, I don't really need to go back to the office this afternoon. Why don't we go back to your place like we used to in the old days?'

Something inside him recoiled from the predatory look in her eyes. 'I – don't think that would be a very good idea.'

'No strings.' She smiled seductively. 'Just for fun. Why not?' Her eyes narrowed as she watched his obvious discomfiture. 'What is it, Gerry? Is there someone new?'

'I haven't said that.'

'No. You're not actually *saying* much at all, are you?' She reached out to cover his hand with hers. 'We had something special, you and I, Gerry. We were damned good together. I still miss you, you know – a lot.'

He withdrew his hand uneasily from hers. 'It's over, Kay. Nothing can change that. As you say, it was good while it lasted. And there's no reason why we can't still be friends . . .'

'Oh spare me the tired old clichés, for God's sake,' she snapped, her eyes flashing fire. 'You know, there's something about you I don't quite get. Why don't you level with me, Gerry – tell me what's going on?'

'Nothing's *going on* as you put it.' He drank the last of his coffee and took out his wallet. 'I'm beginning to think this wasn't such a good idea, Kay.' He took out a note and passed it across the table. 'Perhaps you'd settle the bill for me? I have an appointment this afternoon and I think I should go now, before one of us says something we'll regret.'

'Well, don't let *me* keep you.' She picked up the note and thrust it back at him. 'Here – take this with you. I'll pay. After all, I can afford it. And it was my suggestion. Call me sometime when you're feeling more communicative.'

After he'd left she sat on for a while at the table alone. She ordered another coffee and lit a cigarette, puffing on it furiously. Why in God's name had she subjected herself to humiliation like that? And why was he behaving with such uncharacteristic stiffness? It was blatantly obvious that he had something to hide – chances were it was something he didn't want the media to get hold of if he wouldn't even tell her! She bit her lip angrily. One thing was for sure: no one brushed her off like that without living to regret it.

Chapter Ten

Cathy began her second year at college with renewed enthusiasm. Gerald kept in touch regularly. The architect's report on Cuckoo Lodge was encouraging and he found a builder who, in company with the architect, had been over the place with a fine-tooth comb. Between them, they had come up with some interesting suggestions. Gerald had made a formal offer for the house, and after some negotiations it had been accepted. It was well into the autumn before contracts were drawn up and signed, but as soon as the legal business was completed teams of workmen moved in and made a start on the marathon task of restoring the house.

'They have to install a dampcourse before they can start on anything else,' Gerald explained. 'The house has never had one apparently. You were right about that, Cathy.'

They were sitting round the fire having tea at Chestnut Grove. It was half-term and he had come to ask if Cathy would like to go down to Melfordleigh with him on Sunday to see how the work was progressing. 'It means digging down deep into the foundations and inserting a waterproof membrane. All very technical.' He laughed and Johnny, who had been watching them closely, thought he looked happier than she had ever seen him.

'Then most of the interior plaster has to come off,' he went on. 'The damp has caused it to disintegrate. But that's the exciting part. The builder rang me yesterday to say that it was covering up some very interesting earlier features.'

'So you might get your inglenook after all?' Cathy's eyes were shining. 'I can't wait to see it.'

165

'I warn you, it looked a terrible mess last time I was there,' Gerald said. 'But at least we're getting on. I want you to come so that you can have a chat with the builder, Cathy. I've told him about your en suite bathroom ideas and he's looking forward to meeting you.'

Neither of them saw the look old Mrs Bains exchanged with her daughter and when Cathy had gone out to the car with Gerald later, to see him off, the old lady spoke her mind with characteristic bluntness.

'That girl is getting a sight too keen on that so-called guardian of hers if you ask me,' she said, clicking her knitting needles ferociously. 'I'm not sure I trust him either. Too smart by far for my taste.'

Johnny made light of her mother's misgivings. 'At least he takes an interest in the child,' she said. 'He could just have left her here with us and acknowledged her with a card at birthdays and Christmas. He's her godfather and her guardian, Mother. He's only doing his best!'

Mrs Bains grunted. 'His best for *who*? That's what I'd like to know!' She put down her knitting and leaned forward. 'And I hardly think I have to remind you that Cathy isn't a child any more, Mary. You've seen the look in her eyes when he's here.'

Johnny had seen the look, and it worried her far more than she cared to admit, but she forced herself to laugh. 'Oh, Mother, really! It's hero worship, that's all. Mr Cavelle was her father's oldest friend. He's a musician too so she feels at home with him. He's a father figure to her. That's all.'

'Mmm.' The old lady resumed her knitting, pulling her mouth into a tight line. 'All right. You have it your way. But don't say I didn't warn you,' she added ominously. 'At her age hero worship can soon develop into something more dangerous. And that man has the look of an accomplished philanderer if I'm any judge. You heard the way he was flattering her – making out he wanted her advice about this house

166

of his. What does a girl her age know about such things?'

'She is studying Home Economics, Mother.'

The old lady grunted. 'Huh! Home Economics my foot! Turning her head, that's what he's after. Next thing you know he'll be getting her to go there to live.' She drew her breath in through her teeth with a sharp hissing sound. 'And I don't have to tell you what road that leads to.'

'Mother, really! How can you suggest such a thing?' Johnny was concerned that Cathy might be developing a crush on her guardian but she felt sure that he would never take advantage of it. Whatever any of them might think he was a mature man; an intelligent, talented man whose name was well known. He had a reputation to uphold. Nevertheless, as she gathered the teacups together she promised herself that she would have a quiet word with Cathy sometime soon.

Sunday was bright with golden autumn sunshine and as they drove up to Suffolk Cathy's spirits were high. She looked forward so much to seeing the house again. Gerald seemed so enthusiastic. He hadn't mentioned his illness again and she hadn't asked. He had seemed so much better ever since he became involved in the restoration of Cuckoo Lodge.

When they drove in through the gates she saw at once that work had begun in earnest. The ramshackle corrugated iron garage had been removed and the house was now in full view. It was surrounded by scaffolding.

'They're re-pointing,' Gerald explained as they got out of the car. 'The old lime mortar was crumbling – letting in the weather.'

Cathy saw that all round the perimeter of the house a deep trench had been excavated. Standing looking up at Cuckoo Lodge she was slightly dismayed.

'Poor old house,' she said. 'It looks rather forlorn, doesn't it? I feel as though I shouldn't be looking.'

167

'Why shouldn't you be looking?' Gerald asked.

She lifted her shoulders. 'I don't know. It's the indignity of it – a bit like catching someone in their underwear.'

He laughed and threw an arm around her shoulders. 'You are a funny girl. Just you wait another few months. The "poor old house" as you call it will be positively pristine then. Restored to its former glory as they say.'

'I suppose so.' She looked up at him. 'Can we go inside?'

'Of course. It's perfectly safe. You'll just have to watch your shoes in the mud.'

They picked their way over planks to get to the front door, which Gerald opened with his key.

'This will have to be replaced,' he told her as he unlocked it. 'The wood is rotten. I'm having a replica made by a firm that specialises in them. You were right about the listing. I've had special instructions about the windows too. No knocking the walls about and installing modern "picture" windows.'

Cathy pulled a face. 'God forbid. As if you would.'

Standing in what was to be the house's main reception room Cathy drew in her breath. It looked so much larger now that the plaster was down to the original brickwork and the fireplace had been removed. 'So that's your inglenook,' she said, pointing to the cavernous chimney space.

He nodded happily. 'It will be. Can you imagine it with a massive log fire crackling away? I'm combing antique shops for some genuine fire dogs and a basket. If I can't find any I might have to have them specially made.'

At the back the outbuildings had gone, apart from the barn. And the lean-to kitchen had been demolished. As they went from room to room Cathy watched Gerald's face. His eyes were alight with pleasure as he pointed out the work that was being done. All the depression of previous months had gone. The difference it had made to him was nothing short of miraculous.

168

'Jack Rigby, the builder, is meeting us here after lunch,' he told her. 'It's the kitchen and bathrooms I want you to talk to him about. They're more your province than mine.'

She looked at him with surprise. 'You want *me* to advise the builder? Won't he think it a cheek?'

'Why should he? I'm employing him so I get to choose what I want. And as you are the only family I've got . . .'

'But surely he's the expert?'

'I've only asked him to listen to your ideas. If any of them are impractical I expect he'll tell you.' Gerald laughed at her doubtful expression. 'Cathy, if I still had a wife I'm sure she'd demand to have her say in the kitchen and bathroom. Builders are used to that, I assure you.'

As they walked down the hill the wind coming off the sea was sharp and salty and icy cold. The view today was different from the last time she had been here. Out to sea the waves were crested with white. The boats that were still moored by the sea wall bobbed on the swelling tide, their masts and rigging clicking and creaking in the wind. Overhead seagulls rode the wind, swooping occasionally for food, filling the air with their plaintive haunting cries.

'It's still beautiful, isn't it?' Gerald said as they stood together by the sea wall. 'In a wilder way than before. Most of the boats will be gone soon, taken into dock for the winter months. The artists and weekend fishermen will pack up their palettes and rods till spring, then the place will belong to the locals again.'

'And you'll be one of them soon.' She looked up at him. 'How long will the house take to be finished?'

'Depends on the weather. It's a race against time to get the place weatherproof before the winter sets in. If they can do that they can work on the inside till spring.' He put an arm around her shoulders. 'You look cold.' He laughed. 'Your nose is turning pink. Come on, let's get inside in the warm. I've booked a table.'

Inside the Admiral Nelson it was warm and snug and

the mouth-watering aroma of well-cooked food made Cathy realise how hungry she was. The landlord greeted them like old and valued customers and showed them to the table Gerald had insisted on: Cathy's favourite, the one by the fo'c'sle window that looked out over the sea. But after she'd made her choice from the menu he noticed that she was quiet and thoughtful.

'Is something wrong?' he asked. 'Do you want to change your order?'

'No. I'm fine.' She'd been puzzling over something he had said back at the house and was trying to summon up the courage to ask him about it.

'You're looking rather pensive. Anything worrying you?'

'No . . .' She looked up at him. 'At least . . .'

'Yes – come on.'

'It was just something you said . . .'

'Yes? What did I say?'

She bit her lip. 'You said, if I *still* had a wife . . .'

He smiled ruefully, shaking his head. 'Did I really say that?'

She blushed. 'I know it's none of my business, but it sounded almost as though . . .'

'As though I once had one? Well, it's no secret. Why shouldn't you ask, Cathy? Yes, I was married once. But it was so long ago that I hardly ever think about it now. What I said was a mere slip of the tongue. It must be this business of making a proper home for myself.' When she was silent he leaned across the table, his eyes slightly amused. 'Go on then.'

'What?'

'You want to know about her – so ask.'

She shook her head. 'It's none . . .'

'Of your business? Well, perhaps it is, Cathy,' he told her, his eyes serious. 'Perhaps it has more to do with you – with you and me – than you realise.'

She didn't know what to say. Sometimes he seemed to speak in riddles. 'If – if you want to tell me about it – about her – okay,' she said. 'If not I don't mind. Honestly.'

He reached out to cover her hand with his. 'I *do* want to. Not that there's much to tell. It didn't last very long. We were both very young, you see, very green and inexperienced. Still at college in fact. She was a musician too. We both had lofty ambitions. My grandfather was dead against it, which, as far as I was concerned, was one very good reason for going through with it. We were head over heels in love, or so we convinced ourselves. We had stars in our eyes. Nothing mattered except being together. But a few months of sharing one room and the meagre allowance my grandfather gave me, which he flatly refused to increase, soon put out the stars for us. I think being a wife was a big disillusionment for her.' He smiled wryly. 'They say that when poverty comes in at the door, love flies out of the window, don't they?'

'What happened?'

He smiled. 'The war happened. In a way that made the decision easy for us. She was from New Zealand, you see. Her parents wrote when things began to look bad, insisting that she went home. They added, a trifle half-heartedly, that I was welcome too. But they must have known that no self-respecting British male would desert his country at a time like that. We parted tearfully, vowing eternal love and making God knows what empty promises, but I think we both knew it was the face-saving escape we'd been looking for. We exchanged letters, but gradually they dwindled to the occasional line. Then, a couple of years later I heard from Sarah's solicitor that she was seeking an annulment. It wasn't a great surprise and I didn't contest it.'

'And it didn't hurt? Not at all?'

He looked thoughtful for a moment. 'I'd be lying if I said it didn't dent my ego a little. As I said, I was very young. At that age you're so sure about everything. Discovering you can make mistakes like anyone else can be pretty shattering.

171

But soon afterwards I went off to join ENSA and on the whole I spent the rest of the war quite enjoyably.'

'There must have been other girlfriends?' Cathy said daringly.

'True.' He smiled wryly. 'We all suffer from the rebound syndrome.'

'No one serious though?'

'No.' He paused, and for a moment his eyes clouded. 'No one serious.'

'Don't you miss your music now that you've retired?' she asked.

He shook his head. 'I haven't had time to miss it yet. I've been too busy planning for the future.' He smiled. 'There's so much to look forward to.'

The food arrived and they applied themselves to it. Cathy was learning something new about Gerald every time she saw him. As she ate she wondered if he would mention her moving here with him again. And what Johnny would say if she decided to. Deep down she had the feeling that the decision would be frowned upon. But why? After all she was almost nineteen now. By July she would be finished at college. Qualified with any luck. And Gerald was her legal guardian. Although she would prefer to do it with Johnny's blessing, she didn't really need anyone's permission.

The builder was waiting for them at the house. He was a burly man with a red face and a brusque manner. But it was clear that he knew his business well. He listened politely to Cathy's ideas, pointed out the snags and suggested modifications, while Gerald looked on. A new kitchen was to be built on at the rear of the house. Its position and specifications were decided upon. Jack Rigby made copious notes and sketches which he promised to pass on to the architect and the plumber who would soon need to begin installing the necessary pipes before plastering began.

Dusk was gathering by the time they left for home. As they headed towards London Gerald looked at her.

172

'I'm very proud of you, Cathy.'

She looked at him with surprise. 'I can't think why.'

'You're taking such an interest in Cuckoo Lodge. I'm grateful as well as proud.'

She glanced at him. 'Like you said, I'm your family. You're all the family *I've* got too.'

'The house won't be finished till this time next year. I expect you'll be looking for a job by then.'

'Perhaps. If I pass my exams.'

'Oh, you'll pass all right. I have every confidence in you.' She felt his eyes on her but did not turn to meet them. 'You'll probably rush off to the north of Scotland or somewhere and I shan't see you again.'

Something in his voice made her turn and say fervently, 'I'll never do that. I'll always be here, Gerald. As long as you need me.'

'You mean that?'

'Of course I mean it.'

He was slowing the car. Drawing off the road into a quiet lane, he switched off the engine and turned in his seat to look at her. 'Cathy, I think we should talk.'

Her heart was drumming fast. 'Should we?'

'You know we should. There's been a question hanging over our heads for months now. Ever since that first time we looked at Cuckoo Lodge together and I asked you if you'd come and live there with me.'

She shook her head. 'It wasn't that I didn't want to . . .'

'I know. I could have bitten my tongue out afterwards. It was too soon. I didn't mean to rush you. You wanted to finish your course, naturally.' He picked up her hand and regarded it for a moment, then he held it softly against his cheek. 'Cathy. You know what was in my mind, don't you? Maybe you've known all along. Women seem to have an instinct for these things. And you are a woman now. You're not a little girl any longer.'

She could scarcely breathe. His eyes held hers in the

dim interior of the car. They seemed almost luminous – hypnotic. Was he saying what she thought he was saying? Could she really be sure? So many times she had dreamed of a moment like this, yet she was so afraid of making a fool of herself.

When she didn't reply he turned his head and pressed his lips into the palm of her hand. 'You know what I'm trying so clumsily to say, don't you, Cathy? I'm trying to say I love you.' He smiled wryly. 'You can laugh now if you want to. If all that sounded like the foolish ramblings of a man old enough to be your father, just say so. I don't quite know how it happened. Maybe it shouldn't. So if you're going to tell me to get lost, please do it quickly and put me out of my misery, will you?'

'Gerald.' She reached out to put a finger against his lips. 'Don't. I'm not laughing,' she said softly. 'And I'm not going to tell you to get lost. I *want* to live with you at Melfordleigh. I always have. I want to be with you more than anything else in the world. Since that first time I've been so afraid you wouldn't ask me again.'

He looked into her eyes. 'Is that true? You're not just being kind?'

'Of course I'm not. I wouldn't know how to handle that kind of situation, Gerald. I mean it.'

'Would you mind saying it? Just so that I can be sure.'

She took a deep breath. 'I love you too, Gerald. It's not infatuation. It's not new either. I think I've loved you ever since that time Dad brought me to hear you play for the first time.'

When he kissed her she thought she would drown in happiness. Matthew had kissed her once or twice; clumsy embraces and awkward, embarrassed kisses under the tree by the front gate when they came home from a dance or the pictures. But nothing like this. She wasn't in love with Matthew. It made all the difference.

When Gerald released her, her head was spinning. She

174

felt as though her heart had swelled to fill her whole body. Every nerve tingled – every pulse throbbed. She buried her face against his neck, waiting for her heartbeat to slow and the world to stop spinning.

'Oh, Cathy, I want you so much,' he whispered against her hair. 'Will you marry me?'

She drew back her head to look at him, her eyes wide with wonder. 'Marry you?'

'Of course. What else?'

'Yes. Oh, *yes*.'

'And we'll come and set up home at Cuckoo Lodge as soon as it's ready – run the music school together?'

'I can't think of anything more perfect.'

For a while they sat in silence under the trees, her head on his shoulder. 'I promised myself I'd wait,' he confided. 'Until your course ended; until the house was finished – until you were twenty-one. Then, at the beginning of October when it looked as though a nuclear war might erupt I got to thinking. There's never enough time for the important things – the things we promise ourselves. So often we leave it till it's too late. If there's happiness to be had we should grasp it with both hands while there's still time.'

'I was frightened over the Cuba thing too,' she told him. 'But I had to pretend I wasn't because poor Johnny was so terrified. I don't think she ate or slept until it was over.'

'Understandable. She lost her husband in the war, didn't she? And she has a son of fighting age.' He drew her closer. 'Thank God for the courage of John Kennedy. I daresay the crisis made a lot of people stop and take stock of their lives.' He kissed her forehead and tipped up her chin to look into her eyes. 'Cathy, I think it might be wise to keep this to ourselves just for a while,' he said. 'Mrs Johnson may not approve.'

'Why shouldn't she approve?' Cathy said defensively.

He smiled gently. 'I think you know why. The age gap between us is bound to raise a few eyebrows.'

175

'What if it does?' she said defiantly. 'It's not important. If we don't mind, why should anyone else?'

'Nevertheless, I think it's something we'll have to be prepared for. Let's keep it to ourselves just for now. Say until Christmas – till your birthday.'

She looked up at him. 'We'll get engaged on my birthday?'

He kissed her. 'We're engaged now. We'll announce it on your birthday. I'll buy you a ring then and we'll do it properly.'

'Can I have the ring now?' she asked, her eyes shining eagerly. 'I could wear it on a chain round my neck till Christmas.'

He drew her into his arms and held her close. 'Oh God, Cathy. Sometimes you make me feel so damned old.'

Cathy slept hardly at all that night. Somehow the idea of keeping her engagement to Gerald secret made it all the more exciting. She decided to work extra hard at her Saturday job at the Queen's Head, saving all the money she earned for Christmas presents. This year she wanted to buy Johnny something extra special to show her appreciation for all she had done.

The following day Cathy came home from college to find Johnny alone. Matthew was still at work and Mrs Bains was at her Women's Institute meeting. Johnny was in the kitchen ironing and called out to Cathy as she was making her way upstairs.

'I've got the kettle on for a cup of tea. Do you fancy one, Cathy?'

She leaned over the banisters. 'I've got some homework I'd like to get out of the way first.'

Johnny appeared at the foot of the stairs. 'I'd like to talk to you before the others get home, Cathy,' she said. 'So could you come down now, please?'

With a feeling of foreboding Cathy took off her coat and

176

came back downstairs. In the kitchen two cups and saucers were laid out on the table and the big brown teapot was wearing the blue and white striped cosy Mrs Bains had knitted. Johnny pushed aside the abandoned ironing board, one of Matthew's shirts still spread on it, half-ironed, and drew out a chair.

'Sit down, love.'

It wasn't like Johnny to stop the ironing halfway through. It must be something serious. Cathy looked at her warily. 'Have I done anything wrong?'

'Of course not. I just wanted to have a quiet word while we have the house to ourselves.' Johnny poured the tea, while Cathy looked on, her stomach muscles tightening with apprehension. Deep inside she had an uncomfortable feeling that she knew what Johnny was about to say. She hoped she was wrong.

'I don't want you to think I'm interfering, Cathy,' Johnny began awkwardly. 'But I feel responsible for you and I'd hate to see you get hurt. I know that you and Mr Cavelle are good friends. He's taken his duties as guardian very seriously and that's to his credit.'

She paused and Cathy saw her swallow nervously. 'But I feel I owe it to your dear father to look after your best interests.' She looked up into Cathy's eyes. 'I somehow have the feeling that you're getting a little too fond of him, dear.' Seeing Cathy's jaw drop she hurried on: 'Oh, I know he's a very attractive man with a lot of talent and personality. He's a very romantic sort of person. But he's a great deal older than you, dear. If he knew how you felt he'd probably feel dreadfully embarrassed. So perhaps it would be wiser if you saw a little less of him until you have your feelings under control. I'm sure you know plenty of nice boys of your own age at college who'd love to take you out. And there's Matthew of course. He thinks a lot of you, I know.'

Cathy had an almost irresistible urge to blurt out the truth; that boys of her own age seemed dull and stupid after Gerald – yes, even Matthew; that she and Gerald were already engaged and planning to marry. But, remembering her promise to him, she took a deep breath and said, 'Well, if you think so . . .'

'I do.' Johnny drew a deep, relieved breath. Thank goodness the girl had taken it so well. 'I daresay he's going to be very busy with his new house in Suffolk anyway. Perhaps you could say that you're tied up with your end of term exams, or Christmas shopping – something like that. You needn't tell fibs. I'm sure he'll understand.'

'Yes, Johnny.'

'You didn't mind me saying this to you, did you, dear?'

Cathy got up from the table and replaced her chair carefully under it. 'Of course not.'

Upstairs in her room she wondered how she was going to see Gerald now that she had made this promise to Johnny. And how she would tell him about Johnny's misgivings. Odd that he had already foreseen her disapproval. The following day, during her lunch hour, she telephoned him at the flat.

'Gerald, I need to talk to you,' she said. 'Something has come up that might make it difficult to see you for a while.'

'Does it have anything to do with Mrs Johnson?' he asked perceptively.

'Well – yes.'

'I thought so. Look can you get away this afternoon?'

She felt excitement stir in the pit of her stomach. 'There isn't much on here. I suppose I could say I had a headache and duck out.'

'Right. Go to Edgware underground station. I'll pick you up there at one.'

She arrived with ten minutes to spare and was waiting by the kerb as the car drew up. He smiled reassuringly at her as he pulled out into the traffic. 'Don't look so worried, darling. We'll sort something out.'

She hadn't been to the flat for a long time. Not since the Christmas when she had cooked dinner for them both. It looked the same. And she was happy to see her father's piano still in its place. Seeing her looking wistfully at it, he said, 'We'll take it with us to Melfordleigh when we move. Then you can play it every day if you want to.' Seeing her worried expression, he crossed the room and took her hands. 'What is it, darling? Come and sit down. Tell me about it.'

'Johnny had a talk to me yesterday. She thinks I'm getting too fond of you.'

He smiled. 'Very perceptive of her.'

'She wasn't cross or nasty about it.' Cathy looked up at him. 'She said that if you knew how I felt, you'd probably be embarrassed. She suggested I stop seeing you and go out with Matthew or someone else of . . .'

'Of your own age?' He completed the sentence for her. 'Well, maybe she's right. What do you think? Maybe now that you've had time to think it over you agree with her?'

'Oh, *Gerald*!' She wound her arms around his neck and kissed him. 'I'll tell you what I think. I think anyone who expects me to stop loving you must be mad,' she said vehemently.

After a moment he put her from him with a sigh. 'Oh, Cathy – *Cathy*. Do you have any idea how much I want you?'

She pressed her head against his chest. 'What are we going to do, Gerald? It's six whole weeks till my birthday. I can't stop seeing you for all that time. I'll *die*!'

He drew her down on to the settee beside him and cradled her head against his shoulder. 'Perhaps we should go along with what Johnny wants.'

She twisted her head to look up at him in horror. 'You don't mean that? You *can't*.'

He laughed. 'No, I have to agree, it would be totally unbearable, though I will have to go away again soon, just for a week or so.' For a moment he was silent, then he said, 'How do you feel about a tiny deception – just to keep things on an even keel?'

'Like what?'

'This Saturday job of yours. If you were to stop working at the hotel we could spend Saturday afternoons and evenings together.'

'Oh!' Her eyes lit up and then clouded. 'But someone might see us.'

'Not if you came straight here.'

The corners of her mouth began to lift. 'Oh, Gerald, that would be lovely.' She stopped as she remembered something. 'But I was going to save the money I earned to buy presents.'

He hugged her close. 'That's not a problem. I'll give you what you would have earned.' He looked at her. 'I know you hate being deceitful, darling, and if you don't think it's a good idea . . .'

'If it's the only way we can be together, I don't care.'

'We'll tell everyone at Christmas. Then we won't have to pretend any longer.' He felt in his pocket. 'I almost forgot. I've got something for you.' Taking out a small box he opened it to reveal a ring set with diamonds surrounding a glittering square-cut emerald. 'I chose it because it's the colour of your eyes.' Taking her left hand he slipped the ring on to her finger. She stared at it, then at him, her eyes brimming with tears.

'Oh, Gerald. It's *beautiful* and it fits perfectly. Is it really my engagement ring?'

'It is. It means that you and I have made our commitment. We are pledged to each other. We'll be married as soon as you've finished your course next summer.'

She threw her arms around his neck and hugged him close. 'Oh, I *wish* I could wear it now. I wish I could show it to everyone. Oh, Gerald, I love you so much. I wish I could stay here with you for ever.'

He reached up and took her arms from around his neck, kissing first one hand, then the other. 'But unfortunately you can't, my love. You have to go home now. Look at the time. You'll be missed.'

She sighed. 'I suppose so.'

'I'll come down with you and put you into a taxi. But remember, on Saturday we'll have all afternoon and evening together. That's something to look forward to, isn't it?'

Before she went home she took off her ring and slipped it on to a length of string Gerald found for her, hanging it round her neck under her sweater. It was so exciting to feel it there against her skin all the way home in the cab. She stopped the driver at the corner of the next street to Chestnut Grove and walked the rest of the way. Of course it would be nice to be able to tell people, she mused. But it was almost better keeping it secret.

She went along to the Queen's Head the following day on her way home from college and told them she wouldn't be working there any more. She hated letting them down just when their busy season was getting under way, and felt guilty about deceiving Johnny too. But it was for Gerald, and for him she would have done anything. Every time she thought of spending all afternoon and evening with him at the flat her heart raced with excitement. Everything else was forgotten. Saturday seemed an eternity away.

As soon as she arrived at the flat Cathy put her engagement ring on her finger. She did it in the lift and stood gazing down at its sparkle as she rose to the fourth floor. In the afternoon they listened to music and talked about Cuckoo Lodge, making plans. Later Cathy cooked a meal for which she had shopped carefully on the way there. She made a mixed grill and chips, followed by apple pie and cream, which Gerald proclaimed the best he had ever eaten. Later, as they were washing up together, she said, 'This is what it will be like when

181

we're married. Just the two of us. It's going to be wonderful.'

Gerald put down the plate he was drying. 'I wonder if you know what it means to me to hear you say that, Cathy.' He picked up a towel and carefully dried her hands. 'Leave the rest,' he said, drawing her towards him and placing her arms around his waist. Taking her face between his hands, he kissed her. He felt her trembling beneath his touch and drew her into his arms. 'My lovely Cathy,' he whispered, pulling her hard against him. 'I still can't quite believe you really want to marry me. I keep thinking I'll wake up to find I've dreamed it all.'

She looked up at him. 'How can I prove to you how much I love you?'

'You don't need to feel you have to prove anything.'

'But I want to.' She stood on tiptoe to kiss him. 'I want you to believe without any possible doubt, Gerald,' she whispered. 'We are engaged. If you . . .' She bit her lip, astonished at her own daring. 'If you want to make love . . .'

'Shhh.' He stopped her mouth with a kiss and held her so tightly she could scarcely breathe. 'I don't think you know what you're saying; what you're offering.'

'But I *do*. You said yourself – I'm not a child. And I love you, Gerald.'

For a long moment he looked into her eyes. 'You're really sure?'

'Of course.'

After a moment's hesitation he scooped her up in his arms and carried her to the bedroom. She stood impassive and motionless, shivering with a mixture of excitement and apprehension as he undressed her. Her eyes, huge and luminous, never left his, and as he joined her under the smooth sheets and felt her uncomfortable trembling, he said, 'You're shivering. Are you cold?'

182

She wrapped her arms around him and pressed close. 'No – just excited – and – nervous, I suppose.'

'Don't be.' He kissed her forehead. 'Cathy, don't feel you have to go through with this. It's not too late to stop if you have doubts.'

She buried her face against his shoulder. 'No – please. I haven't . . .'

'I'll try not to hurt you, darling.'

'I know. I know.'

She closed her eyes and tried to relax as he caressed her quivering body. She told herself over and over that it was going to be all right and that as long as she loved him everything would be fine. All the same when it happened she felt every muscle tensing as she bit hard on her lip to keep from crying out.

When it was over tears of disappointment trickled down her cheeks. She had fantasised about this moment – the first time Gerald would make love to her. It was going to be so special – so wonderful – but the painful and hurried coupling that had just taken place between them was so different from her dream. So devastatingly different. She could not believe that this was all there was to it.

Gerald turned to look at her. 'The first time is always difficult, darling,' he said gently touching her cheek. 'Next time it will be so much better you'll hardly believe it.' He stroked her hair and leaned across to kiss her. 'Don't cry, sweetheart.'

'But – but I must have done something wrong. It must have been my fault,' she choked. 'And you must be so disappointed with me.'

'Nonsense.' He laughed softly and drew the covers up over her. 'You'll never know how happy you've made me. And you have no idea of the wonderful life we're going to have together.'

She must have fallen asleep. When she woke she had no idea how long she'd slept or what time it was. Disorientated and drowsy she stared up at the man who stood by the bed looking down at her. 'Gerald . . .?'

He wore his dressing gown and held a steaming cup. 'I've made you some coffee. It's almost time I took you home or I wouldn't have wakened you,' he said, sitting on the edge of the bed. 'You looked so peaceful lying there.'

She sat up. Then, suddenly aware of her nakedness, pulled the sheet up and tucked it around herself as she took the cup from him. 'Thanks.' As she sipped the coffee the memory of what had taken place between them slowly returned. 'I'm sorry,' she whispered, colouring unhappily. 'About what – about – you know . . .'

He took the cup from her. 'That's enough of that.' Very gently he pulled the sheet away from her. 'And please don't hide yourself from me. You're so beautiful.' He bent to kiss her breasts, then, slipping out of his robe, he slid into bed beside her once again and drew her close. At his touch and the feel of his skin against hers she felt excitement stir somewhere in the pit of her stomach, spreading its heat to every fibre of her body; shortening her breath and quickening her heartbeat – turning her blood to molten fire. Some primitive, long dormant instinct seemed suddenly to blossom, taking possession of her as she sank back against the pillows, her arms drawing him down on to her. When his mouth closed on hers the spark deep within her leapt into a white-hot, searing flame. Kisses and caresses were not enough. Her mouth opened hungrily to kiss him as she had never kissed anyone before. She arched her body towards him imploringly.

This time the pain was replaced by a breathtaking delight that was almost as unbearable in its intensity. The sheer surprise of it shocked her and she heard herself cry out, this time with sheer exultation. Together they scaled the heights of sensuous pleasure, relishing every movement, each sensation, until at last together they reached the summit. Tensing beneath him she gave one last convulsive movement, gasping out his name, then lay still, her eyes staring up at him in wonder.

Side by side, their limbs still entwined, they lay staring speechlessly into each other's eyes.

'You didn't believe me, did you?' Gerald said at last, his lips against her hair.

She smiled sleepily. 'Oh, Gerald. I love you so much. I wish we were married now. I wish I could stay here with you like this for ever.'

'So do I. But we aren't married yet, my love, and you can't stay more's the pity.' He rolled off the bed and began to pull on his clothes. 'Unless you want to arouse suspicions you'd better hurry up and dress. Time I took you home.'

He drove her to the end of Chestnut Grove and then stopped the car and switched off the engine.

'Goodnight, my love.' He reached out for her. 'If you only knew what agony it is to let you go.'

She kissed him. 'I do know,' she whispered. 'It's the same for me. I can't wait for next Saturday.'

'That reminds me.' Reaching into his pocket he took out his key ring and pulled off a key. 'Take this,' he said. 'It's my spare. I have to go away for a few days next week. I'll be back on Saturday, but just in case you arrive before me.'

She put the key away carefully in her bag and got out of the car. As she walked the rest of the way she could feel him watching her and turned to wave before the privet hedge cut off her view to the car. Using her own key, she let herself quietly into the house and was already halfway up the stairs when Johnny opened the living room door and came out into the hall to look up at her.

'Cathy. Don't you want to come and have a cup of cocoa with us?'

She felt her cheeks colour as she looked over the banisters. 'Oh – not tonight, thank you,' she said awkwardly. 'I'm a bit tired.'

Johnny frowned. 'Are you all right, dear? You look a bit flushed.'

'I'm fine.'

'You're very late.'

'Yes. I'm sorry.'

'Busy night?'

'What?'

'At the Queen's Head?'

'Oh. Yes. Quite busy.'

Johnny put a foot on the bottom stair. 'Are you sure you're all right, Cathy? There's a lot of flu about and . . .'

'I'm fine, I told you. Look, I'm going to bed now. Goodnight.'

She escaped hurriedly, snapping off the landing light and closing the bedroom door behind her with relief. Leaning against it, she closed her eyes and wrapped her arms around herself, feeling her body tingle afresh as she thought of Gerald and their sensational lovemaking. She didn't want to see or speak to anyone until she'd had time to relive every moment; every single touch, word and sensation. No one, *nothing*, must be allowed to spoil the magic.

At the foot of the stairs Johnny stood looking up into the patch of darkness at the top of the stairs. Cathy's abrupt switching off of the landing light had hurt her. It seemed oddly final. And ominous too; as though instead of the light, it was the loving, trusting relationship between them that was being shut off, perhaps permanently. That hectic light in the girl's eyes, the bloom on her cheeks and the almost tangible aura of arousal she exuded had not been induced by waiting at tables at the Queen's Head. There was only one experience that brought that look to a young girl and Johnny's heart sank with despair.

'Oh, God,' she breathed. 'Oh, God, please let me be wrong.'

* * *

The following Saturday Cathy left home early, saying that she was going up to the West End to do some Christmas shopping and would go straight to the Queen's Head afterwards. The fact that Johnny accepted what she said without question filled her with guilt. She hated telling lies, specially to Johnny of all people. As she travelled up on the underground she wished there was someone in whom she could confide. It would ease her conscience if she could somehow justify what she was doing. But there was no way Johnny would ever understand or condone the intimate relationship that had developed between herself and Gerald. At least, not until they could announce their engagement. And maybe not even then.

When she arrived at the flat Gerald had not returned and she let herself in with the key he had given her. As usual everything was spic and span. A woman came in three times a week to clean and as Gerald had been away the place was meticulously tidy. She took off her coat, then, taking her ring from its hiding place around her neck, she placed it on her finger. Immediately she felt different. Now she was the future Mrs Cavelle. Going into the kitchen she prepared a beef casserole and put it into the oven, then went back into the living room and looked down into the street below. All the Christmas lights were on, giving the already darkening street a glittering magic that made her tingle with excitement. At Christmas they would be telling everyone. At Christmas it would all come true.

When the doorbell sounded it startled her. She turned, hesitating for a moment. Did anyone know she was here? Should she answer it – or what? Then she realised that Gerald must have forgotten his key. He'd guess she was already here to let him in so he wouldn't bother the caretaker. Of course. That must be it. She hurried out into the hall.

'You're a fine one – forgetting your own key. It's a good job I was here to . . .' She stopped short, the rest of the sentence unspoken. A woman stood outside; tall, blonde and very well dressed. She had her back to the door but at the sound of a female voice she turned, eyes as startled as Cathy's.

'My God, who are you?'

Piqued by the woman's abruptness, Cathy flushed. 'Excuse me, but shouldn't I be asking that?'

'Kay Goolden. Where's Gerry?' She peered past Cathy into the flat.

'I'm afraid he's not here.'

'When will he be back?'

'I've no idea.'

'Then I'll wait if you don't mind?' The woman pushed past her into the flat and began to take off her coat. Tossing it on to a chair she turned to Cathy, appraising her frankly with a sweeping look. 'Well, he must be expected or you wouldn't be here, would you? Who are you, by the way? We really should introduce ourselves.'

'I'm Cathy Oldham.'

Kay took a cigarette from a case and lit it, taking her time over the operation. She walked into the living room and sat down, giving Cathy a long appraising look. 'I'm sorry but the name means nothing to me.'

'Neither does yours – to me,' Cathy countered.

Kay smiled and tapped the ash from her cigarette. 'That's not altogether surprising. I used to work for Zenith records, Gerry's recording company. I was in PR.' She smiled. 'I suppose you could call Gerry an old colleague of mine – among other things.' She looked at Cathy, her eyes hard. 'Look, I'd rather like to talk to Gerald privately. Do you think you could make yourself scarce for a couple of hours?'

Cathy felt the hot colour staining her cheeks. Who *was* this woman and what could she possibly want with Gerald now? She said she *used* to work for Zenith. He'd certainly never mentioned her. 'No, I'm sorry but I promised to be here this afternoon. He's expecting me.'

188

Kay waved a dismissive hand. 'That's all right. I'll explain to him.'

'There's no need, because I'm not going anywhere.' Cathy stood her ground. 'But if you want to leave him a message, I'll pass it on.'

The woman ground out her cigarette and stood up, surveying Cathy coldly. 'Just who *are* you anyway?' she demanded. 'And how did you get in here?'

'Gerald gave me a key. And if you really want to know who I am, I'm his fiancée.' Cathy held out her hand triumphantly. 'See?'

Kay's eyes widened as she took in the ring with its obviously expensive square-cut emerald. She was clearly stunned. '*Fiancée?* For Christ's sake! He must be old enough to be your father! How old are you anyway?'

Cathy flushed. 'That's none of your business!'

Kay's eyes swept over her. 'You can't be more than seventeen – eighteen at the most.'

'Nineteen, if you must know.'

'And how did you meet?'

'Through his music.'

Kay threw back her head and gave a brittle laugh. 'My God, has he taken leave of his senses? Giving up a brilliant career for a little teenage groupie.'

'I'm *not* a groupie,' Cathy said hotly. 'I've known Gerald nearly all my life. He and my father were best friends.'

Kay's eyes narrowed as the truth suddenly dawned. So – *this* was the ward that he'd led her to believe was a child. And Gerry was stringing the kid along to believe he'd marry her. Why on earth was he doing it? It was *bizarre*.

'And it isn't because of me that he's given up his career,' Cathy went on hotly. 'It's because of his illness.'

'*Illness?*' Kay peered at her, her attention galvanised. 'What illness?'

Cathy coloured. The woman had rattled her. She'd said more than she should. She shrugged. 'It's nothing serious. A sort of arthritis. It affects his fingers and – and . . .'

Kay felt a spiral of excitement stir within her. Things were beginning to drop into place. That time in New York when he'd been so bad-tempered. He'd almost bitten her head off when she'd suggested that his playing wasn't up to standard. And the day when they'd lunched, he'd been so cagey. She'd known all along that he was hiding something. Her expression adjusted itself to one of solicitude. 'Oh, *poor* Gerry. I'd no idea. How long has this been going on?'

'I don't know. But it isn't important. He's got a new career planned.'

'That's wonderful. And you two are planning to be married?'

'Yes.' Cathy relaxed a little. 'But at the moment it's a secret. We're going to announce it on my birthday just before Christmas.'

'Your twentieth?'

'Well, no. My nineteenth.'

Kay took out another cigarette, surveying Cathy over the flame of her lighter. 'You don't think the age difference is important then?'

'Oh, no. As I said, I've known Gerald since I was a little girl. And we're very much in love.'

'Well, well, how *madly* romantic. My God, I almost forgot.' She opened her handbag and took out an envelope. 'Look, I've brought him an invitation to a flat-warming party I'm giving. I promised him I'd see he got one.'

'You promised him?'

'Yes. When we were having lunch the other day. Didn't he tell you that either? I was telling him all about my new flat. Odd that he never once mentioned you or said a word about getting married. If he had I'd have included you, naturally. You're very welcome of course.'

'Thank you.'

Kay took in Cathy's crestfallen look with satisfaction.

190

'I'll just pop it in the bedroom, shall I? He'll be sure to see it there.' Before Cathy could speak she was already walking across the hall, heading straight for the door. 'Don't worry,' she said over her shoulder. 'I remember where it is.'

Cathy stood waiting, her heart beating fast with resentment. She imagined those sharp eyes examining Gerald's bedroom for signs of female occupation. A moment later Kay returned, a smile still firmly glued to her lips.

'There, that's done. Now, I can see that you'd far rather be here alone for Gerry when he gets back so I'll go. It was so nice meeting you, Cathy – er – Oldham, did you say?' Cathy nodded. Kay pulled on her coat and gloves. 'Tell Gerry I'll give him a ring sometime. He'll probably be tired when he gets home and I'm sure you and he will have more important things to talk about. Good luck, my dear', she said as she reached the door. As it closed behind her she muttered under her breath, '*Believe me, you'll be needing it!*'

It was late when Gerald got home. Cathy had plenty of time to think about Kay and all that she'd said and implied. Time to wonder just how much she and Gerald had meant to each other, and how it had ended – *if* it had ended. He'd never mentioned Kay to her. Obviously she belonged to another part of his life. One that was over. If he meant to forget the past and begin anew, then it was up to her to help him. Questions and accusations would only upset him. That would be playing right into Kay's hands. Besides, it was ancient history.

After careful thought she made up her mind. She wouldn't spoil their time together by mentioning Kay's visit. She would not allow her the satisfaction. Going into the bedroom she stood looking down at the invitation in its white envelope, propped against the bedside lamp where Kay had left it. After a moment's hesitation she picked it up and tore it into small pieces, taking them back to the living room and stowing them away at the bottom of her handbag for safety.

It was barely half an hour later when she heard his key in the lock. Immediately all thoughts of Kay went out of her head. Running out into the hall she threw her arms around him and hugged him hard.

'It's so *good* to come home to a welcome like this,' he whispered holding her close. 'I'm sorry I'm so late, darling. Couldn't be helped. I missed the train I should have caught, then the next one was running late.'

'Never mind. You're here now. I made a casserole for your dinner. It's keeping hot in the oven.'

He kissed the top of her head. 'What would I do without you?'

She watched him eat, thinking how tired he looked. For the first time she noticed that he'd lost weight over the past few months and tonight there were dark circles under his eyes.

'Was it a success?' she asked.

He looked up in surprise. 'Was what a success?'

'Your meeting or whatever. You didn't say where you'd been.'

'Oh, that. Boring and tedious.' He reached out to take her hand. 'The only thing that made it bearable was the thought of coming home to you.'

She smiled. She knew now that she'd been right to ignore Kay's visit and remove the invitation.

The sight of her radiant young face tore at his heart. He couldn't tell her that he'd been to see his consultant in Edinburgh; he didn't want to dwell on the past two days when he'd been through more exhausting tests so that a satisfactory regimen of medication could be worked out. The very thought of it turned his stomach and depressed him. But for the time being at least it was over and, with her help, he could forget it for a while.

After they'd eaten they stacked the dishes into the

dishwasher, then Gerald put on some records and they sat down to relax together. She settled her head happily on his shoulder, telling herself that it wasn't important that they didn't make love. He was tired. It was enough that she could take care of him and love him in this different, special way. This was what it would be like to be married, she told herself contentedly.

At ten Gerald stirred and stretched out the arm that encircled her shoulders to look at his watch. 'Time I took you home, my darling.' He kissed her. 'Much as I hate to let you go.'

'You're not driving all the way to Edgware tonight,' she told him firmly. 'Come down and get me a taxi. I'll be fine.'

'It's no trouble. We only have to take the lift down to the basement carpark.'

She shook her head. 'No. You're tired. I won't hear of it.'

In the hall he helped her into her coat, buttoning it up to the neck and pulling her to him. 'I'm taking no chances with a treasure like you,' he said. 'Can't have you catching cold. Now – are you sure you're going to be all right in a cab?'

'I'll be fine, fusspot.' She slipped her arms around him and raised her face for his kiss.

They went down in the lift and crossed the entrance hall. As they stepped through the doors and out on to the pavement Gerald took her in his arms for a last kiss. Neither of them saw the man waiting in an adjacent doorway with his camera and when the flash came it startled them. Both spun round to stare in wide-eyed astonishment and as they did so the flash was repeated.

'*What the hell* . . .?' Gerald took a step towards the man with the camera but before he had a chance to reach him he had jumped into a car that drew up at the kerb and in seconds was lost among the traffic.

'Who was that?' Cathy asked in alarm.

Gerald shook his head. 'A newspaper photographer. I thought those days were over. He must be behind the times with his information.' He smiled as the taxi he had hailed stopped and he opened the door for her. 'He's going to be so disappointed when he finds I'm not newsworthy any more.'

But as he watched the taxi draw away, he wondered whether somehow they had got hold of the news that he was restoring Cuckoo Lodge. He hoped not. He wasn't yet ready for that particular piece of news to break. Then for a moment his blood turned cold as another thought struck him. Was it possible that the news of his illness had somehow been leaked to the press? If it had he could say goodbye to his coming marriage. What young girl would knowingly marry a man who was terminally ill?

As usual Cathy asked the taxi driver to stop at the end of Chestnut Grove. She paid him with the money Gerald had given her and set out to walk the rest of the way. She was halfway home when she was aware of footsteps behind her. She quickened her own steps, but when the following footsteps quickened too, and a hand descended on her shoulder, she gave a squeak of alarm.

'Cathy! It's all right. It's me, Matthew.'

'Oh!' She looked at him angrily. 'You gave me such a fright. What on earth do you think you're doing?'

'I've been looking for you. Mum was worried when it began to get late so I said I'd walk round to the Queen's Head to meet you.'

'Oh.' Cathy searched his face.

'They said you'd stopped working there a couple of weeks ago.'

'Yes.' She began to walk on.

'So where have you been, Cathy?'

She rounded on him. 'Mind your own business. What has it got to do with you what I do with my Saturdays?'

'Nothing, except when it worries the life out of Mum.' He laid a gentle hand on her arm. 'Look, wait a minute. I want to talk to you before we go in. It's for your own good, Cath.'

She sighed. The look in his eyes was making her uneasy. 'All right, get on with it then. What do you want? It's cold out here.'

'Cath, Mum is terribly worried about you and this pianist chap – Cavelle.'

'Whatever for?'

'She's afraid you're – well, that you're falling for him.'

Under the street lamp Cathy's eyes were defiant as she looked up at him. 'So? What if I am?' she challenged. 'It's my look out, isn't it?'

'She doesn't want you to be hurt, Cath. None of us do.'

'*None* of you? How many people have been discussing my life then?'

He shook his head. 'Only us, the family.' He laid his hands on her shoulders. 'The thing is, Cathy, is it true?'

'Is *what* true? I don't really know what you're talking about.'

He chewed his lip in embarrassment. 'You don't make it any easier, do you? Have you given up your Saturday job to be with him?'

'Okay – yes. What of it?'

'Nothing, if that's what you want. But why does it have to be a secret. That makes people think there's something wrong in it.'

She tossed her head angrily. 'It seems to me that these *people* you keep on about poke their noses into other people's business far too much,' she retorted. 'Now, if you don't mind, I'd like to get inside before I freeze to death.'

'You've changed, Cathy,' he said hurrying to keep up with her. 'You're just not the same girl you used to be.'

'Because I don't go out with *you* any more, you mean?' At the door she turned to him. 'If you dare say anything

195

about me leaving the Queen's Head to Johnny, I'll never speak to you again. Understand?'

'Okay, but I think you're making a mistake.'

She turned her key in the lock. 'Really? Well, who asked you, Matthew Johnson? And who cares what you think anyway?'

'I won't say anything for a little while, Cathy, but I hope you will.' He looked at her, his grey eyes serious. 'If it goes on too long I'll have to . . .'

'It won't. You'll see.' She pushed open the door and went straight upstairs. 'Everything will be clear to all of you very soon.' She looked at him over the banisters. 'Tell Johnny I'm all right and I'm going to bed.'

Her scornful demeanour had put a stop to his questions for the moment and in spite of her unkind remarks to him, she knew that she could trust him not to mention their conversation to his mother. What neither could possibly have foreseen was the bombshell that was about to explode so ferociously about their ears.

Somewhere in Fleet Street a well-known Sunday paper was about to be put to bed. Its showbiz gossip page carried the photograph taken earlier of herself and Gerald kissing outside his flat. It bore the caption:

Retired Pianist to Marry Ward

Underneath, the accompanying comment was both cryptic and cynical.

Concert pianist, Gerald Cavelle, is rumoured to be suffering from a mystery illness that has forced his retirement from the concert platform. He looked far from ill last night, however, as he kissed his fiancée passionately outside his Mayfair flat. Could the secrecy surrounding their engagement possibly have anything to do with the fact that lovely nubile Catherine Oldham is the eighteen-year-old daughter of his best friend?

Chapter Eleven

Christmas at Blake's Folly was dreary. Don, Una and Rosalind spent it alone. They ate turkey and plum pudding, listened to the Queen's speech with their tea and mince pies, and spent the rest of the day staring at the television. To Una it was simply another day – to be got through as best she could, a stepping stone towards New Year's Eve and the party she had spent so much time and trouble organising.

After she had impulsively issued the invitation to Stuart she had begun to panic. She had rashly promised theatrical celebrities. Now where was she to find any? Each night after the light was out and Don's breathing had deepened into gentle snoring, she lay awake, planning, scheming, trying to make lists in her head. Where were the guests to come from, let alone celebrities? As far as she could tell, Don had few friends and none of the acquaintances she had left behind when she married were at all suitable for the kind of gathering she had in mind. There were the models from the show of course. She could ask some of them. But girls like that must lead busy social lives. They would almost certainly be booked up months in advance. She had lost touch with all the show business people she had known during her years on the stage, and anyway, none of them came into the celebrity class. A brief vision of Saucy Stan Stacey popped into her mind. Stan, in his loud checked suit and bowler hat, had appeared at the end of every pier from Land's End to John O'Groats, billed as 'The Comic with the Rubber Face'. She shuddered at the memory of his leering innuendos and suggestive jokes. No, to be completely honest there wasn't one among them she'd wish to be associated with now.

Ben and Freda had made the big time of course. Damn them! If they had still been in England she would even have considered inviting them, such was her desperation. Then, like the answer to her prayers, salvation dropped into her hands in the shape of the *Sunday Recorder*.

That Saturday night she had gone to bed late to toss and turn until the small hours. At eight o'clock next morning she got up and went downstairs to the kitchen to make herself some tea, picking up the Sunday papers from the doormat on her way. As she sat sipping the strong brew she pushed aside Don's *Observer* and opened the *Sunday Recorder*, turning at once to the showbiz gossip page. The photograph of the couple kissing drew her attention and she began to read. Furrowing her brow, she read the piece through again. The name Catherine Oldham rang a bell. Wasn't Rossie at school with a girl of that name? Fancy someone Rossie knew marrying a well-known concert pianist! Her stomach lurched with excitement as an idea suddenly presented itself. She poured a fresh cup of tea and, tucking the paper under her arm, carried it purposefully upstairs.

Tapping on Rosalind's door she called softly, 'Rossie. Are you awake? I've brought you a cup of tea.'

Rosalind sat up, surprised at her mother's sudden thoughtfulness. 'Oh, thanks, Mum.'

'I couldn't sleep so I got up early to make a pot and I thought you might like one.' Una sat down on the edge of the bed and opened the paper. 'You might be interested in this too.' She pointed out the article. 'Isn't this the girl who was in your form at school? The one whose father died a couple of years ago?'

Rosalind reached for her glasses and slipped them on. Taking the paper from her mother, she read the piece with widening eyes. 'Yes, it looks like her. Gerald Cavelle was her father's best friend. He's her guardian. Fancy them getting engaged.' She sat back against the pillows, her face thoughtful. 'She gave up her Saturday job at the Queen's

Head a few weeks ago,' she said. 'This must have been the reason.'

Una was smiling. 'Romantic, isn't it? Just like something out of a James Mason film.' She moistened her lips. 'Rossie, I've had an idea. Why don't you invite them both to our little New Year party? You haven't asked any of your own friends. I've been worrying about that. The party is for all of us, you know. Not just Don and me.'

Rosalind looked doubtful. 'Oh, but I don't know Cathy very well. She might think it funny.'

'Why should she think it funny? You went to school together, didn't you? You worked with her at the hotel.'

'Yes, but we've never been what you'd call close friends.'

'I'm only suggesting you ask her to the party,' Una said exasperatedly. 'Everyone likes parties, don't they? Especially at New Year. And this will be a good one.'

'They might not want to come though.' Rosalind pulled a face. 'I expect people like Gerald Cavelle get invited to all the smart affairs at this time of year. They'll probably be booked.'

'If everyone thought like that no one would ever get invited anywhere!' Una argued. 'You can always ask, can't you? If they can't come they'll tell you. No harm in trying.'

Rosalind had already guessed that Una's real reason for wanting Cathy and her fiancé at the party was to show off. The thought of having to watch her mother parading them round, masquerading as their friend, made her toes curl with embarrassment. She hated the idea of subjecting Cathy to such an ordeal too.

'I don't see her any more now that she's left the Queen's Head,' she said awkwardly. 'I don't see how I'll get the chance . . .'

Una raised her eyes to the ceiling. 'For heaven's *sake*, child. Haven't you ever heard of the telephone?

200

Now – what is the name of the woman she lives with?'

Before she had time to stall Rosalind heard herself saying, 'Johnson.'

'There you are then. Just look up the number in the book.'

Rosalind was stumped for words. It seemed there was no getting out of it.

'Come on, get up and ring her now,' Una urged.

Rosalind shook her head. 'No, Mum. Not on a Sunday. The people she lives with might not like it. I'll do it tomorrow.'

Una raised her eyes to the ceiling. 'Tomorrow, tomorrow. Always tomorrow. You're just like your father. Well, just see that you do it.' She bit back the criticism that rose to her lips and forced herself to smile. 'I mean, it's only right that you should have your own friends at the party, isn't it. I want you to enjoy yourself.'

'I will have Stuart,' Rosalind ventured.

Una glared at her. 'What do you mean, you'll have Stuart?'

'He's my friend. That's what I mean.'

'But *I* asked him, didn't I? You should ask some people too. Really, Rossie, do *try* to make a contribution for once, can't you!'

It took all Rosalind's courage to telephone Cathy. Unwilling to do it with her mother listening, she did it while Una was out shopping the following afternoon. When she asked for Cathy the woman who answered the call sounded suspicious.

'Who is calling?'

'My name is Rosalind Blair.'

'Are you from a newspaper?'

'No!' Rosalind was surprised. 'No, I'm not.'

'Who are you then?'

'Cathy and I were at school together. I'm ringing to ask her to a party.'

'Oh – I see.' There was an audible sigh of relief at the other end. 'Hold on. I'll fetch her.'

'Hello.' Cathy's voice sounded strained and apprehensive.

'Hello, Cathy, it's Rosalind Blair. Congratulations on your – er – engagement.'

'Oh. Thanks.' There was a pause. 'You saw it in the *Sunday Recorder* then?' Cathy's voice was little more than a whisper. 'I wonder how many more did?'

'Yes, I saw it, and I'm very happy for you, Cathy.'

'Are you? You're the first person to say that Rosalind.' There was a pause as Rosalind struggled to pluck up enough courage to come out with the invitation, then Cathy suddenly forestalled her, 'Look, you wouldn't like to meet me somewhere for a coffee, would you?'

Taken aback, Rosalind said, 'Yes, of course I will. I'd like to. Where? And when?'

'Now – if you're free. In the Bluebell. You know, that coffee bar, near St Margaret's?'

'Okay, I know it. I'll be there. It'll take me about twenty minutes.'

'Right. I'll see you there.'

When Rosalind arrived Cathy was already there, waiting at a table by the window from which she had a view of the bus stop. The Bluebell had been a teashop, but now it was under new management and had been turned into an Italian-style coffee bar, complete with an espresso machine that hissed away irritably on the counter. Over cups of frothy coffee they sat looking at each other.

'I just had to get out of the house,' Cathy said. 'Can I tell you something in confidence, Rosalind? I feel that if I don't talk to someone soon I'll go crazy.'

'Of course you can.' Rosalind felt flattered. She would

have thought Carla would have been Cathy's first choice when it came to confidences.

'You said you saw my engagement blown up into a scandal in the paper?'

'Well – yes.'

'I can't tell you how awful it was yesterday morning when the papers came.' When Cathy looked up Rosalind could see the ravages of recent tears on her face. 'It was such a shock. Gerald and I were keeping it a secret you see – until my birthday on the 22nd. But someone must have leaked it to the press. I don't know whether you knew before that Gerald was a well-known concert pianist?'

'Yes, I did know.' Rosalind leaned forward. 'But does it matter all that much that the secret is out? I mean, it's the 19th now. Only a couple of days to go.'

'It's Johnny – Mrs Johnson, whom I live with. She doesn't approve, because of Gerald being a lot older than me.'

'But, is it really any of her business? I mean – she isn't a relative, is she?'

'No, but she brought me up after my – after I lost my mother. She promised Dad before he died that she'd take care of me so I suppose she feels responsible.' Cathy paused to push her hair behind her ears. 'She thinks I've been deceitful, keeping it from her – telling lies about where I was going.' She looked at Rosalind. 'I didn't tell her I'd stopped working at the Queen's Head you see. I've been seeing Gerald instead. Oh, I know it was wrong, but I didn't really have any choice.'

'Oh, I see.' Rosalind thought it was all terribly romantic and exciting, but she could hardly say so when Cathy was so obviously distressed.

'And to make matters worse we've been pestered by the newspapers ever since,' she went on. 'The phone hasn't stopped ringing since yesterday morning. I've *told* her I'm happy and that everything will be all right. Gerald came to see her yesterday too, as soon as he'd seen the paper.

He tried to explain how much in love we are and why we were keeping it quiet. It was exactly *because* he didn't want the newspapers getting hold of it, you see! He promised Johnny he'd look after me, but she's still upset. She says Gerald should have known better and that we must both have known it was wrong or we wouldn't have done it so – so underhandedly.'

Tears began to well up and trickle down her cheeks. 'I feel awful, Rosalind. I didn't want to upset Johnny. I was so happy till this happened. Gerald gave me a beautiful engagement ring. He's restoring a lovely old house in Suffolk and we were going to be married after I'd taken my exams next summer and go there to live. He's going to start a music school – with me to help. But now it's all spoilt.'

Rosalind's heart went out to her. Why should anyone want to spoil two people's happiness? Reaching out she touched Cathy's hand. 'Don't worry. She'll get over it. I'm sure you'll think of a way to put things right.'

'It's all ruined. Nothing can be the same now.' Cathy searched her handbag for a handkerchief and blew her nose.

Rosalind watched her friend's distress for a moment before she asked: 'Is the age difference Mrs Johnson's only objection?'

Cathy sighed. 'No. You probably saw in the article that Gerald isn't well. He's developed a kind of muscular complaint that makes playing difficult, which is why he's taking up teaching instead.'

'And Mrs Johnson thinks . . .'

'She keeps trying to tell me I'm still a child and that I'm taking on a sick man. It isn't true. Gerald *isn't* sick. It's just that he can't play in public any more. If some ordinary person had this thing it wouldn't affect them at all. Gerald is furious that the press somehow found out about that too.'

Rosalind was frowning. 'If you kept it completely secret, how do you think the paper got hold of it? Someone must have told them. Who could it have been if it was neither of you?'

Cathy sighed, her face anguished. 'That's just it, Rosalind. I've got a terrible feeling that it was my fault,' she said miserably. 'When I was alone at Gerald's flat on Saturday afternoon a woman who used to work in public relations for Zenith records came to see him.' She paused, biting her lip. 'I think I might have told her too much. She promised to keep it to herself. She said she was an old friend. I thought it would be all right.'

'Have you told him?'

Cathy stared into her cup. 'No. Do you think I should?'

'It's not for me to say, but I suppose it would be better. He might be blaming someone else. Someone innocent.'

'Oh!' Cathy looked up at her. 'I hadn't thought of that.'

Rosalind looked at her hands that lay spread on the table and saw that they were tightly clenched with tension. 'Poor Cathy. You must love him very much,' she said quietly.

'I do.' Cathy swallowed hard at the lump in her throat. 'And he loves me too. But Johnny just won't *understand*. And he'll be so cross when I tell him what I told this Kay Goolden woman.'

'Surely not,' Rosalind said soothingly. 'It'll all work out, you'll see.'

'I hope so.' Cathy looked at her. 'Thanks, Rosalind. It's good to talk to someone. I know I can trust you.'

Looking into the other girl's eyes Rosalind felt a rush of pride. She'd always admired Cathy so much and the idea of being trusted with such a personal problem, of actually being asked for advice, was almost overwhelming. 'Of course you can trust me,' she said fervently. 'Any time you need a friend, please don't hesitate.' She smiled shyly. 'You know, I've really missed you since you stopped working at the Queen's Head.'

'Me too, Rosalind.' Cathy shook her head. 'Heavens, I haven't let you get a word in, have I? I don't even know what you rang me for.'

To her own surprise Rosalind had almost forgotten about the party. 'Well, after your news it sounds a bit frivolous,' she said apologetically. 'I was ringing to ask you to a New Year's Eve party my mother is giving. But under the circumstances I don't suppose you'll want to think about parties.' Deep inside she was relieved that Una wasn't going to get the opportunity of embarrassing them all. But to her surprise Cathy's face brightened.

'New Year's Eve, did you say?'

'That's right.'

'It might be nice to get out. The atmosphere at home is awful and I've been dreading the rest of the holidays. I'll ask Gerald if he's got anything else planned. He hasn't mentioned anything. I'll let you know as soon as I can.'

Rosalind blushed. 'I think I should warn you ... it might be embarrassing. Mum – well, she makes a fuss of people like your fiancé. You know – likes to show off and all that.'

Cathy laughed. 'Gerald is used to all that, don't worry.' She smiled. 'Thanks for listening, Rosalind. Sorry to heap all my troubles on you.'

'That's all right.'

'What about you? You take your A levels in the spring, don't you?'

'Yes, then it's off to college, I hope.'

'No boyfriend?'

Rosalind hesitated, her cheeks colouring. 'There is someone actually. You'll meet him if you come to the party. His name is Stuart Hamilton and he's a scenic designer.'

'How interesting. I'm glad. Is it serious?'

'Oh, heavens no! I haven't known him very long.'

206

'But you like him – a lot?'

Rosalind blushed. 'I do rather, yes.'

The moment Christmas was out of the way Una began preparing for the party in earnest. She arranged for Hallard's catering department to do the food and spent almost a whole morning on the telephone telling them exactly what she wanted. She even had the piano in the lounge tuned in the hope that Gerald Cavelle might be induced to play for them. What a coup that would be! Then she set about making the house look festive and unearthing all Mrs Blake senior's best china and glass.

Don himself was quite bemused by the frenetic whirlwind of activity. The whole house seemed to be in turmoil. He couldn't remember there being a party at Blake's Folly since he was ten years old. But Una seemed happy. She was in such a good mood in fact that she was almost as charming and affable as when they had first met. To his great relief she appeared to have overcome her violent dislike of the house. He hadn't heard a word about the modern labour-saving bungalow she'd been nagging him to buy since the idea of having a party had first occurred to her. Something for which he was deeply grateful. He was automatically in favour of anything that put that out of her mind. Another good sign was that she had invited all the executive staff from Hallard's. It seemed to indicate that she was settling down at last. Blissfully ignorant of the fact that they had only been added to the guest list to swell the numbers, Don told himself with satisfaction that at last she was beginning to appreciate her position as the wife of one of Hallard's senior executives.

On the evening of the 31st there was a fine covering of snow on the gardens of Jay's Lane. The trees that lined the road sparkled in the glow of the street lamps and lights blazed welcomingly from the windows of Blake's Folly. In the hall a huge Christmas tree, decked with tinsel, baubles and coloured lights, greeted the guests as they arrived, and in the dining room a long table was laid out with every tempting delicacy that Hallard's catering department could provide.

The sliding doors between the lounge and the sitting room behind it had been opened and the carpet covering the woodblock floor had been taken up so that the guests could dance.

Don was wearing his dinner jacket, specially dry-cleaned for the occasion, whilst Una had splashed out on a new evening dress from model gowns: a dazzling creation in scarlet and black.

Upstairs in her room, quivering with excited apprehension, Rosalind dressed and made up with as much care, skill and imagination as she could. Defying her mother, she'd had her hair cut in the short boyish style that Freda had chosen for her, and, to her surprise, in a rare fit of generosity Una had decided that she too should have a new dress from Hallard's. Rosalind had chosen one in sapphire blue watered silk with a short flared skirt and a tight fitting bodice with a stand-up collar. It was the first glamorous dress she had ever owned. She could scarcely believe the difference it made to her confidence and couldn't wait for Stuart of see her in it.

By ten o'clock most of the guests had arrived. Dancing was in full swing and the house was filled with the sound of music and people enjoying themselves. The only guests who had not put in an appearance were Stuart and his flat mate, Cathy and Gerald.

Rosalind hung around unhappily in the hall, her spirits ebbing by the minute and her heart as heavy as lead. Una, no less disappointed, kept peering surreptitiously out of the window, hoping to see a taxi draw up at the gate. It was ironic that the very people for whom the party was being given were the only ones absent. She stared resentfully at all the staff members from Hallard's, each one of them stuffed

208

to the gills with her food and drink, making the most of her lavish hospitality. Trust that lot to turn up for a free booze-up!

On one of her forays to the hall Rosalind almost bumped into her mother on the same mission. Mother and daughter looked at each other in dismay, each of them knowing what was in the other's mind.

'I suppose you *did* ask them?' Una said accusingly.

'Of course I did. And Cathy rang to say they were coming.'

'So where the hell have they got to?' She looked suspiciously at Rosalind. 'You're sure you got the date right?'

'I could hardly get it wrong, could I? There's only one New Year's Eve in a year.'

Una clicked her tongue irritably. 'Such bad form. No apology from them – *nothing*. One would have thought that a person in his position would know better. Then there's Stuart.' Una looked first at her watch, then accusingly at Rosalind. 'It wouldn't surprise me if you'd put him off, you know!'

'Me? How could I possibly have done that?'

'Throwing yourself at him that evening when he took you out,' Una replied. 'You should play things coolly on the first date. I'd have thought you'd know that.'

'I do. And I *didn't*.'

'You should never show how keen you are. It puts a man right . . .' Una's words were interrupted by the sudden ringing of the bell. She gave a startled gasp, pushing Rosalind out of the way in her hurry to open the door. Outside stood Cathy and Gerald and, behind them, coming up the path and clutching a bottle of wine, Stuart, on his own.

Her complaints about their lack of etiquette quite forgotten, Una held out her hands to Cathy and Gerald.

'Catherine! And Mr Cavelle! How *lovely* to see you both. I'm *so* glad you could come.'

209

'I'm so sorry we're late,' Cathy said. 'Gerald had to drive over from the West End and the traffic was dreadful.'

Una waved away her apologies and reached out to pull them inside. 'Not at all. You're not all that late anyway, are you? I'm sure I never noticed the time, we've been having such fun. Now – Rossie will take your coats. Come along in. Everyone is just *dying* to meet you. You must be ready for a drink . . .' Still chattering she led them away, leaving Rosalind to greet Stuart.

Rosalind watched them go. Her mother hadn't given her time to greet her friend. Cathy was wearing a black lace dress that made her look older than her nineteen years and set off her auburn hair dramatically.

Stuart looked at her with a hang-dog expression. 'Oh, dear, am I in the dog-house?' She smiled as she took his coat. 'Not really. Mum was getting worried that her star guests weren't going to show up.'

'I'd have been here earlier but poor old Julian has flu and I had to make him as comfortable as possible before leaving. I wanted to explain to her, but . . .'

'I'd leave her if I were you,' Rosalind advised. 'She'll get round to you in a minute.'

He followed her to the cloakroom with her armful of coats. 'Wasn't that Gerald Cavelle, the concert pianist?' he asked curiously.

She nodded. 'He's engaged to a schoolfriend of mine.'

'Wow! I'm impressed.' He took one of the coats from her. 'Here, let me help you with those.' He looked at her appreciatively. 'You look terrific, Rosalind. I like the dress.'

She blushed with pleasure. 'Thanks. You look very nice yourself.' He did; tall and willowy in his dinner jacket and immaculate white shirt, his blond hair flopping artistically over his brow. 'They're dancing in the lounge,' she said. 'Shall we go in?'

For Rosalind the party began at that moment. Dancing

with Stuart to the radiogram, on the polished floor of the lounge, felt to her like wafting round some fairytale ballroom in the arms of Prince Charming. Closing her eyes she felt as though her feet hardly touched the ground. He was a superb dancer. As they danced his lips brushed her cheek and she could feel his breath, warm and gentle, tantalising her ear.

'I like the new hairstyle,' he whispered. 'You took my advice. That's a terrific compliment, you know.'

'You've got such good taste – artistic taste,' Rosalind said softly.

He drew her closer and as they swayed, Rosalind hummed dreamily to the strains of *Dancing in the Dark*. She thought it was the happiest, most romantic moment of her life.

'Now then, you two. The idea is to mingle.' Una's voice speared through her dream. 'You mustn't monopolise poor Stuart, Rossie.' She put her hand on his shoulder and Rosalind stood aside and watched helplessly as her mother danced Stuart away from her into the midst of the other guests. As they went her heart sank as she heard Una saying, 'Now, I want to hear *all* about this musical you and your friend are writing.'

As she turned away she wondered what plot her mother was hatching up this time.

Cathy looked up at Gerald. His face was drawn and pale and he'd been quiet on the drive over. 'Are you all right?' she asked.

He nodded. 'Just tired, that's all. It's been a hell of a week what with one thing and another. We needn't stay too long, need we?'

'I suppose once they've seen the New Year in we could leave,' she said. They danced in silence for a moment, then she looked up at him again. She'd been trying for days to get up the courage to tell him that the press leak had been her fault. Better do it now before her nerve failed her again,

211

then she could start 1963 with a clear conscience. She cleared her throat. 'Gerald, I've got a confession to make.'

'What can that be?' He smiled down at her.

'It's terrible, I'm afraid. I've been worried sick about it all through Christmas. When I tell you you're going to be so cross.'

'Then maybe you'd better not tell me,' he said wearily. 'At least, not tonight.'

'Oh, but I must,' she insisted. 'It won't wait any longer. That Saturday when I was alone at the flat someone came to see you.'

'Really? Who was that?'

'A woman. Her name was Kay Goolden. She said she was an old friend. She annoyed me a bit, ordering me about – behaving as though she owned the place. She even asked me to make myself scarce because she wanted to speak to you alone.'

He smiled wryly. 'That sounds like Kay. She used to handle my PR at Zenith.'

'Yes. So she said.'

'I think she sometimes felt I was her personal property.'

'Yes – well, I – I'm afraid I told her – that we were . . .'

His brow darkened as he looked down at her. 'Oh, no! You told *Kay* – of all people? Oh, well, that explains everything.'

'I'm sorry, Gerald. I'm afraid I mentioned that you hadn't been well too. I know I had no right. I . . .'

'For God's sake, Cathy! What made you tell her that?'

She felt her cheeks growing hot. 'I told you, it was the way she behaved.' She glanced up at him. 'She suggested that you'd given up your career because of *me*. She called me a groupie! I wasn't having that. It was what she implied about her relationship with you too. She hinted that you were still seeing each other.'

His eyebrows rose. 'The cheek of the woman! I ran into

her one day a few weeks ago and we had lunch. Apart from that I haven't seen her in months.'

Cathy searched his eyes. 'She even made sure I knew that she remembered where your bedroom was.'

'How did she do that?'

'She'd brought something for you – an invitation to a party she was giving. She insisted on putting it by your bed. She went straight to it . . .' She looked at him pleadingly. 'I *asked* her not to tell anyone about us, Gerald. She promised not to.'

'And then she went straight to the press. Well, that's Kay for you. But you weren't to know, were you?' He frowned. 'Invitation, did you say? I never found any invitation.'

'No.' She avoided his eyes. 'I tore it up after she'd gone.'

He laughed and pulled her close. 'Oh, Cathy, you're so sweet. Don't worry about Kay. She and I had something going for a time, but she was too possessive and I finished it a long time ago. This is just her way of hitting back. It's a pity Johnny had to be upset, but it's done now and there's nothing we can do about it. We'll just have to try very hard to make her see that our marriage is going to work.'

She pressed her lips against his cheek. 'Oh, Gerald, it *is* going to work, isn't it? Just think, this time next year we'll be together, spending Christmas and our first New Year at Cuckoo Lodge. It was awful without you over the holiday. And it was the worst birthday I ever had.'

He kissed her. 'I'm sorry we couldn't have spent more time together, darling. This state of affairs can't go on.' He looked thoughtful. 'As a matter of fact I've been wondering if it mightn't be a good idea to bring the wedding forward.'

'Oh, Gerald, that would be marvellous. Do you really think we could? The summer seems an awfully long way off.'

*　　*　　*

213

Una pressed herself close to Stuart as they circled the lounge floor, her cheek close to his. 'It all sounds fabulous,' she told him. 'What a wonderful plot – so original. Your friend Julian must be a very talented writer.'

'He is.' He looked down at her. 'I suppose you recognised the plot? It's really an up-dated musical version of Shakespeare's *Twelfth Night*.'

'Of course. I latched on to that at once,' she lied. 'Such a pity he couldn't come this evening. I was looking forward so much to meeting him.' She giggled. 'Julian, I mean. Not Shakespeare!'

'Yes. He was disappointed.'

'I'd love to read his script when it's finished, Stuart,' she said coyly. 'It might come as a surprise to you when I tell you that I was in the business myself before I married Don.'

'I did know actually,' he said. 'Rosalind told me.'

'Did she?' Una licked her lips carefully and treated him to a glossily seductive smile. 'As a matter of fact I've been wondering if there wasn't some way I could help you,' she said tantalisingly.

His eyes brightened. 'With contacts, you mean?' He looked around the room. 'You did say there would be some show business people here.'

She cleared her throat uneasily. 'Ah – well, New Year is a busy time for most of my showbiz friends. They're all working hard, I'm afraid. Up and down the country in panto and so on. There's dear Gerald, of course, but he's more in the classical line.'

'Yes.' He looked down at her. 'So – in what way do you feel you can help, Mrs Blake?'

She drew in her breath sharply. 'Oh Stuart – Una, *please*. Mrs Blake makes me sound like my own mother-in-law!' To her satisfaction he laughed. 'No, darling. What I wondered was whether some money might help? If you were to take a small theatre in some seaside town next summer season, and do an Out of Town première – persuade a few of the big-wigs from the West End to come and see it – it might get you off to a good start.'

He was staring at her. 'You'd really be prepared to do all that – for us?'

'If I think the play is worthy of it, of course I'd be willing to sponsor you.' She smiled dazzlingly at him. 'I mean, you have all the talent you require, Julian as writer, you on the set designs and costumes, and your other friend writing the music. It should be marvellous.'

'If you put up some money I take it you'd want to take a percentage of the box office by way of repayment?' he said thoughtfully.

Una smiled enigmatically. 'We can thrash out the conditions when I've met your friends and read the play, can't we?'

As midnight drew near Don turned off the music and switched over to the radio for the chimes of Big Ben. Una made sure that everyone's glass was full and they stood in a circle, glasses raised, poised for the birth of a new year. At the first stroke a cheer went up and there were kisses, toasts and good wishes all round. Then they all linked arms for the traditional *Auld Lang Syne*. When the music began again and they took to the floor Cathy laid her head against Gerald's chest.

'I love you so much,' she whispered. 'Can I come back to the flat with you tonight?'

He shook his head. 'Darling, you know that would only aggravate the situation. We'll set the wedding date tomorrow. We'll make it soon.'

'It can't be soon enough for me,' she told him dreamily.

Stuart held out his hand to Rosalind. 'Dance with me?'

Since the first dance with him her mother had made sure she was kept busy handing round snacks and filling glasses. She'd had to watch Stuart dancing with Una most of the evening and felt dejected and disappointed. All the confidence the new dress had brought her had faded and she felt like a dowdy wallflower again. She stared at the hand he offered, then up at him.

'You don't have to be polite. I'm sure you'd rather ask Mum.'

He looked crestfallen. 'Rosalind! Don't be like that.' He took her hand and pulled her towards him. 'I wanted to be with you, really. You're the main reason I came. But your mother has made me the most wonderful offer. I could hardly be rude to her after that, could I?'

Slightly appeased, she allowed him to slide an arm round her waist and draw her on to the dance floor. 'What offer?' she asked.

'Well, it's all very much in the air at the moment, but she just might put up some money so that we can get our musical on,' he told her with barely suppressed excitement.

She stared at him. Where would her mother get that kind of money? she wondered. Presumably from Don. But how would she persuade him to part with it? And what was behind the idea? Knowing Una there was bound to be an ulterior motive. Still, if that was Stuart's only reason for neglecting her all evening, it wasn't important.

'Have you enjoyed the party?' she asked him.

His arm tightened around her waist and he pressed his lips close to her ear. 'I'd have preferred to see more of you. Maybe we can do something about that,' he said. 'Come out with me again soon.'

She felt her heart quicken. 'All right. When?'

'I'll ring you.' He squeezed her tightly. 'I have to go now. Come out to the car with me and say goodnight.'

At the gate, under the shadow of the laurel hedge, he kissed her till she felt her spine turn to jelly. Then he climbed into Julian's Mini and waved her goodnight.

Her feet hardly touching the ground, she walked indoors. In the hall Cathy and Gerald were about to leave. Cathy reached out and put her arms round Rosalind, giving her a hug.

'Happy New Year, Rosalind,' she said, her face radiant. 'Thanks for inviting us to the party. We've had a super time.' She lowered her voice. 'And guess what? Gerald and I are bringing the wedding date forward. We're getting married very soon. I'll make sure you get an invitation.'

Rosalind said goodnight, shook hands with Gerald, then climbed the stairs. It had been a night to remember after all.

It was two-thirty when Una finally joined Don in their bedroom. From the warmth and comfort of the bed he watched her climb out of the splendid red and black evening dress and peel off her black lace bra and panties. Now that he was used to her uninhibited behaviour he had to admit that she really did have a beautiful body. Being on the plump side made her even more voluptuous in his eyes. She looked a lot like the photograph of his mother taken soon after he had been born. Soft and bounteous. He felt excitement mounting.

'You're looking very lovely tonight, Una,' he said huskily as she climbed into bed beside him. He had noticed that she was wearing the sexy black nightgown she had bought for their honeymoon.

'Am I?' Una snuggled down gratefully in the warmth. 'I think the party was a success. Don't you?'

'I do. You're the perfect hostess,' he told her. 'Harry Black, the firm's accountant, told me so more than once.'

As she switched off the bedside lamp Una grimaced. Harry Black, that common little man? What a nerve he had! When he'd danced with her he'd surreptitiously squeezed her bottom. What did he know about anything? Aloud she said, 'Really? How gratifying.' As she felt Don's hands begin to fondle her she gritted her teeth. 'Don – you know the bungalow we've been thinking about?'

217

His heart sank. 'Yes,' he said guardedly.

'Well, I've been thinking. Maybe you're right. After the space we've been used to here, it might feel claustrophobic. So I was wondering if you'd mind if I used a little of the money we would have spent on an investment instead?'

The feel of her warm soft body so close to his was arousing him so much he hardly heard or cared what she was saying.

'Investment? That sounds much more sensible, dear,' he murmured as he pushed her shoulder straps down and began to slide the nightdress over her breasts. 'But tell me about it tomorrow, eh?' His breath was rapid and moist in her ear as he moved over her and muttered urgently, 'I know it's late dear – and you must be tired – but, oh, *Una* . . .'

Resigned, she wriggled out of the nightdress and lay back, preparing herself for the passion to come, consoling herself with the knowledge that if Don was running true to form it would be mercifully short-lived. The really worthwhile things in life were sometimes almost too expensive, she reflected wryly, gazing glassily up at the ceiling.

Chapter Twelve

Gerald found the block of flats without difficulty and took the lift to the top floor. Kay took so long to answer his ring at the bell that he began to think she was out. He was just turning away when she opened the door. She wore a bathrobe and her hair was swathed, turban fashion in a towel.

'Gerald! What a surprise. Come in.' She looked taken aback. 'I'm sorry I was so long. I was in the shower.'

He stood in the spacious hallway while she closed the door. It was certainly a lavish flat. She hadn't exaggerated about that. She turned to him, her face now composed into a smile.

'So – what can I do for you?'

'Don't tell me you haven't guessed why I'm here?'

She took in his grim expression and smiled ruefully. 'You're annoyed.'

'That would be putting it mildly. Why Kay? Why did you do it?'

She shrugged. 'I'm not sure that there was a reason. Why should there be?' She walked through an open door into an exquisitely furnished sitting room. Picking up a silver cigarette box from the glass-topped coffee table she offered it to him. He ignored it.

'You came to the flat and quizzed Cathy – my fiancée. Then, after she'd naively confided in you, you ran straight to the press. Why did you do it Kay?'

She turned to him defiantly. 'Why not? You've always gone all out for publicity.' She looked at him for a moment, registering the determined set of his jaw. 'All right then, if you're set on having a reason I suppose you could say that your fiancée, as you so *quaintly* call her, was so naive that I just couldn't resist it.'

'You really are a bitch, aren't you? Have you no sense of decency at all?'

'Decency?' She lit her cigarette and blew out a cloud of smoke. 'Do you call marrying a kid less than half your age decent? I call it disgusting. It's almost like child molesting.'

'Cathy isn't a child.'

'No? You led me to believe she was though, didn't you? You gave the impression that she was in infant school.'

'I did nothing of the kind.'

'It was what you implied, Gerry. It was what you meant me to believe. Don't deny it.'

He fought to control the rage that bubbled up inside him. 'Why the hell should I want you to believe anything? It's none of your damned business. Why are you so vindictive, Kay? What is it festering away in that devious mind of yours that makes you want to hurt and destroy?'

Her eyes flashed as she viciously stubbed out her half-smoked cigarette. 'There's nothing wrong with my mind – or my body, Gerald,' she said. 'You're the one who's hurting – you're the one who's sick. I knew that in New York. Now I'm sure.'

'Once and for all, I am *not sick*!'

'Really?' Her eyebrows rose. 'Your fiancée seems to think you are. Something muscular, she said. Whatever it is must be bad to make you start behaving so irrationally.'

Suddenly he felt unutterably weary. Sinking down into one of the white leather chairs he said, 'You hurt all the wrong people – people you don't even know, who don't deserve it. You can do what you like to me, I don't matter any more, but Cathy and her family . . .'

'You *do* matter, Gerry!' She crossed the room and sank to her knees in front of him. 'You matter to me. I did it to

220

try and bring you to your senses – make you face up to the sheer stupidity of what you're doing. Why are you throwing yourself and your talent away like this? First you tell me you're about to retire and bury yourself in some frightful dump at the back of beyond, then I hear – second hand – that you're ill and that you're marrying this – this *child*. How do you think it made me feel?'

'Spiteful, apparently.'

'No!' She reached for his hands. 'I really didn't want to hurt you – or anyone else. If I did, then I'm sorry.' She looked into his eyes. 'Tell me, what's it all about? Tell me why you're doing it. Make me understand – if you can!'

He sighed. 'It's simple. I love her.'

She laughed. 'You *fancy* her, you mean. Face it, Gerry, she's every middle-aged man's fantasy with her auburn hair and great big innocent eyes; just as you are every young girl's fairytale dream. The handsome concert pianist with the romantic mystery illness! Get her out of your system, yes. But marriage!' Kay looked into his eyes. 'How long do you think it'll last? How long before the novelty wears off for you both?'

'Maybe it won't have to last.'

She frowned. 'What do you mean? What are you saying, Gerry?'

'Nothing.' He shrugged. 'Who knows how long any marriage will last?'

'I think ours would have lasted,' she said quietly.

He leaned forward and gripped the hands that lay in his. 'You believe that, do you? Well, just tell me this, Kay, would you have given up this marvellous new job of yours with Summit Films? Your fabulous salary and all your hard-won independence? Would you have given up this flat and come with me to live at the back of beyond, as you call it?' He shook his head. 'I don't think so. And as for living with a man with what you call a mystery illness ...' He smiled wryly. 'It just isn't

221

you, Kay. You're hardly the Florence Nightingale type. Why not admit it?'

'Are you saying that you would have asked me if I had been?'

'Who knows?'

'You didn't even give me the chance, did you? Yet you believe that this girl is all of those things – unselfish, caring, ready to give up everything for you, the man she loves?'

'I happen to believe she is, yes.'

'And you think it's fair to expect it of her?'

He stopped short, his eyes suddenly hard as he stared at her. 'What would you know about fairness, Kay?'

She rose and stood looking down at him. 'I know *you*, Gerry. I know and understand you through and through; better than you know yourself probably. I spent a long time building a public image for you. You get to know a person pretty well in the process of doing that. And there's something here that just doesn't fit. What I don't get is why you have to bury yourself in the country.'

'I've changed. I want different things now. My values have altered.'

'We could have stayed here, you and I.' She swept an arm round the room. 'You could have taught here just as well as in the country. There's plenty of room for your piano and I'd be out of your way all day. She leaned towards him, looking into his eyes. 'I could have been a good wife to you without giving anything up. I'm not as selfish as you make me sound, Gerry. I'd have looked after you. And if it's money that's worrying you it needn't have been a problem. I earn enough for both of us.'

'Money is the last of my worries!' he snapped irritably, shaking off the hands that held his. 'Anyway, do you really think I'd ever allow you to keep me, Kay? God forbid! You're not the only one to need independence. At best you'd have swallowed me whole. At worst you'd have grown bored.'

'*That's not true!*' She swung away from him and went to the window, hiding the quick tears and the hurt his remark had inflicted. She wrapped her arms around herself protectively. 'You must have known damned well I'd come back if you'd asked me. I would even now.'

He stood up. 'No, Kay.'

'*Yes!*' She swung round to face him. 'You and I are two of a kind. We complement each other perfectly and you know it.' She went to him and put her arms around him. 'You still want me if you're honest. You want me now. Don't deny it.'

It was true. He couldn't deny that he still found her desirable, seeing her here like this, her face clean of make-up, glowing from the shower. He visualised her skin, damp and fragrant under the bathrobe, and longed for the warm, silken feel of it under his hands; the comfort of her familiar body in his arms. He felt too tired; too weak to argue. She'd always been stronger than him, always able to impose her will on his and bring him into line. It had scared him sometimes in the past. It was one of the main reasons he'd broken with her. And it still worked, even now.

Reaching up suddenly she drew his head down and kissed him hard, her lips parting invitingly, her mouth tender and passionate at the same time. For a moment he resisted, then he pulled the towel from her hair and tangled his fingers in the damp tresses. Holding her face tightly between his hands, he kissed her fiercely, almost brutally.

'Damn you, Kay,' he murmured. 'Damn you to hell!' But in spite of his outward anger he couldn't deny that giving in to what he had been fighting ever since she opened the door to him gave him a soaring sense of release.

She rubbed her cheek against his. 'Come and dry my hair for me like you used to do.' Taking his hand she began to pull him gently towards the bedroom. He went with her willingly.

*　　*　　*

When he awakened the room was dark. Raising himself on one elbow he stared down bemusedly at her. 'Have I been asleep?'

'Yes.' She sat up and switched on the bedside lamp. 'We have to talk, Gerry. What is really wrong with you?'

'Nothing's *wrong*.' He ran a hand through his tousled hair as the memory of his humiliating failure came back to him. 'I was tired, that's all. Maybe I felt a little guilty and inhibited too. I'm sorry if I disappointed you, but I did warn you, Kay. I love Cathy.'

She reached out for a cigarette. 'In my experience most men are completely amoral when it comes to sex,' she said bitterly. 'They take what's on offer. In love or out of it.'

'Don't tar us all with the same brush. I'm not like that.'

'Don't tell me you didn't want to make love to me! You'd been wanting to from the moment you walked in the door.'

Stung by her uncanny insight he hit back. 'Perhaps your technique is beginning to slip, Kay. Sex appeal doesn't last for ever, you know!'

The barb found its mark and she winced. 'Thanks!' Swinging her legs over the edge of the bed, she pulled on her bathrobe, tying the belt tightly. 'What do you think your sweet little fiancée would think if I told her what just happened – or rather *didn't* happen?' she asked, looking down at him.

'She wouldn't believe you.'

Her eyebrows shot up. 'Oh, I see. It's like that, is it? A case of try before you buy!' She frowned. 'Well, maybe you should warn her. Ask yourself seriously, are you really being fair to her – a naive young girl, with God knows what ideals and expectations? She'll be going into this marriage with stars in her eyes, expecting all sorts of things that you can't or won't want to give her. Don't you think she should be warned?'

He sprang up and grasped her by the shoulders, his eyes

burning as they bored into hers. 'You keep away from Cathy, do you hear? Make any more trouble for me and I'll . . .'

'You'll *what*, Gerry?' Her eyes held his with a bold challenge he couldn't meet. She pushed him away. 'Oh, relax. I won't make trouble. It might sound phoney but I really do care too much to do that. I am warning you though. Marry that girl and you'll both regret it. Hire a housekeeper, a nurse, a *whore* if you like. But if you really love the girl as much as you say, don't marry her. If you do you'll ruin her life.'

Chapter Thirteen

The first days of 1963 at Chestnut Grove were difficult for Cathy. Unable to handle the situation downstairs, she stayed in her room for much of the time, but at mealtimes when the family were gathered round the table, the air was thick with an atmosphere of disapproval. Mrs Bains wore an expression of self-righteous satisfaction. She ate in a meaningful silence broken only by the reproachful clicking of her dentures. *I told you it would all end in tears*, was etched in every line of her face. Matthew looked acutely uncomfortable and avoided Cathy's eyes, while Johnny picked at her food, looking downright miserable. Conversation was limited to hopeful comments about the weather from Matthew, and grudging requests to pass the salt.

Finally unable to tolerate the cloud of gloom that had settled over her home a moment longer, Johnny decided that something must be done to put things on a more amicable footing. It seemed that Cathy's proposed marriage to Gerald Cavelle would go ahead whether she approved or not and she could see that if she was not to lose Cathy altogether some kind of compromise must be reached.

One afternoon, just before the new college term began, she made up her mind and as soon as Mrs Bains had nodded off in the armchair for her afternoon snooze she went upstairs and tapped gently on Cathy's door.

'Cathy, can I come in?'

Cathy raised her head from the book she was reading. Johnny's voice was soft but there was a positive tone about it that she recognised of old. It meant that she had no intention of taking no for an answer. Instinctively she drew herself up straight and replied, 'Of course. The door's not locked.'

Johnny stepped inside and closed the door firmly behind her. For a moment the two surveyed each other across the room. For the first time in their long relationship, Johnny felt frighteningly helpless. Cathy was a woman now and out of her control. Was it possible to mend the rift that had opened between them? Was there anything she could do to prevent her from diving headlong into what she saw as an inevitable disaster? She must at least try. She cleared her throat. 'This can't go on, Cathy,' she said. 'I can't take any more of this terrible atmosphere. And frankly I don't see why I should.'

Cathy hung her head, feeling six years old again. 'I know. And I'm sorry. But it really isn't my fault.' She looked up, her eyes brimming with tears. 'I – Gerald and I had planned to tell you about our engagement on my birthday, but the papers got hold of the story before we had the chance.'

'It was the way you lied to me. You've never been deceitful before. I can't help thinking . . .' Johnny broke off, biting her lip. She hadn't meant to begin by reproaching the girl. It was all coming out wrong.

But Cathy was nodding. 'I know. And I hated deceiving you. But I knew you'd take it badly, and I was right, wasn't I? Look – if you'd rather I left . . .'

'*Left?*' Shocked at the idea, Johnny crossed the room and sat down beside her on the bed. 'This is your home, child. At least, for now. Anyway, where would you go?'

Cathy shrugged. 'To Gerald's flat, I suppose.'

'You'd go there and live with him?' Johnny could hardly believe she was hearing right. 'He'd let you do that?'

'No. He's already suggested that we bring the wedding forward.' Cathy turned to look Johnny in the eye. 'He isn't the kind of person you seem to think. He's good and decent and he loves me.'

'Is that why he seduced you? The man who's supposed to

227

be your guardian? The man your father put his trust in to protect and care for you? Do you really think I could ever respect a man like that?' Johnny felt the hot colour rising up from her neck to suffuse her cheeks. She hadn't meant to say it, but now that she had she was glad. It had been festering in her mind for weeks. It was better out in the open.

Cathy's eyes widened and she recoiled as though she'd been slapped. '*Seduced?* I don't know what you mean! It isn't like that.'

'No? Then what do you call it?'

'How did you know anyway?' Cathy asked, her face drained of colour.

Johnny threw up her hands. 'Oh, Cathy, *Cathy*, what do you take me for? I'm not a fool, you know. You can't keep things like that from someone who's known you as long as I have. I know you and Gerald have been lovers. It's been written all over you for weeks.' She broke off as a thought occurred to her. 'You're not expecting his child, are you? That isn't why . . .?'

'*No!*' Cathy's eyes were wide with shock. 'Is that really what you thought? Is it what everyone is thinking? That he's only asked me to marry him because . . .'

'No, of course they aren't.'

'*You* thought so.'

'Cathy, don't you see? You're like my own daughter. Please try to understand how it is for me. Ever since you were no more than a baby I've cared for you; nursed you through all those childhood illnesses; worried about you and loved you like my own child. It's only natural that when something like this happens my instincts tell me.' She spread her hands in a helpless gesture. 'If it had been some young man – some *boy* – I could have tried to talk you out of it – somehow made you see that he wasn't right for you.' Her voice thickened. 'As it is I – I've no right to tell you to do anything. I've never felt so helpless – *so useless* in my life.'

Cathy looked at her. 'You're wrong about one thing, Johnny,' she whispered. 'He didn't seduce me. It was the other way round. But only because I love him so much. I wish I could make you understand what it's like. I want to be with him more than anything else in the world; to belong to him. If anything happened to part us I think I'd want to die. I just wanted everyone to be as happy as I was. I never wanted to make you all miserable.' She could scarcely speak for the lump in her throat and suddenly she threw her arms round Johnny's neck and hugged her. 'Oh, Johnny, I *wish* you could be glad for me.'

Johnny's heart melted as she held the girl who was so dear to her close. Their tears mingled as she said wearily. 'I wish I could too, love. There's nothing I wish more. And I do remember how it feels to be in love, believe me. I'm not that old that I can't remember. It's just that he's so much older than you. What kind of life will you have with him?'

'A happy one. I *promise*!' Cathy pushed her hands against Johnny's shoulders so that she could look into her eyes. 'Oh, *please* say you wish us well. It means so much to me to have you on our side. Next to Gerald you're the most important person in my life. These last couple of weeks have been so awful.'

'I know they have, love.' Johnny looked at her for a long moment. 'What do you think your poor father would have said?' she asked quietly. 'Have you thought about that? The last promise I made him was to take care of you and if I thought I was letting him down . . .'

'Oh, but you're not! He would have been pleased. I know he would,' Cathy said, her eyes shining with confidence. 'Gerald was his best friend. He would have trusted him with his life. He even made him my guardian, didn't he?'

Johnny looked thoughtful. She didn't share Cathy's confidence on that particular issue but there was little point in arguing about it. She looked into the girl's eyes. 'Will you promise me one thing?'

'I'll try,' Cathy said guardedly.

'Will you just stay on at college and take your exams? It's only a few months after all. And that house in Suffolk won't be ready to live in for some time yet by the sound of things.'

'Well – I suppose I could.'

'It wouldn't hurt to wait another six months, would it? Just until the summer term ends. It seems a shame not to take your finals when you've got this far and worked so hard. A qualification is always a good thing to have. You never know when you might need it.' She smiled and took Cathy's hands in hers. 'You could be married from here then – a lovely white wedding with all the trimmings. I'd even make your dress for you if you wanted. And have the reception here. Matthew could give you away. I'd love that, wouldn't you?'

Cathy smiled. 'Oh, Johnny, yes, I would.'

'It's settled then?'

'I'll have to ask Gerald.'

'Of course. You do that. See what he says.' She gave Cathy a hug, then rose and went to the door. 'Come on downstairs now. I'll put the kettle on for a cup of tea.'

'Johnny . . .'

The older woman paused in the doorway. 'Yes, love?'

'Will you ask Mrs Bains to stop looking at me as though I've murdered someone?'

Johnny laughed. 'Mother just feels protective of me because she knows how worried I've been. All mothers are alike. You'll find that out for yourself someday.' She grinned. 'But she'll be fine when I've had a word with her. Just you leave her to me.'

When Matthew came home from work that afternoon and looked into the sitting room he found the three women in his life happily chatting over the teacups. The subject was clearly weddings. Dresses made of lace versus satin? Four bridesmaids or two? And the merits of a sit-down reception as opposed to a finger buffet. As he closed the door and made for the stairs he gave a sigh of relief. Even Gran was smiling. With a bit of luck the pall of gloom that had hung over the house since before Christmas had finally dispersed.

But the following day when Cathy met Gerald and put forward Johnny's suggestion he was less than enthusiastic. 'You don't really want all that fuss, do you?'

She looked at him. 'I thought you'd be pleased. Don't you see, it means that Johnny has come round to the idea?'

His eyebrows came together in a frown. 'I can't see that it's her place to "come round" as you put it. Or to dictate where and when we'll be married,' he said tetchily. 'She's not even a relative. She was only Dan's cleaning woman after all. I thought we were going to bring the wedding forward. I thought you were happy with that.'

'Johnny's always been more than just a cleaning woman,' Cathy said warmly. 'She virtually brought me up. I owe her a lot.' Dismayed, she looked at him. This was their first disagreement. 'I was happy about bringing the wedding forward. I still am in some ways. It's just that Johnny thinks I should finish my course first – take my exams and qualify. And I can see her point.'

'Why? You're never going to need to earn your living in that kind of way.'

'But I might want to get a job sometime. You never know. Johnny says a qualification is always useful.'

His eyes narrowed. 'She still doesn't trust me, does she? What does she think I'll do – run off and abandon you? Leave you penniless?'

'No, of course not. It's just a – kind of safety net – insurance.'

He looked at her for a long moment. 'So now I know what Johnny thinks. How about telling me what *you* think, Cathy?'

Her heart sank. It was so hard, trying to please everyone.

'I want to be with you,' she said simply. 'But I want to do what's right too, what's best – for us, for everyone.'

He shook his head and drew her close. 'You're asking for the impossible, Cathy. In the entire history of the world no one has ever yet succeeded in pleasing everyone. It's your life – your future. It's what *you* want that's important.' He held her at arm's length and looked into her eyes. 'So make up your mind. What do you want?'

'I want what you want.'

He kissed her. 'And *I* want to put my ring on your finger. The sooner the better and with as little fuss as possible.'

He held her close, drawing strength from the warmth and youthful vitality of her body. 'I'd like it to be as soon as possible. We'll have a nice long honeymoon in Switzerland, at a favourite place of mine high in the mountains. Oh, you'll love it, Cathy. I can't wait to show it to you. Meantime I'll arrange with the builders to get a couple of rooms ready for us to come back to at Cuckoo Lodge and we can live in them and supervise the rest of the work on the house.'

He kissed her again. 'Oh, just think of it, darling. Watching the house grow and blossom as the spring turns into summer; making plans. There'll be so much to do. Contacts to make; publicity and booking to organise for the school. There'll be people to see – meetings – entertaining as soon as the house is ready. That's where you'll come into your own. My perfect hostess. It's going to be a wonderful life, darling. Can't you just see it?'

'Can we let Johnny arrange the wedding? It means so much to her.'

He sighed and shook his head at her. 'You're doing it again – trying to please everyone. I'm sorry, darling, but the press are already on to us. If they got wind of a white wedding in deepest suburbia they'd have a field day. They could wreck the whole proceedings for us. No, we'll make it a very quiet affair. A register office – somewhere quiet, off the

232

beaten track would be best. With as few people in the know about the date and location as possible. Afterwards we'll lay on lunch at a local hotel for close friends – that includes the Johnsons of course. You can leave all the arrangements to me.' He kissed the top of her head. 'All you have to do is get yourself a wedding outfit and turn up.'

Cathy tried to swallow her disappointment. 'What about witnesses – someone to give me away – your best man?'

He laughed. 'I don't think there's really any need for any of that. But if there's anyone you want to ask specially, I've no objection.'

'I thought perhaps Matthew. And Carla and Rosalind Blair.'

He shrugged. 'Fine, if that's what will make you happy.' He hugged her. 'It's your wedding, darling.'

As he drew up outside the Johnsons' house she turned to him. 'Are you coming in?'

He shook his head. 'Not today. I'll leave you to tell Johnny what we've planned.' As she made to get out of the car he reached out to draw her back. 'Cathy, wait. I meant to speak to you before – about money.'

She closed the car door and looked at him. 'What about money?'

'I think we should get a few legal loose ends tied up. Restoring the house and putting in all the things we're going to need is going to cost a bomb. I knew it would be expensive but there are some things I hadn't counted for. I take it that you agree that we pool our resources once we're married?'

She laughed. 'Of course, but you're already in charge of my money anyway.'

'Only until the end of next year when you come of age. That arrangement still stands as things are at present and of course I can only do things on *your* behalf. It would be more convenient to have it changed.'

She nodded. 'Whatever you think.'

233

He smiled. 'For instance, it seems rather ludicrous for me to go on making you a monthly allowance, doesn't it? We'll have a joint account at the bank of course. That means you can draw money whenever you need it, without having to ask me. And of course once the flat is sold there'll be no problem.'

'Yes, I see. All right then.'

'To make it legal and above board I'll need your signature on one or two boring old documents,' he said. 'I've made an appointment at the solicitor's for tomorrow afternoon. Is that all right?'

'Yes, fine. Mr MacAlister's?'

'No. I've had everything transferred to James Palmer, my own solicitor. It's more convenient. I'll pick you up at two o'clock.' He drew her towards him and kissed her. 'See you tomorrow then, darling. Don't worry about Johnny. She'll see it our way when you've explained.'

If Johnny was disappointed she didn't say so. And when Mrs Bains opened her mouth to express her own forthright opinion her daughter shot her a warning look that silenced her before she began.

On the day that followed, Gerald's solicitor had all the documents drawn up ready for Cathy to sign at his smart Kensington office. The transaction was over in the space of a few minutes and then they were walking out into the thin February sunshine again and making their way to the bank. Afterwards they went to Gerald's flat where he told her about the arrangements he had already begun to make for their wedding. For Cathy the day had an oddly unreal feel to it. She felt as though the whole thing was out of her control, almost as though it was happening to someone else and she was merely an observer. But then, as she told herself, she knew nothing about financial matters, or about how to arrange a wedding either. If it had been left to her she wouldn't have known where to start.

* * *

234

The wedding took place on a bright Monday morning in early April. The first green leaves of spring were beginning to unfurl on all the trees and Gerald told Cathy that the builders had now completed the two rooms they were to live in on the first floor of Cuckoo Lodge on their return from Switzerland.

Cathy wore a suit of cinnamon linen with a mint green blouse and hat to match. She carried a small posy of pink and cream rosebuds. Matthew, who accompanied her to the register office in the hired car, thought she looked pale, but she insisted that it was only nerves and that she would be fine the moment she saw Gerald.

The ceremony was over almost before she had time to take in her surroundings. She was dimly aware of being ushered into a small room, carpeted in blue and tastefully decked with flowers. There were two rows of chairs on which sat their few guests. The bespectacled registrar gabbled his way through the ceremony in a monotone as though he were conducting an auction sale. Finding herself finally married to Gerald, Cathy allowed herself to be hugged by a tearful Johnny and pecked on the cheek by Matthew. Rosalind squeezed her hands and wished her luck and Carla winked and told her she was lucky to have 'landed herself such a good catch'.

Gerald himself had invited one guest only. Cathy didn't notice her until after the ceremony when she came forward with congratulations. Standing on tiptoe, Kay kissed Gerald's cheek, then turned to Cathy.

'My dear, many, *many* congratulations.' She took both her hands and squeezed them gently. 'I do hope we shall be good friends. And I hope you've forgiven me for getting off on the wrong foot.' She leaned forward to brush Cathy's cheek with cool lips. 'Gerald has very generously invited me to come to Suffolk and see this wonderful house of yours when it's finished. I hope you approve of the invitation?'

Dismayed, Cathy made herself smile. 'Of course. All Gerald's friends are welcome.'

She got through the lunch, hardly tasting the food and declining all but a sip of champagne, then somehow, at last they were on the plane, bound for Switzerland. As they became airborne and safety belts were unfastened she looked at Gerald.

'I can't believe we're actually married and on our way,' she said. 'I thought it would never end.'

He slipped an arm around her and drew her head down on to his shoulder. 'If you found that an ordeal, think how much worse a big church wedding would have been.'

'Gerald – why didn't you tell me you'd invited Kay Goolden?' she asked.

He shrugged. 'It was very much a last-minute thing. She rang me last night. I thought it might be as well to have her on our side.'

'Why did she ring you?'

'Nothing specific. Just a chat.'

'What about?'

'Nothing much. Just gossip. Kay and I have a lot of mutual acquaintants. She used to handle all my publicity as you know.'

'Oh, yes. I knew that all right,' Cathy said wryly.

Gerald chuckled and took her hand. 'That's all water under the bridge now. Forgive and forget, eh? Kay is a good PR woman. When you spilled the beans like that she must have found it irresistible.'

The fact that he was laying the blame for the episode firmly at her door did not escape her. 'Obviously. So – didn't you feel it was risky, telling her we were getting married today? Weren't you afraid she might go to the press again?'

'I knew she wouldn't if she was a guest, which is why I invited her. I thought if I made her part of the conspiracy . . .' He bent to kiss her. 'How did we get into this? Why on earth are we talking about Kay when we're on our way to our honeymoon?'

She relaxed. He was right. They had a wonderful three

weeks ahead of them. Why spoil it with her silly suspicions about Kay?

Switzerland was all that Gerald had promised – and more besides. The view from their hotel window in the little ski resort of Davos enchanted Cathy so much that she couldn't stop looking at it. The mountain tops were still clothed in snow, but the brilliant sunshine turned them pink and gold like sugar frosting. She loved the hospitality of the people and the quaint buildings with their colourfully painted walls. The air was as sparkling and invigorating as champagne and Cathy felt as though she were living in a fairytale that was coming alive. They swam in the indoor heated pool at the hotel; walked the mountain paths; explored the smart little shops that were full of intriguing things; and drank rich, fragrant coffee in the cosy little cafés. Gerald hired a car and took her to Liechtenstein to see the castle, and they went for memorable drives on precipitous mountain roads to villages that looked as though they had stepped straight out of a Disney film. They dined late and danced romantically afterwards in the hotel ballroom with its glittering chandeliers.

Several times they took the ski-lift to the top of the Shatzlap and looked out over what seemed to Cathy the magical, cloud-capped roof of the world; the kind of place where, as a child, she had always imagined Santa Claus lived.

'It's a pity it's a little too late for skiing,' Gerald told her. 'I'd have loved to teach you.'

'Oh, yes. I've always wanted to learn to ski.' Cathy hugged his arm and looked up at him. 'Maybe we can come again next year and do that?'

He didn't meet her eager eyes as he replied: 'Yes – maybe.'

At night, wrapped in each other's arms under the thick duvet they would lie and look out through the open shutters at the sky that looked like black velvet studded with diamonds. And in the mornings they would wake at dawn to watch the sun come up over the mountain tops, bewitching everything it touched with a breathtaking golden beauty.

'I'll remember this for the rest of my life,' she whispered one night when they had just made love. 'I don't know how it's possible to be this happy. Sometimes I feel I shall wake up soon and find it was all a beautiful dream.'

Gerald turned his face away so that she wouldn't see the guilt that filled his eyes. She was like a child, wide-eyed with delight at every new thing. Her unselfish and unquestioning love overwhelmed and terrified him. She had taken to marriage so wholeheartedly, giving herself without reserve. To her, lovemaking was new and exciting. She approached it with an eager, uninhibited adventurousness that enchanted him. He was so lucky. *And so devious*, his conscience insisted. He battled inwardly with the accusing demons that refused to leave him alone. He would make her happy. After all, she was in love with him. It would have broken her heart if he had sent her away. *But had he encouraged her to fall in love for his own gain? And could he live up to her expectations?* He closed his heart resolutely to the answers.

Sometimes he would lie awake watching her as she slept the deep, untroubled sleep of the very young; trying to picture her as an older woman – trying to imagine what it might have been like if he had stayed married to Sarah. Or if he had married Kay. Or if the other – the only true, deep love of his life – could have been his. Until now he had refused to acknowledge to himself that this girl was the next best thing – the nearest he would ever get in this life to the one woman who had meant the world to him; the one woman he'd had no right to. Not that he hadn't been punished in the worst possible way. If there was a God he had taken a terrible revenge for what Gerald had done. But he couldn't be punished any more now. All that was over.

*   *   *

For the last two days of the honeymoon Gerald seemed a little unwell. Cathy fussed over him, but he brushed aside her concern, saying that it was merely the rich food. On the plane on the way home he slept for much of the time and Cathy had the chance to look back and reflect on their first weeks together.

She was happy; happier than she ever remembered being. She had enjoyed her honeymoon so much. Being married to Gerald was her dream come true and their three weeks in Davos had been a wonderful experience in every way. And if Gerald hadn't wanted to make love quite as often as she'd expected him to, it didn't matter, she told herself. They had all their lives in front of them. Some things puzzled her though. Some nights after kissing and caressing her passionately he would turn away abruptly, leaving her bemused and unsatisfied. Was it something she did wrong? Was she too forward? There was no one she could ask. Johnny had volunteered no information about the intimate side of married life and Cathy herself had been too shy to ask. No doubt everything would sort itself out in time, she told herself.

On their return to London they had planned to stay at the flat for a few days before going to Melfordleigh, but on the day of their return Gerald suddenly announced that he had to make a trip up to Edinburgh. Cathy begged to go with him but he was adamant.

'It's business. You'd be bored.'

'What kind of business?'

'Nothing to do with Cuckoo Lodge. Nothing that need concern you.'

'But I could look at the shops. I've never been to Edinburgh,' she told him. 'Besides, I'll miss you.' She went to him and slid her arms around his waist. 'Please take me, Gerald.' She stood on tiptoe to rub her cheek against his, but to her dismay he pushed her away impatiently.

239

'I said no, Cathy. We may be married but we mustn't start living in each other's pockets. I'll be back in a couple of days. If you want something to do you can start looking at furnishings for Cuckoo Lodge. Heaven knows there are enough shops here in the West End.'

He was gone three days, but to Cathy it felt like three months. The flat seemed silent and empty without him. She did as he said – shopped around for fabrics and furnishing ideas. Gerald had said they would engage the services of an interior designer when the time was right. But Cathy wanted to choose the colour schemes and some of the fabrics herself. She wanted to put her own stamp on the house.

When Gerald came home she was eager to show him the swatches of material and samples of wallpaper and carpet she had collected, but he seemed tired and preoccupied.

'I'll look at them tomorrow,' he told her wearily. 'Just now all I want is a hot bath and bed.'

He slept almost as soon as his head touched the pillow; before she had time to tell him how much she had missed him, even before she could whisper the secret suspicion she had been saving up with such excited anticipation.

'Pregnant?' Gerald stared at her across the breakfast table. 'For heaven's sake, Cathy. You *can't* be pregnant already!'

Swallowing her dismay, she smiled at him encouragingly. 'I can. And I think I am. Aren't you pleased?'

He shook his head bemusedly. 'But – we haven't been married a month yet. Surely it's far too soon to know?'

'Well – for sure, yes. But I'm a whole week late and I have this really magic sort of feeling deep inside.' She clasped her hands over her flat stomach. 'Oh, just think, Gerald. It'll be a Christmas baby. Won't that be lovely? It'll make up for all the misery last Christmas.'

'I think we'd better wait and see before we start making plans,' he said guardedly, his brow furrowed. 'I must confess, Cathy, I hadn't planned to start a family. Not

240

at this stage in the proceedings. It isn't the most convenient time to choose.'

'*Convenient?*' Crestfallen, she looked at his dour expression and felt her own happiness slowly beginning to deflate. 'But – if we're going to have children – why not have them now?' She reached across the table to touch his hand. 'You do want children, don't you?'

He drew his hand away. 'Now that you mention it, Cathy, frankly, it's not the most important item on my agenda. We should have talked about it, I suppose. I just assumed . . .' He paused, looking at her face. She looked so downcast. Kay's words came unbidden into his mind. *She'll be expecting all kinds of things you either can't or won't want to give her.* How could he have been so stupid as to take it for granted that she was taking care of contraception herself when the thought of it probably hadn't even entered her head?

As she rose and began to run out of the room he got up and went to her. 'Cathy – don't get upset.' He took her by the shoulders and turned her to him. When she wouldn't look at him he tipped up her chin and saw that there were tears in her eyes. 'Darling, I didn't mean to sound unfeeling. It was just a bit of a shock, that's all. Getting the house finished and the school established is going to mean so much work and planning. You can see what I mean when I say it isn't the right time, can't you?'

She swallowed hard. 'I suppose so. It's just . . .'

He drew her close. 'But if it's happened then there's nothing we can do but make the best of it.' He kissed her forehead. 'And I daresay it will turn out fine in the end.'

She looked up at him. 'I was so pleased. I wanted you to be too.'

'I am. At least, I will be – I expect.' He took out his handkerchief and dabbed at the tears on her cheeks. 'But as I said before, let's wait a few weeks before we start thinking about furnishing a nursery, shall we?'

Her eyes shone up at him through the tears. 'I know you

won't mind once you get used to the idea, Gerald. Once the baby is here you'll love it. And I know you're going to make a wonderful father.'

He held her close, cursing himself for all the fools imaginable. He visualised Kay's sardonic expression when she heard the news that he was to become a father; imagined her incisive comments.

But two days later when Cathy wakened to the familiar dull ache low in her back her heart sank with sick apprehension. For a long time she lay still, willing the inevitable not to have happened. But when she rose and went into the bathroom she knew beyond a doubt that for this month at least, pregnancy had been mere wishful thinking.

Back in the bedroom Gerald did his best to hide his relief as he comforted her. 'Never mind, darling. You know as well as I do that it wasn't the best of times. Once we get the school up and running we'll go all out for a baby if that's what you really want.'

'But – what if I can't have any?' she sobbed. 'What if I lose it again?'

He hugged her close. 'You didn't *lose* it, sweetheart. There wasn't any baby to lose. It was just a little delay, that's all; probably due to your changed lifestyle. As soon as the time is right we'll have as many babies as you want. A whole football team if you like. Just you wait and see.'

Cathy laughed shakily and clung to him. 'Oh, Gerald, I do love you,' she murmured into his shoulder.

He held her close, aghast at the rash promises he had just heard himself making. What on earth was he saying? A child was the one complication he could avoid. And avoid it he would at all costs.

They moved into Cuckoo Lodge the following week. The builders had worked hard during their absence. Two rooms had been completed, a room they would be using as a living room and a bedroom with an ensuite bathroom, both temporarily decorated with plain colourwashed walls and furnished basically with the furniture from the flat. In the ground-floor utility extension the builders had finished work and a firm of kitchen fitters had moved in to install units and cupboards, cooker and other appliances. Meantime, Cathy cooked meals for them on a temporary electric stove and helped Gerald with the advance publicity for the school.

A landscape gardener began work on the garden and the fashionable London interior designer, recommended to Gerald by Kay, a flamboyant little man with a beard and flowing white hair, arrived and spent a day walking round the house, making notes and suggestions for them to mull over.

Looking back later Cathy remembered those first weeks as the happiest of times. Domestically it was like playing house or camping. And acting as Gerald's secretary, planning for the school and discussing the final decor of the house and garden, was like taking part in an exciting and very grown-up adventure.

At last the builders and decorators completed their work and moved out. No more tripping over pots of paint or ladders. The house was finally theirs. Gerald's work routine and programme were arranged and advertisements appeared in the glossy magazines as well as the music journals. There were to be popular weekend seminars where young musicians could come and attend master classes with Gerald and other celebrated musicians. But during the week he planned to coach high-flying young pianists, preparing them for the concert platform. He decided that he would take no more than two resident students at a time and work with them intensively. The first of these, a grave young man called Robert Carr, sent to Gerald by a friend from the Guildhall School of Music, moved in and began work in early-July.

Cathy, in charge of domestic arrangements, engaged a daily cleaning woman and a cook-housekeeper from the village. Maggie Penrose was recommended by Ivor Morris, the Welsh chef at the Admiral Nelson. He told Cathy that he had replaced her when the hotel decided to open its new upmarket restaurant. He knew her to be a good cook and had felt guilty about her ever since, he said. He was anxious to do her a good turn.

Cathy liked Maggie on sight. Short and dumpy with a rosy complexion and fair hair scraped back into a bun, she had a no-nonsense air of reliability. Cathy learned that, like Johnny, she was a widow. She had two teenage children, a boy and a girl, who attended a secondary modern school in nearby Woodbridge. On the day that she came to be interviewed she looked round the gleaming new kitchen approvingly.

'Well now, this is some kitchen. I'd enjoy working in this and no mistake.' She ran her fingertips reverently over the smooth worktops. 'A real pleasure that'd be to keep clean.'

In her rich Suffolk accent she told Cathy frankly that she was a good plain cook, though she wasn't averse to what she called 'a bit of fiddling about' too.

'Nuthin' I like better'n tryin' out fancy new recipes when I got the time – an' the ingredients, o'course. Though I ent no good at the twiddly bits,' she warned. 'Anythin' you wants twiddly bits on you'd have to do it yourself.'

Cathy hid a smile. 'That will be fine, Mrs Penrose,' she said. 'I'm quite happy to do the twiddly bits.' She looked at the woman speculatively. 'There's just one thing. I hope you like music, because you'll be likely to hear a good deal of it if you come to work here? There's a large studio in the barn at the back and another two smaller ones in the house.'

Maggie nodded. 'Oh, the kind of music Mr Cavelle plays is all right,' she said generously. 'It's them twanging *catarrhs* I can't abide. My kids is mad about them new Beatles – 'orrible row if you asks me, with their yeah-yeah-ing! A nice bit of piano music'll make a change. I've always

244

been very partial to that there Semprini m'self. He's classical-like too.'

There were five bedrooms on the upper floors at Cuckoo Lodge, plus the suite of rooms that Cathy and Gerald would share. These consisted of a bedroom, an adjoining dressing room and a bathroom. Gerald insisted that the dressing room must have a divan which would always be made up ready for use.

'It might be necessary for me to work on quite late into the night sometimes,' he explained to Cathy. 'Robert seems to work best late in the day and as you know he isn't an early riser. So as not to wake you I can always sleep in there if I'm late.'

But as time went by she found herself waking to an empty bed more often than not.

Now that summer was at its height Melfordleigh was once more alive with summer visitors. The quay was full of moored boats, their hulls newly painted and their sails furled. The little colony of holiday huts were full of the regular weekend artists who set up their easels daily to produce the souvenir pictures the tourists loved. The air was fresh and salty; the sun sparkled on the rippling water and at low tide the sandbanks gleamed like polished silver.

Cathy often found herself at a loose end now that everything was finished and the school was running smoothly. She spent a lot of time down by the quay, watching the boats and admiring the artists' skill. She loved to watch them capture the sea and sky with a few deft strokes of a brush. Once a week she went into Ipswich to do the week's shopping, but apart from that she had very little to do. Gerald was busy all the time; totally preoccupied with his work. He put so much of himself into his teaching, and she knew of course how important it was to him. But often she was reminded of her lonely childhood, when her father would be busy teaching all week and out playing most nights. At least then she had her schoolfriends for company, and her

245

Saturday music lesson with Dad to look forward to. She found herself thinking of him often and experiencing the aching loss of him afresh. Although she said nothing, it became more and more apparent with each day that passed that Gerald had hardly any time to spare for her at all.

Word had somehow circulated that Gerald Cavelle, the celebrated concert pianist, was living at Cuckoo Lodge. One afternoon Cathy walked up the hill from the quay to find a little group of spectators peering through the gates. As she passed she overheard one of them say, 'We might see him if we're lucky.' As she walked on she reflected wryly that she knew how they felt.

As the end of the summer season approached and the routine at Cuckoo Lodge became established, Cathy found herself thinking more and more of Johnny. She missed the little house in Chestnut Grove and the close family group. When she mentioned the fact to Gerald he looked at her thoughtfully.

'You're not homesick, are you?'

She shook her head. 'No, of course not. I'd like to see them all though. And hear all their news.'

For a moment he looked at her. 'Poor Cathy. It can't be much fun for you. I'll tell you what – as soon as I can see my way clear we'll take a week off and have a holiday.'

Her eyes lit up. 'Oh, Gerald, that would be lovely. When?'

'Well – not yet awhile. When there's a break between students perhaps. We'll see. Meantime, why not invite the Johnsons for a weekend? Robert is going home for a break the weekend after next. It's his birthday, so we'll have a couple of free days. The weather's still warm. I daresay they'd enjoy it.'

Cathy's eyes lit up. 'Oh, Gerald, could I? I'd love Johnny to see what we've done to the house. I'm so proud of it all.'

'Of course. You don't have to ask, darling. It's your

home as well as mine. Ring Johnny today and see if they can make it.'

Johnny was delighted to get Cathy's call. She said that they were all well and, yes, she would love to come for the weekend. Matthew had recently passed his driving test and had bought a second hand car. He'd probably drive them over himself. She'd ring and confirm as soon as she'd checked with him.

She rang back the same evening. She and Matthew would love to come. Mrs Bains felt that the journey would be too much for her. Her rheumatism had been playing her up lately and she really preferred to sleep in her own bed. Cathy swallowed her relief. Mrs Bains had obviously still not forgiven her for depriving Johnny of the white wedding she had planned.

On the following Friday evening Cathy waited with eager anticipation for the first sight of the car and it was just after seven o'clock that Matthew's dark green Austin A40 turned in at the gate. Cathy ran to meet them. She kissed Johnny, hugging her warmly as she got out of the car.

'Oh, it's so *good* to see you,' she said. 'I can't wait to show you everything.'

'Don't I get a kiss too?' Matthew stood grinning beside her and she turned to throw her arms around him.

'Of course. It's lovely to see you too.' She took a hand of each of them and drew them towards the house. 'Come in both of you. Maggie, our cook, has left a meal warming in the oven. It's one of her special casseroles. Almost as good as yours, Johnny.'

Johnny was impressed by the house, especially as she had seen the original photographs and knew what it had been like when they first found it. After supper Cathy took her proudly from room to room, showing her everything and finishing up in their own suite of rooms on the first floor. Johnny took in the spacious bedroom with its built-in wardrobes and tasteful furnishings. She also noted the divan in the dressing room, with Gerald's pyjamas neatly folded on the pillow, and silently speculated over it. Seeing the direction of her glance, Cathy explained hurriedly: 'Gerald sometimes sleeps in here. He works very late with his student at times, you see. He doesn't like to disturb me.'

'Of course,' Johnny said.

Downstairs they sat in the small drawing room, enjoying the view of the garden in the last of the evening sunshine as they drank their coffee.

'You've obviously been busy,' Johnny said. 'It's been quite a year one way and another.'

'It certainly has. Since Gerald and I were married our feet have hardly touched the ground what with all the work on the house and the school to get . . .' Cathy broke off as she saw Matthew beginning to laugh. 'What's the matter?' she asked. 'What have I said?'

'I think Mum was talking about more national matters,' he told her. 'The Profumo scandal for instance. It's taken over the newspaper headlines for months now. And just last month, the sensational mail train robbery.' When Cathy looked blank he explained patiently, 'A gang hijacked a Royal Mail train and got away with over a million pounds. Surely you must have read about it?' His eyebrows shot up in amazement as she shook her head. 'Well – I know the Russians put a woman into space. It wasn't *you*, was it?'

'Don't tease her, Matthew,' Johnny admonished. 'I don't wonder she hasn't had time to read the papers.' She turned to Cathy and patted her hand. 'What you've achieved here is an absolute wonder, dear,' she said. 'You deserve congratulations – both of you.' She smiled at Gerald. 'Take no notice of my son,' she said. 'Teasing Cathy used to be his main hobby. He's forgetting that she's a grown-up married lady now.'

'Matthew is right,' he said. 'We really shouldn't let ourselves get so out of touch with the outside world. Maybe I should get Cathy a television. I'm sure she would enjoy it. I'm afraid she spends quite a lot of time alone in the evenings.'

When Cathy went upstairs with Johnny later to make sure she had everything she needed in her room, the older woman looked at her. The girl seemed well enough. Her skin glowed with the healthy outdoor life she seemed to be leading, and her eyes were clear and bright. When they had first arrived she had looked so radiant, but since the excitement of seeing them had worn off Johnny thought she detected a certain wistfulness about her; a vulnerability. There were tiny lines of strain about her eyes that no nineteen-year-old should have. She sat down on the bed and patted the space beside her.

'Come and talk to me. It seems ages since we had a good chinwag. So – you're happy?'

'Oh, yes.'

'Obviously it's all worked out well. I'm so glad, Cathy.'

'The school is going to be a big success,' she said. 'Gerald has a series of concerts planned for next summer. They'll be in the barn studio and open to the public. The local arts society . . .'

'I meant *you*, dear,' Johnny broke in gently. 'You personally – your marriage. It seems to me there's been very little time so far for you and Gerald to settle down and get to know each other.'

'Oh, but there has. We had a wonderful honeymoon and we work together, don't we? Not so much now that Gerald has started work in earnest, of course, but at the start we did.'

Johnny slipped an arm around her. 'So I was wrong to worry? Well, I couldn't be more glad about it.'

Cathy looked at Johnny hesitantly. 'There was one disappointment. Back in the spring I thought I was going to have a baby. But it turned out to be a false alarm.' She gave a nervous little laugh. 'Just as well, really. As Gerald said, it wasn't the right time.'

Johnny smiled wryly. 'It hardly ever is.'

'But we will have children,' Cathy went on. 'Gerald says we will. That's what I really want. It just hasn't happened yet.'

Johnny slipped an arm around her shoulder and gave her a hug. 'Well – plenty of time, eh?'

Cathy stood up. 'Yes. Plenty of time. Goodnight, Johnny. Sleep well.'

In their room Gerald was preparing for bed. He looked up as she came in. 'Everything all right?'

'Yes, fine. Isn't it good to see Johnny and Matthew again?'

'Yes.' He pulled off his tie and began to unbutton his shirt. 'Oh, by the way, I had a phone call earlier,' he said. 'We'll be having two more guests tomorrow.'

Cathy turned to him, a look of dismay on her face. 'Two more? But this was supposed to be Johnny's weekend. Who's coming?'

'Kay,' he said. 'She's bringing a young pianist she's recently come across. She seems to think he has a rare talent and wants me to hear him play. I thought that as this weekend was free it might be an ideal time.'

'But this weekend *isn't* free,' she said, feeling her colour rise. 'We have guests.'

'Only the Johnsons.'

'They're important to me,' she insisted. 'They're the only family I've got.'

He turned to look at her, his eyes cold. 'No. *I'm* the only family you've got, Cathy. And this is our business – our living. It's at a critical stage of its development. It has to come before everything at the moment. Surely you can understand that?'

'Of course I do.' She turned away. 'But I have worked hard since last spring. I think I'm entitled to one weekend at least away from school business. I haven't seen Johnny for five months. I wanted us to spend the time with her.'

'There's nothing stopping you from spending time with them,' he said sharply. 'They're your guests, not mine. And Kay isn't coming for a social visit. For God's sake, Cathy – she's trying to put some business our way.'

'*Your* way, you mean. And you're right. I'm sure it's not me she's eager to see.'

He looked at her scathingly. 'Oh, don't be so petty.'

'I'm not being petty, wanting you to be with us – with *me* for a change. I hardly ever see you, Gerald.'

'So why, when we have a free weekend, do you invite the Johnsons over?'

She stared at him. 'It was your suggestion!'

'Only because you went on about it so.' He picked up his clothes and began to walk towards the dressing room. Biting her lip, Cathy hurried after him. 'Oh, Gerald – *don't*.'

He turned. 'Don't what?'

'Don't sleep in there again tonight. Stay with me.'

He frowned. 'I'm rather tired. I thought you were too.'

'I miss you,' she said quietly. 'You hardly ever sleep in our bed with me any more.' He stood impassively as she put her arms around him and laid her head against his chest. 'What's wrong? Have I done something to upset you? Is it because I invited Johnny?'

'Of course not. Nothing's wrong. It's just – all the work and the tension of getting the school up and running. I've put everything I have into it. We both have.'

'You haven't stopped loving me, have you? You don't regret marrying me? If I've done something wrong . . .'

'You haven't done anything wrong.' He put his arms reluctantly round her. 'You're just being a silly girl. Imagining things.'

'Then come to bed.' She looked up at him, her green eyes wide and appealing.

He sighed. 'All right.'

* * *

251

Cathy heard the clock on the little church tower overlooking the sea strike two, and turned over for the hundredth time. All she could see of Gerald was the hump that was his back under the covers.

She had tried her best, whispering how much she loved and needed him between kisses, reminding him of his promise that they could try for a baby as soon as the school was running smoothly. But to her bewilderment he hadn't seemed interested in making love. Her body pressed close to his, even her most intimate caresses had failed to arouse him. After a few chaste kisses he had patted her as though she were a recalcitrant child and turned over, urging her to go to sleep. There must be some reason for it, she told herself. In spite of what he said. Did she irritate him? Did he find her distracting? Heaven only knew she was used to living with a musician. She tried to keep out of his way when he was working. Had she stopped being attractive to him for some reason? And, most worrying of all, what could she do about it?

She slept at last as the sky began to lighten, wakening at seven to find herself once again alone in the bed. Gerald was not in the bathroom. He had obviously risen early and gone out. Resignedly, she showered and dressed, then went downstairs to make breakfast for her guests.

Johnny and Matthew were enchanted with Melfordleigh. Cathy had booked her favourite table at the Admiral Nelson. It was to have been a surprise for Gerald too, but now he would have to stay in and wait for his own guests. She had left cold ham and a salad for the three of them in the fridge.

They all enjoyed their day enormously, arriving back at Cuckoo Lodge at six o'clock. After lunch they had gone on a boat trip with one of the old sailors who took visitors around the point by motor cruiser to see the seals basking on their remote sandbank and glimpse the many seabirds that congregated out at the very tip of the point. They had come back windblown and happily tired and as soon as they got in Johnny and Matthew went straight upstairs to change.

Cathy went into the kitchen to make sure that Maggie was happy about having six for dinner instead of four. Coming back she paused at the foot of the stairs. From the small studio came the sound of the piano – a Chopin polonaise. It was being played with a spirit and vitality that seized her attention at once, making her curious to see who the pianist was. She crossed the hall and stood at the half-open door. The studio door was ajar and from where she stood facing the open grand piano, Cathy had a view of the young man who was playing. He was fair-haired with a firm, strong jaw and cheekbones, but his eyes were on the keyboard, his head lowered in concentration, a look of rapture on his face. He was good. Brilliant even. There was little doubt that Gerald would accept him as a student. The piece came to an end and the young man slowly raised his head and looked directly at her. The suddenness of his unblinking dark blue stare startled her and she took a step backwards.

'Thank you, Simon.' Gerald rose and came into view as he moved towards the piano. He caught sight of her. 'Cathy! Come in and say hello to Kay. And meet Simon Posner, who will be joining us here.' He turned to the young man. 'Simon, this is Cathy, my wife.'

Simon rose and came towards her, his hand outstretched. He was well-built, with broad shoulders and long legs. She registered vaguely that he wore jeans and a black sweater over an open-necked shirt, and that there was a fine mist of perspiration on his brow. He was quite young – no more than twenty-two or -three – and he moved with an easy, loose-limbed grace. His handsome, strong-boned face was grave and unsmiling, but the compelling blue eyes held hers almost hypnotically. When he spoke she was surprised to hear that he had a slight foreign accent, though she could not place its origin.

'How do you do, Mrs Cavelle? It is very good of you to have us at short notice like this.'

Acutely aware of her windblown hair and grubby appearance, she put her hand into his and felt the power of the strong fingers as they gripped hers. 'You're welcome,' she said. 'I hope my husband has shown you both to your rooms. Dinner will be ready in about half an hour.' She glanced at Kay, aware that the older woman was watching her closely. She wore her own city idea of country clothes, a Jaeger suit and a long rope of pearls. Cathy forced herself to smile. 'Hello, Kay. How nice to see you again.'

'Hello, Cathy.' She took in the glowing skin and sun-streaked wind-blown hair. 'How *well* you look,' she said, biting back her resentment. 'Marriage and sea air obviously agree with you.' She stood up and came across to link her arm through Simon's. 'This young man is going to be a brilliant international concert star before he's very much older,' she announced. 'And I shall be proud to say that I discovered him. Gerald has agreed to give him the benefit of all his wonderful know-how.' She hugged Simon's arm possessively and gave Cathy a rueful look. 'I've a feeling you're not going to be seeing much of your dear husband over the next few months. In fact, I don't think your life will ever be quite the same again.'

And even Kay did not realise how prophetic or significant her words were to prove.

254

Chapter Fourteen

Dinner was a sociable affair. Kay went out of her way to be particularly charming to Johnny and Matthew and complimented Cathy effusively on the house and on finding such a good cook. She also encouraged Simon to tell them all a little about his background. He told them that his father, anticipating Hitler's invasion of Poland, had fled to England along with his wife and mother-in-law in 1938, shortly before Simon was born, and had immediately joined the RAF. His grandmother was Danuta Polinski, who was a well-known concert pianist in Poland during the twenties and thirties. Simon was still a baby when his father was killed and his mother took up work as a secretary and interpreter at the War Office, leaving him in the care of his grandmother for the rest of the war.

Danuta missed her musical career and the gay social whirl she had enjoyed in Warsaw before the war. Her poor grasp of the English language and her unwillingness to adapt to the British way of life made her rather isolated, but as soon as Simon was big enough to sit at the piano she found a new vocation in teaching him to play.

Simon was without inhibitions when it came to recounting his musical accomplishments and the story of his meteoric progress had everyone enthralled. By the time he was twelve he was giving concerts and when he was sixteen had already begun to teach schoolchildren, saving the money he earned to buy himself a new piano and to help pay his way at college.

In anyone else the lack of modesty would have been obnoxious, but the warmth of Simon's personality more than made up for any hint of boastfulness. He charmed them all with his vivacity, his keen, blue eyes and ready smile. Even Maggie lingered as she drifted in and out to wait on the dinner table, unable to take her eyes off the charismatic young man with the fascinating accent.

After everyone else had said goodnight and gone to bed Gerald invited Kay into the smaller of the two studios, which he also used as an office. Switching on the desk lamp, he took a decanter of brandy and two glasses from a cabinet.

'Well, what do you think of him?' she asked, relaxing into one of the deep leather chairs.

Gerald filled one glass and handed it to her. He took his time over pouring his own drink, considering carefully for a moment before answering. 'Well, he's certainly talented, I'll give you that. Maybe a little on the flamboyant side for my taste, and he does seem to have picked up one or two bad technical habits, but I daresay there's nothing that can't be ironed out.'

'I like his flamboyance. It's part of his personality.'

'You would!' Gerald smiled as he sat down opposite her. 'He's full of himself, isn't he? And what about that rather pseudo accent? Is it cultivated? After all, he was born in this country.'

'He says his grandmother never spoke good English and always insisted that they conversed in Polish at home. As she brought him up, and taught him music, he obviously spoke it most of the time.' She raised an eyebrow at him. 'Anyway, you can't deny that it's terribly attractive and sexy. And it does go with the image of a concert pianist.'

'For those who still see Anton Walbrook in *Dangerous Moonlight* as the archetype!' he said with a smile. 'But then I suppose this is the professional PR view I'm hearing,' he added cynically.

Kay shrugged. 'Perhaps. I'm concerned with what sells – what the public goes for. I'm not ashamed to admit it.'

She got up and went to help herself to another brandy. 'So – will you accept him?'

'Oh yes. I'd be a fool not to, wouldn't I?'

'You can manage two students at once then?'

'Yes. While I'm working with one in the other studio, the second can be in here practising. Both rooms are fairly soundproof. These old walls are thick.' He gave her a wry grin. 'Oh, yes, he's definitely worth teaching. I just hope he hasn't become too arrogant. Doting mum and grandmama, adoring philistine audiences who love that accent and the toothpaste smile.'

'That's not fair, Gerry. And I'm sure he isn't arrogant.'

'How did you find him, by the way?'

'His mother, Anya, is a freelance researcher now. Summit Films hired her to do some Polish background research on a film. She worked with us for about two months. We got along rather well and she was telling me about her son. She's terribly ambitious for him. She took me along to a concert to hear him play. I was impressed and immediately thought of you.'

'That was very thoughtful of you.'

She held up her glass, examining the remaining drops of fiery liquid. 'As a matter of fact I'm thinking of leaving Summit and starting up my own PR agency.'

He smiled. 'And you saw Simon as a potential client! *Ah*, now we're getting to it. I was getting quite worried about you, Kay. Altruism is so uncharacteristic. I was afraid you might be going sentimental in your old age.'

'That's *not* very nice. If you're not careful I'll take him away again.' She laughed. 'Seriously, I can't see anything wrong with a little co-operation, can you?'

'Not at all. It's good business. I'm glad you thought of me.'

'I happen to think he's heading for big things. He could make a fortune for you, you know, once the word gets around that you are his mentor.' He shrugged non-committally and she looked at him searchingly. 'How are you these days, Gerry?'

He gave her a quick glance. 'In what way?'

'You know damn well what way. Healthwise, of course.'

'I'm fine. Never better.'

She opened her mouth to say something, then closed it again. He looked terrible. She had been quite shocked by his appearance when they first arrived. His weight had dropped again and he looked gaunt and grey. In the old days she would have told him so bluntly, nagged him into doing something about it.

'I do hope dear little Tinkerbell isn't wearing you out, darling.' Her attempt at a joke fell flat and she added: 'How does marriage suit you, by the way? *She's* looking remarkably bright-eyed and bushy-tailed. And I must say she's done a fantastic job on the house. It's charming.' She waved a hand around the room. 'All these exposed beams and inglenooks. Very chic!'

He shrugged. 'You said all that at dinner.'

'Did you use Gideon Maidly, the interior designer I recommended, by the way?'

'Yes, partly. He was very good. Expensive though.'

She leaned forward. 'Gerry – what *is* wrong with you, darling? You're obviously ill. Are you seeing anyone about it? Are you having treatment?'

'Which one of these would you like answering?' he asked dryly.

'Any. *All* if possible.'

'Not much point in going into detail or giving you names of conditions you won't know the first thing about. Suffice to say that it's a rare muscular thing.'

'Curable?'

'No, but controllable.'

'So you're on treatment – medication?'

'Got it!'

She shook her head in exasperation. 'Oh, for God's sake, Gerry, do I have to *drag* it out of you?'

He banged his glass down and glared angrily at her. 'I don't know how you've got the bloody nerve to ask me personal questions after what you did last time!'

Suitably chastened she sank back in her chair. 'I wouldn't do that again, Gerry. You have my word on it. It was – I don't know – a mad sort of impulse. I suppose I was shocked and jealous, seeing Cathy and hearing that you and she were engaged. After all, you and I were close. But I know that's no excuse. It was unforgivable and I'm not proud of it.' She leaned forward to touch his hand. 'I'm only asking out of concern for you, darling, I promise. Whatever you tell me will go no further than this room.'

He leaned back in his chair, closing his eyes. 'All right, it's Parkinson's. I see a specialist in Edinburgh at regular intervals. It's a hell of a drag, having to go all that way but he's supposed to be the top man in this particular field. He's done a special research project at the university. I suppose I'm part of it – tests and so on. I have tablets and there are certain things I am advised to avoid.' He opened his eyes and looked at her. 'There are also – certain limitations – functions I find difficult, even sometimes impossible. I'm sure I don't have to spell it out for you.'

'My God, Gerry, I'm sorry.' For a moment they looked at each other, then she asked: 'Is – is there likely to be any improvement?'

He shook his head. 'Probably not.'

'Oh, Gerry. Does Cathy know the full facts – about your illness, I mean?' Again he shook his head and she stared back at him. 'But, shouldn't you tell her? I mean, she must be . . .'

'I don't think I want to discuss this any further.' He stood up abruptly and went to refill his glass. 'Can we talk about something else?'

She rose quickly. 'I'll have another one of those if you

don't mind. I feel I need it. As for discussing it, Gerry, what you're doing is madness. You're simply burying your head in the sand. She has a right to know.' She turned to him. 'If you knew about this, why on earth did you marry her? A girl of that age! It was so cruel!'

'It's none of your bloody business.'

Ignoring his indignant protest, she went on, 'Okay, tell me to mind my own business when it comes to Cathy and your marriage, but what about your work? I mean, if I'm going to be recommending more students, I have a right to know how long you're likely to be able to do this job.'

He threw back his drink in one gulp and rounded on her. 'Do you think I'd have sunk everything I've got into this place if I thought I wasn't up to working for its upkeep?'

'I don't *know*. It seems to me that you've done some pretty inexplicable things over the past year. Marrying a kid young enough to be your daughter when you knew damned well you couldn't be a proper husband to her for a start. For all I know you might have done *anything*! If you won't level with me how would I know?'

For a moment he stared at her, then he sank into his chair again. 'It's not as desperate as all that. I have good days and bad, but if I pace myself carefully I can teach on a full-time basis. My brain's all right, thank God. At least that part of it. It's what they call the motor functions that are affected.'

'And what's the prognosis?'

'What's the prognosis for any of us? What's the expression? *Life's a bitch and then you die!*'

'Oh, Gerry.' She reached out to take his hand again. 'I'm so sorry, darling.'

'Oh, for Christ's sake!' He snatched his hand away. 'There's no need to turn on the soft soap, Kay! It doesn't suit you. I think I prefer you spitting acid.'

'So work is all right. Okay, I'm glad. But you know you have to confide in Cathy, don't you?'

He turned his head away. 'She knows.'

'All of it?'

'There's no need to baffle her with a lot of frightening medical stuff.'

'It might not frighten her. Most women are amazingly strong.' She looked at him. 'Does it frighten *you*?' When he didn't reply she asked: 'Look, Gerry, have you thought? It might be hereditary. Suppose you have a child?'

'We won't.'

She stared at him. 'You mean . . .?'

'I mean – *we won't.*'

'Without telling her why? Without discussing it? Poor Cathy.'

'She's happy enough. Ask her. *Look* at her!' He avoided her accusing eyes. 'I make it up to her as much as I can. She's enjoying her life here. There's no need for you to worry about her or feel sorry for her, Kay. I'll make sure there are more than enough compensations to keep her happy.'

She shook her head. 'I hope you're right, Gerry. I hope to God you're right.'

Chapter Fifteen

Rosalind worked hard through the spring of 1963. So hard that she scarcely noticed how absorbed her mother was. As the time for exams approached she allowed herself only one evening off a week. On this she usually went out with Stuart. Ever since the New Year's Eve party she had known that she was head over heels in love, and the fact that Stuart seemed to feel the same made life complete. Having someone to love gave life a whole new dimension for her. Now she had a purpose in life. Her whole future was channelled afresh. And since her mother had been so preoccupied she had stopped being obstructive about their relationship. In fact she positively encouraged it nowadays.

Their outings were usually to the cinema or, as the weather improved, for a short drive or a walk by the river. They were both short of money and couldn't afford expensive entertainments. Occasionally when Julian was out and Stuart knew that the flat would be empty all evening, he would take her back to Earls Court. It was in Stuart's cramped little bedroom at the flat that they had first made love. For Rosalind it had been so special that every time she thought about the wonderful closeness and intimacy of the precious moments they had spent in each other's arms, her heart swelled with love and pride. At last she felt whole – a real person, who meant something special to someone.

She already knew how precarious Stuart's work was. Until he became an established designer he would be living on a knife edge, waiting for the big break. At the moment he was obliged to accept any temporary job he could find, whether it was in the artistic field or not, curtailing the time he would like to spend on his own work. She told herself that if she found a good job as a hotel manageress she would be able to support him; see him through until his outstanding talent was recognised. She would be so proud to be able to do that for him. Now it was even more important for her to do well. Each evening as soon as she had eaten she would shut herself in her room and revise till the small hours.

For her part, Una was grateful for her daughter's preoccupation with Stuart. Through him she too had a new purpose in her life. Loneliness was a thing of the past. Once more the future beckoned with a glittering promise. All she had to do was play her cards right. Her plans were taking shape and, although there were various hurdles to overcome she was confident that everything would eventually work out to her satisfaction.

Don had been sceptical at first about putting money into something as unpredictable as a play, especially by three unknown young men. But after long hours of discussion and persuasion on Una's part she had finally convinced him that with her behind it, Julian's play could not fail. She had dazzled him with visions of glamorous West End first nights at which they would be honoured guests; dangled the tempting prospect of selling the film rights for huge amounts of money; promised a future gilded with recording contracts and endless royalties. She told him he would be mad to pass up such a chance, and at last he had promised to put the money at her disposal. Now all she had to do was to set the whole thing up and reap the special reward she had in mind.

The moment she had begun to read the script she had felt in her bones that they were on to a good thing. *Sweet Violet* was a modern version of the *Twelfth Night* story, set on a mythical island in the Atlantic, the inhabitants of which were living in a time warp. The story concerned a group of Americans whose private plane made a forced landing on the island and subsequently turned the lives of the islanders upside down.

Intrigued by its originality, Una paid the boys a surprise visit at the flat to tell them how excited she was. Stuart showed her his slightly surreal designs for the costumes and sets, and Brian French, the young musician who had written the score, played some of the music to her. In spite of the condition of the rickety out-of-tune upright piano at the flat, the romantic songs and haunting, evocative themes reinforced Una's conviction that the show was a surefire winner and she promised the boys, somewhat rashly, that she would personally see to it that *Sweet Violet* would get the chance it deserved.

The weeks that followed were spent making fruitless enquiries and regretting her impulsiveness. In truth she had none of the influence she professed to have and the thought of losing face after all she'd said terrified her. They looked up to her so. If she had to climb down and admit defeat now she'd die of shame. But where could she find a theatre to rent? she asked herself. Or a cast with the talent and professional ability to do the play justice?

She'd thought at the beginning that it shouldn't be too difficult when you had the money, but she soon discovered that there were all kinds of snags. To begin with, until she began making enquiries she'd had no idea of the cost of renting a theatre, especially one close enough to London to attract the busy, influential people who mattered. Most of the popular seaside resorts within easy distance were already booked right through the summer season. And even supposing she were lucky enough to find a cheap theatre that wasn't actually falling down, how would she persuade the appropriate people to come and see the show? Who had ever heard of Una Blair? Why should any West End producer put himself out for her and a new play by a bunch of nobodies? It wasn't long before she was forced to face the reality that she couldn't do it alone. So, pocketing her pride, she went along to see Harry Montague, her old agent.

Remembering the old days of walking Charing Cross Road in down-at-heel shoes, she had her hair done and put on her most expensive outfit . . . Then, summoning up all her courage, she sailed up the stairs and into the office like a prima donna, determined to succeed in getting Monty to listen to her or die in the attempt. Luckily the girl in the outer office was new and didn't recognise her, but it still took all of Una's audacity to convince her that she was here to make Harry Montague an offer he couldn't afford to miss. At last the girl, somewhat intimidated by Una's autocratic persistence, buzzed her boss on the intercom to tell him he had an important visitor waiting with a valuable proposition for him.

As she entered the office Harry Montague looked up from his desk with unconcealed dismay. '*Una!* I didn't know it was you. Thought the girl said Blake, not Blair.'

'She did. I've remarried.'

He indicated the chair opposite. 'Well, now you're here what's this all about? I understand you're here to do me some kind of favour.'

Una made herself comfortable in the chair, making a great show of removing the fur stole that Don had bought her for Christmas. 'I certainly am, Monty. As soon as this came up I immediately thought of you.' She accepted a cigarette from the box he offered. 'In spite of the cruel remarks you made to me the last time I was here,' she added, looking at him over the flame of his lighter. Wouldn't hurt to remind him that he owed her one, she told herself.

He smiled blandly. 'Oh, not *cruel*, surely? Frank, I grant you. It's an agent's job to be frank, but never cruel.'

Una shrugged nonchalantly. 'Oh, well, whatever it was, it's water under the bridge now and I'm not one to bear grudges.' She opened her large snakeskin handbag and took out a copy of the script of *Sweet Violet*. 'Some young friends of mine have written this musical play, Monty. I happen to think it's well worth your while taking a look at it. This is only the libretto, of course, but I could let you have a score if you're interested – even arrange for you to hear some of the numbers. And I'm sure you'd be impressed by the set and costume designs.'

Monty picked up the script with a sigh and flicked through it. It was just as he thought. Most of the people who came in to do *him* a favour turned out to be looking for one themselves. He looked up at her inquiringly. 'So what do you want me to do about it when I've read it?' he asked.

'Well – I thought you might know of a theatre they could take on a short lease. Not too far away.'

'You mean they want to do a shop window? Got a cast, have they? If they're amateurs I don't hold out much hope of getting anyone to . . .'

'Exactly!' Una broke in. 'This might mean a lucky break for some of your new up-and-coming hopefuls. When you've read the play you'll see that it's not a project for amateurs. And . . .' She licked her lips. 'You're in a position to ask a few of the people who *matter* to come along and see the show.'

'Mmm. Don't want much, do you?' Harry leaned back in his chair looking thoughtfully at the three names on the script's cover sheet. 'I take it these fellers have got backing? I know I don't have to tell you that hiring a theatre, even a rundown old fleapit, isn't cheap.'

'They have the backing.'

He raised a sceptical eyebrow. 'Cash in hand or just a promise?'

'Cash in hand. No need to worry. It's all legit.'

'Yes, well, I've heard that before. Do you know who's sponsoring them, Una? I mean does their angel have the necessary wings?' He spread his hands expressively. 'Sorry to ask, but if I'm going to help – and I'm not saying I will, mind – I'll have to know what I'm dealing with. I'd need to be sure there isn't a hole in the bucket.'

'The money's not a problem.' She took a deep breath and added with satisfaction, 'If you really want to know, Monty, *I'm* backing them.'

His eyes widened. '*You* are?'

'Yes.' She crossed one leg over the other, displaying the expensive snakeskin shoes that matched her bag. 'I told you I remarried last year. My husband is a very generous man. He has an executive position with a leading West End department store. Hallard's actually,' she told him with smug satisfaction. 'And he's willing to indulge me in this.'

'Oh, *very* nice.' He leaned back in his chair and clasped his hands over his ample stomach. 'So – what's in this for you, Una?' he asked shrewdly.

Una affected shocked surprise. 'For *me*?'

'Forgive my cynicism, but in my experience no one but a fool puts money into a project without some kind of incentive. It can't be profit. You know the business too well to bank on that. So . . .?'

Una sighed. 'These three young men are very talented. Personally, I think there may well *be* a profit, and a handsome one at that. But you're right. I know better than to bank on it.' She gave him a sideways glance. 'I just like being able to help young talent, that's all.'

He looked unconvinced. 'Bored with spending hubby's money?'

Una bridled. 'Look, are you interested or not, Monty? I can always approach another agent if you . . .'

'Calm down.' He waved the script at her. 'Look, I'll read the bloody thing and think about it. Can't say fairer than that, can I? *If* it's got any potential, *if* there are any parts that might interest anyone on my books, and *if* I hear of a half decent theatre that's dark at the moment, I'll maybe think a bit

267

more. Better than that I can't promise at the moment. All right?'

Una tried not to show her relief. At least she was relieved of some of the burden and could actually tell the boys that she had an agent working on it. That would sound impressive. 'Fair enough. Thanks, Monty.' She got to her feet. 'Perhaps you'll give me a ring when you've come to a decision.' She took a card from her bag and put it on his desk. 'The number's on there. I'm home most of the time.'

He glanced at the card, noting the good address with interest. 'Okay, I'll let you know one way or the other.'

'*When*, Monty?'

He sighed impatiently. 'When I've *read* it. I'll give you a bell and tell you what I think.' He held up a warning hand. 'But if I decide it's no deal, Una, you'll have to accept my decision.'

'Of course.' At the door she turned and asked the question that had been clamouring to be asked ever since she walked through the door. 'Oh, by the way, do you still represent Ben and Freda?'

He glanced up at her. 'We're still in touch, but they have an Australian agent now. You did know they were in Australia?'

'Yes, I just wondered . . .'

'They're doing very well. Booked solid for months ahead from what I hear,' he told her. 'Plenty of TV work too. Their kind of act is very popular over there at the moment.' He paused to light a cigar, looking up at Una through the cloud of blue smoke. 'And of course Freda's a real doll. Gorgeous girl. Great voice too,' he added caustically.

Una threw her fur stole carelessly around her shoulders. 'Yes, I suppose she has, if you like that kind of thing. That syrupy stuff is old hat over here now, of course. Well, I'll have to go now. Talk to you soon, Monty.'

He waved his cigar at her. 'Sure.'

When she'd gone he picked up the script and opened it

with curiosity but little enthusiasm. Most of these amateur efforts were a load of old crap. No reason to suppose that this one was any different, but you never knew. No agent worth his salt could afford to miss what might turn out to be a bright new talent. And it took no more than a couple of pages to tell if it had anything or not. No need to waste too much time.

An hour later when his secretary, tired of buzzing him on the intercom, came in to see if he'd fallen asleep, he was still reading.

Rosalind's night off was Friday. At the end of the school week and before her weekend job at the Queen's Head she kept one evening for seeing Stuart. She looked forward to it all week, promising herself that as soon as exams were over she would see him much more often. Not long now before all the revising and hard work were over. She was counting the days to exam time now.

When she heard his ring at the bell downstairs she gave her hair a final flick with the comb and hurried down the stairs. But, as so often happened, Una was there before her. Rosalind was halfway down the stairs when her mother hurried out of the living room and opened the front door with a flourish.

'Stuart darling! Come in. I've got the most marvellous news! I can't *wait* to tell you.' With only a cursory glance at Rosalind she chivvied him into the small breakfast room next to the kitchen. Don was watching TV in the lounge and anyway, this was between Stuart and her and Una wanted to savour the moment she'd looked forward to all day, ever since she got the telephone call. When she saw that Rosalind intended to join them she felt a stab of irritation, but couldn't very well exclude her.

'Come in if you're coming then. And close the door,' she said tetchily. 'We can't hear ourselves think for Don's wretched sports programme.'

Rosalind closed the door and sat on the chair nearest it. Stuart gave her a half-apologetic smile.

'Now,' Una began with relish, 'you'll never guess what. Harry Montague – the agent I told you about – has read the script. He likes the story and thinks it definitely has a lot going for it. He's asked me if he can hear the music next. What do you think of *that*? Isn't it exciting?'

Stuart's face lit up. 'Oh, Una, that's wonderful! We'll have to fix up a date. *Oh!*'

Seeing his face fall, Una asked anxiously, 'What? What's the matter?'

'It's our piano. You know what it's like, Una. We can't really do justice to Brian's music on that awful old thing.'

'I've already thought of that. We'll do it here,' she said triumphantly. 'There's a perfectly good piano going to waste in the lounge. I only had it tuned at Christmas.'

'Oh, that would be marvellous! I can't tell you how grateful we are to you, Una. We could never have got this far without you.'

'Not a bit of it. Talent will out,' she said. 'I just hope it all goes well and that Monty comes up trumps.'

'It won't be your fault if he doesn't. You've done wonders. We're very lucky.'

'So you agree then? I'm to tell Monty to come here?' Una was delighted. It would give her a chance to show Monty that she didn't need the likes of him to help *her* out any more. In fact she'd rub it well in that he was in her debt if *Sweet Violet* got off the ground successfully.

'Yes, please,' Stuart said. 'I'll get the other two over here just as soon as you like. Any time Mr Montague finds convenient.'

Una nodded. 'I'll get on to him first thing Monday morning and I'll let you know what he says.' She looked at Rosalind who was peering surreptitiously at her watch. 'Well, I can see that Rosalind is anxious to be off. Going to the pictures, are you?'

She stood up. 'Yes. It's *Doctor No*. Everyone says it's very good.'

'Then I mustn't keep you,' Una said magnanimously.

But the evening was already spoilt. As far as Stuart was concerned, the exciting news he had just heard already outshone James Bond's outrageous exploits. All the way to the cinema and all through the film he kept talking about the play and how wonderful Una was – how much, how *very* much, they all owed her. So much so that people seated near them began to fidget and *shush* at them angrily.

Later, over coffee in a nearby coffee bar, Stuart was still making excited plans and voicing his uncertainties.

'I wonder if he'll like my costume designs,' he said, chewing his lip. 'They're a bit way out, but then that's the point, you see. The people of St Crispin's have lived such an isolated life that they've devised their own fashions, made dyes and fabrics from plants, woven wool from their own sheep. Each character's costume is individual, you see, reflecting his own personality. And the contrasts with the modern Americans' mass produced clothes is the whole . . .'

'*Stuart!*' Rosalind looked at him. 'Do you realise that you've talked of nothing but the play ever since we left the house this evening?'

'Sorry.' He smiled ruefully at her. 'I suppose I have.'

'I bet you couldn't tell me one single thing about the film we've just seen.'

'I don't suppose I could. But it is frightfully important to us all.' He leaned across to touch her hand. 'And to you too, don't you see?'

'Me?'

'Yes. You've talked of supporting me until I can get established, and believe me, darling, I appreciate it. But if this takes off, I wouldn't need support.'

She stared at him. What exactly did he mean? She'd been looking forward to helping him – showing how much faith

271

she had in him – proving her love. Didn't he know that? Or could he possibly mean something more significant – more exciting? That if the play were a success *he* could support *her*? That they could be married? She felt her cheeks colouring. 'Well, that would be lovely of course. But I don't think I'd want to give up the career I've been working so hard for,' she said slowly. 'At least, not until we had children.'

It was Stuart's turn to colour. '*No!* No, of course not. I just . . .' He looked desperately around. 'Look, what about another coffee? It's not too late yet.'

As he parked Julian's car outside the gate of Blake's Folly she turned to him. 'Thank you for a lovely evening, Stuart.'

'No. Thank you – for listening to me wittering on about the play.' He slid an arm along the back of the seat. 'I'm afraid it's in my mind the whole time these days. Can't seem to think of anything else.'

'I've noticed,' she told him wryly. Then, relenting: 'I don't really mind, Stuart. I just know it's going to be a success.' His preoccupied silence since she'd blurted out that awful thing about having children had made her curl up inside. If only she could turn the clock back – *unsay* it.

He drew her towards him and kissed her. 'The day I met you and Una was the luckiest day of my life.'

'Was it really?' Rosalind looked at him thoughtfully. If only he didn't always have to include her mother. 'I knew then that you had a brilliant talent, you know. Long before I fe– before we started seeing each other.'

He kissed her again, then looked pointedly at his watch. 'Good heavens! Look at the time. Your mother will murder me. She'll be wondering where you are.'

Hurt, Rosalind stared at him. 'We don't want to risk upsetting Mum, do we? Not until *after* she's introduced you to Harry Montague anyway!' She opened the door and jumped out of the car. Stuart followed, hurrying after her up the path to the front door.

272

'Rossie! Wait!' He caught up with her just as she was putting her key in the lock. He grasped her shoulders firmly and turned her to face him. 'What was all that about?'

She looked up at him, eyes bright with hurt tears. 'Sometimes I feel you only take me out to keep in Mum's good books,' she said. 'Well you needn't, you know. She doesn't give a damn for *my* feelings, so you're wasting your time. If you don't want to see me any more, just say so now. You needn't worry. It won't spoil your chances of getting your play put on.'

He shook her gently, then pulled her close. 'Shut up, blockhead! You know none of that is true. I go out with you because I want to.'

'Sometimes I wonder,' she mumbled into the front of his jacket.

'Well, stop wondering at once and kiss me goodnight properly.' He raised her face to his and kissed her, gently at first, then in the passionate intimate way that took her breath away and left her with trembling knees. 'Off you go now and get a good night's sleep,' he told her breezily. 'You work much too hard, you know. I worry about you, you silly little goose.'

She watched with an aching heart as he got back into the car and drove off with a wave. She loved him so much. Too much for her own peace of mind. Did he really love her too? He was so good-looking, so talented. He could surely have any girl he wanted, so why should he want her? And whatever either of them might say, he couldn't risk driving any kind of wedge between himself and the Blake household just now, could he?

It was a week later that the three young men arrived at Blake's Folly for the meeting Una had arranged with Harry Montague. They arrived in Julian's Mini, dressed in their best, neatly groomed and shaven, except for Brian who had a beard. Clutching their copies of the script – in Brian's case the fully orchestrated score, plus his own piano parts – they rang the bell and then stood looking nervously at each other as they waited on the doorstep to be admitted.

Monty was already there. Una had invited him to dinner so that he could meet Don. She felt it was good policy to keep her husband advised and involved, seeing that it was his money that would make the whole project possible. The two men had been polite to each other, though it was clear that neither was completely comfortable in the other's company, and it was a relief to everyone when the meal was over.

Una opened the door and greeted the three warmly, ushering them into the lounge where Monty, Don and Rosalind were already waiting. She offered them coffee first, to break the ice, encouraging small talk. Then, when she felt the atmosphere to be sufficiently relaxed, she invited Brian to present the music of *Sweet Violet* to Monty.

Settling himself at the piano, the stocky, bearded young man played the main themes from the show, then launched into one of the songs, singing the words himself in a growling bass. Listening to his monotonous drone, Una knew that her moment had arrived. Her heart quickening, she rose from her chair and went over to the piano.

'Er – forgive me, Brian, but would it help if I were to sing it for you?' she asked with a beguiling modesty. 'I mean, your voice is . . .'

'I think "lousy" is the word you're looking for.' Brian laughed. 'Please, Mrs Blake, be my guest. I'm only too delighted. Can you follow the music or shall I play it over for you first?'

'No, I can follow,' Una said, positioning herself behind him where she could see the music. She omitted to mention that she couldn't actually *read* music, or that she'd learned the songs by heart from the tape that Stuart had given her, rehearsing the songs privately at every opportunity since with the help of the tape machine in Don's study.

She sang the song through, putting over all of the emotion and pathos the character demanded, just as she

274

had rehearsed it. Monty looked on with shrewd appraisal. He'd always known that her voice hadn't the power or the timbre of the best singers on his books, but for an impromptu rendering it wasn't at all bad, he conceded grudgingly. When the song came to an end everyone clapped and Una blushed, affecting surprise and confusion at their appreciation.

'I just thought Monty might get a better idea of the song's effectiveness with a female voice,' she said modestly.

Sitting quietly in her corner, Rosalind said nothing. Suddenly she knew what all this was about. During the singing of the song everything had dropped into place for her. All Una's altruism, the weeks of selfless striving and scheming, her apparent approval of the relationship between herself and Stuart. Now it all made sense. She looked at the faces of the men around her, all of them totally unsuspecting. Don, gazing with pride and wonder at his talented wife; the three young men, dazzled by yet another new facet of Una's appeal. Even the cynical Monty looked on benignly. It was clear that none of them saw beneath the surface to the real reason for her mother's devoted generosity.

Brian continued with the other songs and Una sang them all, Brian doing his best to join her in the duets. When at last the music came to an end and the buzz of enthusiasm died down, Rosalind was aware of her mother's eyes on her. Sidling over Una hissed in her ear, 'Make some more coffee, will you, Rossie? Really, I'd have thought you'd do it without being asked.'

When she returned from the kitchen with the tray Monty was telling them with guarded optimism that he thought they definitely had a show.

'Mind you,' he warned, 'the public is a funny animal. I've seen surefire hits close in three days flat and real turkeys run and run. There are no cast-iron certainties in this business. But I'm willing to give it a go. Now, there's a little theatre free in Stoke Newington. It's an old music hall and due for demolition. There are plans for one of those new supermarkets. It's not exactly Drury Lane, but at least it still has everything intact and working – well almost. I can get it at a knock-down rent for you from the LCC. Suppose we take it for a month and see how we go?'

The three faces looking at him were alight with enthusiastic disbelief. It was Julian who found his voice first.

'Thanks a lot, Mr Montague. That would be fantastic. Could we see the place sometime?'

'Sure.' Monty paused to light up one of his pungent cigars, drawing a disapproving glare from Don, whose mother had never allowed *anyone* to smoke in the house. Una's 'cool-as-a-mountain-stream' Consulates were bad enough, but *cigars*! She would never have trusted a man who wore a bow tie and a homburg hat either, come to that. Don fumed with resentment. Who did the man think he was – sitting there calmly dispensing *his* money as though it was some sort of largesse?

'I'll give you a bell when I've fixed it all up,' Monty was saying. 'Now, in the meantime, what do you want me to do about casting? Is there some place where you can hold auditions?'

'Have them here if you want,' Una put in.

Monty waved a dismissive hand, scattering cigar ash on the carpet. 'No, no. Too far out of town. Anyway, it looks amateurish. I'll find us a hall somewhere. Shouldn't cost much for a couple of hours or so. Let you know about that too.' He looked at the three eager young faces. 'Just one thing. What do the three of you do for a living?'

Stuart looked at the others. 'Julian works for a solicitor,' he said. 'Brian's in his last year at music college and I've been on the dole ever since I left art school. I take anything I can get.'

'Mmm.' Monty drew on his cigar. 'Well, wouldn't be a good move to give up the day job, Julian. Maybe you can fix it to take some holiday. I'll leave you to sort that out.'

He looked at his watch. 'Better get off, I suppose. I'll be in touch.'

They shook hands all round and Una showed Monty to the door. As she was letting him out he paused and looked at her speculatively.

'Haven't got any ideas about making a comeback, have you, Una?'

She gazed at him with wide, innocent eyes. '*Comeback!* Why on earth would I want to do that, Monty?'

'Just an idea. I thought maybe it was something you might have tucked up that scheming little sleeve of yours.'

'All I want is to help the boys.' She laughed. 'Really, Monty, what an idea! Why on earth would I want to go back to all that hard work and stress when I have a life of leisure here?' She swept an arm expressively round the spacious hallway.

Monty shrugged. 'Who knows why people do things?' As he walked down the path to his car he added under his breath, 'Especially frustrated over-the-hill singers.'

After that things moved fast. Monty was as good as his word. He hired a hall for auditions and notified a group of possibles from among his clientele for the cast. He also inserted an advertisement in *The Stage* just in case. He promised to sit in at the auditions and give the boys the benefit of his experience. The Prince Regent Theatre was hired for the month of July, but as it wasn't being used Monty had obtained permission for the boys to go in beforehand and do any necessary work. It was a good month for tourists, he told the boys. And producers weren't so busy in the summer either. It was also the silly season in the newspaper world and critics might just be tempted out of the Fleet Street pubs to look at something intriguingly fresh by a group of newcomers.

With the help of friends and relatives the three boys cleaned up the theatre and did the necessary repairs.

Brian found enough young musicians from among his fellow students to form a small orchestra who would play for minimum union rates. In their last year they were encouraged to get as much practical experience as they could. And all three looked forward eagerly to the date set for the auditions.

Stuart and Rosalind saw each other hardly at all during the frantic weeks of preparation. Being the only one of the three not busy in the daytime, Stuart was kept fully occupied and seemed to be enjoying every minute. For Rosalind exam time was approaching fast and she was working flat out. They spoke on the telephone regularly, exchanging all their news, and Rosalind looked forward to the time when all the work would be over and they could have some time to themselves again.

It was on the evening before the auditions that Una paid a visit to the flat in Earls Court. Stuart came down to open the door to her and he saw at once that she was upset about something.

'Oh, Stuart, can I come in?' She turned a woebegone face to him. 'I'm afraid I've got something terrible to say to you.'

Full of foreboding he led the way upstairs where Julian was busy at his typewriter, working on some revisions that Monty had suggested. 'There's a fresh pot of coffee on the go, would you like a cup?' Stuart suggested hopefully.

Una nodded and sank into a chair. She said nothing until she had taken a sip of the coffee, then, taking a deep breath, she looked at the two faces watching her anxiously. 'I don't know how to tell you this,' she said. 'I'm so dreadfully sorry.'

Stuart and Julian exchanged worried glances. Una's demeanour suggested only one thing. She was pulling out of the project – their worst nightmare. Stuart braced himself and leaned towards her. 'Please, go on,' he urged. 'Surely it can't be as bad as all that.'

'It *is*.' Una pulled out a handkerchief and snuffled into it briefly. 'It's Don. He says he doesn't see how he can possibly recoup his money and that he must – he has to – *withdraw*.' She said the last word in a hushed whisper. 'Oh God, what can I say?' She looked from one to the other helplessly.

'Not much you can say,' Julian said in a flat voice. 'Without the backing we can't even get off the ground.' He pushed the typewriter away from him in a gesture of finality. 'So – that's that. Finito! All our hard work up the Swanee, as they say.'

Stuart chewed his lip. 'The thing is, we've already hired the theatre. We're probably going to have to pay for that anyway. Then there's all the time we've put in on it. There's the hall too. Auditions tomorrow. Christ! What a mess. We'll be in hock up to our necks over this for years!'

Una sighed. 'I *know*. And I'm so *sorry*, boys, I can't tell you ...' She paused dramatically, twisting her handkerchief between her fingers. Stuart peered at her hopefully.

'What are you thinking, Una? There's something else, isn't there?'

'It's nothing. Just some mad idea Don had. It's too ridiculous even to mention. I couldn't possibly expect you to ...'

'*Tell* us! Anything to save the show,' Stuart urged her.

'Well ...' She swallowed. 'Don has this really silly notion. He started talking about it after the evening when you all came over to play the music for Monty.'

'Yes?'

She had their full attention now and went on: 'He's got the idea that he wouldn't consider the money wasted if – if *I* were in the play. You see, he didn't know me when

279

I was working in the theatre and it's always been his greatest disappointment that he's never seen me perform. That evening when I sang the songs he was . . .' she looked at them from under her lashes '. . . well, quite bowled over, and . . .'

'But that's fine. Just *great*!' Stuart almost shouted. 'It would solve everything, wouldn't it, Julian?'

His reaction was more guarded. 'What part did you have in mind, Mrs Blake?'

'Well, I think I'm mature enough to play Olive, don't you?'

Julian was relieved. If she'd had her heart set on playing the teenaged Violet they might as well have called the whole thing off here and now. Olive, she might handle reasonably well. 'I see,' he said. 'Well, if that's all right with you, Mrs Blake, I'd say that we seem to have saved the day.'

'And we've got you to thank for it, Una – again! What would we do without you?' Almost hysterical with relief, Stuart went to the cupboard. 'I'd say this calls for a little celebration, wouldn't you? Brandy, both of you? Let's drink to the success of *Sweet Violet* and the first member of our cast – Una Blake!'

'Blair,' she corrected, accepting the glass he handed her. 'Blair is my stage name. That's how my public remembers me and that's the name I'd like to see on the programme.'

'Right, Blair it is.' Stuart raised his glass. 'To the success of *Sweet Violet* and to its star, Una Blair!'

The auditions for *Sweet Violet* were held on a Friday afternoon in June. The boys arrived at the hall early, filled with excited anticipation. Monty arrived soon after and found them setting out chairs. Brian had taken the dust sheet off the piano and was running his hands experimentally over the keys.

280

When Stuart announced that the part of Olive had already been cast, Monty's eyebrows almost shot through the top of his head.

'Who've you got?' he asked. 'It's not really on, this, you know. I've got a really good girl lined up who's set her heart on that part.'

'Actually Una's doing it,' Stuart told him.

Monty groaned. 'Christ almighty! I should've guessed! I had an idea she had this in mind. How did she swing it on you?'

'Oh, no, it wasn't like that,' Stuart assured him. 'Her husband – you knew of course that he was putting up the backing – got slightly cold feet. But he said that he was prepared to take the risk if Una played the part.'

'That's what she said, eh?' Monty shook his head, tutting under his breath. So like Una to pass the buck. Obviously this was what she'd had in mind all along. Serve her right if she fell flat on her face on the opening night! Not that these kids deserved a flop. 'Oh, well, if that's the way it is, we'll have to put up with it,' he said resignedly. 'Though I'm not looking forward to telling my girl the part's been cast behind closed doors, I can tell you.'

By the end of the afternoon the play was successfully cast. Even Miriam Gerard, who had had her eye on the part of Olive, accepted a lesser role with good grace. The actors were briefed and a rehearsal schedule handed out by Stuart who had now assumed the position of producer. Julian would direct and Brian would be musical director. They were in business! The three went out that evening to celebrate.

Rosalind went along to the school on the first morning of the exams with a stomach full of butterflies. So much depended on getting good grades. It meant so much to her to do well. No one had wished her good luck this morning. Her mother, totally preoccupied with the play, seemed to have forgotten all about the exams. Stuart too seemed incapable of thinking of anything else. Even her father, who had been writing regularly ever since he and Freda had arrived in Australia, seemed to have dropped the habit lately. She often thought about Cathy and pictured her enjoying her new and exciting life in Suffolk with her handsome husband. She'd looked so happy on her wedding day. It must be so nice to be loved and cherished; to feel so safe and wanted.

But it doesn't matter, Rosalind told herself as she walked to the bus stop. If I do well I'll have only myself to thank. I'll have done it without any support at all. And that's the way I like it. The thought gave her a certain satisfaction, but deep inside she nursed a secret hope that once the play was under way Stuart would turn his attentions to her once more. She couldn't help comparing her mother's indifference to her with the fuss and effort she had gone to on the boys' behalf.

The exams were spread over four days and at the end of that time she felt drained. Walking home from the bus stop on Friday afternoon she felt strangely empty. The pressure was off. It was like having a burden suddenly lifted from her shoulders. She felt strangely light, as though she might blow over and float away in the first puff of wind. Nothing to do now but wait until August for the results and try not to think too much about all the questions she wished she had answered differently.

To fill in the waiting time and earn some money, she'd decided to ask at the Queen's Head if they needed any extra help. Now that she was free from all her studies she could work behind the bar – turn her hand to anything. And it was all good practice for the day when she would manage her own hotel.

She heard the row going on as soon as she put her key into the front door lock. Una and Don were going at it so hard that they didn't even hear her come in. Her heart sank as she paused anxiously halfway up the stairs to eavesdrop.

'Why didn't you ask me first?' Don was demanding. 'How do you think this makes me look? My wife on the stage in some fleapit in Stoke Newington! Sponsored by me too!'

'It makes you look a damn sight better husband than you are!' Una yelled back. 'Anyway they won't know I'm your wife because I'll be using my stage name – Blair.'

'Oh? So *my* name's only good enough for writing on the cheques, is it? That's nice to know!'

'You won't complain when the money comes rolling in, will you?' Una sneered.

'If I don't lose the lot, which is a damned sight more likely! I've been asking around and I reckon I've been taken for a ride. Everyone says that backing a play by a team of unknowns is like throwing money into a bottomless pit!'

'Rubbish! What do any of your cronies know about the theatre anyway? Most of them think that Laurence Olivier is a cigarette manufacturer!'

'You've been planning this all along, haven't you?' Don said. 'You and that common little Montague man – you've set the whole thing up. Me and those three young chaps – just to get yourself back on the bloody stage again. And all at *my* expense!'

'All I ever wanted to do was help the boys. I'm doing it for them,' Una protested. 'They *begged* me to take the part. They seem to think I'll be the making of the show. How could I let them down?'

Don gave a disbelieving grunt. 'This was the only way you could do it, wasn't it. You knew you'd never get another part unless you engineered one. I don't believe they begged you to take the part. As usual you're twisting the truth to suit yourself. And if you mess the thing up I'll stand to lose a fortune.'

'Well thank you *very much* for the vote of confidence!' Una stormed. 'They *do* want me to play the part. Ask them if you don't believe me,' she challenged, knowing that he wouldn't. 'Ever since the evening when they came here with Monty and heard me sing they've been *obsessed* with having me to play Olive. I can't disappoint them now and I'm not going to. You just want me to be shut up in this mausoleum of a house, bored out of my skull all day!'

'Don't be so stupid, Una. I just can't stand the idea of chucking away good money so that my wife can make a fool of herself, that's all.'

From where she stood on the stairs, Rosalind heard her mother striding angrily across the room in the direction of the hall. Quickly she whisked up the stairs out of sight.

From where she stood on the landing she heard Una shout, 'If you've such a poor opinion of my ability, if you think more of the money than you do of me, then perhaps I'd better move out. But don't think you can take your money out of the play now that everything's been settled.'

Don hurried after her. 'Una – listen. Come back, will you? Why do you always have to fly off the handle so?' His voice had taken on the whining conciliatory tone that always meant that she had won. 'If only you'd told me this was what you wanted,' he said. 'If you'd asked – talked to me about it. Why do you always keep things to yourself so? Can't you see, it makes me feel so – so shut out.'

Rosalind slipped into her room and closed the door. The row was all but over. As usual Don had rolled over like a whipped dog. Once more Una had got her own way, devious though it was. She pictured the scene downstairs. Una would probably shed a few winsome tears – enough to make Don feel a brute but not enough to puff up her eyes. Then she'd allow him to kiss her and for the next few days he would give her anything she asked for. Until the next time she did something outrageous.

*　　*　　*

Rehearsals went well. Julian and Brian were pleased with the way the cast was shaping. Stuart and a group of his art school friends had made and painted the scenery and Una had found a woman to make up the costumes. Elaine Frisby, a young divorcee, was a part-time alteration hand at Hallard's. She had given up her place at art school to make an early, disastrous marriage and now she was studying in her spare time and taking what work she could to make ends meet. She had talent and imagination and jumped at this chance to work on a more creative job. The costumes for *Sweet Violet* were a challenge and a delight to her after the mundane every-day tasks she was paid for.

She and Stuart seemed to strike up an instant rapport and with his help and advice she had worked long hours every evening at the sewing machine in her bedsit in Belsize Park. The costumes must be ready in three weeks, which would be hard work, but on the day of the dress rehearsal Elaine arrived at the Prince Regent theatre in a taxi with every costume ready for fitting. Everything was now in place. Cast and production team were on their toes, incandescent with excitement and nerves.

Rosalind arrived home at Blake's Folly to find the house empty. It was ten-thirty, but with Una at the theatre so much of the time Don had taken to having his evening meal at the local pub. As she had her own meals at the Queen's Head and worked unsocial hours the three hardly ever saw each other now that the play's four-week run had started.

As she closed the door behind her and switched on the hall light she saw that there was some mail lying on the doormat. She bent and picked it up. Two bills for Don and a blue air letter, addressed to her in a handwriting she didn't recognise. She carried it through to the kitchen and opened it carefully with the aid of the bread knife. Glancing first at the signature, she saw with surprise that it was from Freda and dated a week ago.

My dear Rosalind,

I am writing with the sad news that Ben was rushed into hospital yesterday morning with a heart attack. The doctors say it was brought on by overwork and strain, but that there is a good chance that he will recover with rest and care.

If you would like to come out, dear, I know he would be so pleased to have you with him. I think it would make a great difference to his recovery. He has been very depressed and dwelling a lot on the past and what he sees as his neglect of you. He is badly in need of the reassurance your presence would give him.

I'd dearly love to be able to send the air fare for you, but I'm not sure how long Ben will need to be in hospital or how much the doctor's and hospital fees will cost us. There is no NHS here and unfortunately we hadn't thought to join a private health scheme. Now that I am responsible for our finances I must take care of the money, especially as we cannot fulfil the rest of the engagements on our tour. I do hope you can understand this, Rossie. Please try to come, but don't worry. He is in good hands.

Hoping perhaps to see you soon.

My love to you,

Freda

Rosalind read the letter through twice more, her eyes blurred by tears. She had blamed her father for not writing when all the time he was ill in hospital – and worrying about her! Heart attacks were serious, weren't they? Even though Freda played it down, her father must be very ill for her to write and ask Rosalind to go over. But how could she go? How much did it cost to fly to Australia? The sea fare was probably cheaper but even that would be beyond her means. Besides, a ship would take ages. By the time she got there Ben could be . . . She bit her lip, thrusting the thought firmly out of her mind. There was only one thing for it. Much as she deplored the prospect, she would have to ask Don for the money. Or at least, ask Una to ask him. She would pay back every penny as soon as she had a job.

Backstage at the Prince Regent there was an air of excitement. Monty had come round in the interval to tell them that Louis Jacobson was in front. Jacobson was a theatrical impresario with a flair for promoting new talent. He had set several new playwrights on the road to success over the past five years and he had a string of successful shows running in the provinces and West End. Monty was very proud of the coup he had pulled off in persuading him to come and see the show.

'So far he likes what he sees,' he told a trembling, pale-faced Julian. 'Get them to give it all they've got in the second act. I'm not promising anything, but by the look on that crabby old face of his, you might just be in with a chance.'

Una arrived home bubbling over with news. Rosalind was in her room but she could hear her mother downstairs, her words tumbling over each other as she told Don about something that had happened at the performance. When she heard her mother coming upstairs Rosalind went out on to the landing to meet her.

'Mum . . .'

'Rossie. Off to bed already? Listen, you'll never guess what happened this evening . . .'

'Mum, I've had a letter.'

'Really? Louis Jacobson came to see the show. And he *liked it*! Afterwards he came back to make Julian a proposition.'

'It was about Dad. He's had a heart attack, Mum. He's very ill.'

Una stopped short to stare at her daughter. Trust Ben to spoil her big moment! 'Heart attacks are nothing nowadays,' she said dispassionately. 'They can put them right just like that.' She snapped her fingers. 'He'll be fine, you'll see. Now – Louis Jacobson has suggested that the show should be a half-hour longer. He's asked Brian to write two more numbers and he's made a few suggestions that Julian is quite excited about. He thinks he can easily incorporate them into the plot and he's going to work on them right away. If we do what LJ suggests and he approves, he's going to send us on tour with the option of going into the West End!' She threw back her head, laughing delightedly. 'Just *think*, Rossie. Una Blair in the West End. It's my dream come true! At last!'

'That's wonderful, Mum. Look, could you ask Don if he'll lend me the money to go over to Australia?'

Una frowned. 'Why on earth do you want to go to Australia?'

'To see Dad, of course. Haven't you been listening to a word I've said?' Rosalind snapped, her nerves stretched to breaking point.

'Don't speak to me like that!' Una walked across the room and twitched angrily at the curtains. 'Here I am with the chance of a lifetime within reach and all you can think about is rushing halfway round the world on some wild goose chase!'

'It isn't a wild goose chase!' Rosalind swallowed her irritation. 'Look, I'm sorry, Mum. I really do hope the show is successful, and I am pleased for you. But I can't help worrying about Dad. Freda says he wants to see me. I *have* to go.'

Una spun round. '*Why?* What has he ever done for you? I'm the one who brought you up – slaved for you – sacrificed my career. If he's ill then all I can say is, he brought it on

288

himself. Booze and women, that's all he ever thought about when we were together!'

'He did pay my school fees. Why are you always so horrible about him? He can't have been that bad!'

When Rosalind began to cry Una crossed the room and shook her shoulder. 'Oh, for heaven's sake, Rossie, don't turn on the waterworks. Your father paid the school fees because I made it impossible for him to refuse. He's always wriggled out of his responsibilities. I'm sure there's no need for you to get in a state. At this very moment he's probably as right as rain again, sitting up in bed swilling beer, likely as not! Oh, why did that wretched woman have to write and worry you – wrecking everything like this?'

'Could you just ask Don?' Rosalind pleaded. 'I'll pay it all back just as soon as I can, I promise. And he can only say no.'

Una sighed. 'I can't ask him for any more money, can I, Rossie?' she said. 'To tell the truth there'll be a few more expenses for the show before we're finished. He's never been that keen on my doing this play anyway and I don't know what he's going to say when I tell him we're going on tour. You do see, don't you?' She looked at her dejected daughter. 'And asking for money to visit my ex-husband isn't really on, now is it?'

Rosalind's shoulders slumped despairingly. 'I suppose not,' she whispered.

All night long she lay sleepless, racking her brain to think of a way to get the money together. Maybe she could borrow it? But from whom? She didn't know anyone who could spare that much. And even if she did, how long would it take her to pay it back? There wasn't even anything she could sell.

Alone in the house next morning she wandered restlessly from room to room, wrestling with her problem. If she were ill she would want someone close to be with her. And being so far from home, in a strange country,

Ben must feel so isolated, even with Freda there. It was her duty to be there. There must be a way. It was only when she stopped pacing and found herself in front of Don's mother's china cabinet that the terrifying idea presented itself.

There had been a big row about the china cabinet when Una wanted to get rid of all the late Mrs Blake's belongings. It was the one article over which Don had stood firm, and won.

'*Mother took a great pride in her collection of Meissen porcelain. She dusted every piece of it every day of her life. Anyway, some of those pieces are very rare. They're worth a fortune.*'

His words echoed in her memory as Rosalind peered through the glass at the delicately modelled figures, painted in exquisite colours. And when the preposterous idea sprang into her head it was with the blinding force of an exploding firework. She caught her breath. *She couldn't do it.* But she must! It could even mean the difference between life and death for her father. And she wanted so much to be with him; to see him again before . . . in case . . .

With slow deliberation she tried the door of the cabinet and found in unlocked. Very carefully she selected one of the treasured pieces. It was formed like a large flower-decked shell, being pulled by four plump cherubs. She held it up to the light. The china was so delicate and translucent that you could see daylight through it; the colours so subtle and clear; the little faces and flowers so perfectly fashioned. It was an exquisite work of art. It must certainly be worth a lot of money. Once his argument had been won she didn't remember seeing Don look at the cabinet again and her mother had never taken any interest in it, dismissing the collection of Meissen as 'dust-gathering junk'. They would never notice if she rearranged the other pieces to fill the gap.

*   *   *

The little man in the antique shop in Chelsea gave her enough for the air fare and a little over. At first he had looked at her suspiciously over his *pince-nez* and asked where she had obtained the piece. The last time he had seen porcelain of such quality and perfection had been in a museum. She told him half-truthfully that it had been left to her by a relative and that she needed the money to go and visit her sick father in Australia. She even showed him Freda's letter. At last he took pity on the pale and trembling young woman. She looked so respectable and the large dark eyes behind the spectacles were so pitifully troubled that it wrenched at his heart. He'd like to think that his own daughters would make such a sacrifice if he were ill.

The money safely in her handbag, Rosalind took a taxi to Stuart's flat. She wanted to tell him about her father and her intention to go to Australia. She even meant to confide in him about the piece of Meissen. She badly needed someone she could trust on whom to unload her guilt. But when Stuart answered the door to find her standing there he looked surprised and flustered.

'Rossie!'

'I'd like to talk to you, Stuart. Is it all right?'

'Talk? Oh, well, if you want to. Come in.'

A little bewildered by his attitude she followed him upstairs, but when she walked into the small living room she saw the reason for his confusion. Stuart was not alone. A young woman sat at her ease on the settee, her shoes kicked off and her feet tucked under her. On the coffee table in front of her were two empty cups and an open portfolio of sketches.

'This is Elaine,' Stuart said. 'We've been discussing her course work. She's studying art – a correspondence course. She works part-time for Hallard's. She made all the costumes for the show.'

'Yes, I know.' Deeply disappointed and disturbed by the

girl's obvious ease, Rosalind made herself smile. She'd heard of Elaine Frisby of course, but never met her. No one had ever mentioned how attractive she was. Her complexion was clear and translucent and her blue eyes were wide and clear. She wore a loose white shirt over jeans and her long blonde hair was tied back in a soft knot on her neck. She looked confident and utterly relaxed. She even offered to make a fresh pot of coffee. Clearly she was totally at home at the flat.

Rosalind shook her head. 'No, thanks. I can't stay.' She looked at Stuart, hoping he would see how much she needed to talk to him – wishing that the girl would take the hint that she wanted to see him alone. Neither of them seemed to sense her silent plea. Or if they did, they ignored it.

Stuart stood diffidently in the doorway. 'So – what can I do for you, Rossie?' he asked in the awkward silence. 'Was there something special or is it just a social visit?'

'I – had to come up to town so I thought I'd drop in.' She looked from one to the other, then at the sketches, scattered over the table and the floor. 'You're talking shop. I won't keep you.'

'Well, if you're sure there's nothing . . . I'll come down with you.' Clearly relieved, Stuart escorted her downstairs. It was almost as though he wanted to be sure she was off the premises, she reflected unhappily. At the street door she turned to him.

'I came to tell you that I'm going to Australia,' she said. 'My father is very ill and he's asking for me.'

'Oh God, Rossie, I'm sorry to hear that.' He patted her shoulder awkwardly. 'Sorry about Elaine being here, but she's only just arrived. I said I'd give her some advice on her work, you see, and . . .'

'Don't worry. You don't have to explain,' she said stiffly.

'What you do is your own business.' She reached for the door but he put out a hand to stop her.

'Rossie! You're not annoyed?'

'Don't make out she hasn't been here before. She looks as though she owns the place!' She turned a face pink with the hurt of betrayal towards him. 'Who you entertain in your own flat is your own affair, but at least have the honesty to be open about it!'

'I never said she hadn't been here before. She made the costumes for the play, for Christ's sake!'

'Yes – well, you and she seem to have a lot in common.'

'That's right we do! Anything wrong with that?' He was clearly annoyed. 'Good God, Rossie, I'm not your personal property, you know!'

Stung, she turned to the door again. 'No, of course you're not. Why should you bother with me any more? After all, you've no further use for me now that you've got Don's money and the play's in production, have you?'

He reached out and grasped her arm. 'Look, Rosalind, why don't you admit that you've never shown the slightest interest in the show? You're even jealous of your own mother ever since we gave her a part in it. All these weeks you haven't even been to one rehearsal.'

'I've been studying. You know that!'

'And while we're on the subject, I'm getting a bit sick of having your step-father's backing thrown in my face every time you feel like it. It's a business arrangement. And none of it is down to you. It's all Una's doing!'

Without waiting to hear more she pulled the door open and ran down the street, tears streaming down her cheeks, oblivious to the curious stares of passers-by.

When Rosalind told the manageress of the Queen's Head the following day that she would have to give in her notice and the reason, her employer was sympathetic.

'There's always a job for you here at the QH, Rosalind,' she said. 'As long as there's a vacancy, of course. If you can give me an idea when you're likely to be back, I'll even keep your job open for you.'

She shook her head. 'I've no idea how long I'll be gone. And if I pass my A levels, I'll be going on to business college in the autumn anyway.' She felt sad at leaving. She'd been happy at the hotel and she liked all the staff. But all she could think about now was her father and how much he needed her. As far as she remembered no one had ever needed her before.

She'd cabled Freda that morning to say that she'd raised the money and was coming out. Now all she had to do was to book her air ticket, pack, and try to explain to her mother where the money for the trip had come from. As it happened she never got that far.

As she let herself into the house that afternoon she heard Don on the telephone in the study. He sounded agitated.

'No, there's no sign of a break in,' he said. 'And nothing else seems to be missing. But the Meissen has definitely gone. Yes, it is valuable – *very* valuable. Irreplaceable in fact. It has sentimental value as well, you see. It belonged to my late mother.'

Rosalind froze to a standstill in the hall. When the police heard they circulated all the antique shops, didn't they? The piece was so distinctive. Surely it would only be a matter of time before she was found out? Her heart began to pound in her throat and she felt as though she were suffocating. *What would they do to her?* Would she be sent to prison? But the thought of facing the police, a prison cell, Don's and her mother's fury and disgust, were all eclipsed by one thought: that of her father's disappointment when he learned that she wasn't coming after all. Maybe he would even hear of her disgrace. The shock would surely make him worse –

it might even bring on another attack and kill him! She rushed into the study where Don was just replacing the receiver.

'Please, don't let the police come. I took the porcelain shell. It wasn't a robbery. It was me!'

For a moment he stared at her ashen face, lost for words, then: '*You?* Whatever for, Rosalind? What in the world did you want with it?'

The words tumbled over one another as she poured out the reason to him. When she had finished he stared at her in amazement.

'Why does no one ever *tell* me anything in this house?' he asked. 'You only had to ask, girl. I would have given you the money if you'd asked me for it.'

'Mum said she couldn't ask you for any more,' she told him. 'Not after the play and everything. And especially as it was for Dad.'

'Are you telling me that your mother *knew* about this?'

'About Dad's illness. Not about the – about what I did.'

'She *knew*, and she did nothing to help you?' Don looked incredulous. 'And you were driven to *this* to get the money for your fare?'

'I haven't spent it – haven't bought my ticket yet,' she told him hesitantly. 'Maybe if I went back to the shop the man would let me buy the piece back.'

'Never mind all that,' Don said decisively. 'First I'll ring the police back and tell them it was all a mistake, then we'll ring the travel agents and book your air ticket.' He reached out to pat her shoulder. 'You and I have never really had a chance to get to know one another, have we?' he said gently. 'I'm not an ogre, you know. And, believe me, I do know what it means to love a parent, Rosalind. You must go to your father as soon as you can. Don't worry, we'll get you there somehow.'

'But the Meissen! The shop where I sold it is in Chelsea.

295

I've got a card.' She found it and gave it to him. 'The man might sell it.'

He took the card brushing her fears aside. 'He won't. It'll be all right. Leave it to me.'

Sick with relief and gratitude, she waited while he telephoned the police again to say that the piece had been found and it was all a mistake. He smiled at her as he replaced the receiver.

'There, that's done.' He rubbed his hands together. 'Now – suppose you go and put the kettle on first, eh? I think we could both do with a cup of tea. Then we'll get your flight arranged.'

Rosalind was in bed and asleep when Una burst in and snapped on the light. Squinting up through sleep-filled eyes she saw her mother standing over her with all the righteous indignation of an avenging angel.

'What the hell did you mean by it?' she demanded. 'Going to Don with your sob story, getting money out of him behind my back? You can just give it back. You're not going to Australia, Rosalind. Do you hear me?'

'I am.' Rosalind sat up in bed, groping on the bedside table for her glasses. 'The air ticket is booked now. And I didn't go to Don with a sob story,' she said. 'Dad's illness just – well, it just came out – by accident. When he heard Don offered me the money at once.'

'Came out by *accident*?' Una threw back her head and laughed mirthlessly. 'Like hell it did! What do you take me for? How could a thing like that come out accidentally? You went behind my back and asked him for the money, you devious little bitch. And after I told you not to as well! You've caused trouble between us again. I've just been accused of being a heartless, uncaring mother! That's nice, isn't it, after all I've done for you?' She folded her arms. 'Well, I'm telling you straight, here and now, that if you go on this hare-brained trip to see your father you can damned well stay there. You won't be welcome in this house any more. So just sleep on *that*, my lady!' And having delivered her exit line she strode out of the room, snapping off the light as she went.

When she'd gone Rosalind lay for a long time staring at the ceiling. She'd go to Australia. And she'd stay there – make a fresh start. Maybe she could find a business college and qualify. But even if she didn't it wouldn't matter. She'd be in a new country, with someone who loved and wanted her. No one here did. Even Stuart didn't love her any more. It was strange to think that Don had been the one to show her kindness when she really needed it. He'd forgiven her for taking the Meissen, lent her the money, and perhaps the kindest of all, he had kept her desperate act from Una. When it came down to it he was the only real friend she had. She'd find work and pay him the money back, she promised herself. She'd owe nothing to anyone – stand on her own feet.

Two days later she was packed and ready. Her air ticket was safe with her passport in her handbag and she stood in the hall, surrounded by her luggage, waiting for the taxi. Una had gone off to the theatre early that morning for a rehearsal call to try out the new numbers without even saying goodbye. But Don had wished her well and pressed a crisp five-pound note into her hand as he left for the office.

'For some magazines and chocolate to pass the long flight time,' he'd said quietly. He bent to kiss her forehead briefly. 'Safe journey, my dear. I hope you find your father recovering well.'

His kind words had brought a lump to her throat. If Una would only give him the chance she'd find him a good and thoughtful husband. But she had always had a talent for bringing out the worst in everyone.

Rosalind looked at her watch and decided there was

time to make herself a cup of coffee before the taxi arrived. Slipping her coat over the banisters she went into the kitchen and put the kettle on.

She heard the front door bell as she was pouring the boiling water into the cup. The taxi was early. Going into the hall she opened the door.

'Cable for Miss Blair.' The boy handed her the envelope.

With trembling fingers she opened it and stared down at the words that danced before her shocked eyes.

Sorry to say Ben passed away ten am July 27th stop Letter following stop Freda.

She shook her head bemusedly. It wasn't true. It couldn't be! It was only a quarter past nine and the cable said ten. It was some kind of horrible sick joke. Then she remembered that Australia was ten hours ahead of English time. It was evening now over there.

The boy cleared his throat and Rosalind looked up, surprised to find him still there.

'Any reply, miss?'

'What? Oh, no. No reply – thank you.'

Slowly she closed the door and stared helplessly at the packed cases standing ready by the front door. Now she had no one. Dad had gone. She wouldn't see him again – ever. There would be no new life in Australia now. No love and no belonging. Just a greater loneliness than ever.

Oddly, the tears wouldn't come. She wanted – needed – to cry but there was a deep, hard coldness inside her that refused to thaw. Uppermost in her mind was the question of where she should go. In a little while a taxi would be here. Where should it take her now? Sitting down on the bottom stair she thought quickly, her mind suddenly crystal clear. Then she rose and went into Don's study. Lifting the telephone, she dialled the number of the Queen's Head and asked for Mrs Gresham, the manageress. When she answered Rosalind explained that she wasn't leaving the country after all – and the reason.

'I'd like to come back to work on a permanent basis if there's a job,' she said. 'I've changed my mind about going to college. There's just one thing though. Would it be possible for me to live in?'

Chapter Sixteen

Autumn at Melfordleigh was beautiful. The summer visitors began to thin out and Cathy found that she could often walk for miles along the sand without seeing a soul. She preferred the dunes. The garden at Cuckoo Lodge seemed melancholy now that summer was over and most of the flowers had gone. The roses hung sad, windblown heads and the bright petals of the dahlias were bruised with early frost. Even this year's brood of baby ducks on the mill stream, which had enchanted her all summer, had grown up and gone.

In November the shocking news of President Kennedy's assassination cast a dark shadow over the whole world. Autumn turned to winter and Christmas loomed once again. Cathy hoped it might be a chance to lift the gloom. Gerald's students, Robert and Simon, were both going home and obviously looking forward to the holiday. Cathy heard their good-natured banter and laughter as she went about her household tasks. She envied them, often wishing she could join in with their youthful camaraderie. But she kept her distance, feeling that Gerald would not approve. She had nursed a fond hope that maybe they'd invite Johnny, Mrs Bains and Matthew to Cuckoo Lodge for Christmas, but when she suggested it to Gerald he shrugged off the idea.

'Didn't you say that the old lady wouldn't travel back in the summer? It isn't likely she'll want to come here in the middle of winter, is it?' he said dismissively.

Cathy had to agree that he was probably right. Johnny wouldn't leave her mother alone at Christmas as she had in the summer. It seemed that they would be spending the holiday alone. She examined the reasons for her crushing disappointment, forced to acknowledge at last that there was something badly wrong with her marriage. All year she had seen so little of Gerald. A year ago the prospect of having him to herself for a few days would have filled her with excited anticipation, so why did she now find herself viewing the prospect with such a heavy heart?

The answer was something she would have preferred not to think about, yet as the end of their first year approached she realised that it was something she must face up to. Instead of growing closer together during the year they had been at Melfordleigh they had been drifting steadily further apart. Gerald was busy with his students. That was as it should be. It was part of their plan and she had been prepared for it. But even during his off duty hours he seemed to have little time for her; indeed, she sometimes wondered if he even noticed she was there. And the fact that she had so little to do made her all the more aware of it. The organising and administrative work she had hoped to do for the school had been taken out of her hands. Gerald had engaged a secretary, a middle-aged woman who came in twice a week to attend to his correspondence. The financial side of things was taken care of by an accountant. If they had been close to a college she might have gone back and finished her Home Economics course. But the nearest one was twenty miles away and the local bus into town ran only twice a week. It would have been impossible for her to get there and back each day.

She spent her days pottering round the house, helping Maggie prepare meals and walking – endlessly walking. By now she knew Melfordleigh as though she had been born there. She talked to the fishermen on the quay; watched the barefoot children sitting on the sea wall, hopefully dangling their bread-baited crablines; acquainted herself with the many kinds of seabirds as they foraged for food on the sandbanks at low tide.

301

Fascinated by the artists, she took up painting, buying materials from an art shop in Ipswich on one of her weekly shopping trips and taking care to work well away from the real artists. She was shy about her amateur, schoolgirlish efforts and afraid of their critical eyes. As the weeks went by she gradually improved and found satisfaction in the challenge of trying to capture the ever changing landscape of sea and sky with the aid of pigment and brushes. It was so much more satisfying than merely taking photographs, but it did not make up for her loneliness, or for the widening gulf in her marriage.

Once winter had truly set in her outdoor activities ground to a standstill. The rain and the relentless icy winds blowing off the North Sea made the dunes a wild, unfriendly place where walking was a bone-chilling ordeal. The gale-force winds were strong enough to lean on and the cold seemed to penetrate the thickest clothing. The yachtsmen and artists had all gone and even the fishermen stopped lingering on the quay to smoke a pipe, gossip and mend their nets.

Christmas was lonely. Without Robert and Simon there was no laughter or friendly chatter to brighten up the house. Cathy missed them even more than she had expected to. She had looked forward so much to this, their first Christmas together, especially after the traumas of last year. But Gerald spent most of his time in the studio, preparing work for next term and arranging next summer's concerts and seminars. He worked late into the night, retiring to his dressing room sometimes during the small hours, long after she was asleep, and sleeping late in the mornings. Cathy occupied herself between the kitchen and the drawing room, where she whiled away the long evenings watching the newly acquired television set that Gerald had bought, she guessed, to keep her amused and out of his way.

Maggie had taken two weeks off to be with her children until the new term began and Cathy missed her big breezy laugh and the village gossip she brought with her each day.

Bad weather kept her confined to the house and when the snow came a few days after Christmas the village was actually cut off for several days so that Robert and Simon were obliged to take a few more days' holiday.

Being shut up in the warm, comfortable house should have been cosy and romantic, especially for two people so recently married. Instead it seemed to make Gerald restless and irritable. He began to snap at her for the smallest thing. Sometimes, when he looked at her, Cathy felt it was almost as though he had difficulty in working out who she was.

The gloomy weeks merged, one into the next, like a slowly grinding treadmill until, to Cathy's relief, the days began to lengthen and the wind from the sea turned noticeably kinder. Wrapped in a thick woolly sweater and gloves, she began once more to take her daily walks down to the quay or along the dunes.

When Robert and Simon returned, Gerald worked them extra hard to make up for the holiday, but in April, just after the builders had moved in to put the finishing touches to the barn, ready for the summer seminars and concerts, Robert announced that he was breaking into his course to go off on a tour of the north of England with a youth orchestra; something of which Gerald strongly disapproved, having intended that the two students would help him with the summer seminars. He warned Robert that he would acquire bad habits and would need to begin all over again. '*If I decide that you're worth taking back*,' he added threateningly.

At the beginning of the spring term, Gerald, much against his better judgement, had agreed to take a few promising sixth-form pupils from the local grammar school at the head's request. But it was a mistake. Their comparative ineptitude stretched his patience to breaking point. Even though the students were keen and worked hard he was intolerant of their shortcomings. Cathy came to dread the days when they came for their lessons. Afterwards Gerald would crash around the house, muttering under his breath and finding fault with everything she did.

Once when he refused his dinner and flung off in a mood she followed him to the studio. Closing the door carefully behind her she stood with her back against it, watching him as he paced up and down in front of the window.

'What's the matter, Gerald?' she asked. 'Why are you so angry?'

He swung round to face her, his face dark. 'Why am I angry? *Why?*' he shouted. 'For God's sake, Cathy! Can't you use your imagination for once? What the hell am I doing? I should be at the peak of my performance – enjoying a successful career – not sitting listening to a lot of acne-covered cretins thumping the piano to a pulp. It's such a criminal waste of my time. They're never going to amount to anything if they live to be a hundred!'

'Oh, Gerald, that's unkind. They're not children. They're intelligent sixth-formers.' She didn't remind him that they were only a year or so younger than she was herself. 'They're really keen and they admire you so much. Besides, from what I can hear they sound very talented.'

'Oh, do they? Well, if you like them so much, *you* bloody well teach them!' He glared at her. 'Anyway, what would *you* know about it?' he added rudely.

'I did grow up with a musician father,' she said quietly.

'Precisely! I mean, you could hardly call what Dan did playing the piano, could you?'

Tears filled her eyes and she turned away. 'That's very cruel, Gerald.'

Instantly he was contrite. 'Oh God, Cathy, I didn't mean that.' He crossed the room and pulled her round to face him, holding her stiff body tightly. 'Dan was a good man and a fine musician.' He threw up his hands in despair. 'It's this bloody illness of mine. I get so *frustrated*, then I take it out on people who don't deserve it.'

'But I thought you wanted to be here at Cuckoo Lodge

– to teach?' she muttered. 'I thought you were tired of the concert circuit and everything to do with it?'

He ran a hand through his hair. 'I was – I *am*. But I still miss it all. I can't help it. It just takes time adjusting.'

'And you've got Simon. Surely he's rewarding? He does sound very good to me, even though my standards aren't as high as yours.'

'*Don't!*' He rubbed his cheek against hers. 'I didn't mean what I said about Dan. You know I didn't. And yes, Simon is good. That's part of the trouble if I'm honest. I see myself in him sometimes and I . . .' He sighed and turned away from her. 'I *envy* him, blast it, with his whole career in front of him. His whole *healthy* life just waiting to be lived!'

'None of us knows what's in store though,' she reminded him. 'You didn't when you were Simon's age.'

'I do now though, don't I?'

'What do you mean?' She looked at him closely, disturbed by his bitter tone, but he shrugged and drew a deep breath.

'Take no notice. I'm just feeling a bit down, that's all. It's probably the medication I'm on. The doctor said – oh, let's forget it.'

'What is this illness you've got, Gerald?' she asked.

He looked at her, his eyes guarded. 'You know what it is.'

'I don't. Not the name of it.'

'What's the difference anyway? You know how it affects me and that's all that matters.'

'Is that what makes you so cross?' she asked him. 'I mean – you would say if it was me, wouldn't you?'

He closed his eyes. 'Oh, Cathy, of course it isn't you. This – this thing I've got stops my muscles from doing what I want them to. That's what makes it so frustrating. It affects my movements as you must have noticed. Sometimes – sometimes I forget things too. It's so maddening!'

She looked at him anxiously. 'Is it painful?'

He shrugged. 'Sometimes worse than others.' He looked at her. 'That's why I sleep in the dressing room. So as not to disturb you when I'm restless.'

'You needn't worry about me. I wouldn't mind you being restless. I miss you, Gerald.'

'I know. I miss you too. But I get tired. Maybe once we've got the place up and running properly . . .'

'But once the summer starts you'll be busier than ever.' She looked at him. 'Are you sure you're not overdoing things? Gerald . . .' She touched his arm. 'Your illness – it won't get worse, will it, darling?'

He shook his head. 'No. Not if I do as I'm told and take the medication. I'll have to go up to Edinburgh to see the consultant again soon. Maybe he'll have good news for me. They're always hoping for some new breakthrough from the research they're doing up there.'

She could see that he was itching to bring the conversation to an end, but there was something else she was determined to say. 'Gerald – I've been meaning to ask you, only you seemed to have so much on your mind. Can we think about starting a baby soon? You did say we might when we were settled.'

His eyes clouded and he turned away. 'You could hardly call us settled yet, could you?'

'When then?'

'I don't know. Maybe when we've got the first summer season over. Let's wait and see, shall we?'

'Yes, but – if you were just to start sleeping in our room again . . .'

'*Leave* it for now, Cathy, there's a good girl.'

The impatient, dismissive note in his voice and the familiar lines that tightened his mouth told her all too plainly that it would be useless to press the subject further. 'At least come and have your dinner,' she said quietly. 'You should eat something. It's not good for you to go without.'

'I'm not hungry,' he said abruptly. 'Tell Maggie to keep it

for me. I might have it later.' He walked towards the door. 'I'm going to work in the other studio for a while. I don't want to be disturbed.'

She watched him turn away from her with despair. 'It's just that I get so lonely sometimes, Gerald,' she said despairingly as he was halfway through the door.

He paused, his head half-turned. 'Why don't you ask Simon to watch the television with you?' he said without looking at her. 'I think he gets lonely too sometimes. He misses Robert and it's dull for him here when he isn't working. Why don't you take him on some of those walks you like so much. I'm sure he could do with the fresh air to blow the cobwebs away.'

For a long moment she stood staring at the empty doorway, her heart heavy with hurt. Didn't he love her at all? Didn't he understand how she felt or what he was doing to her? Didn't he even care?

From that evening on Cathy spent more time in Simon's company. He enjoyed watching programmes on TV with her and when he felt in need of fresh air and some time away from the piano he would accompany her on her walks. He would just tag along without asking and at first she resented him a little. She'd grown used to walking alone and she valued her privacy and the freedom to paint if she felt like it. Besides, just at the moment it made a welcome escape from the builders' intrusion; the mess they made and their constant demands for cups of tea. The open seascape and the tangy air seemed to clear her head and calm her nerves but with Simon along she was obliged to make conversation.

But to her surprise she soon forgot her initial irritation and found herself looking forward to his company. His lively conversation and boyish sense of humour lifted her spirits and refreshed her far more than the hours of solitude. He had a youthful zest for life and looked forward to his future as a concert pianist with a confidence and certainty that made her envious.

307

Lately she had begun to be doubtful about her own future. There seemed no role for her here. Sometimes she felt that Gerald had no need of her at all. His mood swings were so frequent and unpredictable that she often felt as though she were walking on eggshells. She was barely a wife and, as the months went by, it seemed less and less likely that she would ever be a mother either.

For his part, Simon sensed the growing tension between the Cavelles. He was often a witness to Gerald's impatient sniping and cruel criticisms of his young wife. Sometimes his tutor would make oblique references to his wife's restlessness, putting it down to her inability to adjust to the change from London to village life. Simon was surprised and slightly embarrassed when he suggested that it might be beneficial to them both if Simon spent some of his free time with Cathy, indicating that she needed entertaining by someone of her own age to help her settle.

It wasn't hard to imagine how difficult Gerald Cavelle must be to live with. He was a brilliant pianist and coach – the best. Simon knew he was privileged to be taught by him. But he was brutally impatient and mercilessly critical, with his young wife no less than with his students. Simon put up with it, knowing that it was in his best interest to do so. After all, it would not be for long. But he concluded from Cathy's increasingly withdrawn manner that she found her husband's attitude intolerably hurtful.

Often when he was alone in his room he would think about her, wondering how she had come to marry a man so much older. One day, he promised himself, he would pluck up the courage to ask her outright. That day came one spring afternoon when she walked so fast that he had trouble keeping up with her. That morning he had reluctantly witnessed Gerald reducing her to tears because his breakfast egg was too hard and the toast was cold. She had clearly wanted to be alone this afternoon, but he had chosen to ignore her hints and accompany her anyway.

'Do you think you could slow down a bit?' he asked her breathlessly.

She slowed her pace. 'Sorry. I didn't realise.'

'Thanks. It felt more like rushing to catch a train than a leisurely walk.' He glanced at her sideways. 'Walking off a black mood?'

She lifted her shoulders. 'Something like that.' She'd felt so humiliated that morning, being shouted at in front of Simon. His insistence on accompanying her seemed like a further humiliation. She felt he must despise her for not standing up for herself. She despised herself too – more and more lately. In spite of the sunshine and the tangy, sea-fresh promise of summer she longed with a sudden agonising poignance for the happy uncomplicated days when her father was alive.

'Gerald's a lot older than you,' Simon said. 'I daresay that must have its drawbacks.'

His blunt remark felt like a barb, goading her into retaliation.

'Not at all,' she said defensively, quickening her pace even more. 'He's sometimes a little temperamental, but then he's a talented musician. A genius, some people say. You have to make allowances.'

'I'm afraid you'll have to make some for me too,' he said, blowing out his cheeks breathlessly. He threw himself down on the long wiry grass and lay on his back looking up at her. 'You must be fitter than me. I'm totally bushed. How about a little break?' He pulled a piece of grass and began to chew it, squinting up at her with eyes half-closed against the sunlight.

With a resigned sigh she sat down beside him. 'Sorry. And you're right,' she said. 'I was walking off a mood.' She glanced at him, but he had his eyes closed against the glare of the sun. 'I'm sure you know the reason. You heard Gerald shouting at me this morning.'

'I could hardly help it.' He opened his eyes and

glanced sideways at her. 'Why don't you yell back? I would.'

She was sitting up very straight, staring at the horizon. Her eyes were veiled with sadness. The wind blew strands of her long auburn hair across her face and she brushed them back, tucking them carelessly behind her ears. He saw that her skin was already beginning to take on a golden glow and the light sprinkling of freckles across her nose and cheekbones gave her an air of childlike vulnerability. She's *lovely*, he told himself with a small stab of surprise. Why hadn't he noticed before how beautiful she was? He tried to guess at her age. She was probably younger than him.

He missed the company of other young people at college, especially the girls. He'd always been popular with the opposite sex. He prided himself that he had a way with them. He could make them laugh, and that seemed to be the secret of success where girls were concerned. His musical brilliance helped too of course. He knew quite positively and without conceit that he was brilliant. It was a certainty that even Gerald's most scathing criticism could not waver. He still had a lot to learn, he acknowledged that. But one day he would be great and famous. He had always known it.

He chewed thoughtfully on his blade of grass. During the winter it had been easy enough to keep his mind on work. There had been little to distract him. But now spring stirred his blood and heightened his senses. In a way he had envied Robert, going off on his tour; the stimulation of meeting new people and seeing new places. He wondered how much longer he would be able to stand this isolation. He wondered how Cathy stood it too.

Feeling his eyes on her, Cathy turned to look down at him. 'Do you like it here?' she asked with a perception that took his breath away.

'Sitting here by the sea – with you, do you mean?' he asked daringly, his eyes twinkling. 'I like it very much.'

She laughed. And for a moment the bleakness in her

310

eyes disappeared. She looked much younger now – like a teenager.

'You know perfectly well what I mean,' she said. 'Melfordleigh – Cuckoo Lodge. Being coached by Gerald. I'm afraid he's a very hard taskmaster. A perfectionist.'

He nodded. 'I like that. I love to work hard; to be stretched. It's what I'm here for. But I do like to have fun sometimes too and, frankly, there doesn't seem too much of that around.'

'No.' She looked away. 'You must miss your friends.'

He sat up until his face was on a level with hers. 'What about you, Cathy? Do you miss your friends – going out, dances, cinema, the theatre? Having a good time? You used to live in London, didn't you? This place must be one hell of a contrast.'

'Not at all. I love Melfordleigh.' She avoided his eyes, looking out to sea again. 'Anyway, I have Gerald. I'm married.'

'Yes.' The word was loaded with meaning and for a moment neither of them spoke. 'So does all that mean giving up fun?' he asked. 'How sad! Maybe I'll pass on marriage after all.'

She got to her feet and looked down at him. 'I think we should be getting back. Maggie will need a hand with the evening meal and I daresay you should be working.'

She hurried off and he scrambled to his feet and ran after her. 'I've made you angry. I'm sorry. I didn't mean anything, you know.'

'It's perfectly all right.'

'I only thought it might be good for you to have someone to talk to. We all need a friend – someone to unburden ourselves to at times, don't we?'

'I have friends. And a husband, thank you,' she told him icily. 'Gerald is your tutor and I'm his wife. If there's anything you need please don't hesitate to ask, but don't expect me to talk about my husband behind his back.'

311

'I didn't mean you to. You've got me all wrong, Cathy. I'm sorry.' He hung back, allowing her to walk on ahead. This time he'd been too confident of his charm. She made him feel brash and callow. Maybe she was older than she looked. Maybe marriage had made her extra sensitive. Or maybe – just *maybe* – she needed help more than she cared to admit. He shrugged. Oh well, you couldn't win them all. If it was true, if she did want help, she'd come round eventually.

When they reached the quay he caught her up. 'Cathy . . .' He touched her shoulder. 'Look – friends?' He looked into her eyes and saw with dismay that there were tears in their sea-green depths.

She shook her head. 'Of course we're friends, Simon. Please, let's both forget what we said.'

'You mustn't take any notice of me, you know. I'm always putting my foot in it. I was famous for it at college.' He smiled. 'Next time just tell me to take a running jump, eh?'

She smiled ruefully. 'I'll try and remember. But I'll try not to do it when you're standing close to the edge of a cliff.'

He laughed, yet something in her voice made him wonder if her words had a deeper meaning.

In late-May Gerald was due to make another trip to Edinburgh to see the professor. He wanted to get it over with before the first of the weekend seminars, which would start in June. Simon had arranged to pay his mother a visit while he was away and Cathy quite looked forward to having the house to herself for a few days. She had given Maggie some time off so that she could be with her children for half-term. On impulse she had telephoned Johnny to ask if she would like to come and stay with her during Gerald's absence, only to learn that old Mrs Bains had been taken to hospital the previous day following a slight stroke, making it impossible for Johnny to leave London.

312

Gerald left for Scotland by the early train on Wednesday morning. Simon drove them in to Ipswich station, then drove Cathy back to Melfordleigh afterwards. He was due to leave himself later in the day.

At Cuckoo Lodge the house seemed strangely silent and peaceful. Cathy wandered through the rooms, breathing in the peace and quiet. It was strange how much more relaxed she felt with Gerald gone. Even though she saw little of him there was always a tension about the place when he was there.

In the small studio she ran her hands over the keys of her father's piano. It was ages since she'd played. Both studios were usually in use, and besides, she didn't like anyone to hear her. The standard Gerald demanded from all his students was so high that it inhibited her, especially after the cruel remark he had made about her father's playing.

After a few scales to loosen up she began to play a Brahms waltz she had learned as a child. She was very rusty but with no one to hear her she felt relaxed. It was only as the music uncoiled her taut nerves that she realised how tense she had grown over the past months.

As she came to the end the sound of clapping made her turn, startled, towards the doorway.

'What a dark horse you are. I didn't even know you could play!' Simon was leaning in the open doorway, his arms folded.

'Oh! I thought you were upstairs, finishing your packing.' She laughed self-consciously. 'I *don't* play. Not really anyway. Surely you can hear that. My father was a pianist and he used to give me lessons, but neither of us ever pretended I was another Eileen Joyce.'

He wandered into the studio in his casual way and leaned on the piano. 'You're what they call a competent player, I think.'

'Yes.' She smiled wryly. 'That about sums it up. No sparkle. No talent. If I'd lived fifty years ago I'd have

313

taught reluctant school-children to play *The Merry Peasant* and played the harmonium in chapel on Sundays.'

'No you're putting yourself down,' he said. 'Seriously, I'm surprised Gerald hasn't taken you under his wing.'

'Gerald took me *under his wing* as you call it some time ago. Now he has better things to do.' She hadn't meant it to sound bitter, but that was the way it came out. Catching the now familiar note in her voice he leaned forward to look at her for a moment. She felt his eyes searching her face and blushed crimson. Then, as he opened his mouth to say something, the telephone rang.

'Don't move. I'll get it.' He hurried into the hall, closing the studio door behind him. Cathy began to play again, but it was no use, the moment had gone. Her fingers faltered, hitting the wrong notes. She felt inhibited and self-conscious. Maybe when Simon had left and there was no one to hear she could *hammer*, as Gerald called it, to her heart's content. She closed the piano lid regretfully and stood up just as he came back into the room.

'That was my mother,' he told her. 'It seems that she has to go away on one of her research jobs. Short notice. So it looks as though my visit home is off.'

She turned to look at him. 'Oh, Simon, I'm sorry. You must be disappointed.'

He shrugged. 'A bit, I suppose, but it can't be helped.'

'It was such a good chance for you to go home though. Gerald gives you so little time to yourself.' Her face brightened. 'I know. Why don't you ask her to come here one weekend? I'm sure she'd enjoy the concerts, and you could take her out to look at the countryside.'

'You wouldn't mind?'

'Of course not.'

'That's very kind. We'll have to think about that.' He paused, looking at her. 'The immediate problem is, Cathy, what do I do with myself for the next three days?'

She frowned. 'Why – stay here, I suppose.'

He smiled. 'You don't think the locals would gossip? It's a tricky situation with Gerald away, isn't it?'

'I don't see why anyone should object. If it comes to that, how would they know? As for me, I'll be cooking for myself. Might as well cook enough for two. You could work – practise – feel free to use the studio – anything you like.' She laughed. 'Heaven knows the place is big enough.'

'Well, if you're sure . . .'

'I am, of course – unless there's something else you have in mind?'

He looked at her, wondering for one crazy moment if she could read the mad fantasy that was in his mind. She wore a faded blue cotton dress and sandals. Her arms and legs were bare and her bright hair was carelessly tied back in a ponytail. And she clearly hadn't the faintest idea of how desirable she was. For a moment he wondered how it would feel to pull the ribbon from her hair and see it cascade about her shoulders; to take her in his arms and kiss that tremulous mouth till it was bruised and tender; to see his own desire reflected in the fathomless green eyes. To . . .

'No,' he said with a casual lift of his shoulders. 'I'm completely at a loose end.'

She prepared a casserole for dinner, then went out to the mill stream with an apron full of bread and kitchen scraps with which to feed the ducks. They had recently hatched a new brood of adorable ducklings and as she watched them dive and squabble over the scraps she remembered the first time she and Gerald had come to look at Cuckoo Lodge. She had fallen in love with the place even then, in its wild, neglected state. She'd had such hopes – such dreams – about their future here. What had gone wrong with it all? What she had visualised as their home had become something close to a prison. And in so short a time. It had to be her fault. If only she knew how to put things right.

'Greedy little devils, aren't they?' She turned and found

Simon leaning against a nearby willow tree. Suddenly she felt annoyed with him for intruding on her thoughts. Although she refused to admit it to herself, being in close proximity to him made her feel vulnerable and defenceless.

'Every time I turn round you seem to be behind me,' she said, her cheeks pink.

'Sorry! If I'd known you wanted to be alone . . .' He began to walk away and immediately regretting her hasty words, she called out to him.

'No! Simon, come back. I didn't mean . . .'

'Look, if my being here is going to cause you any trouble I can always book into the pub,' he said. 'I thought you seemed quite happy about my staying.'

'I did. I *am*! It's just that I was deep in thought and you made me jump.'

'Deep in thought?' He looked at her. 'Anything you want to share?'

She brushed the crumbs from her hands and smoothed her apron. 'Not really. I was just thinking about – I don't know – silly girlish dreams that don't come true and – you know – things that might have been.'

'Sounds intriguing – and rather wistful.' He smiled, reaching out to take her hand. 'Look, why don't I come and help you in the kitchen? I don't see why you should wait on me. Besides, you might be surprised to find I'm really quite house trained.' He fell into step beside her as she headed back to the house. 'Then maybe you can tell me all about these broken dreams of yours over dinner.'

They ate at the kitchen table, then went to sit in the drawing room. There was a chill to the spring evening air and Cathy put a match to the fire that Maggie had left laid in the grate. Pulling a cushion from one of the chairs, she sat with her back against the settee, her arms linked about her knees as she gazed into the flames.

'When I was little my dad and I used to look for pictures in the fire,' she said.

'You miss him, don't you?'

She nodded. 'He died so young. And so unexpectedly.'

'I never knew my father,' he told her. 'But there have always been lots of photographs and letters from him. My mother and grandmother always tried to keep his memory alive for me.'

She smiled up at him. 'That's nice.'

'So – how did you come to meet Gerald?' he asked, holding his breath against another rebuff.

'He was my father's best friend. They were at college together. Before Dad died he made Gerald my legal guardian.'

So that was it? Simon gave a long, low whistle. 'And you and he fell in love? How romantic.'

'Yes. I suppose it was.'

Into the silence that followed he asked quietly, 'Was? You said *was*. Has the romance faded so soon?'

She sighed. 'You know what Gerald is like. He's very preoccupied with his work. He's finding it hard to adjust to giving up his concert work.'

'Why did he? Give it all up, I mean.'

'He developed a muscular problem. You must have noticed the stiffness in his fingers.'

'Yes. The trembling too. I thought . . .' He looked at her, busy with thoughts and speculations of his own. 'What are you going to do, Cathy?'

She looked at him, her eyes wide with surprise. 'Do?'

'Let's face it. There isn't much of a future for you here. You should at least be looking for a job; a satisfying career to make a life for yourself.'

She turned to look into the fire again. 'I thought I was going to do the administrative work for the school, but Gerald has handed all that over to Mrs French. And an agency in London is handling the bookings for the seminars.'

'Isn't there anything else you want to do?'

317

She shrugged. 'I was at college, studying Home Economics, but we got married before I could qualify.'

'Then why don't you go back and pick up where you left off?'

'I can't. The nearest college is twenty miles away and you know what the public transport is like here.'

'Learn to drive,' he urged. 'I'll teach you if you like.'

She looked uncertain. 'I don't know what Gerald would say.'

'Blow Gerald!' he said vehemently. 'You're entitled to a life. This place is like a morgue. I put up with it because I'll be out of it soon. Besides, I'm enjoying the work. For me it's time well spent, but if I thought I had to stay here for the rest of my life I'd go stark raving mad!'

'Well – that's you,' she said, thrusting out her chin stubbornly. 'Luckily we're not all the same.'

'Face it. You're no different from me, Cathy.' He slid on to the floor beside her. 'You're young and full of vitality. Or you should be at your age. Since I've been here I've watched all the life draining out of you. If you don't start living soon you'll be old before your time.'

She turned her head away from his intense stare. She found his eyes and his closeness even more disturbing now. When she spoke her voice trembled. 'I don't remember asking you for your opinion, Simon,' she said. 'I think you've got a cheek, telling me what I should do with my life.'

His hand reached out and closed around her arm. 'Oh, come on, Cathy. You don't really believe that. I'm only telling you what I think because I *care*. It's a damned awful waste, a lovely girl like you stuck in a Godforsaken hole with a man who doesn't give a damn about you.'

'Who says he doesn't give a damn?' Her cheeks flamed with hot colour, her eyes blazing with anger.

'I do! He snaps at you all the time – takes you for granted. What's more he doesn't care who knows it! He doesn't even *look* at you.' She made to pull away, but his grasp tightened on her arm. 'Running away isn't going to make it any the less true,' he said insistently. 'Be honest – with yourself if not with me. When did he last tell you you were beautiful, eh? When did he last make love to you, Cathy? Can you even remember?'

'How dare you ask questions like that?' She wrenched her arm out of his grasp. She was trembling now. Her own feelings terrifying her, making her defensive. 'Those things are private – secret things between two married people. It's none of your business. How *dare* you?' She scrambled to her feet but he quickly rose to face her, grasping her shoulders.

'Look, we've got to know each other over the past few months, Cathy. I've watched you growing more and more miserable. You're not going to deny that, are you? I don't care what you think of me, but I do care that you're throwing yourself away. Chuck me out if you like. I'll be gone from here soon anyway. Tell me to go to hell. But for God's sake *do* something about your life. Start living before you turn into a cabbage!'

For a moment she stared at him, her eyes wide and her lips trembling. He had just summed up what she'd been trying to suppress for the past months. He had dragged it ruthlessly out into the open and forced her to look at it face to face. She hated what she saw – and hated him for making her see it. But although she tried to break free from his strong grip, his hands held on to her relentlessly.

'Look at me, Cathy.' He bent to look into her eyes. 'Admit it. It's true, isn't it?'

319

Slowly she raised her face to him. It was no use trying to deny that everything he said was true. If she could just make him understand the way it had been. 'I loved him so much,' she whispered. 'I thought he loved me too. I *think* he still does – in his way. I suppose I never thought about what I needed. I never looked beyond the man – beyond Gerald himself. I just thought we'd come here, love each other and live a happy life together for the rest of our days. I saw us running the school and the seminars and concerts – as partners. To me, marriage meant belonging to each other, doing everything together, being in love – for ever.' She looked at him imploringly. 'But he does need me, Simon. He needs me – doesn't he?'

'Maybe. To look after him when he's too ill to work? To go on running things here when he's unable to carry on himself? But is that fair, Cathy? Is it what you expected – what you *want*?'

She turned away. 'I don't want to talk about it any more, Simon. It really isn't any of your business and you're making me feel disloyal. Oh, I know you mean to be kind and I appreciate . . .'

'Kind, my foot!' He grasped her arm, refusing to let her go. 'You're burying your head in the sand. You're young, with a young woman's rights and needs. Why should you . . .?'

'*Stop it!* That's enough!' She shook her head. 'Oh – I wish you'd gone home now. I wish . . .' Her sentence was cut short as he pulled her roughly to him and held her fast. His mouth came down on hers. For a moment she was stunned – unable to believe what was happening. She fought him, her fists drumming against his chest. But his arms held her as firmly as bands of steel and his lips crushed her mouth, cutting off her breath.

320

In spite of her struggles he refused to release her and slowly her fear and anger died, to be replaced by a traitorous excitement that erupted within her like fire. She felt the heat of it sear through her veins, dizzying her brain till her head swam and her knees buckled. Sensing her surrender, the lips that had been so hard and persistent became soft and persuasive, moving sensuously against hers, parting them gently till she heard her own small murmur of assent. Tonight she had been forced to admit so many things she had been trying to deny. Now she acknowledged that one of them was her growing attraction to Simon. For months she had felt drawn to him. He was everything that Gerald wasn't; warm and attentive – young and vitally *alive*. She hated herself for the disloyal thoughts and for the shaming desire that spread through her every nerve like an ignited fuse, but she could stop it no more than she could turn back the tide.

One hand slid down her spine to press her thighs closer to him whilst with the other he began to unbutton her dress. She shivered at the electrifying touch of his hands on her flesh. She knew that she should call a halt now – before it was too late – before things got out of hand. But the blood was pounding in her head and her heart drummed so loudly that she knew he must feel it, just as she could feel his arousal in every tensed muscle, every magnetic beat of his heart. *She wanted him*. There was no denying it. She wanted him more than she had wanted anything for a long time.

She let her head fall back as he slipped her dress from her shoulders and cupped her breasts, his voice thick with longing as he murmured, 'Oh, Cathy, Cathy, you're so lovely – so beautiful!'

In her mind she remembered the nights she had lain awake, waiting and longing for Gerald to come up to their room. The nights she had fallen asleep only to wake to a cold, empty bed next morning.

Together they sank to their knees. Simon pulled the

cushions from the settee and pressed her gently back on to them, then he was beside her, his passion growing as he kissed and caressed every inch of her as reverently as if she were something infinitely precious. Even on that wonderful evening when Gerald had taken her for the first time she had known nothing as headily intoxicating as this. And when at last he imprisoned her beneath him and slipped inside her, his breath warm against her ear as he whispered her name, she thought she would die of pure ecstasy.

Simon was an accomplished lover, bringing her to a feverish climax before surrendering himself. She must have fallen asleep almost instantly, and when she wakened to find her head pillowed on his chest she thought at first that she must be dreaming. Then slowly the reality of what had happened came back. She sat up. The fire was just a pile of cold grey ashes and she could see through the uncurtained window that dawn was already silvering the sky. Simon still slept, limbs spread with an almost childlike abandon over the scattered cushions. His naked body was half-covered by the rug from the settee that he had pulled over them. Very gently she drew it up over him, then gathering up the clothes that lay strewn about the floor, she padded out of the room.

In the kitchen she stood looking out across the dewy garden, shivering a little in the morning chill. But although she was cold her body still tingled with awareness. For the first time in months she felt vibrantly alive. The memory of their recklessly abandoned lovemaking stirred her, quickening her heart afresh. She closed her arms around herself as though to capture the feeling. But she could not silence the accusing word that echoed constantly in her head.

Adultery.

There was no escaping the fact. That was what she had committed. She had been married less than two years and she had slept with another man. What was even more despicable, she had done it while her husband was visiting hospital.

What would her father have thought of her disloyalty, her betrayal? What would Johnny say – Johnny who had tried so hard to warn her not to marry Gerald. She tried to disentangle her confused thoughts. Put some justification on her actions. but she could find none.

So – what happened now? Could she go on as though nothing had happened – live a lie with Gerald? Surely not? After last night nothing could ever be the same again. She tried to examine her feelings. Was she in love with Simon? Did he love her? If he asked her to leave Gerald and go away with him, could she do it with anything approaching a clear conscience?

She put the kettle on then went upstairs to shower and slipped into a sweater and jeans. When she came down again she found Simon in the kitchen frying bacon and eggs. He had dressed hurriedly in the crumpled clothes he had discarded last night. His hair was still tousled and his face was rough with morning stubble, but he looked cheerful and untroubled, whistling to the radio as he worked. He looked up with a smile as she came in.

'One egg or two?'

'Just coffee for me.' She sat down at the table where Simon joined her with his plate piled high. He looked at her quizzically, rubbing a hand over his jaw.

'What's the matter? Do I look that bad? I'll shave and shower when I've had this.'

'It's not that. You look fine.' She frowned at the portable radio, from which a pop group was belting forth its latest hit. *With love – from me – to you*, it blared. 'Could you switch that off, please?'

He switched off the radio and peered at her. 'What's the matter? You're not regretting last night?'

'I can't help feeling guilty, Simon. Surely you can understand that?'

He reached out to touch her hand. 'Don't regret it, Cathy. And don't feel guilty.' He looked into her eyes. 'It was wonderful, wasn't it – for you as well as me?'

She tried not to meet his eyes but found it impossible. 'Yes, it was. I can't deny that.'

'Why should you want to deny it?' He stood up and pulled her to her feet. 'You *know* it was wonderful. And we have two more whole days to enjoy . . .'

'*No!*' She wrenched herself away from him and walked across to the window as if to put as much space between them as possible. 'It won't happen again, Simon. It *mustn't*. At least, not until we've decided what to do. Perhaps you'd better book yourself a room at the pub this morning after all. I need to think.'

He spread his hands, his expression innocently baffled. 'What is there to think about? What harm can it do if I stay now – after last night?' He crossed the kitchen to where she stood. 'Cathy, look at me.' He turned her to face him. 'We're not hurting anyone. Gerald needn't know if you don't want him to. What happened last night was so good – for both of us. It was no big deal. Just fun – delicious fun. Call it a little diversion.'

'Is that all it is to you?' Appalled, she pushed him away. '*A little diversion!* Is that how little you care for other people's feelings?'

He looked shocked. 'I *do* care about you, Cathy. I'd like to see you happy – enjoying the kind of marriage you deserve, but as you told me, it's none of my business. You feel Gerald needs you and you're determined to stay with him. But you and I can still be friends, can't we? Loving friends? I can give you what he can't. It could be the perfect arrangement.'

She felt her heart freeze into a solid block inside her. 'You're saying that you see me as a disappointed, neglected wife?' She said the words slowly and disbelievingly. 'Just ripe for a fling – someone to amuse yourself with until you go back to your friends and the real world.' She

324

backed away from him, shaking her head. 'No, not me, Simon.' She pushed past him and walked to the door. In the doorway she turned. 'Ring the Admiral Nelson now and book yourself a room. I want you to be out of here before I come downstairs again.'

He hurried into the hall after her. 'Cathy . . .' She paused halfway up the stairs to look down at him. The sudden sharpness of his voice captured her attention. 'Cathy – look, Gerald knew damned well that we'd find each other irresistible before long. He's been *throwing* us together. Don't you see that? I believe he meant this to happen. He knows he can't keep you happy and he doesn't mind someone else doing it for him. So there's nothing for you to feel guilty about.'

'That's a *revolting* thing to say!' She ran up the rest of the stairs and went to her bedroom, closing the door and turning the key in the lock. She must put what had happened behind her. Try to forget it. Try to forgive herself and live with the guilt.

Gerald came home from Edinburgh in good spirits. That evening Simon asked him if he could borrow the car, saying that he had to go into Ipswich for the evening. Over dinner Gerald told Cathy about his visit to the consultant.

'There's a surgeon in New Zealand, a colleague of the Professor, who has perfected a procedure that cures this problem of mine,' he told her excitedly. 'No one here is doing it yet, but apparently this man has effected several near miracles. Some patients who were in wheelchairs have been able to walk after the operation.'

Cathy said nothing, but she remembered his claim that his condition would get no worse as long as he took his medication regularly. Obviously he had lied to her about it.

'They're sending my case notes over,' Gerald went on. 'When he's had a chance to study them he'll know whether I can benefit from the operation.'

'When would it be?'

'Probably not till the autumn, which would suit me fine,' he said. 'It will give me time to get this first important season over and assess the results.'

She noticed that he no longer made a pretence of including her when he referred to the business of the school. 'That's good news,' she said. 'Does it mean a complete cure?'

'Apparently. It's a painless operation done under a local anaesthetic, to kill off a tiny portion of the brain that has become over-active.'

She stared at him. 'It sounds horribly dangerous! Are you sure it's all right?'

He laughed. 'Of course I am. It's just a few tiny cells. They're hoping that in time it will be routine everywhere, but for now New Zealand is the place one can get it done!' He reached out to touch her hand. 'Poor Cathy. You haven't had a very nice time since we've been here, have you? I know I don't always treat you as I should, but I have been under a lot of pressure. Once this first season is over, and if this op is a complete success, things should be very different for us. I'll make it up to you, I promise.'

She smiled. 'I know. I hope it all works out, Gerald.'

He stroked her cheek with one finger. 'I might even be able to go back to the concert platform. We might be able to sell up here and go back to London. Who knows?'

'That would be wonderful – if it's what you want.'

'Just think, life could be as it was before. Parties, lots of friends dropping in all the time. You'd like that, wouldn't you?'

She simply nodded. Surely he knew that all she wanted was for things to be as they were before. And he made no mention of the baby she longed for or the close togetherness she missed so much. But if there was a chance he might be completely cured she had to be glad for his sake.

* * *

The first season of weekend seminars and concerts was a great success. In response to the advertising campaign handled by the agency, young musicians from all over the country converged on Melfordleigh by the dozen. Those that couldn't be put up at Cuckoo Lodge found rooms at the Admiral Nelson and in the smaller hotels and guesthouses. The local hoteliers were delighted with the business the school brought them. The house and the barn concert hall rang with music from morning till late at night and in between sessions Gerald 'held court' with young hopefuls who were planning concert careers.

Gerald's agent came down and, after hearing Simon play, signed him up for a concert tour to begin in the autumn. Everyone was busy, enjoying the non-stop activity, and looking round the village. They spilled out into the street and on to the quay, laughing and talking in enthusiastic groups. The only person left out of it all was Cathy. It seemed she had no part in any of it. She worked along with Maggie in the kitchen and helped the extra cleaners they had engaged, but never once did Gerald introduce her as his wife or invite her to play hostess.

In late July he received a letter from the consultant in Edinburgh. Having studied his notes and read the consultant's prognosis Professor Harbage felt that there was a very good chance of the operation being completely successful in his case. He suggested a date in late-November for Gerald's admission to his private clinic in Auckland.

Gerald read the letter to Cathy at the breakfast table.

'It's warm in New Zealand in November, isn't it?' she asked. 'I'll have to remember to pack summer clothes for us both.'

He shook his head. 'There's no need for me to drag you all that way too.'

She looked up at him in surprise. 'But I'd like to come. I've always wanted to see New Zealand and besides, you'll need someone – need me, won't you?'

He smiled and shook his head. 'I'll be fine. I'll need you to be here, looking after the house.'

'We could close up, couldn't we? Simon will have gone off on his tour and the concerts will have finished.'

'There's next year to think about.'

'But I never *do* anything, Gerald,' she insisted. 'You've made sure of that. Other people do all the organising and booking.'

A frown of irritation crossed his brow. 'I can't think why you're complaining. Some wives would give anything to have all the work taken off their shoulders,' he said tetchily. 'If you want the truth, Cathy, we can't really afford for both of us to go. The air fare isn't cheap, you know, let alone hotel bills and so on. The operation will be costly too. It's going to take every penny I've made this season and more besides.'

'I see.' She stood up and began to clear the table. 'Why didn't you say so? You never confide our financial situation to me, do you? So how would I know?'

But the hurt and disappointment of Gerald's apparent rejection was eclipsed by a growing anxiety that refused to go away. For some weeks now Cathy had been trying to ignore the nagging suspicion that she might be pregnant. At first she hadn't taken too much notice. Last time Gerald had assured her that it was due to a change in her lifestyle and when she missed her period she thought that the trauma of her brief affair with Simon must be responsible. But now, after ten weeks, she could ignore the situation no longer. Besides, there were other tell-tale signs. She had been feeling sick in the early mornings and the sight and odour of certain foods made her nauseous.

Whilst one part of her was filled with joyful excitement at the prospect of the baby she had longed for, she was frantic with worry. Gerald would know for sure that the child could not be his. It was months since they had made love. And she knew instinctively that Simon would want nothing to do with it. There seemed little point in telling him anyway. Ever since she had discovered that he was simply amusing himself with her she had avoided him as much as possible.

At last even Gerald began to notice that something was wrong. Looking at her across the breakfast table one morning as she picked at a slice of toast and sipped her half-cold coffee he noticed that she looked unwell. The crop of summer freckles stood out sharply against her pallid skin and her normally bright eyes were dull with anxiety.

'Why don't you go and stay with the Johnsons for a few days?' he said suddenly. Cathy looked up in surprise. 'You've been looking peaky for a couple of weeks,' he went on. 'Maybe a break will do you good.'

The thought of seeing Johnny and sleeping in her old room filled her with nostalgia. 'Oh, Gerald. That would be lovely,' she said. 'I'd love to go.'

'Ring her this morning and lay it on then,' he said. 'Stay as long as you want.'

When she heard Johnny's voice at the other end of the line Cathy's throat tightened so much that she could scarcely speak.

'Hello, Johnny. It's me – Cathy.'

'Cathy! What a lovely surprise! What can I do for you?'

'Can I come and see you, just for a few days?'

'Of course you can. Stay for as long as you like, dear. It'll be lovely to have you. Your old room is always ready for you. You know that.'

'It's not too much trouble?'

'Bless you, no. Matthew's gone up to Bradford on a six-month course and Mother is in a nursing home. I felt bad about letting her go but I couldn't manage her at home

329

any longer. I miss her though, Cathy. I miss you all. It'll be wonderful to have you back.'

Sitting in the train Cathy went over and over what she could say. She had never needed Johnny's advice as desperately as she did now, yet how could she tell her about Simon and the shameful mistake she had made? It was out of the question. Johnny had always had such high moral standards. She would feel so shocked and let down.

The little house in Chestnut Grove was just as she had left it. It seemed smaller and shabbier, but infinitely comfortable and dear. Cathy's old room was spick and span, the bed made up with Johnny's best linen sheets, and the bedspread and curtains freshly laundered. She unpacked and went downstairs to her favourite meal of roast ham with potatoes and broad beans from the garden. Johnny kept eyeing her closely as she ate, and over Cathy's favourite treacle pudding she asked, 'Are you all right? You're not looking very well, dear.'

'We've been so busy,' Cathy said, avoiding her eye. 'Run off our feet with the concerts and everything. It's been a great success. Gerald is so pleased.' She looked up. 'I didn't tell you. He is going to New Zealand in November. There's a surgeon there who has perfected an operation to cure his muscular problem.'

'That's good news. Are you going with him?'

'No.' Cathy looked down at her plate again. 'It's going to be very expensive, you see. The operation will have to be private, of course, and then there will be hotel bills and a lot more besides. We couldn't afford for both of us to go.'

'I see. Then perhaps you could come and stay here while he's away?'

'Oh, Johnny, that would be lovely!' Cathy paused. She had forgotten that by November she would be six months pregnant. There would be no hiding her condition from

330

anyone by then. 'I'd love to come, of course. But I think Gerald wants me to stay at Melfordleigh and look after the house,' she added.

'Then maybe I could come and stay with you instead,' Johnny suggested cheerfully. 'I could spare a few days. Mother hardly recognises me when I go to the nursing home these days and Matthew will still be away. I could easily take a week or so off.'

Cathy flushed, searching her mind frantically for an excuse. 'Yes – that would be nice.' Suddenly she wished she hadn't come. Johnny was so perceptive. She'd already sensed that something was wrong. How would it be possible to keep the truth from her for two whole weeks?

Johnny had arranged to visit Mrs Bains in the nursing home the following day and Cathy was relieved when it was suggested that she take herself Up West on a shopping trip.

'Mother probably won't know you. Her memory is very erratic,' Johnny explained. 'She can sometimes be rather difficult – she gets strange ideas about people she doesn't know. Better for you to remember her as she was.'

They caught the bus together, Cathy alighting at Edgware tube station and catching a train for Oxford Circus. It was nice to be in London again. She wandered along Regent Street, stopping for a cup of coffee in a new coffee bar, then she looked round Liberty's, admiring the exotic jewellery and exquisite materials on display. She was looking at the latest autumn fashions in the window of Dickens and Jones an hour later and thinking about lunch when a voice called her name.

'Cathy! Of all the people to run into!' She turned, startled, to see Carla Maybridge standing behind her. 'I'd have known that red hair anywhere!' The other girl hugged her warmly. 'How *are* you? And how is married life?'

331

'I'm fine, thanks. How are you? You're looking wonderful.'

In actual fact if Carla hadn't seen her first Cathy would probably have walked right past her. The young woman standing before her was a very different Carla from the one she had known two years ago. She had grown her hair long and wore it straight and smooth. The red and black dress she wore was of the latest fashion; it was very short with a geometric pattern. And all her accessories were of expensive-looking cream leather: shoulder bag, gloves, and tight-fitting knee-high boots.

Carla took her arm. 'This is really wonderful. Come and have lunch with me.' She glanced around. 'You are on your own, aren't you?'

'Yes. I've come up to spend a few days with Johnny.'

'Then we must have lunch and a lovely long gossip. I can't wait to hear all about what you and that devastatingly handsome husband of yours have been up to!'

Carla took her arm and dragged her into Dickens and Jones. 'I'm working here,' she explained as she bundled Cathy on to the escalator. 'I model for an agency, modelling outfits in the restaurant. There are four of us and I'm taking my lunch break at the moment.'

'What happened to the A level course and the career in teaching?' Cathy asked as they went up in the lift.

Carla laughed. 'You've got to be joking! The sixth form was the living end. All those rotten little swots with their spotty noses to the grindstone. I couldn't stick the thought of two years of that. I threw the towel in after the first term and managed to get into the modelling school.'

In the top-floor restaurant someone was playing soft romantic music on a white grand piano. They were shown to a table by the window.

'You look as though you've done well,' Cathy said as they settled themselves.

'Not bad.' Carla grinned the old familiar grin and held

out her arms. 'Like the outfit? It's by Mary Quant. She's an absolutely great new designer. Everyone is going to be wearing her clothes soon.'

'What did your parents think of you giving up the A levels?'

Carla pulled a face. 'What do you think? You know Dad, even teaching came a poor second to the bank! But I don't live at home any more. It always was so crowded. Well, you must remember. And as we all grew older it was worse. No privacy anywhere. I got myself a little flat in Fulham – sharing with two other girls. It's no palace but we do each have our own space.' She grinned. 'We have fun too.'

Cathy felt a sharp pang of envy for the happy-go-lucky life Carla clearly led. 'And you like modelling?' she asked.

'Love it. At least there's variety to the work and you get to meet some interesting people.'

They ordered the sole, which the waitress recommended. Carla leaned back in her chair and took a long, critical look at her friend. 'If you don't mind my saying so you could do with taking in hand, my child,' she said with mock severity. 'You're looking distinctly countrified. Why don't we meet up tomorrow? That's my day off. You can get that husband of yours to treat you to some new outfits. There are super new boutiques springing up all over the place in the King's Road. I get a discount at some of them.'

Cathy shook her head. 'I don't think so, thanks, Carla.'

'Why not?' The other girl frowned and leaned towards her. 'What's up, love? You look as though you've got something on your mind.'

Cathy sighed. Carla was her oldest friend. If she didn't confide in someone soon she'd go crazy. 'As a matter of fact – I'm pregnant,' she said softly.

Carla looked at her. 'And you don't want to be, is that it?'

'I *do* want to be. I want a baby very much. But Gerald . . .'

333

'Doesn't?' Carla looked at her, her head on one side. 'He doesn't want anything getting in the way of this new project of his?'

'Something like that.'

'I take it he doesn't know?'

Cathy shook her head miserably. 'No.'

'Surely keeping it from him is unavoidable – unless you're planning to . . .' Carla frowned. 'Look, forgive me if I've got it wrong, Cath, but are you saying that – it isn't his?' When Cathy didn't reply she shook her head. 'God! Poor you. What a mess! How on earth did you get into it, Cath? I mean – an affair is one thing, but . . .' She bit her lip. 'I suppose there's no chance you're wrong?'

'None at all.'

'Well – is there any chance it might actually *be* Gerald's?' When Cathy shook her head again she reached out and touched her wrist. 'Oh, please don't look like that, love. It's not the end of the world.'

'It feels a lot like it,' Cathy said unhappily.

Carla bit her lip. 'Look, I think I might be able to help. How far are you?'

'I don't know. Ten or eleven weeks.'

Carla drew in her breath sharply. 'You're running it a bit fine. Why didn't you do something about it before?'

'I – thought it might be a mistake. That it might all come right. Anyway, I didn't know if there was anything I *could* do.'

Carla looked at her pityingly. 'You always were the naive one when it came to sex, weren't you?'

Their food arrived, but Cathy pushed hers round the plate disconsolately.

'Look – I know of this doctor,' Carla said quietly. 'He's been struck off as a matter of fact, but he's good. One of my flat-mates had a panic like yours a few months ago. He fixed it for her and she was fine. I can get his phone number for you if you like.'

Cathy swallowed hard. 'An *abortion* you mean?' she whispered, her eyes round. 'I *couldn't*, Carla. The idea of it makes me feel sick.'

She shrugged. 'Okay, so what's the alternative? What about this chap – the father? Would he want you to have it?'

'No! I don't want him to know either.'

'You don't love him then?'

'*No!* The whole thing was madness. It should never have happened.'

'Mmm.' Carla smiled wryly. 'Famous last words!' She sighed. 'Well if you change your mind, give me a ring and let me know.' She scribbled her number on a scrap of paper and passed it to Cathy. 'You needn't worry. I can guarantee you'd be safe enough with this doctor. It's not like having it done by some old crone in a back street with a crochet hook. Think about it.' She looked at her watch. 'God! Look at the time. I'll have to fly. Give me the bill. My treat. I'll settle it on my way out.' She patted Cathy's shoulder. 'And cheer up, love. It might never happen. It *won't* if you take my advice.'

Cathy lay awake all that night, thinking about Carla's suggestion. More than anything in the world she longed to have the baby she carried. To give it birth, love it and hold it in her arms. But she had to acknowledge that it was a vain hope. Going through with it was out of the question. She told herself she was being punished for the wrong she had done. But far worse than the fear and the pain of the ordeal she must suffer was the heartache of sacrificing her child.

She tried to comfort herself with the thought that when Gerald was cured perhaps things would be as they were before between them. Then perhaps they would have another child and she could put all this behind her. At least now she was offered a way out. It seemed like providence that she had met Carla today. Perhaps meeting her like that was a sign that she was meant to take her advice.

She rang Carla the following evening while Johnny was making the bedtime cocoa. Next morning she went out to a phone box and rang the doctor's number. A receptionist told her in a brisk, impersonal voice that she could come the day after tomorrow, at two-thirty. She was told the fee for the 'consultation and treatment' which she must pay in cash on the day of her visit. She was given an address in Islington and asked to try to arrive on time.

She arrived early. She had told Johnny she was going to visit a married school friend and might be away till late evening. She had no idea how long the 'treatment' might take. She found the house easily, a crumbling Victorian town house with peeling paintwork and an air of faded respectability. The doctor occupied rooms in the basement, reached by winding steps. A sharp-faced nurse ushered her into a room with fawn wallpaper and uncomfortable chairs upholstered in chipped brown leather. And there she sat, her heart thudding dully in her breast and her stomach churning as though awaiting execution.

When she was shown into the surgery she was reassured by the powerful smell of Dettol and the fact that every-thing appeared to be clinically clean. The doctor was a tired-looking man with stooped shoulders and pale blue eyes behind gold-rimmed spectacles. He enquired about her health and her circumstances – whether there was any chance she might change her mind. But his questions sounded as though they were part of a routine that he had waded wearily through a thousand times before. He reminded her of the risk she was taking and warned her that any complaint she might make would involve her in criminal proceedings too.

The procedure was done surprisingly quickly. She gritted her teeth and submitted to the discomfort and the indignity, eagerly breathing in the gas and air from the mask the nurse held for her. When the doctor had left, the woman helped

336

her down from the table. She gave her some painkillers and a packet of extra thick pads, telling her to expect to bleed heavily for a few days. Then she took the money that Cathy had withdrawn that morning and ushered her out into the street. It was over.

She walked slowly back to the main road feeling cold and stunned as the afternoon traffic thundered by. She reminded herself that it was all over. She wasn't pregnant any more. But try as she would she could not see it as a reprieve. All she could think of was that she had just paid a stranger to kill her child.

She woke in the small hours, the pain gripping her like an iron band. Pulling her knees up to her chest she stuffed a clenched fist into her mouth to stop herself from crying out. As the pain slowly released her she felt the wetness flowing from her. Getting out of bed carefully she went into the bathroom and took two of the tablets the nurse had given her, washing them down with water from her tooth glass. She changed her nightdress and pad and was about to go back to bed when another spasm of violent pain gripped her. This time it was so agonising that she was unable to stop herself from crying out. With one hand against the wall she sank to her knees in the bathroom doorway, both hands clutching her stomach.

Johnny's bedroom door opened and the landing light snapped on. 'Cathy! My dear child!' The shocked face looked down at her. 'Whatever is the matter?'

Johnny helped her back to bed and stood looking down at the white-faced girl anxiously. 'Cathy,' she said gently, 'I believe you're having a miscarriage, dear.' Cathy nodded, her teeth clamped over her lower lip. 'I had my suspicions that you were pregnant when you first arrived,' Johnny went on. 'I think I'd better telephone for a doctor to come and see you. You seem to be losing an awful lot of blood.'

337

'*No!*' Cathy half rose on the bed and grasped Johnny's arm convulsively. 'I'll be all right. I don't want a doctor. *Please*, Johnny!'

The older woman frowned and looked at her doubtfully. 'It would be best, really. A doctor would give you something to help the pain and stop you from haemorrhaging. It could be dangerous, you know. and you might lose your baby – if you haven't already.'

'No – no. I'll be all right – really I will.'

Johnny stood hesitantly in the doorway. 'Shall I send for Gerald then?'

'*No!* Gerald doesn't know – he mustn't. Please do as I say, Johnny.'

'Oh, Cathy.' With a sigh, the older woman sat down on the end of the bed. 'What have you done? Have you been to someone? Have you had this miscarriage induced?'

When Cathy nodded and began to sob Johnny made up her mind. Getting to her feet she worked rapidly. Fetching an armful of Matthew's heavy encyclopaedias from his room she raised the foot of Cathy's bed on the books, then went to the airing cupboard on the landing, returning with a pile of sheets which she proceeded to tear up. As she worked she looked down at Cathy, her mouth set in a grim line.

'I wish I knew who did this to you,' she said. 'And why you felt driven to do it too, but I don't suppose you're going to answer either of those questions.' She drew up a chair and took Cathy's hand. 'Time for talking later. We're in for a long night, child. And I'm warning you now – if the bleeding hasn't eased up by daylight, you're going to hospital whether you like it or not. I'm not having this on my conscience.'

By dawn the worst seemed to be over. As the sun came up Johnny drew back the curtains and went downstairs to make tea, which Cathy drank thirstily, propped up against

338

the pillows, her face grey against their whiteness. Johnny regarded her as she drank.

'Are you going to tell me about it now? I don't want to press you, Cathy, but I really do think you owe me an explanation.'

'I know. And I'll never be able to repay you, Johnny,' she said wearily. 'I'm really sorry to have put you in this awful situation. I wasn't prepared for what happened last night. I thought when I left the – the place where it was done that it was all over.'

'I'd like to get hold of the person who did it,' Johnny said grimly. 'Are you sure everything was properly sterilised? It could be so dangerous.'

'Yes – yes. It's all right, Johnny, I promise.'

'*Why* though?' Johnny looked at her so directly that she could hardly bear to meet the candid eyes. 'Why did you do it? You told me only last summer how much you wanted a baby. So why?'

Bit by bit it all came out; Gerald's moodiness, his refusal to include her in the running of the school, his cold indifference to her physically. Finally the relationship that had sprung up between her and Simon and the fatal night they had spent alone together last May.

'He said Gerald had *meant* it to happen, Johnny,' she said as the tears began to flow. 'He said he'd thrown us together on purpose; that it could be the perfect arrangement. It made me feel so guilty and so – so cheap. I've let you and everyone else down, haven't I?'

Overwhelmed with anger and compassion, Johnny put her arms round the girl and held her close. 'You haven't let anyone down, Cathy love. You've been the victim of two selfish men. I'd like to give Gerald Cavelle a piece of my mind. I wish I could keep you here and take care of you. But you're a grown-up married woman now. He is your husband and this is something you'll have to sort out between you, I'm afraid.' She took out her handkerchief

339

and dried Cathy's tears, just as she had done when she was a small child. 'I do know one thing though, my girl,' she said determinedly. 'You're staying here with me until I'm satisfied you're completely well again. That's one thing I *can* do, and I'm having no arguments about that!'

Chapter Seventeen

Rosalind was eating her breakfast in the staff dining room at the Queen's Head when Bill Kendal, the night porter, came through with the mail.

'One for you, gorgeous,' he said cheekily, dropping the long envelope on to the table in front of her. 'Looks official. Brown job with a window. Don't like the looks of that. What you been up to then, eh?'

Rosalind coloured and pushed the envelope into her pocket. 'None of your business,' she said. 'Isn't it time you were off home?'

Bill assumed a wounded, indignant look. 'Well, I don't know! Try to be friendly round here and look where it gets you!' He nudged her. 'If that there's your exam results I shall expect to be treated, so don't you forget it.'

Smiling at his characteristic cheek, Rosalind finished her breakfast and went through to Reception. She didn't want to open her letter with other staff members looking on. Already the butterflies were beginning to churn her stomach. Could it possibly be her exam results? She could think of no other reason to be getting an official-looking letter.

She'd been lucky in getting the job of receptionist at the Queen's Head. When she'd applied for a job after her father's death Mary Phillips, the girl who had been there ever since Rosalind had first come to work as a Saturday girl, had just handed in her notice. To Rosalind's delight, Mrs Gresham, the manageress had offered her the job, and the room that went with it on a trial basis. After the month was out Mrs Gresham offered her the job permanently and suggested she train at the Queen's Head for management.

But she soon found that the life of a trainee-manageress meant that she was often expected to help out in other departments. As she lived on the premises she was constantly on call. She served behind the bar or in the restaurant – even in the kitchen when they were short-staffed, turning her hand to any task that needed doing. She worked long hours and she suspected that in some ways she was being exploited, but she didn't really mind. She liked being busy and the main thing was that she was learning new things all the time. Anyway, there was nothing else to do in the evenings except sit in her spartan little attic room and listen to the radio.

In the tiny office behind the reception desk she opened the envelope and saw at once with a pang of disappointment that it did not contain her exam results. It came from a firm of London solicitors at an address in Conduit Street and was written on their official-looking headed notepaper. It was short and to the point, requesting her to call into their office concerning her father's estate at her earliest convenience. It was signed by someone called Alan Knight, who she saw from the notepaper, was the firm's head clerk. Glancing at the date she noticed with dismay that the letter had been written almost a month ago. Una must have neglected to send it on until now.

Picking up the telephone she dialled the number on the letter and asked to be put through to the man who had signed it.

'Good morning, Miss Blair, Alan Knight speaking.' The voice was pleasant and not at all intimidating.

'I'm terribly sorry, Mr Knight, but I've only just received your letter,' Rosalind said anxiously. 'I've moved, you see, and it's only just been forwarded to me.'

'Don't worry about the delay, Miss Blair,' he laughed. 'Solicitors don't expect things to happen quickly. Now, when would you like to come in and see us?'

342

'Can you give me some idea of what it's all about?' she asked.

'I thought I made that clear in the letter. It's to acquaint you with the terms of your late father's will.'

Rosalind frowned. 'I know, but it says here his *estate*,' she said hesitantly. The word 'estate' puzzled her. It sounded so affluent – completely unlike Ben who, according to Una, had always done extremely well to make his money last from one pay day to the next. 'Are you sure it's me you want?' she asked. 'I wondered if there was a mistake. You see my father didn't have an estate.'

'Estate is just a legal term,' Alan Knight explained gently. 'It means his worldly goods, if you like. Money, property and so on. Shall we say tomorrow afternoon at three, Miss Blair?'

She agreed, dazedly. Her afternoons were free from two till five. 'Yes,' she said, still mystified. 'I'll be there.'

She arrived with ten minutes to spare at the offices of Turner, Turner and Braybrook the following afternoon, but Alan Knight saw her without delay. He was a tall, willowy man with thick grey hair and kindly blue eyes. Offering her a seat, he put on his glasses and opened the file containing her father's will. For Rosalind there was a strange air of unreality about the situation. Making a will seemed so out of character for Ben. She could hardly believe he had actually gone along to a solicitor and done it.

'As the only child of the late Benjamin Arthur Blair you are his sole beneficiary,' the man was saying.

'Oh.' Rosalind looked up at him blankly. 'I see.'

He turned the page. 'I expect you'll be wanting to know just what it is you have inherited?'

She shook her head. 'As far as I know my father had very little to leave,' she said.

'Not a lot of money, I'm afraid, as you've already anticipated,' said Alan Knight, peering at some accompanying documents. 'His bank account at the time of his death stood at one thousand four hundred pounds.' He glanced up at her. 'Not a fortune certainly.' He cleared his throat. 'However, as well as the money, you inherit the property known as Ivy Cottage in the village of Sherwood Magna, Northamptonshire.' He looked up at her again. 'You did know of the existence of the property, I take it?'

Rosalind had flushed a deep crimson. *The cottage!* She'd completely forgotten about the cottage. But surely Freda should have that? It was half hers. She had helped to restore it – put so much work and love into the task and looked forward to living in it with Ben one day. It wasn't fair. 'I – don't understand,' she said. 'The cottage was only half my father's. He bought it along with his – partner.'

Frowning, Alan Knight looked through the papers in front of him. 'No, there is no mistake. Your father's is the only name on the deed of ownership,' he said. 'It was his property. And now it is yours.'

'You mean it was – it was actually paid for?' Rosalind asked incredulously. 'There was no mortgage?'

'No mortgage.' The man smiled. 'Your father was sole owner of the property and now it is yours, Miss Blair. You are a woman of property, you might say.' He smiled indulgently at his little joke as he took a labelled key from the desk drawer. He handed it to her but she shook her head.

'I don't feel right about this,' she said. 'I must get in touch with my father's partner.' Seeing the man's raised eyebrows she explained, 'Dad was a singer, you see. He and his partner, her name is Freda Morton, toured with a double act: "Ben and Benita Blair".'

'Ah . . .' Light dawned on Alan Knight's face. 'This would be the Miss Morton who was with him in Australia. She is aware of the will, Miss Blair. In fact it was she who contacted us on his death. I'm surprised you haven't heard from her yourself.'

Rosalind sighed. Una would have guessed that anything with an Australian postmark would be from Freda and would conveniently have 'forgotten' to forward it. 'I'm afraid not all of my mail has been reaching me,' she said. 'Have you an address for her? Is she still in Australia?'

'No, she is back in this country.' He rose from his chair. 'If you would like to wait a moment I can find her address for you.' He left the office, to return a few moments later with an address neatly written on a slip of paper.

Outside in the street again Rosalind tried hard to come to terms with the news she had just been given. Ben had left her fourteen hundred pounds – *and* the cottage. But she could feel only guilt over Freda who apparently had been left nothing. Thank goodness she was back in England and that she had her address. She must try to put things straight as soon as she could.

It was as she was coming out of Edgware Underground station an hour later that she saw Cathy Cavelle. She hadn't seen Cathy since the day she'd been married, but the girl walking towards her seemed preoccupied and Rosalind hesitated, unsure if she should intrude. They drew level and were about to pass when Cathy suddenly looked up and saw her. Her face lit up in a smile of genuine pleasure.

'Rosalind! How nice to see you. I wondered if we might run into each other while I was here.'

'How are you, Cathy? Are you staying with Mrs Johnson?'

'Yes. I've been here almost a month. I only meant to stay a fortnight, but I haven't been very well and Johnny persuaded me to take an extra couple of weeks. I'm going back tomorrow.'

'I wish I'd known before. I would have rung you. Are you better now?'

Cathy's eyes clouded for a moment. 'Oh, yes, fine now, thanks,' she said dismissively. 'What about you? You must have taken your exams by now. Any results yet?'

'Not yet. Any day. I'm trying not to think about it.' Rosalind looked round. 'Why don't you come and have tea with me? I work at the Queen's Head now. I live in. We could go up to my room. It's not very smart, but I do have a kettle.'

Cathy smiled. 'That would be lovely.'

In the tiny top-floor room with its sloping ceiling Rosalind made tea and took out a tin of biscuits while Cathy sat in her only armchair.

'You left home then?' she observed, looking round at the threadbare carpet and worn furniture.

Rosalind sighed. 'Yes. Mum and I never did get on. I know this isn't very smart, but it's better this way.'

'What will you do about going to college?'

Rosalind handed her a cup of tea and sat down on the end of the bed with her own. 'I'm working here as receptionist and trainee-manageress. If I pass my As they'll let me go to college on a day-release course.'

'Will that be as good as you wanted?'

Rosalind shrugged. 'I think so. I'm getting lots of practical experience here and I'll have the advantage of having held down a real job when I come to apply for a post.'

'Well, I'm sure Mrs Gresham will give you a good reference,' Cathy said. 'If you ask me, she's lucky to have you.'

Rosalind looked more closely at her friend. Cathy looked pale and much thinner than she remembered. She'd mentioned that she'd been ill. Maybe it was something to do with that. 'Is your husband's music school going well?' she asked. 'I expect you're enjoying life in your lovely house by the sea.'

To Rosalind's surprise Cathy's pale cheeks coloured. 'Yes. Everything is fine, thank you.' She bit into her biscuit, her eyes downcast. 'How is your mother?'

'She's well as far as I know. I don't see much of her now that I've left. She went back into the theatre, you know. She has a major part in a musical play. They're trying out for the West End at the moment. Down in Brighton.'

346

'That's good. And your boyfriend?' Cathy asked. 'Stuart, wasn't it? We met him at the party you gave that New Year's Eve.'

Rosalind took a drink of her tea. 'It didn't last,' she said. 'He was busy with his work and me with my studying. It fizzled out. He found someone who had more in common with him.'

'Oh, that's a shame.'

'Maybe it's just as well. I think he was more interested in Una than me. She got Don to put up the money for the show he was involved with, you see. That's how she came to get a part in it.'

'Oh, Rosalind.' Cathy reached out to touch her arm. 'That must have hurt a lot.'

She nodded. 'It hasn't been the best of years for me. My father died a couple of months ago.'

'Oh, I'm so sorry.'

'He was in Australia at the time. Freda, his partner, wrote and told me he'd had a heart attack and I was going out to see him. I was all packed and ready to leave when the cable came to say – he'd died.' She gave a helpless little shrug.

Cathy's heart went out to the other girl. She'd always seemed so lonely ever since school. Now she was all alone. From what she had seen of Una Blake she seemed a selfish, uncaring mother. Even an absent father was better than none at all. 'I know how it feels to lose your father,' she said softly. 'I still miss my own dad.'

'I never saw much of him of course,' Rosalind said. 'Unlike you I never knew my father while I was growing up. It was only much more recently that we grew closer. He wanted me to go to Australia with him, you know. I wish I had now.' She got up to refill the cups. 'As a matter of fact I've just been to see his solicitor. Dad left me all he had – a little money and a lovely cottage in Northamptonshire. I'm still trying to get over the shock.'

Cathy smiled. 'That's nice. It's good that he cared enough to want to provide for you.'

'Yes, but I always thought that he and his partner bought the cottage jointly. I feel guilty that she has been left out. She was much younger than him but I always thought they might get married. I know she wanted to. I'm going to write and suggest that I sell the cottage and share the proceeds with her.'

'Do you think you should? After all, your father obviously wanted you to have it.'

'I must ask her at least,' Rosalind said. 'She was always very kind to me. And I know she loved Dad very much. She might be feeling betrayed that he left her out.'

Cathy smiled. 'Not many people would be as considerate.'

'What about you?' Rosalind asked, anxious to change the subject. 'What have you been doing with your holiday?'

'Not much. I saw Carla one day. Did you know that she's a model now?'

Rosalind smiled. 'No, but it doesn't surprise me. I never did think she was cut out to teach. She opted out of her A level course in the first term.' She looked up. 'You said you'd been ill? Nothing serious, I hope?'

Cathy shook her head. 'No. I think I was a bit rundown. You know how Johnny fusses. And now that her mother is in a nursing home and Matthew is away she has no one to spoil.'

'I daresay you're longing to get back to your husband. He must be missing you too after almost a month,' Rosalind said wistfully.

'Perhaps.' Cathy hid her face in her teacup. 'He's going to New Zealand in November. I'll be on my own. Why don't you come and stay for a few days?' The invitation slipped out impulsively, startling both girls equally.

Rosalind's eyes widened as she said, 'Well – thanks, Cathy. I don't know if I can get the time off, but if I can I'd really love to come and see the house you told me about.'

Cathy stood up. 'Good. I'll be in touch nearer the time now that I know you're living here.'

Rosalind went downstairs with Cathy to see her out, then returned to her room to get ready to go on duty. As she changed she thought about their meeting. She could hardly believe the change she had seen in Cathy this afternoon. At her wedding she had looked so ecstatically happy; like a young bride should look. In love and looking forward confidently to a happy future. Now she had the appearance of a much older, careworn woman. She looked drawn and unhappy as though there were some deep sadness in her life. Rosalind wondered what could have happened to bring about such a change.

She wrote to Freda that night before she went to bed. The address that the solicitor's clerk had given her was in the Midlands. Maybe Freda's parents lived there. For the first time Rosalind realised how very little she knew about the girl who had become her father's partner.

She had expected to get a reply or a telephone call within a few days, so she was surprised to look up from her typewriter two days later and find herself looking straight into Freda's smiling eyes.

'Hello, Rossie. Do you have a room free?' she asked. 'I'd like to stay for a few nights if that's possible.'

'Certainly.' Rosalind consulted the book that lay open on the desk. 'There's a nice one vacant at the front on the first floor.' She took a key from the board behind her. 'Come on, I'll take you up myself.' She took Freda's case and they went up together in the lift.

'Thank you for your sweet letter,' Freda said, once the door was closed. 'When I read it I had to come and see you right away.' Her eyes filled with tears as she held out her

349

arms. 'Oh, Rossie, I miss Ben so much. You're all I have left of him now.'

Deeply moved, she went into Freda's open arms and the two women clung to each other as the tears flowed.

'He talked about you all the time, you know,' Freda told her. 'He was so proud of the way you'd grown up. He was looking forward so much to your coming out to spend a holiday with us.'

'I wish I could have been in time to see him,' Rosalind whispered. 'I wish – oh, I *wish* I'd come out with you when you asked me. I'll always regret that.'

'No, you mustn't. You wanted to see your exams through. He respected that.' She held Rosalind at arm's length. 'You've taken them?'

'Yes. The results should be through any day now.'

'You'll pass with flying colours, I know you will. Ben knew it too.'

Rosalind looked at her watch apologetically. 'I'm sorry, Freda, but I'll have to get back to Reception now. But I'll be off at two. We could have a late lunch together if you like?'

Over lunch Freda told Rosalind that she would be seeing her agent while in London. 'Monty was shocked to hear about Ben,' she said. 'But I think – *hope* – he has some work lined up for me. When I got your letter I thought I could see him too while I was in town so I gave him a ring. I really need to work, Rossie.'

'I know, Freda. Look – about Dad's will . . .'

'Oh, not for the money,' Freda interrupted. 'I need to work because singing is my life. Without it, I'm nothing, especially now that Ben's gone.' She reached across to lay a hand on Rosalind's arm. 'And before you go any further about this will, Ben and I talked all that through. I know what a tough time you had after your parents parted. Ben always felt really bad about it. He wanted to make it up to

350

you in whatever way he could and we both agreed that he should leave you everything he had, the cottage included. He went along and sorted it all out before we went to Australia.'

'But it was half yours!'

'No. Ben bought it with money he had saved after we started doing well. All I did was persuade him that it was a good investment. He got the place very cheaply.'

'Dad was hopeless with money. You must have persuaded him to save in the first place. You advised him to buy it, and you helped him restore it. You loved it.'

Freda silenced her with a shake of her head. 'No. I loved *him*, Rossie. I had my reward; the six wonderful years we shared. We both wanted the cottage to be yours. It was a good investment. Property is going up and you should get a good price for it. You deserve it, love. So let's hear no more.'

Freda went up to see Harry Montague the following morning and the moment she arrived back at the hotel late in the afternoon Rosalind could see by the look on her face that she had good news.

'I've got an audition for a part in a new musical,' she said excitedly. 'Tomorrow afternoon. I'm sick with nerves just thinking about it. It isn't a big part but I've never done anything on the West End stage before and it would be a marvellous start if only I could get it. I've always wanted to do a musical. Monty has suggested I take a new stage name so that I can make a fresh start as a solo artiste. I've decided on Benita Moore. What do you think? I wanted to keep the Benita part in memory of Ben.'

'It sounds fine to me. Very glamorous.' Rosalind smiled. 'Just like the star of a musical. Dad would have approved. I'll keep my fingers crossed for you. If you get the part and you're going to be working in London we'll be able to see more of each other.'

351

'I know. I thought I might find a little flat somewhere. You could come and stay – make it your home too.' Freda's cheeks were flushed with excitement. 'I mustn't count my chickens, of course, but I've got a really good feeling about this. Maybe things are looking up for us both, Rossie. Maybe we're lucky for each other.' She paused. 'Why don't you come to the audition with me tomorrow?'

Rosalind blushed with pleasure. 'Well – if you're sure I wouldn't be in the way?'

Freda shook her head. 'You know it's high time you stopped selling yourself short, Rossie. Get to know your own worth.'

The following morning the letter Rosalind had been waiting for arrived. For a long time she sat staring at it, unable to bring herself to open the envelope and read the contents. Suppose she had failed? There was no way she could go back and re-take the exams now that she had started working. And without A levels the college wouldn't take her.

Looking at her watch, she saw that she had ten minutes to spare before she went on duty, so, picking up the letter, she went up to the first floor and tapped on Freda's door.

Freda was in her dressing gown, her hair swathed in a towel, but she took one look at Rosalind's worried face and drew her inside.

'What's the matter? You look as if you've seen a ghost.'

Rosalind held out the long envelope. 'This came,' she said, her lip trembling. 'I can't open it. Will you?'

'What is it?' Freda's face cleared. 'Oh! Your exam results.' Turning away she walked across to the window, tearing the envelope open as she went. Rosalind waited, watching and hardly daring to hope as the other woman scanned the sheet of paper inside.

'You've *passed*!' Freda said, turning to her triumphantly. 'And with flying colours just as I knew you would.' She threw her arms round Rosalind and hugged her.

'Congratulations, darling! Now maybe you'll realise that you're a worthwhile person – someone who matters.' She swung Rosalind round in a sudden burst of exuberance. 'Oh, I've a feeling this is going to be a very special day for us, Rossie. A day we'll remember for years to come.'

The auditions were being held in a hall in a street at the back of St Martin's Lane. Freda and Rosalind arrived in plenty of time, but by the time they arrived at the door Freda was a bundle of nerves.

'I'm sure you've nothing to worry about,' Rosalind said, determined to sound reassuring. 'You've got a lovely voice. They'd be mad not to give you the part. What's the name of the play, by the way?'

'It's called *Sweet Violet*,' Freda said. 'Written by a new playwright, Monty says. He was telling me all about it. Apparently it was first put on in a rundown theatre in Stoke Newington, but he managed to persuade Louis Jacobson to go and see the show. He loved it and decided there and then to take it into the West End.' Freda looked at Rosalind's face, which was blank with shock. 'Louis Jacobson is an impresario,' she explained unnecessarily. 'If he has faith in the show you can bet it's a winner.' She frowned. 'Rossie – is anything wrong?'

'No! No, nothing.' She pulled herself together with an effort. 'Let's go in.' Her mind was in turmoil. What was going on? Monty must know how furious Una would be to find herself in the same show as Freda. It was a recipe for disaster. It would make for a terrible working atmosphere and could ruin the show. What could he be thinking of? Would Una be here today? She shrank from the thought of the ensuing confrontation.

But, much to her relief, her mother was nowhere to be seen. Inside the hall two rows of chairs had been set up in front of the platform. There was the usual upright piano, at which sat Brian French. Sitting in the centre of the front row

353

of chairs sat Julian and another, older man whom Rosalind supposed must be Louis Jacobson. To her relief Stuart was not present either.

Freda joined the row of 'hopefuls' waiting to audition, while Rosalind found herself a chair in a dim corner at the back of the hall. They waited. On the stroke of two-thirty Julian stood up and announced that the auditions would begin. One by one, he called up the candidates whose names were on his list. Each in turn they handed their music to Brian, sang a song of their own choice, then read a passage from the libretto and attempted to sight-read one of the songs from the show. When Freda's name was called she walked up on to the platform without the slightest trace of nervousness. Rosalind watched admiringly, wishing she had Freda's looks and poise. Crossing the fingers of both hands, she saw her give her music to Brian and take up her position centre-stage.

The song she had chosen was one Rosalind had heard her sing before. It was *As Long As He Needs Me* from Lionel Bart's musical *Oliver* – and she sang it with a heart-felt emotion that brought a lump to Rosalind's throat. She read from the libretto with aplomb and then attacked the song she had never seen before in a strong, confident voice that Rosalind knew would have made her father proud. There was no doubt in her mind that Freda outshone the rest of the female singers auditioning that afternoon. She was so enthralled that she almost forgot the barrier that lay between Freda and a part in the show.

When she had finished there was a pause, then Julian said, 'Thank you, Miss Moore, we'll be in touch with your agent.' He glanced at his list. 'Harry Montague, isn't it?'

Outside in the street they looked at each other. 'You're sure to get it,' Rosalind said. 'You didn't look a bit nervous and your voice was wonderful. You were miles better than anyone else.'

Freda looked doubtful. 'I don't know about that. When

354

I saw that Jacobson himself was there I almost turned tail and ran. I'm going to try not to think about it.' She linked her arm through Rosalind's. 'Come on, I'm taking you out to tea. We've got your exam results to celebrate if nothing else. And I need something to steady my nerves.'

As they faced each other over the teacups Rosalind wondered whether to tell Freda that Una was playing a leading part in the show she'd just auditioned for. She hated to spoil everything for her. There was, after all, the chance she might not get the part, in which case she need say nothing. On the other hand she couldn't let her accept it first and then find out.

'Rossie – is something wrong? You're very quiet.'

'What?' She looked up with a start. 'Oh, no.'

'Only I've been speaking to you for the last ten minutes and getting no response.'

Rosalind opened her mouth to drop her bombshell – then closed it again. She couldn't do it. She couldn't spoil Freda's happy anticipation. Not today. Maybe tomorrow she'd find the courage to tell her. Who knew what might have happened by tomorrow?

But when they arrived back at the Queen's Head there was a message waiting for Freda. Monty had telephoned and left word for her to ring him as soon as possible. She rang at once from the telephone in Reception, Rosalind looking on apprehensively as she dialled the number.

Monty's secretary put her through immediately. Rosalind heard the rumble of his deep voice at the other end of the line.

'Hello, Monty. I've just got in. You wanted to speak to me?'

Rosalind watched as the other girl's face slowly took on a look of sheer disbelief. 'You're joking! My God, I can't believe it!' she said at last. 'Are you sure it's me they want? I mean, I'm virtually an unknown, apart from the work I did with Ben. This will be the first time I've done a musical play.' While Monty's voice growled on at the other end she smiled and nodded eagerly. 'The contract – you want me to come up to the office and sign it? Of course – when?' She winked gleefully at Rosalind. 'Right, I'll be there.'

At length she put the receiver back on its rest and looked at Rosalind with a stunned expression. 'Oh, Rossie, you're not going to believe this. They've offered me one of the principal roles! It seems that the actress who played Olive at the try-out wasn't really up to it. Jacobson had never really felt she was right for the part. *And they want me to play it!* Can you believe it?' She grabbed Rosalind's hands and squeezed them tightly. 'Oh, isn't it *wonderful*? I told you this would be a day we'd always remember!' She looked at Rosalind's stunned face and laughed uncertainly. 'Well, come on. Aren't you pleased for me?'

Rosalind drew her towards a chair. It was worse than she'd thought. 'Come and sit down,' she said. 'There's something you should know before you sign that contract tomorrow.'

Freda shook her head bemusedly. 'For heaven's sake – what? What's bothering you, Rossie?'

'The other actress – the one they're sacking. I'm afraid it's Una.'

The smile faded from Freda's face and she slumped in her chair. 'Oh, no! What is Monty thinking of? He should have known.' She frowned. 'He *did* know. He purposely didn't tell me, the sly old devil. He knew I wasn't auditioning for a minor role all the time.' She looked at Rosalind. 'Oh my God! What do I do now?'

'I think you should take it,' Rosalind said firmly. 'It isn't your fault they want to sack Una. She manipulated her way into the part anyway. If you don't do it they'll only find someone else – someone who won't be half as good. It's true Monty should have told you. He probably knew that you wouldn't even consider auditioning for it if he did.'

'And he'd have been right. I wouldn't!'

'But Una never considered anyone else's feelings, so why should you?'

Freda looked at Rosalind for a long anxious moment, chewing her lower lip. Then suddenly she nodded decisively. 'You're right,' she said. 'This is my big chance. Why should I lose it?'

Una closed the dressing-room door and sat down to take off her make-up. The show's pre-London run was over. This had been their last night in Brighton. They had a week out before they began fresh rehearsals for the West End opening. Brian had written another two numbers for the show, one of which was for her character. And Julian had re-written the second act curtain. Everyone agreed that the whole show had benefited enormously from the changes. Now she was really on her way to fame and success. Una could hardly wait to see her name up in lights outside the theatre.

She was wiping off the last vestiges of cold cream when there came a tap on the door.

'Come in.' She looked up through the dressing-table mirror, expecting Don. He had come down specially for the show's last night and the party that was to follow. Tomorrow they were leaving for a short holiday in Majorca. She smiled in anticipation. He'd be sure to bring her a bouquet or chocolates tonight; maybe even a piece of jewellery too.

But it was not Don who responded to her call, but Julian. He hovered in the doorway, looking uncomfortable. 'Una. Have you got a minute?' he asked tentatively.

She laughed, turning in her chair. 'All the minutes you want, darling, now that the show is over. Do come in and have a seat.' She got up and went towards the screen in one corner of the room. 'What can I do for you? Okay if we talk while I change?'

'No. I'd rather – look, sit down a moment, Una,' he said uneasily, closing the door carefully behind him. 'I have something important to say to you.'

Something in his tone made her pause and look at him. 'Oh, dear. Did I mess up one of your favourite lines? I haven't been upstaging someone again, have I?'

'No, nothing like that.' Julian swallowed nervously, wishing the next ten minutes could be over. The diplomatic speech he had so carefully rehearsed had completely deserted him. 'You've been absolutely wonderful in the show,' he began. 'And of course we couldn't have got off the ground without Don's support – and yours.'

Una frowned, unhappy at the turn the conversation was taking. 'Do you think you could get to the point, Julian?' she said sharply. 'At this rate we'll both be late for the party. Besides, Don will be waiting.'

'It's all right. I've seen him. I asked him to give us a minute.' Julian slipped one finger inside his collar and swallowed again. 'Right. Well you see, the thing is, we – that is, Louis Jacobson and I – feel that you aren't quite . . . What I mean is that playing the West End can be terribly demanding and . . .'

'And *what*?' Una demanded, facing him challengingly.

He tried again. 'I'm sure you'll agree that over the past few weeks the pressure has been pretty relentless.'

'I don't think I'd agree with that at all,' she said stridently. 'I'm a pro. I hope I can cope.'

'Oh, I'm sure you always do your best. But you've been looking very tired lately and your . . .' He cleared his throat. 'Your voice . . .'

'What about my voice? Are you trying to tell me that I'm not up to playing the part in the West End?' She stood in front of him, hands on hips. 'Well, come on – *are* you?'

'You've been terribly well received, Una,' he lied. 'Very popular and all that – with the cast as well as the public. It's just that Jacobson – well, no, *I* feel you deserve a rest. It isn't only you,' he added hopefully. 'There are one or two other parts that are being recast, for various reasons, and I . . .'

358

'You little *shit!*' Una's face, which had flushed darkly, suddenly drained of all colour. 'You *used* me,' she screamed. 'You were glad enough of the money I got Don to put up, weren't you? I was good enough for your tacky little show then. Now that you've got Jacobson behind you and you don't need my financial support any more you think you can just dump me! Well, you won't get away with it, I promise you!'

'Be reasonable, Una. It happens all the time. Lots of actors who do the pre-London run drop out when the show comes to Town. It's a well-known . . .'

'And what would *you* know about it?' Una spat at him scathingly. 'You're nothing more than a tuppeny-ha'penny bloody *amateur*. Don't you try to tell me what's what. I was in this business when you were still filling your nappies.'

'Well, now that you mention it, that's exactly the point,' he said boldly.

Una drew in her breath with a menacing hiss. 'You're saying I'm *too old?*' She stared at him, her eyes bulging slightly and the veins in her neck standing out. 'Well, let me tell you something, Mr Smartarse. You haven't heard the last of this. By the time I'm done with you, your name will be mud in this business. I'm going to sue you for every penny this show makes. I do have a contract, you know. You can't wriggle out of that.'

'I think you'll find that your contract is up for renewal at the moment,' he said.

She stared at him. 'Does Monty know? Is he in on this too?'

'I believe he knows that we intended not to renew your contract, that's all,' Julian told her. 'According to him you cancelled your agreement with him when you first came into the show. Our decision to recast your part in the show was nothing at all to do with him.' He paused while she took in this piece of information. 'Of course we shall see that Don receives his investment back, plus his share of the profits.'

He began to edge towards the door, but a little too late to escape Una's violent reaction. A scream of pure animal fury accompanied a flying jar of cold cream which struck him a painful and dizzying blow on the temple before falling to the floor. Without another word he fled, slamming the door behind him and leaving Una standing in the middle of the room, trembling and incandescent with rage.

Don, who had been hovering in the corridor, listening apprehensively to the ominous sounds of his wife's disquiet, appeared in the doorway, his anxious face almost hidden behind a huge bouquet of flowers.

'Oh, dear,' he said when he saw Una's scarlet face and quivering mouth. 'What on earth is the matter?'

At the sight of him she burst into floods of noisy tears. 'Take me home!' she hiccupped between sobs. 'Take me home, Don. I've been swindled – robbed! That's what's happened.'

Don looked completely nonplussed. 'But – I thought we were going to this party. Don't you want to go?'

'Go to the *party*?' she wailed. 'When I've been insulted and humiliated? I'll never be able to show my face in the theatre again.' Irritated by his bland, puzzled expression she scowled at him through her tears. 'Oh, for heaven's *sake*, Don, don't you understand? They've kicked me out of the show – dumped me. Told me I'm too old and that my voice is cracking up. Cast me aside like – like some old has-been.'

Amazed though he was, Don couldn't help admiring Julian's pluck. He'd seen him emerge from the dressing room clutching his head. Clearly he hadn't come out of the confrontation entirely unscathed. Don tried hard to keep the smile of relief off his face. He was actually going to have his wife back again. A proper wife who'd be there when he came home from the office every night, with a meal ready and maybe a smile and a kiss, like when Mother was alive. No more empty house and solitary meals. No more driving down to some seaside resort every weekend in order to spend a few hours with his wife. No more sharing her with those awful gushing stage people any more either; for ever kissing and calling each other '*dah-ling*'.

Very carefully he laid the bouquet down on the chair near the door and went to her. Putting his arms gently round her, he patted her tentatively as though she were a recalcitrant terrier.

'There, there, my love,' he said soothingly. 'If they don't appreciate you, I know I certainly do. It'll be so nice to see my little wife waiting for me in the kitchen when I come home at night; to have you all to myself.'

Una pushed him aside with an impatient snort. The very idea of being chained to the kitchen sink at Blakes Folly when she should be starring in the West End, her name in lights, was unbearable. It made her feel physically sick. 'Oh! Oh *shut up*,' she snapped, stamping her foot. 'Honestly, Don. You really do talk the most awful *crap* at times.'

Over the two weeks that followed Freda was busy. Shut away in her room all day she studied the script of the play.

'I want to be word perfect by the first day of rehearsals,' she told Rosalind excitedly. 'This is my big break and I want to make sure I do everything I can to make it a success.'

When the hotel was quiet in the afternoons Mrs Gresham let her use the piano in the bar to rehearse her songs. Secretly the manageress was quite excited herself at the idea of having a West End star staying at the Queen's Head. She planned to put up signed photographs in the bar and reception area once the show had opened.

It wasn't long before the press got to hear about Freda's potential rise to fame. *Sweet Violet*, the new musical, had received more than its share of advance publicity. Louis Jacobson had seen to that. His press office had dug out everything it could on the show's new star, from her humble beginnings in provincial variety theatres to the TV shows she and Ben had taken part in before their departure to

Australia. They had even cabled the Australian Broadcasting Commission's press office for copies of write-ups and reviews of the British singing duo's performances there.

When Freda arrived at the theatre on the first day of rehearsals she was surprised to find several journalists waiting for her at the stage door. Almost before she knew what was happening her photograph had been taken and she had been asked to say 'a few words' for the papers. By the end of the week her picture was on the front page of *The Stage* as well as on the showbiz pages of several national dailies.

'You're a star even before the opening night,' Rosalind told her as they read the reports together.

One or two of the more sensational tabloids had asked personal questions about her relationship with Ben, and she was dismayed to find that one of them reported that they had never married because Ben was still traumatised by his disastrous first marriage. Freda read the article with disbelief.

'I never said that!' she said. 'What on earth will Una say when she sees it?'

'Even if you didn't actually say it, it isn't very far from the truth,' Rosalind said.

Freda sighed. 'Which probably makes it all the more unpalatable. I'm grateful for one thing at least. They haven't dug out the vital connection between us yet.'

Rosalind shrugged. 'It's probably only a matter of time before they do.'

Freda nodded. 'I'm afraid you're right.' She looked sadly at Rosalind. 'I really don't want to make an enemy of her, Rossie,' she said. 'I know how devastated she must be at losing her part just as it was coming into the West End, but it was none of my doing. I wish these people would stop making so much of it.'

Rosalind said nothing. She knew that Una had been Freda's enemy long before this. There was nothing anyone could do to prevent the venomous feelings that would flow when she discovered that Freda had taken her coveted part in the play. For a moment her mind dwelt on kindly, well-meaning Don. He must be having a hell of a time!

'Only a few days to go now till we start rehearsals,' Freda said.

'I expect you'll be wanting to go and see your family before you start rehearsals.'

Freda shook her head. 'There's only my sister in Birmingham. I stayed with her when I first came back from Australia. We've never been close. She's ten years older than me and she has her own family.' She smiled. 'You're the nearest to a family I have now, Rossie.' She looked thoughtful. 'Actually, I've been thinking. How about you and me having a day's shopping?'

Rosalind shrugged. 'If you like. Is there something you particularly want?'

'I was thinking more of you.' Freda laid a hand on Rosalind's shoulder. 'Don't take this the wrong way, darling, but you could make so much more of yourself. If you agree I'd like to help show you how.'

Rosalind smiled. 'It's kind of you, but I'm afraid I'm a bit of a lost cause. I'm not pretty like you. I didn't inherit Una's looks and colouring. All my friends at school were pretty and I got resigned to the fact a long time ago that I'm just a plain Jane, like it or not.'

'That's not true,' Freda said firmly. 'You have good bone structure and beautiful eyes. Your hair is thick and shiny. There's so much you could do to bring out all that potential.'

'Someone else said that once,' Rosalind said wistfully. 'I had my hair cut and bought some new clothes at the time and – and I think I did look better too – for a little while.'

'Was that a boyfriend?' Freda asked gently.

Rosalind nodded. 'Stuart Hamilton. He designed all the sets and costumes for *Sweet Violet*. His friend wrote the

363

play. I met him when he designed a setting for one of Hallard's fashion shows. I think he only pretended to be interested in me so that he could get to know Una and Don better. Don put up the money for the show originally.'

'And Una played a leading part?' Freda's eyes widened. 'Ah! Now I see what you meant when you said that she manipulated her way into the play.'

'It was all a put up job,' Rosalind said unhappily. 'With me in the middle. Stuart used me to get to Don. But Una made sure she was part of the package.'

'And it took Jacobson to sort things out?' Freda nodded. 'Well, I must say that makes me feel slightly better about taking the part from her. Now . . .' She looked at Rosalind challengingly. 'Are you going to let me help transform you?'

She laughed, flattered that someone actually cared enough to want to help improve her appearance. 'I think you're on to a loser, but if you insist . . .'

'I do!'

Rosalind's next full day off was the Friday before rehearsals opened for Freda. They went up to the West End early and Freda took charge from the moment they came out of the underground at Oxford Circus. An expert haircut, a facial and make-up came first. Then they went to look for clothes. Freda picked out colours and styles that Rosalind would never even have considered buying for herself.

'Try it,' she said persuasively. 'Surely you're tired of all those dull browns and navy blues you've been wearing?' Gently but firmly she steered Rosalind towards the changing room. 'Just try some of them on and see what you think. If you don't like them we can put them back.'

But to her surprise Rosalind found that she did like the new styles and colours. She had never realised how good she looked in yellow before; how russet gold brought out the warmth of her eyes; or how surprisingly sophisticated she could look in black. By the time they came out of the shop she had bought a smart black suit and several blouses for work, a dress for evenings and two more dresses for everyday wear – all with the new short skirt length. Shoes followed. Freda scorned the sensible flat-heeled brogues that Rosalind had grown used to wearing in favour of feminine pumps with a pretty trim, and some sandals with higher heels for evenings.

'You have nice legs and feet. Why hide them in those clumpy things?' she scolded.

Over lunch Freda looked at Rosalind's shining eyes across the table. 'You know I was right now, don't you?'

Rosalind smiled. She was already wearing one of the new dresses and, on a visit to the cloakroom, she'd been unable to take her eyes off her reflection in the mirror, astounded at the new image of herself looking boldly back at her. 'Is all this really me?' she asked. 'I mean, will I be able to keep it up?'

'Of course you will,' Freda promised. 'It's just a question of getting into the habit of having your hair trimmed regularly and schooling yourself to the make-up routine. Maybe you could even think about getting some contact lenses too. Or at least some more flattering frames.' She leaned forward, her face serious. 'There's more than just glamorising to all this, Rossie,' she said. 'There's a practical side too. In a way your job is like mine; you're in the public eye most of the time. It's important that you look good. I know how dedicated you are to your work, so you must see the way you present yourself as part of it. Right or wrong, people do judge you by your appearance. And first impressions are vital.'

'I hadn't thought of it like that,' Rosalind said thoughtfully. 'You're right though. I can see that now.' She smiled. 'Thanks, Freda. You're the only person who has ever taken any interest in the way I look. I'm grateful.'

Freda squeezed her hand. 'It's been worth every minute,

love, just to see you blossom into the real you.' She paused. 'There's something else I want to say to you.'

'Yes?'

'What are you going to do with the cottage?'

Rosalind looked away. 'I don't know.'

'Why don't you put it on the market, Rossie? Realise the capital and invest it for your future.'

Rosalind looked up at her. 'I can't bring myself to do that. It meant so much to you and Dad. I'd feel as though I were selling a part of your life. Your dreams.'

'No.' Freda leaned earnestly towards her. 'That time has gone now. The cottage is yours. It's such a waste letting it stand there empty.'

'Would you like to go there again first – stay a few days, take a last look?'

'No.' Freda shook her head firmly. 'It's always a mistake, looking back. Ben and I were happy there. I'd prefer to keep my memories. I'd like to think that someone else might be as happy as we were.' She patted Rosalind's hand. 'Get in touch with an estate agent. Put it on the market, Rossie. I mean it.'

Una was sunning herself on the balcony of their hotel room when Don came back with the English newspapers. He dropped them on to the table beside her and went to find himself a cup of coffee. Idly, Una reached out and picked up the first of them, scanning the front page before turning to the inside. Fashion, gossip, horoscopes, showbiz . . . Suddenly her attention was riveted by a photograph of an attractive blonde. Immediately she sat up, pulling off her sunglasses as a familiar name halfway down the page caught her eye.

The caption over the photograph shouted at her in bold black letters:

Benita's Star In The Ascendant

Beneath it the piece read;

> *Lovely Benita Moore has replaced Una Blair in the role of Olive in Sweet Violet, the new musical that is taking London by storm. By a strange irony Benita also replaced Una six years ago as a singing partner and long-time close companion of Ben Blair, the recently deceased tenor. The partnership enjoyed success on British and Australian TV.*
>
> *Ben Blair began his career in time-honoured way with his wife, Una; first in end-of-pier concert party, then on the variety stage, to find considerable success at last with new partner Benita on TV and stage here and in Australia.*
>
> *It is understood that Una Blair was obliged to step down from her role following the prior to London run owing to problems with her voice. Already the critics are raving about Benita who, with her beautiful bell-like voice, stunning looks and sparkling personality is being hailed as a new Evelyn Laye.*

With a wail of anguish, Una picked up another paper – then another. In every one of them there was a write-up of the show. They ranged from a few guardedly optimistic words in *The Times* to a rave review in the *Daily Mail*. But in all of them Benita's performance was invariably praised to the skies.

When Don reappeared, smiling and refreshed from his coffee, he found his wife pacing the room in a state of near apoplexy.

'Look at *that*!' she shouted, thrusting a paper under his nose. 'And that and *that*!' She threw the other papers across the room where they spread themselves across the carpet like autumn leaves. 'This is that rat Monty's doing.'

'But why?' Don began to pick up the scattered papers. 'Why would he do a thing like that to you? He's your agent after all,' he said, perplexed, shaking his head.

'No, he isn't,' Una said defensively. 'He wanted to represent me again when I took the part in *Sweet Violet*, but I said no. I'd got the part on my own after all, so why should I let him take ten per cent of my earnings?'

Don frowned. 'Wasn't that a little short-sighted, dear?'

'Was it hell! I put him on to the boys and their play. I got him all that. Not that he deserved it. He said some very harsh things to me after Ben and I split up. He didn't want me then, so why should I let him take commission from me when I was on my feet again?'

'And you think this is his way of getting his own back?'

'I'm bloody sure it is!'

'But there's nothing you can do about it. You can't prove it.'

'I can try. My God, I can try. Don't you worry, I'll think of something.' Una picked up one of the papers and flicked frenziedly through it again, her heart quickening dangerously at the sight of Freda's beautiful face and the eulogies of the critics. When she thought of what that woman had taken from her . . . Ben was dead now. She would never see him again, let alone have him back. For the first time the finality of his death hit her and tears filled her eyes. She had loved him. No matter what anyone said, whatever he had done to her when they were married, she had never really stopped loving him. And they might have got back together again if it hadn't been for this Benita or Freda or whatever she called herself. Now, not content with that, she had taken Una's part in the play. Just as she was about to find the fame that had eluded her all these years, this woman had snatched it from under her nose. It was utterly intolerable.

With a sudden piercing scream that terrified the wits out of Don, she threw herself on to the bed and began to weep hysterically, drumming her feet on the quilt and hammering her fists into the pillows, until, to Don's consternation, she gave a gasp, shuddered violently and passed out cold.

* * *

368

Rosalind sat in her seat in the front of the dress circle and watched with pride as Freda took a final curtain call on her own. Although she wasn't, strictly speaking, the main character in the play, she received the greatest acclaim. Brian French's songs suited her voice to perfection and already she had been approached about recording an album of her songs from the show. Monty was currently negotiating the terms of a recording contract.

Rosalind had seen the show three times now. She had been there on the opening night, rigid with nerves and almost as keyed up as Freda herself. She'd enjoyed a more relaxed visit a month later. But tonight was a special occasion. She had heard that morning that Ivy Cottage had been sold for a sum that outshone all her expectations. After tonight's performance she was taking Freda out to celebrate.

Chapter Eighteen

Melfordleigh looked exactly the same as before she had left. Cathy felt a sense of surprise. Somehow she had expected changes, though she could not have said in quite what way. So much had happened in the month she'd been away. It was as though a lifetime had passed.

Johnny had accompanied her to Liverpool Street and seen her on to the train.

'You will write and let me know you got home safely, won't you?' she said, a look of concern in her eyes as the train began to draw out.

Cathy promised that she would, then watched bleakly as the train gathered speed and the homely figure waving from the platform grew smaller and further away.

Looking out of the window from her corner seat as the grimy buildings gave way to fields and trees she felt as though a whole segment of her life had been stripped away; torn from her, leaving a raw and painful scar that she was obliged to keep concealed. In four short weeks she had become a different person. Her own judge and jury, she had been found guilty and sentenced – for the crime she had committed against herself. But now that she was going home she must behave as though nothing had happened. It was going to be the hardest thing she had done in her whole life.

Gerald met her at the station. He greeted her absently, as though he had scarcely missed her. On the drive to Melfordleigh, she gathered from him that the seminars had gone extremely well. The four weekend concerts she had missed had been a great success, and Simon had been

370

working hard in preparation for his concert debut. In fact, everything ran as well in her absence as it did when she was there.

At Cuckoo Lodge, Maggie regaled her with her own version of events. 'Should'a seen some of them music students who came to the jazz concert,' she said, rolling her eyes ceilingwards. 'Long hair and beads. Flared jeans, and some of 'em were wearing them what-ya-call-em – *caffeine* things.'

Cathy hid a smile. 'Caftans, I think.'

Maggie shrugged. 'Well, whatever they're called they look damn' silly on fellers,' she said. 'Makes 'em look a right bunch of jessies. A lot of the serious ones are getting to be as bad too. Little wire glasses some of 'em have taken to wearing.' She formed her fingers into circles, holding them in front of her eyes. 'Just like my old granny. Dunno what the world is coming to, I'll tell you. If my kids start wearing stuff like that they'll get the rough side of my tongue and no mistake.'

She also probed Cathy subtly about the illness that had obliged her to stay on at Johnny's for an extra two weeks.

'Shame, you being poorly while you was on holiday,' she said, peering closely at her. 'You're still looking peaky. Still, I daresay the sea air'll put the roses back. Always works a treat, does our bracing Suffolk air.' She glanced surreptitiously at Cathy out of the corner of her eye as she got on with peeling potatoes. 'What did you say was the matter?'

'I didn't,' Cathy said. 'It was just a touch of summer flu.'

Maggie nodded. 'Ah. Nasty, that can be at this time of year. We'll have to take care of you. Make sure you get plenty of good food and rest.'

Going upstairs later that evening Cathy found Gerald moving his things out of their room into a small one at the end of the corridor that they had deemed too small for visitors or students. Standing in the doorway, she watched him for a moment.

'Why are you moving out of our room, Gerald?' she asked at last.

He glanced round at her. 'With some of the concerts and master classes going on so late I thought I might disturb you. There's a lot to do if I'm to be away for several weeks.'

'You've always slept in the dressing room anyway,' she reminded him. 'It seems a pity to move out. With so many other people around the house, sharing a room is the only chance we ever get to talk privately.'

He looked at her. 'Is there something you want to discuss?'

'No, but it's nice to talk – to be alone together sometimes.'

'I'm sure we can still find enough privacy for that,' he said dismissively. 'The summer season will be over soon. And Simon will be gone in a few weeks' time. We'll have the whole house to ourselves then.'

'But it will be almost time for you to go to New Zealand then.'

He patted her shoulder as he passed on his way out of the room. 'Not quite.'

Her heart rose as she followed him along the landing. 'Does that mean we could take a holiday, Gerald? Perhaps we could go back to Davos. I'd love to go there again.'

'Oh, I don't know about that.'

'Well perhaps somewhere in this country – somewhere we could be together, away from here.'

'I thought you liked this place so much.'

'Everyone deserves a break, surely?'

'I thought you'd just had one. Which reminds me . . .' He frowned as he deposited the armful of clothes he had been carrying on to the bed. 'You seem to have spent an awful lot of money during your stay with Mrs Johnson. I had the bank statement this morning.'

372

She felt the warm blood suffuse her face. 'I know, I meant to mention it. I bought a few new things – clothes.'

'From the amount you got through I'd say you bought enough to stage a fashion show.'

'I hadn't bought anything new since we first married, Gerald. You don't grudge me the money, do you?'

'I wouldn't if we had it. I'm still paying the builders, you know. I don't think you realise just how much the school cost to get off the ground.'

'Perhaps that's because you never discuss anything with me,' she countered.

'There's no reason why I should bother you with it – normally,' he said. 'Then there's the expense of my operation looming. It's going to be some time before we're clear of debt.'

'I see. I'm sorry.'

'Well, now that you know I'm sure you'll be careful.' He glanced at her. 'As a matter of fact I've had a bit of luck. A piece of music I wrote some time ago is about to be published.'

'I didn't know you ever wrote music.'

'As I said, it was some time ago. A rhapsody for piano and orchestra. Once royalties for that start coming in things will be easier. It will help to remind the public that I'm still around too.'

'Congratulations.' She began putting his shirts away in the drawers. 'Gerald, if we can't have a holiday, what shall we do with the two weeks we have before you leave? Perhaps we could see some of the countryside. There seems to have been no time at all for us to be together what with the school and everything.'

He sighed. 'It's a nice idea, but I may have to go up to London for some of that time. As I said, there are things I need to tie up before I leave. I'd rather like to be at Simon's first concert too.'

'I see.' Her heart sank. It was almost as though he was

finding every possible excuse not to spend any time alone with her. 'Maybe Johnny will come and stay with me for a few days.'

'I daresay.'

'I saw Rosalind Blair while I was home,' she went on. 'I thought it might be nice if she could visit while you're away.'

He frowned. 'Rosalind Blair?'

'Yes. She's a school friend. She was at the wedding, remember?'

'An ungainly dark girl? Glasses and frumpy clothes?' He shrugged. 'If you're desperate for company invite her by all means.'

The weeks passed drearily. Gerald was fully occupied with coaching Simon and preparing for his approaching absence. Cathy walked on the dunes. Sometimes she took her paints and tried to lose herself in the hobby, but somehow the pleasure seemed to have gone out of it. Would Gerald's operation really change anything between them? What had she done to make him fall so completely out of love with her? Would there ever really be a new start now that he had changed so much? Once he was well again would he want to go back to his old life and his friends, especially Kay?

Although she tried hard not to think of it, her mind was constantly haunted by thoughts of the baby she might have had. In the bleak small hours of her lonely wakeful nights the questions and speculations heaped one upon the other. Would her child have been a boy or a girl? Would it have looked like her? Would her father's grandchild have inherited his gentle nature and his musical talent? Now she would never know and it seemed unbearably, intolerably sad. In the dark empty hours she longed for the comfort of Gerald's arms; the closeness they had once shared which seemed now a thing of the past. Sometimes she thought she would never recover from the feeling of loss.

374

Before she had returned to Melfordleigh, Johnny insisted on taking her to a doctor to make sure no damage had been done. The doctor, a stranger in another part of London whom she had paid for a private consultation, had examined her thoroughly. If he had been suspicious about the reason for her miscarriage he had not shown it. To her relief he had pronounced her well, if a little anaemic. But no amount of probings or medicine – not even Johnny's wise counselling – could come anywhere near healing the deep wound in her heart. Had she made the sacrifice for nothing? Could Gerald possibly have loved her any the less if he had known of her adultery?

Late one afternoon at the beginning of October she was walking back towards the village when she saw a figure coming towards her. Too late she recognised Simon. Lately he had grown his hair longer and taken to wearing the slim-fitting shirts and flared jeans so despised by Maggie. He raised a hand to wave to her. Reluctantly she acknowledged the greeting and stood still, resigned, waiting for him to catch her up.

'Thought I might find you out here,' he said. 'I've been wanting to talk to you. I'm off next week as you know and I thought I might not get another chance.'

She kept on walking. 'I don't think you and I really have anything to talk about, Simon.'

'I think we do.' He put out a hand to stop her and she turned and looked at him. 'Sit down a moment,' he said. 'There's no hurry to get back, is there?'

'No, except . . .' She shivered. 'It gets cold in the afternoons now.' Reluctantly she sat down among the tall, wiry grass, wrapping her arms around herself.

He lowered himself beside her. 'Are you all right, Cathy?'

'Of course. Why wouldn't I be?'

'Anyone with half an eye can see you're not happy. And you don't look well either.'

'Well, that's my problem, isn't it?'

'It's not because of me, is it? You're not angry – about what happened between us?'

'No.' She glanced quickly at him. Was it possible that he had guessed? 'It's ancient history. It wasn't important anyway.'

'I know you regret it, but I want you to know that I don't. It was something special to me, Cathy. Even if I did handle it clumsily.' He looked at her. 'I meant what I said, you know. You should never have married Gerald. He isn't right for you.'

'And I meant what *I* said; that it's none of your business.' She wished with all her heart that it was time for him to leave. There would be no peace until then. Every time she was forced to look at him she was reminded of the child they had conceived.

For a moment he was silent, then he turned to her and said, 'You know she's going to New Zealand with him, don't you?'

Her head snapped round to look at him. 'Who?'

'Kay, of course. Who else? Oh, look, Cathy, I know I probably shouldn't be telling you this, but she was here while you were away. Ostensibly it was to see me and arrange the publicity for the tour, but anyone can see that there's something going on between her and Gerald. She's flying out with him on the fourth. I heard her mention it. Oh, not purposely to be with him. It's true that she does have business of her own there. But nevertheless . . .'

'Gerald is ill. He's going to New Zealand for an operation. You know all that,' she said. 'We can't afford for me to go too, so if Kay has to go to New Zealand on business it's good that she should keep him company.' She turned to glare angrily at him. 'Why are you so determined to make trouble between us?' She got up and began to walk away very fast, but he scrambled to his feet and was soon walking beside her.

'I'm not trying to make trouble. If it's all as innocent as you say, why didn't you know about it?'

'I *did*!' she protested unconvincingly. Tears of humiliation sprang to her eyes and Simon grasped her arm and swung her round to face him.

'Cathy! Believe it or not, I do *care* about you. I happen to think you're getting a raw deal and I don't like to see you being deceived.'

'Maybe it's no more than I deserve,' she said bitterly. 'After all, we – *I* deceived him, didn't I?'

'You think I'm being disloyal, don't you?'

'Since you ask, I think you could show more loyalty and respect to the man who has devoted more than a year of his life to your career,' she said. 'You owe him that at least.'

He walked beside her in silence for a moment. 'I meant it when I said I wanted us to be friends,' he said at last.

'*Friends?*' She stopped and turned to face him, her mind in turmoil. If he only knew! At that moment she longed to tell him of the price she had paid for a moment's vulnerability; of the heartbreaking sacrifice, the risk and pain she had put herself through. She stopped herself just in time. 'I don't want to hear any of this, Simon,' she said, her voice trembling. 'When I need help to sort out my life I'll ask someone and it won't be you. If we don't speak again I hope your concert tour – and your future career – is a success. Now will you please leave me alone?'

Simon left for his concert tour ten days later and on the following Monday Gerald began to pack. He planned to go to London first then on to Manchester where Simon was to make his debut. He would fly to New Zealand from there.

'You won't be back then?' Cathy asked as she helped him choose the clothes he would take.

'It hardly seems worth it. I can tie up a lot of loose ends while I'm in town, then fly out from Manchester the day after the concert.'

'Shall I come with you? To London, I mean.'

He turned to stare at her. 'Why?'

'I thought – you might like to have me with you,' she said quietly. 'We see so little of each other and you'll be away at least six weeks altogether.'

He fastened the case he had finished packing and turned to look at her. As their eyes met his face relaxed a little. 'I'm sorry, Cathy. All this hasn't been much fun for you, has it?' He put his arms around her awkwardly, as though she were a stranger. 'I really can't see much point in you coming to London though. You'd be bored, sitting alone for hours while I was out.'

'I daresay Johnny would put us up if I asked her,' she said hopefully.

He shook his head firmly. 'No, Cathy.'

'What is this business you have to do?' she asked.

'It's mostly to do with the school,' he told her vaguely. 'And I have to see James Kendrick, my agent, too. There is talk of a première of my rhapsody. Erhart Froebel the conductor is looking for new works to perform at a special concert he's planning for next year's Proms. James thought it might be nice if Simon could be the soloist and he's going to try to arrange a meeting between the three of us.'

'So – where will you stay?' she asked.

'With a friend.'

'Which friend?'

Gerald frowned impatiently, his moment of compassion forgotten. 'Oh, for heaven's sake, Cathy! Does it matter?'

The house seemed bleak when everyone had gone. Once again Melfordleigh seemed to be settling down for winter. Maggie had reluctantly asked for time off. Her widowed father, who lived on the other side of Ipswich, had just come out of hospital following an operation and she wanted to bring him to stay with her for a while. Cathy didn't need her anyway, so she agreed.

'Are you sure you won't mind being in this great place all on your own?' Maggie asked her anxiously.

Assuming a cheerfulness she did not feel, Cathy assured her that she would not, adding that even when the house was full she was alone.

Lying in bed in the empty house, listening to the north wind buffeting the chimneys, she thought about what Simon had told her. Was Kay really going to New Zealand with Gerald? Perhaps she was the 'friend' he was staying with in London. Next morning, obsessed with the desire to find out, she looked through the address book in the study for Kay's telephone number. For a long moment she sat staring uncertainly at the telephone. She was behaving like a suspicious wife and despised herself for it. Then, making up her mind, she reached out and dialled the number with trembling fingers. After several rings she was about to put the receiver down when it was lifted. A male voice answered by repeating the number. The voice was unmistakably Gerald's. Without speaking she dropped the receiver back on to its rest, her heart thudding dully in her chest. So it was true.

Sick with the thoughts that tormented her and desperate for company to block them out, she rang Johnny.

'Gerald left two days ago. You did say you'd come and stay.'

'Oh, Cathy.' Johnny's voice was apologetic. 'I'm sorry, love. It's impossible at the moment. Mother was rushed into hospital yesterday. It's another stroke, I'm afraid, and they aren't very optimistic this time. I have to be close at hand.'

'Of course. I understand. Poor Johnny. I'm so sorry.'

She sat for a long time in front of the telephone, then she picked up the receiver again and dialled the number of the Queen's Head. It was Rosalind who answered.

'Queen's Head. Reception. Can I help you?'

'Rosalind? It's Cathy Cavelle.'

'Cathy! How are you?'

'I'm fine, thanks. Look, how about coming for that visit? Can you get any time off?'

'I'd love to come, Cathy. I am due some time in lieu of overtime, and it's half term at college next week. I'm not sure how long I have off though. Can I get back to you?'

'Of course. I'll wait to hear from you.'

Rosalind rang back an hour later with the news that she could have a week off beginning the following Saturday. She sounded pleased and excited, but no less so than Cathy. Delighted at having something to do, she ran upstairs to get a room ready, choosing one that had a view of the garden and got the morning sun.

She met the train at Ipswich. Standing eagerly on the platform as it drew alongside, she watched the passengers disembark. Rosalind, to her disappointment, did not seem to be among them. She was just turning away when she felt a hand on her sleeve.

'Cathy.'

Turning, she was surprised to see her friend standing there – but a very different Rosalind from the one she had seen only a few weeks before. This tall slim girl in the smart tailored suit, with her hair cut in a sleek style, her face expertly made-up and minus the glasses she had always worn, looked totally different. The overall improvement was so overwhelming that Cathy felt it would be tactless to mention it.

'Rosalind!' she laughed. 'I didn't recognise you without your glasses.'

'Contact lenses,' she explained. 'They take a bit of getting used to, but I think the effect is worth it.'

Cathy took her case and drew her towards the barrier. 'Come on,' she said. 'We'll get a taxi. I can't wait to hear all your news.'

The taxi dropped them at the gate of Cuckoo Lodge and Rosalind stood staring in stunned amazement at the lovely old house with its mellow red brickwork glowing gently in the watery autumn sunshine.

'Oh, Cathy,' she exclaimed. 'I'd no idea it was so beautiful. You must be so proud of it.'

Cathy smiled. 'If you're interested I'll show you the photographs that were taken before the restoration work began.'

Inside Rosalind was entranced by the spacious drawing room with its inglenook fireplace and low-beamed ceiling. She was impressed by the studios, and the kitchen delighted her.

'You've managed to keep the character of the place whilst including all the up-to-date mod cons,' she said, looking round at the gleaming worktops, the cupboards and the Aga in its tiled recess.

'A bit of a cheat really,' Cathy told her. 'This part of the house is completely new. You should have seen the state of the old kitchen. I think it was added in Victorian times and it would have given you nightmares.'

Upstairs Rosalind looked into all the rooms with their pretty furnishings and bright colour schemes, expressing her approval again and again. 'Did you have a hand in the design?' she asked.

'Partly. We had the advice of a professional, but I chose most of the colour schemes and fabrics myself.'

It all seemed so long ago that she could scarcely remember the fun and excitement of it any more. The home she had helped so lovingly to restore now felt alien to her – almost like a prison sometimes. And Gerald's music school, the dream project they had planned together that had once excited her so much, now seemed like something that had nothing to do with her.

Her pensiveness did not escape Rosalind. Again she saw the sad, wistful expression that had clouded the other girl's face the last time they had met. There was something not quite right about her life. Rosalind wished they knew each other well enough for her to try and help.

Cathy suddenly smiled and took her arm. 'Come and see the barn. It's been converted into a concert hall. Then I'll show you the garden and the mill stream. Do you like ducks?'

Rosalind laughed. 'Yes.'

'Good. We'll take some scraps and you can feed them.'

Later that evening, after they had eaten and Rosalind had seen and marvelled at the photographs of Cuckoo Lodge in its original derelict state, the girls settled down before a log fire in the drawing room and Rosalind told Cathy her news – about her father's will and selling the cottage.

'I've never had any real money of my own before,' she said. 'It's a strange feeling. I've invested it for the moment, but I feel I should do something meaningful with it. Something that Dad would have approved of; that would have made him proud of me.'

'Do you have anything in mind?' Cathy asked.

'What I really want – what I've always wanted – is to buy a hotel of my own,' Rosalind said wistfully. 'If I could find a house, somewhere like this for instance, and turn it into a small hotel that would be marvellous. But the money I got for the cottage isn't nearly enough for that kind of ambitious enterprise.' She sighed. 'Isn't it funny? In some ways it seems such a lot of money, yet it isn't nearly enough to do what I really want.'

'You don't have to put down all of the money,' Cathy pointed out. 'You could get a mortgage, and probably a bank loan to start your business if you could convince the bank that it was a worthwhile venture.'

Rosalind nodded. 'I've learned a lot about management since I've been at the Queen's Head and college. Perhaps I'm not really quite adventurous enough. The idea of taking that kind of risk terrifies me. Supposing it all went wrong and I lost the money?'

'I'm sure you wouldn't.'

Rosalind shook her head. 'It would be an awfully big thing to take on by myself. I don't think I'd have the confidence.' She went on to tell Cathy about Freda's return to England and, listening to the warmth and affection in the other girl's voice, Cathy realised how much of an influence Ben Blair's singing partner was on Rosalind. A good one too by the sound of it. Clearly it was Freda who was responsible for the change in Rosalind's appearance and the new self-confidence she exuded. Cathy found herself wishing she could meet the woman who cared enough about Ben Blair's daughter to take her under her wing.

'Freda has real talent. She's been lucky enough to get a major part in a musical play in the West End,' Rosalind was saying. She went on to explain how Freda had been cast in the part her mother had lost in *Sweet Violet*.

'Oh, dear, that must have been awkward for you,' Cathy said sympathetically. 'How did your mother take it?'

'I haven't seen her. She hasn't been in touch since I left home, so I don't really know,' Rosalind said. She pulled a wry face. 'I can imagine though. She'll have been bitterly disappointed at missing playing in the West End. It was always her dream to see her name up in lights.' She sighed. 'It won't have helped when she found out that Freda was taking her part over either. I daresay poor Don is bearing the brunt of it.'

'You and your step-father got along all right in the end then?'

Rosalind blushed. 'I'm ashamed to say that I misjudged him,' she said. 'I have a lot to be grateful to him for. It wasn't his fault that I left home.' She paused, wishing she knew Cathy well enough to confide in her about the shameful stealing of the Meissen figure. It was something she had been too ashamed even to tell Freda. Maybe someday, if she was lucky, she would find a friend in whom to confide. Someone she could be sure would understand and forgive.

'So maybe it's as well you're not at home at the moment,' Cathy said with a smile.

'Yes – although . . .' Rosalind glanced wistfully round her. 'Being here in your lovely home makes me dread going back to that dingy little room of mine at the Queen's Head. It felt like a haven at first, but now it's beginning to depress me.'

Cathy could well imagine that it was. She had only been in Rosalind's room once but she knew that the lack of space, the threadbare brown carpet and porridge-coloured walls would depress her too if she was obliged to live there. 'You could use some of your legacy to buy a flat,' she suggested. But Rosalind shook her head.

'I want to save the money for the future.'

Cathy nodded. 'Well, you're always welcome here whenever you can take some time off,' she said with a smile. 'I'll be glad of the company. I get lonely sometimes when Gerald is working.'

When it was time for Rosalind to leave both girls were sorry. The week had flown so quickly and they had enjoyed each other's company so much. Cathy had enjoyed showing Rosalind the village; the quay and the dunes, the little craft shops and art galleries. Once they had lunched at the Admiral Nelson, but most evenings they had cooked together in the kitchen at Cuckoo Lodge. For Cathy it was a treat to have someone to cook for, and to have the kitchen to herself, though she did not tell Rosalind that. It would have sounded so strange that she rarely cooked a meal for her husband and did not have full access to many of the rooms in her own home.

That week Cathy had seen a side of Rosalind she never knew existed. She had always liked the quiet, slightly nervous girl, but had never realised they had so much in common or shared so many opinions. When they said goodbye at the station, promising to write and keep in touch, what had been a casual acquaintanceship had developed into

384

a warm friendship. It was with genuine regret that Cathy waved goodbye and went back to Melfordleigh and the empty house.

Cathy had booked a call to the hospital in Auckland for early on the morning following the day scheduled for Gerald's operation. She was up bright and early on the day in question and as she made coffee in the kitchen she reflected that it would now be eight p.m. in New Zealand, whilst here it was still breakfast time. A whole world separated herself and Gerald. A whole world – and so much more. She had received two postcards from him since he left. One from Manchester, telling her of the success of Simon's first concert; the other was posted soon after his arrival in New Zealand, giving her the date of his operation.

She was just finishing her breakfast when the telephone rang. The hospital receptionist put her call straight through to the ward where a Sister told her briskly that Gerald was resting comfortably after a good night's sleep. As far as could be ascertained the operation had been a complete success and so far he was doing very well.

Cathy replaced the receiver with a sigh of relief. So – the first hurdle was over. Would this operation really turn Gerald into a different person? Would his love for her return, or would he want to turn back the clock, pick up the threads of his old life again? Only time would tell. With luck he would be home for Christmas. She must start preparing for it. Christmas had become an unlucky time for her over the past few years. Somehow something bad always seemed to happen at this time of year. But perhaps now she had reached a turning-point. Perhaps this year would be the happiest Christmas she had known since the last she had shared with Dad.

Cathy telephoned the people on the list he had left, noting with some irony that Kay's name was not included. Her first call was to James Kendrick, his agent. He was delighted at the news.

'I'm glad you've called, Cathy,' he said. 'There has been quite a bit of interest in Gerald's rhapsody. You probably know that Simon is to be the soloist at its first performance next August?'

'No, I didn't know,' she said dryly.

'Yes. We finalised the details while he was here a couple of weeks ago. As you know, word soon gets around on the grapevine and enquiries have been coming in ever since. I wondered if he had any more copies?'

Cathy shook her head. 'I've no idea. I suppose I could have a look though.'

'I'd be grateful if you would. The original is with Froebel at the moment and I'm still waiting for the first batch of copies from the publisher to arrive. I don't want to let any opportunities slip.'

'I'll have a look and ring you back, James.'

When she had finished her calls Cathy looked through the music library Gerald kept stored in files in the study, but she could find no more copies of his composition. Knowing that he would almost certainly not have parted with the only copy she tried to think where it might be. He had said it was something he had written some years ago. Could there be another copy in one of the boxes stored in the attic? She pictured the boxes stacked away in the roof space and shrank from the thought of searching them. Some had come from her home, some from Gerald's flat. Most of them contained little-used things they had meant to sort out long ago. Somehow they had never got round to it, but she had very little else to do. It would be a good opportunity to deal with a long delayed chore.

On the landing she pulled down the extending ladder that led up into the attic and climbed into the void. When the house was restored Gerald had made sure the attic was wired for electric light and the floor was boarded. Finding the switch, Cathy made her way over to the corner where the boxes were stacked. Luckily they were all labelled with either her name or Gerald's. The first one she searched was full of books, which she carefully repacked and put aside. The next contained a mixture; magazines, newspaper clippings and press cuttings of Gerald's, some of them dating back more than twenty years. There was a thick manilla document wallet too. Glancing at the contents she saw that it contained some hand-written manuscripts. Perhaps the one she was looking for was among them. She put it to one side.

It was then that she noticed, right at the bottom of the packing case, an old cigar box full of letters. She took one out and looked at the envelope. It had Gerald's name and an unfamiliar address written on it in faded ink. The writing looked feminine. There were others in the box, a dozen or more of them, all with the same handwriting. After a moment's hesitation she took the letter out of the envelope in her hand. Inside was a sheet of notepaper, lilac-coloured and faintly scented. There was no address, but it was dated 20 August 1945. It read:

My darling
　So the war is over at last. That terrible new atomic bomb they've dropped on Japan. It's like some frightening apocalypse. So much suffering and death makes life seem so much more precious. Fifty-five million killed in the war, so they say. What a tragic waste. But in a way it has helped to make up my mind, my love. Life is too short to resist the way fate intended us to live it. I've finally decided, my darling, to do as you say. I'll come to you. Now that peace has come your career can begin and I want more than anything else in the world to be your help and support. I want you to have the success you deserve.

We'll be together, just the two of us. I'll get a job and work for us both so that you can go back to college and study for the great career you must surely have.

I can't pretend that it won't be a dreadful wrench, Gerald, leaving everything behind. Leaving my darling baby will be the hardest thing I have ever done. But when we are settled perhaps I can have her to live with us. Whatever happens I can't bear to lose you. You are all I have ever wanted. I long to be close to you where I belong. To feel your arms around me and to know we need never part again. I can only pray that they will understand one day and that they will find it in their hearts to forgive me.

Please let me know as soon as you can what arrangements you have made so that we can start making plans.

My heart is always with you.

Ever your loving Jenny.

For a long moment Cathy sat staring at the signature on the bottom of the letter. *Jenny.* Gerald had said that his wife's name was Sarah and that his marriage had ended at the beginning of the war. This letter was dated 1945. She tried to ignore the vile suspicion hovering like a dark evil shadow in the corner of her mind. Surely it could not be possible . . .? The thought repelled her, churning her stomach and quickening her heart. Not wanting proof, yet unable to resist the temptation to find out, she took out another letter. It was dated a year later.

Gerald

I'm sorry we quarrelled last weekend. I hate having our precious time together spoilt, but I really can't believe that you meant to be so heartless. You promised that I could have Catherine to live with

us. If Daniel agreed to a divorce I would almost
certainly get custody of her, but you won't let me
ask him. If I were free we could be married. Why
are you so adamant about not getting a divorce –
and not telling Daniel I am with you? I came to
you willingly. Are you ashamed of our love?

The only way I can have Catherine with me now
is to throw myself on Daniel's mercy and beg. But
you even refuse to let me do this! Already I have
lost more than a year of her life. I will be a stranger
to her if I don't do something to get her back soon.
Please try to understand what it means to me. How
it breaks my heart to be parted from her. Will you
please try to come home from college this weekend
so that we can talk?

Yours,
Jenny

Cathy sat down on her heels. So it was true. Gerald had
been her mother's lover; the man she had deserted her
husband and child for. And Dad had never known. He
couldn't have. And through all those years Gerald had
continued to masquerade as his friend.

Bitter, angry tears scalded her eyes. Jenny, her mother,
had loved and wanted her after all. It had been Gerald who
had kept them apart. How could he have been so cruel?
But what was the rest of the story? What had happened to
Jenny? Maybe the rest of the letters in the box held some
clues. Painful though it was she felt compelled to read them.
Taking out another she saw that it was headed Trouville,
France, May 1947. It read:

Oh my darling,
How I miss you! So much. So very much.
I have settled in well here. Your friends the
Labeque family are very nice and the children

are sweet and very well behaved. You would be surprised at how well they speak English already. The little girl, Suzanne, reminds me so much of my little Catherine. She has the same green eyes and coppery hair. She is almost five, not much older than Catherine must be now. I can hardly believe that my baby will soon be going to school.

I hope your concert went well, my darling. How I would have loved to be there. It would have made me so proud to see you make your debut. But, as you said, this is best. It is not for long. Daniel would never think of trying to find me here in France and as I am living en famille, the money I earn is all mine. I will enclose as much as I can to help pay your tutor what you owe him.

I hope you will be able to come over soon. Madame Labeque says you are welcome any time. I long so much to see you, darling.

Always yours,
Jenny

At the bottom of the letter there was a postscript. It read:

Monsieur Labeque is teaching me to drive so that I can take the children to school. When I am proficient I am to have the use of Madame's car. Isn't that generous? It feels very strange to be driving on the wrong side of the road though! All my love – J

Cathy stared down at the faded writing for a long time. He had sent her to work as an au-pair in France – because, as she suggested in the letter, Daniel might try to find her? Or had it been so that she would not be tempted to try to see her little daughter and press for divorce?

There were other letters in the same vein. Slowly it became clear that Gerald had been too busy, or too occupied with his newfound success, to go over to France to see the woman who loved him. No doubt by this time he had become bored with her selfless devotion. He was afraid she would grow tired of waiting – obtain a divorce and be free for the marriage he had promised but had no intention of fulfilling. He had successfully got her out of the way.

Finally there was just one more letter at the bottom of the box. This time in a strange handwriting and penned in uncertain English. It was headed: Trouville, France, August 1948

My dear Gerald

Following the cable sent yesterday.

I cannot tell you how very sorry I was to be the bearer of such bad news. Your friend, Mrs Jenny Oldham, was taken to hospital following a crash made as she was returning from taking the children to school. Surgery was performed, but sadly she did not recover. I cabled and am writing to you as I have found no address for her husband or family among her effects. Can you please inform her relatives and make known for me the arrangements they would wish for her enterrement as soon as possible? Again, I am so sorry to write with such sad news. Madeleine and I would be happy to see you when you are next in France.

Yours in great sympathie.

Armand Labeque

With a feeling of overwhelming sadness, Cathy replaced the letters in the box and covered them with the rest of the papers from the packing case. Then she went downstairs. For a long time she sat in the kitchen, numb with shock at the discovery she had made. Gerald had been the one who had broken up her family all those years ago. He had seduced her mother and then, bored with her and irritated

391

by her constant longing for her child, had packed her off to his friends in France. But why did he not send her back to her husband? Perhaps he had been afraid that the scandal might become public and tarnish his glamorous image – threaten his promising career as a concert pianist. He had taken Jenny away from the husband and child who loved and needed her, cynically allowed her to support him through his studies, then neglected her, leaving her to die among strangers.

The sound of the telephone ringing in the study jerked her out of the daze she was in and sent her hurrying to the study to answer it. It was James Kendrick. His voice sounded so normal and ordinary that she felt as though she had just wakened from a bad dream.

'Ah, Cathy. I thought I'd better give you a call. I now have some proof copies of Gerald's rhapsody. They arrived from the publisher's just after lunch. So if you've been tearing the place to pieces you can relax. Besides, I daresay he wouldn't want to part with his own original copy.'

'Oh.' With an enormous effort Cathy pulled her scattered thoughts together. 'Oh, yes the manuscript. I have been looking but I didn't find another copy. Thank you for letting me know, James.'

'Quite all right. No more news of Gerald?'

'What? Oh, no. No more news.'

'Well, it's early days, isn't it? And the worst is over. Let me know when you hear anything. Take care, Cathy. 'Bye.'

'Goodbye.'

For a long time she sat on the edge of the chair in the study, trying to take in the full implications of the discovery she had just made – trying to make some sense of her life. But all she could think of was the baby she had sacrificed for Gerald's sake.

Cathy did not ring the hospital in New Zealand again. She could not bring herself to do it. But a week later a cheerful letter arrived from Gerald. He was recovering well, he told her. In fact he had not felt so well for a long time. The operation was nothing short of a miracle. His weakened muscles were already stronger and daily physiotherapy was helping enormously. The surgeon was delighted with his progress and would allow him out of hospital in another week's time. He would need to stay in Auckland for a further two weeks, however, to convalesce and would need to see the surgeon again for a final check before flying home. The only piece of news that did not concern his health was that he had heard from James Kendrick that the final arrangements for the première of his rhapsody at next season's Promenade Concerts had been made.

> I shall look forward to next summer now with renewed enthusiasm. Who knows? Perhaps I too will be playing at next season's proms. Already my mind is buzzing with plans and ideas.

Already Cathy sensed that they did not include her. Perhaps they never had.

Maggie dropped in to see her at least twice a week.

'I don't know how you stand it, alone in this great place,' she remarked one bleak day in early-December. 'I mean, the place is usually full of people. It must be strange.' She peered into Cathy's wan face with concern. 'You know where I live if you want a bit of company, don't you? You'll have to take us as you find us, mind. Teenagers make such a muck of the place. Fast as you clean up, there they are with their clothes all over the place and their records blaring out, driving you up the pole.' She grinned good-naturedly. 'Still, the kettle's always on.'

Cathy smiled, touched by the older woman's concern. 'You must be busy, with your father there and two growing children to look after?'

Maggie laughed. 'Bless you, I'm used to that. One day they'll be gone, so better make the most of it while I've still got them. Dad's going on fine now. He's very independent – already started whittling about going home. He's quite a help to me: does a bit of shopping and washing up; pushes the Hoover round.' She patted Cathy's arm. 'Mr Cavelle be home soon now, will he?'

'In time for Christmas, I think,' she said dully. 'I haven't heard anything definite yet. It's summer over there now so he'll feel the cold when he gets back.'

'You'll have to take good care of him. Get the place well warmed up.' Maggie looked out of the window at the wintry day outside. 'Could do with a bit of sunshine myself,' she said. 'And so could you by the look of you. You'll have to get him to take you away somewhere for a nice holiday when he gets back. Before next season's rush begins.'

Before next season's rush. The words had an empty ring to Cathy. Bleakly she wondered where she would be by then.

By the second week in December Cathy was ready for Christmas. She had decided to wait until Gerald was completely well again before confronting him with her discovery. Maybe he had some explanation. Perhaps he deeply regretted what had happened all those years ago. After all, he had kept Jenny's letters. Cathy would give him the chance to put his side of the story.

The following Friday was a bleak, wintry day, the wind churning the sea into boiling fury and the sky strewn with ragged clouds. Maggie was back. She had just begun preparing Gerald's study for what she called a 'good bottoming' in preparation for his return. Cathy was on her way upstairs when she heard the crunch of car wheels on the gravel outside. Looking out of the landing window she was astonished to see Kay getting out of her car. She wore a full-length ranch mink coat, which she hugged closely round her as she made a dash for the front porch.

Maggie, who had heard her arrival too, was just coming out of the study, her hair tied up in a scarf, when Cathy ran down the stairs.

'It's all right, Maggie. I'll get it,' she called on her way. As she pulled open the door her heart was beating unevenly. What on earth could bring Kay all the way from London? Had something happened to Gerald?

The moment the door was open Kay almost fell in through it. 'God, what a place!' she gasped. 'You can hardly breathe for the wind out there. I don't know how you stand it.'

'Hello, Kay,' Cathy said dryly. 'What a surprise. Can I do something for you?'

Kay was taking off her coat and untying the scarf from her hair. 'A cup of coffee would be nice,' she said. 'A gin and tonic would be even better.' She threw the coat over a chair and looked Cathy in the eye. 'But I haven't come all this way to socialise. We have to talk, Cathy.' She looked around her. 'You are alone, I take it?'

'Apart from Maggie.' Cathy's stomach churned uneasily. 'Is it serious – bad news?'

Kay looked at her oddly. 'Perhaps we could go somewhere where we won't be disturbed? I'd rather we weren't overheard.'

Without a word Cathy led the way into the drawing room and closed the door. She could hear the sound of the vacuum cleaner coming from behind the closed study door, Maggie's voice rising above it with a spirited rendering of *If You Were the Only Girl In The World*. She turned to Kay who had already made herself comfortable in a chair near the fire.

'Would you like that drink first?'

She shook her head. For the first time she looked edgy. 'I think we'd better get this over,' she said. 'Sit down, Cathy.'

In spite of the fact that she resented being told what

to do in her own home, Cathy sat in the chair opposite and looked expectantly at the other woman. Kay opened her bag and took out a cigarette. As she lit it Cathy saw that her hands trembled slightly. She drew deeply on it and blew out a thin stream of smoke before she said: 'The fact is, Gerald won't be coming home.'

Cathy's heart missed a beat. 'Something's gone wrong? His treatment . . .?'

'No, no! Nothing like that,' Kay said with an impatient shake of her head. 'Look, there's really only one way to say this, Cathy. He wants a divorce. He's leaving you.'

'I see.' She found that she was icily calm. 'And is there a reason? Am I to be allowed to hear it? I take it you know?'

Kay drew hard on her cigarette and threw back her head defiantly. 'Of course. He intends to marry me. We've been close for years, Cathy. I'm sure you know that. We should have married a long time ago. He needs me. I understand him as no one else ever could. When he married you he wasn't in his right mind. His illness clouded his judgement.'

'Really?' Cathy felt detached – unreal. It was such a bizarre situation. 'In what way?'

Kay shrugged. 'Maybe he saw it as clutching at life while there was still time. Now that he's well again and thinking rationally he knows it was a terrible mistake – for you both.'

'In other words, he's regained his sanity and turned back to you?'

Kay looked hard at Cathy. 'I must say you're taking it all very coolly.'

'Perhaps there's something you should know, Kay,' she said. 'Something I've only just discovered for myself. Gerald is a liar and a cheat. His only real consideration is himself and his career. Twenty years ago he broke up a marriage, split a family and caused a lot of suffering and heartbreak. How do you think I felt when I found out recently that the family was mine? That the woman he ran away with was my mother? The wife of Gerald's best friend.'

For a long moment the two looked at each other. Then Kay said: 'I know.'

Cathy stared at her. 'You know?'

'Yes.' She ground out her cigarette. 'He told me the whole story a few days ago. I've been in New Zealand myself, Cathy. I had to go over on business, so I was able to be with him. Gerald and I have talked a lot over the past weeks. Serious illness makes people do a lot of soul searching. It was good I was there for him. He married you for a variety of reasons. You reminded him of her – Jenny. Maybe it was partly out of some wish to put right the wrong he did; partly some vague notion of regaining his lost youth. Who knows? As I said before, he wasn't himself. But all it did was give him an inflated sense of guilt and bring back memories he'd hoped were dead and buried. Now he wants to turn back the clock and return to his concert career.'

'I see. Just like that? As though I didn't exist.' Cathy looked around her. 'And what about all this? What about this house and the school, the people booked for next year's seminars and concerts? The pupils he has lined up for his return?'

Kay waved a dismissive hand. 'You can cancel them, can't you? As soon as he's back in circulation Gerald will see to it that the house is put up for sale and that you're all right financially, of course.'

'Oh, yes, that's Gerald's way isn't it? To cancel everything he's bored with. Turn over a new page in the Cavelle saga and begin a new chapter. Never mind the trail of havoc he leaves behind.'

'I tried to tell him it was wrong at the time, Cathy. He did you a grave disservice and he knows it now. He's trying to make amends, so why not let him? Oh, come now – can you honestly say he made you happy?'

'That's not the point. A marriage is between two people

and so is the breaking of it. Why couldn't Gerald have talked to me about this himself?'

'It's better this way. He isn't up to it yet. He knows he can rely on me to handle it tactfully.'

'He's lucky to have you. I'm beginning to see it now,' Cathy said dryly. 'What happens next then?'

'First we're going to have a holiday together. Right away from everything and everyone.'

'From me, you mean. From Melfordleigh and me.'

'Don't be bitter.' Kay reached out a tentative hand to touch Cathy's arm. 'Why not cut your losses and make a new start? You're still so young. You have your whole life in front of you. As for your mother . . . it was all so long ago. And it takes two, you know. She ran out on you and your father. Jenny had to be at least fifty per cent to blame.'

'Don't you *dare* speak my mother's name!' Cathy was on her feet, her cheeks pink and her eyes blazing. 'You know *nothing* about her or the suffering Gerald put her and my father through. She wanted to have me with her. She probably wanted to come back to us, but he wouldn't let her. He was afraid of a scandal. He thought he might be named in a divorce case. He wasn't risking that. So he sent her abroad and she died there. Convenient, wasn't it? And poor Dad never even knew that Gerald – his so-called best friend – was the cause of it all.'

'He did try to make amends, you know,' Kay said quietly. 'He even bought music from your father to pay for your school fees.'

'He did *what*?' Cathy's colour faded.

'Bought compositions of your father's. Little jingles he knew would never be published. To finance your education at some private school. He did it to try to make up for what had happened. So don't judge him too harshly, Cathy. None of us is perfect – not even you, I daresay.'

She flushed warmly, stung to silence as she wondered if

Simon had said anything to Kay about their brief affair. The other woman rose to her feet.

'I think perhaps I'd better go now.' She walked to the door, then turned. 'I wouldn't get any vindictive ideas about refusing to divorce him,' she said. 'He isn't coming back anyway, so it wouldn't make any difference, except to you.' She paused. 'I'm sure you'll see that this is best for everyone – when you've had time to calm down.'

Cathy stood perfectly still. Above the beat of her own heart she heard Kay's footsteps cross the hall. With crystal clarity she heard the slam of the front door, the clunk of the car door, then the crunch of gravel as Kay drove away.

Very slowly she sank on to the chair again and felt the tension slowly seep from her body. So – her marriage, her mockery of a marriage, was over. She was left to pick up the pieces. But there were some pieces that could never be reassembled; some shattered fragments of her life whose sharp edges would hurt her for ever.

Chapter Nineteen

When Rosalind returned to the Queen's Head she missed Cathy and Cuckoo Lodge even more than she had expected to. She had loved Melfordleigh and the natural beauty of the Suffolk coastline. The house had impressed her too. She envied Cathy in so many ways. She had so much: a lovely home and a husband she adored. Belonging to someone who loved you in return must be very special, though an underlying unease about Cathy still haunted Rosalind. There was something she couldn't quite put a finger on. Although the other girl had made her welcome and seemed genuinely glad of her company, the feeling that she was putting a brave face on some hidden unhappiness was always present. It was in the way she looked when she thought no one was observing her; in the wistful sadness lurking in the lovely green eyes. It tugged at Rosalind's heart, making her long to ask what was troubling her and try to help. If only Cathy had trusted her enough to confide it would have encouraged her to unburden herself about the shameful secret she herself was trying to forget. Telling someone was something she found she needed more and more as the months passed.

In spite of her nostalgia for the fresh sea air and Cathy's company, she continued to enjoy her work at the hotel and her days at college. Each week she learned a new facet of the hotel business and she was grateful to Mrs Gresham for allowing her the opportunity of working in so many parts of the hotel. She had tried her hand in every department now, from the kitchen, restaurant and bar to the bedrooms; from catering to housekeeping; admin to personnel. She realised that studying at college alone could never have provided her with so much practical experience.

She had seen little of Freda since the opening of *Sweet Violet*. The unsocial hours they both worked left few opportunities for meeting. The show had enjoyed rave reviews and there was even talk of taking it to Broadway some time in the coming year. How proud Ben would have been of the girl he had discovered and loved so much. Since the opening of the show Freda's photograph had appeared on the cover of *Applause*, a popular show business magazine, and there had been interviews and profiles in several glossy women's magazines too. Rosalind had cut them all out and lovingly pasted them into a scrap-book.

Although there weren't many opportunities for them to meet, Freda often telephoned and kept in touch and occasionally, on Rosalind's day off, they would lunch together. Freda had recently taken a cosy little flat in Holland Park and loved to spend her free time cooking and pottering.

Rosalind had read in the papers that Julian Travers and Brian French had completed a new musical, which would be going straight into the West End and was already in rehearsal. Freda told her that Stuart would not be doing the designs for this one. He no longer shared a flat with Julian. Both had moved to smarter flats closer to the West End and Stuart had been offered a permanent job with a television company.

As Christmas approached a party was arranged backstage for the cast and friends of *Sweet Violet*. Rosalind was invited but she told Freda she couldn't possibly go. The Queen's Head was busy now with the Christmas rush. The restaurant was booked solid, mainly with dinner dances and private firms' Christmas functions. Most of the accommodation was booked too, as many people liked to stay over after a party and she explained to Freda that she couldn't ask for time off. But a few days later when Mrs Gresham heard about the party she insisted that Rosalind must go.

'I hear it doesn't start until after the performance,' she said. 'Miss Moore rang me and explained. She says you are the only family she has and she wants you to be there very much.' As Rosalind opened her mouth to protest she held up her hand. 'No arguments. I'm going to insist that you go, Rosalind. You'll enjoy it so much, meeting all those celebrities, and you've worked so hard here. You deserve it.'

Rosalind had mixed feelings. In a way she was excited about the party, but, truth to tell, she was half-afraid of walking into a room full of such glamorous people. They were all so confident and accomplished, even the chorus girls exuded a charisma that made her feel plain and insignificant. But Mrs Gresham was adamant that she must go and Rosalind knew Freda wanted her to be there. So, swallowing her misgivings, she went out to buy a new dress, determined that at least Freda would not be ashamed of the way she looked.

It was arranged that after the party Rosalind should stay at Freda's flat for the night, and as the following day was Sunday and her day off they could spend some time together.

Rosalind arrived at the stage door at half-past ten, soon after the final curtain. Freda was in her dressing room. She had already changed into a stunning dress of white silk, embroidered with beads and sequins, and had just finished putting on fresh make-up when Rosalind arrived. She looked up at her through the dressing-table mirror, her face breaking into a smile.

'Rossie. You look lovely!' She got up and held out her hands, admiring the slim black dress with its short flared skirt and ribbon sleeves. 'And you've had your hair cut too!' She turned Rosalind round, admiring the new swinging jaw-length bob. 'Sit down and let me make up your eyes for you,' she invited. 'I've got a new eye shadow that will make them look enormous.'

Very skilfully she shadowed Rosalind's dark eyes in soft shades of brown and beige, accentuating them with liner and mascara. 'There,' she said, standing back to admire her work in the mirror. 'You look fabulous.' She held out her hand. 'Now – come and meet the rest of the cast.' She laughed, giving Rosalind a quick hug. 'And don't look so terrified. Relax, darling. I want you to have a good time.'

On the stage the set had been taken down. A long table was laden with a sumptuous buffet and in one corner a bar had been set up. Whoever was in charge of music had put on a Dusty Springfield record and already several couples were dancing. Rosalind shrank as the familiar shyness engulfed her. She'd looked forward to this evening so much, convincing herself that she had conquered her old insecurities, yet now her one desire was to turn tail and run away.

Freda, feeling the reluctance in the sudden dampness of the hand she held, grasped it tightly, refusing to allow Rosalind to give way to her nervousness. At the bar she asked for two large gin and tonics and pressed one into Rosalind's trembling hand.

'Drink that,' she ordered. 'It'll make you feel relaxed in no time.' She cast her eyes around for a face that would be familiar to Rosalind. 'Look, there's Julian over there,' she said. 'You know him. And there's Brian with him. Come on. I'll take you over.'

Freda tapped Julian on the shoulder. 'Look who's here. I know you've met Rosalind before.'

He turned and looked at her. 'Of course. How nice to see you,' he said, holding out his hand and taking hers warmly. 'How is your mother?'

She gave him an apologetic smile. 'I don't really know. I left home some time ago and we don't keep in touch.'

'I can't say I blame you,' Julian said wryly. 'Though I

suppose I shouldn't say that.' He turned back towards the group he had been talking to. 'Let me introduce you. Brian you know of course. This is Paul Greirson, our musical director, and . . .' He tapped the shoulder of a man whose back was turned towards them. 'Stuart – look who's here.'

The man turned and Rosalind found herself suddenly face to face with Stuart. The shock made her heart quicken uncomfortably. Knowing that he was no longer involved with Julian and Brian, it hadn't occurred to her that he might be at the party. If it had she would probably not have come. Now there was no escape. Tentatively she offered her hand which he took, looking at her with an expression of frank astonishment.

'Hello, Rossie. How marvellous to see you again. How are you?'

'I'm fine, thank you.'

The others in the group seemed suddenly to melt away and she found herself left with Stuart. He looked very handsome. He had grown his fair hair longer in the current fashion and the dinner jacket and frilled evening shirt he wore were well cut and looked expensive. He was staring at her with open admiration. So many times she had visualised a chance meeting such as this and wondered how she would react, but now that she had recovered from the initial shock of seeing him again she found that her emotions remained surprisingly cool.

'I didn't recognise you for a moment,' he was saying. 'You look absolutely wonderful.'

She took a sip of her drink, trying to ignore the back-handed compliment. 'Thank you. I hear you've landed rather a good job. Congratulations.'

'Thanks. Yes it is going rather well. Working for TV is very exciting. What are you doing?'

'Training for hotel management, just as I always meant to,' she said. 'Boringly predictable, that's me.'

'Oh, I wouldn't say that,' he said with an appraising smile. 'I wouldn't say that at all. Will you dance?' Without waiting for her assent, he took the glass from her hand and put it on a nearby table, leading her on to the space reserved for dancing.

In his arms as they circled to a romantic tune, Rosalind was amazed at her own coolness. Just a short time ago she had thought herself deeply in love with this young man; her world had fallen apart when he had dropped her so callously in favour of someone else. Yet now when she looked at him she saw only a shallow, slightly foppish young man; self-centred and ineffectual, certainly unworthy of the tears she had shed for him. To prove it, both to him and to herself, she asked casually: 'How is Elaine?'

He looked blank.

'Elaine Frisby,' she prompted. 'The girl who made the costumes for *Sweet Violet*.'

Light dawned in the lazy blue eyes. 'Oh, *that* Elaine,' he said. 'I haven't seen her for ages.' He looked round at the other dancers. 'She might be here this evening, I suppose.' He smiled down at her. 'How is Una?'

Rosalind smiled wryly. 'I wouldn't know. I left home some time ago. Soon after my father died. We haven't made contact since.'

'Pity she never made it to the West End with the show,' he said casually. 'Jacobson always felt she was wrong for the role, you know. Between you and me, he couldn't wait to get rid of her. It sounds harsh, I know, but you can't afford sentiment with such a huge financial investment at stake. And I must say that Freda is an enormous improvement. She has a fantastic voice and brings such vibrance and vitality to the part.'

'Yes, she does, doesn't she?' Rosalind looked at him. 'I'm very proud of her. But Una and Don did get the three of you off the ground, didn't they?' she said dryly. 'I'm sure none of you will ever wish to forget that.'

To her amusement and secret satisfaction he actually blushed.

When the music stopped she made an excuse and went to find Freda, relieved that an unhappy chapter of her past had been successfully brought to its conclusion. To her relief Stuart avoided her for the rest of the evening.

After that first dance she found to her astonishment that she was in demand. She hardly sat one dance out. Even Stephen Troy, the male lead from the cast, asked her to dance, and Freda told her later that several young men had asked her who her attractive friend was. Rosalind suspected her of making it up to boost her confidence, but nevertheless she was quietly pleased with herself. The party she had dreaded turned out to be most enjoyable and she was sorry when it came to an end.

She and Freda spent a quiet Sunday relaxing until it was time for Rosalind to catch her train. Freda travelled with her as far as Tottenham Court Road underground station and waved her off, promising to ring her again before Christmas. She was going up to Birmingham to spend the two days she had off with her sister so this would be the last they would see of each other till the New Year.

As Rosalind sat in the train, her thoughts on last night's party and the coming holiday, she was suddenly aware that the glamorous blonde girl in the seat opposite was staring at her. She looked up and instantly recognised Carla Maybridge. She wore a striking black velvet coat whose huge fur collar framed her blonde head and exquisitely made-up face. Below it her long legs were encased in shiny black patent boots. She smiled in surprised recognition.

'It really *is* you, isn't it – Rosalind Blair? I couldn't make up my mind at first.'

'Hello, Carla. Haven't seen you for ages.'

'You look fabulous.' Secretly impressed by the transformation in Rosalind, Carla moved across to join her, engaging her in what was mainly a one-sided diatribe about her own madly gay social life and her success in modelling. 'I'm going home to see the folks,' she explained. 'I don't see them very often and when I found I was free this Sunday, I thought I'd better make the effort.'

'You won't be going home for Christmas then?'

Carla shook her head. 'God forbid! All my lot seem to have hordes of kids. You can't hear yourself *think* for the noise. Screaming babies wall to wall and sticky fingers all over your clothes! It's just not my scene. No, they're going to have to exist without their Auntie Carlie this year. I'm off to Austria instead. A whole bunch of us are going – boys and girls.' She smiled in anticipation. 'A little ski lodge high in the mountains. Log fires and après ski parties. I can't *wait*! A lot more fun than washing up endless greasy dishes and fishing the nut shells out of the loose covers.' She looked inquiringly at Rosalind. 'What are you doing these days?'

'I work at the Queen's Head. I'm a trainee manager,' Rosalind told her. 'I'll be working over Christmas. It's our busiest time.'

'God, how dreary! Poor old you.' Carla's expression transmitted her opinion of hotel management as a career. Although, she mused, it seemed to have made poor old Rosalind pull up her socks on the appearance front. Still very conservative, of course, but certainly an improvement on the plain, lumpy schoolgirl in specs and baggy cardigans. Her legs weren't bad either, now that one could actually see them.

Thinking of school reminded her of her recent meeting with Cathy. She said, 'I saw Cathy Oldham last summer, or Cathy Cavelle as she is now. Said she was up here for a couple of weeks' holiday.' She looked at Rosalind inquiringly. 'Did you happen to run into her at all?'

'Yes, I did as a matter of fact. Actually she invited me to go and stay with her in Suffolk. I went a few weeks ago. We had a lovely time.'

'*Really?*' Carla bridled. She'd received no such invitation and after the good turn she'd done her too. She raised an eyebrow at Rosalind. 'I see. So – as you've become such close friends I expect she told you about her little trauma.'

'No. What trauma?'

'She didn't tell you about her abortion? Well, I *am* surprised.'

'Cathy?' Rosalind frowned. 'Surely, you must be mistaken?'

'I don't think so, unless of course she decided not to go through with it. In that case she must be going ahead with her pregnancy.'

'She wasn't pregnant when I saw her last.'

'Oh well, in that case there's no mistake.'

Rosalind shook her head. 'Are you sure – about Cathy? I mean, it doesn't sound like her at all. It wouldn't do to go spreading stories like that if it isn't true.'

'I only know what she told me,' Carla said defensively. 'For all I know perhaps everything resolved itself without any help. And I'm not *spreading stories* as you put it. I only mentioned it because you and she have obviously become close friends.' Carla felt distinctly uncomfortable. She'd clearly said too much. As the train rumbled to a halt at Hendon Central she seized her opportunity of escape and edged towards the door. 'Look, I can't stop now. I'm getting off here. Have a call to make. Someone else I have to drop in on before going home. *Super* to see you, Rosalind. Have a good Christmas. 'Bye.' And with a waft of Chanel and a swish of fur-trimmed velvet she was gone.

The casual remark gave Rosalind plenty to think about. So much in fact that she almost went past her own station. Had Cathy really been pregnant last summer? She certainly hadn't looked at all well. If she had lost a baby it would explain a great deal. Poor Cathy. No wonder she looked sad and wistful.

When she arrived back at the Queen's Head Mrs Gresham came out of her office and met her in the hallway.

'Rosalind, you have a visitor. She's been here for over an hour. She spent a lot of that time in the bar, but I've put her in your room to wait for you. I had to use the pass key. I hope you don't mind?'

'No. Not at all.' Rosalind looked mystified. 'Who is it?'

'It's your mother, dear,' Mrs Gresham said quietly. 'And I'm afraid she seems a little – er – under the weather. I told her you might be some time but she insisted on waiting.'

Rosalind was quaking with apprehension as she pushed open the door of her room and went in. At once she could see what Mrs Gresham had meant by 'under the weather'. Una had obviously been drinking. Rosalind could smell the alcohol from here. No wonder the staff were anxious to get her out of the bar.

On closer inspection she saw that her mother had lost weight. Her skin looked sallow and her features sharp and haggard. When she saw Rosalind she stared at her accusingly.

'Where the hell have you been?' she demanded stridently. 'I've been stuck in this poky little room for hours! That snooty manageress woman made me come up here. Who does she think she is?'

'Sunday is my day off,' Rosalind said. 'And I think Mrs Gresham thought you'd be more comfortable in here.'

'I rang last night and said I'd be coming along at six. I think you might have made the effort to be here.'

'I wasn't here, so I didn't get the message. What's wrong, Mum? Why are you here?'

Una affected a wounded expression. 'Why am I here? That's a nice thing to greet me with, isn't it? I hope I have the right to visit my own daughter.' When Rosalind didn't reply she said, 'I want you to come home, Rossie. It's as simple as that. I want us to make up our differences.'

Rosalind's heart sank. Una's whining tone and maudlin expression didn't fool her. There was more to her sudden request for a reconciliation than met the eye and Rosalind knew from experience that whatever it was would not be to her advantage. She sank on to the chair opposite. 'Why, Mum? What's gone wrong?'

'Does there have to be something wrong for me to want my own daughter home with me again?'

'Why now?'

Una shrugged. 'It's Christmas. It's the time for families, isn't it?'

Rosalind sighed. 'I can't come home now, Mum. This is our busiest time. I'll be working all over the holiday.'

'Afterwards then. Say you give in your notice now and come home in January?'

'Give in my notice?' Rosalind stared at her. 'You're asking me to give up my job? I can't. I'm training for management. I go to college two days a week and I work here the rest of the time.'

'But surely if your family needs you . . .?'

'What's all this about, Mum? Why don't you just tell me? Is it Don? Have you left him?'

Una grunted. 'Huh! Chance'd be a fine thing. Look, Rossie, I've got the offer of work – up north. It's important to me. I want to take it.'

'A show?'

'No.' Una avoided her eyes. 'Just, you know, singing.'

'A tour?'

'Not exactly. Cabaret – I suppose you could say. Clubs, the northern circuit.'

'Oh, Mum, you've done clubs before. It didn't work out.'

'This is different,' Una insisted. 'Northern clubland is different now. Industry and mining are booming up there apparently. There's a lot of money around nowadays. Working men's clubs are very different places to what they were years ago. Sophisticated; glamorous even. The pay is good too. I'd get top billing. I want to do it, Rossie.'

410

'So – what's the problem?'

Una sighed and twisted her fingers in her lap. 'It's Don. He's planning to retire from Hallard's next year and he wants me to retire with him. He says he's had enough of being on his own, but I'm fairly sure I could get him to agree to a compromise. I'm going to suggest that he lets me have this one last try. If I make it, well and good. If I don't, then I'll do as he says and retire.'

'So?'

'I'm pretty sure he'd agree if I got you to come home and look after him while I'm away.'

Rosalind stared at her mother in disbelief. 'You want me to give up my training and my job so that you can go on a short tour of northern working men's clubs? Mum, why don't you face up to reality? You've got a lovely home and a good husband. You could have a life of leisure. He'd do anything for you – give you anything you wanted, you know he would. But it's *you* he wants with him, not me. I've heard about these northern clubs from some of the guests here. They might look glamorous, but the audiences are as tough as before. They'd destroy you.'

'You can't know that! You're just saying it to get out of your duty. You're as selfish as you always were, Rossie. You're your bloody father all over again.' Una stared at her daughter, for the first time taking in her new appearance. She assessed the smart, understated suit, the hairstyle and make-up. Her eyes narrowed. 'You've been seeing *her*, haven't you? That Morton bitch?'

'Freda? I've seen her, yes.'

'More than just *seen* her by the look of this!' Una sprang to her feet and revealed something hidden behind her in the chair. It was the scrapbook filled with Freda's press cuttings. She must have been looking through while she waited. She threw it at Rosalind's feet.

'The pair of you have ganged up, why not admit it?' Her eyes flashed dangerously as they swept Rosalind from head

411

to foot. 'You always did let her influence you, didn't you? She's been trying to tart you up again too by the look of you. That cow took my big chance away from me; snatched my part just as we were going into Town with the show.' She narrowed her eyes at Rosalind. 'But of course you *know* all that, don't you? I daresay the pair of you had a bloody good laugh at my expense. I wouldn't put it past you to have put her up to it in the first place. Just to get back at me.' Her voice had risen shrilly and Rosalind stepped forward.

'Mum! Keep your voice down, please. The residents will hear and think we're having a row.'

'A row?' Una swayed unsteadily. 'Well, what if we are having a sodding row? It's none of their business. Let them think what they bloody well like. I'll shout if I want to. I'll say what I like to my selfish bitch of a daughter.' She stepped up to Rosalind and wagged a finger in her face. 'You *owe* me, Rossie. You betrayed me – you and that treacherous slut. She took the man I loved, then she stole my chance of success. Now she's poisoned my daughter's mind against me.' Her face crumpled and she choked on a sob. 'You owe me, Rossie. So are you going to come home and give me one last chance? *Are you?*'

'*No, I'm not!*' Rosalind's voice was strong and firm as she stood her ground and looked her mother in the eye. She was slightly shorter than Una but as she spoke her mother seemed to shrink visibly before her eyes. 'Face facts, Mum,' she went on. 'Freda didn't take Dad from you. They met long after you'd parted. No one stole your part either. Mr Jacobson recast it. When Freda went to the audition she didn't even know you were in the play. It was open to anyone and she got it. And as for poisoning my mind . . .' She stopped herself from saying what was in her mind. A row would get them nowhere. She reached out to touch Una's arm gently. 'Oh, Mum, why don't you give up? Let go. Don't risk making a fool of yourself. You've got so much and you're throwing it all away. I won't come home and let you do it to yourself. I wouldn't even if it *didn't* mean sacrificing all I've worked for.'

Speechless, Una stood looking at her daughter, her face working with anger. For a moment Rosalind thought she was about to collapse. Then she took a deep breath and pulled herself together. 'All right,' she said at last. 'You just think of yourself. Just stay here in your pathetic little job. You're no more than a servant if only you knew it!'

'Are you saying that what you're offering me is better?' Rosalind asked coolly.

Una snatched her handbag from the chair where she'd been sitting and headed for the door. 'Have it your way then. But don't think you've heard the last of this, my girl, because you haven't. No one tells me I'm a fool and gets away with it, especially the ungrateful child I sacrificed everything for.'

As the door closed behind her Rosalind felt all the old insecurities and inhibitions flood back. Why did Una always manage to make her feel guilty when she knew she had nothing to feel guilty about?

When Don opened the front door and saw Una standing on the doorstep his first reaction was relief. She'd been gone for hours and he was just wondering if he should go out and start looking for her.

'Una . . .' he began.

She swept past him into the hall. 'There's a taxi waiting,' she said abruptly. 'He wants paying. See to it, will you? My head's splitting.'

When he came back in he found her sitting slumped in a corner of the settee, one hand clutching her head. Kneeling, he eased the shoes from her feet. 'You're frozen, love. Where have you been? I was so worried.'

'I've been to see that daughter of mine,' she said bitterly. 'I thought we might make up our differences. I invited her to come home again – for Christmas. Maybe for good.'

'Really? Oh, I'm so glad, dear. What did she say?'

413

'You might well ask. Threw the invitation in my face. I might as well have stayed at home in the warm and saved my breath,' Una said. 'I've humiliated myself for nothing. And you should have heard some of the things she said. It's all that Morton bitch's doing. Hand in glove they are. Rosalind even keeps all her press cuttings pasted into a book.' She choked on a self-pitying sob. 'She never kept *my* press cuttings, never gave a damn about my career.'

'Never mind. Let me make you a nice cup of tea and get you an aspirin, eh?'

She nodded. 'Yes. And make it strong. In fact, don't bother. I'll have a brandy instead.'

As he put the glass into her hand, he sat down on the settee beside her. 'I know you must feel hurt and disappointed about Rosalind, dear. But she's a young woman now and she has her own life to live.' He took her free hand and held it tenderly. 'I daresay she sees Freda as more of a friend. After all, they are of an age, aren't they?'

She glared at him. 'You're saying I'm old, are you? Over the hill?'

'Of course I'm not. I'm just pointing out that we all have our own futures to think of.' He squeezed her hand and leaned closer. 'Just think of the marvellous time we'll have when I retire. We can spend a lot of our time travelling abroad, all winter if you like; follow the sun as they say. We can go to the theatre, join the golf club and socialise more – anything that takes your fancy. Just the two of us. All mothers have to let go at some stage, you know, dear.'

'You're a fine one to talk about mothers letting go,' she snapped, snatching her hand away. 'Yours still hasn't let go from the other side of the grave! I've told you, Don, I'm not as old as you. I've got no intention of retiring. I still want to *work*. I've had this offer to do the northern clubs and I really want to do it.'

He sighed. He had made his views plain, or so he thought. Heaven only knew they'd been over it enough times. He

414

couldn't face living with the person Una became after experiencing a failure. His life had been hell on earth after her exclusion from the cast of *Sweet Violet* – and since. He had come to dread those magazine articles and cover pictures of Freda Morton, or Benita Moore as she was known. Every time Una read one of those interviews it threw her into a black depression for days, especially if her ex-husband's name happened to be included. It was true that Mother had tended to dominate him when she was alive, but at least she'd had his best interests at heart. Mother was devoted to him whilst Una cared only for herself. Every instinct told him that if he gave in over this latest issue he would never know another moment's peace as long as they were together.

'*No*, Una,' he said as firmly as he knew how to. 'I'm sorry, but I'm putting my foot down. If you want to go rushing up and down the country again then you'll do it without my support.' He looked at her white face. 'It's you I'm thinking of if only you could see it. Those northern audiences are tough and demanding. They'd tear you apart. And you know what another failure would do to you.'

'Why must you take it for granted I'd fail just because that woman manipulated me out last time?' She turned to stare at him accusingly. 'You've been talking to *her*, haven't you? Rossie? She said the very same thing! You've been meeting. You've cooked this up between you.'

'No.' He shook his head. 'I haven't set eyes on Rosalind since . . .'

'Since when? Since you gave her the money to go to Australia? Is that what you were going to say?'

'No. She didn't go to Australia.'

'But she *was* going. And you did give her the money – behind my back too. That was disloyal of you, Don. It was what caused the row that split us up.' She turned in her seat to look at him. 'You could say yes to *her*, couldn't you? You gave her the money when you knew I didn't want her to go.

415

The devious little bitch went snivelling to you behind my back and you caved in and gave it to her, just like that.' She snapped her fingers.

'It wasn't like that, Una. She never asked.'

'Oh, no?' she sneered. 'It all came out by accident, didn't it? Lucky accident for *her*, wasn't it?'

'Believe it or not, it's the truth, Una.' For a long moment their eyes locked. Don held her gaze, his grey eyes unfaltering. It was Una who looked away first. But she wasn't convinced. There was something more behind this and she'd get to the bottom of it if it was the last thing she did. And if she wasn't going to be allowed her chance to make her name in the northern clubs then Don was going to have to make some concessions.

'All right,' she said at last. 'If I'm going to be kept like a bloody prisoner in this mausoleum of your mother's, I'll need to redecorate it.'

Don gave a sigh of relief. He'd dreaded putting his foot down but it seemed to have worked. 'All right, if that's what you want.'

'I do!' She looked at him. 'It hasn't been done since we were first married. And when I say redecorated I mean completely, mind. Furniture, carpets, curtains. The kitchen re-fitted, new bathroom, the lot. All done by a professional designer too. No amateurs or cowboys.'

Don tried not to wince as he did some rapid panic-stricken mental arithmetic. 'If that's what it takes to make you happy,' he said haltingly.

'It does. I'll make a start tomorrow.'

'But we're only a few days off Christmas.'

'Sod Christmas! We'll spend that in a hotel.' She got up and began to walk around the room. 'When I'm done with this house your beloved mother wouldn't know it,' she said spitefully. 'I'll see to it that there isn't one thing of hers left. I think it's high time *she* let go, don't you Don?'

Una was as good as her word. The following day she

went from room to room, notebook in hand, jotting down her ideas. Then she sat down with the telephone book and made a list of all the interior designers in the area. She was determined to transform the place, to get rid of every last vestige of the late Mrs Blake senior. On a separate piece of paper she made a note of the few pieces of Mrs Blake's furniture that Don had insisted on keeping. She would telephone a saleroom to collect the horrid antiquated monstrosities. The sooner they were out of the house, the sooner Don would know that this time she meant business.

She thought she had noted everything when she remembered the display cabinet. Don had stuck out for that, but now it would definitely have to go. But what about the contents? He had always insisted that his mother's collection of Meissen porcelain was extremely valuable. Perhaps she should contact an antique dealer about it.

Opening the glass door Una looked at the delicate figurines with dislike. She'd always hated fussy fragile things that broke if you so much as breathed on them. But nevertheless, she respected them for their value. She peered closer, frowning. If she wasn't very much mistaken there was a piece missing. Yes, there was a gap on the top shelf and the outline of its base could clearly be seen on the glass support. She took a step back and racked her brain as she tried to remember what it had been like. If she remembered correctly it had been the largest piece in the collection – a ghastly thing shaped like a shell. Yes, that was it. It had sugary flowers and four fat naked children with insipid expressions. Nauseating! But the question was, where had it gone? Don would never have sold it. He didn't need the money. Anyway, if he'd been that hard up he would surely have sold the whole collection.

Her eyes narrowed. Had he sold it so that he could give Rosalind the money for her fare to Australia? Yes, that must be it – so that Una wouldn't notice that the amount had been withdrawn from their bank account. Her suspicions well and truly aroused, she went into the study and began to rummage in his desk. There would be something – a receipt, a bill of sale, an auctioneer's invoice. When she knew the date of the sale she would know for sure she was right. But although she searched thoroughly she found nothing until, right at the back of the little stamp drawer, she found a small card. Printed on it in heavy black German text were the words:

Pegasus Antiques
Furniture, antiquarian books and objects d'art
Prop. Arnold Corbett. 125 Bently Street, Chelsea

Una found the little shop without difficulty. The old-fashioned door-bell tinkled as she went in and she wrinkled her nose at the familiar musty smell of old books and furniture. Why on earth anyone wanted to pay good money for dead people's cast-offs was beyond her. But the elderly man behind the counter seemed clean and tidy enough. He looked up at her over his half-moon glasses with a benign smile.

'Good morning, madam. Can I help you?'

'I don't know. I'm looking for a particular piece of china. An ornament. I have reason to believe that you might have bought it.'

'Well, I do often buy china and porcelain. Could you perhaps describe it for me?'

Una did her best to describe the piece, adding as an afterthought, 'I believe it was rather special. Meissen, I think.'

'Ah.' The man's face cleared. 'There was a piece recently that answered to that description. But if you were wanting to buy it, I'm afraid it was sold almost immediately. I have a client who is a keen collector of Meissen, you see. He was delighted with it and snapped it up at . . .'

'Yes, *yes*,' Una snapped impatiently. 'I didn't want

to buy it. All I really want to know is, who sold it to you?'

The man looked uncomfortable. 'Well, I don't normally . . .'

'It may well have been stolen for all I know,' Una put in sharply. 'It's missing, you see. But I found your card, so I think it may have been a member of my family, which would clear the mystery up and make everything all right.' She looked him in the eye. 'I don't want to have to go to the police, do I? Receiving carries a rather high penalty, I believe.'

'Ah – I see. No, indeed. Bringing in the police would be most unpleasant. Well now, let me see. I'm afraid I don't have a name for the person.'

'A description would do.' Una was beginning to lose her patience. Why couldn't the old fool just spit it out? 'Was it a man, for instance?' she prompted. 'A middle-aged man?'

'Oh, no.' For the first time the man sounded positive. 'Definitely not a man. A young woman.' He half-closed his eyes, recalling. 'Dark hair and eyes. Spectacles. A very pale face as I remember. If my memory serves me right I believe she said the piece belonged to a deceased relative. She needed the money to visit her sick father in Australia.'

Una gasped. So *that* was it! 'Did she now? Thank you, Mr Corbett,' she said on her way to the door. 'Thank you *very* much.'

'Not at all, madam. Happy to have been of help.'

'You'll never know just how *much* of a help you've been,' Una murmured under her breath.

In a nearby café she digested the shocking revelation. Rosalind had stolen the Meissen. She must have done. Don would never have given it to her. He'd rather have given her the money. Then he must have found out. *And he had let her keep the money and said nothing about it.*

She could hardly believe it, yet it all fitted now that she knew the truth. Rosalind's sudden announcement that she

419

was going to Australia, then her impulsive departure from home after Ben's death. Well, they were going to have to pay for their sly little piece of deception, Don and Rosalind. And she would be the one setting the price!

'She took it, didn't she? The lying little thief stole one of your mother's precious ornaments and you let her get away with it!'

When Don arrived home from work that evening Una was standing in the hall waiting for him. Even before he had a chance to remove his coat she had begun her accusing tirade.

'If I'd done a thing like that you'd have kicked me out, lock, stock and barrel. But not her. Oh, no! Not little miss butter-wouldn't-melt!' She stood in front of him, hands on hips, demanding an explanation. 'What's been going on, Don? I'm sick and tired of having the wool pulled over my eyes. What do you think I am – stupid or something?'

'It isn't the way you think,' he began. 'If you'll just calm down and let me explain.' He made to move towards the living room but she barred his way.

'There's only one thing I want to know,' she said. 'Did she take that ornament or didn't she?'

Don winced. 'Well, yes, but . . .'

'With or without your permission?'

'I told you, it wasn't . . .'

'*With or without, Don?*'

'Without. But as soon as she'd done it she was sorry,' he added hurriedly. 'She confessed to me and . . .'

'And you let her keep the money.' Una shook her head. 'You *fool*! You're as bad as she is. You deceived me, the pair of you. And to think I was willing to give up my career. First I made sacrifices for her, then you. And all the time you were both deceiving me rotten.'

'Una, see sense. The poor girl was desperate. She needed the money to go and see her father. She'd never have done it otherwise, you must know that. If you'd only told me – if you'd let her ask, I'd have given her the plane fare happily.'

'Well, now you can *happily* make amends by letting me go and take that job,' she told him. 'I've already been in touch with my agent and said I'll go so there's nothing you can do about it now, Don.' As she spoke she was pulling her coat on. The last button fastened, she turned to him. 'And now I'm going to cook *her* goose for her. I'm going to make that little swindler wish she'd been straight with me.'

Rosalind was helping out behind the bar when Una strode into the lounge of the Queen's Head. Pushing her way to the front of the crowd she said stridently, 'I want a word with you, madam.'

The man Rosalind had been serving swung round. 'Do you *mind*? I'm being served at the moment. Wait your turn, can't you?'

'Mind your own business,' Una said, elbowing him out of the way. 'She's my daughter and I need to see her urgently on private family business, so take your drink and push off.'

The man paid for his drink and moved away with a resentful look.

Acutely embarrassed, Rosalind leaned across the bar. 'I'm on duty, Mum,' she whispered. 'Can't it wait?'

'No, it can't. I need to speak to you now.'

Afraid Una might make a scene, Rosalind asked the other girl serving to cover for her, lifted the bar flap and took her mother's arm, steering her away from the curious eyes turned in their direction. 'We can go up to my room,' she said, her heart thudding with apprehension. 'But I can only take five minutes off.'

'We'll see about that!' Una's expression smouldered unpleasantly. 'When you've heard what I have to say you might need time to take stock of the situation.' As they went up together in the lift Rosalind's heart was heavy as she wondered what was in store for her this time. She didn't have to wait long to find out. The moment the door of her room closed behind them Una came straight to the point, leaving her in no doubt about the reason for her untimely visit.

'You're a thief! You took one of Don's mother's valuable ornaments to pay for your air fare to Australia.' She held up her hand. 'Don't make things worse by trying to deny it. The man in the shop where you sold it described you to a tee, and now Don has confirmed it too.' She had the satisfaction of seeing Rosalind's face turn paper white as she sank down on the chair by the door.

'How did you find out?' she whispered.

'Never mind that. I *know*. That's all that matters to you.'

'What – are you going to do?' Rosalind asked, her stomach churning unpleasantly.

'That depends on you.'

'What do you want?'

'I want you to give in your notice here and come home. You and Don seem to be thick. Thick as *thieves*, you could say!' She laughed dryly. 'So you might as well come and keep house for him while I'm away.'

'How long would that be for?'

Una shrugged. 'I've no idea. It could be for a very long time. I hope it will!'

Rosalind sighed. It was her worst nightmare come true. But she couldn't throw away her future without some sort of fight. 'I can't do that, Mum. Frankly I don't see why I should. I asked for your help and you refused. I had to do something to get to see Dad.'

Una laughed unpleasantly. 'Oh, yes. You're your father's daughter all right.'

'And after all, the Meissen was Don's, not yours. I confessed to him what I'd done. He understood how much I needed the money and he promised me everything would be all right. He said he was going to buy the piece back.'

'Well, he couldn't,' Una told her with satisfaction.

'Oh.' Rosalind bit her lip. 'I'm sorry about that.'

'Apparently the man sold it almost immediately. That's how I found out. I noticed it was missing.'

'But I know Don wouldn't go to the police,' Rosalind said. 'He wouldn't have me charged with theft.'

'Don't rely on it,' Una said grimly. 'He would if I told him to, make no mistake about that. But don't worry. Unlike you, I wouldn't stoop so low as to betray a blood relative.'

Rosalind swallowed hard. 'I can't give up my job and my training. Not indefinitely as you seem to be asking.'

'I see. In that case I'll have no alternative than to tell Mrs Gresham the real reason you had to leave home so suddenly. I didn't expect to have to resort to that, Rossie. I was sure you'd want to do the right thing and help out; put your family first.'

Rosalind stared at her, white-faced. 'You – you wouldn't,' she whispered. But even as she said it, she knew that Una would if she had to.

'I'm sure she'd feel that it would be too risky to employ a compulsive thief in a reputable hotel like this.' Una surveyed her daughter, arms folded. 'So you might as well come home while you still have a roof over your head. It's time to make your mind up, Rossie. The offer won't stay open for ever.'

Rosalind stared at her mother incredulously. 'Why are you doing this, Mum? Why are you punishing me? You know how hard I worked to get my A levels. This job is important to me.'

'You'll get another one easily enough. Hotel skivvying jobs are ten a penny,' Una sneered. 'You ask why I'm doing it? Well, if you want to know the truth, Rosalind, I'm sick and tired of your disloyalty. You and that scheming Morton bitch have had a good laugh at my expense. Well, now you can laugh this off together. I wonder if she'll be there to help *you* find a job when you need it.' She turned, her hand on the door handle. 'Come to think of it, I wonder what your precious Freda would think of you if she knew you were light-fingered. Turn awkward and I might even have to let *her* know too.' She opened the door. 'You can move your things into Blake's Folly whenever you like. I'm off to Huddersfield the day after Boxing Day, thank God! I'll tell Don to expect you.'

Mrs Gresham looked at Rosalind across the desk in her office. 'Leave? But I thought you were so happy with us, Rosalind.'

'I was – I am, Mrs Gresham. It's just that there are family problems and I have to go home and help out.'

'Well, if there's anything I can do to help in any way, just say so,' Mrs Gresham said anxiously. 'It seems such a pity to leave when you've settled into your training programme so nicely.'

Rosalind swallowed hard at the lump in her throat. 'It's just that my mother has to be away from home for some time and she needs me to take care of things there.'

The manageress frowned. 'If you don't mind my saying so, Rosalind, I think that's rather inconsiderate of her. She must know how important your training is to you. Surely she could engage a housekeeper? How long will this situation last? I couldn't keep your job open indefinitely, of course, but perhaps for a month or so.'

'I – don't know.' Rosalind looked down unhappily at the hands clenched together in her lap. 'Probably for quite a long time. You'd better find someone else, I think.'

There was silence as she struggled to control her emotions. The older woman watched helplessly, waiting for further explanation. When it did not come she said gently: 'Rosalind, if there is anything wrong – anything

424

you want to talk about – I can assure you it will not go beyond these walls. Forgive me, dear, but if there is some problem, something personal, I'd like to think you could trust me to help. I really hate losing you like this. It seems such a sad waste.'

'No. I – I'm sorry, but no.' Rosalind stood up and backed towards the door, afraid that if she didn't get out of the room at once she might burst into tears and blurt it all out. She couldn't risk seeing the look of incredulous shock – the disillusionment on the face of the woman who had been so kind to her. Much better to leave while she was still respected. 'You can't help,' she said. 'No one can. If it's all right with you I'll leave the day after Boxing Day.' And she left the office hurriedly, leaving the manageress shaking her head.

Christmas at the Queen's Head was frenetically busy, but Rosalind was glad to be rushed off her feet. It gave her no time to think about her ruined career prospects. When she crept up to her room at night she was too tired to do anything but fall into bed and sleep.

On the day after Boxing Day she packed, said a hurried goodbye to the rest of the staff and a regretful Mrs Gresham and took a taxi to Blake's Folly. She found Don alone staring moodily out of the drawing-room window at the deserted garden.

'Mum's gone then?' she said, looking round.

He nodded. 'Yes. Early this morning. I'm sorry about this, Rosalind. I assure you, it was none of my doing.' He turned to look at her. 'I didn't tell her voluntarily about the Meissen. She found out; saw that it was missing and put two and two together. Una was always good at that,' he added bitterly. He looked at her with genuine anxiety. 'I feel responsible for your giving up your job. I really don't need you to keep house for me. I told Una that, but she was adamant – said that her conscience wouldn't allow you to stay in a position of responsibility after what you'd ...' he trailed off, looking away.

'It's all right, Don. I know,' she said.

He turned quickly. 'Look, when I said I didn't need you, I wasn't ... I mean, you know you're perfectly welcome to stay. This is your home after all. I just didn't want you to feel obligated.'

'I know. I haven't anywhere else to go just now,' she said. 'If I could just stay here till I find another job?'

'Of course, my dear. Naturally. But couldn't you just tell your present employer that you've changed your mind and go back? Una wouldn't know. And once she's engrossed in this new job of hers she'll probably forget all about it.'

Rosalind sighed. Don obviously didn't know of Una's threat to tell Mrs Gresham everything. 'No, I can't do that,' she said. 'It doesn't matter. I didn't really want to work there any more anyway.'

'Oh, I see.' He looked relieved. 'Well, I suppose we may as well make the best of it. Shall we start by having a cup of coffee? Then we can work out some kind of routine.'

As they sat together over coffee at the kitchen table Don told her dejectedly that he doubted whether Una would return. 'I think our marriage is probably over, Rosalind,' he said. 'I've tried my hardest to please her, but I've come to the conclusion that my way of life isn't hers and never will be.'

'It's since she went back into the theatre,' Rosalind said. 'Before that she'd settled down; resigned herself to other work. She quite enjoyed her job at Hallard's – until Stuart and Julian came on the scene.'

'Now she's driven by this manic ambition to make the big time,' he said with a sigh. 'The trouble is, I'm afraid she's fooling herself. I'm terribly afraid that history will repeat itself. And what will become of her then, I dread to think.' He looked up at her bleakly. 'The trouble is that in spite of everything I still love her.'

426

'If she fails this time maybe she'll come home and settle down again,' Rosalind said without conviction.

Don sighed. 'Well – maybe. But I've decided. I'll be here for her one more time, Rosalind. If she still wants me, that is. After that . . .' He lifted his shoulders helplessly. 'After that, I'm going to have to admit defeat.'

Upstairs in her old room Rosalind unpacked her clothes and put them away. Then she went downstairs and began to prepare a meal for Don and herself. When they had eaten he asked hesitantly if she would like to watch television with him for a while.

'I don't want you to feel you have to spend your free time with me,' he said. 'You must live your own life – do as you please. Maybe we could turn one of the other bedrooms into a sitting room for you so that you can entertain your friends. I don't want you to feel that you're shut up with only an old man for company. It's not right.'

Rosalind was too touched by his kindness and concern to tell him that she didn't have any friends. She'd been too busy at the Queen's Head to have any social life.

'I can't think why Una insisted that you should come and keep house for me,' he went on earnestly. 'But at least it's good to know that she cared enough to want to see me looked after.' He smiled at her. 'And I have an idea that she thought I could keep an eye on you too; that we'd look after each other. It proves to me that she does still care for me – for us both. I'm sure that underneath that brittle exterior she's as soft and caring as any other wife and mother.'

Rosalind said nothing. She had no intention of disillusioning Don any further by telling him the bitter truth.

By the time the nine o'clock news began she was already yawning. Over Christmas she had worked long and hard and she was tired. She was about to make her excuses and say goodnight when a news item suddenly caught her attention. She leaned forward in her chair, concentrating

427

on the screen. The newsreader was talking about an air crash that had occurred the previous day – somewhere in the Swiss Alps.

'It is now thought that the crash was caused by severe weather causing ice to form on the plane's wings,' he announced. 'There were no survivors of the crash and it has now been confirmed that among the casualties was Gerald Cavelle, the internationally renowned concert pianist who was to have spent a holiday in Switzerland following a stay in a New Zealand hospital. A tribute to the pianist follows this news bulletin.'

Shocked, Rosalind turned to stare at Don. 'That's Cathy's husband,' she said. 'Cathy, my school friend. Don't you remember? She brought him to a party here just before they were married.'

'Of course. I remember them both,' Don told her. 'Poor child. What a terrible thing to happen.'

'They spent their honeymoon in Switzerland.' Rosalind froze, her hand flying to her mouth as a thought occurred to her. Suppose Cathy was with him? Suppose she had been killed too?

'Do you know her family?' Don asked.

Rosalind shook her head. 'She has no family. Just the people she lived with after her father died. I'll telephone Mrs Johnson first thing tomorrow. I must find out whether Cathy was with him.'

Chapter Twenty

It was late afternoon when Matthew drove into the centre of the little market town and pulled over to the side of the road.

'Better have a look at the map,' he said, looking anxiously out at the darkening winter sky. 'The weather seems to be getting worse and it's almost dark too.' He leaned forward, peering through the windscreen. 'I seem to remember we have to turn off just after Wickham Market and I don't want to miss the turning. We could be wandering around in the dark all night on these country roads.'

Rosalind spread out the map on the dashboard and pointed. 'We're here. I think that's the turning you're after, about three miles along the road.' She looked at him. 'Last time I came it was by train, so I'm not much help, I'm afraid.'

He smiled at her. 'You've done wonders. I wouldn't like to have made the trip alone. I have driven to Melfordleigh before, but that was a year last September. It all looked very different on a fine summer afternoon with the sun shining.'

Rosalind had met Matthew only once before, at Cathy's wedding. When they first set out on the drive to Suffolk they had been slightly shy of one another but the shared journey with its attendant difficulties had soon broken the ice. By the time they got as far as Wickham Market they were talking easily and felt as though they had known each other all their lives.

* * *

After hearing about the air crash on television the previous night Rosalind had decided to go over to the Johnsons' house first thing the next morning. Mary Johnson answered the door looking pale and haggard from worry and lack of sleep. She invited Rosalind into the living room.

'When I heard the news about Gerald Cavelle on television last night I was so worried in case Cathy was with him,' she explained. 'I had to come over and find out.'

'No, thank God, she wasn't,' Johnny told her. 'I spoke to her just a few days ago when I rang to wish her a happy birthday. I had thought that Gerald would try to get home for that. But she said she was alone and that she'd be spending Christmas alone at Melfordleigh too.' She shook her head. 'Heaven knows what Gerald came to be doing on a plane to Switzerland. I just knew at the time that something was wrong. I could hear it in her voice. But she kept insisting that everything was all right.' Johnny sighed. 'I tried to get her to come here to us for Christmas, but she wouldn't. As it happens, with Mother so ill in hospital it wouldn't have been a very happy occasion. I've been ringing her number ever since I heard the dreadful news,' she went on. 'But I can't get any reply.'

'I'll go to Melfordleigh,' Rosalind said decisively. 'Cathy's going to need someone. I know I'm not as close as you are, but as you say, someone should be with her.'

Johnny looked at her with relief. 'Oh, I'd be so grateful if you would, dear. Mother is so ill. I have to stay here in case she takes a sudden turn for the worse. But are you sure you can get the time off?'

'That's not a problem. I've given up my job,' Rosalind told her. 'I've come home to keep house for my step-father while my mother is away, but he can manage without me for a few days. In fact he suggested it himself. I'll get on the first train I can.'

'No need,' Johnny said quickly. 'Matthew is home and he has some leave due. He'll take you. He was going anyway, to bring Cathy back here to stay with us, but he was reluctant to go alone.' She smiled ruefully. 'You know how awkward men are on occasions like this.' She shook her head. 'My poor Cathy. Heaven knows what this will have done to her.'

'I could go right away if that's all right?' Rosalind said.

Johnny looked doubtful. 'I think we should make sure she's actually there first. I don't want you to have a wasted journey. Matthew thinks she's probably taken the telephone off the hook to avoid being pestered by the press. If I can't get any reply from the house today I might contact the local police and ask them to make tactful enquiries for me.' She smiled at Rosalind. 'I can't tell you what a relief it is that someone is going to her. If you'd like to go home and prepare I'll telephone you as soon as I have any news.'

Rosalind did as Johnny suggested. Back at Blake's Folly she packed a bag and set about making sure Don had plenty of food prepared, though he assured her that he could always eat at the local pub if he ran out.

Johnny's call came late that afternoon.

'I had to get in touch with the police in the end,' she said. 'It was as Matthew thought – the phone was off the hook. Cathy is there, but apart from the daily woman no one has seen her. Matthew will come and pick you up at ten tomorrow morning if that's all right?'

'I'll be waiting.'

'I've told him to bring her back with him, if she'll come.' Rosalind heard her sigh at the other end of the line. 'Oh dear, troubles never come singly, do they?'

It was already dark by the time they reached Melfordleigh; the dense inky darkness of the countryside that neither of them was used to. As they travelled along the country lanes the twin beams of the headlights picked up the slanting shafts of rain and the wet glisten of the road. On either side tall hedges obscured their view and Rosalind saw only too well

431

what Matthew had meant about getting lost. But as they crested the hill and dipped down into Melfordleigh they saw with relief the lighted windows of the village houses winking a warm welcome.

As Matthew nosed the car into the gateway of Cuckoo Lodge Rosalind hopped out, a newspaper held over her head against the driving rain, and ran to open the gate. The house was in darkness and they looked apprehensively at each other as they stood under the porch.

'I hope she's in,' Matthew said. He rang the bell and together they listened to it echoing emptily through the house. After a few moments the porch lantern went on and the front door opened an inch or two. A round-faced woman peered out.

'Who is it?' she asked warily.

'Matthew Johnson and Rosalind Blair,' he said. 'We're friends of Mrs Cavelle and we've come to see her. Is she at home?'

Maggie held the door open and beckoned them in with a sigh of relief. 'Sorry about that,' she said. 'But you wouldn't believe the nosy parkers we've had sniffing round here. Reporters mostly.' She shook her head. 'Like vultures, they are, taking advantage of folks's grief to fill their papers.' She looked at their rain-spotted coats. 'Take off them wet things and give them to me. I'll hang them up by the Aga to dry. And you must be spittin' feathers for a nice cup of tea. I'll get the kettle on this minute.'

'Where is Cathy?' Rosalind asked as they followed Maggie to the kitchen. 'How is she?'

Maggie closed the door carefully. 'Won't come out of her room. Soon as I heard the news on telly I got on my bike and came straight round. She seemed – I don't know, numb, I suppose you'd call it. Made one or two phone calls, cool as you please. Took a few more yesterday. Mr Cavelle's agent and people like that I think they were.

432

Then the papers started pestering. After that she took to her room and stayed there.'

Matthew looked concerned. 'She is – all right, isn't she?'

'Oh, bless you, yes. I mean, she hasn't locked the door or nothing. I've been taking her meals up and she's even eaten a little bit. As my dad was at home to stay with the kids I moved in here with her – didn't seem right, her being left all alone at a time like this.'

'That was very kind of you,' Matthew said. 'My mother has suggested that we take Cathy back with us to London.'

Maggie nodded. 'Good idea. She needs her friends round her.' The kettle began to whistle and she made the tea. 'I'll get a couple of rooms ready for you,' she said as she poured three cups. 'Then I'll get off home, seein' as you're here. Leave you to it like.'

They sat drinking their tea while Maggie went up to tell Cathy they were here. 'I suppose you've known Cathy a long time?' Rosalind said, looking at Matthew across the kitchen table.

He looked up. 'Only since she came to live with us after her father died. She was sixteen then and I resented her like mad to begin with. Mother seemed to be making such a fuss of her. I suppose I felt a bit pushed out.' He grinned sheepishly. 'Well, I was only a teenager myself at the time. But pretty soon we grew to be like brother and sister.' He sipped his tea thoughtfully. 'Between you and me, Rosalind, she never should have married Cavelle. Mother was worried to death at the time. She always knew it would end in tears.'

Rosalind looked up, shocked to hear him voicing such an opinion at a time like this. 'But they loved each other,' she protested. 'They were so happy. No one could have foreseen a tragedy like this. It must be devastating for her.'

'I don't think they were all that happy actually,' Matthew said. 'Cathy was so much younger than him. I think she was dazzled by his fame and all that success.'

433

Rosalind shook her head. 'Surely not? Cathy was far too sensible for that.'

'I don't know. Mother felt she was looking for a father figure. Maybe she was right. I had a feeling something wasn't quite right the last time I saw her.' He sipped his tea. 'Between you and me, I have a feeling that something happened during Cathy's visit last summer. I wasn't at home at the time and Mother hasn't actually said anything but I've had the distinct impression that she was disturbed about Cathy's well-being.'

Rosalind frowned, reminded of Carla's hints about a pregnancy. 'Well, whatever happened it's over now,' she said. 'And in the worst possible way. She's going to need our support in any . . .' She broke off as the door opened and Cathy came in. She wore a dark skirt and sweater which accentuated her pallor and the hollows under her eyes and cheekbones. Her bright hair was tied back and looped at the nape of her neck. She looked very young and very vulnerable. But in spite of her gaunt appearance she seemed composed and greeted them warmly.

'Rosalind and Matthew! How good to see you both.'

'Mother was worried,' he said, going to her. 'You know how she is. She's been trying to ring you ever since we heard the news on TV. She wanted to come down herself only Gran is very poorly.' He reached out a hand and patted her awkwardly on the shoulder. 'We're all – you know, really sorry about what's happened.'

'Thank you, Matthew.' Cathy frowned. 'I should have realised that you would have heard about the crash. I should have rung Johnny. It's just that the last couple of days have been a nightmare what with the press and everyone. Can you imagine people jostling each other for interviews at a time like this?'

'They're so insensitive,' Matthew agreed. He slipped a finger inside his collar. Cathy looked so cool and normal that it unnerved him. Tears would have been embarrassing and

434

hard to cope with, but this icy calm was worse if anything. 'Well, I'll – er – go and bring in the bags,' he said, eager to escape. 'Shall I take them straight upstairs?'

'Yes. You'll find Maggie up there. She'll show you where to put them.'

When he had gone Rosalind got up and crossed the room to Cathy. 'Mrs Johnson wants us to take you home,' she said. 'Cathy – we're here now. If there's anything either of us can do . . . If you want to talk about it . . .'

'I don't!' Cathy turned away. 'My marriage is over, Rosalind. I've got to get used to it. Gerald has gone. I'm on my own now.'

Rosalind felt her blood chill at Cathy's unnatural calm. 'But – there must be things to see to; things we can help you with? What – what about the – arrangements – the . . .'

'The funeral? That's all being taken care of by James Kendrick, Gerald's agent. He and Kay Goolden are organising it all. It will be very quiet, next week in London. But there is to be a memorial service later, probably in the Savoy Chapel.' She looked up at Rosalind with eyes like the winter sea. 'They've taken it out of my hands.'

Rosalind swallowed, trying to see through this hard, icy barrier Cathy had put up to the real feelings beneath. 'Oh. I see. That's good of them. It must be a – relief.'

'Oh, yes. They've organised it all down to the last detail, like some kind of glossy PR exercise. Kay used to do all Gerald's PR, you know.'

'Yes, I remember.' Rosalind felt uneasy. She also seemed to remember that it was the Goolden woman who had leaked Cathy and Gerald's engagement to the press and caused untold trouble for her. 'In that case why don't you close up the house and come back to London with us tomorrow? Mrs Johnson is longing to look after you and there's nothing to stay here for, is there?'

'No. Maybe there never was.' Cathy looked at Rosalind as though she were seeing her for the first time and her expression relaxed a little. 'Thank you for coming, Rosalind. It was kind of you to think of me. I'll have to be in London for the funeral, so yes, maybe I will come back with you and Matthew.' She gave herself a little shake as though coming out of a dream. 'I'm forgetting myself. Have you eaten? You and Matthew have had a long drive. What must you be thinking? I'll make you something.'

'No, don't bother. We'll go to the pub. The Admiral Nelson, isn't it? All three of us? It will do you good to get out of the house for a while.'

Cathy shook her head. 'I'd rather not. I'm not hungry and I don't feel up to facing people – not yet. But don't let me stop you.' She turned towards the door. 'I'd better go and put a match to the fire in the drawing room. It hasn't been lit since Gerald left.'

As she went out she passed Maggie in the doorway with hardly a glance.

'Well, your rooms are ready,' the housekeeper said. 'I'll get off home now that she's got some company.' As she buttoned her coat she looked at Rosalind and lowered her voice. 'I don't like the look of her,' she whispered. 'It takes people in funny ways sometimes. She's heading for some kind of reaction if you ask me. Simmering away like a little pressure cooker. I've put you in the room next to hers – just in case.' She tied a plastic rainhood firmly over her hair. 'Well, I'll be off and brave the elephants as my son used to say when he was a little 'un. My address is on the phone pad if you want me.' She paused in the doorway. 'Oh, by the way, there's a casserole in the fridge. It just wants warming up. I made it for dinner but all she wanted was an omelette. Shame to let it go to waste. G'night, then.'

'Goodnight. And thank you.'

Rosalind went to the fridge and took out the covered dish, putting it into the Aga's oven gratefully. She and Matthew hadn't eaten since the sandwich lunch Johnny had packed for them and they were both hungry. She found plates and cutlery easily enough and was laying the table as he came in.

'That smells good. I could eat the proverbial horse.' He rubbed his chilled fingers and held them out over the heat of the Aga. 'What did you make of Cathy?'

'I don't know. Maggie says she's heading for some kind of reaction.'

'Sooner we get her home the better if you ask me,' Matthew said. 'Mother will know what to do, she always does.' He nodded towards the table. 'Have you persuaded her to eat with us?'

'I thought I'd try,' Rosalind told him. 'Though maybe we should just leave her for tonight.'

Cathy did not appear again, and after they had eaten Rosalind and Matthew decided to call it a day and retired to their respective rooms. It had been a long cold day and they were both weary. Rosalind was pleasantly surprised to find that Maggie had thoughtfully put an electric blanket in her bed, and, snuggling down in the warm, lavender-scented softness, she soon found her eyes closing in sleep.

She had no idea what wakened her. For a moment as she lay there in the unfamiliar bed she could not make out where she was. The rain had stopped and the night sky had cleared. The moon was shining in at the window, flooding the room with its milky light. Then she heard it – the sound that must have wakened her; the sound of sobbing. And it was coming from next door. From Cathy's room.

Getting out of bed, she pulled on her dressing gown and tiptoed out on to the landing. For a moment she stood outside Cathy's door, wondering what to do. Should she go in and try to comfort her, or would she rather be left alone? Then she heard the sound again; muffled as though it came from under the bedclothes. It sounded so heartbroken; so lonely and forlorn, almost childlike. Rosalind didn't stop to think again. Opening

437

the door quietly she went in and crossed the room to the bed.

'Cathy,' she whispered. 'Cathy – please let me help. I can't bear to hear you crying all alone like this.'

She sat up at once, brushing at her wet cheeks with her knuckles and struggling to control her emotions. 'I'm sorry. I didn't mean to wake you,' she said fumbling under the pillow for a handkerchief. 'Please go back to bed, Rosalind. I'm all right – really.'

'No, you're not.' Rosalind laid a hand on her arm. 'It's right that you should grieve,' she said. 'But not alone like this. Not when I'm here to share it. I know it must be terrible for you, losing your husband . . .'

'But it isn't!' Cathy burst out. 'He wasn't my husband, you see. We didn't have a marriage. Not a real one.' She blew her nose. 'And – and just before Christmas, after he was sure that his operation was successful, he sent word to me that he wanted a divorce. He didn't come and ask himself. He sent word with Kay Goolden – the woman he intended to marry.'

Rosalind was stunned. Just for a moment she wondered if Cathy was in her right mind. Surely what she was saying could not be true? Surely no one could be so cruel and heartless? Then she remembered what Johnny had said about her strangeness on the telephone – about spending Christmas alone. Lost for adequate words, she reached out and took both of Cathy's hands in hers. 'Oh my God, Cathy. How awful for you.'

'He and Kay were going to meet in Switzerland – to have a holiday there together. In Davos, the place where he and I spent our honeymoon.'

Rosalind drew in her breath sharply. 'Oh, Cathy, you must have been so hurt. Oh, if only you'd got in touch. You really should have talked to someone about it.'

'I couldn't.' Cathy was shivering violently now. She looked at Rosalind with dark, hollowed eyes. 'His asking me for a divorce wasn't the worst thing, you see. If he'd come home I was going to have to leave him anyway – because of something I'd found out.'

She told Rosalind of the discovery she had made in the attic that fateful afternoon. About what happened between Gerald and her mother all those years ago; about the break-up of her parents' marriage and the disillusionment and failure of her own, ending with the brief affair that had led to the pregnancy she had been forced to terminate. The words came haltingly at first, then gained momentum as though a flood of emotion had been released. And as she poured it all out, the bitterness, guilt and regret that had tangled together into a brutal snare over the past weeks, gradually loosened its stranglehold on her.

'And the worst – the *terrible* – part that hurts so badly is that it was all for nothing, Rosalind,' she said, choking on the words. 'I gave up the baby I wanted so much for *nothing*. Gerald never really cared for me at all. I believe he wanted me off his hands almost as soon as he married me. And as soon as he was healthy again he decided to dump me. Why he married me in the first place I can't understand. I've gone over and over it, trying to make some sense of it. Trying to find a reason. Perhaps I reminded him a little of my mother and he thought marrying me was a way of making amends; in the same way as he must have thought buying Daddy's music to help pay my school fees was making amends.'

She shook her head angrily. 'I don't really know what was in Gerald's head. I've given up trying to work it out. All I do know is that it was all a mistake. A disastrous mistake. And now I'm left to pay the price for the rest of my life.' She laid her head on Rosalind's shoulder as fresh tears coursed down her cheeks. 'And now – I know this sounds awful – now he's dead and – and I'm not even allowed to hate him!'

'Of course it isn't awful.' Rosalind held her close, letting her weep out all the bitterness and grief against her shoulder.

Through the other girl's thin nightdress she felt her birdlike thinness and was consumed by pity for the friend she had always admired and envied so much. Cathy, who had seemed to have the best of everything life had to offer, had secretly suffered this terrible hurt and double betrayal. Suffered it all alone. Rosalind had a sudden vivid memory of the New Year party she and Gerald had attended at Blake's Folly; the starry, almost incandescent happiness in Cathy's eyes that night as she looked forward so eagerly to marrying the man she loved. The memory made her own eyes fill with tears of pity.

At last Cathy stopped crying. Her breathing returned to normal and she composed herself. 'You won't mention any of this to Johnny, will you?' she said. 'Or breathe a word of it to Matthew?'

'Of course I won't.'

Cathy took a long shuddering breath as she dried her eyes. 'Johnny knows about the baby, of course, but not the rest. I'll tell her in my own good time. For now I'd rather it was just between you and me.'

'Of course.' Rosalind looked at her. There was a little colour in her cheeks now and her eyes looked less haunted. 'Do you feel better now?'

Cathy nodded. 'Much better, thanks to you.'

Rosalind smiled. 'There's nothing to thank me for. I'm glad I was here – that I could be a friend to you.'

Next morning Cathy appeared at the breakfast table looking much more like her old self. While Matthew took the car to the local garage for petrol she and Rosalind walked round the house together, making sure that everywhere was secured.

'I'll drop a note in at Maggie's house on the way,' Cathy said. 'She has a key and she'll look in each day and make sure everything is all right.'

'What will you do?' Rosalind asked. 'Afterwards, I mean. Will you live here, or sell the place?'

Cathy shrugged. 'It's the only home I've got. It's much too big of course. I suppose the sensible thing would be to sell it. I haven't really thought about it. I'll have to think about getting a job too. Most of our money was tied up in this place and we still owe some of the money for the building work.'

Rosalind looked thoughtful. 'I wouldn't imagine there are many jobs to be had down here, except in the holiday season.'

'You're right. I don't suppose it's practical to think of staying here.' Cathy looked around her and sighed. 'I do love this place though. It was such fun, seeing it rise from its derelict state. I hate the thought of abandoning it again – going back to London.'

'It would make a marvellous hotel,' Rosalind said. 'Or a conference centre. That barn conversion would make a fantastic conference hall.'

Matthew arrived back and whistled from the hall below. Cathy took a last look round and smiled wistfully at Rosalind. 'Maybe someone will buy it with that in mind,' she said. 'I'll have to remember your idea when I advertise it. Come on, we'd better go or Matthew will be cross. He's always hated being kept waiting.'

Cathy settled into her old room at Johnny's, happy to get away from the scene of so much trauma; to give in and let motherly Johnny fuss over her for a while. Gerald's interment took place a week later at a quiet little church in Hampstead. There were few people present and it was a private affair, kept out of the public eye, unlike the planned memorial service which was scheduled for three weeks later, to be followed by a reception at the Savoy. Cathy dreaded the theatrically staged affair with its invited galaxy of celebrities and show business razzmatazz. It hung over her head like the Sword of Damocles during the three intervening weeks. She knew it would be impossible to put the past behind her until it was over.

On the day she dressed carefully, knowing that the press and TV would be out in force. Whatever had happened she would not let herself down. She had chosen a charcoal grey suit and dressed her hair in a smooth chignon topped by a black velvet pillbox hat. Johnny and Rosalind would be going along with her and Matthew had taken the day off and would arrive in time to drive them.

When they arrived the host of glamorous guests had already begun to assemble. Almost at once Cathy spotted Simon with an older woman whom she took to be his mother. He had written to her after the crash and she had replied briefly and politely. She had no wish to see him today and to her relief he made no attempt to speak to her. Kay arrived with James Kendrick and his wife. She looked elegant in black and white, but her face, half hidden by the wide brim of her hat, still bore the traces of recent tears. Cathy found to her own surprise that she felt nothing but a detached pity for the older woman. She had wanted Gerald for so long and to have him taken from her a second time must have been a cruel blow. She moved impulsively towards her, but Johnny, who now knew of Gerald's betrayal and the proposed divorce, steered her tactfully in the opposite direction, away from Kay and from the threatened attention of the press, gathering in packs around the main entrance to the chapel.

Leaving the front pews to the celebrities, the four of them sat quietly and anonymously in a pew near the back. They sang the hymns and listened to the florid eulogy that traced Gerald's career and triumphs – the courage with which he faced his illness and the subsequent collapse of this brilliant musical career – to the cruel irony of his accidental death. A well-known violinist who had been one of Gerald's college friends spoke of him in glowing terms after which Simon moved to the grand piano which had been placed below the pulpit and played an arrangement of the theme of the emotive last movement from Rachmaninov's Second Piano Concerto.

Cathy sat and listened to it all, trying not to notice the whirring of the TV cameras at the back of the chapel; trying not to think about the darker side of Gerald that no one would ever guess at. Rosalind sat on one side of her, Johnny on the other. From time to time they glanced at her, but neither touched her, sensing the carefully controlled emotions, wound as tightly as a coiled spring, admiring her strength and dignity. For her part Cathy was infinitely grateful for their tacit support.

But it was as they came out of the chapel that the real ordeal began. The reporters and TV cameras were there in force. They crowded eagerly round the doors as they opened, snapping frenziedly at the many celebrities as they emerged. Somehow Rosalind and Johnny were borne ahead by the rest of the crowd, but Cathy found herself trapped by a group of reporters. As Matthew grasped her arm firmly in an attempt to steer her out of the way, she was almost blinded by the flash of a camera. One hand went up instinctively to protect her eyes and when she removed it she found herself surrounded by reporters firing a volley of bewildering questions at her.

'How long had you been married, Mrs Cavelle?'

'Are there any children of the marriage?'

'Have you any plans to continue with the music centre in Suffolk?'

'How did you feel when you heard about the air crash?'

Then a steely-eyed woman reporter pushed forward till she was standing directly in front of Cathy.

'Tell me, Mrs Cavelle. Is there any truth in the rumour that your husband was planning to divorce you?'

Seeing her look of shock and distress, the panic in her eyes, Matthew took her arm. 'Leave her alone,' he shouted angrily. 'Can't you see you're upsetting her?'

Cathy felt as though her feet hardly touched the ground as he pushed her along in front of him, heading for the hotel. The sea of faces that parted for them seemed to melt and merge one into the other, and everything around her began to swim out of focus. From somewhere a long way off she heard a man's voice call out, 'Careful! She's going to faint!' There was a roaring in her ears and she felt arms catch her as everything went black.

When she came round she thought at first she must be dreaming. She seemed to be in a small room – an office of some kind. She was lying back in a chair and a strange young man was sitting beside her, gently chafing her hands. He had dark brown hair and concerned brown eyes. When he saw that she was coming round he smiled.

'Hi there. Welcome back.' As she tried to get up he put out a hand to stop her. 'It's all right, don't get up yet. You passed out for a moment, that's all. Luckily I happened to be there at the time. Your brother has gone to get you a glass of water.'

'How silly of me.' She struggled into a sitting position. 'I don't think I've ever fainted before.' She wondered uneasily if the man was someone she should remember. 'Please don't feel you have to stay,' she said, embarrassed at the furore she seemed to be causing. 'I'm quite all right now, really.'

'It's okay. All in the day's work.' He smiled. 'I'm a doctor. I told your brother I'd stay till he got back.'

'Matthew's not my brother. Thank you for staying with me, but I don't need a doctor – really.' She racked her brain feverishly to remember who he was. Could he have attended one of the master classes at Melfordleigh – stayed at Cuckoo Lodge? He had an accent she couldn't quite place. 'I promise you I'll be fine now,' she assured him.

'There's no way I'm going to leave you alone,' he

444

said firmly. 'I mean, that'd look pretty ungallant now, wouldn't it?'

'Have we met?' she asked. 'I'm sorry but I don't remember . . .'

'No reason why you should.' He shook his head. 'I'm forgetting my manners. I should have introduced myself. I'm Paul Franklin. Doctor Paul Franklin.'

Relieved, she took the large firm hand he offered. 'How do you do? I'm Catherine Cavelle,' she returned.

His smile was replaced by a puzzled frown as he stared at her intently.

'Did you know Gerald?' she asked. Suddenly she placed the accent. 'Ah – you must be from New Zealand. Are you from the hospital?'

'I qualified in a New Zealand hospital,' he told her. 'Which is hardly surprising, seeing that I was born and grew up there.'

'So you . . .' Whatever Cathy had been about to say was cut short by the arrival of Johnny, closely followed by Matthew and Rosalind.

'Cathy! Are you all right?' Johnny asked, bustling in and putting a glass of water into her hand. 'Those dreadful reporters. Like jackals with their horrible questions. It really shouldn't be allowed. Now – Matthew's brought the car round so if you're feeling up to it I suggest we all get off home.'

'I'm fine now, Johnny. There's no need to fuss.' She got to her feet. 'This is Doctor Franklin. He very kindly kept me company while Matthew went to find you.'

Johnny turned to the young man. 'Oh, dear, do forgive me, Doctor Franklin. How rude you must think me. Matthew told me how kind you'd been. It was so lucky you happened to be passing when Cathy fainted.'

'Not at all. I did nothing.' He smiled at Cathy. 'I can see you're in good hands now so I'll go. I hope you feel better soon.' As Matthew and Johnny escorted her out of

445

the room he turned to Rosalind. 'Excuse me. Am I right in thinking that's Gerald Cavelle's daughter?'

Rosalind looked surprised. 'Heavens, no! She's his widow.'

'His *widow*?' Paul Franklin's jaw dropped in surprise and just for a moment he seemed lost for words. But as Rosalind made to follow the others he stopped her.

'Look, I have to see her again. I wonder if you could tell me where I can get in touch with her?'

Rosalind looked doubtful. 'Well – I don't know if I should give that kind of information to a comparative stranger.'

'Oh, I'm not a stranger,' he said. 'I promise you I'm not. And it really is very important that I speak to her.' He spread his hands. 'I'd talk to her now but I'm sure you'll agree this is neither the time nor the place.'

'No.' Rosalind looked at the tall young man in the dark suit. He looked so sincere, so earnest. What should she do? 'Suppose I gave you a telephone number where you can contact her? Would that do?'

His dark eyes smiled their relief. 'Oh, that would be marvellous.'

Rosalind tore a page from the back of her diary and scribbled the Johnson's phone number on it. 'You'll be able to reach her here for the next week or so. It will be up to her, of course. I can't guarantee that she'll see you.'

'Of course. I understand that. Thanks a lot, Miss . . .'

'Just call me Rosalind.'

'Thanks, Rosalind.' He paused. 'Oh – another thing. I'd be grateful if you were to prepare her, tell her that I'll be calling her in a couple of days' time. I think I can safely say that she and I will have a great deal to talk about.'

Rosalind bit her lip anxiously as she watched him walk away. What interest could this young Doctor Franklin have in Cathy? Had she done the right thing?

* * *

Cathy wakened on the morning following the memorial service feeling stronger than she had for months. Over breakfast she told Johnny that she would be going up to Kensington to see James Palmer, Gerald's solicitor, as he had written requesting she should. It was time she set about sorting out her financial affairs.

When Johnny knew what she planned she asked if Cathy would like her to go along too, but she refused.

'I'm going to have to start doing things by myself,' she said. 'So I may as well begin now.'

Johnny watched her go from the window of the front room, her heart going out to the slender figure in the dark grey coat, walking bravely up the street with her head held high. She was so young to have been through such trauma. She longed to help and support her but knew that Cathy was right to tackle it by herself. There would be many things to face alone in the years to come. Johnny knew very well that however much she wished, she would not always be around to help her. Briefly she wondered what the future held for the girl who was a beloved daughter to her in all but name. Surely Gerald Cavelle would have left her well provided for? At least she would not have to worry about money.

But Johnny was soon to be proved wrong.

When Cathy learned that she was Gerald's sole beneficiary and that he had left her the house she was relieved. But her relief was to be short-lived. The solicitor quickly followed the statement by telling her that there was still a large mortgage on the house and more money owed to the builders for the restoration work, plus other amounts outstanding for furnishings, advertising and other sundries.

'All Gerald's business documents including unpaid bills were placed by him in a safety deposit box at the bank,' he told her. 'Before he left for New Zealand he sent me a key, along with instructions to deal with things if anything were to happen.'

Cathy felt the colour leave her face. So she couldn't even

447

be trusted with that? 'Will my own money meet the debts?' she asked in a small voice.

The solicitor looked puzzled. 'Your money? But you had a joint bank account. Everything was transferred to that at the time of the marriage.'

'But there was the money my father left me – from the sale of our house,' she said. 'Gerald said he had invested that for me.'

Clearly uncomfortable, the man cleared his throat. 'Invested it, yes, Mrs Cavelle – in Cuckoo Lodge and the establishing of the music school at Melfordleigh.'

She stared at him. 'You mean it's – all been spent – used up? It's gone?'

'I'm very much afraid so, yes.'

A feeling of panic quickened her heartbeat. 'But – I didn't know. I wasn't asked – never gave my permission.' She shook her head. 'Surely . . .'

The man took a document from the file in front of him and passed it across the desk to her. 'This is your signature, isn't it?'

She stared down at the name signed on the bottom line and remembered the day Gerald had brought her here to this office to sign it. He had said it was for joint ownership of the house. But he hadn't mentioned that her own money was to be tied up in it.

James Palmer was looking at her with some concern. 'Surely your husband explained it to you?' he said. 'You must have been aware . . .'

'Yes!' Suddenly she felt foolish and naive. How stupid the solicitor must think her. She made herself laugh. 'Of course, I remember now. How silly of me.'

The man looked at her sympathetically. She was so young to be widowed, let alone burdened with a massive debt like this. 'I assume you'll sell the house and effects?' he asked. 'It is what I would strongly advise.'

448

'Yes.' She nodded dazedly. 'It seems the only thing I can do.'

'Do you wish me to write to all the creditors and explain the situation?' he asked. 'I'll ask them to give you time to sell the property, though I must warn you that if they press for immediate payment we shall have to go for voluntary bankruptcy?' He saw the look of wide-eyed fear and distress on Cathy's face and added quickly, 'I'm sure they will all agree to wait a while. It will be to their advantage to do so. I'll make sure they know that.'

Outside in the street the sun was shining; thin lemon-coloured winter sunshine that somehow made the cold wind blowing down Kensington High Street feel even keener. Cathy shivered and pulled her coat collar up. What was she to do? She was penniless. The owner of a great house, yet no home. An overwhelming number of debts and no money with which to pay them. She had thought when Gerald died that he could hurt her no more. How wrong she had been.

As she pulled on her glove the emerald in her engagement ring flashed in the sunlight. At least she still had that, she comforted herself. It had ceased to be a symbol of Gerald's love a long time ago. Now at least it would provide enough money for her to live on for a while.

Chapter Twenty-One

It was the day after her interview with the solicitor that Paul Franklin telephoned and asked to meet Cathy. Still numb with shock about her financial situation her first impulse had been to refuse. She had hesitated, racking her brain for a polite excuse, but Paul was so persuasive that in the end she had promised to ring him back. When she asked Johnny's advice on the matter the older woman had suggested that she invite him to the house.

'I don't know who he is or what he can possibly want to see you about,' she said. 'But I think you'd be well advised to meet him on your own territory. Ask him to come here to tea.'

Cathy rang Paul back the next day with the invitation which he accepted delightedly.

Although there had been a fall of snow during the night, the sun was shining and Johnny's comfortable sitting room was warm and homely with a bright fire burning in the grate and its window looking on to the sparkling white garden outside. Johnny welcomed Paul and showed him into the sitting room where Cathy was waiting, then she left the two of them to talk.

'It was very good of you to invite me,' he said as he took the chair Cathy offered, close to the fire. 'I can't get over the snow out there. You know, this is the first time I've seen it.' He laughed a little self-consciously. 'It must sound crazy to you, but I haven't been able to stop looking at it ever since I first drew the curtains this morning.'

'I'm afraid the novelty will soon wear off once it gets to the slushy stage,' Cathy warned him. There was a pause as she watched him rub his chilled fingers and hold them to the blaze. She cleared her throat.

'So – what was it you wanted to speak to me about, Doctor Franklin?'

'Oh, please call me Paul.' He looked up and their eyes met. 'I guess I should get to the point,' he said uneasily. 'I don't want to take up too much of your time. I don't want to intrude either.' He looked at her uncertainly. 'I don't know how much you know about Gerald's life? I mean – the part before you were married; before you met.'

'Quite a lot as it happens,' Cathy said. 'He and my father had been close friends since they were students. When my father died he made Gerald my legal guardian.'

'And you fell in love and married?' He smiled. 'How romantic.' Cathy gave a small non-committal shrug and he went on. 'So you must have known that he was married once before? A long time before.'

'Of course I knew.' Cathy tried to hide the unease she felt. Why all these questions? Could Gerald somehow have been in this young doctor's debt? Was there even more to uncover about his past? Was she going to spend her entire life discovering things about that other, darker side of Gerald he had so successfully hidden?

'I don't quite understand where this is leading,' she said. 'Do you know something I don't know about Gerald? Have you come to drop some kind of bombshell?'

'No – well . . .' He smiled ruefully. 'It rather depends on how you see it.' He paused, looking at her apprehensively. 'I guess there's no way to break a thing like this gently,' he said. 'Gerald Cavelle is – was – my father.'

For a long moment Cathy stared disbelievingly into the grave brown eyes. There had to be some mistake. Gerald had no son – no children at all. 'You say you're his *son*?' She shook her head. 'But your name – Paul Franklin?'

'Franklin is my mother's maiden name. She reverted to it after they divorced. It isn't surprising you didn't know

451

about me. Gerald himself didn't know I existed until just a few weeks ago. He and my mother parted in 1939, just before the war began. When she went home to Auckland she didn't know that she was already expecting me.'

'And she never told him?'

'No. I think she was afraid he might make demands if he knew about me. Seems she wanted him out of her life. It was never a good marriage. For years she let me believe my dad had died in the war. I was eighteen before she told me the truth.'

'How strange that must have felt.' Cathy was looking at him, searching his features for some resemblance to Gerald. Apart from his build and colouring, she found none.

He smiled wryly. 'You can say that again! By then he was a well-known concert pianist. A big name in the world of classical music. Once I knew who he was he started to be something of an obsession with me – an idol if you like. I began to collect all his records – magazine articles – pictures. Once, when I heard that he was touring Australia, I saved up and bought a plane ticket to go and hear him play.' He shook his head. 'I was so damned *proud*. I wanted to turn around and tell everyone he was my dad. For weeks before I went I fantasised about how I'd go round and surprise him afterwards and we'd be reunited. But when it actually came to the crunch I just couldn't get up the nerve, I chickened out – just came home without seeing him.' He smiled ruefully. 'Much to Ma's relief, I might add. I think she was scared I might bring him back with me.'

'So – did you ever meet him?'

Paul nodded. 'Oh, yes – finally. When I heard on the hospital grapevine that he was in Auckland, having surgery in Professor Harbage's clinic, I had to go and see him. Even Ma couldn't help but agree when she knew he was ill.'

'He must have been very surprised,' Cathy whispered.

'Oh, he was.' Paul smiled. 'We only met that one time,

but I think he liked me. I like to think he was pleased to know about me.'

'Did he tell you he was married?'

'No. And I certainly never expected him to have a wife as young as you. When you told me your name the other day I thought you must be his daughter. I thought I was discovering a half-sister!'

Cathy smiled. 'Sorry to disappoint you.'

'Oh, no!' Paul coloured. 'Not at all! I'm *glad* really. I mean – oh, God, I'm sorry.' He shook his head. 'I've put my big foot in it again. I'm always doing that.'

'No, you haven't. Did you come all the way over here just for the memorial service?' Cathy asked.

'Oh, no. I'm here to complete my studies. I'm hoping to specialise in cardiology, you see. As soon as I knew there was a chance to come over and work at one of your great teaching hospitals, I applied. It's so exciting all the pioneering work they're doing now with transplants. I wanted to be in on all of it.' He looked up shyly. 'It was a kind of scholarship. I got it for qualifying with highish marks.'

'Congratulations.'

'But I didn't hear I'd won it till after the air crash.'

'So Gerald never knew?'

'No, more's the pity. It seemed such a marvellous chance in every way. To study and to see more of him too. Hear him play again, maybe. He'd told me about the fine old house by the sea where he was holding master classes and teaching. I hoped I might get a chance to see that too.' He sighed. 'Sadly I only got here in time to attend his memorial service.'

Cathy felt her heart contract for this young man who had wanted so badly to know his father. 'And your mother?' she asked.

He shrugged. 'She was thrilled about the scholarship of course. Not so keen for me to spend time with Gerald though,' he admitted. 'They parted on bitter terms. When

I was born she didn't even give me his name, so you can guess how strongly she felt.' He sighed. 'When she saw that I was determined to get to know him while I was in England she was pretty upset. I regret that now, specially under the circumstances.'

'But you had a right to find out who your father was,' Cathy said. 'And you must have been proud of his brilliant talent. Have you inherited it?'

'*No!*' He laughed and shook his head. 'Oh, I play a bit, but Ma is the musician. She teaches music at the local college.'

He glanced at her hesitantly. 'Is there a chance I could maybe visit Suffolk and see Cuckoo Lodge?'

Cathy sighed. It was the request she'd been dreading. 'I don't know Paul. The truth is, I'm going to have to sell the house. I don't know what my future plans will be at the moment.'

He nodded. 'I understand. But I'd really like to see it before you sell. If that's at all possible. See the place where he lived and worked. It'd mean a lot to me.'

'Well – I'll think about it and let you know,' she said non-committally.

Johnny came in with the tea trolley and Paul jumped to his feet to help her, his eyes lighting up like a small boy's when they lighted on the plates loaded with sandwiches and three kinds of home-made cake.

'Hey, you really shouldn't have gone to so much trouble, Mrs Johnson, but I must say it looks wonderful!'

When he had gone Johnny glanced at Cathy as they washed up together. Ever since Paul Franklin left she'd been quiet and pensive.

'He's nice,' she said. 'You haven't told me what he wanted. Did you find out who he is?'

Cathy picked up a plate and dried it thoughtfully. 'He's Gerald's son.'

Johnny stopped to stare at her. 'Did you say his *son*?'

'From his first marriage,' Cathy explained. 'It was before the war and it only lasted a short time. Paul's mother went home to New Zealand when the war broke out. She didn't realise that she was pregnant until after they parted. She never told Gerald. He didn't know about Paul till he went over there to have his operation.'

Johnny shook her head. 'How many more secrets in that man's past? I wonder. So, what did Paul want? Will you be seeing him again?'

'He wants to see Cuckoo Lodge. He wants to find out as much as he can about the father he never knew and I think he sees me as some kind of link.'

'Will you take him to Suffolk?'

Cathy looked at Johnny with clouded eyes. 'How can I? Gerald was some kind of idol to him. How can I smash that? I wouldn't have the heart to tell him what kind of man his father really was, and I was never any good at pretending. Better to leave things as they are.'

Johnny looked doubtful. 'Surely it wouldn't hurt to let him see the house where his father lived?'

Cathy sighed. 'That would mean I'd have to go back myself and I don't want to do that.'

Johnny looked shocked. 'But you have to Cathy. You know that, even if it's only to pack up and put the place on the market.'

She sighed. 'I know. I've imposed on your hospitality for far too long.'

'Imposed on my hospitality!' Johnny looked shocked. 'You know very well that you're family to me, Cathy. I think of you as a daughter, so don't let me hear you saying things like that.' She dried her hands and hung up the tea towel. 'You must know that you're welcome to stay here for as long as you want,' she said. 'Having you here has been a treat for me. I've been at such a loose end with Mother in hospital and Matthew away so much.'

455

'I know, Johnny.' Cathy bit her lip, feeling ashamed of the thoughtless remark. 'I'm sorry. Nevertheless, you're right. It is time I started thinking about the future.'

Johnny was peering at her. 'You don't hate Melfordleigh that much, do you?'

'I don't hate it at all. I love it. It's just the memories. The pain and disillusionment I went through there; the mistakes I made. The – the loss. I can't help thinking that there must have been some way I could have done things better, differently – made it all work.'

'You couldn't,' Johnny said putting a hand on her arm. 'Forgive me for reminding you, love, but you know now why Gerald married you. He was your guardian – obliged to care for you until you were twenty-one. And marrying you was just a legal way to get his hands on the money your father left you so that he could buy Cuckoo Lodge and set up the school. But what's done can't be undone. It's over now and you have to try to put it behind you and start making plans. You won't do that by running away and I think you know it.'

She looked at the doubt and anxiety etched on Cathy's face. 'Look, I tell you what – why don't you take Rosalind with you? She's a sensible girl and you seem to get along together. Then you could invite Paul to go and stay for a weekend. Kill two birds with one stone as it were. No need to shatter his dream of the father he never knew. You can put on a bit of an act just for a couple of days for his sake, can't you? You'll probably never have to see him again once you've done it.'

Cathy went round to see Rosalind next morning with her proposition. Rosalind's face broke into a smile when she answered the door. Over coffee Cathy told her about Paul Franklin's visit and his revelation about who he was, explaining that he wanted to visit Melfordleigh.

'It's all going to be rather difficult,' she said. 'And I

wondered if you'd be free to come down too? I know you like it there and it would help me out.'

Rosalind smiled. 'Oh, Cathy, I'd love to come. Keeping house for Don is okay. He's so kind and considerate, but it gets lonely and boring by myself in the house all day. I miss the life and the bustle of the Queen's Head and all the people I used to work with even more than I expected to.'

'There's one thing I don't understand,' Cathy said. 'Why did you let your mother browbeat you into giving up your job and your training course just so that she could go and take this job?'

Rosalind looked at her for a long moment. This was something she'd been dreading, but she knew she owed it to Cathy to confess. 'She – found out about something I did,' she said haltingly. 'She threatened to go to Mrs Gresham and tell her. I had no choice.'

Cathy looked puzzled. 'But what could you possibly have done that was so terrible?'

Rosalind couldn't look at her. 'I – stole something. One of Don's mother's antique porcelain figures. I needed the money to go to Australia when Dad was ill. Mum wouldn't help. She wouldn't even ask Don to lend me the money. I was desperate, Cathy! I'd have done almost anything.' She looked up fearfully but saw only compassion in the other girl's eyes. 'Don found out almost at once of course. He missed the piece and notified the police so I had to tell him. He was marvellous about it and gave me the money anyway. But he wasn't able to buy the figure back and eventually Mum found out.'

Cathy reached out and took both her hands. 'Oh, poor Rossie.'

'So now you know the worst about me,' she said. 'You know what sort of person I am.'

'I know that you were desperate to see your father, and that you put yourself into a dangerous situation because of it. And I know that your mother used it against you. I'd

457

say you'd been punished more than enough.' She reached out to take both Rosalind's hands. 'We all make mistakes. Sometimes we're pushed into doing desperate things that are completely against our characters. I know that all too well.'

Rosalind looked relieved. 'I'm so glad I've told you. Maybe now I can start to forgive myself.' She paused. 'There's something else I have to tell you – if you don't already know. I've been seeing – someone since Christmas.'

Cathy smiled. 'Matthew, you mean?' She knew that since Rosalind and Matthew had made the trip to Melfordleigh they had been out together a few times. Matthew had confided as much to her on his weekend visits home.

Rosalind coloured. 'That's right. He's taken me to the theatre once and out to dinner twice.' She looked at Cathy. 'You know that he's looking for another job now that he's qualified? Well, he rang me yesterday and said that he's being interviewed for one in a practice in Ipswich next Friday.'

Cathy's eyes widened with surprise. 'Ipswich? I don't think even Johnny knows about that. He must feel you're rather special to confide in you.'

'Oh, no! I daresay he just wanted to keep it to himself until there was something positive to tell,' she said.

Cathy was looking closely at her. 'You like him, don't you, Rossie?'

'Yes, I do.' Rosalind's colour deepened. 'He's the first man I've ever felt I could trust. I can relax with him. He's so easy to talk to. He seems to understand. I've even told him about the porcelain figure. I thought he might not want to see me again after that, but I had to be honest with him.'

'And it made no difference? I'm really pleased,' Cathy said sincerely. 'You and he are ideally suited. You're both quiet and deep-thinking. You both . . .'

'Hey, stop it!' Rosalind stopped her with an embarrassed

laugh. 'We're just friends, that's all. You'll be choosing the bridesmaids' dresses in a minute!'

Cathy joined in the laughter, noticing how pretty Rosalind was with her eyes shining and her cheeks pink. This was the first time Cathy had seen her looking really happy. 'I'll tell you what,' she said. 'We'll go down to Melfordleigh next Friday and take Paul along. Then, as Matthew will already be in the area, why don't we ask him to come and join us there for the weekend?' She sighed. 'It may be the last time any of us has a chance to stay there. I'll be putting the house on the market next week.'

'Oh.' Rosalind's face dropped. 'That's a shame. Don't you want to live there any more?'

'It just wouldn't be practical,' Cathy told her. 'It's much too big. I couldn't keep it going as a music school, and anyway, I'll have to get a job of some kind. Gerald left me nothing but a pile of debts, you see. Everything we both had went into the house and the school.'

'Oh, no. I didn't realise. Poor Cathy.'

'I can't blame him for that,' she said quickly. 'After all, he never expected that plane to crash, did he? If we'd been divorced as he planned, Cuckoo Lodge would have been sold anyway, so it seems it was on the cards all along.' She looked at Rosalind. 'By the way – what I told you about Gerald and our marriage, the divorce and everything from the past . . . I don't want Paul to know any of it. He's built up such an ideal image of his father, I don't want to disillusion him. There isn't any point. Now that Gerald is dead there's no reason he need ever know.'

'Of course. Just as you say,' Rosalind promised.

'This weekend will be for Paul's benefit,' Cathy went on. 'I was lucky. I had a wonderful father and I was close to him for sixteen years. Paul had only newspaper clippings and records, so I think I owe him that.'

* * *

When she telephoned Paul and invited him to Melfordleigh for the weekend he was overjoyed.

'I can't tell you how much it means to me, Cathy,' he said excitedly. 'To see the place where he lived; the house he loved. To be able to touch his things – play his piano. Thanks, Cathy. I can't tell you how much I'll look forward to it.'

Cathy had intended that they should travel to Suffolk by train, but Paul had telephoned to say that he'd hired a car for the weekend. 'I thought that way I'd be able to see more of the countryside,' he explained. 'While I'm here I intend to see as much of Britain as I can.'

He picked her and Rosalind up the following Friday evening. Cathy had written to Maggie and asked her to open up the house and when they arrived they found fires lit and the rooms ready for them. Matthew was already there, sitting in the drawing room with his feet up on the brass fender.

'Hi!' he said when they walked in. 'Your housekeeper let me in, Cath. She told me to tell you that there's a meal waiting in the oven if you're hungry.'

Rosalind stood in front of him, trying to assess his mood. 'Well,' she said. 'Are you going to tell us how the interview went? Is there any news?'

'Not really.' Matthew stood up and stretched his arms above his head with exaggerated nonchalance. 'Unless you want to say hello to the new junior solicitor in the firm of Hawkins, Hawkins and Mather.'

Rosalind gave a whoop of delight and threw her arms around him. 'Oh, *Matthew*! That's wonderful.'

Cathy echoed Rosalind's congratulations and Paul shook his hand. Then, sensing that they wanted to be alone, Cathy took Paul's arm and steered him towards the kitchen.

'Come and help me dish up this meal,' she invited. 'It's too dark to see much now but tomorrow I'll show you round the house and the village.'

* * *

Saturday morning dawned bright and clear. Although it was still only late-February the weather was mild and springlike and as soon as they had breakfasted Matthew and Rosalind wrapped up in their warmest clothes and went for a walk down to the quay. Sitting on the wall and looking out across the calm water Rosalind said suddenly: 'Matthew. About two o'clock this morning I woke up with this crazy idea.'

He laughed. 'How crazy?'

'I don't know. Impossibly crazy perhaps. That's what I want you to tell me.'

He smiled and slipped an arm around her shoulders. 'Then you'd better explain it to me, hadn't you?'

'Cathy says she has to sell Cuckoo Lodge.'

'That's right. Gerald died owing quite a lot of money.' He looked at her, one eyebrow raised. 'Don't tell me you're thinking of buying it?'

Rosalind bit her lip. 'There – I knew you'd think it was crazy. Oh, well, it *was* two in the morning when I thought of it.'

'No, wait.' He was frowning. 'I mean, what would you do with it?'

'I've always wanted a hotel,' she told him simply. 'It's been my ambition ever since I was a little girl. Cuckoo Lodge would be perfect. Even the name is just right. But you're right. It's a mad idea.'

'Hang on, I didn't say that. It was a surprise, that's all.' He looked at her thoughtfully. 'Do you think you could do it? You must think there's a possibility.'

'I feel fairly confident that I could run it. What I don't know is whether I'd have enough money. I told you my dad left me a cottage? Dad and Freda had done a lot of work on it – made it really nice. I sold it for a good price as a weekend retreat.'

'Well, Cuckoo Lodge is equipped for guests,' he said. 'There'd be nothing for you to buy and no alterations to be

461

made. But . . .' He looked at her. 'Even if you had enough money for the deposit and could get a mortgage, it would be hard work, you know. You'd have staff to pay. You couldn't run it alone. It could be years before you saw any profit.'

'I realise that. But if I just made enough to live on I'd be happy. It would be *my* business, you see – and my home too. I'd be working for myself; answerable to no one. Doing what I've always dreamed of doing.' She turned her face up to his, eyes shining with excited enthusiasm. 'I want it, Matthew. What would I have to do to get it?'

Catching some of her excitement, he hugged her closer. 'Well – first you'd have to find out what sort of price Cathy is hoping to get for the place. You'd probably need a bank loan to start the business. For that you'd have to work out a business plan – present a set of figures so that the bank could see you know what you're doing. Then there'd be a mortgage to fix up.'

'I'm sure I could do the business plan. I lay awake for hours last night working all that out in my head . . .' Suddenly the light went out of Rosalind's eyes and her face dropped.

'What? What's the matter?'

'No bank would give me a loan though, would they, Matthew? I wouldn't get a mortgage either. Not after – after what I did.'

'You've got to put that behind you, Rossie,' he said sternly. 'It was something you did out of desperation – a private matter, between you and your step-father. He accepted your explanation and understood. You gave the money back to him and he forgave you. As it was never reported to the police there's no record. No one even knows about it apart from you and your parents.'

She sighed. 'That's right, I suppose.'

'Of course it is. Your mother was simply playing on your conscience when she bullied you into giving up your job.' He drew her close. 'You've got to try to forget it, darling.'

She looked up at him. 'I don't think I ever will.'

'But you *must*. You can't let one incident like that ruin your life.' He bent and kissed her. 'If that is the worst mistake you ever make you'll be doing well.' He jumped down from the wall and held out his hands to her. 'Come on, I'll treat you to lunch at the Admiral Nelson, then we'll go back and ask Cathy what she thinks of your plan.'

Paul wanted to see everything, each room in the house, the grounds and garden, ending with the converted barn where the concerts and master classes had been held. He stood in the auditorium, looking at the shallow stage and the rows of seats, enthralled by everything he saw.

'And you helped with it all?' he said, looking round him in admiration. 'All the restoration, the decor and everything? I can't imagine why anyone would want to give it all up.'

'I've no choice, Paul,' she told him. 'Gerald died still owing a lot of money. It has to be paid back.'

Back in the house she left him running his fingers experimentally over the keyboard of Gerald's piano in the larger of the two studios while she went to make coffee. When she came back he turned to her, his eyes bright with an idea.

'Why don't you keep the place on, Cathy – open it up as a kind of shrine to Gerald?' he said. 'All the people who were his fans could come to pay homage; to see his home and all the things he lived and worked with. Like Elgar's birthplace in Worcestershire. I've been there. Hundreds of visitors go to see that every year. You could still run concerts in the barn to help finance the place. You said you were going to have to get a job, so why not right here?'

Cathy's heart sank. How could she tell him why the idea appalled her so? 'It would be too much of a gamble, Paul,' she said gently. 'Elgar was a great composer. His music will live on. Gerald was a concert pianist. Oh, a brilliant one, I grant you, but others will follow him. People soon forget. Maybe there would be a few visitors the first summer. After that it would run at a loss.' She looked at his crestfallen face. 'I'm sorry, Paul, but I couldn't afford it. Gerald's creditors are pressing for their money. They need to be paid now, otherwise I'll have to settle for bankruptcy and I don't want that.'

'I never meant for you to do it alone.' He reached for her hands. 'Look, Cathy. I have some money. My grandfather left me some. I'd willingly put it into a project like this. Gerald was a composer too. There's his rhapsody and maybe there are more compositions that he never showed to anyone.' He pressed her hands. 'Please – at least think about it.'

She pulled her hands away and walked to the window. 'I don't have to think about it, Paul. I need to sell. If you want to buy Cuckoo Lodge and do it yourself, I can't stop you. But I couldn't take on a project like the one you suggest.'

There was a long pause as she stared unseeingly out of the window, but she could still feel his eyes on her back. 'And if I were to ask you why you're so against it?' he said at last.

She turned to face him. 'I've told you why. I'm not against it as such. It's just that I don't think it would work.' She looked down at her hands. 'And I don't want to be a part of anything like that.'

He got up from the piano and went towards her, his eyes searching hers uneasily. 'Were you unhappy with him? Is that it?'

She shook her head. 'I was much too young – too immature for marriage. Oh, it was my fault. I was warned but I ignored the warnings, refused to see the difficulties.' She sighed. 'You needn't concern yourself with that.' She looked at him. 'Paul – please don't put your money into Cuckoo Lodge. You'd lose it all and I'd hate to feel responsible for that.'

But he wasn't listening. 'You say I shouldn't be concerned that your marriage was unhappy, Cathy,' he said quietly, 'but I am. Ever since the day I first saw you I've known there was something about you – some deep unhappiness. I wish I knew what it was. I wish there was something I could do . . .'

'There isn't. And I'm fine.' She forced a smile. 'How morbid we're getting. Come on, let's go down and look at the village before it decides to rain.'

But already the sky was overcast and by the time they reached the quay the rain had begun. The water in the harbour that had been so smooth and calm was choppy now, the rising wind whipping it into angry little wavelets that slapped against the harbour wall. They ran to the Admiral Nelson for cover and found Matthew and Rosalind sitting in the lounge overlooking the quay.

'We were just going to have lunch, why don't you join us?' Matthew suggested. He looked at Cathy. 'Rossie has an idea she wants to put to you anyway.'

Paul, who was utterly enchanted by the quaint old pub, went off to the bar to buy drinks and Rosalind leaned across the table. 'Cathy – what would you say if I told you I want to buy Cuckoo Lodge?' she asked, trying in vain to suppress the excitement in her voice.

Cathy's eyebrows rose. 'I'd say that at this rate I shan't have to advertise. Yours is the second offer I've had this morning.'

'The second?' Rosalind's face dropped. 'Whose was the other?'

'Paul's. But he was only half serious and I think I've talked him out of it,' Cathy told her. 'He wanted to turn the place into some kind of living memorial to Gerald.' Rosalind and Matthew stared at her in silence. 'I know,' she said. 'It would never work. He'd be pouring money into a bottomless pit and I told him so. But you, Rossie – what would you do with it?'

465

'I'd open it as a hotel,' Rosalind told her. 'We've just been talking to the landlord here. Apparently this is the only residential place in the village apart from the bed and breakfast places and the holiday cottages. He turns people away all the time, so I wouldn't be short of business.' She leaned forward, her eyes shining. 'And as for the off-season, remember what I said about letting the place out for conferences – using the barn as a conference hall?'

'I do indeed,' Cathy said guardedly. 'It's a lovely idea but . . .'

'There's the money I've been saving,' Rosalind went on, anticipating the next question, 'that I got from the sale of the cottage, remember? Matthew thinks it might be enough for the deposit. He's going to help me apply for a bank loan and a mortgage.'

'You should get the place valued first, Cath,' he put in cautiously.

'Yes, I know. Well, if you're serious I'll start doing something about it first thing on Monday morning.'

By the time Paul came back to the table with the tray of drinks he found the other three in good spirits. He took the news that Rosalind meant to make an offer for Cuckoo Lodge resignedly, but later that afternoon, as he and Cathy were walking on the dunes after the rain had stopped, he said: 'I'd like to take something of Gerald's home with me when I go.' He sighed. 'I suppose I have to admit that buying the house was kind of a stupid idea when I live on the other side of the world – just a pipe dream really. All the same . . .'

Cathy turned to him. 'I'd like you to have his piano.'

'His *piano*?' He stopped in his tracks and turned to her. 'You mean you wouldn't *mind*?'

'Not at all. It should be yours by right.'

'Oh, Cathy. I don't know what to say. That's so generous.'

'Of course transporting it might be a problem.'

466

'Never mind that. I'll get it home somehow.' He looked at her. 'I'd like you to come over and see Auckland sometime, Cathy. I think you'd like it there. Of course we don't have olde worlde pubs or wild, windswept coastlines like this, but it is beautiful and I have to say that our weather has yours licked.' He grinned disarmingly. 'The natives are friendly too. What do you say?'

She smiled. 'It sounds nice, but I've got an awful lot of planning to do, Paul. A whole new life to sort out for myself.'

He stopped walking and reached out to take her hand. 'Look, you're not saying that this weekend – I mean – it won't be the last we'll see of each other, will it?'

She shook her head, acutely aware of the hand that held hers. 'I don't know, Paul. You have your studies at the hospital. I have so much to attend to. Maybe it would be best.'

'I don't agree.' He was looking at her with earnest brown eyes. 'I'm going to be here for a whole year. Surely we could see something of each other during that time? I'd really like us to get to know one another better.'

'Well – maybe.'

'And don't forget that Gerald's rhapsody gets its first performance in August at the Promenade Concerts. We just have to go and hear that together.'

'Well . . .' She couldn't meet the compelling eyes that looked into hers. 'I – just don't know,' she hedged. 'It's a long time ahead. Six whole months. Let's leave it for now, shall we?'

She made to move away but he held on to her hand. 'Look – maybe this is the wrong time to be saying this and I'll be putting my foot in it all over again, but we only have these two days so I want you to know how I feel. It's as though I've known you for years, Cathy, not just days. We have so much in common. We can't just say goodbye and leave it at that.'

467

She'd sensed this coming and now she felt something very close to panic tightening her throat. 'Paul, we don't really know each other at all. You know nothing about me. You think that because I was married to your father we automatically have things in common . . .'

'No, you've got it all wrong.' He was shaking his head. 'It isn't just that. I . . .'

'I'm probably nothing like you think.' She pulled her hand forcibly from his grasp. 'I don't want to talk about it any more, Paul. Let's go back. It's beginning to get dark and I'm cold.'

Sleep did not come easily to Cathy that night. The weekend was proving so much more traumatic than she'd imagined. Paul clearly saw his father as some kind of saintly genius and her as his adjunct – the closest link he could form – which was why he wanted to cling to her. Keeping up the charade of Gerald's honour and integrity was becoming more of a strain with each passing hour. As she tossed and turned she wished fervently that the weekend could be at an end so that they could leave for London again. As for Paul's suggestion that they see each other again during his stay in England, that was the hardest thing to cope with. She liked him so much. She found his warm personality, his sense of humour and his dark good looks attractive and infinitely appealing. In any other circumstances, if he had been anyone other than Gerald's son, she would happily have agreed to see him again. As it was, how could she allow him to get any closer without revealing the unpalatable truth about his father?

It was early next morning when she was wakened by someone tapping on her bedroom door.

'Can I come in?' Rosalind put her head round the door. 'I know it's early but there's something I need to talk to you about.'

Cathy sat up, rubbing the sleep from her eyes and

yawning. It had been four o'clock by the time sleep had finally claimed her. Her head felt heavy and her eyes ached. 'Come in and sit down,' she invited. 'Don't tell me you've had another brilliant idea.'

'I have as a matter of fact.' Rosalind perched on the end of the bed drawing up her knees and hugging them. 'I don't know what it is about this place but I feel a different person here – so alive and full of vitality. It must be the air.'

Cathy smiled. Privately she felt that Rosalind's good humour had more to do with Matthew than Melfordleigh. 'Okay, are you going to tell me about it then?' she said through another yawn.

'Right. I can't imagine why I didn't think of this before. It's been staring us in the face all the time.'

'Mmm? What has?'

'You've been saying that you need to look for a job, right?'

'Right. I do – and soon.'

'Well, the answer is obvious. Why don't we go into partnership – run Cuckoo Lodge together? After all we get along together, don't we? I've had experience and training in hotel work and you did your Home Economics course.'

'Well, yes, I suppose you're right.' Cathy was suddenly wide awake and staring at her friend. The idea was so simple and so obvious that there must surely be some snag. 'But – but would it really work?' she stammered.

'It could. I'm sure it could. We'd have to work out the details, of course, but if the money I've got would pay off what Gerald owed we could count that as my share of the business, then we could start with a clean sheet; run the place as a hotel, each draw a salary and pay the existing mortgage off out of our profits. We might not even need a bank loan. It's perfect, Cathy!'

She felt her heart leap with excitement, and had to force herself to be cautious. 'On the face of it, yes, but it all

469

sounds a bit too good to be true. 'Have you spoken to Matthew about it?'

'Yes, last night. I kept him up till the small hours. He says that if my money is enough to settle the debts, and if you agree of course, he doesn't see why it shouldn't work out fine. He's even offered to draw up a proper partnership agreement for us so that everything is fair. He says he'll do all the legal work for us as a gift.'

Cathy was smiling now, her weariness forgotten. 'Oh, Rossie, wouldn't it be fun? I hardly dare think about it. Do you *really* think we could make a go of it?'

'I've told you, I'm sure we could. I've worked it all out. If we got a move on and advertised we could have a good first season *this* year. The landlord of the Admiral Nelson will send us his overflow if we ask him. I sounded him out yesterday – without giving anything away, of course. And while we're doing that we could be advertising and booking conferences for the winter months. And the beauty of it is that as the place already belongs to you, there'll be no waiting for contracts to be finalised. We could start right away! As soon as you like.'

Cathy jumped out of bed and pulled on her dressing gown. 'Let's go and get Matthew up this minute and start working out the details,' she said excitedly.

Rosalind laid a hand on her arm. 'Cathy – what about Paul?'

'What about him?'

'He's going to feel rather left out of all this, isn't he? Especially when he wanted the place himself. Do you think we should wait and talk about it later, when we're alone?'

Cathy sank back on to the bed again with a sigh. 'I suppose you're right.' She looked at Rosalind. 'I don't know what to do about him, Rossie. He wants us to go on seeing each other. He's going to be over here for a whole year. It's going to be so difficult to avoid him.'

'Why should you want to?' she asked. 'He's so nice and he's obviously very taken with you.'

'But he's Gerald's son.'

'Biologically, maybe, but that's all. They never knew each other, did they?'

'But he thinks of him as some kind of hero. I couldn't keep up that kind of pretence.'

'Then don't. Tell him the truth.'

Cathy stared at her. 'How could I?'

'Why not? We all have to cope with the truth at some time, Cathy. It's part of growing up, isn't it?' She leaned forward. 'If you can't bear to hurt him then you must care about him a little. If that's the case you'll want to go on seeing him. I don't see why you should let a thing like that stand in your way.'

Cathy shook her head, her eyes troubled. 'I keep thinking of Dad and how much he meant to me,' she said. 'I was so lucky to have had him all the time I was growing up. All Paul has is this image he's built. How can I shatter that?'

'What about *your* images, Cathy? You believed in Gerald, didn't you? He was a hero to you too once. You gave your life to him, and you had to find out the hard way. And what about me? My mother did her best to poison my memories of my father. I knew he wasn't perfect but it didn't make any difference. I loved him the way he was.' She touched Cathy's arm. 'Even with all Gerald's faults he was a musical genius. Paul can still be proud of that.'

'I know that what you're saying is right,' Cathy said. 'I just don't want to be the one to tell him.'

'Because you think he'll hate you for pulling down his dream? And having him hate you is the last thing you want?'

For a long moment they stared at each other. Rosalind had interpreted Cathy's thoughts with uncanny accuracy, but she wasn't sure she was ready to face them. 'You're right,' she said at last. 'It would be better to wait until

471

the three of us are alone. Today we'll just relax and enjoy ourselves.'

'Okay, only don't bury your head in the sand,' Rosalind warned. 'Don't spend the rest of your life throwing away chances of happiness. They don't come along so often that we can afford to waste them.'

The four of them spent the day pleasantly enough. The weather was fine again and over breakfast Paul suggested a drive inland.

'Might as well make the most of the car while I've got it,' he said. 'See a bit of Suffolk. I'm really keen to take a look at these ancient Brecklands I've heard so much about.'

Although he asked Rosalind and Matthew to go too, they declined. Matthew had telephoned some married friends in nearby Woodbridge to tell them about his new job and they had invited him to take Rosalind along to lunch. They left soon after eleven and Cathy and Paul set out soon after. As they drove along the lanes in the winter sunshine Cathy was quiet. She felt stupid and tongue-tied and the more she searched her mind for some intelligent topic, the blanker it became. For a while Paul struggled to make conversation.

'I think I might buy myself a car to use while I'm here,' he said. 'It'd be cheaper than hiring and it would certainly help me to see more of the countryside in my spare time.' He glanced at her. 'I could always sell it when it's time to head for home again.'

'Yes. That sounds like a good idea.'

'If I do that will you come out in it with me?' he asked, glancing at her.

She looked at him. 'If you do what?'

'Buy a car. I'll need someone to show me the way around.'

She sighed. 'Look Paul, there's something I should tell you. I'm planning to go into partnership with Rosalind and run Cuckoo Lodge as a small hotel.'

'That's a great idea.' He looked slightly puzzled. 'You're not still worried about my crazy idea for the place, are you?'

'No. What I mean is that I won't be living in London any more. We – you and I will be a long way apart.'

'So what's new?' He drew the car into the side of the quiet country road and turned in his seat to look at her. 'We've been a long way apart ever since we met, Cathy. And it seems to me that's the way you want it to be.'

'You're wrong. I don't, not really. It's just with you being Gerald's son. It makes things – difficult.'

'I don't see why. I know you and he weren't happy together, but that has nothing to do with you and me. There's no reason why we shouldn't get along.' When she didn't reply he reached out to cup her chin, turning her head towards him so that she was forced to look at him. 'Well, is there?'

'No. No, of course not.'

'Then why do you hold me at arm's length like this?'

'I think you've already made up your mind about what kind of person I am,' she said.

He shook his head. 'Okay, so maybe I'm wrong about you. I don't happen to think I am, but I'd like the chance to find out. Can't you at least give me that?'

She opened her mouth to start to tell him, then closed it again. If she were to tell him the truth – the whole truth – not only must she indict Gerald but herself as well. She had been far from blameless, and suddenly she knew that Rosalind was right: she could not bear Paul to be disillusioned about her. She sighed and shook her head.

'It's no use. I'm sorry but I don't want to have this conversation with you, Paul,' she said. 'Perhaps we'd better go home now.'

His face was dark with angry frustration as he started up the engine again. 'Okay, if that's the way you want it,' he said tightly. 'I think I finally got the message.'

473

For a while they drove in silence, then in a vain attempt to put things on to a friendly footing, she said, 'When we get back to London I'll arrange for the piano to be moved and put into storage. Is that all right?'

'Do what you like with it. It's not important,' he said raggedly. 'I don't give a damn any more.'

For the rest of the way back to Melfordleigh Cathy was rigid with misery. Paul sat silent and stony-faced beside her, clearly hurt and bewildered by her attitude. Sending him away like this, giving him all the wrong ideas, was the last thing she wanted to do. But what other course was there?

After tea they locked up the house and set off on the journey home. Cathy announced that as Matthew was going to spend a few days with his mother she would travel with him.

Rosalind drew her aside. 'Have you and Paul had a row?' she asked.

'No, but I just can't face being alone with him any more this weekend.'

'Well, you can't let him drive back on his own. It looks so rude,' Rosalind admonished, clearly shocked at her behaviour. 'I'd better go with him if you won't.'

They said their farewells at the gate and Cathy climbed into Matthew's car, acutely aware that she was upsetting everyone's arrangements. Noticing her pensive silence Matthew kept glancing at her and after a few miles asked if she was all right.

'Not regretting your decision to go in with Rossie, are you?'

She shook her head. 'No. I'm looking forward to it.'

'Then why are you so fed up?' He glanced at her. 'Come on, Cath, we've known each other too long for play-acting. Does it have something to do with Paul?'

She nodded, swallowing hard at the lump in her throat.

'He seems like a good bloke.'

'Yes, he is.'

474

'Are you going to see him again?'

'No.'

Matthew glanced sideways at Cathy's pale stricken face. She obviously didn't want to talk about it. He gave up trying to work out what had gone wrong and concentrated all his attention on the road ahead. Although he had grown up in a house of women he'd never been very good at understanding them. Cathy especially had always been hard for him to puzzle out. He congratulated himself that Rosalind seemed less complicated.

Rosalind was suffering a silent travelling companion too. Paul's face was grim as he gripped the steering wheel with white-knuckled hands, staring at the empty road with unnecessary concentration.

'Did you enjoy seeing your father's house?' she asked.

'Yes, thanks.'

'We were lucky with the weather.'

'Yes.'

'Apart from the shower yesterday.' She looked at him. 'Did you know that East Anglia has the lowest rainfall in the country?'

'No. Really?'

'Look, Paul – about Cathy . . .'

He turned to stare at her. 'If you're going to tell me to lay off, I already got the message,' he said bitterly. 'She thinks I'm a creep.'

'That's not true!'

'Well, whatever, she doesn't want to know.'

'You're wrong there too. She likes you very much.'

'Oh, really? You could have fooled me! What's she like with folks she doesn't like?'

'It's just that she's had a bad time. Maybe it's all a bit too soon for her.'

'I only wanted to see her again, damn it . . . for us to get to know one another,' he said bleakly.

'I know. And I'm sorry.' Rosalind sat in silence, struggling with her conscience. What had happened between these two people was nothing to do with her. Or was it? Cathy was her best friend – soon to be her business partner. She was unhappy and so was Paul. If she were to tell him the truth about what held Cathy back, would she be interfering in what didn't concern her? He might take it badly in which case she would make matters worse. On the other hand . . . Should she keep her mouth firmly closed and mind her own business? Yes, she should. She *really* should mind her own business.

'Paul – would you pull over and stop, please?' She glanced at him, her heart thudding dully in her chest.

He looked surprised. 'Is something wrong?'

'Something is very wrong,' she told him. 'But with Cathy, not with me. I've decided that I'm going to try and put it right – even if it's none of my business. Someone has to.' She looked at him apprehensively. 'And, Paul, I'd better warn you – you may not like what I'm going to tell you, so be prepared.'

When Paul dropped Rosalind off at Blake's Folly she was surprised to see most of the lights blazing. It was unusual. Normally when Don was alone, he ate in the kitchen and sat in the little breakfast room which was easy to heat. Taking her weekend case from the back seat, she thanked Paul and ran up the path, opening the door with her own key. Inside the front door she stopped short. At the bottom of the stairs various pieces of luggage were strewn carelessly around, and as Rosalind closed the front door she heard Una's voice. She sounded upset.

'Why don't you just go ahead and say it? *I told you so. Serves you right*. You'd have every right to.'

'I shan't say anything of the kind,' Don replied mildly. 'I'm just grateful you've come home.'

The voices came from the sitting room and through the

half-open door Rosalind could see her mother, her hair awry and her mascara running unheeded down her cheeks as she stood facing her husband.

'Oh, Don. I don't deserve a husband like you,' she sobbed, fumbling for a handkerchief in her handbag. 'I've made such a mess of everything. I can't tell you how awful it was. Those horrible coarse audiences! They talked and laughed all through my act, then complained that they couldn't *hear* me! In one place they actually *threw* things!'

Don pulled out a large white handkerchief and put it into her trembling hands. 'Poor love,' he said, taking her tenderly in his arms. 'What things? Were you hurt?'

'Well, no. Not hurt. It was mostly bread rolls, but it was so *humiliating*. Imagine – me, Una Blair – a West End star being pelted with bread rolls!'

'Never mind. It's all over now,' he said soothingly. 'You're home where you belong and I'm glad.'

Una nestled her head against his chest. 'Oh, Don, so am I. I've been such a silly vain fool.' She looked up at him with brimming eyes. 'Where is Rossie?'

'She's gone away for the weekend with her friend Cathy,' he told her. 'I thought the break would do her good. She's a good girl, Una. One of the best. She's worked really hard since you've been away.'

'Oh, well, I'm glad she made herself useful.' She looked up at him with appealing brown eyes. 'You won't tell her my tour was a failure, will you?' she begged.

'Of course I won't. Not if you don't want me to.'

'And, Don – do you think we could still go on that cruise you were planning? I'm so tired.'

Rosalind tiptoed back to the front door, opened it and closed it again with a bang.

'Hello!' she called. 'I'm home, Don!'

He and Una came out into the hall together, smiling and hand in hand. Rosalind put down her case and affected surprise.

477

'Mum! How are you?'

'I'm fine. Exhausted of course after the tour. Had a nice weekend have you? Don told me you'd gone away with Cathy.'

'It was very nice. Well, you'll be wanting to talk. I'll go up now then.'

She was almost ready for bed when there was a tap on the door and Una slipped into the room. 'Just thought I'd come and have a chat,' she said, sitting down. 'Don and I have been making plans. As soon as he retires next month we're off on a long cruise. Don says you've been a great help to him while I've been away. As you've nowhere else to go you can stay on here and mind the house for us while we're away.'

'That won't be possible, Mum. I'm going into business with Cathy. We're planning to start almost immediately.'

Una sat up very straight and stared at her daughter. 'Business? What business?'

'You must have heard that Gerald Cavelle was killed in a plane crash.'

'Yes, I heard. Dreadful of course, but I don't see . . .'

'She and I are going to run her house in Melfordleigh as a hotel.'

Una smirked. 'Oh, is *that* what you mean by business? You're going to work for her – as a domestic.'

'No. We're going into partnership.'

Una sighed patiently. 'Correct me if I'm wrong, but I've always understood that to go into partnership you have to put up some money?'

'That's right.'

'So where will you get that money, may I ask?'

'Dad left me his cottage. The one he bought in Northamptonshire. I sold it for quite a good price.'

Una's face turned bright pink. 'Ben left – left *you* that cottage?' she spluttered. 'But – but what about me? I was his wife!'

'No, Mum. You're Don's wife.'

Una sprang to her feet. 'Don't be so insolent, you devious little bitch! You've had all that money ever since Ben died and you said nothing to me about it. How could you?'

'I was working at the Queen's Head when I found out. We hadn't been in touch. I didn't think you'd be interested.'

Una paused, her eyes narrowing. 'I'd have thought that a celebrity like Gerald Cavelle would have left his wife well provided for,' she said. 'Why does she have to take in lodgers?'

'She's not taking in *lodgers*, she's turning Cuckoo Lodge into an hotel,' Rosalind said patiently.

Una laughed. 'What's the difference? It could hardly have a better name, could it?' she said scathingly. 'You're the cuckoo if you ask me. You're getting taken for a ride if you could only see it. Know what they say – a fool and his money . . .'

'The partnership is all being drawn up legally,' Rosalind said, swallowing down the anger slowly mounting inside her. 'It's being done tomorrow. It's all going ahead, Mum, whatever you say. And it's going to be a success.'

'I see. So you're walking out now that you don't need free board and lodgings any more?'

'I had a good job, Mum. You forced me to give it up because it suited you. And I think I've worked quite hard for my board and lodging, as you put it.'

'It was a tuppeny-ha'penny job and you know it,' Una said unrepentantly. 'Which reminds me – what would Cathy Cavelle say, I wonder, if she knew that her prospective business partner was a common thief?'

'She knows I took the Meissen. She also knows that I took it out of sheer desperation – when no one else would help me when Dad was ill.'

Rosalind saw the door open quietly and Don appeared in the doorway. Una, who had her back to the door, went on, 'I can see now why you were so keen to be at your father's

479

bedside. Still, he left you the cottage anyway, so it hardly matters any more, does it? I suppose I should be thankful that scheming Morton cow didn't get her hot greedy little hands on it. That must have been a blow for her.'

'Will you come downstairs now, Una?'

She sprang up, scarlet-faced, and turned to him. 'Don! How long have you been there? I didn't hear . . .'

'That is painfully obvious.' His face was dark as thunder. 'Come downstairs, I want to talk to you. I think it's high time you and I had a little chat. If you're really planning to stay this time, I'm going to need to lay down a few rules. And if when you've heard them you don't agree, I suggest that you take the luggage that's still down in the hall and leave again before you create any more trouble.'

The colour drained from Una's face as she stared first at Rosalind and then at Don. Her eyes bulged and her mouth worked as though she was about to let loose a stream of invective. Rosalind braced herself, but the tirade never came. Instead Una walked meekly to the door and through it on to the landing.

Before he closed the door behind him Don turned to Rosalind and, to her surprise, closed one eye in a triumphant, conspiratorial wink.

Rosalind unpacked her weekend case and put her things away. Would Don really succeed in taming Una? Somehow she thought he would. Una must know by now the elusive stardom she had longed for would never be hers and Rosalind thought she was wise enough to settle for what Don had to offer.

It wasn't until she was in bed with the light out that Rosalind allowed herself to think back over the journey home and the revelations she had made to Paul about his father. When she first began to speak his reaction had been distinctly cool. He had refused to look at her and as she stumbled on her blood had chilled with misgivings.

'He should never have married Cathy,' she told him. 'I

don't suppose you know that when he was killed he was on his way to meet another woman – the woman he intended to marry? He had already left Cathy. He'd sent this other woman to ask for a divorce. And that wasn't the only way he had betrayed Cathy. He – wasn't a real husband. He shut her out in every possible way. He made her very unhappy.' She paused. She had already said too much. Far too much. Yet there was so much more she could have told him about Gerald's coldness and his betrayal – its disastrous consequences. When she looked up again she saw that Paul was looking at her.

'What you're saying isn't entirely new,' he said quietly. 'I've heard it all before – from my mother. Years ago he treated her in much the same way. She always said that he put all his emotional energy into his music. There was never anything left over for relationships. When they were first married they were very poor. They lived on her money – the allowance she got from her parents. Once he didn't need it any more . . .' He lifted his shoulders helplessly. 'She never really got over the way he treated her. Because of it she never married again.' He sighed wistfully. 'All the same, I'd still like to have known him. You only have one father.'

'I know.' Rosalind sighed. 'I'm sorry. I shouldn't have said anything. It's none of my business really. It's just that Cathy is my friend and I know it hurt her to have to pretend to you. She's a very honest person.'

He sighed. 'Do you think that was the reason she brushed me off?'

'I'm sure it was. She didn't want to disillusion you.'

'So . . .' He looked at her with new hope in his eyes. 'So you're saying that if I . . .'

'I'm not saying anything, Paul. I've absolutely no right to. I just wanted to put right the misunderstanding

481

between you, that's all. What you do about it now is up to you.'

She turned over and punched her pillow. She hoped to heaven she'd done the right thing. But even if she hadn't it was too late to change anything now.

Chapter Twenty-Two

'We could do gourmet dinners in the winter months,' Rosalind said. 'I learned some very good recipes from the chef at the Queen's Head when I was there. That reminds me, do you think we could afford to keep Maggie on to help us? Oh, and I thought we might make a special arrangement with the boatmen on the quay to run trips out to the point to see the seal colony. You know, a reduced rate for parties. Now . . .' She placed a piece of paper on the table between them. 'I've made a list of the best magazines and papers to advertise in. Look.' She pointed. 'These at the bottom are the ones that specialise in conference venues.'

'Hang on!' Matthew raised a hand to stop her flow of excited chatter. 'There are a few other things to sort out before we get to that stage!' he told her with a rueful smile. 'Boring little legal details for instance.'

The three of them were seated around Johnny's dining table, making plans for the future of Cuckoo Lodge. Rosalind's excitement was infectious. Her cheeks were pink and her eyes shone with enthusiasm as she looked from one to the other.

'Oh, I know all that,' she said impatiently. 'But I don't think either of you realises that this is my dream that is coming true. I've got a perfect right to be excited!'

Matthew reached for her hand and gave it a squeeze. 'Of course you have. It's just that there are a few hurdles to be got over first.'

They had already established that the money Rosalind had received from the sale of the cottage, plus what Cathy had got from the sale of her emerald engagement ring, would be enough to pay off Gerald's creditors. Matthew had made an appointment to see Gerald's solicitor and arrange for the settlement of outstanding debts. But he had yet to draw up a satisfactory legal partnership for them both to sign.

'The one disadvantage of not needing a bank loan,' Matthew said thoughtfully, 'is that a bank manager would vet your business proposal and know whether it covered everything. I'm not sufficiently experienced in business matters, especially the hotel trade, to say. Is there anyone who's experienced in the trade who'd have a look at your figures and give you advice?'

The girls were silent for a moment, then Cathy looked up. 'What about Mrs Gresham at the Queen's Head?'

Rosalind's eyes brightened. 'Of course! Why didn't I think of her? Shall we go along this afternoon and see her, Cathy?'

'Of course.' She got up from the table. 'I'll go and give her a ring now and make an appointment.'

Mrs Gresham turned out to be just what they needed. She brought up several items the girls hadn't thought of, but applauded them on their enterprise and seemed optimistic for its success. Rosalind's business plan impressed her too.

'I'm glad to see that you learned something useful while you were with us,' she said with a smile. 'I only wish you could have stayed on to take over from me when I retire in a couple of years' time.'

On the way home Rosalind decided that at least one of them should learn to drive. 'We'll get a ticket for one of those cash and carry places and get our supplies cheaper than we could at the shops,' she said. 'But the nearest one is bound to be miles away so we'll be missing out if we don't drive.'

Cathy smiled to herself. The change in Rosalind since they'd begun to plan their new partnership was incredible.

For the first time in her life she found herself required to act as a steadying influence, constantly pulling Rosalind up and making her take things one step at a time. Sometimes it was a bit like riding a runaway horse. 'Can we afford to buy a car though?' she asked cautiously.

'We can't afford not to!' Rosalind retorted. 'And for that we *will* need a bank loan, but that shouldn't be a problem. Oh, it's all so exciting. I can't wait to get started.'

'Me neither,' Cathy agreed. 'I thought we might put the first advertisement in next week and if we ask Matthew very nicely perhaps he'll give us some driving lessons?'

They parted when they got to Rosalind's bus stop and Cathy walked the rest of the way home to Chestnut Grove, her mind busy with plans. The small front gardens in the Grove were bursting with promise. Daffodil bulbs were thrusting their spears above the ground and here and there yellow and purple crocuses flaunted their brightness. They seemed to Cathy to symbolise a new beginning.

As she turned in at the gate her thoughts were of Rosalind's idea that they should buy a car. She remembered how much she had longed to learn to drive at Melfordleigh and wondered how long it would take to learn. She let herself into the house and hung up her coat in the hall. From the living room came the muted buzz of voices. Johnny hadn't mentioned that she was expecting a visitor and she wondered vaguely who it could be. So when she opened the door and saw Paul sitting in the chair by the fireplace her heart gave a lurch. He stood up when she came in.

'Hello, Cathy.'

'Paul! Hello.' Her heart had begun to beat unevenly and she felt the colour warm her cheeks. She'd thought when they left Melfordleigh that she wouldn't see him again. Part of her had ached with sadness at the thought while another part had told her firmly that it was best to forget him.

Acutely aware of the tense atmosphere, Johnny got up from her chair. 'Ah, there you are then. Doctor Franklin has been waiting for almost an hour, Cathy.' She looked uncertainly from one to the other. 'Well – I'll leave you to talk.' She moved to the door. 'If you'll excuse me, I should be getting the meal started.'

'Of course. Thank you for letting me wait, Mrs Johnson,' Paul said politely.

As the door closed Cathy looked at him. 'Is there something I can do for you, Paul?' she asked coolly. She was annoyed – with herself for showing her vulnerability and with him for coming here uninvited.

'I had to come – whether you wanted me to or not.' His voice was low and harsh as he looked into her eyes. 'Rosalind told me the way it was between you and Gerald. On the drive home from Melfordleigh.'

'She told you? I don't . . .'

'Cathy – why didn't *you* tell me? I always knew he wasn't good at relationships. I never had any illusions about what he was like. God knows my mother went on enough about the way he used people. But I always secretly thought it might have been partly her fault. I thought in your case he might have been different.'

Cathy was shaking her head incredulously. 'Rosalind *told* you? I can't believe it!'

'Yes. Look, don't be angry with her. She did it for you. She knew you'd never tell me yourself.'

'She had no right.' Cathy turned away. 'I didn't tell you because it was none of your business. Besides, I didn't want to spoil your image of the ideal father.'

'I didn't have one. Not in that sense.'

Cathy turned back to look at him, wondering just how much he really knew. 'Rosalind shouldn't have said anything.'

'I'm very glad she did. I understand now why you were so cool. The important thing is that it's all cleared up. We can be friends now, without any misunderstandings.' He cleared his throat. 'Cathy, now that all that is out in the open, can we see each other again? After all, there's no reason why not.'

'I'm going to be very busy with organising the new business,' she hedged. 'I really don't know. Besides, you will be busy too and . . .'

'*Cathy!*' He took a step towards her. 'Listen. I'm not taking no for an answer any more.'

'Just – just how much did Rosalind tell you?'

'That you and Gerald weren't happy. That he shut you out of his life and was planning to divorce you. She told me about the letters you found too; about the affair Gerald had with your mother all those years ago.' He took a step towards her, his arms outstretched. 'What a terrible shock that must have been for you. I'm so sorry, Cathy.'

It was no use. Now that he knew half the truth she would have to tell him everything. There was no other way. She stepped back from his outstretched arms. 'Yes, it was, but there's more than that, Paul, much more, and you'd better know all of it.' She turned away, afraid to see the look on his face when she told him the whole truth.

'She told you that Gerald shut me out of his life – rejected me. Did she tell you how his rejection destroyed me?' she asked quietly. 'Did she tell you that I turned to someone else – another man – because of it? That I would have had his child if I hadn't – hadn't . . .'

'Cathy! What are you saying?'

'I was so *lonely*,' she told him, struggling to control her voice. 'So lonely and so unloved – unwanted. I felt it had to be my fault – that there must be something terribly wrong with me to make him so indifferent. So – when someone came along and – treated me like a woman it was like coming alive again. I . . .' She shook her head. 'I gave in. I was so weak and feeble that I allowed myself to be taken in by insincere flattery and lies. When I found I was pregnant I didn't know what to do. I wanted the baby more than anything in the world, yet I knew I couldn't have it.'

487

Her voice choked on the words. She was crying now, tears coursing down her cheeks to drip unheeded from her chin. 'I had to abort my child, Paul, to keep my infidelity from Gerald. Can you imagine what that did to me? Especially when I found that he had actually encouraged the affair to keep me quiet and occupied – as though I were some bothersome, fractious child in need of amusement. Since he died I've discovered that I made the sacrifice for nothing. Gerald only married me to gain control of the money my father left me. He never cared anything for me at all.'

For a long moment there was silence. She longed to escape from the room without having to see his reaction, but it was as though she was rooted to the floor. She stood staring out of the window, noticing small insignificant things like the tiny buds on the lilac tree; a bird pecking at some unseen insects on the lawn; a solitary dry brown leaf, a relic from last summer – a dead past. Then she felt his hands on her shoulders as he gently turned her towards him.

'Cathy, what can I say? I had no idea you'd gone through this – this terrible trauma.'

She couldn't look at him but kept her head down. 'Well, now you know all about me and why I tried to save you the disillusionment of finding out. People are seldom what they seem are they? If you want to go now and forget we ever met, I'll understand.'

'*Go?* What are you saying? What do you take me for, Cathy? Now that you've trusted me with this confidence, leaving you is the last thing I want to do. Do you think I don't know what it must have cost you to tell me all that? To relive it?'

For the first time she looked up and searched his eyes. She saw compassion and understanding there. No trace of blame or reproach.

'Now I'm going to tell *you* something,' he said with a smile. 'When I first saw you at the memorial service I was completely stunned. I couldn't take my eyes off you.

I thought you were the most beautiful girl I'd ever seen and I spent most of the time trying to work out some way I could find out who you were – how I could get to speak to you. I'd just decided it was hopeless when you fainted in all that crush and I saw an opportunity to help, I just couldn't believe my luck. It was as though fate had stepped in. Don't you see, Cathy? The way I felt then had absolutely nothing to do with the fact that you were Gerald's wife. Nothing to do with the fact that he was my father. And nothing has changed. Anything that happened in the past to either of us is totally irrelevant. All I care about is that we're here, you and me. Together. I want to try and make up for what you've been through, Cathy. Will you let me?'

'Why should you want to?'

'*Why?* Do I really have to tell you why?' Reaching out he took her face very firmly in both hands and raised it towards him, kissing her gently. 'Does that tell you anything about why?'

The kiss told Cathy a lot of things. It told her that she was fighting a losing battle; that his touch and the feel of his lips on hers meant more than she could ever have imagined it would. When Gerald died she had told herself she would never trust enough to give her love to another man but she hadn't bargained for the tumult that Paul aroused in her. The pounding of her heart and the clamour of her senses.

'You know I'm going away,' she said breathlessly. 'To live and work in Melfordleigh with Rosalind.'

He laughed. 'It's hardly a million miles away. I'll come down – at every possible opportunity – even if it's only for a couple of hours. I want to spend time with you, Cathy. I want us to have time to discover each other. And I'm warning you, I won't be turned away. I won't take no for an answer, because I know deep down that we can have something good together.' He drew her closer and kissed her again, this time with all the depth and passion he had held at bay. She felt the tension seep out of her as she relaxed

489

in his arms. She allowed herself the luxury of response, her lips parting for him, her arms holding him close, her fingers in his hair. It was like coming home; like a long cool drink after the heat of the day. His arms were warm and safe. In that moment nothing else seemed to matter. Yet even in her response a warning voice somewhere deep inside told her to take care. Hearts were so easy to break and so hard to mend and hers seemed especially fragile.

'I'll come to Melfordleigh as often as I can,' he whispered. 'Will you like that? Will you look forward to seeing me?'

'Yes. Of course I will.'

'Cathy . . .' He looked into her eyes. 'Cathy, I . . .'

'*No.*' She stopped him from completing the sentence, her fingers against his lips. 'Don't say it. We have a long way to go yet before either of us can say that.'

'Why?' He took her fingers from his lips and held them against his cheek. 'When can I say it?'

'I don't know. One day perhaps. When we're both sure beyond a shadow of a doubt.'

'I am now.'

'No. Not yet. It's just a word, Paul, too easy to say and too hard to live up to. It's important to me to wait.'

By April Cuckoo Lodge had had its first Bank Holiday weekend, for which, thanks to a brief spell of beautiful weather and a sudden rush of visitors, all their rooms had been full. It had been slightly nerve-racking. Would anything go wrong? Would their visitors be comfortable and satisfied that they were getting good value? They needn't have worried. With Maggie's placid good sense and capability in the kitchen, they pulled through. Everyone went home happily and after that it was plain sailing. The landlord of the Admiral Nelson sent along any customers who enquired about good accommodation and by the beginning of June they had fallen into a comfortable and happy working routine.

Matthew, now settled in the new legal practice in Ipswich, was a regular weekend guest, sleeping good-naturedly on any camp bed or settee that happened to be available. Paul too made regular, sometimes unheralded, appearances whenever he could snatch some time off, driving down in the middle-aged Ford Consul he had bought.

Rosalind's enthusiasm knew no bounds. She was full of plans for the future. She suggested that when they'd saved enough they might build an annexe so that they could take more visitors.

'The reception rooms are big enough to take more,' she pointed out. 'The dining room could take at least three more tables. And it's just as easy to cook for twenty as ten so why not?'

'Before we think of building annexes we could probably convert the attics into a couple more rooms,' Cathy said practically. 'It might be worth getting a builder in to look at them.'

Rosalind's plans for expansion included turning the larger of the two studios, now vacated by Gerald's grand piano, into a restaurant for non-residents with a carvery and salad bar. She was arranging to apply for a licence to serve alcohol too. Her energy often left Cathy breathless. She had never seen her friend happier or more fulfilled. And she guessed that Cuckoo Lodge was only partly responsible for the transformation. She felt sure it was only a matter of time before Rosalind and Matthew would announce their engagement.

One weekend in late June Paul managed three whole days off. The weather was glorious and after dinner on his first evening he and Cathy walked down to the quay together. The sea was smooth and glassy with only the merest swell to sway the boats moored in the harbour. Above them the cloudless sky was a serene, milky blue and the air was clear and tangy.

Paul took a deep breath. 'Ah – that's so good after

London,' he said. 'I take back all I said about your weather. Nothing to touch a perfect English summer evening.' He looked at Cathy. 'It's great to be here like this. I miss you,' he said softly, taking her hand. 'A whole lot more than you realise. I miss your amazing hair and those green eyes; your laugh and the way your mouth curves. Sometimes I think I must be mad to stay up there away from you.'

'Your work is important. You know it is,' she told him practically.

'I only wish I could give my mind to it,' he said wryly. 'At the moment I can't think of much else but you.' He bent to kiss her, then pulled her arm through his as they walked. 'Cathy, the Promenade Concerts start next month. I've been looking forward to going to the Albert Hall and hearing the première performance of Gerald's rhapsody.' He looked down at her. 'You will come with me, won't you?'

She sighed. 'I know I said I might come, but we're fully booked at Cuckoo Lodge. I don't see how I can leave Rossie with all the work.'

'I've already thought of that,' he told her. 'I've spoken to Matthew and he's promised to come and help that weekend. As a matter of fact he had an idea. It seems that Rossie's friend Freda will be off to America with the cast of her play in a few weeks' time. Apparently she's invited Rossie and Matthew up to a farewell performance and a party, but Rossie has the same doubts you've just expressed – about leaving you to cope alone. This way you could repay the favour.' He looked at her doubtful face and squeezed her hand. 'Oh, please say yes, Cathy. I'm sure Maggie would put in a few extra hours too, if you asked her.' He bent to look into her eyes persuasively. 'You must agree that it's kind of a special occasion. You might think that's a strange way to look at it, but if it wasn't for Gerald we wouldn't be here now.'

'You're still very proud of him, aren't you?'

'Do you mind? Does that hurt?'

'No, of course not.' She squeezed his hand, 'It's as it should be. He was your father – and a musical genius. It will be a very special occasion as you say.'

'So you'll come?'

She smiled. 'Yes, I'll come with you, Paul.'

To the amusement of two fishermen who were unloading their boat close by, he lifted her off her feet and swung her round. '*Great!* You're wonderful, Cathy! The most wonderful girl in the world and I . . .'

She shook her head. 'Shhh. Remember what we said?'

He shook his head in frustration and they walked on for a while in silence. 'You still don't really know how you feel about me, do you?' he asked at length. 'I wonder if you know how that makes me feel?'

'I know that I look forward to seeing you and I love being with you,' she told him. 'You're the nicest, kindest and most sincere man I've ever known.'

He pulled a face. 'God! That sounds so damned tame. Don't you know that a man likes to be thought exciting and irresistible; wild and fiery and passionate and . . .' He stopped as she began to giggle. 'Don't *laugh*,' he said woundedly. 'I'm not joking, Cathy. Nice, kind and sincere sounds more like an agony aunt or a cocker spaniel than a lover.' He stopped walking and pulled her round to face him. 'I want to be your lover, Cathy,' he said angrily. 'Don't you realise that I want to sweep you off your feet? I want to pick you up and carry you off to bed and make love to you until you beg for mercy.' He looked into her eyes and she saw the deep hurt and frustration there. 'I'm just like any other man. *I want you.* And if you won't let me say what I really mean – what's in my heart – that will just have to do.'

'Oh, Paul, I'm sorry.' She drew his head down to hers and kissed him. 'I know how you feel and I know I'm being unfair to you. If only I could make you understand. I – I *think* I feel as you do. It's just that I'm afraid to trust those feelings, desperately afraid of being hurt. And afraid of hurting you too.'

'So . . .' He lifted his shoulders helplessly. 'What do I have to do to prove that you can trust me – and trust what you feel yourself?' he asked exasperatedly.

She sighed. 'That's just it. I don't know.' She shook her head. 'It really isn't fair. I realise that. Maybe you should give up on me. I wouldn't blame you if you wanted to.'

For a long moment he looked down at her. 'You know, sometimes I almost wish I could,' he said. 'Most of the time I'm afraid you're going to tell me to get lost – that I'll lose you. Sometimes I even wish you would. At least I'd know where I was. If you are going to do that, Cathy, I'd rather you did it now.'

'I can't blame you for feeling that way.' She slipped her arm through his and hugged it close. 'Let's not spoil the time we have by arguing. I've planned so much for us to do.'

But Paul's obvious discontentment with their relationship had set the mood for the weekend. For the rest of the time he was quiet and by the time he left on Monday morning Cathy was uneasily aware that she was about to lose him. Later that afternoon she confided her fear to Rosalind as they worked together in the kitchen.

'I can't see the problem,' she said. 'You do love him, don't you? It's obvious to me by the way you look at him.'

'Yes, I do. And then again, I don't know. I'm not sure I know what love is any more. I know that he makes me happy; that I want to be with him; that each time we part is harder than the last. But is that enough?'

Rosalind shook her head. 'What else is there?'

'I felt all that for Gerald. I was so *sure*, Rossie. I wouldn't listen to anyone. I thought he loved me too, but in the end all the promises were empty. The people who warned me were right. Our marriage just – disintegrated, like dust.' She sighed. 'Now I'm completely confused. Did I ever really love him at all? If I had, how could I have turned to anyone else?'

'Because he neglected you.'

But Cathy shook her head helplessly. 'If only there was some way of knowing for sure.'

The local builder Rosalind had asked to give them an estimate for converting the attic telephoned two days later to ask if it would be convenient for him to come and assess the job the following day.

'There's still a lot of junk up there,' Cathy said. 'Things of Gerald's and mine that have been packed away ever since we first came here. I've been putting off sorting through it for ages. I'd better go up and do it before he comes.'

'Shall I give you a hand?' Rosalind asked. But Cathy shook her head.

'I'd rather do it alone.' She was remembering the last time she'd looked through the boxes in the attic. The letters from her mother were still there. Now she would be forced to make a decision about what to do with them.

Seeing her pensive look, Rosalind touched her hand. 'I forgot about those boxes,' she said. 'Shall I ring and put the builder off? After all, there's no hurry, is there?'

'No. It's time it was all cleared up,' Cathy said decisively. 'Time I stopped putting it off. Besides, there's nothing to be gained from hanging on to a lot of rubbish.'

'But you won't throw everything away, will you?' Rosalind was looking at her. 'You might regret it if you decide too quickly. Would you like me to help you go through it?'

But on her own insistence Cathy was alone when she climbed the loft ladder that afternoon. Now that she had made up her mind she was determined to lay the ghosts from the past once and for all.

There were fewer boxes than she remembered. Her own things were fairly impersonal. Most of the odds and ends

495

from the house in Laburnum Close had been destroyed before she and Gerald married. The contents of Gerald's boxes on the other hand were more difficult to sort. She began by putting the box of letters to one side. She would take them downstairs and read them just once more before burning them. There were some old clothes which she put aside for the Salvation Army. Then the box of books; she would have to look through them – perhaps donate them to the local library. Then she came to the manilla folder that contained the hand-written music manuscripts which she now knew to be her father's. On the afternoon when she had found her mother's letters she had abandoned these. Now Kay's cold words came back to her: *Gerald tried to make amends, you know. He even bought some of your father's compositions to pay for your school fees. Little jingles that would never have been published.*

Slowly she opened the folder and looked at the manuscripts. Seeing her father's neat, sloping handwriting again brought quick tears that stung her eyes and blurred her vision. If only he had said that he couldn't afford to send her to St Margaret's, she wouldn't have minded. All those hours spent teaching and composing these so-called jingles. They had been for her – to give her what she had set her heart on. And she hadn't even known.

Downstairs the house was quiet. It was a warm, sunny day and all their visitors were out. Maggie, having prepared the vegetables for the evening meal, had gone home for the afternoon and Rosalind had gone into Woodbridge on the bus. Cathy went into the small studio, now used as a sitting room, where her father's baby grand piano still stood under the window and sat down on the stool. Through the open window came the scents of summer, honeysuckle and roses and the clove pinks that grew in clumps at the edge of the drive. The curtains moved gently in the breeze and a solitary bee buzzed against the window pane.

She hadn't played for months and her fingers felt stiff as

she ran them over the keys. The piano could do with tuning, she told herself. Dad would have been horrified. He was always so particular about the instrument's maintenance. Opening the folder she drew out the first of the manuscripts and, to her surprise, saw her own name written on the title page. 'Cathy's Theme' was written in capitals at the top. Then, in brackets (For my darling daughter). Her throat tightened. Why had he never told her he had written something specially for her? Why had he never played it for her?

She raised the music stand and rested the manuscript against it. Her fingers faltered a little over the first notes, then gradually, to her delight, she found that the music was familiar. As the tune slowly came back to her, her fingers relaxed and slipped easily into the nostalgic melody. She had heard it so many times before, when Dad was alone, working away at the piano in his studio back in the childhood days that seemed so far away. Kay had been wrong to describe his work as unpublishable jingles. This one was good – very good. It was heartachingly evocative; wistful and haunting. Maybe he could have made money with it if he had submitted it to a publisher – made his name even. But that was so typical of Dad. He had never had any real confidence in himself. She came to the end, paused, then played it through once more, savouring the unforgettable theme and brilliantly simple harmonies. She would cherish it always, she told herself. Whenever she wanted to feel close to him she could always get it out and play it. When she heard the front door slam and Rosalind's voice call out to her she rose and put the manuscript away carefully inside the piano stool. Just for now she would say nothing, she decided. 'Cathy's Theme' would be her secret.

The builder announced that he could make three rooms out of the roof space. And as the floor was already boarded and the electricity supply connected it would not be too difficult.

He left, promising to send in his estimate as soon as he could. Rosalind was excited.

'I thought we could make those rooms into our own summer quarters,' she said. 'A room each and a bathroom. Because, you see, we could hardly expect visitors to use a loft ladder, could we? Then we'd have two more rooms to let.'

Cathy laughed. 'I have an idea that you and Matthew will be married before those attic rooms are ready,' she said, privately wondering just how much their marriage would alter the position. But Rosalind was shaking her head.

'Whatever happened I'd never want to give up Cuckoo Lodge,' she said. 'The first time I saw this place I loved it, and on the day we moved in it was like coming home. This is my dream, Cathy. Matthew knows that. This is the first real home I've ever had, and it's my career too. It's all I've ever wanted.'

Paul telephoned to say that he had bought the tickets for the Promenade Concert and booked Cathy a room at a nearby hotel. But on the morning she was to leave for London she found herself feeling nervous and apprehensive.

'I wish I didn't have to go,' she told Rosalind over breakfast. 'It's going to bring back so many unwanted memories.'

'Just go to the concert and enjoy being with Paul,' Rosalind advised. 'Try and think of it as any other concert.'

But in spite of her misgivings, Cathy felt a little thrill of excitement as the afternoon train drew in to Liverpool Street Station. One slight disappointment was that Paul was working at the hospital until later so he wasn't able to meet her. He had arranged to pick her up later and take her out to dinner before the concert.

She took a taxi to the hotel and found she had plenty of time to shower and change into the new dress she had bought specially for the occasion. It was made of a beautifully soft silky material in a silvery green that matched her eyes. The skirt was of the new mid-calf length, swirling around her legs and setting off her black patent sandals. She dressed her hair in a French pleat and clipped on a pair of diamante earrings which were her only jewellery.

Paul arrived on time, looking handsome in black tie and dinner jacket. Apart from the suit he had worn for the memorial service it was the only formal clothing she had ever seen him wear. It suited him and she told him so. He looked pleased.

'Not as much as that dress suits you,' he told her. 'You look like some kind of wood nymph, all russet and green.'

It was a warm evening and they ate at a little bistro at a table in the open air. The food was good and the atmosphere relaxed. Cathy couldn't help wishing they could stay there all evening instead of going to the concert. But she said nothing. This evening was so important for Paul and she would do nothing to spoil the occasion for him.

It was a long time since she had been in the Albert Hall and she was awed anew by its vastness and Victorian splendour. Paul was impressed too as he gazed up at tier upon tier of crimson draped boxes and gilt ornamentation. They settled in their seats and Cathy opened her programme. Rhapsody for Piano and Orchestra by Gerald Cavelle was the third item on the programme and would not be played until after the interval. She breathed a sigh of relief when she read that the soloist was not Simon after all, but another well-known pianist who, the programme told her, was also responsible for arranging the piece for piano and orchestra. The brief programme notes outlined Gerald's career and mentioned his tragic death in an air crash. As she read them, Cathy wondered at her strange feeling of detachment. It was as though she were reading about a total stranger.

The familiar frisson of excitement rippled through the audience as the musicians began to take up their positions on the platform and tune their instruments. The leader arrived, acknowledging the flutter of applause with a discreet little bow before taking his place. Finally the conductor, Erhart Froebel strode on to the platform, immaculately attired in white tie and tails.

As she applauded, Cathy was reminded poignantly of the concert her father had taken her to when she was twelve; the first time she had seen her childhood idol, Gerald Cavelle and heard him play. Instinctively she reached for Paul's hand. He returned the pressure of her fingers, smiled reassuringly as the lights were lowered and the conductor raised his baton.

When the first half of the concert ended and the lights went up for the interval they made their way to the bar. Standing amidst the crush waiting for Paul to get her a drink, Cathy heard a familiar voice at her side.

'*Cathy!* How nice to see you!' Carla looked at her most glamorous in an exquisite creation of white and silver. At her elbow stood a tall distinguished looking man of about fifty. 'It's good to see you back in circulation, darling,' she gushed. 'I was so sad about your loss.' She turned to the man at her side. 'May I introduce you to Adam Meynard? Adam, this is Cathy Cavelle, one of my oldest friends.' The man nodded polite acknowledgement. When he'd gone to join the queue at the bar, Carla leaned toward Cathy confidentially. 'Isn't he *gorgeous*? One of the best photographers in the business. Met him on an assignment in Paris and he was *completely* bowled over! He's taking me to New York next month. You wouldn't *believe* what he has planned for me and . . .' She broke off as Paul rejoined them.

'This is Doctor Paul Franklin, Carla.' Cathy turned to Paul. 'Carla, an old schoolfriend of Rosalind's and mine.'

As Paul offered his hand Carla's face was a study. Her eyes flicked over him with unconcealed admiration as she flashed him her most dazzling smile. 'Well, *hello*. How lovely to meet you!' Rejoined by her escort she took a sip of her drink and leaned towards Cathy. 'Well, *well*! Didn't waste much time, did you darling?' She gave them a little wave as they moved away. 'Watch for me in all the glossies,' she called. 'Adam says he's going to make me a star!'

Paul and Cathy looked at each other in stunned silence as the couple were swallowed up by the press of people, then simultaneously they burst out laughing.

As they resumed their seats Cathy felt her nerves begin to jangle once again. Seeing Carla had provided a welcome little diversion but now she was reminded that the music they had come to hear, Gerald's rhapsody, was about to be played.

The conductor led the soloist on to the platform and the applause died down as he settled himself at the piano. She stole a look at Paul's face. It was eager with anticipation and she felt her heart contract for him. He looked so young, so vulnerable and suddenly she felt a closeness, a sweet affinity with him. Reaching out as the lights dimmed she took his hand and smiled at him. He smiled back, his dark eyes holding hers for a second before the conductor's baton came down and the music began.

As the first few bars of exquisite melody flowed from soloist and orchestra Cathy's heart almost lurched to a stop. Even with the skilful and elaborate orchestration she could not fail to recognise the piece being played – not as 'Rhapsody' by Gerald Cavelle, but as 'Cathy's Theme' by Daniel Oldham. Gerald had stolen it – passed it off as his own. How *dared* he? It was the ultimate infidelity – the final act of betrayal. The bitterness of bile filled her throat and mouth. She wanted to leap to her feet and scream that it was all a terrible deception. That Gerald Cavelle was a thief, a liar, a *cheat*! That the man who should be receiving the acclaim was her father. Inside the pain of it tore her apart as she silently cried his name over and over. *Daddy – Oh, Daddy – Daddy. I'm sorry. So sorry.* Hot tears streamed down her cheeks at the injustice as the music swelled and pulsed through her, its sweetness melting her bones while its bitterness broke her heart into a million pieces.

Then she turned and saw the look on Paul's face. It was radiant with pride and delight. Catching her look, seeing the glimmer of tears in her eyes, he smiled and reached for her hand.

'Isn't it just – *wonderful*?' he whispered, shaking his head as adequate words escaped him.

As she watched him she felt her anger slowly evaporate. Gerald may not have written this music, but he hadn't stolen it either. Daniel had sold it to him; sold it so that he could give Cathy the things he wanted her to have. He would never have published the music himself; probably never even have played it to anyone. This way at least it would live on to be enjoyed. And Gerald couldn't possibly have imagined the pleasure it would bring to Paul, the son he had never known. Gerald Cavelle was dead and so was Daniel Oldham. Things like credit, success and acclaim meant nothing to them any more. But Paul was alive and so was she. Between them, the two fathers had left them a legacy of love and life to share. Things that were infinitely more precious than riches.

The music came to an end and the audience roared its approval in a storm of applause. The soloist and conductor acknowledged their appreciation with smiles and bows; the applause continued, refusing to let the soloist leave the platform. Gerald Cavelle's rhapsody was an outstanding success. Tomorrow the record companies would be clamouring to buy the recording rights. The royalties would pour in and the dishonoured debts and broken promises that Gerald Cavelle had left behind would be no more than an insignificant memory, eclipsed by this newfound fame. It was strangely ironic, Cathy told herself, that fate often had a roundabout way of settling scores.

As the applause began to die Paul was pulling at her hand. 'Shall we slip out?' he said urgently. In the corridor he looked at her. His eyes were still shining and his cheeks flushed. 'I

502

couldn't have sat through another piece of music,' he said, 'however good. I'm far too excited.' He grasped both her hands. 'Oh, Cathy – *Cathy*! Wasn't it marvellous? I had no idea he was as brilliant as that. Why on earth didn't he take up composing before? He could have been even more famous as a composer.' He pulled her close and kissed her. 'God! I think this must be the proudest moment of my life.'

She smiled and said nothing. She'd already made up her mind to let him go on believing the music was Gerald's. It was to be her gift to him. But a gift he must never know about. A sacrifice she could make from the depths of her heart only for the man she loved.

Paul said he wanted to end the evening by the river, so they took a taxi to the Embankment and stood looking out over the black satin water in the mellow warmth of the summer night. The sky was clear, bright with a thousand stars; the river shimmering with reflected lights. A magic night. The kind of night that gave rise to memories.

Cathy touched his hand as it lay on the parapet. 'Paul. There's something I have to tell you.'

He turned to look at her, his dark eyes slightly apprehensive. 'What is it?'

'Just that I love you, that's all.'

For a long moment he stared at her. Then, 'Just? Did you say *just*?' He let out his breath on a shaky, tremulous laugh. 'I thought you were about to shatter my evening by telling me you didn't want to see me again. All evening I've had this awful feeling that you only came to the concert with me as a final gesture because you were about to send me packing.' He took her shoulders and turned her towards him. 'Would you mind saying it again for me?' he asked. 'Just in case I didn't hear it right the first time.'

'I love you, Paul Franklin,' she said softly. 'I think – no, I'm *sure* now that I always have.'

'Again,' he demanded.

She was laughing now, though tears were not very far away. 'You haven't told me yet.'

'Only because you refused to let me. You know I love you, Cathy. With all my heart. For ever. I've loved you since the first moment I set eyes on you. And, I believe, even before that. Somehow I think you've always been there, waiting for me in the shadowy corners of my dreams.' He kissed her and for a long moment they clung to each other. 'But what made you so sure, tonight of all nights?' he asked at last.

She smiled gently as she hid her tear-dewed face against his shoulder. 'I think it might have had something to do with the music,' she said. 'Though don't ask me how.' She looked up at him with shining eyes. 'And now do you think you could walk me back to the hotel, please? I think we have some catching up to do.'

He drew her close and kissed her long and deeply. 'I said this was the proudest night of my life,' he said huskily. 'I never expected it to be the happiest too.'

Pressed close to each other, their arms entwined, they walked all the way back to the hotel. And beneath their feet the pavement sparkled with stardust.

Thursday's Child

Chapter 1

'Yes, but where are we going?'

Fleur's voice was tinged with impatience as her friend Bobby held on to her arm and hurried her along the street.

'Not much further. You'll see.'

Fleur shook off the other girl's hand and stopped walking. 'Look, Bobby. I've still got some packing to do. I want to catch an early train in the morning, 'cause I've got to find a place to stay when I get there. I've got no time for pratting about.'

Bobby looked hurt. 'Sounds like you can't wait to get away from us all,' she said.

'It's not that.' Fleur relented. 'Oh – all right then.' She sighed indulgently. 'Let's get it over with. But just one drink – right?'

'Right.' They'd stopped outside the Royal Albert and Bobby's big brown eyes danced with excitement. 'Okay. Now, close your eyes.'

'Oh, come *on!*'

'No, close them. You've got to.'

Fleur sighed and did as she was told, allowing Bobby to lead her by the arm. She was aware of being taken inside the pub and led down a corridor. A door

1

was opened and she was pushed inside. When she opened her eyes the sight that met them took her breath away.

The function room of the Royal Albert had been decorated with balloons and streamers and there, assembled in front of her were all the friends and neighbours she had grown up with. Many of her schoolfriends were there; neighbours from Brightman Lane and the flats, including Bobby's brothers and sisters and her mum, Ada. The Wallaces from the fish bar were there; the Smiths from the shop; Hosein and Melini Patel and many others. At her entrance into the room they all clapped and cheered, making her blush with embarrassment. Hands reached out for her and led her into the room as Bobby's elder brother, who was in charge of the disco, put on Fleur's current favourite record, 'Lady In Red'.

'Now you know why I made you wear your red dress,' Bobby said delightedly.

'And why *you're* all dressed up. I thought it was a bit over the top for a quick drink at The Royal.'

'Yeah. Great, eh?' Bobby was already dancing to the music. She never could resist a rhythmic beat.

Fleur looked affectionately at her vivacious friend in the tiny skin-tight black lycra mini skirt. Her crinkly black hair was drawn tightly back into tiny plaits and the bright yellow cropped top she wore exposed six inches of golden brown midriff. 'Oh Bobby. Did you really do all this for me?'

'It was my idea. Mine and Mum's,' Bobby admitted with a grin. 'But we had plenty of help. We couldn't let you go without doing something and once they knew everyone offered to pitch in,' she said. 'A lot of people round here are fond of you, you know. They wanted the chance to say goodbye properly.'

'Including me. Come and dance. Fleur.' Gary

Johnson reached out to take Fleur's hand and led her into the throng of dancers. 'So – you're really going then?' he said as they danced. 'Tell you the truth I thought you might bottle out when it came to the crunch. Seems I underestimated you!'

Fleur smiled. She and Gary had gone out together for a while earlier that year. They'd known each other since schooldays. He worked for a computer firm, a nice, hard-working guy, just the kind that Dolly, her grandmother, would have approved of. Good looking too. Fleur knew that some of their friends had seen them as an item. But she didn't intend to get into a serious relationship with anyone. Not yet. Too many girls she knew were already saddled with babies and debt. There were things she needed to do before that day came and she'd always made that clear to Gary. She smiled at him.

'I need to get away from Hackney,' she said. 'It's what Grandma wanted. Me too. I think I always have.'

'I think so too,' he said perceptively. He smiled down at her. 'Going to find yourself – that the idea?'

She glanced up quickly to see if he was laughing at her. He wasn't. The smile in his eyes was wistful as if he sensed that there was more to her leaving than she'd ever tell him.

'There's no need, you know. It's like Bobby said. Folks round here like you. They take you at face value. Just look around you. All the proof you need is right here.'

'I know.' Fleur shrugged. 'I can't explain, Gary. It's more to do with never knowing my parents than with colour.'

He shrugged. 'Okay – whatever you want. It's your life. But I'll miss you,' he said softly.

'I'll miss you too – all of you. Maybe I'll come back someday. Who knows? Everything changes though,

3

Gary. Grandma's gone. Bobby will be off to college soon. Nothing stays the same.'

'Some things do.' He smiled, shrugging resignedly. 'S'pose you're right though.'

It was a happy evening, ending at midnight with Bobby making a short speech and presenting Fleur with a present they'd all clubbed together to buy. The main gift was a leather writing case complete with stationery and pens. 'To make sure you don't forget to write,' Bobby said with an impish grin. In another tiny box wrapped in gold paper Fleur found a little amber heart pendant on a silver chain from Bobby and Ada. Everyone hugged Fleur and wished her well before they left, then Gary and Bobby walked her home.

When they had gone she stood in the almost empty flat and tried to imagine what it would be like not to live here any more, not to see her friends each day.

It was a warm night and from the street below the accustomed roar of traffic from Hackney Road and the familiar smells floated up to Fleur through the open window. There were just a few last chores to be done. Most of her belongings were packed in two suitcases, the last few sticks of furniture would be collected tomorrow. In the morning she would leave here for ever. She tried hard to view her future positively, swallowing the chill of uncertainty she had felt ever since her grandmother died, strengthened by this evening's touching farewell party. *It will be a challenge, an adventure*, she told herself. But the uncertain child that still lingered somewhere deep inside her wept for the loss of comfort and love and security.

It seemed such a very short time since she and Bobby had played down there in those streets, taking it in turn to ride Bobby's brother's ancient rusting bike, begging the boys to let them join in their games of street football, swinging on the lamp posts and swapping the

4

treasures that children love to collect. This street in the East End was the only playground Fleur had ever known. It had been her home for all of her nineteen years.

It was here in the cramped little flat two floors above the Smiths' grocer's shop that she had shared her life with her grandparents, London-born Dolly Sylvester and her West Indian husband, Maurice. Like so many other East End families, the Sylvesters had been poor, but Fleur's childhood had been a happy one. What she had lacked in luxuries had been more than made up for by the love Dolly and Maurice had lavished on her. Now both her grandparents were gone and life must change. Tomorrow she would say goodbye to the East End and all her friends and leave her childhood behind for ever.

Fleur had been three years old before she had realised that children were supposed to have a mother and father as well as grandparents. When she had asked Grandma where hers were she had been told that they were away working hard and that she would see them some day soon when they came home. She knew that her father's name was Dean and that he was the Sylvesters' only child. She also knew that he earned his living by playing the guitar and had left home in 1966 to make his name in the world of pop music.

When his talent had first begun to show itself Dolly and Maurice had been immensely proud of their handsome son. They were convinced that he had inherited his talent for music from his Jamaican father, to whom rhythm came as naturally as breathing. Maurice would tap a rhythm out instinctively with anything that came to hand, and although he had never had a lesson in his life, could coax a tune out of anything from a comb and paper to a trombone.

Eager to encourage his son's gift for music, Maurice had put in as much overtime as he could get on his job as a labourer for British Rail in order to give him the best possible chance of success. Dolly had done her share too, putting in extra shifts at The Royal Albert where she worked in the kitchen, and using her culinary skills catering for local weddings and other informal festivities.

By the time Dean was eighteen he had formed his own group, playing first in the pubs and at small local gigs. Two years later, full of the brash confidence of youth, he had left home and set out to make his fortune.

It had been big, gentle Grandpa Maurice who had told Fleur all this, taking his small granddaughter onto his knee, his molasses-dark eyes smiling and the deep voice, that still held the warmth of the Caribbean sun, throbbing with pride.

'Your daddy will be famous one day, sugarplum,' he told her confidently. 'Then he'll take us all back to Jamaica for a holiday and you can meet *aa-all* your cousins and aunts and uncles. So many of them. What a party we'll all have then!' He would throw back his big head with its tight mass of greying curls and chuckle with delighted anticipation. 'Oh you're going to *love* it there, sugar. The sun always shines and the sea is so blue and warm.' His brown eyes would grow soft with reminiscence. 'Maybe we'll even stay – make our home there when your daddy comes home.'

Dolly, although equally proud of her son, listened to it all with silent scepticism as she went about her work in the kitchen. She did not share her husband's optimism or his illusions about their son. Maurice had always spoiled Dean. She knew why. He had wanted a better life for the boy than he had had as the eldest of a family of nine hungry, barefoot children growing up in

6

his native Jamaica. He wanted his son to be given the chance to foster his talent and he thought, naively, that one day Dean would share his good fortune with the parents who had sacrificed so much to give him that chance, in the same way that he still scraped together what little money he could afford to send home to his aged mother.

But so far all Dean had given them was Fleur, his illegitimate daughter. Another mouth to feed out of their meagre earnings while he went on his self-seeking way without a qualm. As for Fleur's mother, it had been left to Dolly to fill in the details and answer the endless questions fired at her by her increasingly curious granddaughter.

'What's my mum like, Grandma?'

'Well – I haven't seen her for a long time. She was very young when you were born,' Dolly said as she rolled out pastry at the kitchen table.

'What's her name?' Standing on a stool on the other side of the kitchen table, Fleur rolled out her own ball of pastry till it was grey and leathery. She had asked all these questions before, but she never seemed to tire of hearing the answers, and she always knew at once if her grandmother dared to vary them in the smallest detail.

'Her name is Julia, lovie. You already know that.' Dolly looked at the child. The little triangular face with its intelligent brown eyes and the unruly mop of black curls reminded her sharply of Dean at the same age. He'd been such a beautiful little boy, so loving and sweet. The man he'd grown into seemed like quite another person. But at least he had given them Fleur to make up for the disappointment.

The little girl did not resemble her mother at all. Julia had been blonde and delicately built, whilst her daughter, already sturdy and tall for her age, showed signs of

7

growing into a tall, statuesque woman. Fleur was bright and clever too, missing nothing with her sharp ears and those huge dark, enquiring eyes. The hurtful truth could not be kept from her for ever, but Dolly vowed she would protect her for as long as she could.

'I like that name.' Fleur said, her head on one side. 'Why am I called Fleur, Grandma? No one in my class is called Fleur and Bobby says it's a funny name.'

' 'Course it's not funny,' Dolly said indignantly. 'It's different and it's special. It's French, see? It means flower.'

'Bobby's name sounds funny, doesn't it, Grandma? It's like a boy's name.'

Fleur's best friend, Bobby, was Dolly's oldest friend's youngest child. 'Bobby's real name is Roberta,' Dolly explained. 'She was named after her daddy. None of us can help our names. We have to have what our mums and dads give us.'

'So why did I get called Fleur, Grandma?'

'Your mum chose the name because it reminded her of the Flower Children.'

'Who are the Flower Children?'

Dolly sighed. Fleur's questions seemed endless. Satisfying her curiosity was like trying to fill a bottomless pit. She always tried to answer the child's questions as best she could, assuming that she was too young to understand what had really happened, but she was acutely aware that with each year that passed the time was rapidly approaching when Fleur would no longer be satisfied with half-truths. She was unsure herself what it was that the strangely garbed people with flowers in their unkempt hair and beards had really stood for. In her view the philosophy of the free-living hippies seemed to be to take what they wanted from life regardless of who it upset. They had certainly played a big part in leading Dean astray, of

8

that she was convinced.

'*Grandma!* Who are the Flower Children?'

Dolly looked up and saw that Fleur's bright eyes were still upon her, waiting for an answer; she went on: 'Oh yes, the Flower Children. Well, they were all the rage at the time when you were born,' she explained. 'They dressed up in long frocks, liked bright colours and wore flowers in their hair, and they liked to gather together and listen to the kind of music your daddy played. Your mum and daddy met at one of their festivals. And that's why your mum gave you the name of Fleur.'

'I think they sound nice.' Fleur looked up at her grandmother and startled her by asking, 'Is my mum white, like you, Grandma? Or black, like Grandpa?'

'She's white – like me.' Dolly avoided the child's eyes, busying herself with her baking.

'So – when will she come and see me, Grandma – soon?'

Dolly avoided the bright enquiring eyes. 'Maybe, lovie, maybe,' she said.

'Why doesn't she write to me, Grandma?'

Dolly shook her head. 'I expect she leaves that to your dad, lovie.'

From time to time postcards arrived from Dean. They all had brightly coloured pictures of exotic places, the names of which meant little to Fleur. She would study the gaudy pictures carefully, then turn the cards over and touch the spidery writing on the reverse side with her fingertips as though by so doing she could somehow communicate with her unknown father. Dolly would pin all the postcards up on the dresser shelves in the kitchen so that everyone could see them and Fleur knew that her grandma would have liked to write back. Later, when she had mastered her letters sufficiently she longed to write to him herself. But there never seemed to be an address to which they could write on any of his cards. The brief messages Dean scrawled on the backs of the cards would read *'Appearing here for two nights'* or *'Played a one night stand at this theatre'*. So even if they had tried to write he would have left long before the letters could have reached him. Dolly kept hoping that he would eventually get back to London and come and see them, but he never did. Neither, to her fury, did he ever remember the child's birthday or send her a Christmas present.

There was just the one photograph of Dean. It stood on the living room mantelpiece in a frame decorated with flowers. In it he carried his electric guitar and wore his thick black curly hair very long. He had on flared jeans embroidered with silver thread and a brightly coloured shirt with full sleeves. Fleur knew the photograph so well that she could picture every detail of it when she closed her eyes. He wasn't black like Grandpa. His skin was brown as though he'd spent a long time in the sun. It was several shades darker than her own. Once she had asked why there were no photographs of her mum. Grandma had explained that Julie had gone away before any could be taken.

Fleur was twelve when Grandpa Maurice was killed in a tragic accident on the railway. She was stunned and deeply saddened by her grandfather's death, but Dolly was totally devastated. Her first instinct had been to send for Dean, but she had no way of contacting him. The last they had heard of him was a postcard to say that he had split from the group and was going to California to look for work in the clubs there. She made endless inquiries of all his old friends but none of them knew where he was. No one had heard from him. It was almost as though he had vanished into thin air. Then one evening about six months later Dolly answered a knock on the door to find the local parish

10

priest standing outside. He was closeted with Dolly in the living room for almost an hour and when he had gone Fleur learned that he had come to tell her that Dean had died.

Apparently it had been almost two months ago that he had been found dying in the room he had rented in a cheap lodging house in a run-down area of Los Angeles. It had taken all this time to trace his original home address.

The priest had told Dolly as gently as he could that Dean had been out of work and living rough for some months and that his death was attributed to malnutrition coupled with drug abuse. Later Dolly broke the news to Fleur, though she could not bring herself to tell the child the full sordid facts.

Fleur felt sad for Grandma's sake. She knew that it was terrible for Grandma to lose her son, and it should be equally bad for her to lose her father. Yet how could she mourn a man she had never known?

Apart from Fleur, Dolly's only comfort during this time of grief was her friend Ada. The two women, both now widows, would sit at the kitchen table in the Sylvesters' flat, drinking endless cups of tea and talking about happier times, while the two girls played quietly in the living room. Ada Morris had six other children, the youngest of whom was already fourteen when Bobby was born. Bobby's older brothers and sisters alternately spoiled and bullied her and she loved to escape to the comparative peace and quiet of the Sylvesters' flat to play with Fleur.

Fleur grew up very quickly after the news of Dean's death. She worried about her grandmother. The shock about Dean coming so close on the heels of Grandpa's death seemed to have turned her into an old woman

11

overnight. Dolly had always enjoyed her job at The Royal Albert Hotel where she was a cook, but with Maurice gone money was short and she took all the extra work she could. Luckily her party catering was popular and, guided by her grandmother, Fleur helped out with the work as much as she could as she grew older. But during the four years that followed she watched her grandmother's health failing inch by inch. The catering being spasmodic, Dolly was obliged to look for extra work. She took on a regular office cleaning job, and rose at the crack of dawn, leaving the flat before Fleur was awake each morning.

Fleur watched helplessly as Dolly grew increasingly tired and frail from grief and hard work. Once, when she collapsed downstairs in the shop, Ethel Smith sent for the doctor. He told Dolly she must ease up. Fleur had overheard him when he had finished examining her upstairs in the flat.

'That old ticker of yours isn't what it was, Dolly,' he said gently. 'Your blood pressure is higher than I'd like it to be too. Take this as a warning. Ease up now, my dear, before it's too late.'

The words, *before it's too late*, made Fleur's blood run cold as she stood outside the half open door of Dolly's bedroom. Losing Grandpa had been terrible. It would be unbearable to lose Grandma as well. She made up her mind there and then. She and Bobby had taken their O levels that summer. They'd both done well and planned to go on to A levels and then, if they were lucky enough, perhaps to university. But at sixteen Fleur knew that she could legally leave school and get a job. Her decision to do so horrified Bobby.

'What'll you do though?' she asked.

Fleur shrugged. 'I could take over Grandma's job at the pub,' she said. 'I think I can cook almost as well as her now. I could probably do the catering work too.'

Bobby looked crestfallen. 'If you want to do something in that line you could go in for hotel management,' she said. 'Take a proper college course. You can't throw away everything you've worked for. We've both worked so hard. It'll be awful if you leave now. It won't be the same without you, Fleur.'

Fleur shook her head sadly. 'I know. I'll miss you too – and school. But I can't let Grandma struggle on when I could be helping her, can I? You still have your mum to help you. Now that all your brothers and sisters have left home they'll help you too. I don't think Grandma could ever have managed to keep me there anyway.' The girls hugged each other and cried a little in their disappointment.

'But we'll always be friends, won't we?' Bobby said earnestly. 'We'll always keep in touch no matter what happens.'

' 'Course we will,' Fleur promised.

But if Bobby was upset by Fleur's decision to leave school, Dolly was appalled. She enlisted the help of Fleur's teacher to try to get her to change her mind. There was so much to be gained by staying on, at least for two more years. But the girl would not be deterred.

'What's the good of a lot of bits of paper if I lose you, Grandma?' she said. 'Mrs Wallace at the fish bar on Hackney Road has offered me a job. It isn't very good pay but if you keep teaching me all you know about cooking I might be able to take over your job in the kitchen at The Royal Albert when I'm eighteen. I could help out behind the bar too. The girls there get tips as well as wages.'

Dolly was mortified. She felt she was letting her granddaughter down. Fleur had grown into such a lovely girl. Although still in her early teens she had fulfilled her promise of statuesque womanhood. She was tall and well built, stunningly attractive with her

13

honey-warm complexion and glossy black hair. She and Maurice had pinned such hopes on the grand-daughter who had already more than made up for her father's shortcomings. They'd wanted something better for her than a job in a fish and chip shop.

'No, love – no,' she said weakly, shaking her head and rubbing Fleur's hand between both of hers. 'Your grandpa would be so disappointed if he knew I'd let you leave school, 'specially to go an' serve in a pub.'

'It's not for ever,' Fleur assured her. 'I'll get some-thing better as soon as I can and I can always take my A levels at night school. In the meantime you can at least give up that awful cleaning job and have a lie in of a morning.'

Dolly was sad, but proud of the girl at the same time. She might look like Dean but at least she hadn't inher-ited her father's selfishness. Maybe there was some-thing in what she said; if she had a rest she would get her strength back, then, as soon as she felt herself again she would see to it that Fleur went back and completed her education.

For a while after Maurice's death and the news of her father's demise, Fleur had moved in to share her grand-mother's room so that she wouldn't feel lonely at night and it was after the light was out that Dolly began little by little to tell her the story of how she came to be born. Her conscience pricked her. The girl had sacrificed a lot. The least she was entitled to was the truth. She should know the full story about her parents while there was still time. Somehow Dolly found it easier to tell in the dark.

'Your grandpa and I didn't even know Dean had a girlfriend till he brought her home that time,' she said. 'He told us they'd met the previous summer at a pop

14

festival on the Isle of Wight. By the time we met her she'd been on the road with the group for four months. They came for a weekend. At least that's what Dean said it would be. Then when he got me on my own he broke the news that Julia was expecting and he wanted to leave her with us for a while.'

Fleur turned her head on the pillow to look at her grandmother's dim profile. 'I see – so they weren't married then?'

Dolly reached for her hand and gave it a squeeze. 'No, love. Dean had promised that they would be – after his tour was over. I expect he meant it too – at the time. He was always making promises he couldn't keep. Somehow or other, more important things always came along and got in the way. He told me that Julia had got tired of touring round in that ropey old van they used. She used to get very sick and the smell of the petrol and the bumping around was making her ill. He said it would only be for a little while. To begin with he used to write to her and even sent a bit of money now and again. He came home a couple of times. Just flying visits. Then he stopped coming home and gradually the letters and the money stopped.'

Fleur bit her lip, trying to imagine what it must have been like. 'That must have made her very unhappy.'

'Oh yes, it did. We used to feel so helpless, your grandpa and me, lying awake at nights hearing the poor gel crying herself to sleep through the wall. We felt guilty too, after all, it was our boy who was the cause of it. But we never had an address for him what with the group bein' on the move all the time, so we couldn't even write and tell him to come home.'

'So – what happened?' Fleur whispered.

'Well, eventually you were born. We took Julia along to the London Hospital down at Whitechapel late on Wednesday night and I stayed there with her till you were born early next morning.' Fleur felt her hand squeezed tightly. 'Such a dear little baby you were. Just like my Dean when he was born. Tight black curls and big dark eyes. Brought it all back, it did. Thursday's child, I told Julia. Remember the old rhyme? "Thursday's child has far to go." '

'And what about Julia – my mum? Was she pleased when I was born?'

Dolly paused. 'She was only a kid,' she sighed. 'No older than you are now and she was already unhappy. I thought she might settle down once she'd had you – be happier with a little baby of her own to look after.' Again she sighed. 'She wasn't though – just got even more miserable and restless. I think she was homesick. She started to talk a lot about her mum and dad – told me all about this lovely house they had at the place where she come from. Elvemere, it was called. 'Course, I always knew she was used to something a lot better than what we had,' Dolly said without resentment. 'You could tell she'd 'ad a good education. I reckon she was hardly out of school when she met Dean, I don't know why she wanted to leave a nice home like she had and go rattlin' round the country in an old beat-up van. But then my Dean could turn any gel's head with his looks and his music.' Dolly sighed. 'I think she regretted it soon enough though. Life in the East End must've been a real eye-opener after what she was used to.'

'Didn't Dean – my dad ever come back?'

Dolly nodded. 'Just the once!'

'To see me?'

'It was just after you were born. I don't know exactly what he and Julia said to each other but he told me before he left that he'd tried to get Julia to go home to her own folks. He said it had all been a mistake and that he wasn't ready to be a father. I tried to talk to him

– make him see sense and face up to his responsibilities, but he was so obsessed with his career – couldn't see no further than the next gig as he called it. He was so sure he was going to make the big time – fame and fortune.' Dolly sighed. 'Well, he gave Julia what money he had and told her he wasn't coming back any more.'

'What did she do?'

'What could she do, love? She couldn't work. I don't think she'd ever done a hand's turn. All she knew was what she'd learned at the posh school she'd been to. So it all fell to your grandpa and me to provide. Oh, we didn't mind. We loved you and we got quite fond of poor little Julia too. But I won't pretend it wasn't hard. Your grandpa was always makin' excuses for Dean; sayin' he'd change his mind when he'd had time to think straight. Couldn't believe his precious son could've done anything wrong. But I knew what he was up to all right. Off with some new girl, more like. Drinkin' and livin' it up with his show-biz mates. Julia knew it too, though she never said nothin'.' Dolly shook her head, muttering to herself under her breath. 'Always had a selfish streak, that boy. I don't know where he got it from. Not me, and certainly not your grandpa.' She took a deep breath and continued, 'Anyway, in the end even your grandpa got the message. Dean had dumped Julia and you and cleared off, knowing that we'd see no harm'd come to her. He knew we was both a soft touch when it came to kids.'

'What happened to Julia then?'

'Ah, well . . .' Dolly fell silent for a moment. 'I should've seen it coming, I suppose. In the end she couldn't take no more. She'd always hated it here in the East End and after Dean told her he wasn't coming back I s'pose she just got to the end of her tether. One morning – you were about three months old at the time

17

– we got up and found you in your cot, alone in the room. Julia's bed was empty; neatly made with a note pinned to the pillow. She'd gone off home to her parents, she said. Thanked us for all we'd done and asked us to forgive her. Begged us to take care of you and not let you go to strangers.'

'You mean she – she didn't want me?' Fleur swallowed hard at the lump that had suddenly risen in her throat. 'Wasn't she going to come back for me – not ever?'

'She never made any false promises,' Dolly said noncommittally.

'But – how could she do that?' Fleur asked angrily. 'If I had a baby I'd never just walk away and leave it. I *couldn't!*' She sat up in bed. 'You're saying she abandoned me, aren't you, Grandma? All those years when I kept on hoping she'd come and see me and all the time she couldn't care less. She never wanted me – she'd probably even forgotten she ever had me, hadn't she? She didn't give a damn! That's it, isn't it?'

Dolly squeezed her hand. 'Now, now. Don't take on love. None of us knows what we might do if we was really desperate. It won't do no good gettin' angry about it either.'

'But didn't it make you angry? Didn't you want to go and bring her back?'

'It don't do to judge folks, Fleur. You'll learn that as you get older.' Dolly's eyes glistened moistly in the dimness. 'I'd watched that poor gel going downhill for eight months. She was fretting her heart out over Dean and the mistake she'd made. She was heartbroken, homesick an' scared stiff of the future. I reckon she got to the stage where she couldn't see no other way out. I couldn't find it in my heart to blame her for leaving. It was Dean I was angry with, but he wasn't coming back to face up to his responsibilities, was he?'

'But she – Julia could have taken me home with her, couldn't she?'

'Think about it, love. How could she turn up on her mum and dad's doorstep with a baby? It would've been a terrible shock for them – a disgrace too.' Dolly sat up and switched on the bedside light. 'See, Julia 'ad let on to her mum an' dad that she had a good job in London and was sharin' a flat with two other girls, you see.' She shook her head. 'I expect she hoped she'd be married by the time she had to face them and it would have been too late then to do anything about it.'

'So – she hadn't told them about Dean then – or me?' Very slowly the truth was dawning on Fleur. Dolly was trying to let her down lightly. 'It wasn't just that she had a baby and no husband, was it?' she said. 'What you're really saying is that she'd have been ashamed of – of my colour.'

Dolly winced. She'd racked her mind to think of a way to put it that wouldn't hurt. 'Not ashamed, love – not of you. But it's like I said. It would have shocked her parents – made life difficult for them all,' she said awkwardly. 'People who live in them little places are narrow-minded. Up here in London it might have been different.'

'No it wouldn't,' Fleur said quietly. 'There's prejudice everywhere. You know that as well as I do. It hasn't changed much since you married Grandpa, has it?'

Dolly sighed. It was true of course. Her own family had turned their backs on her when she refused to give Maurice up. That had been one of the main reasons she'd understood and sympathised with Julia. 'Your mum was very young,' she said. 'She loved Dean – trusted him and he'd let her down, left her high and dry with a baby on her hands. It was very different with your grandpa and me. No one could've had a better, truer man. I never regretted marryin' 'im for a minute. Everything he ever did was for us – his family and I loved him till the day he died. I still do and I always will.' She sighed, lapsing again into audible thoughts. 'Why Dean couldn't have been more like his dad I don't know,' she muttered. 'Maybe it was our fault for lovin' him too much. For spoiling him.'

Becoming acquainted with the fact that Dean had never cared enough to want to be a father to her, and her mother was too ashamed to acknowledge her existence affected Fleur deeply. Her grandparents had been wonderful. But neither her mother nor her father could have known for sure that they would keep and bring her up. For all they knew she could have ended up in care, or been shunted round a series of indifferent foster homes. Her confidence suffered. Just what and who was she? Neither black nor white; despised and rejected by her own parents. Where and to whom did she really belong?

It was only as Fleur grew older that she became increasingly aware of racial prejudice. There were certain people who made a point of creating situations where fights would erupt. Racist elements among their society who got their pleasure out of seeing someone weaker than themselves suffer. But Fleur had always seen these for what they were: dangerously inadequate people, needing someone to victimise because brutality was their one twisted claim to dominance.

Not that she had ever suffered this kind of prejudice herself. Her honey-coloured skin, black curly hair and brown eyes had a look more of the Mediterranean than the Caribbean and, as she grew up, her cheerful nature and strong personality had always made her popular. But after she had learned the truth about her parents' betrayal she became subdued. She grew defensive and quick to sense criticism. She had always hated any kind of bullying, but now she was fiercely protective. Any kind of injustice infuriated her, a trait that was brought to the fore one Friday evening when she was serving behind the counter at Wallace's Fish Bar.

From her place at the end of the counter she saw a young Asian boy being bullied in the street outside. Four skinheads with brawny tattooed arms were jeering and pushing him around, clearly trying to make him retaliate with their racist jibes and threatening behaviour. Fleur knew the boy. Hosein was a quiet studious boy in his late teens. He lived with his Pakistani family in Brightman Lane and Fleur had been in the same class as his younger sister Melini. She knew that he was studying law and worked hard at a part time job as a waiter to help his parents.

Serving the queue that snaked around the shop, she kept an eye on the group outside the steamy window until suddenly she heard one of the thugs shout a racist obscenity and land a blow that sent the boy sprawling into the gutter. Blazing with anger she abruptly abandoned the woman she was serving and ran round the counter, pushing her way through the startled customers and out into the street.

'What the bloody hell do you think you're doing?' she demanded, her dark eyes flashing as she brandished the fish slice still in her hand. 'What kind of lousy wimps are you? Four of you and one of him – and he's smaller than you too!'

The thugs turned to stare at her in shocked surprise, momentarily speechless. Then one of them took a step forward, leering at her. 'Who're you callin' wimps?' He looked her up and down and turned to the others. 'What d'ya reckon – is she another Paki slag or what?'

The others closed in on her menacingly. 'Wimps, are

21

we? So whatcher gonna do about it then?' the ring-leader challenged. 'Make men of us all?'

The others laughed raucously and, encouraged, he stepped right up to stand in front of her. 'Come on then, get 'em off and give us a treat. Bet you could take us all on, couldn't ye?' He spread his arms and thrust his pelvis forward suggestively. 'Me first! Comin' round the back with me then, eh? Gonna show us what you c'n do! Never know, maybe we c'n teach you a trick or two. I bet you been gang-banged loads a times!'

As the other three cat-called and whistled, Fleur felt a prickle of fear down her spine, but she stood her ground, calling to Hosein to make himself scarce. Her challenger's leering face was thrust close to hers now and his appearance repelled her. His small, pale eyes glinted sadistically and there was a swastika tattooed on one unshaven, spotty cheek. She saw that there was a hoop through one nostril as well as the one through his left earlobe. Adrenaline surged through her veins like fire, fuelling her anger.

'Yeah? Teach me a trick or two, could you?' she said, throwing caution to the winds. 'Well, s'pose I teach you one first?' Stepping aside to avoid his clutching hands, she lashed out at him with the fish slice. The implement was made of sturdy stainless steel and Fleur swung it with considerable force catching him a clanging blow on the side of his shaven head. The mean eyes watered with pain and he let out a piercing yell, clasping one hand to his head and shooting her a look of purest hatred.

'*Shit!* You bloody little *cow*! I'll . . .' He broke off to finger his ear gingerly, muttering under his breath.

Fleur's instinct for self-preservation urged her to turn and run, but she stood her ground, knowing that it would be fatal to show any sign of weakness now. She wondered briefly if any of the chip shop customers would intervene to help her should the rest of the gang decide to set about her. She'd noticed with relief that young Hosein had taken her advice and vanished into the night. Then she saw to her surprise that her victim's three companions also seemed to have faded away. A moment later the reason presented itself in the form of a dark uniformed figure who loomed up behind the wounded skinhead, who was tenderly prodding his ear and muttering dark threats.

'Having a spot of bother, miss?' The policeman was clearly trying not to grin, which replaced her relief at seeing him with annoyance.

'Oh, *there* you are then, *officer*!' she said, her eyes flashing. 'Good at turning up when the trouble's all over, you lot, aren't you? Maybe you should go and see if you can find the poor young kid these creeps were thumping! Four of 'em onto one.'

The chip shop queue, their appetites temporarily forgotten, had spilled out onto the pavement by now and one or two of them spoke up on Fleur's behalf.

'Real guts that gel's got.'

'Wants a medal if you ask me!'

The injured skinhead, burning with indignity, spoke up. 'I want her nicked!' He pointed an accusing finger at Fleur. 'She's a bleedin' maniac! Just attacked me, she 'as – for nothin'! If I got caught with an offensive weapon I'd get banged to rights. No danger!' He held out a grubby finger. 'Look, I'm bleedin'. Reckon I need an ambulance.'

The policeman turned sternly to Fleur, sucking in his breath sharply. 'Attack with an offensive weapon is it? That's serious. Let's have a look then. Come on, hand it over.' He took the fish slice from Fleur's hand and examined it carefully. 'Well now, that's some weapon!' He turned to the skinhead. 'Nearly brain you with it, did she sonny?' He shook his head, tutting in mock

23

sympathy. 'Clipped round the ear by a young gel with a fish slice. Oh yeah, I reckon you've got a good case there.' He pulled out his radio. 'Still want an ambulance do we?'

His support gone, the skinhead slunk away, muttering obscenities under his breath as he elbowed his way through the jeering crowd. The policeman looked at Fleur as the crowd began to disperse, his eyes concerned.

'You all right, love?'

Fleur tossed her head, trying to ignore the reaction that was beginning to set in. She found she was trembling, visualising for the first time what might have happened had it not been for the policeman's intervention. 'I'm fine, thanks. Can't stand to see them ganging up like that.'

'No? Well, just the same, I wouldn't recommend tangling with the likes of that lot,' he said. 'You're lucky they didn't pull a knife on you.'

'Like to see 'em try!' she said with a bravado she didn't feel.

'*I* wouldn't. Seen too many knifings for my liking. I know we can't be everywhere at once as you've already pointed out,' he said with a wry smile. 'But next time try dialling nine-nine-nine instead, eh?' He paused as he moved away. 'And I'd watch my back for a day or two now if I were you.'

Back inside the shop Harry Wallace eyed Fleur wryly. 'I 'ope you ain't gonna make a habit of that kinda thing,' he said. 'Half o' them customers never come back after your little frac-arse out there. Some of 'em conveniently forgot to pay for what they'd 'ad an' all.'

His wife, Marj, was more sympathetic. 'Leave the kid alone, 'Arry. It was brave, what she done.' She peered into Fleur's face. 'Wanna go 'ome, luv? You look a bit green round the gills.'

24

'I'm all right, thanks,' Fleur told her. 'I'd rather stay till closing time. Grandma'll think something's wrong if I go home early.'

But if Harry Wallace was worrying about a lack of trade he had no need. The word had spread like wild-fire and for the rest of the evening the shop was crowded with people curious for a glimpse of the hero-ine who had stood up to four skinheads armed only with a fish slice. Wallace's Fish Bar had never done such good business. Urged by his wife to make amends, Harry pushed a parcel into Fleur's hands as she was putting on her coat.

'For your gran an' you,' he said with a wink. 'I know Dolly likes a fish supper. Tell 'er this one's on me.'

The policeman's warning to Fleur was not made merely to frighten her. He'd seen the sadistic retribu-tion doled out by these thugs too many times to speak lightly. Fleur remembered his warning when she became aware of being followed on her way home from work. Often there were scufflings and footsteps behind her as she walked, sometimes a muted whistle or half-heard call. She guessed that it was the gang of skin-heads and although their unseen presence unnerved her she tried to tell herself that scaring her was all they meant to do. If she stuck it out and showed no fear they'd eventually get bored and turn their attention to someone else.

Fleur said nothing to her grandmother about the incident with the skinheads and Dolly might never have known about it had it not been for Hosein's conscience. A few days later, feeling bad about leaving her to face the skinheads alone, he came round to the Sylvesters' flat to apologise and to thank her. Fleur had already left for work and it was Dolly who answered the door to him and heard the story of his attack from his own lips When Fleur arrived home late that evening her grandmother was waiting for her.

'Don't you ever do nothing like that again!' she said. 'Okay, I know you wanted to help the lad. I saw the nasty bruise where those thugs hit him. He come round 'cause he felt bad about leggin' it and leavin' you, otherwise I might never 'ave 'eard. Why didn't you tell me?'

'It wasn't important, Grandma,' Fleur said lightly, taking off her coat. 'I'd forgotten by the time I got home.'

'Don't you lie to me, gel!' Dolly's face was pink with anguish. 'You've always been too quick to stick your neck out for other people. It was all right when you was a kid at school, but this is something else. It ain't for the likes o' you to go fightin' other folks's battles for 'em, putting yourself in that kind of danger!'

Fleur hung up her coat and turned to her grandmother. 'Who else then, Grandma? There were at least eight men in the chip shop when it happened, and they weren't doing anything. Someone had to.'

'Not you though. Not any more. Promise me!' Dolly demanded. 'Promise me you won't do nothing like that *ever* again!'

'All *right*, Grandma. I'm big enough to look after myself. No need to go on about it.'

'Yes there is!' Dolly drew a long shuddering breath and lowered herself into a chair. 'Life round 'ere ain't what it was when I was a gel. Them days we looked after one another. Nobody never locked their street doors and you knew who you could trust. Now there's never a week goes by without we 'ears about a muggin' or a knifin'. It's like livin' in the jungle – every man for 'imself and the sooner you faces that fact my gel, the better.'

'I can't *be* like that, Grandma. If more people stood up for what's right things'd have to get better.'

26

'I wish I believed that.' Dolly drew in her breath sharply and clasped one hand to her side. 'Listen love, I want you to promise me something. It's been on my mind for a long time now.'

Alarmed at her grandmother's sudden pallor, Fleur sat down beside her and took her hand. 'What is it, Grandma? I didn't mean to upset you. I wasn't even going to tell you about it. I won't do anything like it again if you say so. It was just that . . .'

But Dolly was shaking her head. 'It ain't that . . .' She took a deep breath and squeezed Fleur's hand. 'Look, I want you to promise that if anything 'appens to me you won't stay on round 'ere.'

Fleur frowned. 'But – where else would I go? Anyway, nothing's going to happen to you.'

'It will love – bound to sooner or later. You're a grown woman now and it's time to face facts. My heart's not strong – angina, the doctor says. I've known it for a long time. I could go any time an' I don't want to have to worry about what's going to happen to you.' She shook her head at Fleur's worried frown. 'Don't look at me like that. It don't bother me – not that part. What does worry me is the thought of you bein' left 'ere on your own.'

'But there's always Bobby and her family. I know they'd help me.'

Dolly shook her head. 'You know as well as I do that Bobby will be goin' off to college soon. Ada deserves some time to herself after bringin' up all them kids.'

'So, what's the alternative?'

'I want you to promise me you'll go and find your mum.'

'Go and *what*?' Fleur stared at her incredulously. 'You're *joking*!'

Dolly shook her head. 'No. She left her address in the note she left. I know she never wanted you adopted

27

or to go to a foster home. I reckon if you was in trouble – an' you was to go and see her – she'd help you. Maybe she's even been *hoping* you'd go all these years.'

'I bet she hasn't!' Fleur said. 'It was *years* ago she said that, when I was a baby. I expect she felt guilty, going off and leaving me with you like that. Who was she to say what should happen? She didn't want me, did she?'

'It don't matter how long ago it was,' Dolly insisted, her blue eyes dark with anxiety behind the spectacles. 'You're still 'er daughter and nothing can't change that. Julia come from a good family. There's no shortage of money there. She'll see you right. She owes you that much.'

'I don't *need* help, specially not from *her*!' Fleur said indignantly. 'I'm strong and healthy. I can work for myself. I . . .' She caught sight of her grandmother's anguished face and stopped, bending forward to stroke the white hair. 'Oh, look, Grandma, nothing's going to happen to you for years and years.'

'All the same, I'd rest easy if I knew you were going to be all right.'

'I *will* be,' Fleur said firmly. 'Maybe one of these days I'll even go and look Julia up too, just out of curiosity. Who knows?'

'That ain't good enough gel. I want you to promise me faithfully.' Dolly squeezed Fleur's hand imploringly till the girl nodded.

'Okay, Grandma. If you say so. I promise.'

Sighing with relief, Dolly heaved herself to her feet and went to the bedroom, returning a few minutes later with a scrap of paper. 'Here's the address. I've looked after it all these years so mind you keep it somewhere safe.' She pressed it into Fleur's hand. 'And don't forget your promise now, will you, gel? Don't stay round 'ere. It's no place for a young gel on 'er own.'

Fleur kissed her cheek. 'Okay, I promise. Now let's

28

stop being morbid and forget all about it, shall we?' Later she pushed the paper into the back of her underwear drawer, reflecting that Julia had most probably forgotten by now that she had ever had an illegitimate daughter.

It was just four weeks later that Fleur arrived home late one evening to find the flat strangely silent. She called out as she always did, 'Grandma! I'm home! What's for supper?'

As she hung up her outdoor clothes she sniffed. There was no welcoming smell of cooking. Normally at this time of the evening Dolly could be heard singing along to one of Grandpa's records. He had a collection of big band numbers from the fifties and Dolly loved them. She always left the kitchen door open so that she could hear the music above the sizzling of the chip pan. Tonight the kitchen door was firmly shut and the old-fashioned radiogram that Grandpa Maurice had been so proud of stood silent in its corner, the lid closed and Dolly's prized potted fern standing on the top.

Fleur stood for a moment, prevented from moving by the sudden icy dread that froze her muscles. Slowly, with feet of lead, she crossed the hall to the bedroom and stood fearfully in the half open doorway. Without entering she could see Dolly's reflection in the mirror of the dressing table on the opposite side of the room. The old lady half sat, half lay on the bed, supported by the headboard. She was still fully dressed, the print overall she always wore in the kitchen covering her skirt and blouse. Her glasses were slightly awry and on her face was an expression of gentle surprise, as though someone had just given her a piece of unexpected news.

'Grandma . . . ?' Fleur took a step into the room and turned to look down at the old woman slumped across the bed. Then her hand flew to her mouth to stifle her

cry of anguish. *'Grandma* – oh, no – *no!'* The moment
she had dreaded – that she had refused to accept would
ever happen, had come. She knew even without touching her that Dolly was dead.

It was two days after the funeral that Ethel Smith came
up to the flat to speak to Fleur.

'Are you all right, love?'

'Yes, thanks, Mrs Smith.'

'Managin' okay?'

'Fine.'

Ethel sighed. What she had to say wasn't going to be
easy, especially under the circumstances. 'I – er –
wondered if you had any plans?' she asked tentatively.

Fleur frowned. 'What kind of plans?'

'Well – this flat for a start. It's a bit big for one and I
wondered if you might find the rent hard to find now
there's only you.' She cleared her throat. 'Had you
thought of applyin' for one of them council flats down
Tower Hamlets?'

'Well, no. I hadn't.'

Ethel bit her lip. There was nothing for it but to come
out with it straight. 'Fact is love, Alf and me are retirin'.
We're goin' down to Kent – bought a little place near
Maidstone. Well, Alf's never been keen on the business
as you know.'

'I see. So you've sold the shop?' Fleur tried not to
think of the implications.

'Well – not exactly.' Ethel licked her lips. 'My daughter's husband lost his job a few months ago. He worked
at Ford's and he got made redundant. He can't seem to
find nothing else, so they're going to sell their house at
Dagenham and come and run the business for us.
Trouble is, they'll be needin' these rooms up 'ere as well
as our flat. With the kids there's five of 'em altogether,
see?'

30

'Oh.' Fleur swallowed hard. The flat wasn't exactly a palace but it was the only home she had ever known. Grandpa Maurice, Dolly and she had been happy here. Now she would have to find somewhere else to live. Somewhere she could afford. The prospect was daunting to say the least.

'I feel terrible askin' you to leave,' Ethel was saying. 'Specially with you just havin' lost your gran and everything, but I can't see no other way round it. Kath and Jim have got three kiddies to think of, see? They've been havin' a real struggle and it'll mean a lot to them to have a job and a secure roof over their heads.'

'Yes, of course.' Fleur took a deep breath. 'When do you want me to leave, Mrs Smith?'

'Oh, no mad rush,' Ethel said, trying to hide her relief. 'Shall we say the beginnin' of next month?'

Fleur gasped. That gave her only three weeks and she knew that her prospect of getting a council flat in that time, especially as a single teenaged girl was practically nil. Forcing a smile, she nodded. 'I'll start looking round for something else right away.'

Ethel looked around her. 'If you're not takin' the furniture p'raps I could buy some of it off you? The place we've bought is bigger than our flat downstairs and we'll be needin' a few more things. Would that help you?'

Fleur brightened. Dolly had some good pieces of furniture. It was old-fashioned, but solid and well made. There was no way she could manage to keep any of it herself. 'Well, yes, it might,' she said. 'Providing you're willing to pay me what it's worth.' Some of the light came back into her eyes. If Ethel thought she could rip her off she had another think coming! She'd go down the market and check out the price of second hand furniture. It wouldn't do to let the woman think she was a push-over. 'After all, Mrs Smith,' she went on, 'I'll need to get the best price I can, seeing as you're chucking me out!'

That night Fleur lay awake into the small hours trying to make some kind of plan. Even if she'd been able to stay on at the flat her job at Wallace's Fish Bar would not be enough to pay the rent, feed and clothe her. Yet jobs for someone with her lack of experience were few and far between. It was expensive, living in London, even in the East End. Dolly had left her everything she owned, but the little money there was in her Post Office account plus what Fleur could get for the furniture would not last long.

Sometimes she wondered about her father. Had the daily grind of life in the East End been his reason for his leaving? Had he used his gift for music as a passport to a better life? And did he ever achieve success? Had he ever spared a thought for the girl he had abandoned or the child he had seen only once?

Every day of the following week Fleur raked the papers for a flat to let, but they were all too expensive, even the bed-sits. She looked for jobs too and even went after one or two, but either she had no experience or she was dismissed sight-unseen as 'over-qualified' because of her eight O levels. At last in desperation she asked Harry Wallace if he could give her some extra hours. He shook his head.

'Matter of fact, love, we were about to ask you if we could put you on short time,' he said. 'Business has fallen off something chronic these past few months. Marj had to stand off the cleaner last week. We just can't afford to pay her no more.'

The stab of insecurity Fleur had felt when Ethel Smith had asked her to vacate the flat grew into a feeling of near panic. 'Only I've lost my flat,' she said bleakly. 'And everything else I've looked at is so expensive.'

Marj had come into the shop. She'd been listening to the conversation as she buttoned her overall and now she joined in. 'If I was your age I'd get out of London, love,' she said. 'A young gel like you with no ties could go anywhere. What have you got to lose?'

But Fleur lifted her shoulders uncertainly. 'I'd rather stay here,' she said. 'I was born here. It's all I know. I expect I'll find something if I keep looking.'

That night on her way home there were no footsteps following Fleur as she walked home. As she turned the corner into Brightman Lane everything was quiet, just a few residents returning from a night out at the pub and the endless muted roar of the traffic on Hackney Road. Before entering the narrow alleyway between the buildings that led to the flat's entrance, she paused under the street lamp, fumbling in her bag for her key and the torch she always carried. It was pitch dark in the passage and it wasn't until she had stopped in front of the door and inserted the key in the lock that she was chillingly aware that she was not alone. Instinct told her that someone had stepped out of the shadows and now stood close behind her. When he spoke quietly to her she felt his breath, hot on the back of her neck and her blood ran cold.

'Ullo darlin'. You an' me've got a little business to settle. Remember me, do ya?'

Fleur would have recognised the voice anywhere. Her heart beating fast, she wrestled with the key in a vain attempt at forestalling him, but before she could get the door open he grasped her by the shoulders and turned her round, pinning her against the wall.

'Oh no you don't!' He laughed hoarsely and thrust his face close to hers, breathing beer fumes into her face. 'Thought you could make a prat outa me, didn't you?' he hissed. 'Well I'm gonna show you what happens to gels who try an' get clever with me.'

'My grandmother's expecting me. She'll ring the police.'

He laughed in her face. 'Who're you tryin' to kid? The old cow's dead. You buried 'er more'n a month ago. 'Sides, you ain't even got a phone. Whatcher take me for – stupid or somethin'?' He spat the words at her and she felt her face spattered with moisture. Pinning her body against the wall with his own he forced his mouth on hers, prizing her lips apart with his hard tongue and thrusting it into her mouth. Fleur struggled, feeling her stomach heave as his teeth ground against hers. The nauseating taste of him made her gag. She pushed frantically against his shoulders as his hands clawed at her buttons, tearing her blouse open. Then she felt one rough hand painfully squeezing her breast as he pressed himself even closer. 'Come on.' He forced his knee between her legs and his breath rasped in her ear. 'I've been lookin' forward to this for weeks.'

Fleur wrestled with every ounce of strength that was in her and when he thrust his tongue into her mouth a second time she clamped her teeth down on it hard till she tasted blood.

'Ooow! Vicious *bitch*!' One big hard hand around her throat, he jerked her towards him, then propelled her backwards to the end of the passage where the dustbins stood. 'Wanna play rough, do you?' Forcing her off balance, her back against one of the bins he squeezed her throat so tightly that she could scarcely breathe, let alone scream, and with his other hand he ripped her jeans undone. To her horror she felt his fingers snake inside her panties and heard his breath rasp with lust as they made contact with her naked skin.

She struggled frantically, dislodging the dustbin lid so that they both staggered sideways, but the hand around her throat tightened its strangling grip on her till she felt herself beginning to pass out.

She gulped in air through her open mouth in a desperate attempt to gain strength and suddenly she realised that the torch she had taken from her bag was still clutched in her hand. It was a large nightwatchman's torch that had belonged to Grandpa. Dolly had always insisted on her carrying it when she had to walk home alone at night. She managed to get her arm free and brought the torch down hard against the side of her attacker's neck. He gave a surprised grunt, then as he moved back slightly she brought her knee up between his legs with as much force as she could. At once the hand around her throat relaxed its hold. He let out a scream of pain and doubled up. Pushing him to one side with a deafening clatter of overturned dustbins, she scrambled as fast as she could to the door, clutching her torn jeans around her. Finding the key still in the lock almost made her weep with gratitude. Already she could hear the cries of pain turning to roars of reprisal and she knew she had only seconds.

She turned the key, pushed the door open and slipped inside, shooting the bolts at top and bottom and leaning against it breathlessly, weak with relief. Outside the skinhead's bellowed obscenities and violent poundings reverberated through her body and she stepped backwards to sink onto the bottom stair, one hand over her mouth and her eyes fixed on the vibrating door, praying that the hinges would hold. Then there was a pause.

The letter box rattled, making her start with fright. 'You're for it now, you snotty tart!' he yelled through the aperture. 'Better watch your back from now on, 'cause I'm gonna get you. You can bet on it! Next time I'll slice that face o' yours – cut you so bad no one won't never wanna *look* at you again, you *bitch*!'

For what felt like an eternity she sat there in the dark, numb with shock. She remembered with dismay that her handbag still lay out there in the alleyway. It contained a week's wages, paid to her this evening. She owed that money to Ethel Smith for the rent, but she guessed that by now even if the bag was still there it would have been emptied of everything of any value.

Finally she found the strength to climb the stairs. Once inside the flat she went to the window and peered down into the street. To her relief it was empty. She drew the curtains and switched on the light. It was then that her stomach began to churn. A moment later, one hand over her mouth, she made a dash for the lavatory where she threw up violently.

In the kitchen as she filled the kettle with shaking hands and set it on the gas stove, tears began to trickle down her cheeks. For the first time in her life she felt vulnerable and utterly alone. She wept for her grandparents and even for the father she had never known, knowing that she would never be able to tell anyone what had happened this evening. It was all too shameful – too sordid and dirty.

At last the tears stopped and she made herself a promise. 'I won't let them win,' she vowed between clenched teeth. 'I won't be beaten!' But she also knew that in a way they already had won. Dolly had been right. She must leave Brightman Lane and the East End if she was to make a worthwhile life for herself.

In the end Fleur put most of her grandparents' furniture into a saleroom. She was pleasantly surprised at the figure it fetched. The auctioneer told her that some of it was Edwardian and coming into vogue again.

Grandpa's radiogram and records she sold to Ethel Smith who had taken a fancy to them. And the chest of drawers from the bedroom she gave to Ada Morris as a keepsake. It was only when she was removing the last of her own things from the chest of drawers that Fleur came across the piece of paper with her mother's address written on it. She smoothed it out and glanced at it. The notepaper was discoloured and dog-eared, the ink faded, but the writing was still clear enough.

> Miss Julia Philips,
> Gresham House,
> St Paul's Green,
> Elvemere,
> Cambridgeshire.

Her first impulse was to tear it into bits and throw it into the bin, then she changed her mind and put it into the box along with Dean's photograph and the postcards he had sent. These few scraps of yellowing card and paper were her only proof that she had ever had two parents. For a moment she stood pondering. Her mother, Julia Philips, would be pushing forty by now. She would more than likely have married and left this Elvemere place in Cambridgeshire long ago.

Out of curiosity she looked up Elvemere on the map and found that it was only an hour's train journey from London. Why shouldn't she go there? she asked herself. Dolly had said it was a nice place and it was as good as anywhere to start a new life. If Julia Philips was still there it might even be interesting to see what she was like and what she had made of her life. From a distance, of course. She had no intention of contacting her. Who needed a mother like her?

'I don't need anyone's help to survive,' she told herself. 'I've lost my family, my home and my job and I've survived an attempted rape. Nothing worse than that can happen to me. I'll make it in the end and when I do I'll have no one to thank but myself.'

37

Fleur shivered slightly as she stood there at the window. There was little time left for sleep now. It was almost morning, and now that the time had come to leave she didn't feel quite so brave. These streets might be dirty, noisy and sometimes dangerous, but they were all she had ever known. They were where her friends were. Was she mad to go to a strange town where no one knew her? Crazy even to think of looking for the mother who had wanted to be rid of her? Yet she knew that if she didn't go she would always wonder what she might have found – might have achieved. This was her watershed – her turning point. Now there was no going back.

Chapter 2

Vernon Grant nosed his silver BMW in through the double gates of his parents' house and glanced at his wife. As always she looked immaculate, her blonde hair expertly dressed and her make-up flawless. The dress she wore was her usual style, a dark blue thing, classily plain and obviously expensive. No man could have had a more attractive wife or a better hostess to entertain his business associates. He certainly couldn't fault her on appearance. The trouble with Julia was she couldn't take criticism. She just wouldn't be told. He drew the car to a smooth halt under the huge flowering cherry tree that was the centre-piece of the Grants' front garden and turned to her.

'Try not to make an atmosphere tonight of all nights, Ju. Remember it's Mother's and Dad's anniversary.'

'In that case, why choose tonight to pick a quarrel?' she returned without looking at him.

He sighed. 'All I said was that you should have asked me first before going ahead with this hare-brained idea.'

She turned to look at him. 'Why should I need your permission to put up for the council? It's hardly going to affect you, is it? You're hardly ever at home. Charlotte doesn't need me around any more. And everyone else seems to think I'd be an asset.' Her eyes were bright with something he hadn't seen in them before: defiance. It irritated him intensely.

'Not permission – *advice*. Christ, Julia, are you really so naive that you can't see that they're taking advantage of you? And by *everyone*, I suppose you mean the Maitland woman?'

'Councillor Eleanor Maitland? Among others, yes.'

Vernon sighed again. 'Look, Julia, this is a crucial by-election. If they don't get another Conservative in this time they'll lose their majority and no one else has come forward. Added to that the Labour bloke is popular. You're there to make up the numbers, can't you see that? God! It infuriates me to think you can be taken in like this. If you don't get in – and you won't – think of the laugh they'll have. At my expense too! What kind of an idiot do you think it'll make me look in front of my business associates?'

'I don't believe they're taking advantage of me,' she said stubbornly. 'Surely if they thought I wouldn't get in, they wouldn't have asked me? And why should it do you any harm? It could even do you some good.'

'Oh, I see. I suppose you're going to get on the planning committee and see that GPC gets all the plum contracts? Do me a favour! Why don't you just stick to your Townswomen's Guild and your committees and leave the serious stuff to those who are capable of handling it?'

She rounded on him indignantly. 'I'm not the complete moron you seem to take me for, Vernon. I do know enough to declare an interest should anything concerning GPC come up.'

He shrugged. 'If you take my advice, you'll stand down before you make a fool of yourself. You won't get elected anyway.'

Julia bit back an angry retort. Maybe Vernon was in

for a few surprises. Eleanor Maitland had convinced her that she was capable of being a good councillor. She'd persuaded Julia to stand and she intended to do justice to the older woman's confidence in her. She smiled at her husband. 'In that case, you have nothing to worry about then, do you? Shall we go in?'

His hand shot out and grasped her wrist. 'In a minute. I want to talk to you about Charlotte first. You know Mother's going to be very disappointed that she isn't with us this evening. Why on earth did you say she could go out with her friends when you knew Mother would be expecting her at this family dinner?'

Julia sighed. Once Vernon got the bit between his teeth there was no stopping him. He'd bring up every grievance he could think of. 'It was arranged ages ago,' she said patiently. 'Her friends from school agreed last winter that they'd have a meal out to celebrate the exam results – whatever they were. And as it happens they've all got good reason to celebrate.'

'But you *knew* Mother was planning this anniversary dinner.'

'Charlotte's growing up, Vernon. She's not a child any more, to be told what to do and where to go.'

'She's sixteen, for God's sake. In my book that's still a kid!'

'This is a once in a lifetime thing. She's worked hard and done well. She's already agreed to come into the business with you.'

Vernon snorted indignantly. 'She's *agreed*, has she? That's good of her. Most teenagers would give their eye teeth for a job like that with a secure future assured.'

'I know, but she'd have hated us for making her come with us tonight when all her friends were off enjoying themselves.'

'Ah, now we're coming to it, aren't we?' he sneered. 'Anything to be your daughter's best chum. You'll

41

regret the way you let that girl wind you round her little finger, Ju. You really will have to try to develop some backbone!'

Perhaps I already have, she said inwardly. Maybe putting up for this by-election is just what I need. Aloud she said, 'We're here for your mother's and father's party, so shall we try to forget my shortcomings for once?'

He got out of the car and slammed the door.

Julia picked up her beaded evening bag from the dashboard. Getting out of the car, she smoothed down the skirt of her dress and followed her husband to the front door of her in-laws' house. It had always been like this. Vernon would have his say and then shut her up on some pretext or other before she had a chance to put her side of the argument. Well, things were going to change. She'd made her mind up to that and he was going to have to get used to it.

Queen's Lodge, Vernon's parents' house, was an imposing mock-Tudor villa which Charlie Grant had built himself in the early sixties when his building firm had first begun to prosper. Charlie had started out as a humble bricklayer and had met his Lancashire-born wife Louise one summer when he was spending a working holiday on her father's farm. Twelve years later when his wealthy father-in-law died he had started his own building firm with the help of his wife's inheritance.

Queen's Lodge had been built to show the public in general that Charlie Grant, the scruffy kid with the backside hanging out of his pants, had made it. It had five bedrooms, two bathrooms and three reception rooms, and its black beams and sparkling latticed windows cocked a snook at the world, Charlie's defiant proof of his rise to success. Inside, the furnishings leant heavily towards Gothic Baronial. The decor favoured flocked wallpapers in reds and blues and most of the furniture was heavily carved, custom-made reproduction Jacobean.

Julia usually found the place intensely depressing. But this evening it had a festive, almost cheerful atmosphere. The windows were thrown open to the warm summer evening sunshine and Louise Grant, her mother-in-law, had obviously done her best. Bowls of flowers were everywhere, scenting the air with their fragrance, and there was an appetising aroma of food coming from the kitchen.

Louise came out on to the porch to greet them, her heavy figure swathed in rose pink lace. Pink was one of her favourite colours, though it did nothing for her rather florid colouring. Her blue-rinsed hair was fluffed out in a girlish halo and she wore a five-strand pearl necklace and earrings to match – her anniversary present from Charlie. She greeted Vernon warmly.

'Lovely to see you, Vernie, chuck.' She'd never quite managed to lose her northern accent or to cure herself of the habit of calling her son 'Vernie chuck' even though she knew it made him wince with embarrassment. She kissed him before turning her attention to Julia.

'What a pretty little frock,' she said, eyes glinting as they swept up and down her daughter-in-law's Versace original. 'That will have cost Vernie a penny or two, I know.' She slipped an arm round her daughter-in-law and gave a little shudder. 'Julia, love, you're nothing but skin and bone. You could do with putting on a bit of weight.' She regarded her thoughtfully. 'Have you ever considered getting yourself a padded bra, lovie?' As they went in through the front door, Vernon ahead of them, she said, 'Our Vernie looks right worn out. Are you sure he's eating properly?'

In the lounge Charlie was over by the cocktail

cabinet, dispensing the drinks. In late middle age he looked every inch the prosperous businessman with his florid complexion and thick white hair. His thickening middle was carefully disguised by the expensively tailored dark grey suit he wore. He looked up as they appeared in the doorway.

'There you are then! Late as usual!' He beckoned to them impatiently. 'Well, come on then. Come in, dammit! Don't stand in the doorway like a set of jugs. I've already poured you each a G and T.' As he put Julia's glass into her hand he bent towards her. 'Looking lovely, m' dear. If I were only twenty years younger, eh?' He winked and nudged her so hard she almost spilled her drink. It was his usual joke, and although she was used to it, it never failed to set her teeth on edge.

It was a small family gathering. Julia's parents, May and Harry Philips, were already there, sitting uneasily on opposite sides of the room. May Philips was an older, faded version of her daughter. Slightly built and still slim, she was a complete contrast to plump, overblown Louise. She wore a plain black dress, its only adornment, a small diamond clip that had belonged to her mother. Convent-educated May, whose late father had been the local doctor, had caused quite a stir some forty years previously when she had married Harry Philips, a poorly paid young electrician from the wrong side of town.

Harry, a small, balding man with glasses and a placid, genial expression, was Charlie's business partner in Grant Philips Construction Ltd. The two families had been drawn together by Vernon's and Julia's marriage seventeen years ago, and the business partnership had been established soon after.

Harry had gone to work for a small firm of electrical engineers when he left school at fourteen. He had risen

44

to the position of manager and finally bought his employer out on his retirement. Later, with the aid of a bank loan, he had expanded into plumbing and heating. Then, after the marriage of their respective children, Philips Electrics and Grant and Son Builders had joined forces to form Grant Philips Construction, with Vernon, newly out of business college, as the new firm's business manager.

They couldn't have chosen a better time to amalgamate. Once an agricultural area, Elvemere was turning to industry and, foreseeing the need for housing estates to accommodate the influx of workers, GPC had invested heavily in the large parcels of local agricultural land made redundant by EEC regulations. They had tendered for all of the new industrial buildings on the massive new trading park and, thanks to Vernon's negotiating skills, had been contracted to build eighty percent of them. Their latest and most adventurous venture was the building of upmarket luxury homes in the town's leafier suburbs, to attract the rising class of young executives. In seventeen years Grant Philips Construction had grown to become the largest building contractor in the county.

On the window seat sat Vernon's divorced sister, Kathleen, a tall, spiky woman who ran a stud farm on the outskirts of town. Her long hair, normally tied back with an elastic band, hung over one shoulder in a loose plait, schoolgirl fashion, and her angular figure, normally clad in jodhpurs and flannel shirts, looked slightly incongruous in a black skirt and frilly white blouse. As Julia took a seat next to her, May Philips looked at her daughter over the rim of her glass and knew at once by the expression in Julia's eyes that something was wrong. She and Vernon must have had another row. She could always tell. She smiled – she hoped reassuringly.

'Such a pity that Charlotte couldn't be here,' Louise said, sitting down heavily on the other side of Julia. 'Our only granddaughter. I did hope she'd be with us.'

'She asked me to say how sorry she was to miss it,' Julia said diplomatically, 'but she and her friends had arranged this meal out together months ago. It will be the last time they'll all be together, you see. Some of them will be moving on to college next term.'

'Charlotte did so well, didn't she?' May said placatingly, beaming at Louise with a nervous little laugh. 'Ten GCSEs and most of them As and Bs. And isn't it exciting that she'll be joining the family business? It seems only yesterday that she was a tiny . . .'

'Paper qualifications don't cut any ice with me,' Charlie said bluntly. 'I never had any and I don't think I've done so badly. I'd have taken my own granddaughter into the business whether she had any or not. She'll be nothing but a nuisance to start with, with or without GCSEs!' He threw a reproachful glance at his daughter-in-law. 'I had hoped the two of you would produce a lad to take over the business when we're gone, but there, you didn't, and it's too late now, I suppose.'

He sloshed a generous measure of whisky into his glass as though to reinforce his point. 'And another thing: when we were kids we'd have been made to put our grandparents first! Youngsters nowadays don't seem to be brought up to have respect for their elders and betters. Still . . .' He tossed back his treble whisky and burped softly. 'That's progress for you, more's the pity.' He looked at his watch, then at his wife. 'What about some food then, Mother? Isn't it time you ran along to the kitchen and got that lass to put on her cap and apron?' He rubbed his hands and looked round at them. 'Don't know about you lot but my stomach's rumbling fit to wake the dead.'

Louise had put on a sumptuous meal and hired a woman to serve it. Prawn cocktails to start, roast turkey with all the trimmings, followed by sherry trifle, and cheese and biscuits. Charlie dispensed the wine with the air of a connoisseur, a light Chablis with the starter, a rosé with the main course and a sweet Sauternes with the dessert. When May Philips protested at his refilling her glass for the fourth time, Charlie insisted.

'Come on, woman, it's our anniversary. We don't want any wet blankets here tonight.' He filled her glass to the brim. 'I've got no time for gentility meself,' he announced, reinforcing the statement with a barely stifled burp. 'An occasion like this deserves a slap-up blow-out with plenty of good quality booze. And this stuff . . .' he held the bottle aloft '. . . is the business. Twenty quid a bottle.'

He sat down, smiling benignly round at them. 'Well, what do you think of Mother's present from me then?' He waved his fork in the direction of his wife's necklace. 'You've not said, any of you. A couple of grand that little lot set me back. And that was at cost too! Got a mate in the jewellery trade. Nothing but the best for my Lou. Wouldn't be where I am today but for her.' He raised his glass to his wife, sitting at the other end of the table. 'To Lou,' he said. 'To Mother, God bless her.'

The others reiterated the toast while Louise, blushing, waved a plump, heavily ringed hand at them. 'Get away with you all,' she said. 'I told Gladys to serve coffee in the lounge so let's go and get it, shall we?'

As they filed out of the dining room Julia looked surreptitiously at her watch. It was almost ten o'clock. How long before she could decently suggest leaving? she wondered, as she made her excuses and went upstairs.

In Louise's bedroom with its half tester bed draped in pink flounces she applied lipstick at the dressing

47

table. The door opened and her mother slipped into the room and leaned against it exhaustedly.

'Oh, dear, that meal,' she said. 'So rich, and so much of it. I'm so full I can hardly move, but one daren't refuse anything. They get so offended.' She hiccuped gently. 'Oh, excuse me. I'm afraid I'm a little tipsy too. All that wine that Charles kept insisting on pouring. I never could drink more than half a glass, as you know, and I must have had at least four.'

Julia smiled at her. The fact that she doggedly persisted in calling Charlie Grant 'Charles' irritated him intensely and was the main reason why he always tried so hard to make her feel uncomfortable.

May sat down on the end of Lousie's bed and peered at her daughter's reflection in the mirror. 'Are you all right, dear? You look pale and I thought you looked strained when you first arrived.'

'I'm fine. I suppose it's worrying about Charlotte's exam results but that's all over now.'

May examined her nails. 'Er – you and Vernon – you're – all right?'

'We're fine.'

'You do know, don't you, darling,' May said earnestly, 'that Daddy and I are always there if you're in need of – you know, someone to talk to?'

Julia got up from the dressing table and bent to kiss her mother's cheek. 'I do know and I'm grateful.'

'I know that things are sometimes – well, difficult for you. I do so want to see you happy.'

'I know. And I am.' Julia offered an arm to her mother. 'Shall we go down now?'

In the lounge Charlie was passing round liqueurs. He pounced on May the moment she entered the room. 'Ah, there you are. Come on, sit down and make yourself comfy. I know what *you* like – cherry brandy, eh? Just suits you, May. I've always said you were like a

48

little cherry blossom, so small and dainty.' He pinched her cheek playfully. His face was glowing and red from the wine he'd drunk and he was becoming more outspoken by the minute. 'Mind you,' he went on with a deep-throated chuckle, 'I never went much for little women myself. Always liked plenty to get hold of, haven't I, Mother?'

Louise bridled. 'Behave yourself, Charlie. You're making poor May blush.'

But he swept aside her protest. 'Rubbish! May knows it's only my fun. We're all family and friends here.'

Kathleen, who'd hardly spoken all evening, lit a cigarette. As she exhaled the smoke she said casually, 'I hear you're going in for local politics, Julia?'

Everyone turned to stare at Julia who blushed hotly. Charlie's benign smile vanished and he glowered across the room at her.

'*Never!* Well?' he demanded. 'Is it true? Are you?'

'Well, yes.' Julia cleared her throat, resenting the embarrassment and the sudden inexplicable guilt she felt. 'As a matter of fact, I'm standing at the by-election in October.'

'You mean you're hoping to take Jack Martin's place?' Charlie stared at her. 'Old Jack was on the Town Council for more than forty years. If he hadn't dropped dead he'd have been on it still.'

'He'd been ailing for a good few years, I believe,' Julia said coolly. 'I understand he hadn't been at a council meeting at all for the past year and he'd been absent from a good many before that.'

Charlie's colour deepened. 'Are you criticising Jack Martin?' he challenged. 'Jack was one of my oldest friends. He was on that council when you were no more'n a glint in your father's eye. Well, I'll tell you this, lass, you'll go a long way to better him. Chairman

49

of the planning committee for years, Jack was. We've got him to thank for a lot of our successes and . . .'

'Never mind that now, Dad,' Vernon put in. 'It's only something Julia's been *thinking* of. Chances are she'll change her mind once she learns of all the hard work that's involved. Anyway, it's unlikely she'd ever get elected.'

'I should just think not!' Charlie said, pouring himself another brandy. 'And I'm surprised at you for allowing it, Vernon. Won't get my vote, I'll tell you that now, Julia. Women in politics! I've never held with it.'

'We do happen to have a woman Prime Minister, Father,' Kathleen put in with a wry smile.

'Maggie Thatcher's a one off,' Charlie waved his glass at his daughter. 'She's got a man's mind. Once she's finished you'll not see another like her in many a long year. And a good thing too if you ask me. Women are on this earth for three things. To be good wives, bring up children and to give a man a good . . .'

'That'll *do*, Charlie,' Louise interrupted, her cheeks pink. 'I think we've heard enough on the subject for one night.' She glared reproachfully at Julia, as though Charlie's outburst had been her fault. 'I'm sure Julia has far too much to do at home to want to get herself mixed up with the council anyway. If you take my advice, Julia, you'll leave all the argy-bargying to the menfolk and get on with your own job. I saw the way Vernie tucked in to his dinner tonight. Maybe now that Charlotte's off hand, you'll have more time to cook nice meals for the two of you.'

Seeing her sister-in-law's rising colour, Kathleen got to her feet. 'I'll have to be off,' she said abruptly in an attempt to defuse the situation. 'I've got a mare due to drop a foal at any time and I don't like to be away too long.' In the hall as they saw her off Kathleen bent towards Julia and said in an undertone, 'Sorry if I dropped you in it, but I daresay criticism is something you're going to have to get used to if you're serious about standing for the council. Good luck with it if you do. You'll get my vote, for what it's worth. Time someone got in among all those old fogies and started stirring things up a bit.'

Julia smiled at her. 'Thanks, Kath. I'll remember that.'

'And tell Charlotte to come round and see the new foal whenever she likes.'

'I will. She'll be thrilled.'

The party broke up soon after that. May, glad of the excuse to get away, pleaded a headache, and soon after that Julia and Vernon said their goodnights too.

In the car as they fastened their seat belts, Vernon looked at Julia. 'Satisfied, are you?'

'I don't know what you mean.'

'No? You only managed to ruin the evening with your radical views.'

Julia laughed. 'Radical? Just because I happen to think that councillors are supposed to attend meetings? And might I remind you that it was Kath who brought the subject up, not me? She happens to be on my side.'

'Your side!' Vernon sneered as he started the car. 'My sister would be on the side of anyone about to trouble,' he said bitterly. 'She thinks people are there to be schooled, like those horses of hers. Now she hasn't got a husband of her own to push around she's doing her best to disrupt other people's lives. No doubt she saw it as trying to liven the evening up.'

Julia smiled ruefully into the darkness. 'And what's wrong with that?' she muttered under her breath.

As Harry Philips drove his Rover in through the gates of Gresham House he turned to look at his wife in concern. 'All right, dear? Head still bad, is it?'

'I haven't really got a headache at all,' May confessed. 'But I would have if we'd stayed much longer. Charles really is the limit. He's so vulgar. And we really must take a dose of liver salts when we get in, if we want to get a wink of sleep tonight. That meal was enough to give anyone indigestion for a month!'

Harry chuckled. 'I know what you mean. Hardly what you'd call health food, was it? Still, Lou's a good sort at heart. I'm sure she did her best. I suppose it's what they're used to.'

May sighed. Lou could be a real bitch with her snide remarks, but Harry always saw the best in everyone. Sometimes she thought he was too mild, especially where the business was concerned. Charles and Vernon always seemed to be the ones making the important decisions. Harry just did the donkey work and smoothed the men down when Charles upset them. He'd averted industrial action more than once after Charles's abrasive manner had upset things, but he never took any credit for his diplomacy. She laid a hand on his arm. 'They say it's a pity you can't choose your relatives,' she said. 'It seems to me that the same applies to business partners.'

In the hall as she took off her coat she asked, 'Harry – did you think Julia seemed upset?'

He shook his head. 'Can't say I noticed. I thought she was looking especially nice this evening.'

'And what was all that about her standing for the council?' May said, a frown creasing her brow. 'I'd have thought she had enough on her plate with that large house and all her committees.'

Harry patted her shoulder and smiled benignly. 'I shouldn't worry about her if I were you, dear. You know Julia. She'll do what she wants to do in the end whatever we say. She always has. And you've always worried about her unnecessarily, haven't you?

Remember that time she left home and worked in London for over a year? I told you then she'd come home when she was ready and she did, didn't she?'

'I daresay you're right, dear.' But May was remembering the girl who came home to them, so changed and withdrawn. She'd never told Harry about the times she had got up in the night and heard Julia sobbing into her pillow. He hadn't seen the girl undressed as she had and noticed the way her ribs showed through her flesh and how pitifully thin she'd grown. She took off her coat, patting her hair thoughtfully in the hall mirror. 'Do you think she and Vernon are happy?' she asked. 'You know, sometimes I wonder if we threw them together all those years ago. We were so anxious to get her safely married to someone suitable at the time, weren't we?'

'And who could be more suitable than Vernon?' Harry's eyes looked startled behind his spectacles. 'I must say it's never struck me that we threw them together. I've always thought how lucky it was that they met and fell in love just at the right time.'

'Well – yes.' May was remembering the dinner parties and barbecues she had thrown, making sure that the Grants and their good-looking son were invited; how much she had hoped and prayed to see her wayward daughter comfortably settled.

'They were an ideal couple and very much in love. I'm sure they still are,' Harry went on. 'After all, look at what they've got: a lovely daughter and a beautiful home. A prosperous business and no money worries. Oh, no, I'm sure they're happy.'

May sighed. 'I expect you're right, dear. You usually are.'

In the pink bedroom at Queen's Lodge Charlie and Louise were getting ready for bed. Louise sat at the dressing table in her pink lace négligée, creaming her face. 'Was it really all right?' she asked. 'People don't seem to eat like they used to. May just picked at everything like a bird. I remember when I was at home on the farm we'd have great joints and piles of vegetables and it'd all get eaten. Nowadays all they seem to want to do is nibble at lettuce leaves and a bit of tomato.'

Charlie, resplendent in purple striped pyjamas, climbed into bed and thumped his pillow into submission. 'Stop whittling, Lou. It was a grand meal. Anyway, May and Harry always look as if a damn good meal would kill them, and as for our Vernon . . .'

Louise swung round. 'You noticed it too, did you? I told Julia straight. Our Vernie's looking right poorly, I said. Are you sure he's eating properly? But I don't think she took the hint. Sometimes I think she's a bit thick. All that rubbish about cholesterol and cardia vasica – what d'you call it! If you ask me it's just an excuse not to cook properly.' She wiped off the last of the cleansing cream and picked up her hair brush. 'What did you make of that business about her standing for the council?'

Charlie grunted. 'Nothing but a bloody fad! I blame Vernon,' he said. 'He should put his foot down; give her a thick ear if needs be.' He began to chuckle as his wife removed her négligée to reveal the filmy nightdress beneath. 'Failing that, a good seeing to. That'd keep her happy. She looks frigid if you ask me!'

'*Charlie!*'

He reached out to pull her on to the bed. 'Come off it, Lou. You're not frigid, I'm happy to say. Come on, you know you love it, and it *is* our anniversary, so how about it?'

Fleur turned over in the narrow bed, closed her eyes tightly and tried hard to sleep. It felt so odd, lying in this bed in an unfamiliar room, knowing that tomorrow morning when she woke and looked out of the window everything outside would be new and strange. Before she slept she'd written a quick letter to Bobby, giving her her new address. The act of writing to her friend had somehow made things feel more settled and less unreal. The train journey from London to Elvemere had taken less than an hour, yet she might as well have been on another planet and already she felt disorientated and homesick.

Her first priority had been finding somewhere to sleep. Outside the station she spotted a policeman and asked him if he knew of any cheap lodgings.

'You could try Mrs Franks at number thirteen Victoria Gardens. She'll put you up, love,' he said kindly. 'I happen to know she's got a room vacant at the moment. It's not posh, mind, but it's clean and cheap. Tell her PC Roberts sent you.'

'Can you tell me how to get there?' Fleur asked.

He pointed across the road. 'If you get on a number four bus over there, it'll drop you off at the park gates. Ask again when you get there. It isn't far.'

Victoria Gardens consisted of a crescent of three-storey terraced houses with a green in the centre encircled by iron railings. It had been built by local tradesmen and merchants in the middle of the nine-teenth century at the height of the town's prosperity and had once been a fashionable residential area. But with the advent of the motor car it had fallen out of vogue in favour of the suburbs and now the place had a sad, neglected air. The front doors that once gleamed with immaculate black paintwork and shin-ing brasses were scuffed and peeling. The central green, once meticulously manicured and planted with flowering shrubs, was now a tangle of weeds and rough grass, a hunting ground for the local cats and a dump for empty bottles and used fish and chip wrappings.

Fleur found number thirteen and stood looking up at it before mounting the front steps. The windows were dulled by grease from decades of passing traffic and she could see very little through the greying net curtains. She knocked hopefully on the front door and after a short interval a door below in the area opened and a woman in a blue nylon overall stuck her head out and peered up.

'Can you come down here, love?' she said without removing the cigarette from her mouth. 'Save my legs, eh?' As Fleur descended the area steps the woman looked her over critically, guessing that she'd be after the room. They never stayed vacant for long, but Ivy Franks generally preferred male lodgers, they weren't so much trouble. In her experience young women were always wanting to come down to the kitchen to wash their smalls or cook fussy meals. They left long hairs in the bathroom plughole and spent far too long in the bath. Then there were the boyfriends ... She could write a book about the love life of some of her female ex-lodgers. You had to be careful of all that. It soon got the place a bad name.

'Yes? What can I do for you then?'

'I've just arrived from London,' Fleur explained. 'I asked a policeman at the station. PC Roberts, he said his name was. And he said you had a room vacant?' She looked hopefully at the woman whose wary eyes were permanently narrowed by smoke from the cigarette which dangled from the corner of her mouth. She wore a bright red lipstick, applied in an exaggerated Cupid's bow and her frizzy hair was a dubious shade of auburn.

'Well now, I dunno where he got that idea from,' she said guardedly. 'Come from London, eh?' The narrowed eyes took in the short skirt and shapely legs. Could she be on the game? You never could be sure nowadays, and you couldn't be too careful who you let your rooms to.

'Got a job then, have you?' she asked, subjecting Fleur's features and the luxuriant mane of dark hair to embarrassingly close scrutiny.

'Well, no. I'll be looking for one though.'

'So, if you've not come here to work, what brings you to Elvemere?' Ivy asked bluntly.

'I'm here to look up some relatives.' The reply slipped out glibly on impulse. Fleur didn't like the suspicious way the woman was eyeing her and it was the most respectable reason she could think of.

Ivy Franks's face brightened. 'Oh, I see. So it'll only be temp'ry then, will it?'

'I expect so, yes.'

Ivy held the door open. 'In that case, you might as well come in.'

Fleur followed the woman inside with relief. It was past seven o'clock and she hadn't looked forward to searching for digs in a strange town after dark. Inside the basement kitchen of number thirteen it was dim but cheerful. An ancient Aga provided a warm atmosphere. There was a large table in the centre of the room, two comfortable shabby armchairs and a dresser. In one corner there was an archway through which she could see a sink and kitchen cabinet.

'I live down here,' Ivy explained. 'All the rooms upstairs except my bedroom are let to my "perms".'

Fleur frowned. 'Perms?'

'Permanent paying guests,' Ivy supplied. 'There are two flats at the back,' she said proudly. 'Big bedsits with their own facilities. They're more expensive, of course. Young Robbie – PC Roberts lived in one of them before he got married last year. He said there was no privacy at the Section House.' She removed the cigarette stub for a moment. 'Mind you, I don't encourage my tenants to entertain visitors of the opposite sex,' she warned. 'At the moment I've got a bank clerk in one and the manager of a hardware shop in the other. Most of my perms are business gentlemen, you see. I don't normally take young women.' She sniffed and folded her arms. 'But as you say it's only temp'ry . . .'

'I don't do food,' Ivy warned. 'There are gas rings in the rooms and if you've got an electric kettle you can use that. Electric's on a meter.'

'Er – how much?' Fleur asked.

Ivy raised an eyebrow. 'Better have a dekko at the room first, hadn't you?'

The vacant room was at the top of the house and looked out over the central green with its jungle of overgrown shrubs and rusting railings. From up here it looked even more squalid. It was a long, narrow room and held a single bed, a dressing table and chair, a wardrobe and a marble-topped wash stand which doubled as a worktop and table. On the floor was linoleum covered by a narrow strip of threadbare carpet.

'The bathroom's on the floor below,' Ivy told her. 'I've had a shower put in to keep the costs low. It takes less time too,' she added meaningfully. 'There's always a queue for the bathroom of a morning. And in the interests of my gentlemen, I'd be obliged if you wouldn't hang your undies in there. There's a yard at the back with a line.' She named a rent at which Fleur heaved a sigh of relief. It might not be luxurious but at least she could afford it. Until her money ran out.

'I'll take it,' she said.

'Right. Want to go and collect your stuff then?'

'There's only the two cases I brought with me,' Fleur told her. 'I'll come down and get them.'

At the bottom of the stairs Ivy turned to look at her new lodger, her sharp features relaxing into a smile. 'I was just going to make myself a cup of tea,' she said. 'Fancy one, do you?'

Fleur smiled. 'I'd love one. Thanks.'

'Right. You just get them things upstairs and come right down to the kitchen.' There was something intriguing about this girl. She had a foreign look about her that Ivy couldn't place. She could be Spanish or even Cypriot or Maltese. Yet she reckoned she had relatives here in Elvemere. Maybe over tea Ivy could find out who she was and who these relations were she'd spoken of.

'So, you'll be looking for work then?' Ivy poured Fleur a cup of strong tea and passed the biscuit tin across the chenille-covered table.

'Yes.'

'In what line would that be?'

'I'll take anything,' Fleur told her. 'In London I worked in a fish and chip shop, but only because it was all I could get. I'd like to get something better if I could.'

'Waitressing?'

'What I'd really like would be to train for something. I got eight O levels before I left school. I would have stayed on for my As but my grandmother was ill so I left school to help her.'

'Granny from foreign parts, was she?' Ivy asked slyly.

'No. A Londoner.'

'I see.' Ivy sipped her tea, peering speculatively at Fleur over the rim of her cup. 'Mum and Dad?'

'My grandmother brought me up,' Fleur said.

'So how's she managing without you?'

'She died a few weeks ago.'

'I see. I'm sorry to hear that.' Ivy lit a fresh cigarette

from the stub of the old one and squinted at Fleur through the cloud of exhaled smoke. 'So now you've come to look up the rest of your family?'

'Well, distant relatives really. Yes – probably. But mainly to make a new start.'

'What would their name be then – these relatives? I mean, I might even know them. Same as yours, is it, Sylvester?'

'Er – yes, that's right,' Fleur lied. She realised now that the woman had only offered her tea so that she could quiz her for information.

'But I lost touch with them years ago, so they might not even live here any more.'

Ivy screwed up her face thoughtfully. 'Sylvester. Would that be a foreign name then?'

'Not as far as I know.'

'Well, I can't say I've ever heard of any Sylvesters in these parts. Still I don't know everybody, do I?' She cackled hoarsely. 'They do say the Salvation Army are good at finding lost relatives.'

'Oh – well, I shall have to think about that.'

As soon as she could Fleur made her excuses and left. As she came up the basement stairs into the hallway she met a young man on his way in. He smiled at her. 'Hello there. Have you just taken the top floor front?'

'That's right, Fleur Sylvester.' She held out her hand and he shook it.

'Tom Markham.' He looked at her appreciatively. 'Well, I must say, it'll be a treat to see a feminine face around here for once.' He lowered his voice. 'It's not too bad here as long as you don't intend to spend the rest of your life in the place. Watch the old girl though. The News Of The World, we call her. She knows everyone's business. Take a tip from me and don't tell her anything unless you want the whole town to know about it.'

Fleur laughed. 'I'd already gathered that.'

He had a nice, unremarkable face with warm brown eyes and floppy brown hair. It was cheering to see a friendly face, but he disappeared into one of the first-floor rooms and when she had climbed the next flight to the top floor and closed the door it hit her quite suddenly how alone she was. Had she done the right thing? Fleur asked herself as she stood at the window looking down into the litter-strewn green. This place looked hardly any more salubrious than Brightman Lane. Would she have done better to have stayed in London where she knew people and everything was familiar? Then she remembered the street fights, the racism and muggings. No. She'd been right to take Grandma's advice and make a fresh start. The future was in her own hands now. And her first priority was to get a job. Things would surely be better once she had settled down.

Fleur spent most of that first week familiarising herself with the layout of the town. On her first morning she discovered to her satisfaction that Victoria Gardens was within easy walking distance of the town centre, which would save on bus fares. At the first newsagent's she came to she invested in a street map and took it into a café to study over a cup of coffee and a doughnut. Soon she knew her way around. The Market Square, the Town Hall, the Cathedral and the town's bright new shopping mall soon became familiar territory.

She liked what she saw. For the most part, Elvemere was clean and spacious, a fascinating mixture of the very old and the brand new. It had wide streets with bright, well-stocked shops and plenty of trees and flowers. And everywhere the towering presence of the great Cathedral was like a protective patriarch, enfolding the town in its embrace.

The Cathedral had been a surprise. Somehow she hadn't expected a town as small as Elvemere to have a great medieval cathedral at its heart. She'd always thought that only large cities had cathedrals.

She often reminded herself that this was the place where her mother belonged. She would have known these streets as a child, probably walked these very pavements and looked in these shop windows every day. Sometimes she found herself wondering what Julia was like and what she had made of her life. It struck her once with a small shock that they could pass each other in the street and not realise it.

She invested some of her precious money in an electric kettle, a small saucepan and a toaster. She had to have the means of making herself a cheap meal, eating out was out of the question. Each day she went to the Job Centre and studied the cards displayed there. There were plenty of vacancies for shop assistants and filing clerks, but although Fleur wasn't completely clear exactly what it was she wanted, she knew she wanted something with more of a challenge to it than any of them. She longed for a job that had a future prospects for improvement; something that would fire her imagination and bring satisfaction. But jobs in this category were clearly going to be hard to find and Fleur's meagre savings were dwindling fast. In the end she was obliged to apply for a job stacking shelves in the town's largest supermarket.

She had been there a little over a month and had almost given up hope of finding anything better when she spotted something that intrigued her in the Situations Vacant column of the local evening paper. The advertiser wanted a general assistant to help in a catering firm. *'The applicant should preferably have some experience in the catering trade, should be willing to work flexible hours and versatile enough to juggle several tasks at*

once,' the ad read. *'Initiative and common sense essential.'*
Something about the way it was worded stirred Fleur's
interest. She had a little experience of the catering
trade, helping Dolly with her party buffets. Perhaps
that would count in her favour?

Fleur went out to a telephone box to ring the number
given in the paper. The pay phone at number thirteen
had been installed at the top of the basement stairs and
she had already learned that Ivy Franks always left her
door open so that she could eavesdrop on all her
lodgers' conversations.

A woman with a pleasant voice answered her call
and an appointment was arranged for the following
evening after work. For the first time since she had
arrived in Elvemere, Fleur went to bed that night in a
hopeful frame of mind.

Sally Arden was forty-nine and had started her catering
business twenty years previously when her husband
died suddenly, leaving her a penniless widow with a
young son to bring up. Desperate to make some money
to keep her home going she had begun in a small way,
working from her own kitchen and catering for friends'
parties and small functions. But word had soon spread
and her business had gone from strength to strength.
Now she ran a successful outside catering firm, providing buffets and meals for everything from weddings to
boardroom lunches.

She explained all this to Fleur as she interviewed her
in the office at her pleasant suburban home. 'I started
working from home when my son Peter was little and
it's become a habit,' she said. 'It's handy too as I still do
all the cooking myself. I can answer the telephone
while I'm busy in the kitchen.'

'How many other staff have you got?' Fleur asked.

'None. I still do most of the work myself,' Sally

63

smiled. 'I hire my waitresses on a casual part-time basis and I drive the van myself. But I must admit that I do get tired more easily than I used to and my son has finally convinced me that I really do need a permanent assistant.'

'What would the job involve?' Fleur asked.

Sally laughed. 'A bit of everything, I suppose. I do a lot of preparation in advance, storing food in the freezer, so to begin with you'd probably find yourself spending all day making sandwiches or filling vol-au-vents. On the other hand, I'd need you to answer the telephone when I'm not here – take bookings, that kind of thing.' She smiled. 'When we had a function on I'd need you to come along with me to help set everything up, maybe double as a waitress if we were short-handed, and generally run around for me. That would mean working unsocial hours, I'm afraid. Of course I'd pay you the going rate for overtime, or we could arrange time off in lieu, whatever you preferred.'

Fleur smiled. 'I don't know anyone in Elvemere, so I don't have any social life at the moment. I haven't worked in the catering trade before, but my grandmother used to cater for parties and I usually helped her,' she said frankly. 'I'm quite a good cook too. My grandmother taught me.' She paused, glancing at her prospective employer hopefully. 'My grandfather was from Jamaica and I can make some Caribbean dishes. So maybe when I've got the sandwiches right I could learn to do something more ambitious?'

Sally looked at the girl's eager face and warmed towards her. 'Of course the job can go much further than that if you want it to,' she said. 'If you were interested, I could teach you to cook some of the more adventurous dishes, and eventually how to interview clients and assess their needs – make suggestions, create menus, all that. Then there's the business side of things: the ordering, accounts and book keeping. Can you drive – use a computer?'

Fleur shook her head, her cheeks flushing with excitement. 'No, but I'd love to try all of those things. I'm sure I could learn.'

Sally nodded. 'I'm sure you could too. We can sort out driving lessons and some evening classes for you. And, of course, the more responsibility you can take, the more you'll earn, so it will be worth your while.' She liked the look of the girl. She was intelligent and keen to learn. She was very young, of course, but for all her youth there was an air about her – a presence that Sally found impressive. If she could be trained to work in all branches of the job she could prove an invaluable asset in time. Sally stood up and held out her hand. 'Well, Fleur, you seem prepared to be flexible. If you really think you'd like it we could give it a go. Shall we say a month's trial?'

It was beginning to rain when Fleur got off the bus at the park gates and by the time she reached the Gardens it was coming down fast, large cold drops that quickly penetrated her light summer clothes. Her head down, she ran all the way to number thirteen and had just reached the front door when she bumped into someone coming the other way.

'Oh! I'm sorry. I...' Looking up, she saw Tom Markham smiling down at her. 'Oh, it's you.'

He looked at her thin clothes and took her arm. 'Better get in before you get soaked.' Inside she took off her jacket and shook the raindrops from it. Tom looked at her. 'You seem pleased with yourself.'

She smiled at him. 'I've just got a job.'

'I thought you already had one. Whenever I see you you're rushing off somewhere. We've hardly spoken since the night you arrived.'

She pulled a face. 'I don't call stacking supermarket shelves a job. It's more of a punishment. Anyway, it was only temporary. To keep me going and pay the rent. This is something much better.'

He looked at her glowing cheeks and shining dark eyes. 'Look, do you want to come and tell me about it?' He held out the large newspaper-wrapped parcel he was carrying. 'I've just been out for some fish and chips and I always get too many.'

She hesitated, wondering how Ivy Franks would feel about her going into Tom's room. She had made her disapproval of 'entertaining' only too plain. Besides, since the attack Fleur had fought off she had found herself instinctively avoiding being alone with a man.

'Come on. You'd be doing me a favour by helping me eat them,' Tom urged. 'I'll only put on weight and you wouldn't want that on your conscience, would you?'

She laughed. 'Okay then. You're on.' Tom was nice and she was going to have to overcome her apprehension sometime, and it would be great to be able to tell someone about her good luck instead of shutting herself away alone for the rest of the evening.

Tom's room on the first floor was larger than hers. It had a three-quarter bed and an armchair. Best of all it had its own wash basin. She looked around. 'This is better than my room.'

He filled the kettle and plugged it in, then began to unwrap the fish and chips. 'There are some plates in the bottom of the wardrobe, if you wouldn't mind,' he said. 'There isn't anywhere else to keep them.' He grinned. 'It's hardly The Ritz, is it?'

'It is compared to mine,' Fleur told him. 'You've even got a gas fire. I don't know what I'll do when the weather gets cold.'

Tom struck a match and the fire popped into life.

'Old Poison Ivy will find you an electric fire if you're still here in the winter. But I expect you will have moved on to pastures new with this fabulous new job of yours.' He pointed to the chair. 'Hang your jacket over that to dry,' he invited.

Over supper he told her that he worked as a reporter on the local paper. He'd been born in Elvemere, but spent much of his childhood away at school.

'My dad died when I was ten and my mother went to live with her parents in Yorkshire. My grandfather paid for me to go to boarding school.' He grinned. 'To get me out of the way, I think. They were getting on in years and I was a bit of a tearaway. I did my training on a Yorkshire paper, but I always wanted to come back here so when the vacancy came up on the *Elvemere Clarion*, I applied.'

'It must be interesting, working for a paper?' Fleur remarked.

'Very, even if the hours are terrible. But you were going to tell me about this marvellous job you've landed?'

She shook her head. 'It isn't a marvellous job yet, but it will be. It's with Arden Catering and I'll have a chance to build it up, to learn to drive and work with a computer. Best of all it's working with food and people, both of which I like.'

'I think you might have landed on your feet,' Tom told her. 'Everybody in Elvemere knows Arden Catering. Mrs Arden is a very successful lady. She does all the best weddings in the district, engagement parties and so on, plus all the council functions.' He grinned. 'Everything I ever cover for the *Clarion* seems to be catered for by Mrs Arden. There's a lot of one-upmanship here, you know. I imagine it's become quite trendy to have Arden Catering providing the nosh for your do.'

Fleur's eyes were shining. 'It sounds as if I'm in for a fascinating time.'

'You'll be in for a busy time by the sound of it, what with your driving lessons and your evening classes.'

Tom made coffee after they'd eaten and they sat near the gas fire, their hands round the warm mugs, relaxing and getting to know one another. 'What made you leave London and come here?' he asked.

'My grandmother died and I didn't fancy staying on alone.'

'Why Elvemere though?'

She shrugged. 'Stuck a pin in the map?' she offered.

'Well, your pin struck lucky for me,' he said. 'I've got nothing in common with the two other guys here and working the odd hours that I do, I don't have much social life. It gets lonely sometimes. So if you ever have any time off from all your studying . . .'

'Yes – er . . .' Suddenly Fleur felt a twinge of uncertainty. She glanced at the clock and stood up, handing him her empty mug. 'It's getting late. I'd better go,' she said. 'Thanks for supper and the coffee.'

Tom put both mugs down on the mantelpiece and looked at her anxiously. 'Look, I didn't mean anything, Fleur. I'm not trying to push or anything. It's just that it'd be nice to have someone friendly around.'

Embarrassed, she began to back towards the door. 'Of course. I know. Yes, it would.'

'Look – Fleur.' He reached out to touch her arm. 'If you want company any time, I'm here. Just knock on the door. I won't hassle you. Right?'

She smiled, feeling awkward and foolish. 'Of course, Tom. And – thanks.'

'I've got the car. It's only a clapped-out Metro, but I could take you for a run down to the coast one Sunday – if you'd like that?'

'Yes. That might be nice. Goodnight, Tom.'

Later, tucked up in bed, Fleur thought about Tom, and their talk over supper, his offer of friendship and tentative invitation. She felt slightly ashamed. She'd always been more than able to stand up for herself, so why had she behaved so stupidly? The man who had attacked her had been a vicious thug. It had been a frightening, humiliating incident, but she had survived and it was unlikely to happen again. Tom was so different; decent and kind. She was going to have to start trusting men again. If she didn't she'd become warped and paranoid. As she closed her eyes she made up her mind to take him up on his offer of a trip to the sea.

Chapter 3

Canvassing was an eye-opener for Julia. She could not believe that she had lived in Elvemere all her life and not known of the conditions under which some people lived. On some of the council estates she was shocked to find that there were homes where there was no floor covering and hardly any furniture. It was the kind of poverty she had previously thought existed only in inner city areas, not prosperous small towns like Elvemere.

It was a far cry from the luxurious home she took so much for granted and she felt slightly ashamed. Yet in spite of her smart outfit and generally affluent appearance, she was greeted for the most part with respect and politeness. There were people who were rude, of course. She had been prepared for that. But she found that most of the rudeness came from the people who had all they needed in life and – if Councillor Eleanor Maitland was correct – never bothered to vote anyway.

Eleanor Maitland was in her mid-sixties. She had been on the council for more than twenty years and was well known for her outspoken views and her toughness. She had taken Julia under her wing from the first and had generously offered to accompany her on the first few forays into the unknown world of political canvassing.

'You'll need a thick skin, my dear,' she said, pulling on her sensible tweed coat and ramming the familiar brown felt hat down over her steel-grey hair. 'A thick skin and a lot of determination. Not only with the voters either,' she added. 'You'll find some of your fellow councillors are hard nuts to crack. It helps to do your homework well – make sure you're damned well right. Don't let the buggers grind you down, in other words.'

Councillor Maitland's gritty obstinacy and doggedness in getting what she wanted for the people she represented had earned her the nickname 'Old Brillo'. It alluded not only to her tightly permed grey hair, but also her abrasive manner. She confided in Julia that not only was she perfectly aware of the nickname, she was actually proud of it.

'I may be a dyed in the wool Tory, my dear, but I stand for the underprivileged. They can't speak up for themselves but I bloody well can. I was one of them myself once and I know what I'm talking about.'

It was no accident that on their first day out together she took Julia to the streets she had never ventured into before, to show her the class from which she herself sprang. In spite of the poverty Julia found there was pride and dignity here too, a resigned acceptance that tugged at her heart-strings and a desire for betterment against all the odds: qualities that unearthed old memories for her.

But, as always, there was another side to the coin. There were those who felt the world owed them a living and would milk the system for all they could get. There were the resentful, suspicious ones; tough unshaven men in string vests who used the kind of language that made Julia's toes curl, and expressed

71

their views of the Tory Party, and Mrs Thatcher in particular, in highly colourful terms. Eleanor was equal to them all.

'All right, lad. Keep your hair on,' she'd bellow good-naturedly. 'Tory we might be but we're on your side, can't you see that? Party politics count for nothing when it comes to local government. We're here to do our best to try and put things right for you, so just watch your language and show a bit of respect.'

Julia admired her enormously. Privately she felt that she could never be as tough or as outspoken as Eleanor if she lived to be a hundred. All the same she was inspired enough to want to try. From Eleanor she learned to handle the insults and swearing with dignity; how to cope with the awkward ones and convince the waverers. There were some it was wisest to walk away from, and those who, with patience and sincerity, could be won over. Eleanor showed her how to spot the difference.

After a particularly gruelling evening of canvassing Eleanor asked Julia in for a much needed cup of tea when she dropped her off outside her house.

'I reckon you can go it alone now, lass,' she said as she filled the kettle. 'You don't need me to hold your hand any more.'

Eleanor still lived in the little house she and her husband had shared since the day they married. It was a tiny terraced cottage in a row originally built for railway workers. It had two rooms upstairs and two down and few modern conveniences, but Eleanor had made it homely and warm. There were hanging baskets and brightly planted tubs in the back yard and her little living-kitchen was bright and welcoming with its yellow curtains and geraniums on the window sill. Looking around her, Julia noticed that the bookcase was full of biographies of eminent statesmen and books written by campaigning politicians.

Eleanor drew the curtains on the gathering darkness outside and turned to look at Julia's doubtful face. 'Don't worry, you're doing fine.'

'I hope you're right.'

'I am!' Eleanor plonked a tray of tea down on the table between them. 'You know, I'm pinning a lot of hope on you, my dear. I can't go on forever. Old Jack Martin's death set me off thinking. I've been on Elvemere Town Council for almost as long as he was and I hope I've done a bit of good in that time. I'd like to think there'd be some like-minded person to carry on the work when the time comes for me to pop my clogs.' She smiled at Julia. 'You've got the background and the education I never had. You've got the *words*. All I ever had was a bloody loud voice and teeth like a bulldog.'

'I don't think anyone will ever replace you,' Julia said with an affectionate smile, 'but I'm deeply flattered that you have so much confidence in me.'

'You'll be all right, lass,' Eleanor said, nodding to herself as she poured tea into willow pattern cups. 'Of course there are those no one will ever help. You'll have to get used to having your teeth kicked in and your heart broken for your trouble. But just keep on believing in the human race, that's the secret. There's an old saying: To be in the weakest camp is to be in the strongest school. Just remember that.'

'I will.' Julia pulled her canvassing schedule out of the bag that contained her leaflets. 'Well, if I'm flying solo I might as well start right away.' She unfolded the paper and spread it on the table between them. 'I think I'll make a start on Victoria Gardens. I can drop the leaflets off on my way home and follow them up tomorrow evening.'

Eleanor smiled. 'That's the spirit, lass.'

As she saw Julia off on the doorstep, she said, 'Oh,

by the way. I don't know if you realise it but Victoria Gardens is due for redevelopment.'

'They're surely not thinking of pulling it down?'

'No, they can't. The houses are listed, but the place has been getting steadily more rundown these past years. The plan is to buy up all the occupied houses and renovate the whole place – turn the ground floors into offices and maybe have some luxury flats above. The council's got some vague thoughts about turning a section of it into a health centre – maybe even a new library.'

'I see.'

'But that's all under your hat, understand?' Eleanor tapped the side of her nose. 'I'm only telling you so that you'll be careful what you say when you're round there. Don't make any promises.'

'Right. I won't.'

Julia parked her car near the park gates and set off to drop her leaflets. As she walked round Victoria Gardens she saw what Eleanor had meant about the place being rundown. It was years since she had visited the place. Her school friend, Joanna Bloom, had once lived at number twelve with her family. In those days the houses had been well-kept and the central green neatly maintained with flowers and shrubs.

It was a long time since Julia had thought about Joanna and her Bohemian family. The friendship had been ill-advised; even the teachers at school had tried to warn her against it, but she had been drawn to the other girl like a fly to a spider's web. It had been Joanna who had first persuaded her to rebel against her parents' protectiveness; Joanna who had introduced her to the delights of disco dancing and the heady excitement of pop music. Eventually Joanna had been at the root of her downfall and the secret tragedy that had changed her life and left an indelible blemish on her memory. Julia had never quite forgiven her for that. But it was years since she last saw Joanna. When she had returned to Elvemere the family had packed and gone – no one knew where.

As she pushed a leaflet through the letter box of number twelve she saw that the house was very different from when the Blooms had occupied it. There was a rusty bicycle propped against the wall down in the basement area; the steps were muddied and the paintwork chipped. When the Blooms had occupied the house the front door had been painted purple, and bright orange curtains had hung at the windows. Inside there had been no carpets, just varnished boards and rush matting, and Julia seemed to remember that all the furniture had been made of bleached pine.

As she went from house to house she found herself remembering so many things about Joanna and her family, things she had almost forgotten. Mrs Bloom with her braided hair and colourful caftans, and Joanna's bearded, sandalled father. She had loved the disorganised chaos in which they had lived, the carefree, casual atmosphere that was so different from what seemed to her the stiflingly ordered life her parents led. The Blooms went to bed, ate and partied just as the mood took them. Joanna and her two older brothers came and went as they pleased, owned their own keys and followed no rules except those they made for themselves. As both boys were musical their home always rang with the strains of the guitar or the latest hits on disc. Joanna's father was an artist so there was always an odour of turpentine and linseed oil in the air. Julia had found it all exotic and exciting.

Joanna was allowed to do all the things Julia was not. She wore mini skirts and daring tops with bare midriffs – later, when the ethnic look came in, she drifted around in Indian cotton skirts that swept the floor and masses of jangling silver bracelets. Her chestnut hair was long and silky straight in the favourite style of the sixties and her green eyes, made up with heavy liner and thick mascara, had the brooding, soot and treacle look that Julia longed to achieve for herself.

May and Harry Philips were so afraid of the modern hippy culture with its shocking sexual permissiveness that they hardly let their daughter out of their sight and monitored her wardrobe carefully. But their claustrophobic watchfulness only served to drive a wedge between them and Julia. The more she saw of the Blooms and their way of life, the more defiant and rebellious she became. She'd persuaded her parents to let her take a Saturday job in a hairdresser's and with her wages bought some fashionable clothes which she kept at Joanna's and changed into whenever she was allowed out.

It was quite dark by the time Julia had delivered all her leaflets. It had begun to rain too and she was grateful for the warmth of her car. She spent a few minutes arranging her cards in order for the following day's canvassing, then switched on the ignition and headed for home.

As soon as she opened the front door she heard Vernon's voice raised in anger and Charlotte's shrill response.

'You can't tell me what to do. I'm an adult now and it's my decision. If I want to spend my free time working with horses then I *will*, and you can't stop me!'

There was a loud slam as Charlotte banged her bedroom door and Julia gave a sigh of dismay as she began to take off her outdoor things. When she came out of the cloakroom Vernon was coming down the stairs, his face dark with fury.

'That girl! I've always said you're too soft with her.

She might have finished at school but she's still got a lot of studying to do, I keep reminding her of it, but will she listen?'

'She does need to have some recreation too,' Julia pointed out. 'I think riding and caring for the horses is good for her. It helps her confidence and develops her sense of responsibility.'

Vernon snorted. 'Huh! As far as I can see she needs no help in the confidence department. And Kath is hardly the best influence on her responsibility-wise. She positively encourages that rebellious attitude of hers.' He looked at her. 'Where have you been, by the way? I have to go out and we should have eaten half an hour ago.'

'Dinner's all ready. I cooked it this morning. It only needs warming in the microwave. I'll see to it now. I did tell you I'd be out canvassing.'

'Did you? Well, I've no time now.' He tapped at his watch. 'I'll have to get a sandwich at the pub after the meeting.'

'In case you want to know, I'm doing rather well with the canvassing,' she told him pointedly as he gathered his briefcase and car keys from the hall table. 'Eleanor says I'm ready to go out on my own from now on.'

'In other words, she's fed up with trailing round with you, eh?' He aimed a kiss in the direction of her cheek. 'Well, if you're really set on putting yourself through this fiasco . . .' He looked at his watch again. 'God! Look at the time. I must go. See you later.'

In the kitchen Julia took the lasagne she'd prepared that afternoon out of the fridge and put it into the microwave. Vernon hadn't said what meeting it was he was going to. She had her suspicions that there was no meeting. He'd been wearing his favourite shirt and had reeked of expensive aftershave. That usually meant only one thing: he was seeing someone again. The signs were all there: the extra meetings, the late nights and unscheduled weekend conferences, the hurried phone calls. Not to mention the tell-tale perfume that lingered about his clothes and in his car. His affairs were usually short-lived and she had become resigned to them, riding out the mingled feelings of anger, humiliation and rejection they gave her. When they had first started, soon after Charlotte was born, she'd tried confronting him. He had brazened it out, scorning her tears and accusing her of being paranoid. Adamantly denying everything.

She began to make a salad. As Vernon would not be joining them she laid the table in the kitchen, then went into the hall to call Charlotte. When the girl joined her Julia could see traces of angry tears on her cheeks.

'I wish you wouldn't antagonise Daddy,' she said. 'There are better ways of getting round him. You know arguing always makes him lose his temper.'

Charlotte helped herself to lasagne and salad. 'Why should I have to wheedle and coax to get him to let me do something so harmless?' she said rebelliously. 'Anyone'd think I was asking to throw a drugs and sex orgy or something! All I want is to spend my weekends and free time helping Auntie Kath.' She turned large blue eyes on her mother. 'I did as Dad asked and gave up working at the stables till the exams were over. Surely he can't object now I've left school? You will get him to say yes, won't you?'

'I'll try.'

Charlotte stuck out her chin stubbornly. 'Well, you can jolly well tell him that I'm doing it, whether he likes it or not. I've agreed to work at GPC to please him and learn boring computing and book keeping at evening classes. Isn't that enough for him?'

Julia looked up at her daughter. 'I thought you were happy with that?'

Charlotte poked at her food. 'Well, I'm not – not really. You've no idea how stultifying it is. They treat me like the office girl. *"Go and make the tea, Charlotte."* *"Pop round to the post office, will you?"* They never stop! No one would ever think I was the boss's granddaughter. And I've got to put up with it when all my friends are going off to college or taking their As.'

'But you didn't want to stay on, did you?'

'I'm not academic, Mum. It was a real struggle getting my GCSEs. You know what I really wanted was to go into partnership with Auntie Kath. All I've ever wanted to do was to work with horses, but we both know there's no way Dad would ever agree to that, is there?'

'He just thinks you have a good brain and should put it to better use.'

'Oh, yes? Like running around making tea all day and sitting staring at a flickering computer screen every evening in some stuffy classroom?'

'It won't always be like that. He's actually very proud of you, Charlotte. And he was so pleased when you agreed to join the firm. He's looking to the future,' Julia told her. 'He wants you to begin at the bottom, like he did. One day you could find yourself running the business.'

'Oh, big deal!' she said, unimpressed. 'It's every girl's dream, isn't it – the construction business! What it's really about is that he and Granddad have always been pissed-off that I'm not a boy.'

'Don't talk like that,' Julia said with a sigh.

'Well, it's true,' Charlotte insisted. 'That and the fact that he and Auntie Kath have never got on. This is a way of getting back at her too.'

'He wouldn't dream of being so petty,' Julia said unconvincingly. 'Look, I'll speak to him later about it.

I'm sure he won't mind you going to the stables in your free time if he's approached reasonably.'

'Okay, thanks.' Charlotte helped herself to more salad and ate in silence, obviously appeased. 'How did you get on with your canvassing?' she asked.

Julia smiled. 'I thought you'd never ask! Very well, actually. Tomorrow I'm going solo. Councillor Maitland said she thinks I'm ready to canvass on my own.'

'Really? That's great!' Charlotte swallowed the last mouthful then pushed her chair back. 'Look, I'm sorry, Mum. I'd love to stay and hear all about it but it's the first of these wretched evening classes tonight and I'll be late if I don't go.'

Julia washed up the dinner things by hand. Two place settings hardly justified using the dish-washer. As she worked she heard the sounds of her daughter's hasty preparation for departure and replied to her call as she left, banging the front door behind her. The house settled into silence around her.

It was a solid, well-built house, architect-designed and built by Charlie Grant for them as a wedding present. It had every modern convenience and was equipped with the finest fittings that money could buy. In the hope that his son and daughter-in-law would provide him with several grandchildren Charlie had supplied them with five bedrooms. The house was far too large for the three of them and Julia had never really liked it. The design was unimaginative and even after eighteen years it still looked raw and new with its red brick exterior and large flat windows. But she knew better than to suggest a move to something smaller and more stylishly designed. Charlie and Louise would be scandalised and Vernon would be irritated. It would never happen and it wasn't worth the furore which suggesting it would create.

Julia ran her home and coped with the garden alone, enjoying it as a relaxing hobby. But she could see that if she was elected to the Council she was going to have to think about getting more help, both indoors and out. It was something she hadn't broached with Vernon as yet. He was of much the same view as his father – that a woman's place was, if not permanently in the home, then certainly taking sole responsibility for everything in it.

Her leaflet drop in Victoria Gardens had stirred up old memories and as she washed up Julia let her mind drift back to the late-sixties when she and Joanna had been friends. It had been such an exciting time – 'flower power', 'love and peace', the music of The Beatles and The Rolling Stones, the freedom of the new kind of dancing, so different from the sedate and laboured ball-room dancing they learned at school. And somehow the fact that she was deceiving her parents had made it all the more thrilling.

She and Joanna went to a disco at least once a week and sometimes she would stay at Victoria Gardens for a whole weekend, sharing Joanna's bedroom where the walls were plastered with Andy Warhol posters and pictures of all her pop favourites. On those occasions they would stay out till after midnight. Joanna was boy crazy and used to boast of her sexual exploits, claiming to have had sex with dozens of boys. Julia, with her straight-laced upbringing, had been secretly shocked at the time. Her views were more romantic and idealistic. In spite of the so-called permissive age, she still felt it was wrong to give yourself completely to a person you didn't love, and said so. Joanna laughed.

'It's just a game, you sweet old-fashioned thing,' she laughed. 'A wonderful game. You don't know what you're missing.'

And gradually even Julia had discovered that under

the intoxicating influence of a rhythmic beat, strobe lights and the Bacardi and Coke that Joanna had taught her to drink, there was a certain honeyed sweetness to kisses and petting, even with someone she hardly knew. As Joanna had said, it was all a game, and anyway she never let things go too far, even if she did tell the occasional white lie to Joanna.

It had been in the summer of 1970 that Joanna had announced her intention to go to the Isle of Wight for the rock festival. She took it for granted that her friend would go too. When Julia hesitated and shook her head doubtfully, Joanna tossed her long hair petulantly.

'Please yourself, but I shall go of course. It's going to be fabulous. The Stones will be there, Procul Harem, Jimi Hendrix and loads of others. Imagine actually seeing and hearing them in the flesh! If you don't come you'll miss out on something fantastic.'

The more Julia thought about it, the more she longed to go. She racked her brain for a way to get her parents to agree and in the end she came up with an idea. The English mistress at school was getting up a weekend party to go to see an open-air production of *A Midsummer Night's Dream* in London. It was August and Julia had left school at the end of the summer term but she was still entitled to go. She asked and her parents agreed readily. Their daughter could come to no possible harm under the eagle eye of the elderly Miss Grimshaw. Luckily for Julia it did not occur to them to telephone and check that their daughter had in fact booked.

The two girls hitch-hiked down to Lymington and caught the ferry across to Yarmouth, both of them in a state of high excitement. From Yarmouth it was only a short journey to Afton Down, Freshwater.

To Julia the festival was a revelation. There on the clifftop, in a tiny place renowned for its Victorian values, every pop star she had ever heard of seemed to be assembled. And the mass of young people that grew hour by hour dazed her completely. Joanna took it all in her stride, pointing out the celebrities to her friend as they wandered wide-eyed through the crowds.

'Look, there's Joan Baez – Jim Morrison. I've just seen Tiny Tim and – you'll never guess – *Keith Moon!*'

'Where are we going to sleep?' Julia asked. 'Most people seem to have brought tents and things.'

Joanna looked at her askance. 'Sleep? How can you even think of sleeping? Oh, I expect we'll find some place to snuggle down when and if the music ever stops,' she said airily. 'Who knows?' She grinned. 'We might get lucky and get to share some gorgeous guy's sleeping bag!'

The weekend became a blur to Julia; an amalgam of pulsating music, good-natured pushing, discomfort, and at times downright squalor. There were times when she was chilled to the bone and others when she was so hungry her stomach hurt. The sanitary facilities were adequate but only just. There was certainly no place to take time over one's appearance, and for the most part people were grubby and dishevelled. But no one seemed to care. The sight and sounds of artists like Miles Davis and Jimi Hendrix, with his exotic personality and colourful clothes, soon made Julia forget her discomfort. She and Joanna spent the first night huddled together under a blanket someone had lent them, hardly able to sleep for the mixture of cold, damp and excitement. But it was on the morning of the second day that Julia met Dean Sylvester. After that the rest of the festival became a mere sideshow for her.

'Need any help?' She'd been looking for some breakfast when the voice behind her spoke.

She turned and recognised the lead guitarist from a minor group called The Sylvas who had impressed both girls the night before when they had heard them play. He was a tall young man with dark skin and a mane of black curls. Julia thought him quite the most attractive man she had ever seen. She felt herself blush hotly as he looked down at her appraisingly, his lips curved in amusement.

'We – I was looking for something to eat,' she said.

'The kitchen's over that way.' He pointed. 'Come on, I'll show you.' With an air of complete assurance he took her hand and they began to walk. Julia was astounded. He was so casual and relaxed. It was as though they'd always known each other. And he had a wonderful accent that sent thrilling shivers up and down her spine.

'Enjoying the festival?' He looked down at her with warm melting brown eyes that turned her knees to jelly.

'Oh, yes. We saw your group perform last night. You were fabulous.'

He threw back his handsome dark head and laughed delightedly. 'Great! For that I'll buy you a sausage!'

They ate breakfast together and talked. Julia couldn't get over it. That a man as good-looking as Dean Sylvester should not only notice but want to spend time with her was amazing. His conversation was riveting. He knew so much about pop music, and about all the other artists at the festival. He'd met them all – even performed with some of them – and she listened with rapt attention as he recounted little personal anecdotes about them. The life he led, travelling from place to place and performing with his group, sounded fascinating. And while he spoke he held her hand, or draped an arm around her shoulders. It felt wonderful.

They spent most of that day together. When he was playing he made sure she had a place near the front, flashing her the occasional 'special' smile. When he wasn't he would escort her to where all the most exciting action was. It was almost evening before Joanna caught up with Julia again. She was far from happy.

'Where on earth have you been?' she demanded indignantly. 'You went off to get us some breakfast and that was the last I saw of you!'

'Sorry. I met this marvellous boy.'

'What boy?'

'His name is Dean Sylvester. He's the lead guitarist with that group we saw last night, The Sylvas.'

Joanna's face was a study. 'The tall black guy?'

'He isn't black.'

'Yes, he is – well, partly anyway. Bet you anything. He looks a lot like Jimi Hendrix.' Joanna pouted, clearly resentful. 'What on earth did he want with you?'

Julia blushed. 'Thanks! You'd better ask him. He's coming over.'

But although Joanna tried hard, fluttering her eyelashes and using all her wiles to attract Dean's attention, she did not succeed. To her fury, he had eyes only for Julia.

In the small hours of the following morning, when everything was comparatively quiet, they walked hand in hand round the perimeter of the ground, and in the shade of a group of trees Dean took her in his arms and kissed her. It was the most exciting kiss Julia had ever experienced. She wanted it to go on forever. The previous evening some of the people they'd been with had passed round a joint. Joanna had persuaded her to try a few puffs and she had found the effect surprisingly pleasant. It made her feel relaxed and dreamy. But Dean's kisses were better than any drug – infinitely more exhilarating. Her knees seemed to turn to water as she clung to him.

'You're not going back to find your friend, are you?' he whispered, his warm breath tickling her ear.

She sighed. 'We've only got one blanket between us. It was cold last night.'

'Haven't you got a tent?'

'No.'

He chuckled and pulled her closer. 'I have. I've got a sleeping bag too. Share it with me and I promise I won't let you get cold.'

Julia stood with her hands in the cooling washing up water, her eyes far away as she remembered Dean and that first night together. Never in a thousand years could anyone have prepared her for the ecstatic delight of making love with him. He was gentle, especially when he realised that it was the first time for her. But later, as dawn was breaking and all her shyness and inhibitions had melted, her passion had matched his. By morning she had known that she was hopelessly in love. In spite of Joanna's insistence that sex was just a game, something that you enjoyed and forgot, like a bar of chocolate or a can of Coke, she had known by morning that there could never be any other man for her but Dean.

Even now after all these years she could still conjure up the breathtaking thrill his lips had the power to create, the explosion of sensations she felt at the touch of his hands. Closing her eyes, she allowed herself to visualise his handsome face, the golden skin and beautifully moulded features, the midnight-dark eyes and glorious mass of curling hair. If only he could have turned out to be the man she'd thought he was. If only the tragic disillusionment that had come later had . . .

The shrill of the telephone startled her out of her dream, jerking her thoughts abruptly back to the present, and she hurriedly dried her hands and went into the hall to answer it.

Charlotte had enrolled at the local further education college for computer studies and book keeping, neither of which aroused her enthusiasm in the slightest. The college, a sprawling red brick complex, was only a ten-minute cycle ride from home and she arrived with time to spare. Parking her bicycle, she went inside to join the other students crowded round the information board in the front hall, all of them checking to see which room their particular course was to be held in. As she scanned the board she became aware of another girl standing beside her.

Charlotte turned with a smile. 'Hi. What have you enrolled for?'

'Computer studies. It's in Room B-six.'

'I'm doing that too.' Charlotte looked at her with interest. She guessed that the other girl was a few years older. She looked her over enviously, admiring her figure and striking looks. 'Shall we go up?' she asked companionably.

'If you like.'

As they went up the stairs together, Charlotte said, 'I haven't seen you around.'

'I've only just come here to live,' Fleur told her. 'From London.'

'You've left London to come and live *here*?' Charlotte looked at her in amazement. 'You'll find it a bit tame. I'd give anything to go and work up in London.'

'It isn't all it's cracked up to be,' Fleur said. 'Going up on a day trip or a holiday is one thing. Living there is something else. I lived in the East End.'

Charlotte had already guessed that. She watched the new soap *East Enders* regularly and had recognised the accent. 'Oh. What's it like – rough?'

'A bit.' Fleur smiled.

Charlotte was fascinated by this attractive older girl with her exotic looks and fascinating way of speaking. She looked so sophisticated and worldly. Why on earth had she wanted to come and bury herself in a dump like Elvemere? Surely she could have had a much more exciting life in London? 'Seriously, though, what made you come here?' she asked.

Fleur shrugged. 'Why anywhere?' she said evasively.

'You must have had a reason though. I shouldn't think many people have actually ever heard of this place.'

Fleur resorted to the answer she'd given Tom. 'I stuck a pin in the map.'

'Really? No kidding.' Charlotte was intrigued. It all sounded so wonderfully free and adventurous. 'Have you got a job then?'

'Yes. With a catering firm,' Fleur told her proudly. 'I'm going to learn everything from the cooking to the business side so that I can eventually be my employer's right-hand woman.'

'Wow!' Charlotte was impressed. It sounded a whole lot more interesting than the construction business. 'I have to work in my granddad's office,' she said. 'It's so boring you wouldn't believe. I really wanted to work with horses. My aunt has riding stables and I go there and help her whenever I can.' She looked at Fleur. 'You like the catering trade, do you?'

'Yes, I do.'

'Are your parents pleased?'

'Haven't got any. My grandma brought me up. When she died I thought it was time to move out – make a fresh start.' They had reached their room and Fleur turned to the inquisitive younger girl with a smile, relieved that the cross-examination would have to stop. 'Right then. Shall we go in?'

When the class was over and the students began to

file out Charlotte pushed her way to the front to catch her new friend before she disappeared. There was no one else in the class she fancied making friends with. All of the boys were spotty and gauche and she didn't know any of the other girls.

'Hi! How did you get on?' she asked breathlessly, catching up with Fleur at the bottom of the stairs.

'Oh, all right, I suppose. I never liked computers much at school but now that I have a reason to be computer literate, as they call it, it makes all the difference.'

'There's a canteen place here,' Charlotte said. 'Fancy a coffee?'

Fleur hesitated, then smiled. 'All right, if you like.'

Over coffee they exchanged names. Charlotte thought the name, Fleur was beautiful. 'I wish I had a pretty name,' she said, stirring her coffee. 'I was christened Charlotte Harriet, would you believe? After both my grandfathers. Isn't it the absolute *pits*?'

Fleur laughed. 'I expect people call you Charlie.'

'Good heavens, no!' Charlotte looked shocked. 'That's what my granddad is called, so at least I've been spared that.' She took a sip of her coffee, studying Fleur over the rim of her cup. 'So – tell me about yourself. I don't get to meet many Londoners.' She licked her lips and asked the question she'd been wanting to ask all evening. 'You're not actually English, are you? I mean – not, well, completely.'

'My grandfather was West Indian,' Fleur told her. 'Apart from that I'm English. I was born here and so was my father. In fact until I came here I'd never been out of London, apart from a day trip to Southend.'

'West Indian, eh?' Charlotte rested her chin on her cupped hands and looked at Fleur. 'How fascinating. You're very beautiful,' she said candidly. 'I'd give anything for hair like that. And those eyes. I've always wanted brown eyes. They're more – I don't know mysterious, I suppose.'

Embarrassed by the girl's scrutiny, Fleur looked up at the clock on the wall opposite. 'I'll have to go,' she said. 'There's a bus at half-past and if I miss it, I'll have to wait half an hour.'

'Of course.' Charlotte sprang to her feet, gathering her books together. 'I'm starting driving lessons the moment I'm seventeen. When I've passed my test I expect Mum will let me borrow her car. I'll be able to give you a lift home then.' She fell into step with Fleur's long-legged strides. 'Where do you live by the way?'

'Victoria Gardens.'

'In a flat?'

'A room.'

Charlotte sighed with envy. The girl had it made. A room of her own, a job and the independence and freedom to organise her own life. It sounded marvellous. 'I wish I were in your shoes,' she said wistfully. 'I bet you have no one telling you what time to be in and what you can and can't do.' They had reached the main entrance and she paused to pull on her jacket. 'My bike's over there in the bike sheds. See you next week then?'

'I expect so.' Fleur watched the other girl hurry off with a wry little smile then turned towards the bus stop thinking wistfully of the obvious contrast between the two of them. She wouldn't mind going home to a mother who was waiting eagerly to hear how the class had gone; who had a tasty supper ready and a hot water bottle warming her bed. Briefly she wondered how a cosseted girl like Charlotte would cope with living alone in a cramped single room, making her own scratch meals and sleeping in a narrow, lumpy bed. The girl had no idea. She didn't know she was born!

But as Fleur began to walk towards the bus stop she

reflected that there was a certain engaging charm about pretty little Charlotte Grant. She was like a friendly puppy; bouncy and uninhibited taking it for granted that her company would be welcome. That kind of confident personality only came from a stable home background, she told herself sadly.

Fleur's first week at her new job was mainly routine. She buttered bread till her arms ached, learned how to mix the various fillings, wrap, pack and label for the freezer. She also became acquainted with the appointments book in the office so she could deal with bookings if Sally was out. But on Saturday evening the monotony of the week's routine was relieved when she attended her first function, a twenty-first birthday party in one of the town's smartest suburbs.

At the client's home Sally quickly showed her how to assemble the long trestle tables, to spread the snowy cloths so that they fell exactly to the ground and arrange the coloured swags. Sally always took along her own silver candelabra and flower arrangements as well as cutlery and napkins, and she showed Fleur how to fold them deftly into pretty shapes. She learned how to arrange the food attractively on dishes and lay it all out on the tables. Later, wearing the smart black skirt and white blouse that Sally had provided for her, and with her hair carefully plaited and tamed, she circulated along with the hired waitresses among the guests with trays of wine.

At the end of the evening Sally complimented her. 'You're picking it all up very well, Fleur,' she said. 'Several people have asked me who my attractive new assistant is. You have a very pleasant way with people.'

Fleur found herself unable to stop smiling. She had enjoyed the evening very much. Getting the job with

Sally was a real piece of luck. For the first time she felt she had made the right move in coming to Elvemere. Even the chore of packing everything up afterwards seemed pleasurable. She was looking forward to tomorrow with anticipation. This was the Sunday that Tom was taking her down to the sea for the day.

'Oh, I *love* the country,' Fleur said, looking out of the car window as they drove, admiring the gently undulating Norfolk landscape. They had left the busy dual carriageway now and were on the quieter country roads. The trees were beginning to turn from green to gold and the fields were already brown with newly turned furrows.

'I hardly ever saw trees and fields in London,' she told Tom. 'Oh, it's so fresh! You can really breathe out here.' She rolled down the window and took a deep draught of the air. 'Mmm – I believe I can smell the sea already!'

Tom laughed. 'That'll be the muck spreading,' he joked. 'They do a lot of it at this time of year.' He glanced at the girl sitting beside him. She really was quite beautiful with her warm olive skin and flashing dark eyes, alive with excitement. Ivy had hinted at some kind of mystery attached to her new lodger. She had told him with an air of gloomy foreboding that in her opinion Fleur had *foreign blood*. Her inquisitive remarks had led him to believe that she suspected him of knowing more about Fleur than she did. Obviously the old girl had observed their growing friendship with a more than casual interest and was hoping he would be able to satisfy her curiosity. She had certainly looked disappointed when he told her he knew no more than she did. Nevertheless, his natural journalist's interest made him wonder about Fleur, her background and sudden unheralded arrival in Elvemere.

'So – you're glad you chose this neck of the woods now, are you?'

She turned to him with a smile. 'Yes. I like my new job and the town.' She paused. 'I'd like somewhere better to live though. I'm not looking forward to spending the winter in that poky little room.' She looked at him. 'I've been meaning to ask, who lives in the room on the first floor at the back – the one with the little balcony?'

On her trips into the back yard to peg out her washing she had been intrigued by the little white-painted wrought-iron balcony. She indulged herself with dreams of what it would be like to occupy the room behind it. There were two half-glazed doors opening out on to the balcony and she imagined herself sitting out there on warm summer evenings or Sunday mornings with her coffee. If it were hers she would put out hanging baskets and trailing ivy – perhaps even buy herself a sun lounger and use it for sunbathing. She had never known the pleasure of a garden, but that balcony would be the next best thing. There must be a nice view over the park from up there too.

'It's one of the flats. Derek Jones lives in it,' Tom told her. 'He's the tall thin guy with the moustache. He manages the hardware shop in the High Street. Ivy tells me he's divorced. But he's moving out shortly – to share a house along with a friend apparently.'

'Really?' Fleur bit her lip with excitement. 'Would she let it to me, do you think?'

'If you want it, you'd better ask quickly.' Tom looked doubtful. 'And I warn you, she doesn't usually keep female tenants permanently.'

'I know. The rent might be more than I can afford too,' Fleur said.

'I've no idea what she charges for the flats. You'd have to ask.' Tom pointed as they rounded a bend in the road. 'Hey, look, there you are – the sea.'

Fleur sat up straight, peering intently through the windscreen. There it was, a shining silver ribbon etched against the blue of the sky in the distance. She drew in her breath sharply. 'Oh! Isn't it lovely? I can't wait to get there.'

Tom laughed and pressed his foot firmly on the accelerator. 'Right. Have you there in five minutes flat!'

Fleur hadn't know quite what to expect of the Norfolk coastline. She had known it would not be like Southend but she had not been prepared for its wild beauty. She was enchanted by the many different kinds of seabirds, crowded together to feed on the saltmarsh as they drove along the coast road. And, as they entered the little fishing village of Ormsburgh, the delightful brick and flint cottages, built around the tiny harbour.

For what was left of the morning they explored the streets which converged on the harbour, and Fleur marvelled at the colourful cottage gardens, overblown now, but still bright with dahlias, asters and chrysanthemums. In the tiny natural harbour, boats were moored, tossing gently on the incoming tide, their sails furled, whilst out to sea the waves rolled in, capped with white foam. Fleur was enchanted by it all.

'Can we walk along there?' She pointed to the dunes. 'Is it safe?'

' 'Course it is.' Tom took her hand. 'I know this bit of the coast like the back of my hand. We used to come here for holidays when I was a kid.' It was impossible not to catch some of her enthusiasm. Even though the place was a familiar childhood haunt to him he found that he was seeing it afresh, through her eyes. 'We can walk as far as you like. Don't you want to eat first though?' he asked. 'I know I do.'

It was only with reluctance that she allowed herself to be drawn inside a harbourside pub for lunch. But even there she was intrigued by her surroundings. The centuries-old walls were whitewashed and the heavy oak beams black with the smoke of the years. Small round tables with wheel-back chairs were clustered around a huge open fireplace in which burned a fragrant log fire. Behind the bar stood a smiling land-lord and his wife, waiting to serve them.

Tom ordered ploughman's lunches for both of them and it was only then that Fleur realised how hungry she was. She applied herself with zest to the ripe Stilton cheese, salad and home-made crusty bread.

'So you want to go for a walk after lunch?' Tom asked.

Fleur nodded. 'Yes, please. I want to see it all.'

'I warn you, walking on soft sand can be tiring.'

'I don't care.'

An hour later, replete with lunch and the local real ale, they began their walk. Tom admired Fleur's stamina as she strode along beside him. As she walked her cheeks were whipped to a glow by the wind and her eyes shone.

'You never told me your real reason for choosing Elvemere,' he said.

'I told you – I stuck a pin in the map.'

'Ivy mentioned that you had relatives here.'

She turned to look at him, her eyes clouding. 'What else has she been saying about me?'

'Nothing. Just that. It's not true then?'

Fleur paused. 'It might be.'

'That's rather an oblique remark.'

She stopped and sank down on a hummock of wiry grass. 'Let's have a breather, shall we?'

'Suits me.' He sat down beside her and pulled himself a long blade of grass, looking at her thoughtfully as he wound the wiry length around his finger. 'Was it just something you told her to keep her quiet then?'

'About having relatives here? No, not exactly.' She paused, following his example and pulling herself a piece of grass. 'As a matter of fact, my mother came from here.'

He stared at her. 'Your mother?'

'Yes. I don't remember her. She left me with my grandparents when I was a baby. They brought me up. Before my grandmother died she made me promise to try and find her. But that's only partly why I chose Elvemere. If I ever do look for her it'll only be because of my promise. There's absolutely no reason why I should want to find a mother who couldn't care less about me. Anyway, for all I know she probably left here years ago.'

'I see. What about your father?' Tom asked casually. He was trying hard to hide his rising curiosity. Whether Fleur knew it or not she had come here because of her mother, and one day she would have to face the fact. But he sensed that she might be put off if he showed too much curiosity.

'My dad?' She shrugged. 'Haven't a clue. He abandoned my mother before I was born, and he died soon after.'

For a long moment they were both silent. Fleur looked at the sea and wondered at its vastness. This morning in the distance it had looked so dreamy and idyllic. Later with its little white waves it seemed almost playful. Now it looked hostile and threatening. It made her shudder a little.

But Tom's curiosity would not let him alone. It rubbed insistently like a stone in his shoe. 'Your father – was he . . . ?'

'Half-West Indian.' She turned to look straight into his eyes. 'My grandfather was black. That's what you and Ivy have been dying to know, isn't it? Well, you can tell her now. And I daresay that when she knows that

96

she'll be sure to turn down my request for the flat.' She got up and brushed down her jeans. 'But I'll tell you this – my grandpa was the finest man I've ever known. He was kind and honest and good and I loved him very much.' She began to walk back towards the village. 'You were right, Tom,' she said over her shoulder. 'Walking on these dunes is harder than I thought.'

He had to run to catch up with her. 'Fleur – wait. I didn't mean to pry. And I wasn't trying to find out about your private affairs. If I was clumsy and I upset you, I'm sorry. Really sorry.'

She walked on for a moment without speaking, then turned and he saw the brightness in her eyes. 'It's okay, Tom,' she said softly. 'It doesn't matter.'

He caught her by the shoulders and pulled her round to face him. 'Yes, it does matter! I wasn't trying to find out so that I could tell Ivy. Surely you didn't think that?'

'I don't know what I thought.' She shook her head. 'No, of course I didn't.'

'You don't have to be so defensive. I'm sure you've every reason to be proud of your grandfather. Look, Fleur, you do trust me, don't you? I wouldn't do or say anything that would hurt you.' He brushed a strand of windblown hair away from her face and cupped her face between his hands, looking deep into her eyes. 'You do believe that, don't you?'

Eventually she nodded. 'Yes. I trust you, Tom.'

'I'm glad.' He took her hand. 'Hey, they do fantastic cream teas at the Lifeboat Café. I could murder one, couldn't you?'

She laughed. 'You bet!'

By the time they got back to Victoria Gardens it was dusk and a chill wind had replaced the balmy breeze.

Fleur shivered a little as she got out of the car. 'Thanks for a lovely day, Tom.'

He bent his head to look up at her. 'Don't run off like that. I thought we'd have a coffee or a nightcap when I've put the car away.'

'Oh, all right then.'

Tom rented a lock-up garage a couple of streets away and as he drove off Fleur let herself into the house. She'd only just closed the front door when Ivy poked her head round the corner of the basement stairs.

'Have a nice day at Ormsburgh, did you, Miss Sylvester?'

'Lovely, thanks. And please call me Fleur.'

Ever since she had first arrived, Ivy had steadfastly refused to call Fleur by her christian name.

She emerged into the hall and Fleur saw that she was wearing her fur fabric jacket and pearl stud earrings. 'I've just come in myself – been out to tea with my friend, Mrs Jennings,' she volunteered. 'A real lady, Mary is – fallen on hard times since her husband died. He was a gambler, you know.' She shook her head and drew in her breath with a hissing sound. '*Terrible*. Poor Mary never knew what she was going to have to manage on at the end of each week when he was alive, then when he passed on she was left without a penny. She has to go out cleaning now to eke out her pension. Shocking, isn't it? Especially at her age.'

'Yes, that's very sad.'

Ivy folded her arms and leaned against the side of the stairs, clearly preparing herself for a long gossip. 'She only cleans for the best people, of course. Three days a week she goes to Mrs Charlie Grant. That's Grant Philips the builders, you know. Lovely place they've got. Every modern convenience – carpets up to your ankles! Mary says it's a pleasure to work there, and Mrs Grant is ever so generous with her.'

'That's nice.' Fleur put one foot on the stairs. 'Well – better go, I suppose.'

Ivy peered at her. 'Early night then, is it? Tired after all that fresh air?'

'No. It's just . . .'

The front door opened and Tom came in, rubbing his hands together briskly. 'Brrr, the evenings are getting really chilly now. Never mind, that coffee will soon . . .' As his eyes adjusted to the dim light in the hallway he noticed his landlady standing in the dark recess near the basement stairs. 'Oh, hello, Ivy. Didn't see you there.'

'Evening, Tom. *Well*,' she smirked, 'sorry if I've kept you, Miss Sylvester. I expect you'll be wanting to go up and – er – take your things off.'

'What was all that about?' Tom asked with a grin as they reached the top of the stairs.

'Oh, nothing much,' Fleur stopped outside his door, her face still burning at Ivy's suggestive remark. 'Look, Tom, I'm a bit tired. It must have been all that fresh air. I think I'll leave the coffee for tonight, if you don't mind.'

'Hey, come on.' He reached out to touch her shoulder. 'It's not what Ivy said, is it? You know what she's like – always making pointed remarks. Take no notice. She doesn't mean anything.'

'I know. It's not that . . .'

'Well, if you're sure?'

'I am – really. Another time, eh?'

He paused, then stepped closer. 'I've been meaning to ask you, Fleur, did you leave anyone special back in London? Is there a boyfriend? If there is . . .'

'No!' His face was very close to hers and she turned her head away, her heart pounding uneasily. To her annoyance the memory of the attack she had suffered still affected her. She forced herself to swallow the panic that rose in her chest, reminding herself firmly that Tom was nice. He was decent. Not like that animal. 'No, there's no one,' she said.

'Any special reason?'

What did he mean by that? 'No. I just never seemed to have time for socialising.'

'Well, I won't pretend I'm not pleased about that.' He bent his head to rub his cheek against hers. 'Goodnight then, Fleur. And thanks for coming out with me today. I enjoyed it very much. More than you know.' He looked into her eyes. 'Can we do it again some time?'

'Yes. Yes, I'd like that.'

'And maybe next time we can have that nightcap?'

'Yes mayb—' The word was stifled as his lips covered hers. It was a chaste kiss, soft and undemanding. She should have enjoyed it, but she couldn't submerge the spectre that had haunted her for weeks. The violent image of her sadistic attacker, bent on inflicting pain and humiliation, rose again behind her closed eyelids. Once again she could feel his rough hands on her flesh and the evil smell of him filled her nostrils. She bore it as long as she could, then, with a strangled gasp she pushed Tom away, holding her hands protectively in front of her.

'I – I'm sorry. I have to go. I'm sorry, Tom – *sorry*.' She backed away and ran up the stairs to her own room, shutting her eyes to the dismayed look on his face. Closing the door of her room, she leaned against it as she waited for her heartbeat to slow and the tumult of nauseated panic to cease. What she'd done was unforgivable. She'd hurt him without meaning to. And after he'd treated her so well. What she'd just done had ruined the delightful day they'd just spent together. But the feeling of revulsion had been so strong, so inescapable. It seemed to swallow her up, squeezing the breath from her body until she thought she would suffocate. It was triggered by Ivy's knowing smirk and suggestive remark, then Tom's unwitting entrapment of her as she stood with her back to the wall, her escape blocked by his body.

When would the memory ever go away? she asked herself despairingly. When would she feel free to form a normal relationship again?

She lay awake for a long time, thinking regretfully of Tom and wondering how she could explain her strange behaviour, make it up to him. But it was only as she was drifting into sleep that something quite unrelated that Ivy had said suddenly rang a bell in the back of her mind. She had mentioned that her friend Mrs Jennings worked for a family named Grant. She had heard that name somewhere recently – but where? Then she remembered the young girl in the computer class. Her name was Grant. On the brink of sleep Fleur wondered drowsily whether she was from the same family.

Chapter 4

Julia parked the car under a street lamp and stepped out into the rain. This was the last evening. Just one more street to canvass and then it would be in the laps of the gods, or rather the voters. One more night of uncertainty before tomorrow.

Polling day! The very thought of it made her stomach churn with apprehension. Although Eleanor had urged her to be positive, she kept guarding against disappointment by telling herself that she wouldn't really mind if she didn't get in.

Putting up for the council had been much harder than she'd envisaged. She'd certainly worked hard, but over the weeks of canvassing she had learned that wasn't enough. She had at least to appear strong – to convince people, make them believe she was sincere. And she was. She genuinely wanted to represent them as best she could, to serve her community, although for now she wasn't committed to any particular cause. The trouble was that everyone seemed to want something different. How did you convince them all that you had their best interests at heart when a lot of the time you didn't agree with their views? When it came to the crunch you could only really be yourself and if that wasn't enough, then so be it. Twenty-four hours from now she would know just how convincing she'd been.

She had left the Mapleton Estate till last and the notorious Scrimshaw Street was the very last on the list. She locked the car carefully, put up her umbrella and lowered her head against the lashing rain as she stepped out along the puddled pavement.

Scrimshaw Street was unfamiliar territory, as so many of the other streets had been. She was beginning to realise how little she knew about the town she had grown up in, or the people who lived in it. This street was lined on either side with mean little red brick council houses, built between the wars. Many of the council estates she had canvassed were well kept, with neat gardens and fresh curtains at the windows. Some of the tenants had bought their houses and took a pride in them, paid their mortgage and council tax regularly and kept control over their pets and children. Not so here in Scrimshaw Street. Eleanor had warned her what to expect here, and now Julia saw that she hadn't exaggerated. Most of the front gardens were overgrown and strewn with rubbish, broken and discarded toys and rusting bicycles. Derelict-looking cars were parked on the pavements and the atmosphere of despair and apathy was almost tangible. The only advantage was that being a wet evening the street was free from marauding children.

Julia stood with her hand on the gate of number one, hesitating. From the cards attached to her clipboard she saw that the tenant here was a Miss Brownlow. Glancing up, she saw that there were no lights on. Maybe she was out. She was tired and it was getting late. Was it really worth canvassing a street like this? she wondered. Would these people actually bother to turn out to the polling station tomorrow? From the look of things they had little to lose or gain from exercising their right to vote, especially for a mere by-election. But this was the last street so she might as well go ahead now that she was here. She pushed open the rickety gate, walked up the path and knocked.

Somewhere inside she could hear a baby crying. She was struggling to hold on to her clipboard while folding her umbrella when the door opened an inch or two. She looked up to see a young girl looking at her enquiringly through the gap.

'Yes?'

'Good evening. Miss Brownlow?'

'That's right.'

Julia went into the routine that felt almost parrot-like by now. 'Hello, I'm Julia Grant, your Conservative candidate at the by-election tomorrow,' she said. Holding her umbrella and clipboard in one hand, she extended her fingers through the four-inch opening. The girl ignored them but Julia smiled and managed to hold her eyes. 'I'm sorry to call so late and I don't want to take up your time, but I wonder – can I count on your vote?'

The door closed abruptly and for a moment she thought she was being summarily snubbed, but the next moment she heard the chain being released and to her surprise the girl opened the door and held it wide. 'You'd better come in,' she said. 'You look as if you're getting wet out there.'

A little taken aback, Julia shook the raindrops from her umbrella and stepped inside. The poverty of the little house shocked her. There was no floor covering, even on the stairs, and the dark brown paintwork was chipped and peeling. The only light came from candles stuck into bottles, and shadows danced and leaped as the draught from the door stirred the flames. Julia saw now that the girl was no more than eighteen. She was very thin and her long fair hair was tied back with a piece of tape. Her skirt and cardigan, although clean and tidy, were clearly far from new. In the hall stood a pram in which a baby stirred restlessly.

'Go through,' the girl invited. 'Sorry about the mess but I couldn't get the washing dry today.'

There was a small fire burning in the living-room grate. Around it was a clothes horse hung with gently steaming nappies and baby clothes. Although spotless, the room was furnished very basically with a table, two chairs and one armchair covered in faded tapestry which the girl now indicated to Julia.

'Take the weight off your feet for a minute.' She looked towards the door. 'I put the baby out in the hall. The steam from the washing makes him chesty,' she said.

'Yes. Yes, I see.' Embarrassed, Julia sat down and looked again at her clipboard.

'Do you live here alone, Miss Brownlow?'

'That's right. Just me and baby. It's Tracey, by the way. Can I get you a coffee? I was just going to have one.'

'I don't want to put you to any trouble. I only came because . . .'

'It isn't any trouble,' the girl interrupted. 'It's nice to have a bit of company to tell you the truth.' Without waiting for Julia's reply she went into the kitchen and came back with two mugs on a tin tray. 'I've got a little spirit stove,' she explained. 'So that when they cut off the electric I can still manage.'

Julia took the mug from her, suddenly understanding the candlelight. 'They've cut off your electricity supply? But that's terrible! Do they know you have a tiny baby?'

'Oh, yes.' Tracey sounded resigned. 'But you can't have what you can't pay for and that's all about it. I just can't seem to manage on the benefit money and if I got a job I'd have to pay someone to look after baby.'

105

'How old is he?'

'Three months.' The girl sat on one of the chairs and pushed a stray strand of hair behind her ears. 'To tell you the truth, I wouldn't trust any of them round here with him anyway,' she said. 'Only interested in the money, they are. Know how to charge too! And God knows what they'd do with him once my back was turned.'

Julia took a sip of her coffee and tried to hide her horror and distress at the girl's plight. 'What about the baby's father?' she ventured. 'Wouldn't he pay something towards his child's keep? Couldn't the Child Support Agency make him?'

Tracey lifted her shoulders in a small helpless gesture. 'They'd have to find him first,' she said. 'Soon as he knew I was pregnant, he took off. I haven't seen him since, and if his mates know where he is they're not saying.'

'Your parents then?'

Tracey gave a wry little grin. 'There's only Mum and she don't want to know. She don't want her new boyfriend to know she's got a daughter my age. He's younger than her, see? She's frightened of losing him. She says I'll just have to manage the same as what she did.' Tracey looked around her with a resigned sigh. 'I know I was dead lucky to get this place, and once I get myself sorted I'll make it nice. I just need to be able to find a job where I can take Damian.'

'Damian?'

'My baby.' As though on cue he began to cry again and Tracey got up and went into the hall, returning with the child in her arms. 'He's hungry. Do you mind?'

'Not at all. Please go ahead.' Julia watched as the girl unbuttoned her blouse and gave one breast to the hungry baby who sucked greedily, his big blue eyes fixed on his mother's face and his fuzz of fair hair transformed by the flickering candlelight into a shining halo. As he fed he made satisfied little grunting noises and suddenly a memory that Julia thought she had buried forever flooded back with sharp and painful clarity.

She hadn't breast fed Charlotte, but she'd fed Dean's child, Fleur, for the first few weeks of her life. Now, watching the young mother and child wrapped in the sharing of this intimate and tender moment, she felt a lump tighten her throat and quick tears stung her eyes.

Tracey looked up at her. 'They wanted me to have him adopted when he was born,' she said, 'but how could I? Look at him. It's not his fault he's here, is it? I'd *never* part with him, whatever they did to me. He's all I've got.' She wrapped her cardigan round the baby's head and hugged him closer. 'I'm not a tart you know. I trusted his dad. I really loved him.'

As she transferred the child to her other breast her eyes were dreamy. 'We spent hours planning the way it'd all be when Rick found a job. We were going to get married with me in a lovely white dress – in a church and everything. I'd was training to be a hairdresser. I was good at it too. I had a job and I used to go to college one day every week. I had to give all that up to have Damian.' Her eyes hardened. 'Still, better off without a guy who lets you down like that, eh? We'll get through somehow, Damie and me.' She looked at Julia hopefully. 'I hadn't even thought about voting tomorrow, but if you could do something about getting some of the factories round here to have crèches so's single mums like me could go back to work and take the kids with us, I'd vote for you then all right, no sweat. I can think of a good many others round here who would too.'

Julia felt ashamed not to be able to promise. 'If I'm elected I'll certainly do all I can,' she said. 'It's a shame, being forced to live like this when you're willing to work.' She opened her handbag, fumbling for her cheque book. 'Look, how much is your electricity bill?'

Tracey flushed and waved her hand. 'No! Please, I wasn't looking for no handouts. I don't want you to think I was whingeing. My Giro comes any day now and then I'll pay it. We'll be all right, really.'

'Have you had anything to eat today?'

Tracey nodded. 'I'm okay – honest. Soon as the Giro comes I'll go round the supermarket, do a big shop.'

They went into the hall together and suddenly Tracey put the baby into her arms.

'Here, just hold him a minute while I straighten the pram, will you?'

Julia held the sleepy baby while Tracey rearranged the blankets. The warm feel of his fragile little body through the shawl and the sweet milky scent of him tugged at her heart.

'Thanks.' Tracey took him back, tucking him up warmly in his pram. 'Goodnight, Mrs Grant.' She opened the front door for Julia. 'It was really nice meeting you. Good luck for tomorrow. Us single mums want more like you sticking up for us.'

Julia sat in the car and watched the curtain of rain that streamed down the windscreen. What would that young woman say if she knew just how much they had in common? The difference was that Tracey had the guts to stand by her child, to struggle to keep him, while Julia had abandoned her baby in favour of an easy, soft life. If that girl knew what she was really like she wouldn't vote for her in a thousand years!

Holding the tiny baby in her arms had been so evocative, reminding her of things she hadn't even thought of for years. Suddenly she was back in Brightman Lane, Hackney, with Dolly and Maurice

Sylvester, in the cramped little flat over the shop where Dean had taken her after those three terrible months of touring with the group.

When Dean had impulsively asked her to stay with him after the Isle of Wight pop festival she had been delirious with happiness. Swearing Joanna to secrecy, she had telephoned her parents with a story about the old schoolfriend she had met during the weekend school trip to London, the job she had been offered and the flat she would share with two other girls who were now university students. They'd been a little apprehensive at first about the suddenness of her leaving home, but she'd talked them round. She'd felt a little ashamed at the readiness with which they had believed her lies, but the heady prospect of being with Dean, of being part of his career and helping him climb the spangled ladder to stardom, had eclipsed any guilt she might have felt.

She could not have foreseen the squalor and disquiet of the weeks that followed. The snatched meals and boredom of waiting around for endless hours while Dean was at concerts, rehearsals or just out searching for an agent or anyone who would give the group a recording contract. Worst of all, sharing accommodation with a series of fellow artists in flats that seemed to grow progressively more squalid. Sometimes, when a gig went on till the small hours, they even used the van as sleeping quarters, all of them sharing the confined space. At times like this it was only Julia who suffered from the extreme discomfort. The other members of the group, including Dean, were usually too stoned, either on drink or dope, to notice.

After the first few weeks of ecstatic lovemaking it was only too clear from Dean's attitude that for him the novelty had worn off. He'd even begun to hint that maybe she'd be better off at home. Julia was devastated. She was disillusioned with the kind of life they were living. It was not what she had been led to expect; a fact of which she constantly reminded him. She repeatedly pointed out that it could all be remedied if they just got a little place of their own. Why didn't he want to please her when he had said he loved her so much? she demanded.

Dean grew impatient with her, tired of her constant complaints. He was bored with her and did nothing to conceal the fact. She whined and nagged day and night, her nerves torn to shreds by his indifference. And the more she nagged, the more he ignored her. Only the other members of the group seemed affected by her truculence and soon they began to complain about it to Dean.

When she first discovered she was pregnant she thought that surely Dean would now be shaken into making a commitment? The realisation that he had no intention of doing any such thing brought her to the brink of panic. How could she have a baby when they had no proper home? When she asked him this, and he casually suggested that she should have an abortion, she became almost hysterical.

Finally the other members of the group gave Dean an ultimatum: either she went or they did. That was when, in sheer desperation, he took her to Hackney, to his parents, Dolly and Maurice.

Julia sat in her car outside the little house in Scrimshaw Street, the rest of her canvassing forgotten. Oblivious to the damp and cold, she made herself relive that May evening at the hospital when Dolly had sat with her all night, sharing the pain while holding her hand and telling her how proud she was of her, and how much she and Maurice looked forward to the grandchild they would hold in their arms tomorrow. Kind-hearted

110

Dolly, and Maurice with his gentle face and soft brown eyes, were good people, the best. But even Dolly couldn't help her bear that other pain – far worse than the pangs of childbirth. The excruciating, heartbreaking pain of knowing that Dean didn't want her, had never really loved her – couldn't care less whether she lived or died. And, in spite of Dolly's reassurance, Julia sensed that he wasn't coming back for her.

She remembered the weary weeks that followed, the sleepless nights, the endless routine of feeds, bathing and washing clothes for a child for whom she could feel nothing. The little girl with black curly hair, dark eyes and olive skin who was so like Dean and whose grandparents doted on her, was merely the symbol of her own folly and wasted life.

Week followed week and her belief that Dean must know the baby was born and come for them became an obsession. Then at last he came, unheralded one weekend, only to tell her that this would be the last time. He should never have taken her away from her own environment, he told her. Their relationship had been doomed from the start. His career was what he wanted to concentrate on – the only important thing in his life. He had been offered the chance to go to America and wanted to take it.

'Go home, Julia,' he had urged her. 'Go home where you belong and take the baby with you. I'm not cut out to be a husband and father. I don't think I ever will be.'

The cruel words rang in her head long after Dean had left. Every time she looked at the child she felt mocked and cheated – trapped into an endless round of poverty and helplessness. Homesickness for her parents and the comfortable life she had given up ate into her soul like acid until she was reduced to a mental and physical wreck, unable to eat, sleep or even think logically.

111

The decision to leave the child with Dolly and Maurice, to go home and make a fresh start, hadn't seemed momentous at the time. It had come to her in the early hours of one morning as she lay awake after another sleepless night. The thought had hit her with a blinding clarity. Suddenly it all seemed ridiculously simple – like a revelation. It was the answer to all her problems and she couldn't imagine why she hadn't thought of it before. She had always known that taking Fleur home with her was out of the question. Her parents were still happily under the impression that she had a job in London and was sharing a flat with friends. She had written regularly, her letters filled with fabrications about the good job she had, the happy and fulfilled life she was enjoying. Arriving home with a baby of mixed blood would shock them more than words could tell. None of them would ever survive the stares and the gossip of all their acquaintances in Elvemere. It would ruin everything: her father's business, her mother's social standing in the town. Julia could not subject them to it.

She had done it without giving herself time to think, rising early and writing the note, packing her few clothes. As she stood looking down at the sleeping dark-haired baby, she had felt a slight pang, no more. She knew that Fleur would be cared for and loved here with her grandparents. She had no fears about that. No one could love her more than they did. This was where she belonged, with her own people. Julia, her mother, belonged elsewhere.

She had been home for almost a week before it hit her. She missed her baby with a crippling guilt and an ache in her heart that was almost unendurable. The tight bud of mother-love, that had never fully opened, suddenly flowered with as much pain as birth and death combined. It was almost as though she had left a

112

part of herself behind. The anguish was made worse by the fact that there was no one she could tell, no one to confide in. Every time she saw a pram she had to force herself to resist looking into it. Children at play brought a lump to her throat, as did the sight of a pregnant woman or a young couple absorbed in their new baby. And all the time she had to hide these feelings, suppress her agony and force herself to smile.

Meeting Vernon had helped a little. Handsome and personable, newly home from university and fired with ideas for the family business, he had lifted her spirits and restored her confidence. Her parents were pleased at their friendship and so were Vernon's. The two of them were almost precipitated into marriage, urged on by the prospective merging of the two firms. Julia had allowed herself to be carried along on the tide of approval. Life with Vernon would be safe and comfortable. She did not feel the headlong excitement she had experienced with Dean, but it didn't matter. Marriage to Vernon would be safe. Never again need she know heartbreak or loss. Little did she know!

Their engagement was a foregone conclusion and within a year they were married. It had taken years and another baby girl in her arms finally to obliterate the pain of losing Dean and baby Fleur. But tonight she had remembered the way she had felt as though it were yesterday. Tracey Brownlow had made her realise anew how despicable, how cowardly, her action had been. Tracey would never abandon her child. She would stand by him whatever happened. And when he grew up he would be proud of his mother and all that she had sacrificed to keep him. If only Julia could have had an ounce of Tracey's courage all those years ago, how different life might have been. But perhaps it was not too late? If she were to be elected tomorrow, maybe she could try to pay back the debt she owed.

Starting the car, she began to head for home. On the corner of the next road a fish and chip shop was doing good business. The bright lights from its windows shone out through the driving rain, making the pavements glisten. On impulse Julia stopped the car and got out to join the queue.

Ten minutes later she was knocking on the door of number one Scrimshaw Street again. Tracey opened the door a crack and peered out into the gloom.

'Who is it? Oh, Mrs Grant!'

Julia thrust the newspaper-wrapped parcel into her arms. 'Here, have supper on me,' she said. 'You have to keep your strength up for Damian's sake.' And before Tracey could argue she had fled to the shelter of the car, started the engine and headed once more for home.

It was almost midnight the following night before the count was completed. Julia had been up since seven, dividing her day between the polling station and party committee rooms. She had been here in the school hall since nine o'clock when the polling stations closed. She had watched the sealed black ballot boxes arrive and seen their contents tipped onto the waiting tables. Sitting mesmerised, she had watched as the tellers sorted the papers and bundled them, later meticulously recording the votes on the forms provided. She had watched as the column with her own name at the top lengthened. Success became at first hopeful, then likely. Finally the knot in her stomach tightened as that likelihood became a definite possibility.

She had applied for two tickets to attend the count, hoping that Vernon and Charlotte would accompany and support her, but both had announced that they were too busy so in the end her parents had come. Harry and May sat on their hard chairs at the back of the hall, looking weary as the waiting hours ticked by.

114

But now the final lull had arrived and the tellers sat back, rubbing their stiff necks and heaving sighs of relief as they waited for the Recording Officer to make his final calculations.

Harry and May roused themselves at the prospect that the result was at last imminent, welcoming Julia, who joined them looking pale and tense. May reached into the bag she had brought and produced a flask of hot coffee. She poured it into three mugs, handing her daughter and husband one each.

'Here, I'm sure we can all do with this.'

But before Julia could raise the mug to her lips, the Recording Officer rose from his seat in the centre of the hall and nodded to the four candidates to join him. On trembling legs, Julia crossed the hall to where the small hopeful huddle had gathered. It was through a daze that she heard him tell her she had received the greatest number of votes and was therefore the elected candidate.

The other three melted away and, in a kind of dream, she was mounting the steps of the platform for the announcement. A storm of applause greeted it and the first person to congratulate her was Eleanor Maitland.

Flinging her arms around her she said, 'Well done, girl. You're going to be the best councillor Elvemere has ever seen. Sock it to them, lass! Drag them into the twenty-first century. *I know you can do it!*'

Julia knew then that she had been handed the biggest challenge of her life. Briefly she heard an echo of Tracey Brownlow's words. *Us single mums want more like you sticking up for us.* Till last night she'd had no special cause to fight for. Now she had. People were counting on her. She wouldn't – couldn't – let them down.

At the back of the hall May Philips looked at her husband with a smile. 'Well, Harry, she's done it. Aren't you proud?'

115

He sighed and pushed at the bridge of his glasses. 'Of course I'm proud, dear,' he said. 'She's done well – very well.' But privately he was remembering Charlie Grant's words and wondering just what his daughter had let herself in for.

Chapter 5

'Well, I think that about wraps it up for tonight, unless there's any other business?'

Vernon, who was chairing Grant Philips Construction's monthly board meeting, looked up at his father and father-in-law, hoping that neither of them would bring anything further up. He had an urgent appointment at eight and it was already twenty to.

Charlie Grant cleared his throat and nodded to the secretary taking the minutes. 'Right, that's it, Jennifer, lass. You can go now.'

'Thank you, Mr Grant.' The girl closed her notebook and left. When the door had closed behind her and his father remained seated, taking out his pipe and tobacco pouch, Vernon's heart sank.

'Now then – there's this business about Victoria Gardens,' the older man began, packing tobacco carefully into his pipe.

Vernon groaned inwardly as he glanced at his watch. He'd certainly be late if they got onto that. 'Nothing's been settled about that, Dad,' he said. 'It's only a wild rumour as yet.'

'Don't you believe it.' Charlie waved him to silence. 'It'll go ahead all right. I had it on good authority –

from Jack Martin, not long before his last heart attack – that the Gardens were definitely scheduled for redevelopment.' He frowned impatiently at the two doubtful faces opposite him. 'You have to get in on these things before they become public knowledge,' he said, accentuating his remark with a thump on the table. 'How do you think we've been successful in all our other council ventures? By getting inside information and then getting off our arses before anyone else. That's how!'

Harry Philips frowned. 'Do you think perhaps it was just a bit of guessing on Jack's part, Charlie? After all, he hadn't been attending council meetings regularly for some time and might have been out of touch or got the wrong end of the stick – anything.'

'Not Jack,' Charlie said vehemently. 'In all the years I knew him he was never out of touch. He was very seldom wrong about anything either. Had a nose for these things did Jack. He may have been badly over the last couple of years but he was far from senile. Now . . .' He leaned his arms on the table. 'His information was that there's to be a new library built on the town side of the gardens and a health centre on the side nearest the park. In between, there'll be offices at ground level – solicitors, accountants, that kind of thing. All top-class professional people, 'cause from what I can make out the rents'll be upper limit. Then, this health centre – it's to be the kind of place where they have everything under one roof. You know, dentists, doctors, physio-what-d'you-call-'ems. You know, like a kind of health *supermarket*.' Pleased with his own joke he leaned back, waving his pipe at them expansively. 'That whole area will be completely refurbished. The job'll be worth a packet. If we get in sharp like, we could get that contract, and the money we make out of it will help finance the new executive estate at Meadowlands. Plans for that should be passed at the next meeting.'

'But we haven't done that kind of thing before, Dad,' Vernon pointed out. 'It'd take ages and we want to get on with the Meadowlands project.'

'So – we take on more men,' his father said.

Vernon frowned. 'Yes, but so far we've always built from scratch. Those buildings are listed so we wouldn't have a free hand. We'd have to abide by strict specifications. And another thing: once you start pulling old buildings like that about, you never know what you're letting yourself in for. We could end up out of pocket.'

'Never!' Charlie leaned back and lit his pipe. 'Trouble with you, Vernon, is you've got no vision. You might be good at the business side of things, but it's *vision* you want! The ability to see ahead like I've always had. Make no mistake, we wouldn't be sitting round this table now if it hadn't been for my business instincts. Just you get that architect feller we used for Meadowlands to do some preliminary plans, lad. He'll know all about listed buildings – what you can pull down and what you can't. He should do, he bloody charges enough! You get on and cost the job out and I'll drop hints in all the right places. Then we'll sit back and wait till the time's right.'

'When it's announced officially, you mean?'

'Oh, before that, lad. *Long* before. You can leave that part to me.' Charlie tapped the side of his nose. 'I'll get wind of it on the grapevine.'

'At a Lodge meeting, you mean?' Vernon said with a wry smile.

'All right, but don't knock it! I mean GPC to be first in with a chance. If our ideas are original and the estimate pleases them we'll get the job. We can juggle with the figures when we've got them good and interested.' He puffed hard on his pipe, then blew out a cloud of smoke and looked at the other two. 'I mean it. I've set my heart on this one. Handle it right and we'll get

Meadowlands off the ground without having to go cap in hand to the bank, so think on.'

Vernon nodded. He had to admit that getting the contract for Victoria Gardens would certainly be a coup. And if his father's business methods were less than ethical, they certainly weren't new. 'Right, I'll get onto it.' He looked from one to the other of the older men. 'Well, if that's all . . .'

'What about the new secretary?' Harry asked. 'We haven't talked about that at all yet. I seem to remember at the last meeting there were about a dozen applications. Don't we need to make a shortlist – arrange a date for interviewing? After all, Jennifer's notice will be up the week after next.'

'I've already chosen a secretary,' Vernon said, shuffling his papers. 'Someone I know was among the applicants. She's very competent and experienced – up with all the latest computer skills. In fact, I think she'll make a very good PA once she's settled in.'

Harry frowned. 'You mean, you've already engaged her?'

'Subject to a few loose ends, yes.'

'Isn't that rather irregular, Vernon?' He looked across the table at his partner. 'Did you know about it, Charlie?'

He shrugged. 'Not till now, but it's Vernon who'll have to work with the woman most of the time and if he's happy with her, I'm content to trust his judgement.' He glanced at his son. 'Who is it anyway? Anyone I know?'

'I don't think so. Her name is Mrs Hanson. She lived in Elvemere as a young girl, until she married and went to live in America. Recently she was divorced and now she's come back to settle here.'

'An older woman then?'

Vernon lifted his shoulders. 'Well – older than

120

Jennifer. Who can tell nowadays? At least she won't be running off to start a family.'

'That's a point.' Charlie sucked on his pipe and regarded his son speculatively. One of Vernie's old flames? Ah, well, it was nothing to do with him, or with Harry Philips either if it came to that. Just so long as you kept your private life and business in separate watertight compartments and didn't mess around with other men's wives, nothing could go too badly wrong. At least, that had always been his maxim. Aloud he said, 'Right then. If there's nothing more I suggest we all retire to The Hat and Feathers for a little libation, as they say.'

'Not for me tonight, Dad,' Vernon said, gathering up his papers and pushing them into his briefcase. 'I've got to be somewhere else and I'm already late. See you at the office tomorrow. Goodnight.'

In the car park of the GPC building the two older men got into Charlie's Mercedes and headed towards the town and their favourite hostelry.

'A great pity we've lost old Jack, you know,' Charlie said thoughtfully as he negotiated the traffic in the town centre. 'A good friend and ally, he was. We'll miss him.' He glanced at his partner. 'Julia's done well to get in. Pleased, was she?'

Harry nodded. 'According to her mother she's working very hard at it already. Out all hours apparently. Seems she's taking her duties very seriously.'

'Mmm. Let's hope she remembers which side her bread is buttered, 'specially as she's on the planning committee,' Charlie said dryly. 'She could be a big help to us if she plays her cards right.'

Harry bit his lip. He'd been secretly dismayed when he heard that his daughter was to be involved with planning. Privately he considered it bad enough her being elected to the Town Council, but being on the planning committee would put her in an impossible situation. Charlie had absolutely no scruples when it came to business. When he decided to put the pressure on he could be quite ruthless. In his book anything was fair and the word 'corruption' simply wasn't in his vocabulary. Although to his shame Harry had benefited amply from his partner's devious methods in the past, he had no wish to see his daughter mixed up in them.

'I hear that Councillor Mrs Maitland has been a great help to her,' he said into the silence.

'Lena Maitland, eh?' Charlie gave a snorting chuckle. 'There was a lass for you, if ever there was one. I could tell you a tale or two about her! She and I almost got engaged once, you know. Oh, years ago when we were both n'more than kids. Chucked me for that Jim Maitland. A plate-layer on the railway! I ask you! Real choked I was at the time. Still, reckon I had a lucky escape, eh? She's turned into a right old battle-axe since. Left-wing as they come, even if she does pretend to be Tory.'

Charlie turned into the car park of The Hat and Feathers and neatly parked the Merc in his favourite space. 'You want to have a word with your Julia, Harry lad,' he said, unfastening his seat belt. 'You know, father to daughter, like. I've warned our Vernon – wives want keeping under your thumb. Give these modern lasses an inch and before you know it they've taken the whole of the bloody M1! Maybe you could tip her the wink about this council thing; point her in the right direction.' He punched Harry's shoulder play-fully. 'Young chaps nowadays can't hold a candle to us old 'uns when it comes to knowing how to handle a woman, eh, Harry lad?'

'No, well . . .' Harry Philips coughed nervously. 'I daresay you're right.' He turned to look at his partner.

'About this new secretary ... Don't you think we should make a proper shortlist and interview everyone? It doesn't seem very fair the way Vernon's handling it.'

Charlie turned to look at him. 'Like I said, he will be working with her most of the time so let him have the choice. You see, Harry, the trouble with Vernon is that he's got no imagination. He can't see any further than a balance sheet. Sometimes he complains we don't give him enough say in things, so I reckon this is a good way to let him think he's making a decision.' He nudged Harry in the ribs and winked broadly. 'Take my tip and let him have his head on this one, Harry. It'll keep him quiet – for the time being at least.'

After Vernon had watched the two older men drive away he got into his own car and drove off in the opposite direction. His destination was the Fairwoods Country Club and Motel halfway between Elvemere and Merifield, the nearest village.

When he drew onto the forecourt he felt a little frisson of excitement at the thought of the coming meeting with Jo Hanson. So far they'd only spoken on the telephone and that was when he'd suggested meeting away from the office instead of the usual formal interview. The Fairwoods Country Club had been her idea. It was where she'd been staying since her recent return to England.

When he'd received her application and read the little note she'd enclosed in a separate sealed envelope he'd been surprised. He hadn't seen her for something like twenty years, just before she'd run off with an American airman and got married.

They'd had a brief, torrid affair the year before he had married Julia – when he was twenty-three and just beginning to work for his father. Jo had been seventeen at the time, but more exciting and passionate than any other girl he'd known. Certainly more experienced. Their affair had been too frenetic and fiery to last and had burned itself out after a couple of months, after which the American serviceman had loomed onto the horizon, presumably sweeping her off her feet. But Vernon had never forgotten Jo. She wasn't the kind of girl a man easily forgets.

Switching off the engine, he adjusted the rearview mirror to examine his reflection, wondering if she would think he had changed. Taking out his comb, he flicked it through his hair, grateful it was still thick and wavy. The streaks of silver over his ears were attractive and sophisticated, he had been told. Sexy even. Anyway forty-three wasn't exactly over the hill, was it? He was in his prime.

Would she have changed? he wondered. He pictured the long thick hair, a rich dark red like old mahogany, and the sultry green eyes that could burn with passion or flash with temper. Oh, yes, Jo had been a powerfully attractive woman, even at seventeen. Had marriage and divorce dimmed and disillusioned her, or would her experience of life have brought a fascinating new depth to her character? There was only one way to find out, he told himself.

He saw her at once, sitting alone at a table in the corner of the garden bar were they had arranged to meet. She didn't see him at first and he had time to observe her from the doorway. She looked a little older, more mature, but it suited her. The lines of her jaw and cheekbones, softly blurred in her teens, were now sharper and more defined, deepening the shadows under cheekbones and eyes. And the hair . . . He was pleased to see that its colour was as rich as before. The style was different, of course. He missed the luxuriant waist-length sweep he remembered, but the short sophisticated feathery style she wore now accentuated the new sensual contours of her face.

She turned towards the door, saw him and lifted her hand. As he returned her wave and crossed the room towards her he saw that her eyes were the same. Large and lustrous, a deep, deep green, the heavy lids giving them that mysterious brooding look he remembered so well. He felt his stomach lurch.

She stood up and held out her hand. 'Vernon. How lovely to see you again after all these years.'

He shook her hand. 'Jo. How are you?' He took in the charcoal grey suit and silky cream shirt, the understated gold jewellery. Her taste in clothes had matured too, along with her figure; a little more rounded, perhaps, but still as stunning and alluring as ever.

'I'm fine. It was very good of you to agree to meet me here. So much nicer than a formal interview.' She sat down again and indicated the chair next to her. 'I took the liberty of getting you a whisky and dry ginger. That used to be your favourite, didn't it?'

'Still is. Fancy you remembering.' He sat down and lifted the glass, intrigued by the slight trans-Atlantic accent she had acquired. He remembered the way those husky tones had once had the power to make his heart race.

'Here's to the future. I hope you're going to like working at GPC.'

'I'm sure I shall. I must say it was marvellous of you to offer me the job so promptly. Are you sure it's all right with your father?'

Vernon felt his colour heighten. Did she imagine he was still running around like an office boy as he had been before she left? 'I don't need his permission,' he said stiffly. 'I'm the firm's general manager now.'

'Of course. I'm sorry.' He was aware of her, watching him from under lowered lids as she took a sip of her own drink. 'I've brought you my references,' she said, opening her handbag. 'They're all from my previous employers in the States, of course, but you could always ring them for quick confirmation.'

'I wouldn't dream of it.' He waved away the handful of letters she passed him. 'Put them away. If I can't take the word of an old friend . . .'

'So – when would you like me to start?'

'In two weeks' time, if that's all right? Meantime you must come into the office one day soon and look round – let Jennifer acquaint you with the routine.'

'Jennifer?'

'My present secretary. The girl who's leaving. She's getting married and going to live down south. She's been with me since leaving school and she's very good, but now that I'm replacing her I'm looking for someone who can eventually take more responsibility – work on her own initiative, more of a PA in other words. We're taking on more and more work all the time, you see. There are plans for going much further out of town. I have to be away from the office more and I need someone capable to leave in charge.'

She smiled. 'Sounds fascinating.'

'Your salary will be adjusted once that happens, of course.'

'Of course.'

'I'm sure you'll make a very capable PA.'

'It's in line with the work I've been doing over in the States. I was with a real-estate company in Denver for the past two years, so I hope I shall live up to your expectations.'

'I'm sure you will.'

She regarded him in that direct way of hers that made his spine tingle. 'What have you been doing all these years, Vernon?' she asked. 'It's so long since I left Elvemere, I've got an awful lot of catching up to do.'

'Well, as you must have realised, the family firm has expanded. I'll have to take you on a guided tour of all our sites.'

'I've certainly noticed a lot of changes. I'd hardly have recognised the place, the town has grown so.'

'We've been responsible for a large part of that. I daresay you've seen the new industrial estate? We were heavily involved in that. We've been very successful since we merged with Philips Electricals.'

'Yes, I wondered about the Philips part. That wouldn't be the Harry Philips who used to have the little electrical shop in the High Street, would it?'

'That's right. He branched out into plumbing and heating later. When Dad heard he was planning to expand, he offered him a partnership.'

'Well, well! His daughter Julia and I were friends at school. I wonder what became of her?'

Vernon cleared his throat. 'As a matter of fact, I – er – married her.'

She threw back her head and laughed. 'I *see*! A family merger in more ways than one. How is she?'

'As a matter of fact she's just been elected to the Town Council,' Vernon told her. 'She's so busy I hardly ever see her these days.'

She looked at him speculatively. 'Do I detect a slight note of resentment?'

He laughed. 'Good heavens, no,' he lied. 'Julia and I have always done our own thing. I've always believed that women should use their skills and talents in whatever way they can.'

'I see. Any little Grants?'

'One. A daughter, Charlotte.'

'Congratulations!'

'Oh, she's hardly little any more – sixteen – just passed her GCSEs.'

'And going into the family business?'

127

'Yes, but I'm insisting she does it from the bottom up, just like I had to.'

'In this day and age?' She looked at him, one eyebrow raised. 'Are educated young people still willing to join their family businesses on those terms?'

'Oh, yes! She's quite happy about it. She's a bright girl. She knows she can only benefit in the long run.' Vernon wasn't too keen on the way the conversation was going. It made him feel very attached and very old. 'But that's enough about me,' he said with a light laugh. He leaned forward and treated her to his special intimate smile. 'What about you, Jo? What brought you back to Elvemere?'

'I'd had enough of America, especially after my second divorce.' She glanced up at him. 'Oh, yes, I'm afraid marriage has been a bit of a non-starter as far as I'm concerned. I've decided to concentrate on my career from now on.'

'So you decided to come home.'

'Yes. I was never all that keen on life in the States anyway. Somehow I never really seemed to fit in. I think I've always been essentially British.'

He tossed back the last of his drink. 'Well, their loss is our gain. Another drink?'

She looked at her watch. 'No time, I'm afraid. I'll have to be going.'

'Oh. You're not still living here then?'

'No.'

To his considerable disappointment she began to gather up her bag and gloves. 'I'll walk you to your car,' he said quickly.

As they crossed the forecourt he wondered where she was going. Did she have a date – was there already a new man? 'You've found somewhere permanent to live then?' he asked. 'If you'd told me you were looking I could have helped you.'

'I've bought a house in Hazel Grove just off the Merifield Road. Do you know it?'

Vernon grinned. 'I should do. It's one of ours. We built that estate soon after we merged. They're nice houses. Small but well-planned.'

'Yes, compact and warm. That's one thing one gets used to in the States. Central heating and air conditioning are counted as necessities over there. I moved in last week.' She turned to smile at him as she unlocked the door of a little scarlet Mazda. 'I'll have to give a house warming party. You must bring your family round. It'd be fun to see Julia again.'

Vernon watched as she settled herself into the driving seat and fastened her seat belt. 'Give me a ring and say when you'd like to come into the office and look round,' he shouted, stepping back as she started to move the car forward.

She smiled up at him through the window. 'I will – soon. 'Bye, Vernon. And thanks again.'

Walking to his own car he felt flat. The meeting had disappointed him. She'd given not the slightest indication that she remembered the passionate affair they'd enjoyed. He sighed. He'd been fooling himself. What had he expected? He reflected that he had probably been one of many such lovers in those far off days. Why should she have remembered him? Since then she had been halfway round the world and had two husbands, whilst he had scarcely stirred from Elvemere, Grant Philips Construction and Julia. As he headed back to Elvemere he wondered whether to tell his wife that her schoolfriend, the former Joanna Bloom, was back in town? Then, for reasons he was reluctant to acknowledge, he decided against it.

'I'd like to stay on permanently, if that's all right with you, Mrs Franks?'

129

Fleur had come down to the basement flat to pay her rent and felt that the time was right to broach the subject of the flat. Her little room under the eaves was bitterly cold now that the winter was close on the heels of autumn. Derek Jones had already moved out and she knew the flat hadn't been advertised yet.

Ivy looked up from counting the notes in her hand and took the half-smoked cigarette from her mouth. 'Oh, you would, would you?'

'But not in the room I'm in now.' Fleur took a deep breath. 'I hear you haven't advertised Mr Jones's flat.'

'Oh?' Ivy's eyes narrowed. 'And where did you hear that?'

'You mean, you have?'

'I might and I might not have. But what would you want with a flat anyway?'

'I could make more of a home of it,' Fleur said. 'And I like the little balcony. I've seen it from the garden.'

'Mmm, I daresay you would like it – along with a good many others.' Ivy stuffed the notes into her capacious handbag, put the smouldering cigarette back between her lips and folded her arms. 'I could let that flat ten times over if I'd a mind to. And I seem to remember telling you I was only letting you have that room on a tem'pry basis.'

'That's right. Which is why I'd like to rent the flat,' Fleur said firmly. 'I've got a steady job and I'm willing to pay the same rent as Mr Jones.'

'Oh! I expect you know what that is too, do you?'

'Not exactly, but obviously I'd expect it to be more than I pay now.'

'Too right it is! In fact I was thinking of putting it up,' Ivy said. 'I could double what I ask for that flat if I'd a mind to. My trouble is, I'm my own worst enemy. Too soft by half, I am.'

Fleur turned away, trying to hide the irritation she

felt. Ivy was playing her like a fish on a line and she wasn't having it. 'I see,' she said. 'In that case, I'd better give you my notice. I don't want any favours, Mrs Franks, but now that the winter is almost here I'll have to find something more comfortable.' At the door she turned. 'Shall we say a fortnight's notice as from today?' She was almost through the door when Ivy said, 'Hang on – wait a minute! You're a bit sharp off the mark, aren't you? You might give a body a chance to think, springing things on me like that.' She regarded Fleur speculatively. 'I expect you want to stay here to be near your feller. That it?'

Fleur frowned. 'Feller?'

Ivy winked. 'Come off it. You know who I mean. Young Tom.' She smirked. 'Planning some romantic little candle-lit suppers for two, are you?'

'I just want somewhere to live, Mrs Franks – somewhere a bit better than where I am now. It has nothing to do with Tom.'

'Why has he been dropping hints about you then?'

Fleur felt her colour rise. 'What kind of hints?'

'About how he hoped you'd be staying on permanent like.' Ivy nodded and grinned knowingly. 'Reminding me what a nice girl you are and what a good tenant; hinting that he'd like me to let you stay here.'

Fleur felt resentment pricking at her. What made Tom think he had the right to speak on her behalf? She could fight her own corner. 'I did mention it to him, but you're quite wrong, Mrs Franks. Tom and I are friends – nothing more,' she said. 'I'd no idea he'd said anything to you, and if you're putting the rent up it'll probably be out of my reach anyway so maybe I should forget it.'

'Now then, no need to get uppity,' Ivy chided. She looked at Fleur's indignant expression for a moment, then said, 'Okay. I've got used to you now and you've been a good tenant so far. Better the devil you know, I suppose. You can have it for what Derek paid. That suit you?'

Fleur's heart gave an excited leap, but she kept her voice level. 'Thank you, Mrs Franks, that'll be fine.'

'You can move your stuff in any time you like seein' it's empty and you're all paid up.' She treated Fleur to one of her rare smiles. 'You're right to keep that young Tom in his place,' she said. 'Too much casual sex these days, if you ask me. Only starts 'em thinking they own you. Oh, and by the way, I think it's time you started calling me Ivy like the others.'

'Of course. There's just one thing . . .'

Ivy lit a new cigarette from the disintegrating stub of the old one, squinting up sideways at Fleur as she did so. 'Go on then. I can always say no.'

'Would you mind if I decorated it? The flat, I mean.'

Ivy gave a cackle of laughter. 'Why should I mind that? S'long as you don't want to paint it black with pink spots, you can do as you like.'

Fleur was settling down well to her job with Arden Catering. As well as the evening classes in computer studies, she had begun a course of driving lessons. She had very little free time but that was the way she liked it.

Sally Arden had discovered that Fleur had a light hand with pastry and taught her to make the quiches that she was famous for as well as some of her other celebrated recipes. In return Fleur had given Sally some of the Caribbean recipes she had learned from her grandfather which Dolly had cooked regularly when they were together as a family in Hackney.

As they worked together in the gleaming kitchen

that Sally had built onto her home. Fleur learned more about her new employer; about the brief marriage that had ended so tragically and her dedication to her only son, Peter, whom she had worked so hard to send to his father's old school just as they'd always planned. Peter Arden was now an under manager in a large London hotel.

'He could have done anything,' Sally told her. 'Medicine, law, journalism. But that was what he'd always wanted. Of course I insisted that he must do it the right way,' she added. 'He took a course in business and hotel management at college after leaving school, then he went to work in a large hotel in Switzerland for a year. He's had experience in every in every department from the kitchens up. He could turn his hand to the job of anyone in the hotel from the maître d' and chef to the manager's secretary or receptionist.'

'He sounds very efficient,' Fleur said.

'Oh, he is. He has the charm and diplomacy to go with it too. And the good looks,' Sally added. 'I'll show you his photograph some time.'

But Fleur had already seen Peter Arden's photograph. It was once when Sally had forgotten her reading glasses and sent Fleur up to her bedroom for them. Out of a silver frame on the little table beside her bed a handsome dark-haired young man smiled. His hair was thick and well-groomed and his eyes a soft, twinkling hazel like his mother's. Fleur had guessed at the time that he must be Peter.

As Christmas approached Arden Catering grew very busy indeed. As well as the usual parties there were the more formal buffet dances and executive Christmas lunches, given by various local firms. One of these was a boardroom lunch at the premises of Grant Philips Construction on the industrial estate.

They arrived early with their assortment of boxes

and equipment, and were shown up to the boardroom by an exquisitely groomed woman with red hair. Fleur set to work, laying the long table with Sally's snowy damask cloth and elegant cutlery and glasses. Working quickly and deftly as she'd learned, she folded the napkins into water lily shapes and set the pretty flower arrangement of bronze and yellow chrysanthemums in the centre of the table.

When it was done she joined Sally in the small adjoining kitchen where she was carving the pre-cooked turkey and unpacking the vegetables from their insulated boxes. In places like this where there were no cooking facilities, a hot lunch was more of a challenge, but Sally had the task worked out to a fine art.

'You can change now, if you like,' she told Fleur over her shoulder as she put plates to warm in the microwave they took everywhere with them. 'Then take the wine out of the cool box and uncork it. By the time I've dished up they'll be ready for their pre-lunch drinks.'

At exactly twelve-forty-five the door opened and the party came in. They seemed to be in a jovial mood and Fleur was waiting with her tray of drinks: sherry, dry and medium, orange juice or mineral water. There were two older men, whom she took to be Mr Grant and Mr Philips; a younger, rather suave-looking man in what looked like an Armani suit; the elegant woman who had shown them to the boardroom; and two other men whom she gathered were a senior sales executive and a transport manager. They took drinks from her tray and chatted in a relaxed way. Fleur was just about to go back into the kitchen when the man in the designer suit stepped in front of her.

'*Hello* there! I don't think I've seen you before.'

She smiled. 'No, I've only worked with Mrs Arden since October.'

He gave her an appraising look. 'And unless I'm mistaken you don't come from around here.'

'No. From London.'

He nodded wisely. 'I knew it. The young women in this part of the world just haven't the style. I could see at once . . .'

'I'm sorry but I'll have to go,' Fleur said, edging away. 'There's only Mrs Arden and me and I think your meal is ready to serve.'

'My dear, of course. Thoughtless of me. What's your name?'

'Fleur.'

He smiled. 'Charming. Well, Fleur, we don't stand on ceremony here so there's no need to be afraid.'

'I'm not!'

He laid a warm hand on her arm. 'My wife and I were thinking of having a party at our home for New Year. If we engage Mrs Arden to do the catering, I shall insist on making it a condition that you'll be coming along too.'

'I see – er – thank you, but I would anyway.'

'Well, isn't that a stroke of luck? I shall speak to her about it this evening.'

Fleur went quickly into the kitchen with her empty tray and closed the door. Sally looked at her flushed face.

'Did you have a job to get away?'

'You saw then? Who was that man who was talking to me?'

'That's Vernon Grant. He's the boss's son and general manager of GPC. He's got a bit of an eye for a pretty girl, so I hear.' She laughed. 'But you've just discovered that! I'm sure you can cope.'

Fleur said nothing, deciding that the man's behaviour must be an occupational hazard. She served the starter, a delicious concoction of prawns and grapefruit.

135

Vernon Grant kept giving her encouraging smiles as she worked her way round the table. To her embarrassment he even attempted once to draw her into the conversation. She suspected that he'd already taken more than a glass or two of something alcoholic before the party began. Beside him sat his private secretary, the sophisticated red-head with the slight American accent whose name she now knew was Mrs Hanson. She looked increasingly annoyed each time her boss addressed Fleur with such familiarity, and twice she saw her lay a discreetly restraining hand on his wrist and give him a reproachful look.

In the kitchen she told Sally of the embarrassing situation. 'I wish he'd stop,' she said. 'Can't he see that I'm just trying to do my job? I'm being discreet and unobtrusive just like you've taught me, but he isn't making it very easy.'

Sally smiled. 'Don't worry. This is the first time you've encountered a man like that but I'm afraid it won't be the last. Try to ignore it.'

'I think he's had a bit too much to drink.'

'I'm sure he has,' Sally said wryly. 'Just keep reminding yourself of how awful he's going to feel when he's sober.'

'And his secretary looks so annoyed,' Fleur said, watching as Sally sliced the delicious home-made chocolate gâteau.

The older woman paused in her work and frowned thoughtfully. 'You know, I have the oddest feeling I've seen that woman somewhere before. It's been bothering me ever since we arrived. Apparently she's fairly new here – been living in America. But I could have sworn . . .'

'I wouldn't have thought there were many like her around,' Fleur remarked as she loaded her tray with plates. 'If you'd met her before, you'd remember.'

'Yes, and if you ask me she's got trouble written all over her,' Sally said quietly.

Joanna Hanson drove her car into the garage and unclasped her seat belt. Vernon turned to her.

'It's very good of you to do this for me, Jo, but I would have been perfectly all right.'

'All right my foot,' she said bluntly. 'The police are especially vigilant at this time of year and you must be way over the limit. I'll make you a pot of strong black coffee and then later, when you've sobered up enough, I'll drive you back to the yard to get your own car.'

Vernon got out of the car and followed her into the house. As she unlocked the front door and they stepped into the hall, he looked around with admiration. She had made good use of mirrors to enhance the space in the small square hall. Twin gilt-framed ones were placed on either side, facing each other and reflecting light from the window, and the rose pink carpet and white walls helped provide a warm welcoming feel to the house. 'Well, I must say, this is very nice,' he said, nodding his approval.

'I'm glad you like it.' She took off her coat and held out her hand for his. 'I like nice things. My parents favoured a rather spartan way of living. My tastes are a little more affluent. My last divorce settlement was generous, so why not?'

'Why not indeeed!' Vernon walked through into the living room where glass doors gave onto a circular conservatory filled with green plants and cane furniture. The living-room chairs and carpets were of soft cream leather, strewn with pastel-coloured cushions, and the walls and lampshades were a delicate shade of peach. He noticed that there were two original paintings by lesser French Impressionists on the walls. As he sank into one of the cream leather chairs Joanna slid a

CD of Vivaldi's *Four Seasons* into a music centre discreetly concealed on a book shelf and a moment later the lush string music billowed into the room.

He leaned back to close his eyes. 'Mmm, very restful.'

'I'll make you that coffee,' she said.

After a few minutes he got up and followed her through to the kitchen. The decor here was in pale shades too: ivory cupboards and worktops, beige and white ceramic tiles on the floor. Only the curtains added a splash of colour with their design of sunflowers.

The coffee machine was already bubbling and Joanna had laid a tray with cups and put a jug of milk into the microwave to heat. Vernon looked around him with interest.

'Funny, although we built these houses, I've never been into one of them after it was occupied,' he remarked. 'Except for the show house, this is the first one I've ever seen furnished.'

She glanced at him. 'I don't suppose there's any reason why you should.' She turned to look at him. 'Vernon, don't you think you should ring your wife? She'll be wondering where you are.'

He leaned against the worktop and folded his arms. 'She's sure to be out,' he said gloomily. 'Since she got elected to the council she's hardly ever in.'

The microwave pinged and Joanna took out the jug of milk and set it on the tray. 'Poor Vernon. Are you feeling terribly deprived?'

He shrugged. 'Not particularly. I must admit I don't enjoy eating alone, though.'

'What about little Charlotte?'

'She's hardly ever there either.' He looked at her. 'It isn't easy, you know, living in a house of women. They gang up on you.'

She picked up the tray and headed for the living room again. 'I'm sure that can't be true.'

When they were seated on the settee with the coffee table drawn up before them, Joanna looked at him. 'If you don't mind me saying so, Vernon, I really don't think you should drink so much.'

He looked at her. 'Give me one good reason . . .'

'Because you can't handle it,' she told him bluntly. 'Well, you did ask. Take this lunchtime, for instance.'

'What about this lunchtime?'

'Chatting up the waitress. Couldn't you see you were only embarrassing the poor girl?'

'Was I?'

'Of course you were. Then saying you were going to engage that catering firm for a New Year party at home.'

'What's wrong with that? Julia will be far too busy to bother with catering for her own parties now she's on the council.'

'Oh, she *asked* you to book them, did she?'

'No – but she'd want me to. It'll be a surprise.'

'And if she's already booked another firm?' He stared at her. 'There, see what I mean?' she added. 'You're so used to making decisions in the office, Vernon. You're overworked – showing all the signs of executive stress. It's a good job you've got me to help you now.'

'Believe me, I know that. I'm already wondering how I managed before you came,' he said. 'I can't tell you how wonderful it is to have someone sympathetic to talk things over with.'

'Don't you ever talk to Julia about business, Vernon?'

He shrugged his shoulders. 'Julia and I stopped talking – about business or anything else – years ago.'

She poured the coffee, put milk into her own and gave him his black. 'There, drink that. It'll clear your head.'

139

He sipped the strong brew, looking at her thoughtfully as he did so. 'Now if I was married to someone like you, Jo . . .' She laid a hand on his arm.

'Vernon, tell me something. I noticed that none of the wives are on the board of directors. Is there any reason?'

He shook his head. 'Only that Dad is old-fashioned about things like that,' he told her. 'Doesn't believe that women have heads for business. Ma has some shares in the firm – well, she put up so much of the money in the beginning. But she's never taken up her position as a shareholder. It's largely on paper, for tax purposes, I suppose.'

'You mean, she doesn't demand to have her say – doesn't use her vote on any proposals?'

'Well, no.'

'And what about Julia?'

'She's never asked. But even if she had, I could hardly demand she had a seat when Ma hasn't.'

'Are there any shares for sale, Vernon?' She looked at him closely.

'We're not a public company, you know.'

'I know, but that doesn't stop people from investing in GPC, does it?'

'I suppose not. I've never thought about it. No one outside the family has ever offered.'

'Well, I'm offering now.'

He stared at her. 'Are you serious?'

'Never more so. I told you my divorce settlement was generous. What better firm to invest in than the one I'm working for?'

'I'd have to put it to the next meeting. And I'm not sure that it would be acceptable to have an employee holding shares.'

'Some firms actually *offer* their employees shares. It makes them feel they have a stake in their company's future.'

'Well, just leave it with me. It won't be till after Christmas now.'

She leaned across and covered his hand with hers. 'Are you feeling more relaxed?'

He smiled. 'A little. This is a very relaxing room.'

She stood and picked up the tray. 'Tell you what, why don't you go upstairs and have a lie down for an hour? I'll wash these cups and tidy up a bit. I'll call you at six o'clock.' At the foot of the stairs she directed him. 'It's the door facing you at the top of the stairs. Help yourself.'

When Vernon opened the door at the top of the stairs he found himself in what was obviously Joanna's bedroom. It was decorated in dove grey and pink, with fitted cupboards and dressing table in ivory and silver. He took off his jacket and trousers and slid under the frilled coverlet. Minutes later he was fast asleep.

When he awoke it was dark. He was about to reach out to switch on the bedside lamp when the door opened and Joanna came in. He saw that she wore a dressing gown, or rather a négligée. It floated around her as she came into the room, the light from the landing silhouetting the outline of her body through the filmy material.

'Don't switch on the light,' she said. 'I'll draw the curtains first.' She pulled the cord and the velvet drapes swung across, enveloping the room in a cosy intimacy. She turned to him. 'That's better. You can switch on the light now, if you like. I've just had a bath. Would you like one before you go home?' She sat down on the bed and looked at him and as she did so the years rolled away. She was even more beautiful now than she had been at seventeen. He sat up in the bed and raked a hand through his hair, acutely conscious of his dishevelled appearance.

'Sounds like a good idea,' he said.

'It seems odd, seeing you in my bed.' She reached out to touch his cheek. 'It's all so long ago, isn't it, Vernon?'

He swallowed hard. 'I – thought you'd forgotten all that.'

She smiled. 'Oh, no. I could never forget, could you?'

'No. It was too special.'

'Was it really? Was I someone special to you, Vernon – or just another little bimbo?'

'You were never that.'

'No?' She leaned towards him and the soft lace and chiffon of her négligée fell away. Her breasts were clearly visible and he caught his breath. Her lips brushed his. 'You're still a very attractive man,' she breathed against the corner of his mouth. 'Even more attractive than you were all those years ago. But I expect you know that. I expect there have been dozens more since me – since Julia even.'

It was a question rather than a statement and he looked into the direct green eyes that were so close to his. 'There have been a few. I might as well be honest.'

'For me too,' she said. 'But at our age experience is everything, don't you agree? We have no illusions, no expectations. Just desires and needs.' She slipped her arms around his neck and kissed him. 'I suppose you'd better get up now,' she said as their lips parted. 'Julia will be worrying about you.'

'To hell with Julia,' he said raggedly as he pulled her roughly to him again.

The flat on the first floor of thirteen Victoria Gardens was really no more than a glorified bed-sit. It had been converted from what had once been an elegant first-floor drawing room. The deep fireplace alcove had been made into a bedroom area, the fireplace itself being boarded up and disguised as a dressing table. There was a built-in wardrobe and just enough room for a single bed and bedside table. The whole area was closed off from the rest of the room by heavy curtains. Another corner was partitioned and equipped as a tiny kitchenette, with a sink, cooker and cupboard.

What was left of the room was spacious and airy, the best part in Fleur's eyes being the French windows that gave onto the little balcony overlooking the garden.

After she moved in Fleur spent every spare moment decorating. Tom helped, but by now he knew her well enough to respect her independence and only gave his assistance when invited to. She painted the walls of the living room white and bought a brightly coloured floral border which she applied at waist level. 'To help lower the ceiling,' as she explained to Tom on the Sunday afternoon before Christmas when she invited him in to see her finished work.

He laughed. 'How can you *lower the ceiling* and why would you want to?'

'Because this room was once much larger,' she told him patiently. 'So now that it's been chopped up, it looks out of proportion. The border helps rebalance it.'

He saw that she was right and was impressed. He had to admit that she seemed to have an instinct for interior decoration. The whole place had been completely transformed since Derek Jones had lived in it.

She had papered the bedroom area with a pretty sprigged paper and bought herself a duvet cover and pillow cases to match. She'd also found a pretty table lamp with a soft pink shade that gave the room a soft warm light. The whole effect was completed by the two coats of brilliant white paint with which she had covered the dingy beige woodwork.

'When I can afford it, I'd like to get a new carpet and

143

some covers for the armchairs,' she told Tom as she looked around the room with satisfaction. 'There's one of those discount warehouses out at Merifield. I'd like to have a look sometime.'

'Well, if you're serious, I'll take you,' he said. 'But surely you don't want to waste your money on a rented flat? You never know, you might want to move to something better in a year or two – even buy a place of your own.'

'I shan't,' she said firmly. 'I like it here. It's just the right size for me and I'd never get anywhere as cheap. Just as soon as the spring comes I'm going to transform the balcony. Just you wait and see.' She hugged her arms around herself gleefully. 'I'm *really* looking forward to that. I'm going to paint the wrought iron-work white and I'll have hanging baskets and tubs. A whole riot of colour. My own little corner. Maybe I'll get some of those wind-chimes to hang up, to play me to sleep on warm summer nights.'

He grinned. Her enthusiasm was so infectious that it was impossible not to be affected by it. 'You and your old balcony,' he teased. 'Well, when you're lugging bags of compost up the stairs and hanging from the railings by your eyelashes with a paintbrush in your teeth, maybe you'll let me help?'

'I'll manage, thanks.'

He regarded the stubborn set of her mouth, a little wounded by her rejection. It was impossible not to admire the stoic, independent way in which she struggled to manage alone. He just wished she'd unbend a little towards him. They'd known one another almost three months now and yet, to his disappointment, their relationship was no closer than when they'd first met.

'Miss Emancipation, aren't you?' He reached out to brush her cheek with his knuckles, his eyes wistful. 'I wish you'd let me inside that reinforced steel barrier sometimes, Fleur. I mean it when I say I want to help, you know. There are no conditions – no strings. I just want to do things for you because I like you very much.'

'I know, Tom. And it isn't that I don't appreciate it. I like you too, really.'

'Then why?' He took a step towards her and put his hands on her shoulders. Immediately he felt her stiffen just as she always did at his touch and for a second anger warmed his blood and sharpened his voice.

'You see? There you go again! Am I really so repulsive to you, Fleur? If I am you only have to say so and I'll . . .'

'Oh, please don't be angry, Tom. It isn't that.' His sudden abruptness disturbed her and she drew away, turning towards the window. 'It's not what you think, but I can't explain. Don't ask me. Maybe – maybe it would be better if you left now.'

For a moment he stood looking at her straight, unyielding back, wondering whether to do as she asked and leave. But if he left now it would be for the last time, and somehow, in spite of her apparent coolness, he knew that neither of them wanted that. He had to make her trust him if they were ever going to get anywhere and he sensed that they had arrived at a watershed.

He moved to stand behind her as she looked down into the rambling garden below. Her arms were wrapped protectively around herself and he looked at the tense fingers that clutched each upper arm.

'Did something happen to you, Fleur?' he asked softly. 'Is it something to do with your childhood – the time before you came here?'

'I had a *wonderful* childhood!' She spun round to face him, her eyes bright and defensive. 'No one could have had a better family. I miss them very much and . . .'

'And *what*?' He put his hands on her shoulders, firmly this time, drawing her towards him. 'Tell me, Fleur. Did you love someone? Did he hurt you? Is that why you ran away?'

'*I didn't run away!*' She tried to push him away, but he held her fast. She lowered her eyes, refusing to meet his insistent gaze. 'Let me go, Tom. You've got no right to question me like this.'

'Maybe not but I still think we should talk,' he insisted. 'Come and sit down, Fleur. I'm your friend. You can trust me, I promise you that. There's something bothering you. It's eating at you and it's time you got it off your chest – for your own sake.'

The feel of his hands on her shoulders was sending spirals of panic through her chest, making her want to scream. She could feel her breathing become so shallow it was making her hot and dizzy. As the room began to spin she opened her mouth to shout at him to leave her alone – to go away and mind his own business. But as she looked into his eyes and saw the respect and genuine concern in them the words died in her throat. Suddenly she realised how long it was since she'd shared her anxieties with another human being; how long since she had confided in anyone or poured out her innermost fears. She felt the panic and tension slowly seep out of her like air from a burst balloon and suddenly, without warning, tears welled up in her eyes and began to trickle down her cheeks.

She laid her head against his chest. 'Oh, Tom, I'm sorry. I never meant to hurt you. You don't deserve this.'

'You haven't hurt me.' His arms closed gently around her. 'I just wish *you* weren't hurting so much. Darling, can't you tell me why you're so reluctant to trust me? You must know how much I care about you by now.' He led her to one of the armchairs and knelt beside her, holding both her hands.

'You're right,' she said slowly, her mouth dry. 'It was something that happened – just before I left Hackney. And I suppose I did run away.' Her hands gripped his tightly. 'I never ran away from anything in my whole life till then, Tom, and I despise myself for it.'

'Maybe if you tell me about it you can stop running,' he said gently. 'At least in your mind.'

'I told you that I promised my grandmother to come and look for my mother,' she began. 'But I don't think I ever would have come to Elvemere if it hadn't been for . . .' She paused, biting her lips.

'Yes. Go on.'

'I stopped a gang of skinheads from beating up an Asian boy one night. It was outside the fish and chip shop where I worked.'

He smiled. 'That sounds like you.'

'A policeman happened to come along and I made the leader of the gang look silly in front of him.' She shuddered. 'They don't let you get away with a thing like that. Not where I come from. I suppose I should have known they'd try to get even.'

He held her hands tightly. 'What happened?'

'Nothing for a while. Except that I suspected that someone had been following me home for some time. I guessed it was them – or rather him. I thought he was just trying to intimidate me, scare me to get his own back. Then, one night, a few weeks after Grandma died, he was waiting for me. He cornered me in the alley next to the flat where we lived.' She raised huge haunted eyes to his and he felt his blood turn to ice. 'He attacked me. He tried – tried to . . .' She broke off as her mouth dried again.

'Say it, Fleur,' he urged. 'Get it out in the open once and for all, that's the only way you'll ever be free of it.'

She swallowed hard and took a deep breath. 'He

147

tried to rape me. He didn't, though. I fought him off. I had a heavy torch with me and I managed to hit him with it, then I kicked him – where it hurt most. Somehow – I'll never know how – I managed to get indoors before he recovered.'

The expression on her face told him she was reliving the terror of that night and he drew her into his arms and held her close. 'My poor Fleur,' he whispered, stroking the thick soft curls. 'But he didn't succeed. That's the important thing. You won. Just hang onto that.'

'But he *did* win,' she insisted. 'He drove me out of my own home. I was afraid to stay there alone after that. Don't you understand, Tom? Afraid is something I've never been, and I can't forgive myself for it!'

'You didn't report it to the police?'

She shook her head. 'It would have been his word against mine. I've heard of girls who report attacks like that. Everyone blames them – says they asked for it. And I felt bad enough as it was. Dirty and disgraced. I didn't *want* anyone to know. You're the first person I've ever told. All I wanted at the time was to get as far away as possible.'

'So you came to find your mother?'

'No.' She shook her head adamantly. 'I came to Elvemere because it was the only place I could think of.'

'Fleur.' He took her face between his hands and looked into her eyes. 'Listen, if you want to find her, I can help. It wouldn't be difficult. I have access to the archives at the paper. There'd be a report of her marriage or clues of some sort – bound to be in a town this size. If you could just give me as many details as you can . . .'

'*No!*' Fleur shook her head. 'There isn't any point, Tom. The time when I needed a mother is long past.

148

I've got a job I love and my own home. I'm my own person and I'm happy. I don't need *anyone* now.'

He shook his head slowly. 'We all need someone, Fleur. You're no exception.'

For a long moment she looked at him, then she let out a long shuddering breath as the last of the tension left her. 'Thanks, Tom.'

'Don't thank me. The offer is there. All you have to do is ask. As for the rest, I'm proud to be the only person you've told,' he said. 'And you can rest assured that nothing you've said will go further than this room. All I want now is to make it up to you – if you'll let me? In whatever way I can.' Very slowly and tenderly he drew her towards him and kissed her. This time her lips were soft and responsive, melting into his. He pulled her to her feet and for the first time her arms went round him and he felt her body relax in his arms. For a long time she stood in the circle of his arms, just holding and being held.

'Only a few days till Christmas,' he said looking at her. 'What are you going to do about it?'

'I haven't given it a thought,' she confessed. 'I suppose I've deliberately pushed it to the back of my mind. It hasn't been hard, Sally and I have been so busy. Last year I still had Grandma.' She smiled reminiscently. 'She loved Christmas. Even though I wasn't a kid any more she still hid my present and made me hang up a stocking. We still had a tree and decorated the flat. She belonged to a Christmas Club – saved up for it for months so we could have all the things she loved.'

'You must miss her.'

'I do.' She looked at him. 'You must be planning to go and spend it with your mother.'

'No. Mum's met someone and wrote to say he's taking her away for Christmas.' He smiled. 'I'm glad for her. She spent years nursing my grandparents and it's time she had a life of her own again.'

'Do you like him, this man?'

He shrugged. 'Haven't met him yet, but if he makes her happy, who am I to say whether I like him or not? The fact is, Fleur, it looks as if you and I are both at a loose end for Christmas, so how about sharing it?'

She smiled, feeling suddenly light as a bubble. 'Oh, Tom, that would be lovely! Spending Christmas here will make the flat feel like a real home!'

Chapter 6

The New Year began for Arden Catering on the afternoon of December 31st with preparations for the party at the home of Mr and Mrs Vernon Grant. Sally had taken the booking when Fleur was out and she had only noticed it in the book the day before they closed for the Christmas holiday. She'd been surprised to see that in spite of his obviously tipsy mood Vernon Grant had obviously meant it when he said he would be booking Arden Catering for a party at his home. Sally was surprised too.

'Mrs Grant junior has always done the catering for her own parties,' she remarked as they packed the van. 'But I suppose her time must be fully taken up now she's been elected to the Town Council.'

Fleur rarely had time to read the local paper and, as she had not been in Elvemere long enough to qualify for a vote, the local by-election had not particularly interested her. She looked up as she carefully stowed the microwave in its padded box into the van. 'The Town Council? That sounds important.'

Sally gave a rueful grin. 'That's what a lot of them like to think,' she said. 'If you ask me these local councils have had their day. If things were run at County level there wouldn't be so much wheeling and dealing going on.'

'Wheeling and dealing?' Fleur shook her head. The complexity of small-town politics was unfamiliar territory to her and at that particular moment she was more concerned with making sure her change of clothes and the little vanity case she always used was in the van before she climbed into the passenger seat. But instead of getting into the driving seat beside her, Sally stood at the window and said, 'Not there, Fleur. I'd like you to drive this evening.'

She felt her cheeks burning and her heart quickened with a mixture of excitement and apprehension. 'Oh! Do you really think I should?'

'I don't see why not. You've been having lessons for several weeks now and I seem to remember you telling me you'd applied for your test.'

'That's right,' Fleur told her. 'I'm taking it next month.'

'Then what are you waiting for? The sooner you get behind the wheel and get as much practice as you can, the better. From now on you can consider yourself Arden Catering's official driver.'

'What about the L plates though?'

Sally laughed. 'No problem. I found a pair at the back of a shelf in the garage the other day. They're the ones Peter used when he was learning. I always knew they'd come in useful. Just wait a second while I attach them.'

Fleur enjoyed the drive across town to the suburb where the Grants lived. It was a pleasant district, and although it was winter and the trees were bare she could well imagine how leafy and delightful it would be in summer. As she drove into the drive of the large square house and parked carefully and unobtrusively close to the side entrance, Sally turned to her with a smile.

'Well done! You should pass the test first time if that's a sample. And while we're on the subject of tests, unless you particularly want to continue, I don't think you need any more computer classes. You're managing very nicely on what you've already learned. I was very impressed the other day when I went to check and saw that you'd updated all our customer files.'

For the past few weeks, while she wasn't working in the kitchen, Sally had encouraged Fleur to use the computer in the office and she had devised a new method of keeping track of their stocks, making it easier to see at a glance what provisions they needed to reorder. She'd also invented a system for circularising clients in order to up-date them on their services. She'd viewed it as more of an experiment than anything else and now blushed with pleasure at Sally's appreciation.

'Thanks. They were just some ideas I had.'

'No, thank *you*. They work extremely well. You've worked very hard since you've been with me, Fleur, and come up with some very sound ideas. I sometimes wonder how I ever managed without you.'

They began to unload the van and carry the equipment inside. Fleur looked round the Grants' kitchen admiringly. It was large and spacious, fitted with light oak cupboards and smooth green-tiled worktops with concealed lighting. It was equipped with every kind of gadget and modern convenience imaginable. 'I wish all the kitchens we had to work in were like this,' she remarked.

'No shortage of money here,' Sally told her. 'Grant Philips made their pile out of the building boom, though apparently Charlie Grant was a poor boy who made good. There are those who say he did it on his wife's money, but he must have had the know-how and the business acumen to make it work.'

As they made the final preparations Sally asked what kind of Christmas Fleur had had.

'Fairly quiet. It was nice spending some time in my new flat,' she said. 'Tom shared Christmas Day with me as he wasn't going home. We had turkey and a tree – all the usual things. He brought his portable telly with him and we watched some of the shows, and in the afternoon we went for a walk down by the river.'

'Tom – that's the boyfriend, is it?'

'He's a neighbour. He has a room in the same house and he's a journalist on the local paper. He's just a friend.'

As they worked on in silence Fleur wondered why she had been so quick to deny any kind of affection between herself and Tom. Christmas Day had been a delight. They had bought each other small presents and spent the day together, quietly enjoying each other's company. He'd been sensitive and considerate, careful not to push their new understanding too far. There had been kisses, and they'd held hands, but he had made no attempt to take their relationship further. As Tom was on duty for the paper on Boxing Day, covering various sporting events, he'd had only one day off and now he had gone up to Yorkshire at his mother's invitation, to spend the New Year with her and no doubt to be introduced to the new man in her life. Somewhat to her dismay Fleur was finding that she missed him a lot more than she had expected to.

'He has no family then?'

'Who?' Fleur realised that Sally was still talking about Tom. 'Oh, Tom. There's just his mother, she lives up North.'

'But he spent Christmas with you?'

'Only because he had to work on Boxing Day and his mother was going away. He's taking some holiday and spending a couple of weeks with her now.'

Sally smiled a little at Fleur's defensiveness. 'You do like him though?'

'Yes, of course I like him.'

'I'm glad.' Sally smiled. 'You should have more social life, Fleur. I worry about that sometimes. With us working the hours we do.'

'Tom works strange hours too. Did Peter come home to spend the holiday with you?' she asked, anxious to change the subject.

Sally shook her head. 'Working in the hotel business, it was his busiest time. He's coming home for a few days at the end of January when the seasonal rush is over. It's a dead time for catering too and so far there are no functions booked, but there'll be plenty for you to do in the office and the kitchen.' She laughed. 'You needn't worry, I shan't be laying you off.'

The buffet table was to be laid out in the dining room which was decorated with evergreens and a large Christmas tree decked out in red and gold. Sally put the finishing touches to her flower arrangement while Fleur changed out of her jeans into her dress and did her hair. She had just joined Sally in the dining room when the door opened and a woman came in. She wore a plain but exquisitely cut black evening dress and her delicate bone structure was enhanced by the expert cut of her blonde hair. Her only jewellery was a single diamond on a fine gold chain and earrings to match. Sally looked up with a smile.

'Good evening, Mrs Grant. I hope everything is to your satisfaction?'

Julia looked around the room briefly and nodded. 'It all looks very nice indeed.' She looked at her watch. 'The guests will be arriving soon. You will be ready to serve them drinks?'

'Of course. Hot punch as you requested as well as the usual choice of sherry and fruit juice.'

155

'That's fine. I thought we'd eat at about half-past ten. We'll open the connecting doors between here and the drawing room just before.' Julia cast an eye over the table then turned away as the door bell was heard. 'It all looks delicious. I'm sure it's all going to be a great success. Thank you.'

Fleur looked at Sally. 'So that's Mrs Grant.'

'*Councillor* Mrs Grant now,' Sally reminded her.

The large drawing room was beginning to fill and Fleur was circulating with her tray of drinks when Charlotte suddenly appeared. She wore more make-up than usual and her hair was a glorious explosion of tiny spirals. Over her glittery party dress with its minuscule puffball skirt she carried a coat. 'Anyone seen Mum?' she asked no one in particular. 'Oh, *Fleur*. What are you doing here?'

'I work for Mrs Arden, remember?'

'Yes, of course you do. I suppose I might have known.' She pulled a face. 'Doesn't she give you New Year's Eve off?'

Fleur smiled. 'I'd rather be working.'

'You've got to be kidding! I'd rather be anywhere than here,' Charlotte said, lowering her voice. 'Did you ever see such a collection of wrinklies? I'm off to the Dramatic Society bash. A lot of my friends are members and they always put on a good party for New Year.'

'Well, I hope you have a good time.'

Charlotte laughed. 'I intend to! Gotta go. See you at college next term.'

'Well, no. I won't be coming back.'

'Oh – you're kidding?' Charlotte frowned. 'Lucky you! Still, I'm not surprised. I wish I'd picked up computing as quickly as you. I was always a complete prat at it at school and I'm not much better now. I reckon I'll still be there when I'm as old as this lot! Oh well, see you around, I expect. Happy New Year, Fleur!'

She waved a carefree hand and disappeared into the throng of party guests.

Charlie and Louise Grant were the first guests to arrive and as soon as Charlie had made sure his wife was busy talking to Vernon, he buttonholed his daughter-in-law.

'So – I hear you've wangled yourself onto the planning committee then?'

'There was no wangle about it. I was asked to be on it.'

'Never mind. Just as long as you use the opportunity to help your family, eh?' Charlie took a sip of his drink and eyed her thoughtfully. 'No doubt you'll have heard about this redevelopment planned for Victoria Gardens. So what's to do about it then? When are things likely to start moving?'

Julia sighed. 'Father, you know I can't discuss things like that with members of the public.'

'*Members of the public!*' His florid complexion deepened to purple. 'I'm your bloody father-in-law, for Christ's sake, girl! Not some faceless punter.'

'I know that, but you're still a member of the public as far as the council is concerned.' As more guests began to arrive she seized the excuse to escape with some relief. 'If you don't mind, I'll have to leave you for a moment. Perhaps there'll be a chance to talk later?'

He watched her go resentfully. He'd never really liked his daughter-in-law. Stuck up little bitch! If it hadn't been for the chance of that merger he might have tried to warn Vernon off. Who did she think she was? Just because her grandfather was a doctor and she'd been to some snotty private school. He had a pretty good idea the marriage wasn't a roaring success either, especially now that she'd got herself elected to the council. And the way Vernon looked at that new

157

secretary or Personal Assistant or whatever he called her proved his point. What did she *personally* assist him with? wondered Charlie. If he wasn't getting his leg over there Charlie was a Dutchman! He'd be a damned fool not to after all! Charlie looked around the room. The fact that the lovely Jo Hanson was noticeably absent from this little soiree went some way to proving his point.

His eyes lighted on his wife on the other side of the room. Louise was talking to May Philips. He always enjoyed pulling old May's leg – taking her down a peg. Almost as stuck up as her daughter. It was a damned good thing old Harry was down to earth. He was ridiculously easy-going too. Never put up much of a fight about anything, silly old sod.

'Now then, May,' said Charlie, swaggering over to join the two women. He was rewarded with a warm blush from his partner's wife who could read all the signs that Charlie was out to embarrass her.

'Good evening, Charles.'

May's insistence on calling him that never failed to set his teeth on edge. Who did she think he was – the heir to the throne? He noticed that she was wearing a dress of coffee-coloured lace. It had a flesh-coloured underslip which intrigued him. He stared pointedly at her bust. 'You're looking 'specially sexy tonight, m' dear,' he said, watching with satisfaction as the colour spread to the roots of her hair. He took a step closer and lowered his voice to an undertone. 'Between friends, is that your skin I can see through all those holes?'

May's face turned crimson. 'Indeed it is *not*!'

He chuckled. 'Pity. Thought for a minute you'd come out without your bust bodice. I like to see a woman with a good bosom on her. Lou will bear me out in that, won't you, Lou?'

His wife gave him a push. 'Behave yourself, Charlie.'

She nodded towards his glass. 'How many of those have you had?'

'Not enough yet, lass. When I've had enough I start chasing women and saying outrageous things!' He chuckled, holding up his glass to May. 'Here's to ladies with lovely curves. Long may they quiver.'

Kathleen Grant had arrived at the party when it seemed to be in full swing, and now wished she hadn't come at all. Family parties were one thing, this was something else. There was hardly anyone she knew here. It seemed that even Charlotte had escaped.

She stood on the fringe of the group looking acutely uncomfortable. The chignon she had forced her long hair into was coming down and the long black velvet dress that did little to enhance her tall thin figure had seen better days. If only she had worn something less formal. The other women were wearing more festive dresses in pretty colours. She felt positively funereal. The fact was that she never really felt at ease in anything other than jodhpurs and sweaters. Looking round at the assembled guests, all chattering and clearly enjoying themselves, she wished again that she'd stayed at home. This really wasn't her scene at all.

'Can I offer you a drink?'

Kath looked up to see a young woman standing before her. She was striking-looking with a beautiful golden complexion, dark eyes and curling black hair. Her short black dress revealed long shapely legs in sheer black stockings which reminded Kath painfully of the reason she preferred jodhpurs and had worn a long dress this evening. Years of riding and the outdoor life had given her the muscular legs of a carthorse. Suddenly she became aware that the girl was still holding out her tray and smiling.

'Drink?'

'Oh! Yes – thank you.'

'There's hot punch,' Fleur said, indicating the sugar-frosted glasses. 'Or there's sherry – medium and dry, or orange juice.'

'The punch looks nice.' Kath took a glass and sipped at it. 'You're new, aren't you?' she said, wanting to hang onto the girl for as long as she could. 'I mean – I haven't seen you around before.'

'I've been here a few months,' Fleur said. 'I moved here from London last autumn.'

'I see. Like this job?'

'Very much, thank you.'

'I'm Kathleen Grant, by the way. Vernon is my brother.'

'Oh, you must be the lady who owns the stables. Charlotte has told me a lot about you.'

Kath smiled and began to relax. 'You know Charlotte?'

'Yes. We met at evening classes. We've both been doing computer studies.'

'I'm very fond of Charlotte,' Kath said. 'I once cherished fond hopes that she might come and work for me when she left school, but her father had other ideas.'

'Yes. She told me that.' Fleur looked around uneasily. She had no wish to be overheard discussing the party's host and could see several people whose glasses were empty. 'I'm sorry but I'll have to go now,' she said with an apologetic smile. 'It was nice meeting you.'

'Yes. Maybe we'll . . .' Kath trailed off, seeing Vernon frowning at her reproachfully. He came across the room towards her.

'Hello, Kath. Can't you find anyone to talk to?'

'I don't know anyone here.'

'You know Julia, me, Ma and Father and the Philipses. You don't have to hob-nob with the hired help.'

'She's a very nice girl.'

'That's hardly the point. I daresay she'd like to get on with what she's being paid to do. Come and talk to Ma. She says you haven't been round to see her for weeks.'

'I wouldn't have thought you'd be too worried about that!'

'No? Well, since you've brought up the subject of family problems, I'd be grateful if you'd discourage Charlotte from spending all her spare time round at the stables. She has a lot to learn and I want her to get on with it.'

'I don't ask her to come, Vernon. I can't help it if she loves working with horses.'

'It wouldn't have anything to do with the fact that she's cheap labour, would it? Oh, don't think you can pull the wool over my eyes, Kath. I know how devious you can be and I won't have my daughter exploited.'

She flushed angrily. 'And just what is it *you're* doing? She seems to be nothing more than an errand girl at your office.'

Vernon's nostrils flared and the colour left his face. 'Mind your own bloody business and leave my daughter alone,' he hissed at her between clenched teeth. 'You just can't stop meddling in other people's lives, can you? First it was Julia and her crazy local government fad. Now it's Charlotte. Just because you couldn't hang onto that husband of yours for long enough to persuade him to get you pregnant!'

As he turned on his heel and walked away Kath felt herself shaking with fury and frustration. It was so like Vernon to make a vile remark like that in a situation when she couldn't retaliate without making a scene. She took a long drink of her punch and tried to swallow her fury with it. *Damn Vernon to hell!* He'd always been a perfect little shit, ever since he was a small child. The moment her parents had produced a son they'd had little time for her, a fact which he quickly latched onto. As a boy he'd lied about her, told tales and got her into trouble at every possible opportunity. She could see his angelic little face now, smirking with satisfaction as he watched her being smacked and sent to bed without supper for something *he'd* done. And as they'd grown older the situation had worsened. Vernon had seemed to have all the advantages. While she'd grown into a gangling, ungainly teenager, he had developed into a debonair and outwardly charming young man. His success with the opposite sex had been phenomenal. He had delighted their parents by marrying the right girl and opening up the opportunity for a family merger for the business, whereas all Kath had achieved was a childless failed marriage and a riding school that barely paid its way.

She decided she must leave. No one would notice her absence anyway. She put down her glass and began to move towards the door, but Julia caught her in the hall as she was putting on her coat.

'Kath! I'm sorry I haven't had time to have a word with you before. It's lovely to see you. It's been ages.'

'Don't worry, Vernon has already had a *word* with me, as you put it,' Kath said, her lips still quivering. 'It was nice of you to invite me, Julia, and I know *you* mean it when you say you're pleased to see me. I wanted to come if only to congratulate you on getting elected. But I think it would be better if I left now – before there's an atmosphere.'

Julia's heart sank. Vernon and his sister had never hit it off and of course Kath was right when she said that their animosity would create an atmosphere. It seemed impossible for them to be in the same room without sparks flying. But she liked her sister-in-law and hated the thought of her going home alone and upset on New Year's Eve.

'Take no notice of him,' she said hopefully. 'Do stay. I'm sure your mother wouldn't want you to leave. Come and say hello to her and your father at least.'

Kathleen shook her head. 'I'd rather just slip away quietly, if you don't mind.' She bent to kiss Julia's cheek. 'Thank you for inviting me. Goodnight.'

'Well – if you really must. I'll ring you. We'll have coffee or lunch some time soon.' Julia watched her sister-in-law go with genuine regret. Kath had had a difficult, disappointing life. It wasn't her fault that she was sometimes touchy. Surely Vernon could have made an effort for once?

On the far side of the room Charlie nudged his wife. 'Bloody hell, I've just seen our Kathleen. What the flippin' heck has she got on? She looks like a flaming stick of liquorice!'

Louise shook her head. 'Don't be so cruel, Charlie. It's not her fault she's no fashion sense. Where is she? I must go and have a word with her.' But Charlie grabbed her arm.

'I think she's leaving. Let her go. If she stays and knocks back a few she'll start airing those barmy left-wing ideas of hers. Better let well alone. We don't want her embarrassing us, do we? She's better off stopping at home with those damned nags of hers. Come to think of it, she gets more like them every time I see her!'

As he spoke his eye was drawn to a middle-aged woman who had just arrived. He detached himself from his wife and made his way across the room towards her.

'Well! As I live and breathe. If it isn't little Lena Maitland!'

Eleanor turned to look at him. 'Hello, Charlie. Not so little nowadays! And no one has called me Lena for years.'

'I daresay.' He put his empty glass on the tray of a

passing waitress and took a full one. 'A lot of water has gone down the plughole since you and I were snogging behind the bike sheds, Lena. How have you been then, eh, lass?'

'I've been fine. Busy of course. No need to ask how you've been.'

'Not so bad – not so bad at all, thanks. I hear you've been giving our Julia a bit of a bunk up. Good of you, that.'

'I set her off in the right direction, that was all. She's a very bright and capable woman. She doesn't need any help from me.'

'Oh, I'm sure she'll make a damned fine councillor given time. I daresay they're lucky to get her.'

'Too true.' Eleanor smiled ruefully. She'd heard a little about Charlie's resistance to his daughter-in-law's ambitions in local politics from Julia herself. What was the old hypocrite up to?

Charlie took a swig of his drink and shuddered slightly. *Ugh! Sherry!* A woman's tipple if ever there was one. Tasted like bloody cough syrup. Where did they keep the hard stuff? he wondered. He regarded Eleanor speculatively over the rim of his glass. She would be about two years younger than him, but she'd worn well. She was still a handsome woman. He could still fancy a bit of slap and tickle with her, especially if it proved worthwhile. It didn't look as if he was going to get much inside information out of Julia. Have to box clever though. Lena was nobody's fool.

'Tell you what, Lena,' He lowered his voice conspiratorially. 'You and I will have to have a bite of supper one of these evenings, just the two of us. Catch up on all the old gossip.'

'My door is always open. I'm your councillor, in case you've forgotten,' she reminded him. 'I represent your ward.'

'Yes, yes, I know all that. I was thinking more on friendly lines,' Charlie said with a sly wink. 'I'll give you a ring in a day or two, eh? I'm sure you can – what's the expression these days? – find a window in your busy schedule for a friend as old as me.' He chuckled to himself as he tossed back the last of the despised sherry. That was the tactic. Don't *ask* them, tell them what you're going to do – and then do it.

Fleur was on her way through the hall to the kitchen to refill her tray when Vernon caught her.

'Well, hello there – Fleur, isn't it?'

'Good evening, sir.'

'Oh, surely there's no need to be so formal? We're almost old friends, aren't we?' She made herself smile. 'That's better!' He took a step towards her. 'Anyone ever tell you you've got a lovely smile, Fleur?'

She edged towards the kitchen door. 'I'd better go and . . .'

'Don't run away. Look, I just wanted to apologise for my sister. She was the tall woman in black velvet who was monopolising you. She's a bit of an odd-ball. All she cares about is horses. People don't really rate for much with her. I hope she didn't keep you from your work?'

'Not at all.' His nerve almost took her breath away. After the remorseless way he had chatted her up at the boardroom lunch! 'I didn't realise she took me for a horse.'

'*What?*' He stared at her, then saw the joke. 'Oh – I see what you mean!'

'And I thought she was very nice actually.'

'Really? Oh, well, that's all right then.'

'Vernon! There you are.' Julia stood in the doorway. 'I've been looking for you. I want to announce that we're about to eat. Are you coming?'

He moved away looking sheepish. 'Right. Just coming. I was just – just . . .' He looked at Fleur. 'So if you could make sure the wine is really well chilled?' he said with a change of tone.

'Of course, sir.'

He walked past Julia into the dining room. She looked at Fleur. 'Is everything all right?'

'Yes, thank you. I'll tell Mrs Arden you're ready for us to serve the buffet now, shall I?'

'I'd be glad if you would. And as my husband says, the wine should be well chilled, especially the champagne.'

'It's been on ice ever since we arrived.'

'I thought it would be, knowing how efficient Mrs Arden is.' Julia took a step towards her, her eyes puzzled. 'Excuse me, but haven't I seen you somewhere before?'

'Not that I remember.'

'You haven't been with Mrs Arden for long then?'

'Just since September.'

'Oh, I must be mistaken then. I could have sworn . . . Wait a minute, you didn't come to my daughter's last birthday party, did you?'

'No. I'm new to Elvemere.'

Julia looked puzzled. 'Odd. I'm sure we've met somewhere. Never mind.' She shook her head. 'We'll open the double doors between the two rooms now and then you can serve.'

'Certainly.'

'You really mustn't mind Charlie's teasing.' Louise was looking at May Philips with some concern. Charlie had really gone over the top tonight. He'd made a target of poor May ever since she'd arrived, and he'd flirted with that Councillor Maitland woman and generally made a nuisance of himself with his outspoken remarks. She intended to give him a piece of her mind when they got home.

May sniffed. 'A joke is a joke, Louise,' she said in wounded tones, 'but the remark he made about my dress was really quite offensive.'

'I know it might've seemed that way, love, but he doesn't mean anything, you know. It's just his idea of fun.' Louise laid a placatory hand on the other woman's arm. 'He was brought up in a very outspoken home. I was too if it comes to that. Us Northerners don't mince words, you know.'

'But you do know where to draw the line, Louise. Charles doesn't seem to give a fig for people's feelings.'

'Ah – now that's something I've been meaning to mention to you,' she said.

'Feelings?' May looked nonplussed.

'No. The way you always call him *Charles*. I think I ought to tell you that he hates it. It might be the reason why he goads you like he does.'

'I was brought up to call people by their proper names,' May said stiffly. 'It's only polite and courteous.'

'Mebbe so, but it isn't very *friendly*, is it? See, Charlie thinks you're being – well, stuffy, and it gets up his nose.'

'I can't help the way I was brought up any more than he can,' May said pointedly.

'But everyone calls him Charlie. They always have. Even his mum called him that.'

'Yes. Well, I'll try to remember,' May said. 'Now I think I'd better go and find Harry. I can see Julia is about to tell us that supper is being served.'

Louise watched her go with a sigh. May had been like this for as long as she had known her and that was a good few years. She'd never be any different now. Her old dad would have described her as toffee-nosed. She could hear him now explaining to her the difference between gentry and snobs. *'There are them as was*

*born wi' a silver spoon in their gobs and them as looks as if
they was born wi' a stink under their nebs. It pays to know
t'difference.'* She smiled to herself as she moved with the
rest of the guests towards the dining room. May was
definitely one of them wi' a stink under her neb!

At midnight everyone gathered for the chimes of Big
Ben, toasted each other and sang 'Auld Lang Syne'. As
soon as everyone had begun to drink again Vernon
sneaked away upstairs to the bedroom he shared with
Julia. Closing the door carefully, he lifted the telephone
and dialled. After a moment or two he was rewarded
with the sound of Jo's sleepy voice.

'Hello – who is it?'

'It's me, darling, just calling to wish you Happy New
Year.'

'I was asleep,' she told him petulantly. 'Did you have
to?'

'Don't be cross. I miss you,' he whispered.

'I bet you do. You sound drunk. I expect you've been
having a whale of a time – never given me a thought.'

'That's not true. Would I be ringing you now if it
were?' He cradled the receiver close to his ear. 'I wish I
was there with you now.'

'Then what are you waiting for?'

'Be reasonable, darling. You know I can't come now.
I really wish I could, though. When we're apart, just
thinking of what you do to me nearly drives me mad.
It's sheer torture.'

'I'll let you demonstrate that next time you're here,'
she said with a husky laugh.

'Tomorrow?' he asked, encouraged. 'Can I see you
tomorrow?'

'I suppose you can try.'

'I can't promise a time or anything, but I'll come
round when I can.'

'In that case, darling, you'll have to take the risk that I might well be out, won't you?'

'Yes, but I . . .' Vernon found himself holding a dead line. Joanna had hung up.

It was one-thirty when the last of the party guests departed. Sally and Fleur had already cleared away the leftovers, washed up and packed most of their equipment. There was just the table to dismantle and pack away. As they stood in the kitchen waiting Sally explained to Fleur who the guests were.

'The big man with the white hair was Mr Grant Senior and the lady in the pink dress with the sequin embroidery and all the jewellery was his wife.'

Fleur smiled. She'd already gathered that. Mr Charlie Grant was as bad as his son, though less subtle. Twice he had pinched her bottom as she circulated with her drinks tray, but she had decided to say nothing about that, assessing for herself that he'd obviously had more than enough to drink.

'Then the dignified little woman in the coffee lace is Mrs Philips. Her husband is the nice dapper little man with the thinning grey hair and gold-rimmed glasses. They are Mrs Grant Junior's parents.'

Fleur looked up with interest. 'Oh, her name was Philips before she was married then?'

'That's right. May Philips was Doctor Geoffrey Bishop's only daughter. He was Elvemere's best loved GP some years ago. She was his receptionist and they were very close. It caused a bit of a sensation when she married Harry Philips.'

'Why was that?'

'He was just a poor electrician in those days,' Sally explained. 'I was still at school at the time but I still remember the talk. But Harry turned out to be a local lad who made good and Doctor Bishop came round to it in the end. The Philipses still live in the family home, Gresham House, a big Victorian place on St Paul's Green. It always used to be known as Doctor's House when I was a child.'

For the past hour Fleur had been stifling yawns and longing for her bed, but now she was suddenly wide awake. *Gresham House*. Surely that was the name of the house on the scrap of paper with her mother's address scribbled on it? *Philips – Julia Philips!* Was it possible that the woman she had spoken to earlier this evemng was the same one who had abandoned her illegitimate baby daughter in the East End of London twenty years ago?

Fleur pictured the cool attractive woman in her elegant home, surrounded by family and guests. The very thought seemed ludicrous. Yet the more she thought about it, the more she realised that too many details fitted for it to be a mistake. She had actually seen and spoken to her mother this very evening and been unaware of it. She had never meant to seek her mother out when she came to Elvemere, yet it seemed that fate had somehow stepped in and found her anyway. The question was – now that she knew, what did she do about it?

Chapter 7

It began to snow again as Julia turned into Scrimshaw Street. The covering of white that gave most things a sparkling, pure look merely made the mean little pebble-dashed houses appear grimmer and even more uninviting than before. As Julia stood shivering on the doorstep she fervently hoped that Tracey had found the money to pay her electricity bill. It must be freezing inside. She turned up the collar of her sheepskin coat against the falling flakes and put the suitcase she was carrying down on the step.

The curtain twitched and Tracey's face appeared momentarily at the front room window before she opened the door. She looked pale and hollow-eyed as she greeted Julia. 'Come in out of the cold, Mrs Grant. Sorry to keep you waiting, only Damie isn't very well.'

Julia could hear the baby's fretful wailing as she stepped into the hall. 'Poor little boy. Has he got a cold?' she asked. 'I've brought a few things for you,' she said. 'I don't want you to think I'm unloading all my unwanted rubbish onto you, but Charlotte, my daughter, is about your size and she's so wasteful with her clothes. Most of these are almost new.'

Tracey smiled and some of the colour seemed to come back to her cheeks. 'It's very good of you, Mrs

Grant. I'm ever so grateful. Come through.'

In the living room Julia was glad to see that a bright fire was burning. 'You applied for the extra benefit I told you about then?' she said. Tracey nodded.

'They never let on about these things till you ask, do they? It isn't much but it does help.' She watched with eager eyes as Julia opened the suitcase, exclaiming with delight at the soft woollens and other barely worn garments cast off by Charlotte. Picking up a red cashmere sweater, she held it to her cheek.

'Oh, Mrs Grant, this is lovely! Are you sure your daughter doesn't want it?'

Julia smiled. 'That colour is just right for you, and yes, I'm quite sure. Charlotte asked me to drop them off at the Oxfam shop this morning but I thought you might like to have first pick. Whatever you don't fancy can still go there.'

'Will you stay and have a coffee?'

Julia shook her head. 'I'm meeting a friend in town in ten minutes. I just thought I'd pop in on you first.' She looked at the girl's pale face. 'You're looking very tired, Tracey.'

'I know. I've had some sleepless nights with Damian. It started as a bit of a sniffle but now it's gone on his chest.'

Julia looked into the pram at the baby who had settled into a restless sleep. He looked flushed and she could hear him wheezing softly as he breathed. 'Have you taken him to the doctor?'

'No. I know I should but I haven't liked to take him out in this weather. It's about a mile to walk and the air's been so cold and frosty. I just kept hoping he'd pick up.'

'When I've seen my friend, I'll come back and take you,' Julia said.

Tracey shook her head. 'Oh, no, I couldn't . . .'

'Yes, you could. No arguing. It's for Damian and it won't take long. The doctor will probably put him on some antibiotics – have him well again in no time.' She looked at the girl with concern. 'Maybe we should ask him to check you over too? You look as though you could do with a tonic. Are you sure you're all right?'

'Yeah – yeah, I'm fine.'

'Getting enough to eat? Warm enough?'

Tears welled up in Tracey's eyes and she sat down suddenly on the only armchair. 'Oh, Mrs Grant – I wasn't going to say anything but it's Rick.'

Julia frowned. 'Rick?'

'Damie's dad.'

'He's back? You've seen him again?'

'Oh, yes, I've seen him.' Tracey said bitterly. 'Turns out he's been inside all this time. Breaking and entering – says it weren't his fault. He got mixed up with the wrong people, apparently. Anyway, he's out now and he's got no job and nowhere to go.'

Julia began to see. 'So he thought he could move in with you?'

'That's it. He says it ain't fair that I've got a house and money to live on when he's got nothing. He says I owe him.'

'That's ridiculous. You owe him nothing.'

'There's no way I want him back, Mrs Grant, but he keeps on and on coming round. He makes sure the neighbours hear too – banging on the door, shouting and going on till I let him in. I'm so ashamed.'

'You must tell the police,' Julia said.

'He says if I do, he'll tell them I'm on the game – that I ill treat Damie – and then they'll take him away from me.' Tracey began to cry, her thin shoulders slumped and her hands over her face.

Julia watched her helplessly. Patting her shoulder in an attempt to reassure her, she said, 'Anyone can see

173

that you don't ill treat your baby, Tracey. And you know that I'd vouch for your character any time.' Opening her bag, she pressed a clean handkerchief into Tracey's hand. 'Here, dry your tears.'

'Thanks.' She blew her nose. 'You've been so kind, Mrs Grant, but you don't know what Rick's like.'

'I can't see that there's any way he can do what he threatens. It's all bluff.'

Tracey turned haunted eyes to hers. 'I haven't told you the worst. He said that if I make it tough for him he'll make sure Damie's got the bruises to prove what he says is true.'

'He said *what*?' Julia was shocked.

'He says he's desperate enough to do that, and that if I force him to it'll be my fault! He really scares me, Mrs Grant. He's not the same person he used to be. His eyes look wild and strange and he shouts and acts really violent. I reckon he must be on something.'

'Drugs, you mean?' Julia was seriously concerned now. 'Look, Tracey, I've got to go now but I'll be back later. I'll take you and Damian to the doctor's and then I think we should go and see Social Services and ask what they can advise.'

'*No!*' Tracey was twisting the handkerchief between her fingers. 'Look, I don't want to get him into trouble. That'll only make things worse. Maybe if I tell him about you – warn him off – he'll keep away.'

'I think we both know that he won't, don't we, Tracey?'

They looked at each other for a long moment, then Tracey took a deep breath and made herself smile. 'Look, Mrs Grant, I feel a lot better now I've told you, but there's no need to go making a big thing of it. Rick never used to be bad. I daresay he never meant what he said. He'll probably calm down when he's had time to think. He might never come back again. Maybe he'll get

174

a job – go away, anything. I shouldn't have said anything to you. Let's just forget it, shall we?'

Outside as she got into the car Julia's heart ached for the girl and her child. They had looked so vulnerable in the cold, bare little house. She couldn't stop herself thinking that but for the grace of God and a good family home she might easily have been in the same position.

Sitting at the wheel, her eyes staring unseeingly through the windscreen at the soft flakes of snow, she remembered the child she had left. She had been a strong healthy little baby. But suppose she had become ill like Damian? In her mind she heard a baby's pitiful crying and saw the little tear-stained face and arms held out to her. Suppose her baby had died? She would never have known. There was no way she could ever find out. Taking a deep breath, she shook off the tortured thoughts and turned the ignition key. She would help Tracey all she could. It was almost as though she were being given a second chance. At least she could see that this girl was not driven to take the drastic action she had.

Julia found Eleanor waiting for her at a corner table in The Apple Tree, the small restaurant near the Cathedral where they often met. She hurried across to her.

'Sorry I'm a bit late, Eleanor. I went to visit Tracey Brownlow and found her in a bit of a state.'

Eleanor smiled. 'It's all right. You're a councillor now. Your time isn't completely your own any more.' She poured Julia a strong cup of coffee from the pot she'd already ordered.

'Her baby is poorly and I promised to go back later and take her to the doctor's.'

'Can't she take him herself?'

'She would have done but it's a long walk and he has

what sounds very much like bronchitis to me, poor little scrap. She quite rightly didn't want to take him out in the cold air.'

'I know you feel she's a deserving case, Julia, but you mustn't let yourself get too involved, you know,' Eleanor warned. 'People will put on you if they think you're a soft touch.'

'Not Tracey. She's a very independent young woman.' Julia dropped sugar into her cup and stirred thoughtfully, wondering whether to ask for the older woman's advice. Seeing her worried expression, Eleanor said, 'What is it? Some kind of problem?'

'Yes, I'm rather concerned for her. It's the ex-boyfriend, the child's father. It appears he's been in prison and now he's out and pestering Tracey to take him in.'

Eleanor shook her head. 'If you take my advice you'll keep out of it, Julia. Next thing you know he'll be living with her and you'll be labelled an interfering busybody.'

'It's not quite that simple. It sounds as though he's on drugs,' Julia said. 'He's threatening the baby; using him to get at her. And if she gives in and lets him move in, I think she and the baby will be seriously at risk.'

'Oh, dear, poor child.' Eleanor sighed and sipped her coffee thoughtfully. 'Of course what we badly need here in Elvemere is a women's refuge.'

'You mean there isn't one?'

Eleanor shook her head. 'I've been trying to get one for a couple of years, but it's hopeless. Everyone just seems to want to shut their eyes to the fact that there are battered wives and kids in Elvemere. It doesn't go with their image of the tranquil life of a cathedral town.'

'Maybe it's time the issue was raised again. We could try, couldn't we?'

'Maybe. With your help they might start taking notice. But I wouldn't hold my breath if I were you!'

'We could lobby some of the other women councillors,' Julia suggested. 'You said Victoria Gardens was going to be redeveloped. Couldn't the council rent us one of those houses as a temporary measure? I noticed there were two or three empty when I was canvassing.'

'That's a good idea, but I doubt if you'll persuade the council to spend any money on it. It would need furnishing and decorating for a start, then there'd be heating and lighting. It costs more than you think – a lot more.'

'Surely Social Services and local charities would help, and I'm certain we could get volunteers to help – even some of the women themselves. There's something else I'd like to raise too: the problem of young mothers who can't go to work because the factories don't have crèche facilities,' Julia said. 'It would save so much in State benefits if only employers would provide this simple service. If people were made aware of the problem . . .' She broke off as she saw Eleanor's rueful smile.

'I'm afraid you've got an awful lot to learn about people, Julia, lass,' she said. ' 'Specially those with money and power. It's one thing getting them to recognise a problem – quite another getting them to put their money, or their application, where their mouth is.'

'Yes, but surely . . .' Julia broke off as a woman who had just come into the restaurant attracted her attention. Something about the way she held her head and the chestnut hair triggered recollections. Then suddenly the memory clicked into place and she realised she was looking at someone she hadn't seen for more than twenty years. 'My God!' she exclaimed.

Eleanor looked up and followed her gaze. 'What? Who is it?'

'Joanna Bloom! I'm almost sure that the woman who just came in – the one who's just sat down at the corner table – is an old schoolfriend of mine.'

'Really?' Eleanor smiled. 'Well, what are you waiting for? Go over and say hello. I've got to go now anyway.' She gathered up her gloves and various bags of shopping. 'See you at the meeting on Wednesday.' She reached across the table to pat Julia's hand. 'Good luck with the Brownlow girl, and remember what I said – keep your distance.'

Julia watched Eleanor leave and poured herself another coffee, her eyes still on the woman in the far corner. What if she went over and it wasn't Joanna after all? But if it wasn't then this woman bore her an uncanny resemblance. She was older, of course, more mature, but then she would be. Her hair was different and her style of dress much more conservative, but still . . .

Sensing someone's scrutiny, the woman turned and looked directly into Julia's eyes. Their gaze held for a moment, then Julia smiled and the woman rose and came across.

Standing by the table she said, 'It *is*, isn't it? You're Julia Philips.'

'Hello, Joanna. I recognised you the moment you came in. You haven't really changed at all.'

'Nor you!' Joanna laughed. 'What a fantastic piece of luck, meeting you like this. I've been meaning to look you up ever since I got back to Elvemere, although I didn't really expect you to be here still.'

'How long have you been back?'

'Not long.'

'Please, sit down and join me.' Julia looked at her watch, remembering Tracey. 'I don't have long but I'm dying to know what you've been doing all these years.'

They ordered another pot of coffee and Joanna lit a cigarette 'I've been in America for the past eighteen years,' she volunteered when the waitress had withdrawn. 'I'm afraid I've two failed marriages behind me, both to Americans. After my last divorce I suddenly got this yen to come home, so here I am.' She shrugged. 'That's all. Nothing exciting really. I see you're married,' she observed, looking at Julia's left hand.

'Yes, I married Vernon Grant, remember him? We have a sixteen-year-old daughter, Charlotte, so I've been busy looking after her since she was born, but I've just been elected to the Town Council.'

'Of course! I didn't connect the new Councillor Mrs Grant with the little Julia Philips I went to school with.' Joanna leaned across the table. 'I take it your mad passionate affair with the pop guitarist fizzled out?'

'Yes.' Julia coloured. 'No one knows about that so I'd be glad if . . .'

'I'd keep it under my hat?' Joanna laughed. 'My dear, what do you take me for? Heaven knows there are plenty of skeletons in my closet.' She chuckled huskily as she stubbed out her cigarette. 'God! We were a pair of wild little devils in those days, weren't we?'

Julia nodded half-heartedly and looked away. 'I suppose we were. It was the age we grew up in, I daresay.'

'The crazy permissive sixties.' Joanna sighed. 'What fun it all was. I'd do it all again, given the chance, wouldn't you?'

'Not really.' Julia picked up the bill and began to gather her things together. 'It's been lovely seeing you again, Joanna, but I have to go now. Council business.'

'Of course. Mustn't keep you from your good works, must I? We'll have to get together and have a girls' night out some time, eh? I'm sure there's a good club around someplace where we could have some laughs and relive some of the old days. I'll give you a buzz, shall I?'

'Yes – fine. Bye then, Joanna.'

'Bye.'

Joanna smiled as she watched Julia go. Now that she had met the competition she felt more confident than ever. Poor hidebound, suburban-minded little Julia. She'd always been so scared to try her wings – until that weekend at the Isle of Wight Festival when she'd fallen like a ton of bricks for that dishy exotic-looking guitarist. What was his name? Shane, Wayne? No Dean – that was it! Dean Sylvester. What had *really* happened after she ran off with him? Joanna wondered. Had she discovered the heady delights of flying – or flown too close to the sun and singed her feathers badly? One thing was as sure as hell: she didn't want to talk about it. Did Vernon know about her escapade? Obviously not. She poured herself another coffee and mulled over the interesting possibilities of his accidentally finding out. Then she decided that for the moment that was one trick she'd keep up her sleeve.

Tracey emerged from the doctor's surgery looking relieved.

'It's only a slight chest infection,' she told Julia. 'I've got a prescription for some penicillin and Doctor Moss thinks he'll be as right as rain in a couple of days' time.'

In the car Julia glanced at the girl sitting beside her. 'Did you ask him to take a look at you?'

'No.' Tracey shook her head. 'I'll be fine now I know that Damie's okay.'

'I've been thinking, Tracey, you need a job and I need someone to help me now that I'm out so much on Council business. How would you feel about doing some cleaning for me? You could bring Damian with you of course.'

Tracey looked at her. 'It's ever so good of you, Mrs Grant, but it's this benefit problem. I'd lose my Family Credit.'

'I'll pay you below the ceiling,' Julia said. 'It won't affect that. And if I want to give you something extra occasionally, to get things for the baby, then that's between you and me.'

Tracey's cheeks turned pink with pleasure. 'Well, I'd love that, if you're sure?'

Julia smiled. 'I am. So that's settled then. You can start as soon as Damian's better and fit to go out again.'

'Apart from anything else, it'd be great to get out of the house for a few hours each day.'

Julia glanced at her. She looked so young and so vulnerable sitting there clutching the baby. By 'getting out of the house' Julia took her to mean out of the way of Rick and his demands. This way she would be able to keep an eye on them both. She smiled as she drew up outside the house in Scrimshaw Street, convinced she'd done the right thing. 'Just give me a ring when you're ready to start, Tracey,' she said. 'And feel free to ring me if there's any kind of problem too, won't you?'

Fleur took her driving test on the last Wednesday in January. Luckily the worst of the snow had thawed and the day dawned crisp, dry and sunny. After an early breakfast her driving instructor took her out for a warm-up drive before dropping her off at the test centre.

'Don't look so worried!' he urged her 'You're going to pass with flying colours. Next time I see you, you'll be smiling all over your face.'

She swallowed hard. 'I hope you're right.'

'I *am* right.' He looked at his watch. 'Well, this is it. Good luck!'

Fleur got out of the car and walked up the steps,

wishing that Tom could have been here. She had purposely kept the date of her test from him, afraid that he might postpone his holiday. If she passed she would be able to surprise him when he came home.

As she gave her name at the desk and felt her heartbeat quicken she took a firm hold on herself. *You're not on trial for your life*, she admonished herself. *It's only a driving test. Pull yourself together!*

'Miss Sylvester?'

A portly, stern-looking man in a tweed cap and trench coat was peering enquiringly at her.

'That's right.'

'Will you come with me, please?'

Forty minutes later Fleur emerged from the driving school car feeling dazed and disbelieving. She'd convinced herself that she'd got all the Highway Code answers wrong and still couldn't quite believe she had actually passed. She tried to recall the formal and impersonal phrase the examiner had used, intoning the words as a matter of habit. *'I am pleased to tell you that you have achieved the standard necessary and passed your Ministry of Transport driving test.'* As though it was a mere matter of routine!

She was still standing on the pavement looking dazed when a voice behind her said, 'Hi! You must be Fleur.'

Turning, she saw a tall young man smiling at her and recognised him at once from his photograph. She'd known Sally was expecting her son home today but hadn't expected to meet him like this. 'Y-yes,' she said shakily.

He held out his hand. 'I'm Peter Arden.'

'I know. I – I mean – hello.'

He laughed at her bewildered expression and

pointed to the slip of paper in her hand. 'I take it you've passed?'

'Yes.' She shook her head. 'I'm still trying to take it in. It's amazing.'

'Not from what I've heard.' He nodded towards a smart little sports car standing at the kerb. 'I've come to take you home.' He raised an eyebrow at her. 'Want to drive?'

She looked at the pristine little car and shook her head vigorously. 'No! I'd probably crash the way I feel at the moment. That would ruin everything, wouldn't it?'

He smiled. 'Okay, I'll let you off.'

As she fastened her seat belt, she said, 'I live in Victoria Gardens, do you know it?'

'Yes, but I'm not taking you there,' he told her. 'Mum has prepared a special celebration lunch for you.'

'But she didn't know I'd pass.'

'She was pretty confident you would. But she reckoned that if by some unlucky chance you didn't, you'd need consoling anyway.'

'Your mother is a wonderful woman,' Fleur told him. 'She's been so kind to me.'

He grinned. 'She is a pretty remarkable woman, but from what I hear she's found her ideal assistant.'

'I love the job. That makes it easy.'

'I've been taking a look at the work you've done on the computer,' he said. 'Mum never really got the hang of it, you know, but now that she's got you she's beginning to reap the benefit.'

Fleur blushed with pleasure at the compliments. This was turning out to be her day!

Sally was waiting for them. The table in her dining room was spread with her best cloth and laid with her finest crystal, silver and china, and the delicious aromas drifting through from the kitchen made Fleur's mouth water. Sally hugged her warmly when Peter announced that she'd passed her test.

'Congratulations! You've done so well. Barely five months since you joined me and look what you've achieved already.'

'With your help,' Fleur reminded her.

'Nonsense. I'm lucky to have you.' Sally poured three glasses of wine and raised hers. 'Here's to our future success! And I can tell you now that from this week on you'll be getting an extra little something in your pay packet.'

The lunch was delicious with all three of them in a celebratory mood. Afterwards Sally insisted that Fleur must take the rest of the day off, instructing Peter to drive her home. In the car he glanced at her.

'Well, I have to say that you look a lot more cheerful than when I picked you up this morning,' he remarked. 'You looked lost then. Now you're positively glowing.'

She smiled happily. 'It's been a day I shan't forget in a hurry. When I think of the way things were for me just six months ago, I can hardly believe my luck.'

When Peter stopped the car outside number thirteen Victoria Gardens she turned to him. 'Thanks for bringing me home.' When he hesitated she said, 'I suppose – I mean – would you like to come up for a cup of tea?'

He laughed. 'Why not? I'd love to.'

He seemed impressed by the flat and her plans for it.

'I can't wait for the spring,' she told him as they stood at the window. 'I'm going to make a feature of the balcony. Paint the wrought ironwork white and have hanging baskets and things. I can just see myself having breakfast out here on warm summer mornings.'

'Yes, I can see that it could be very pleasant.' He looked at her. 'Fleur – Mum's appointment book doesn't seem too full for the next few days so I know you're not busy. Will you have dinner with me one evening before I go back to London?'

Her eyes widened with surprise. '*Me?* Well, yes. Yes, I'd like that.'

'So would I.' He stood looking at her with open admiration till she felt her cheeks flush.

'I – I'll put the kettle on,' she said, turning away. 'We'll have that tea.'

Over the teacups he told her a little about his job as under manager at the large London hotel where he worked, and his ambition to take over as manager one day. His enthusiasm for his work matched her own. She found her mind wandering as he spoke. He was so good-looking. She wondered what kind of social life he had in London and how many smart, attractive girls he knew – and why he clearly thought she had no social life of her own beyond work. It also occurred to her to wonder what Sally's reaction would be to their going out to dinner.

Ever since the New Year party at the Grants' house she'd had mixed feelings about her own background. Discovering who her mother was, suddenly and by accident like that, had plunged her even deeper into the identity crisis she'd struggled with for most of her life. It was just as Dolly had said: Julia Grant née Philips had clearly been born into an upper-middle-class family. She was used to an easy, comfortable way of life, had never had to worry about trivialities like paying bills or where the next meal was coming from. So being thrust headlong into the Sylvesters' lifestyle must have been traumatic to say the least. Life in the meagre little flat in Hackney was so far removed from her own comfortable life that she had been prepared to abandon her child in order to get away from it. Surely a person as shallow as that could have little character? Why should anyone want to waste sentiments like love or respect on a woman so weak and ineffectual that she had set more store on physical comforts than the welfare of her own child? Julia Grant did not deserve to be her mother, Fleur told herself stoutly. She was *lucky* to have been brought up by Dolly and Maurice Sylvester. They were each of them worth a dozen Julia Grants! She would make something of herself; she would succeed without any help from her.

Yet in spite of what the positive side of her mind told her she found herself unable to shake thoughts of Julia out of her head. When she closed her eyes at night the cool, assured voice rang again in her ears and she saw the slim, graceful figure, the delicately boned face and blonde hair, so very different from her own. It seemed so strange to think she had stood in the same room as her natural mother, near enough to smell her expensive perfume, close enough to have been able to reach out and touch her, while at the time neither of them had been aware of it.

The disturbing feelings and emotions she went through were a total enigma to Fleur; a bewildering tangle she found impossible to unravel. She longed to talk to someone about them, yet she could not bring herself to tell anyone about her discovery, not even Tom. It was all too close – too intensely personal. Was it hatred that was preventing her from forgetting Julia Grant? Did something deep inside her crave for revenge? Or was there some other, inexplicable reason why thoughts of Julia refused to leave her dreams and waking hours?

'A penny for them?' Peter was looking at her closely.

She shook her head, focusing her eyes on him. 'What?'

'You were miles away.'

'Oh, sorry. It's been quite a day.'

'You're tired. Time I was going anyway.' He stood

up. 'I'll see you tomorrow, I expect?'

'Yes. I'll be at work as usual.'

'I'll look forward to seeing you.' He took her hand and held it for a moment. 'Goodbye, Fleur.'

The following morning Peter told her that he had booked a table for that evening at the Fairwoods Country Club in Merifield. It all sounded very grand and she began to have doubts. He had booked it without asking her if she was free and she wasn't at all sure that she wanted to be taken for granted. Besides, she didn't have a thing suitable to wear to a place like that. But in the end Peter's charm won.

'I know it's short notice,' he said with his special smile. 'I should really have asked you first. But I'll be gone the day after tomorrow and I'd really like us to spend an evening together.'

'That's all right. As it happens I've nothing else planned,' she heard herself saying.

In her lunch hour she took the bus into town and looked around the boutiques. Luckily she'd just received her pay cheque and she decided that if she went easy on food this week she could afford a new dress as well as the rent. The choice wasn't easy, but she finally chose a soft wool dress in glowing garnet red. By a stroke of luck it was left over from the winter sale which was just ending and she was thrilled to find that she could afford a pair of shoes to match.

Peter picked her up at eight o'clock that evening and they drove out to Merifield. He admired the new dress, telling her how well the colour suited her. Privately she thought he looked very handsome in his dark grey suit and impeccable shirt and tie but she was too diffident to tell him so.

The restaurant was plushy, with soft lighting and discreet music playing in the background, and there was a small dance floor in the centre of the room. The waiter showed them to their table and gave them each a menu. Fleur glanced at the prices and almost gasped with shock, but a glance at Peter's cool assurance told her that he was obviously quite used to eating in expensive restaurants.

She concentrated on the various dishes on the menu, mentally translating the names of the dishes from what she could remember from her schoolgirl French. She eventually decided on a seafood cocktail to start, with *Coq au vin* to follow. Peter ordered the same.

By the time they reached dessert several couples had got up to dance and the tiny dance floor was filling up. Peter looked at her inquiringly. 'Would you like to dance while we wait for our dessert?'

Fleur stood up and took his hand. She thought this kind of dancing only happened in old films. It seemed unreal and almost laughable, but when Peter's arm encircled her and they began to move in time to the music on the crowded little floor she soon forgot her misgivings and began to enjoy herself.

'I'm afraid it's too crowded for proper dancing,' he said. 'At least, the kind you get at a disco.'

She smiled at him. 'It doesn't matter. I don't like discos much anyway. All that noise. You can't hear yourself think!'

He laughed and rubbed his cheek against hers. 'Thank you for coming out with me this evening, Fleur,' he said softly. 'I'm really enjoying myself. I hope you are too?'

'I am. Thank you for asking me.'

'I think my mother was very lucky to find you.'

'I'm the lucky one,' Fleur told him. 'She offered me a job just when I needed one badly. I love working for her.'

'She's very fond of you, you know,' he said softly. 'Concerned because she's afraid you don't have enough fun.' His arm tightened around her waist.

Fleur made no reply. Was this evening just a thank you for being a good employee? she wondered. Had Sally persuaded her son to give her poor hard-worked assistant an evening out? As he smiled down at her she quickly admonished herself for the ungrateful thought.

It was as they were sitting down again that she noticed a couple who had just come in. A waiter was showing them to a table tucked discreetly away in a quiet corner on the far side of the room. Although the lighting was dim she recognised the man as Vernon Grant. The woman, on the other hand, certainly wasn't Julia. She had short red hair and wore a beautifully cut dress in a stunning shade of green. Fleur racked her brain to remember where she had seen her before. Then it came to her. Of course! She was Vernon Grant's personal assistant. She had been at the Grant Philips Construction company's Christmas boardroom lunch.

Peter ordered liqueurs with their coffee and Fleur felt relaxed as she sipped the thick, sweet liquid. She wondered now why she had felt so apprehensive about coming here this evening and why she had been so suspicious of Peter's motives in asking her out. As they circled the small floor once again she couldn't remember enjoying herself so much. Then suddenly she was shocked to see it was after midnight.

'I hadn't realised it was so late. The evening has gone so quickly! I really should go,' she said apologetically.

He looked amused. 'All right, Cinderella. I'll settle the bill while you get your coat.'

Outside the air was frosty and sharp. Stars twinkled in the sky and the moon was almost full. Her spirits buoyed by the good food, the wine and Peter's company, Fleur looked up and took a deep breath of the fresh, frosty air. 'Oh! What a beautiful night!'

'Isn't it?' He slipped an arm around her waist and

drew her close as they walked. When they reached the car he turned her towards him. 'I've enjoyed your company very much, Fleur. I'll be visiting again soon and I'd like us to see more of each other.'

She smiled. 'I'd like that too.'

When he drew her gently towards him she did not resist. His arms were firm, holding her close, and his mouth on hers was warm and sensual. 'You're lovely, Fleur,' he whispered. He kissed her again and when their lips parted, he whispered, 'You know what's happened, don't you?'

'Happened?'

'It began yesterday, didn't it? One of those special, rare once-in-a-lifetime things – the minute we met. Don't say you weren't aware of it too?'

'I – don't . . .' She was unable to finish the sentence. She'd certainly felt attracted to him, but if she'd allowed herself to think of it at all she would have assumed that it was wishful thinking – imagination. What he was implying had a slightly unreal, dream-like feel to it. He gave her no time to think about it. His mouth was on hers again and she allowed her lips to part eagerly for his kiss as he unbuttoned her coat and pulled her closer.

'Oh, Fleur, I wonder if you want me as much as I want you?'

The hard warmth of his body pressed close to hers was intoxicating and she let her head fall back as his lips moved from her mouth to her neck, pausing sensuously at the little pulse that throbbed at the base of her throat.

He took her face between his hands, looking into her eyes. 'I can't take you home,' he said breathlessly, 'and perhaps your place isn't such a good idea either. Will you wait in the car while I see if they've got a room here?'

Suddenly she came down to earth. The euphoria of the past moments evaporated abruptly as she realised what he had in mind. She stared at him. *'No!'*

He looked surprised. 'But why?'

She pulled away from him, shaking her head. 'I don't know. It just – doesn't feel right. It makes me feel like a . . . I think I'd like to go home now, if you don't mind.'

His face fell. 'Of course. Just as you wish. I'm sorry.' He let her go abruptly and unlocked the car door. They got in and for a moment or two sat silently side by side. Then he turned to her.

'I'm an insensitive idiot, rushing you like that. It must have sounded almost insulting to you, Fleur. I'm sorry. Can you forgive me?'

'Yes. Yes, it's all right.' She was stiff with misery. He thought she was easy. A mixed-race cockney girl might be a new experience for him. What was it his type called it? *A bit of rough?* She cringed with humiliation at the thought. She had thought him so attractive – been so flattered when he had asked her out for dinner. She had let him kiss her – almost believed . . . She shuddered.

He was looking at her. 'Fleur?'

She shook her head. 'Look, I know people – some girls – do this kind of thing, but I'm not one of them.' She broke off. She sounded so stuffy and prudish. There was no way she could begin to explain how she felt so she might as well give up trying. He probably wouldn't be interested anyway. 'Please, could you just drive me home?'

'Of course. Anything you say.' He started the car and backed it out of the parking space. As they turned and headed for the entrance gates the car's headlights raked the forecourt. In the brief flash from the lights Fleur saw a couple walking hand in hand towards the

191

country club chalets. She had only a momentary glimpse, but it was enough to recognise them. It was Vernon Grant and his PA, Jo Hanson.

Councillor Harold Jeffries, Mayor and chairman of Elvemere Town Council, looked at his watch and cleared his throat. 'I think that concludes our meeting for tonight, ladies and gentlemen.' He glanced at the Town Clerk who was taking the minutes. 'So unless there is any other business . . .'

'There is something I'd like to bring up.' Julia's voice shook slightly as she rose to her feet and all eyes turned on her. This was the first time she had actually spoken since being elected. She had told Eleanor she would keep quiet until she had something of importance to say. Now she definitely felt she had.

'Yes, Councillor Grant?' Councillor Jeffries glared at her over the tops of his spectacles in the manner he reserved for new councillors who threatened to get too big for their boots He hoped she wasn't planning anything lengthy. *Sports Night* was on TV and he'd just catch it if he started out now.

Julia took a deep breath. 'It has only just come to my attention that there is no women's refuge in Elvemere.'

A general rumble went round the council chamber and someone said, 'There's one in Merifield.'

'Merifield is ten miles away,' Julia remarked. 'A woman with small children and no transport can't go that far.'

'Why not? What's wrong with public transport?'

'In the middle of the night? When she's traumatised by a violent husband or partner?'

A buzz of disapproval went round and the chairman tapped his gavel. 'This is an issue which has been brought up before, Councillor. It was intensively discussed and at the time we all agreed that it was out of the question. It would be exceptionally expensive and I personally do not feel that the cost would be justified.'

'I think it would,' Julia said boldly. 'How many of the councillors here have actually looked into this need? Battered wives and violent men are not confined to large inner city areas,' she said. 'Neither are single mothers.'

'They're a drain on our resources already!' shouted a voice at the back.

Julia's colour rose. 'Mainly because of the men who have deserted them and reneged on their responsibilities!' she said. 'And in many cases these young women have no wish to be a drain on anyone. They would like to work and be independent. In some cases they have been trained in skills – often paid for out of our taxes – which are being wasted. If employers would only provide crèche facilities . . .'

Her words were lost in the ensuing uproar and Eleanor who sat beside her whispered, 'Now you've done it! At least seventy percent of the council is made up of employers of one sort or another.'

'Then I hope they're listening,' said Julia unrepentantly.

Once again the chairman banged his gavel. 'These are issues that need careful analysis and debate,' he said.

'If I might make a suggestion?' Julia was on her feet again. Her blood was up now, her eyes shining and her cheeks pink. Without waiting for permission she went on. 'There are two empty properties in Victoria Gardens. One of them might be rented by the council and used as a women's refuge. I'm sure that I could get voluntary help and the various local charities would . . .'

'The area known as Victoria Gardens is already

under discussion for redevelopment, as I believe you are aware, Councillor?'

'I know, but as a temporary measure – surely . . .'

'I'm sure that everyone will agree that this is not a matter that can be discussed at such short notice and with so little information available.'

There were calls of, 'Hear, hear!'

'Then can it be put on the agenda for a future meeting?'

Councillor Jeffries spluttered into his handkerchief, blew his nose loudly and glared furiously at Julia. 'Your remarks have been minuted, Councillor Grant. There are a great many other issues associated with your proposal which need to be considered.' Before Julia could speak again his gavel came down for the last time. 'I now bring this meeting to a close.' He glanced up at the ancient council chamber clock. 'At nine-thirty-five precisely.' Damn and blast the woman! By the time he got home now *Sports Night* would be all but over.

As they filed out of the large semi-circular council chamber Eleanor gave Julia a pat on the back. 'Well done!'

She pulled a face. 'I didn't get very far with it, did I?'

'You raised the matter. That's the important part,' Eleanor said. 'I purposely kept quiet and let you get on with it, but when it's formally brought up you can count on my support. And, as you say, we'll lobby some of the other women councillors in the meantime. Coffee?' she looked at Julia enquiringly. 'My place if you like. Or we could go to The Feathers for a drink.'

'I'd love to but I feel I should get home,' Julia said. 'I don't get to see as much of Charlotte as I'd like. Vernon's sister Kath sees more of her than I do. Charlotte spends every spare minute round at the stables and I daresay she'll be there even more when the lighter nights arrive.'

'How is the Brownlow girl?' Eleanor asked.

'The baby is better,' Julia told her. 'Unfortunately the child's father is still causing problems, demanding money she can't afford to give him. I just hope he doesn't do something violent. We really do need that refuge, you know, Eleanor.'

'I know, my dear. And we'll get it, you just see. If we stick together we'll win through in the end.'

Charlotte was already in when Julia got home. She was in her room, watching television. Julia asked her if she wanted a hot drink but she said no. She seemed disinclined to talk either, much to Julia's disappointment. As her daughter grew older the gulf between them seemed to be widening. She watched a little TV herself downstairs in the living room, trying to unwind after the meeting, but her mind was so full of her plans that she found it impossible to concentrate and switched it off. She looked at her watch. Half-past eleven. Vernon was very late. She decided to go up.

She didn't know how long she had been asleep when he came in. She woke to hear him stealthily creeping around, undressing in the dark, and reached out to switch on the bedside lamp. Half in, half out of his underpants, he looked up, startled.

'Oh! I thought you were asleep – didn't want to wake you.'

'What time is it?' She peered sleepily at the face of the alarm clock by the bed. 'Two-thirty! Where have you been till now?'

'Round at Dad's. Where did you think I'd been?' He pulled on his pyjamas and went into the bathroom. 'We had a lot to discuss.'

'You must have done. Was Daddy there?'

'No.' The tap running and tooth-cleaning sounds drowned his next remark. He turned off the bathroom light and came back, climbing into bed beside her.

195

'What were you discussing?' she asked.

He punched his pillow and lay down with his back to her. 'For heaven's sake, Ju, it's late. I'm sure you wouldn't be interested but if you really need a blow by blow account, could we have it in the morning?'

'If you like.' Julia was vaguely aware of a scent that certainly wasn't his usual aftershave. It was a feminine perfume, though not one she had ever used herself. She sniffed. It was familiar yet elusive. Who was it this time? she wondered resignedly. Switching off the bedside lamp she lay on her back, staring up into the darkness. Although he had the duvet over his head she could tell that Vernon was awake too.

'Do you know who I saw a few weeks ago?' she asked.

'No idea,' he grunted.

'Joanna Bloom. Remember her? Only her name is something else now. Hinton ... Hampson or something. She's been divorced twice – been living in America.'

He paused then said, 'Really?' After another pause he turned over and she felt his breath on her cheek. 'It's funny your mentioning her. I meant to tell you. She applied for a job at GPC and got it. She's working as – working in the office. But then, I suppose she told you that?'

'No, she didn't.' Julia frowned into the darkness. 'How odd. I wonder why?'

'God knows.' Vernon punched his pillow again. 'She's only just started. Maybe she didn't even know she'd got the job at the time.'

'Maybe not.'

'Better get some sleep then.' He pecked her cheek and turned over again. ' 'Night.'

'Goodnight.' She remembered now where she'd smelt that perfume before.

Fleur was busy cleaning the flat on Sunday morning when there was a knock on her door. She opened it to find Peter Arden standing outside on the landing. Her heart quickened with surprise.

'*Oh*, hello.'

'Your landlady said it was all right to come up. I hope you don't mind?'

'No.' She was slightly at a loss to know what to do next when he suddenly produced a bouquet of flowers from behind his back.

'I brought you these.' He grinned disarmingly at her nonplussed expression. 'Well, I suggest that you either put them in water or hit me over the head with them.'

She laughed, taking the bronze and yellow chrysanthemums from him. 'They're lovely. Thank you. Would you like some coffee? I was just going to make some.'

'I thought you'd never ask. That would be very nice. Thanks.'

As she put the flowers into her one and only vase she said, 'I thought you were going back to London today?'

'I am, but I wanted to come and see you first.'

'There was no need.'

'I think there was. I wanted to say how sorry I am for the mess I made of things on Friday evening, Fleur.'

'That's all right. I'd already forgotten it,' she lied.

'Then will you come out to lunch with me before I leave? Give me the chance to make a new start?'

She hesitated. She'd been going to wash her hair and catch up on some jobs. Besides, she wasn't exactly sure just how she felt about him yet, or whether a new start was what she wanted.

'Please come,' he said.

She looked at his contrite face and appealing brown eyes and capitulated. The least she could do was to give him a chance to make amends. 'Okay,' she said. 'Can you give me about ten minutes to change?'

They drove out to a small country pub that Peter said had a reputation for good food, and ate roast beef and Yorkshire pudding. As she attacked the meal with relish Fleur couldn't help thinking of the frozen meat pie she had planned to defrost for lunch.

'When I first came to Elvemere I had this freezing cold little room at the top of the house,' she told him. 'All I had was a kettle and a toaster so you can imagine what kind of meals I had.'

He regarded her across the table. His first impression of her, with her fiery gypsy eyes and endless legs, could not have been more wrong. He saw now that the light in her eyes and the firm set of those luscious lips belonged to a girl determined to get the best she could from life. He admired that, and at the same time found her air of assurance challenging. There was also an intriguing air of mystery about her.

'Tell me, why did you come to Elvemere?' he asked.

'Mainly to get away from London after my grand-mother died.'

'But why here?'

'I'd heard the name.' She shrugged. 'It seemed as good a place as any other.'

'And you have no family at all now?'

'Who needs family?' The moment the words had left her lips and she saw the spark of curiosity brighten his eyes she regretted them.

'That sounds intriguing,' he said. 'Are there some skeletons rattling around in your family cupboard then?'

'Not at all, as far as I know. I only meant that I intend to stand on my own feet.'

'I see.' He looked at his watch apologetically. 'I'm sorry, Fleur but I'll have to take you home now. I'm on duty this evening so I'll have to be on my way.'

As they drew up outside thirteen Victoria Gardens he turned to her. 'I won't get a chance to visit again for some time unfortunately.'

She nodded. 'I understand.' Was this the polite brush-off, intended so as not to leave her working relationship with his mother strained?

He leaned towards her and kissed her softly. 'What I said on Friday – about something special happening between us – it wasn't just a line, you know. I meant it.' He reached out to draw her closer. 'I really do want to see you again, Fleur. I'm going to have a problem waiting till my next visit. Can I ring you?'

'You could, but there's only the communal phone in the hall. It isn't very private.'

He looked into her eyes. 'Is there any chance you might come up to London – stay for a weekend? We could have a good time. I could book you a room at the hotel – get tickets for a show. Please say you'll come.'

'Well – I don't know.'

'Will you at least think about it?'

'Yes. All right. I'll think about it.'

'I'll ring you in a few days to see if you've made up your mind.' He kissed her again.

She stood waving on the pavement as he drove away. On Friday evening she'd been so disappointed in him, but today everything had been different. Now she believed he was sincere. She drew in a deep breath of the cold winter air and found that it tasted like champagne. It made her feel as light as air. Victoria Gardens with its rusty iron railings and ragged frost-bleached grass was suddenly transformed and the raw damp wind felt as warm as a spring breeze. She climbed the narrow stairs on dancing feet, happier than she ever remembered feeling. As she took out her key to unlock the flat a voice from behind her spoke.

'Hi there, dreamy! I'm home.' Turning, she came face to face with Tom. 'It's great to see you. I've missed you so much.' He was looking at her expectantly. 'That's your cue to say you've missed me too,' he prompted. 'Well – do I get a kiss?'

She smiled. 'Of course I missed you. Did you have a good time?' She put her hands on his shoulders and gave him a peck on the cheek.

He drew back his head and looked at her ruefully. 'Is that all the welcome I get? Here I am, back after spending two weeks in the frozen North, missing my girl-friend like crazy, and all I get from her is a chilly little peck on the cheek?'

It took an effort to stop herself from retorting that she wasn't his girlfriend. Instead she said, 'Sorry, Tom. You took me by surprise. Look, come in and have some tea – tell me all about your holiday.'

He followed her into the flat, only slightly mollified. He felt puzzled and uneasy. There was something about Fleur, something he couldn't quite pin down. Then his eyes fell on the vase of flowers by the window; expensive flowers, their rich glowing colours brightening the cold winter light. Something had happened in his absence, and he had the distinct feeling that it wasn't to his advantage.

Chapter 8

'So – did you ask them?'

They were driving towards Merifield and Vernon glanced apprehensively at Joanna. It was the question he'd been dreading. 'I mentioned that you had some money to invest and that you'd like to give GPC the benefit.'

'Yes, and . . .'

'You have to take these things a step at a time, you know.'

'Yes?' When he didn't reply she gave an impatient little snort.

'So are you going to tell me what they said?'

'Dad says he doesn't believe in employees having a financial interest in the firm.'

'What do you mean, *Dad* says? Don't the rest of you get any say?'

'Of course we do.'

'All right then, what did *you* say?'

Vernon drew the car onto the forecourt of the Fairwoods Country Club and switched off the engine. He'd been nursing the vain hope that they could put off this discussion until the end of their weekly rendezvous. 'I pointed out that we could always do with extra resources, of course, and Harry agreed with me. But it wasn't any use. When Dad has made up his mind about something, there's no moving him.'

'But he's in a minority of one! Don't you have the chance to vote on proposals?'

'Look, Jo, even if he agreed to accept your investment, he'd never agree to you taking a seat on the board. He's old-fashioned about that kind of thing. Julia's mother put some money into the firm when they merged but she doesn't have a directorship either.'

'*What?*' Joanna stared at him. 'Why do these women put up with it? Your father is more than old-fashioned, he's a bloody dinosaur! I blame the rest of you for standing for it. As for you and Harry Philips, you're just a pair of yes men. I can't believe you just sit there like a couple of nodding dogs and let him have things all his own way?'

'We don't – not all the time. Dad did build the firm, remember, Jo. He has the largest financial share in the business and he does know what he's talking about.'

'And you have the necessary negotiating skills to get his projects off the ground. Wake up, Vernon! Where would the firm be today if you hadn't pulled off all the land deals? It's time you made him sit up and take notice for a change instead of sitting there and agreeing with everything he says.'

'Maybe so,' he mumbled non-commitally, and looked at her enquiringly. 'Let's not spoil our time together talking business, Jo. Now – do you want to eat first or . . .'

'I'm not at all sure that I want any *or* tonight,' she said petulantly.

He ran a hand through his hair. 'Oh, for God's sake, don't tell me you're going to sulk about it? This business has nothing to do with our relationship. We agreed on that.' He reached out for her but she pushed his hand away. She could hardly say so, but as far as she

202

was concerned it had *everything* to do with their relationship. 'I'm sorry, Vern, but I don't feel like it tonight. I've had a splitting headache all day.'

'I see. You might have said so before we drove all the way out here. Do you want me to drive you home then?'

'Yes. I think that would be best.'

As he turned the car he said, 'By the way, I've been meaning to ask you, why didn't you tell me you'd seen Julia?'

'I didn't think it was important.' She turned on him irritably. 'Do I have to report back to you on who I've seen every time I go into town?'

'When it's my wife I would have thought you might mention it, yes. And why didn't you tell her you were working for GPC?'

'Because it was obvious she didn't know, that's why. She didn't even know I was back in England!' She turned to look him squarely in the eyes. 'If it comes to that, why didn't *you* tell her?'

'We don't discuss the firm much, I told you that. I didn't think she'd be interested.'

'Well then, there's your answer – neither did I.'

'Didn't it occur to you that once she did know she might think it odd you hadn't mentioned it?'

She turned to him. 'Vernon, Julia is your problem. What she thinks *odd* is a matter of supreme indifference to me! Now, are you going to drive me home or do I have to call a cab?'

The drive back to Joanna's house was silent and strained. When Vernon stopped the car outside her house, he turned to her. 'Do I get a nightcap?'

'If you want to make it yourself.' She got out of the car and strode up the front path. Vernon locked the car and followed. They normally spent their evenings together at Fairwoods to avoid the attention of Joanna's neighbours and he was acutely conscious of the BMW's conspicuous gleaming silver bulk standing outside the house. 'Would you like me to put the car in the garage?' he asked as she unlocked the front door.

'*My* car is in the garage,' she told him brusquely. 'Besides you won't be staying long enough to cause any gossip, will you?'

Once inside the house she took off her coat and headed for the stairs. 'You know where the kitchen is,' she said over her shoulder. 'I don't know what you're having but I'll have a coffee.'

He'd made it by the time she reappeared. She had changed out of the suit she wore for the office into jeans and a sweater and had removed all her make-up. Vernon poured the coffee and handed her a cup. 'Don't be like this, Jo,' he said. 'If you make an atmosphere in the office tomorrow everyone will notice. They'll start to think there's something going on.'

She laughed dryly. 'Then they'd be wrong, wouldn't they?'

'Look, it's only that I'm treading carefully over your investment,' he said, 'using a little diplomacy. I'm sure I'll get Dad to accept it eventually.'

'*Really?* How kind of him,' she said caustically. 'That's not what you said earlier. You said that once he'd made his mind up there was no moving him.'

He winced. How could he have said that? He ran a hand through his hair. 'What I meant was that you can't bulldoze him into things. You have to be tactful with Dad. Once he'd agreed to accept your investment we'll let him think it's his idea to invite you onto the board.'

'Maybe you'd rather I tried a bit of feminine guile,' she said with a little smile. 'He obviously thinks that women were only put on earth for one purpose. What do you think, Vernon? Is it worth a try?'

'Don't be flippant!' He moved across to sit beside her

on the settee. 'Just give it a bit more time, Jo. I promise you I'll get you in eventually.' He slid an arm around her. 'Come on, don't let's waste the time we have to spend together. You're surely not going to let this one little setback spoil what we've got, are you?'

She remained stiff and unyielding in his arms as he kissed her, offering no response to the hand that pushed up her sweater and fumbled with the fastening of her bra.

'Oh, Jo, let's go upstairs,' he murmured, his breath warm and moist against her neck. 'It seems ages since last week. I can't wait to . . .'

'Well, I'm sorry, but you're going to have to, Vern.' She pushed him away and stood up, straightening her sweater and smoothing her hair. 'I'm tired and I think you should go now. You know I don't like people seeing your car standing outside. And neither should you. It's careless and indiscreet.'

'Let's go back to the Fairwoods then. It's not too late.'

'No!' She was suddenly irritated by the sight of him sitting there on the settee with his crestfallen expression and untidy hair. She went into the hall and returned a moment later with his coat. 'Goodnight, Vernon.' She held it out to him. 'And for goodness' sake, do something about your hair before you get home. It's standing on end.'

Getting up, he snatched the coat from her hands, his face dark with anger as he self-consciously smoothed his ruffled hair. 'If you want that seat on the board you're going the wrong way about it, Jo,' he warned.

'Really? If that's a threat it's a pretty empty one. You don't seem to have much clout with the firm from what I can see.' Her eyes narrowed. 'And while we're on the subject, Vernon, if you want the luxury of a discreet mistress, I'd say that *you* were going the wrong way about it!' She strode to the door and flung it open. 'Drive carefully,' she called after him. 'But then you always do, don't you?'

The house was in darkness when he let himself in. His heart sank. It was like this most nights now. No wonder he looked elsewhere for amusement, he told himself self-pityingly. There was a light showing under Charlotte's door, but he didn't go in. His daughter and he were barely speaking these days. She persisted in defying him, going off to his sister's stables at every possible opportunity. He was convinced that she did it to spite him, and Kath encouraged her, revelling in the girl's defiance. At the office Charlotte was sullen and moody, doing the minimum of work with the maximum of resentment. If only she could have been a boy, life would have been so much easier.

As for Julia, she was always busy with her council business. If she wasn't out at some meeting or other she was working on something at home. There was no family life in the house any more. And now Jo had started to be difficult. It was the last straw. Until tonight he had at least had these Thursday evenings to look forward to. There had to be some way he could persuade his father to accept her onto the board of directors. He locked up and began to ascend the stairs. It had been a bloody awful day. Might as well have an early night and write it off.

To his surprise Julia was awake. She was sitting up in bed and had obviously been working on some papers. A council agenda and her reading glasses lay on the duvet. Now she was watching a documentary on the portable TV. She looked up, surprised when he came in.

'Hello. You're early.' She snapped off the TV with the remote control.

'I know. Chap I was meeting couldn't make it.

Something about his car breaking down.'

'I see. Well, an early night will do you good.'

He looked at her. She wore a filmy nightgown in a flattering shade of pink trimmed with black lace and she'd done something different with her hair. Had it cut, restyled or whatever they called it. 'Everything all right?' he asked her.

'Fine thanks.'

'Charlotte okay?'

'Seems to be.'

'Right.'

In the bathroom he hurriedly undressed, showered and brushed his teeth. When he emerged she'd already put out the light on her side of the bed and was lying down. He climbed in beside her and switched off his own light.

'You're looking very lovely tonight, Ju,' he said quietly into the darkness. Reaching out he put a hand on her thigh and rolled her towards him. 'It's ages since we made love. There never seems to be time or an opportunity these days.'

'You're so often late.' She paused. 'I thought you'd lost interest.'

'Ju! How could you think that?' His hand travelled upwards to cup her breast and he raised himself to lean over her. 'We really should make more time for each other, shouldn't we?'

'I suppose we should.'

'I do still find you attractive, you know – very much so. You've kept your figure and you always look nice.' He kissed her and pulled up the silky material of her nightdress to stroke her hip and slide his hand over the smooth curve of her stomach. Pushing the gown above her breasts he nibbled at the soft nipples and felt them harden at the touch of his tongue. 'You're a very desirable woman, Ju. You still excite me,' he whispered huskily. Unable to contain his arousal any longer, he moved urgently over her acquiescent body and entered her in one strong thrust.

Perversely, Joanna's angry, vindictive rejection had excited him more than her normal eager response, creating an urge to vent his anger on her in a sexual way. He had left her house in a highly aroused and frustrated state. Had that parting shot of hers about driving carefully held a snide criticism? he wondered. He recalled the comment about him and Harry being nodding dogs and smarted. How he wished now that he'd insisted on staying and proving to her that he was no pushover to be manipulated and threatened. He would have shown her who was boss. Nodding dog indeed!

Now, as Julia lay submissively beneath him, he envisaged overpowering Joanna, imagined her cries – first of alarm at his anger and the power of his masculine dominance, then of ecstatic response as she happily surrendered to his passion. Julia's surprised compliance was a poor substitute for the splendidly explosive climax he and Jo would have achieved, but it was better than nothing.

He came quickly and rolled away. 'Sorry about that,' he gasped. 'It's been so long, hasn't it? We could try again if you like, but I'm not sure if I . . .'

'It's all right,' she said quickly. 'I'm fine, honestly.'

Julia lay on her back staring up at the ceiling. What had happened she wondered, to make Vernon feel amorous towards her tonight? Was she standing in for someone? Was that someone Joanna? And if so – why?

She lay quite still, listening tensely as his laboured breathing slowed and then deepened. Released from his pent-up frustration, he was already asleep while she felt only revulsion mingled with a sense of treachery. Getting up quietly she went into the bathroom and pulled off her crumpled nightdress, dropping it into the soiled linen basket. Then she showered away all traces of Vernon's duplicity.

As she lay on the brink of sleep, memories of Dean returned unbidden to haunt her last waking thoughts. Those first blissful weeks they had shared seemed so long ago. Like all half-buried memories the barbs and the sharp edges of the ill-fated affair had become blurred and softened by time. She forgot the squalor, the discomfort and neglect, remembering only the blissful nights when there was nothing but love.

Dean may have proved false in the end but at least for a little while he had made her feel vibrant and alive – a passionate flesh and blood woman. Vernon only ever made her feel used and exploited. He had always been a selfish, uncaring lover, concerned only with his own gratification. She was so used to his ways now that it was hard to believe she had once known an intense, all-consuming love. Far easier to believe was the bitter pain of the final betrayal that had ended it all. She thought guiltily of the baby girl she had abandoned, Dean's child; then briefly of pathetic little Tracey Brownlow, struggling with the potentially dangerous results of her own folly, bravely making the kind of sacrifices that she herself had shirked.

Perhaps she deserved the reward she had reaped. Her marriage had been dead for years, but there was no way she would ever be able to end it while the two families were so closely intertwined in the business. Happy or unhappy, she was trapped.

Fleur was alone in the office when the telephone rang. 'Good morning, Arden Catering. Can I help you?'

'Fleur! It's me, Peter.'

'Peter!' Her heart quickened at the sound of his voice. 'If you want your mother, I'm afraid she isn't in.

She's snatched a free hour to go to the hairdresser's.'

'No, it's you I want. I'm glad I've caught you alone. Any chance of coming up to London next weekend?'

She caught her breath. So soon! She had half thought his invitation was a spur-of-the-moment idea he'd forget once he was back in his own environment. 'Well, I don't know,' she hedged. 'I don't *think* we've got any functions booked but I'll have to have a look in the book.'

'Come off it, Fleur. You know there are no bookings. Mum has arranged to go away next weekend and she kept it clear. I checked when I was home.'

Fleur frowned, a hint of resentment prickling. If he'd known there were no bookings, why hadn't he asked her before he left? He was taking her for granted again. 'Then can you wait till I see if *I* have anything booked?' she said. 'I do have a life of my own too, you know.'

'Of course. I'm sorry, Fleur. I would have mentioned it before but I had to check my work rota. I couldn't do that till I got back.'

'No. I see.' She held the phone away from her, one hand over the mouthpiece. What should she do? He sounded sincere. She wanted to go and yet . . . She counted to fifty, then she took her hand from the receiver.

'Peter? Ah, you're still there. Sorry to keep you. As it happens I do seem to be free next weekend.'

'That's great!' He sounded genuinely delighted.

'So – what did you have in mind?'

'I thought you could come up on Friday evening and stay until Sunday evening,' he said. 'I'll book you in here at The Ascot. It's my weekend off. I'll get tickets for a show for Saturday evening. Is there anything you particularly fancy seeing?'

Fleur's heart stirred with excitement. 'Oh, well, as a matter of fact I'd love to see *Phantom of the Opera*,' she said.

'Right. *Phantom* it is.'

'Unless you've already seen it?' she said quickly.

'No need to worry about that. I've already looked up the trains and there's one that gets in to Liverpool Street at seven-twenty. I'll meet you, all right?'

'Yes, fine.'

'I'm looking forward very much to seeing you again, Fleur,' he said softly.

'Are you? That's nice,' she said.

'Look, just one thing, Fleur. No need to mention the weekend to Mum, okay?'

She frowned. 'If you say so. But why?'

'It's just that I've always liked to keep my private life separate and you know what mothers are like.'

'I don't actually, but of course I won't say anything if you don't want me to.'

'Thanks. See you on Friday evening then. Can't wait. 'Bye, darling.'

'Goodbye, Peter.'

Fleur sat looking at the telephone for several minutes after she'd hung up, that 'Bye, darling' still echoing in her ears. Was she right to go up to London and spend a weekend with Peter? She wanted to very much. Ever since he'd gone back she thought about him constantly. But why not tell Sally? It felt wrong. What was the real reason he didn't want her to know? It wasn't as though there was anything to hide. Did he feel that she might disapprove? She quickly dismissed her concern, telling herself that Peter must have his own reasons. She put the thought out of her head and began looking forward to the weekend.

She saw him as soon as she got off the train, standing head and shoulders above everyone as he stood at the barrier. He didn't see her right away and for a moment she watched him raking the faces of all the passengers as they passed him. Then he spotted her and his face lit up.

'Fleur!' He held out his arms and she went into them. Passers by smiled at the sight of the handsome young couple embracing. 'It seems ages since I saw you,' he said, looking down into her face. 'Let me take your case. I've got the car. Or are you hungry? We can have something to eat now if you want?'

'No.' She laughed. 'I can wait till later, thanks. It is good to see you, Peter. I've looked forward to it all week.'

'Me too.' He put her case down again and drew her into his arms, kissing her. She struggled free, laughing and embarrassed. 'People are looking.'

'Let them.' He put an arm around her, pulling her close to his side as they walked. 'They're only jealous, especially the men.'

The Ascot was a small but elegant hotel overlooking Green Park. As they went in through the revolving door Fleur was impressed by its slightly old-fashioned air of affluent gentility. The decor was stylish yet discreet, the carpets deep and the lighting soft. At the reception desk she signed in and then they went up in the silent lift to the third floor. Peter opened the door for her with a flourish.

'Welcome to The Ascot, madam.'

Fleur looked around the comfortable room with delight. There was a large bed with a draped satin cover and quilted headboard. The built-in furniture was white and gilt and there was a lovely view of the park through the two long windows. Through the open bathroom door she glimpsed gleaming tiles, a pink suite and soft cream carpet. She turned to look at him.

'Oh, Peter, it's lovely!'

'There's TV and radio. A hair dryer if you need it, and tea and coffee-making facilities.' He smiled at her.

'Not that you'll be spending much time in here. I've got all sorts of things planned for us.'

She threw her arms around his neck. 'Oh, Peter, I never expected anything this grand. Do you know, I've never actually been in a hotel before, let alone one like this.' She peered at him doubtfully. 'It isn't costing you a fortune, I hope?'

He laughed. 'That's something you needn't bother your head about. I'm under manager, remember? I do have certain perks. Now, I'll leave you to unpack. Pick you up in an hour and we'll have dinner here. All right?'

She made the most of the hour, taking a luxurious bath in the elegant bathroom and changing into the dark red dress she had bought for their dinner date at New Year. When he knocked on the door she ran to open it, her cheeks flushed with anticipation. His admiring expression told her all that she wanted to know.

They dined downstairs in the hotel dining room where the food was even more delicious than that at the Fairwoods Country Club. Fleur enjoyed every mouthful. Peter had ordered wine, choosing carefully from the wine list. She found it sweet and refreshing and she lost count of how many times he refilled her glass. By the time they had finished Fleur felt pleasantly relaxed. When Peter asked her if she would like to go onto a club and dance she was surprised.

'It's eleven o'clock,' she said.

He laughed. 'You're in danger of sounding like a country cousin, my sweet,' he said. 'The night is still young.'

He took her to an intimate little club well known for its jazz and they danced in the dim, smoky atmosphere, pressed close together and barely moving on the tiny crowded floor. Fleur had more to drink. She hardly knew what was in her glass except that it never seemed to be empty but it didn't seem to matter very much.

They finally arrived back at The Ascot at two a.m. Fleur felt as though her feet hardly touched the ground and Peter collected her key from the night porter and escorted her up to her floor.

Turning the key in the lock he pushed open the door for her. She smiled at him. 'Aren't you coming in? I can make you a cup of coffee.'

Inside the room she groped around for the light switch and suddenly the situation seemed overwhelmingly funny. She began to giggle. 'Peter – where are you? I can't find you. It's dark and . . .'

In the darkness she stumbled against him. His arms closed around her and he held her close.

'I believe you're ever so slightly drunk, my darling,' he whispered in her ear.

'No, I'm not,' she said indignantly. 'How can I be?' She wound her arms around his neck. 'It's just that I need to hold onto you because – because I can't seem to stand up very well.'

He put his arm behind her knees and scooped her up. The room seemed to spin around her dizzily until she felt herself deposited on the softness of the bed. Peter switched on the bedside lamp and smiled down at her in the soft diffused light.

'There, that's better. Now I can see you.' He kicked off his shoes and lay down beside her, pulling her into his arms again.

She smiled hazily, snuggling against him. 'Mmm. That's comfy. I like it here – being with you – like this.' The room was still spinning as her lips parted eagerly for his kiss and when he began to undress her she felt her heartbeat quicken. The sensation of his hands exploring her body was heady and sensuous. It made her ache for more, and when he left her for a few

214

moments to undress she received him back with open arms, thrilling to the touch of his naked flesh against hers – offering herself with avid abandonment.

Looking down at her Peter held both her hands in his. 'Better get something sorted out first sweetheart,' he said. 'You're on the Pill I take it?'

She stared up at him. 'No.'

He smiled reassuringly. 'Okay, just as long as I know. Wouldn't do to take any risks, would it?'

It didn't occur to Fleur to be surprised that he had come prepared with condoms. And if he was surprised to find her a virgin he didn't say so. To begin with he was as gentle as his arousal allowed, but when they made love for the second time he found her less submissive, assuming a more assertive role and delighting him with her uninhibited passion. Dawn was breaking before they finally slept, their exhausted limbs entwined amidst a tangle of crumpled sheets.

Fleur was the first to waken. For a few moments she could not make out where she was, then she turned and saw Peter's head on the pillow beside her and slowly the events of the previous night came back to her. She blushed as she remembered the abandoned sensuality of the night before and decided to get up before Peter wakened. But as she was starting to get out of bed he stirred and opened his eyes.

'Hello, beautiful,' he said sleepily, throwing a restricting arm across her. 'Where do you think you're going?'

'I was going to get dressed,' she said.

'I prefer you as you are.' He raised himself on one elbow to look down at her. 'You know, you could be a model, Fleur. You have the most beautiful body. Those page three girls have absolutely nothing on you.'

She shook her head and tried to sit up. 'Peter – don't. You're embarrassing me. I want to get up.'

He laughed softly. 'You weren't embarrassed last night. And there's no hurry to get up. We have all day.' He pressed her back against the pillows and began to kiss her breasts, circling each nipple with his tongue until he drew little moans of pleasure from her. 'All day to make love, my darling,' he whispered seductively into the hollow of her throat as his hands caressed her. 'Isn't that a delicious prospect?'

Although the effects of the vodka had long since faded, her head was beginning to spin again. Peter's lovemaking was far more intoxicating than any alcohol and under the irresistible persuasion of his teasing, questing lips and fingers she abandoned her inhibitions once again, giving herself up to her own clamouring urges.

At the theatre that evening they sat hand in hand. Fleur was enraptured by the ambience, the music and romance of the story, the sheer spectacle of it all. But as much as she enjoyed the show she was impatient to be alone with Peter again. Afterwards they went back to the hotel to eat a late dinner, then up to Fleur's room where they fell eagerly into each other's arms again.

Long after Peter had fallen asleep Fleur lay awake, her body still tingling, every nerve singing, vitally alive and glowing from their lovemaking. These two days had been a revelation. She would not have believed it was possible to feel like this. Till now love and desire was something she had only read about. If she'd given them any thought at all it was to doubt their existence – to believe they were nothing but fantasy. Something dreamed up by authors in order to sell books. Now she knew better. Everything the books said was right. She was in love with Peter, in love for the first and last time. So much in love with him that she would have done anything he asked.

She thought of Sally and wondered what she would

think when she knew they had spent this weekend together. Surely she would not be angry at the small deception, especially when she realised how much in love they were? She raised herself on one elbow to look down at Peter's sleeping face. He was so handsome. She loved him so much that just looking at him like this brought a lump to her throat. It was hard to believe that so much happiness was possible.

At the station the following afternoon he saw her onto the train and kissed her goodbye.

'When shall I see you again?' she asked, holding onto his hand till the very last minute.

'I'll ring you,' he said. 'I don't know when I'll be free again, but I'll ring.'

As the train began to move she asked, 'Peter – will you write to me?' She visualised the pleasure of getting a letter from him – reading the special intimate things he might write, writing back.

He laughed and shrugged his shoulders. 'I might. I'll see. I'm not very good at putting my thoughts on paper.'

'Just a few lines, please.'

He was walking with the moving train, but the distance between them was lengthening and she was forced at last to let go of the hand she held. There was something odd about him this afternoon. This morning when they first wakened he had been as warm and passionate as before, making love to her even more urgently because it would be the last opportunity for a while. But ever since lunch he had seemed restrained, almost distant, as though he was locked up inside himself, afraid to display his feelings. Perhaps he felt as sad as she did at saying goodbye. As the train reached the end of the platform she leaned out of the window to wave, but to her dismay he had already turned and started to walk away.

She sat down in her corner seat, puzzled and slightly troubled. Why couldn't he have stayed until the train had gone? But he was a man, wasn't he? Men were sometimes reluctant to reveal the depth of their feelings. Maybe he wanted to be by himself. Tomorrow, or maybe the next day, he would telephone and everything would be all right. And they would write to each other – wonderful poetic letters that would almost make up for the distance between them.

She closed her eyes, beginning already to compose her first letter to him – shutting out the other occupants of the carriage along with the rest of the world. Enclosed in her own private world she indulged herself with thoughts of Peter, reliving the blissful two days and nights they had shared.

Eleanor Maitland was making her bedtime drink that Sunday night when a knock on her front door made her look up in surprise. She slipped the chain on and opened it a crack to peer out cautiously into the darkness.

'Who is it?'

'It all right, Lena, it's me, Charlie Grant.'

'Charlie?' Eleanor closed the door and slipped off the chain, opening it again to reveal her childhood friend standing on the doorstep. 'I hope there's nothing wrong?'

'No, no. Nothing to worry about. I was passing and I thought you might like to see this.' He tapped a flat brown paper parcel under his arm. 'Well, are you going to ask me in, lass, or do I have to stand here and freeze?'

'Sorry, Charlie.' She opened the door. 'Come in, of course. I was just making myself some cocoa, would you like some?'

He pulled a face. 'Cocoa? I'll pass on that, if you don't mind. I always say it's only for old maids and invalids.'

218

'I might still have a drop of whisky in the cupboard, left over from Christmas.'

He grinned. 'Now you're talking!'

In the living room she took the whisky bottle from the sideboard cupboard and poured him a glass. 'Well – are you going to show me what's in the parcel then?'

'Oh, yes. I almost forgot.' He removed the paper and held up his offering. 'I found this the other day when I was having a bit of a clear out. An old school photograph, look. You and I are both on it. Your Jim an' all. I thought you might like to have it so I've had it framed for you.'

'Oh, Charlie!' Eleanor took the photograph and studied it carefully, her eyes misty. 'How thoughtful of you.' She sighed as she looked at the rows of childish faces ranged in tiers against the background of the Victorian school building. 'It all seems so long ago, doesn't it?'

'It does that.' He stood looking around him. 'Fancy you still living here, Lena,' he said. 'How many years is it?'

'Forty-two,' she told him. 'The last fifteen alone. It suits me, this little place. All my memories are here. Moving to some big posh house is all very well, but we're not all rolling in money like some I might mention, Charlie Grant.'

He sipped his whisky and smacked his lips appreciatively. 'Mmm – don't know about rolling in it. Not as well off as some folk think,' he said, making himself comfortable in the armchair by the fire. 'Thing is, Lena, strictly between ourselves, I'm hoping to get the contract for the redevelopment of Victoria Gardens. Our plans for Meadowlands Park have been passed okay. It's going to be the most upmarket project we've ever tackled, is that, but it's going to stretch our resources to the limit and the bank could prove to be tricky over the loan we need to get things up and running.'

'Oh? Why's that?'

'Oh, don't get me wrong, they haven't turned us down,' he went on. 'Our credit's good, but we still have a substantial loan outstanding and it'd be a lot more comfortable not to have to ask. The Victoria Gardens contract would just about save our bacon if you know what I mean.'

She nodded. 'I do. But I don't quite see how I can help, Charlie.'

He cleared his throat. 'Well, all I really need to know is, when are they likely to offer the job for tender and what kind of sum are they prepared to spend on it? Julia's on the planning committee, of course, but you know what new brooms are like. She's as tight as a tick. Can't get a dicky bird out of her.' He leaned forward towards her. 'You're on the finance and general purposes committee aren't you? You must have some idea. Now, Lena, I'm sure you know that anything that passes from you to me will be strictly between ourselves. Goes without saying, eh?' He winked.

'Yes, it does, Charlie, but I'm afraid there's nothing I can tell you.'

His jaw dropped. 'Oh, come on, lass. We go back a long way. Surely you can do me a small favour like this? I wouldn't ask if it wasn't vital.'

'I know you wouldn't, but I really can't help, Charlie.' She paused, biting her lip. 'But as you say, we do go back a long way and there is one piece of advice I can give you, off the record.'

'Yes?'

'Give the whole idea up.'

'Give it up! Why?'

She sighed. 'I shouldn't be telling you this but it'll be public knowledge very soon anyway. The plans for redeveloping Victoria Gardens have been abandoned, or at least shelved for the foreseeable future. Since the community charge came in the budgets have gone haywire. The council won't be making any major changes until they've have had time to sort out a new financial programme.'

Charlie stood up and put his glass down on the mantelpiece with the thump of finality. For a moment he stood staring pensively into the fire, then he looked up at her. 'I appreciate your telling me this, Lena,' he said. 'You're a pal.'

'I'm just sorry it had to be bad news, Charlie.'

He nodded thoughtfully. 'Don't know about that. Forewarned is forearmed, as they say. You might have done me more of a favour than you realise.' He stepped up to her and put his arms round her waist, then he kissed her full on the mouth. 'You always were a grand lass, Lena. Thanks. And thanks for the whisky too.'

Fleur was letting herself into the flat when a step on the stairs made her turn. As his head came level with the landing Tom's face lit up with pleasure at seeing her.

'Hi! You're back then.'

'Yes, I'm back.' She was irritated. She'd hoped to get in without being seen. All she wanted was to be by herself. Now Tom would expect to be invited in to hear all about the weekend she was supposed to have spent in Hackney with her grandmother's friend.

'How was it then?'

'Fine, thanks.'

'I'll make you a coffee, if you like?'

'It's all right. I can make one for myself.' His hurt expression immediately made her regret her terse reply.

'I just thought you might not have any milk,' he said apologetically.

'I like it black anyway.'

'Right then.' He backed away. 'I'll leave you to unpack in peace.'

She relented. 'No. Look, sorry if I was sharp, don't go.' She took her key out of the lock and pushed the door open. 'Come in. Tell me all the latest gossip.'

As she took off her coat, he busied himself filling the kettle and plugging it in. 'You had a good time then? You look positively blooming.'

'Thanks.' She came and stood with her back to the worktop in the tiny kitchen. 'Look, Tom, there's something I think I should tell you.'

He turned to look enquiringly at her in the act of pouring hot water into the mugs. 'Yes?'

'I didn't quite tell you the truth – about this weekend, I mean.'

'No?' He handed her a mug of black coffee.

'I didn't go to Hackney. I stayed at The Ascot Hotel in Park Lane.'

'Wow! Very posh. Don't tell me you've won a . . .'

'With Peter Arden. Sally's son.'

'Oh!'

'Yes. We – I'm in love with him, Tom.'

He stood looking at her. 'What you're saying is that you slept with him.'

'Please, don't make it sound sleazy. It isn't. I'm really happy. Happier than I ever thought possible.'

'Really? I'm glad for you.' He put his untouched coffee down on the worktop. 'Right then. If there's nothing else you want to tell me, I'll go.'

'Please, Tom, don't be difficult about it. Don't spoil it for me.'

'*Difficult?* What the hell do you expect?' He rounded on her. 'Do you want me to stay so that you can tell me all the intimate details and gloat? So that you can enjoy watching me curl up with misery. Is that it?'

'Misery?' She stared at him, shocked and dismayed

222

by his reaction. '*No!* Tom, how can you say that?'

'Oh, come on! You must have known how I felt about you,' he said, his voice thick with emotion. 'Ever since you first came here I've hoped that we might get closer. I've waited, thinking you were still traumatised over your bad experience. I've been patient, waiting for you to come to me when you were ready, in your own time. What a prize bloody *idiot* I was! This Arden guy crooks his little finger and you go haring off to London. He wines and dines you and before you know it – bingo! He's got you into bed! Simple as that!'

'It wasn't like that, Tom. You're making it all sound cheap and sordid.'

'Then how was it? You haven't known him five minutes. How can you be in love with someone you hardly know?'

'I don't know. I just *am!*'

'I see. There's nothing more to be said then, is there?' He walked to the door. 'Goodnight, Fleur.'

'Tom – wait. Don't go like that. I still want us to be . . .'

He spun round to look at her, stopping her words with his wounded expression. '*Friends?* Is that what you were going to say?' His eyes were bright with anguish. 'For Christ's sake, spare me that old chestnut, Fleur. At least have the decency to spare me that!'

Vernon's weekend had been hellish. He hadn't seen Joanna since their quarrel and he could only guess at what was going through her mind. He'd spent Saturday on the golf course and Julia had invited both sets of parents round for the day on Sunday so there was no escape. After they had eaten a late lunch his father took him to one side.

'Can we have a word, Vern?' He glanced around him and lowered his voice. 'In private, I mean. Perhaps we

223

could go to your study?'

'Of course.' Inside the study Charlie took the high-backed leather swivel chair behind Vernon's desk, leaving him to draw up a hard chair for himself opposite. It was typical and Vernon tried unsuccessfully to rise above the resentment that rankled. He looked enquiringly at his father.

'What is it, Dad? Problems?'

Charlie lit his pipe and regarded his son through a cloud of blue smoke. 'How much cash was Mrs Hanson thinking of investing with GPC?'

Vernon's eyebrows rose in surprise. 'I don't know.'

'You don't *know*?' Charlie glared at him. 'You come to a board meeting with an investment proposal without knowing how much the punter's got to invest? Well, I think you'd better find out then, don't you?'

'But you turned the offer down,' Vernon protested.

'Yes – well, something's come to my attention since that meeting.' Charlie regarded the glowing bowl of his pipe. 'We won't be getting the contract for the Victoria Gardens redevelopment so if there's any extra cash going, I think maybe we should look into it.'

'Why won't we be getting the contract?'

'They're shelving the project. Seems the community charge has thrown the council's budget out of kilter. Oh, they might do it at some later stage but that'll be too late for us. I want to get Meadowlands under way before the bubble bursts. I want it doing *now!*' He thumped the desk to reinforce his statement.

'I think I should warn you, if she invests money she's going to want a directorship,' Vernon pointed out.

'Is she now? Doesn't want much, does she? Damned cheeky bitch. Well, we'll meet that one when we come to it.'

Vernon shifted uneasily on his hard chair. 'Look, shouldn't Harry be in on all this?'

Charlie waved his pipe, scattering hot ash across the pristine desk top. 'We'll let him in on it when I've tested the ground. You know what an old woman he is, forever putting obstacles in the way. Now . . .' He leaned forward. 'When can you find out what she's thinking of investing with us?'

'Why don't you ask her yourself?'

Charlie grinned knowingly. 'She's your personal assistant. You're the one with the – what shall we call it? – *intimate inside knowledge*.' He leaned back, enjoying his son's obvious discomfort. 'No, what I mean is, ask casually. I don't want her getting her hopes up. If she's got nowt but a few piddlin' hundred to put in it won't be worth bothering with, and certainly not worth a directorship. I can't help thinking that if she was that well off she wouldn't be living in Hazel Grove and working for us.' He gave Vernon a meaningful look. 'Not even as your PA. But you did mention a substantial divorce settlement so maybe it's worth asking.'

'I'll sound her out in the morning.'

Charlie stood up. 'Right. Do that. And let me know as soon as you can.' He walked to the door. 'Better get back now before the womenfolk send out a search party!'

As Vernon parked the BMW in his parking space, Joanna's little red Mazda pulled up beside him. Opening the window he gestured to her to do the same. She frowned at him as she wound the window down and he noticed that she still looked far from happy.

'What is it, Vernon?'

'I want to talk to you.'

She got out of the car and locked the door. 'There's nothing to talk about.'

'Yes, there is. Get in here with me for a minute. I don't want to talk in the office with all the staff flapping their ears.'

Something about the urgency of his tone made her hesitate. Slipping her keys into her handbag, she walked round the car and got into the passenger seat. 'Well?' She raised her eyebrows at him challengingly.

'I have to ask you something.'

'Go on then – ask.'

'How much were you thinking of investing with GPC?'

Her eyes flickered and he knew he'd got her full attention. 'Why do you want to know?'

'Isn't that obvious?'

'Your father has agreed?'

'He might. I've been working on him all weekend. He just might agree when he's satisfied himself as to just how . . .' he cleared his throat, '. . . how serious you are.'

'*Seriously* serious.' Joanna leaned back against the seat. 'I know that the company is trying to launch into up-market residential properties starting with Meadowlands Park,' she said slowly. 'I know how much initial investment these ventures require from my own experience in real estate, and I also know that GPC has a lot of cash tied up in land, materials, not to mention payments still outstanding on an existing bank loan.'

He nodded. 'You've done your homework, obviously.'

'Well, it is part of my job after all. The fact remains, GPC's cash flow is strictly limited.'

'True. So?'

'So I thought perhaps five hundred K might help for starters.'

He stared at her, his eyes popping, momentarily stunned into silence. 'Five hundred thou'? Half a *million*? You're joking!'

'I'm not in the habit of joking about large sums of

money. And there's more where that came from.' She smiled. 'I don't want to appear vulgar, do I?'

'But – so *much*? I mean how – where . . . ?'

'Where did I get it? I told you I had a good settlement from my ex. He happened to own the real-estate business I worked for and he made quite a lot of money out of it. I made good and sure that I had my own share of the business, so I had that as well as my settlement. I sold it before I left the States – at a very good profit, I might add.' She laughed. 'Don't worry, Vernon. The money is there all right. It's all kosher, legal and above board.'

He closed his gaping mouth and took a deep breath. 'But the house you bought. And the car, your job here, your lifestyle . . .'

'Isn't that of a wealthy woman? You're right, Vernon. But living a life of pampered luxury isn't what I want. I consider myself far too young to spend my time and money on luxury cruises and face-lifts,' she told him. 'I like money for what it can do. I want to make it work for me. I love a challenge. It's what life is all about as far as I'm concerned right now. Pampered luxury can come later.'

He nodded. 'I think you should see Dad as soon as possible.'

'What about my seat on the board?'

He smiled wryly. 'I think you hold the trump card as far as that's concerned,' he said. As she made to get out of the car he laid a hand on her arm. 'And what about us, Jo? Are we still on? Am I forgiven?'

Glancing round the car park to make sure they were not observed, she leaned across and kissed him, her mouth moist and seductive and the pressure of her hand warm on his thigh. He reached out to pull her closer.

'Oh, Jo, I've had a hell of a weekend. I was so

worried you might not want . . .'

'Shhh.' Very gently she extricated herself from his arms. 'Later darling. Business first, pleasure later. Maybe we could meet at the Fairwoods this evening?'

'Yes. I'll ring and make a booking.'

She smiled her sultry smile at him, running the tip of her tongue along her upper lip. 'Then I can show you just how grateful I really am.'

Fleur watched for the postman every morning, running downstairs as soon as she heard the rattle of the letter-box, but to her disappointment there was no letter from Peter. She decided to write to him anyway, but it wasn't as easy as she'd thought. Putting down in words what she felt was so difficult. When she read it through afterwards it all sounded so schoolgirlish and inadequate. She kept the letter that finally satisfied her, slipping it into a drawer and promising herself that she'd post it if she didn't hear from him by next weekend.

Arden Catering had gone through the usual post-Christmas lull and now the bookings were beginning to come in again. Through the lull Sally and she had been working hard, stocking up the freezers so that when the functions began again they would have plenty of ready-prepared foods to draw on. Each afternoon Fleur worked in the office, making sure the paperwork, orders and accounts were up to date. But being restricted to the kitchen and the office had become tedious and by the time they set out for their first party, a twenty-first birthday celebration, both were glad to be back in harness.

As they loaded the van Fleur wondered whether Sally had heard from Peter. His lack of communication had made her uneasy. She wondered whether he was all right. She had telephoned The Ascot twice to find out why she hadn't heard from him, to be told on the first occasion that he was out; on the second that he was too busy to come to the telephone. Finally she decided to come right out and ask Sally.

'Have you heard from Peter lately?' She tried to sound as casual as she could as she climbed into the van's driving seat.

'Yes, I had a long letter from him just this morning,' she said as she fastened her seat belt. 'As a matter of fact he sprung some rather surprising news on me.' She turned to look at Fleur. 'How would you feel about managing on your own for a few days?'

'You're planning to go away? When?'

'In April. Peter has announced that he's getting married and he wants me to go over to Switzerland for the big day.' She turned to smile at Fleur. 'Thanks to your efficiency I shall be quite confident to leave you in sole charge, as long as you're happy about it.'

'Yes . . .' Fleur's mouth had dried so that speaking was difficult. 'Yes, of course,' she said. She ran her tongue over her dry lips and took a deep breath. 'I'd no idea that Peter was engaged.'

'Neither did I. Not officially anyway. Lorraine is Swiss. They met when he was working in Switzerland and she was working in London until recently.' She smiled. 'She's a really lovely girl. I've met her several times. Her father has a lovely hotel on the outskirts of Geneva. She and Peter have been seeing each other for about two years, but I didn't know it was this serious until now.'

'I see.' Fleur had to grip the steering wheel tightly to stop her hands from shaking.

'It seems that the wedding is to be in a little church by the lake,' Sally went on. 'It will be so beautiful there in the spring. So romantic.'

Numb with shock, Fleur scarcely heard as Sally chattered on excitedly about her future daughter-in-law. It was like a slap in the face, hearing so suddenly that Peter was to be married. He had never even mentioned a girlfriend. But then he hadn't given much away at all, especially about himself. How could she have been so easily taken in? Surely there had to be some mistake, she told herself disbelievingly – a misunderstanding?

'She's going to make the perfect daughter-in-law,' Sally was saying. 'I've always wanted a daughter so naturally I can hardly wait. When they're married they're hoping to run a hotel of their own in Switzerland. Lorraine's father has already started looking out for one for them. She turned and noticed Fleur's shocked expression for the first time. 'Fleur! Are you all right, dear?'

She shook her head and forced a smile. 'I'm fine. It's just – just a surprise, that's all.'

'You're not worried about managing on your own? It will only be for a few days. And it won't be for a while yet.'

'No. I'm not worried at all.' Fleur swallowed hard at the lump in her throat that threatened to choke her.

'I could always get someone in to help you if you're at all doubtful.'

'No, really, I'll look forward to it. Fleur swallowed hard and turned to smile at her employer. 'Congratulations, Sally,' she said. 'I'm very happy for you.'

Chapter 9

Charlie Grant leaned back in his chair. The pad before him on the desk was covered with calculations and his heart was pounding with excitement. When Vernon had named the sum the Hanson woman was thinking of sinking into the business, he'd been floored. *Gobsmacked!* His mind had been on overdrive ever since. What couldn't GPC do with that kind of input? Especially just now! It meant that the idea that had been in his mind ever since his visit to Lena was an actual possibility. This could turn out to be the biggest opportunity he'd ever been offered.

It would need to be handled carefully, of course, he told himself, drumming his fingers on the desk, especially in view of who the investor was, but the breathtaking idea that filled his mind eclipsed all his reservations. The thing was to get on with it. Strike while the iron was hot. No good dithering about till things went off the boil. If he waited for Harry and Vernon to ruminate over his idea and come up with all the inevitable objections it would be too late. Vernon he could easily sway. It was Harry who was the fly in the ointment. He was always so afraid to try anything new and daring. No, best to have all the loose ends tied up and put it to them both as a package – a *fait accompli*.

231

After all, he was really only obliged to consult them over incurring debts, not investments.

A couple of confidential phone calls to his solicitor had reassured him on the few possible stumbling blocks and cleared up some vital queries. Now everything looked set fair. He rubbed his hands together gleefully. It couldn't be better. He buzzed his secretary.

'Ask Mrs Hanson to come in here, will you, Phyllis? And then see that I'm not disturbed for half an hour.'

He looked up when Joanna walked into the office. She was a damned good-looking woman right enough. No wonder Vernon was taken with her. But her money was far more attractive than her face and figure – to him at any rate. Better not let her think he was snatching her hand off though. The impression he would convey was that they were doing *her* a favour by letting her into the firm. He gave her his most affable smile.

'Have a seat, Mrs Hanson. Or may I call you Joanna?'

'Please do.' She sat in the chair opposite, crossing her shapely legs. She looked as cool as a cucumber. But then she had every right to.

Charlie leaned back. 'Vernon tells me you have some spare cash you'd like to invest with us. We feel very flattered that you have so much faith in the firm.'

'Does that mean you're accepting my offer?'

She didn't beat about the bush! But that was all to the good. 'In principal, yes,' he said cagily. 'Though there will be a few technicalities to iron out, of course. As a matter of fact I have a new project in mind and the input of fresh money could be a help.'

'The Meadowlands Park Estate, you mean?'

'Ah, no.' Charlie smiled and tapped the side of his nose. 'Better than that. Something even more ambitious. What I have in mind will finance Meadowlands and bring all of us a substantial income for many years to come,' he said. 'But I don't want to say anything further on the subject till my partners and I have had a meeting to discuss the possibility.'

'I take it that I will be invited to this meeting, Mr Grant?'

He glanced at her. One look into those calculating green eyes told him that she was not a woman to be trifled with. There was no pulling the wool over her eyes either. She already worked for Vernon and had access to the firm's books, so she was well aware of their delicately balanced financial situation. She knew exactly what she was doing right down to the last detail. He reminded himself to have a private word of warning in Vernon's ear about her. A woman like this could eat him for breakfast and be looking around for afters before he knew what had hit him. He cleared his throat. 'Is that what you'd like?'

'I'd go further than that, Mr Grant. In fact I'd like it to be perfectly clear from the start that unless I have an active partnership, the deal is off.'

Charlie gritted his teeth and kept the benign smile resolutely glued in place. 'I had thought a director-ship . . .'

'I hardly think so, Mr Grant. Theoretically, any employee can be a director. With the kind of investment I'm prepared to offer . . .'

Charlie held up his hand. 'All right, lass. Fair enough. A partnership it shall be.'

'With the accompanying bonuses, reimbursements and expenses, of course. I would also like to be appointed Company Secretary,' she said coolly.

Charlie's eyes bulged with astonishment. *'Oh!* I thought you'd want to give up your status as an employee.'

'Oh, no, Mr Grant. I have no intention of becoming some kind of sleeping partner. I would hope to play a much more useful part in the firm's running.'

Charlie was completely thrown. 'Well, I don't know . . .'

'You need have no worries. I can assure you that I am up to the job. You are aware of my experience in real-estate management.'

'I am. Yes.'

'And I have to say that I feel a partnership is a small return in view of the risk I'm taking.'

'You drive a hard bargain, lass.'

'Not at all.' Joanna smiled icily. 'I think it's best to put our cards on the table so that we know exactly where we each stand right from the outset, don't you?'

'Oh, by all means.' Charlie fiddled with the pencils in the pen tray on his desk. 'Er – in view of the terms you're asking for I shall have to speak to my son and my partner before I accept your offer, of course.'

'Really?' She looked surprised. 'Surely you're not obliged to do that, Mr Grant. As chairman of the company you are surely authorised to accept investments at your own discretion?'

'Ah . . .' Charlie coughed. 'Well, yes, of course you're right. I see we'll have a lot to discuss, Miss – er – Joanna. I'll call a board meeting for tomorrow and introduce you then.'

'I shall need to be reassured of the terms before I attend any meeting, Mr Grant,' she told him. 'And I would also like to have prior knowledge of this new project you're planning before I make my final decision to invest. After all, it is a lot of money.'

He stared at her, momentarily rendered speechless. *Bloody cheek!* This woman was going to need very careful handling. He was half tempted to tell her what she could do with her money and chuck her out here and now. Then he remembered how much she was offering and the exciting plan already more than half worked out in his mind.

'As a matter of fact, you're the first person I've mentioned it to,' he told her. 'Even Vernon doesn't know about it yet, and you want me to confide in you?'

She smiled. 'I'm afraid so, yes. You can be sure that it will be strictly between ourselves, especially if it's to be my money financing it.'

'Company money,' he corrected her. Nevertheless, he saw her point. 'All right then,' he said at last. 'Stay behind after work this evening and I'll tell you a bit about it. I'll agree to the terms you've mentioned, provisionally of course, and we'll work out the details of your partnership. But you must understand that your acceptance into the company must be above board. The whole thing must at least *appear* to be finalised at the meeting. Then, all things being equal, we'll get you registered and have my solicitor draw up an agreement.'

She smiled triumphantly. 'I knew you'd see it in a positive way, Mr Grant.'

'I'll see you here in my office after work then.' Charlie made a note on his pad and buzzed the inter-com to let her know that the interview was at an end. No harm in reminding her that he was still the one in charge.

She stood up and came round the desk, offering her hand. 'Thank you, Mr Grant. I'm sure neither of us is going to regret the decision.'

He stood up, taking her hand briefly. 'I trust not, my dear. I trust not.'

He watched her walk from the room with resentment fermenting inside him like rising yeast. She'd got a bloody nerve, screwing him to the floor like that. But she'd got what he wanted so he was going to have to bite his tongue and make her look tempting to the others. It was going to take all the bravado he could muster.

Fleur stood in the draughty hallway at thirteen Victoria Gardens, the receiver of the payphone in her hand as she waited patiently. It was several minutes since the receptionist at The Ascot had gone to find Peter. It was a good job she had brought plenty of change with her. Any moment now her time would run out.

This was the third time she'd tried to ring him since Sally had mentioned his engagement. She kept telling herself that there had to be some simple explanation. Perhaps he hadn't told his mother that he had broken off the engagement. He seemed to keep his private life very much to himself. Maybe he had been putting it off, afraid that she would be disappointed – upset. There was a click at the other end and the receptionist's voice spoke.

'Miss Sylvester?'

'Yes, I'm still here.'

'I'm sorry but Mr Arden isn't answering his office phone or the one in his flat.'

'Oh, could you please try and find him for me?' Fleur begged. 'I've been trying to get him all week and it's very important.'

'Well, I'll try and find out whether he's in the hotel.'

She had only just gone when Fleur saw the digital readout flashing. Her time was up. She hastily put more money in before she was cut off. These pay phones seemed to eat the money.

'Having trouble, are you, dear?'

She turned and saw to her dismay that Ivy was standing at the top of the basement stairs, half hidden in the shadows, her eyes glinting with curiosity. 'No – just waiting,' she said. 'It's a long-distance call. A private one.'

236

Impervious to subtleties, Ivy ignored the hint. In fact the news that the call was private only increased her curiosity. 'Oh dear,' she said. 'You haven't had bad news, I hope?'

'No, nothing like that.'

The front door opened and Tom came in, bringing with him a gust of raw February air. His leather jacket was spattered with rain. He glanced at her and then at Ivy. 'Everything all right?'

'It's just Fleur,' Ivy said. 'She's making an important long-distance call. Seems to be having a bit of trouble getting through.'

'I *am* through,' Fleur said through clenched teeth, her nerves shredded. 'I'm just waiting for – for the person I'm ringing to come to the phone.'

Summing up the situation, Tom walked to the top of the basement stairs and took Ivy's arm firmly. 'You were asking me to have a look at your television the other day,' he said. 'Why don't I come down with you now, before I take my coat off?'

They had just disappeared down the basement stairs when she heard the telephone click and Peter's voice at the other end made her heart leap with relief.

'Fleur? What's wrong? I was in a meeting.' He sounded irritable. 'Is there something wrong with Mother?'

'No, nothing like that. Sally's fine. I'm sorry, Peter, but I had to speak to you,' she said breathlessly. 'I've been trying to get you all week.'

'Yes?'

His abruptness made her feel tongue-tied. 'I – you didn't write,' she said lamely.

'I told you, I'm no good at putting thoughts down on paper. You haven't dragged me out of a meeting just to say that, surely?'

'No.' She took a deep breath. 'Peter, I think there's

237

some kind of misunderstanding here. Your mother seems to think that you're engaged – getting married in April. To a Swiss girl called Lorraine.'

'Oh.' There was a small silence, then he said. 'So – what of it?'

Her heart turned to ice as she clutched the receiver. 'You mean – it's true?'

'Yes, it's true.' He sounded irritated. 'My mother would hardly have made it up, would she?'

'But I thought – I thought maybe there was some mistake – that she'd got hold of the wrong idea.'

'Look, I'm sorry if you think I should have told you, Fleur, but we had a great time together, didn't we?' he said. 'You surely didn't think there was any more to it than that?'

She swallowed. It was like a horrible dream. Soon she'd wake up and find it was all nonsense. 'But I *did*, Peter!' She felt her cheeks growing hot as the full implication of the situation hit her. 'Did you imagine I was the kind of girl who'd spend a weekend with just anyone?' Her mind was whirling with images of the two of them in that hotel room, naked in each other's arms – making frenzied, abandoned love, totally immersed in one another. And all the time it had meant nothing – less than nothing to him. He had simply been using her, amusing himself while his fiancée was absent.

'Fleur, look, let's be realistic about this. It was no big deal,' he was saying unbelievably in her ear. 'We both enjoyed ourselves, didn't we? You had a luxury weekend, good food and wine, a show. I thought you understood from the start that it was just fun – time out for us both.'

She could hardly believe what she was hearing. He made it sound as though it had been some kind of deal – sex in return for a good time. She opened her mouth

238

to speak, but no sound would come from her constricted throat.

'For heaven's sake, Fleur,' he went on. 'Get real for God's sake! You got as much out of it as I did, so what are you complaining about? There's no harm done. We haven't hurt anyone.'

A dozen angry retorts sprang to her mind, but they all died before she could voice them. Clearly there was nothing she could say that would make any impression on him. He would not be interested in her hurt feelings and she was already too ashamed to risk more humiliation.

She took a deep breath to steady her voice. 'I'm sorry, Peter. We seem to have got our wires crossed. I don't want to be in your debt. I'll send you the money for my room and for the theatre ticket.'

'Oh, my God!' She heard him groan impatiently. 'Don't be so bourgeois. I don't want your money. It was fun – a laugh, that's all. Look, I think you're a great girl. You don't owe me anything.'

Her hand tightened round the receiver. The word 'bourgeois' had stung her acutely. He probably thought she was too ignorant to know what it meant.

'A laugh. That's how you see it?'

'Yes, of course. Let's just remember it like that. I thought you were a modern, liberal-minded girl.'

'Let's face it, Peter, we both know what you thought I was.'

'You're over reacting,' he said coldly. 'But if you feel that way, it's your problem, not mine. And if I were you I wouldn't get any ideas about running to my mother and playing the wronged little innocent.'

'Don't worry. I think far too much of Sally to let her know what kind of man her son is!' Still shaking with anger she hung up and rested her burning forehead against the cold wall, feeling as though the pain inside her chest would suffocate her. She'd been a challenge to him, nothing more. She wouldn't sleep with him on their first date and he couldn't resist trying again to prove to himself how irresistible he was. And she had fallen for it, taken the bait like a fool. She could still scarcely believe she could have been so naive.

Another of Ivy's tenants came in, nodded 'good evening' to her and went on his way up the stairs. As soon as it was quiet again Fleur lifted the receiver and dialled the hotel's number again. When the receptionist answered she enquired as to the cost of a weekend stay at The Ascot plus the cost of a theatre ticket. When the girl told her she caught her breath. It was more – much more than she had thought.

Upstairs in the flat she took out the tin in which she had been saving money for the balcony. Ever since she moved in she had been putting her spare change in the tin ready for the day when she would buy the paint, the hanging baskets and plants for what she thought of as her little corner of heaven. She sat on the bed and counted the money. It was about half what she needed. She would have to live cheaply all next month, but she was determined not to be in Peter Arden's debt. Hot tears stung her eyes and thickened her throat. She swallowed hard and dashed away the wetness with the back of her hand. She *wouldn't* cry for him. He wasn't worth it. But the hurt and humiliation wouldn't go away. It was worse than the shame and outrage of what had happened in the alley all those months ago in Hackney. At least her attacker had made his intentions to hurt and humiliate perfectly clear. That skinhead had had more integrity than Peter Arden, the first man she had trustingly given her love to. She had always thought herself streetwise, a good judge of character, yet it seemed she was more naive than a babe in arms.

At last she gave in and let the tears trickle unchecked down her cheeks. Keeling over sideways on the bed, she drew up her knees and wrapped her arms around herself until she was curled into a tight ball. What was it about her that made people see her as some kind of expendable commodity, to be used and tossed aside? Why did she appear so insignificant and worthless?

A sudden soft tapping on the door startled her. She sat up and brushed the tears from her face with her fingers. It would probably be Ivy, come to probe, having scented a juicy piece of gossip. She sat quite still. If she ignored her she might go away.

But a moment later the knock was repeated and Tom's voice said softly, 'Fleur, are you in there? Are you all right?'

She stood up and went across to the door, smoothing her hair as she went. 'Yes – yes, I'm fine.' Standing close to the door she sensed that he was still on the other side and after a moment's hesitation she unlocked it. Ivy had ears like a bat. If she heard them she'd be up in a minute herself. Opening the door a couple of inches she looked out at him. 'It's all right. I'm fine, really.'

He peered at her. 'You don't look it. What's wrong, Fleur? Can I do anything?'

She opened the door and let him in. 'I'm all right. But thanks for asking.' She made herself smile at him. 'Would you like a coffee?'

He stood looking at her, unconvinced, his eyes searching hers. 'Do you want to talk about it?'

She turned away to fill the kettle, busying herself with mugs and the milk bottle. 'It's just – oh, nothing really. A little disappointment, you could say. I'll get over it.'

'It's him, isn't it? Arden. He's let you down.'

She turned to look at him, her chin held high and her eyes dry. 'Not really. I read him wrong, that's all. I thought our relationship meant something – was worth more.'

'What's he done?'

She shrugged. 'He hasn't actually done anything. I found out that he's engaged – getting married in April.' She waved a hand at him as though to erase the angry expression from his face. 'No, Tom, it's *me*. People are more open-minded nowadays. I was brought up by my grandmother. She always believed that love was a precious gift that you only gave to someone special. I suppose that's just stuffy and old-fashioned nowadays.'

'I don't happen to think so.'

'I didn't understand that the time Peter and I spent together – what happened between us – was just meant to be for amusement. I should have seen it for what it was and taken it lightly. It's my fault. I've been naive and stupid.'

'No, you haven't! Don't say that.' Longing to comfort her, he took a step towards her then stopped, his hands clenched at his sides. 'Look, I've always respected your privacy, Fleur, so I'm not going to force my company on you. I won't invade your space, but you know where I am if you need me. Right?'

She nodded. 'Thanks, Tom.' The kettle boiled and she made the coffee, handing him a mug, glad of something to keep him a few minutes longer.

As he sipped the hot brew he looked at her. 'Why don't you try to trace your real mother?' he said. 'I think you need to, Fleur. I think it's what you came here for, whether you realise it or not. And I don't think you're ever going to be really happy till you do it. You see, even if you don't actually contact her you'd . . .'

'I know who she is,' she interrupted.

He stared at her. 'You *do*? But how . . . ?'

'By accident as it happens. I knew her maiden name,

you see. We came face to face at a party we catered for just after Christmas. Sally was giving me the background of the guests there and Ju— her name came up.'

'And you're leaving it at that? You don't intend to take it further?'

She shook her head. 'She wouldn't want that, Tom.'

'There's no way you can know that for sure.'

She shook her head. 'It's obvious. She has a happy marriage, another daughter, a comfortable lifestyle. People look up to her.' She smiled wryly. 'If she was ashamed to own me all those years ago, just think how devastated she'd be if I suddenly turned up now!'

'Are you going to tell me her name?'

She shook her head. 'No, Tom.'

'You can't trust me – because I'm a newspaper man?'

'No. I'm not going to tell you because I'm determined to forget it. I need to build a life of my own. I want to be my own person. I can't do that if I have a shadow hanging over me.'

Tom drank the last of his coffee and put his mug down. 'I understand. At least, I *don't* but I do respect your decision.' He stood up. 'I meant what I said, Fleur. If you need me, just call. Goodnight.'

'Goodnight, Tom. And thanks.'

She sat for a long time just staring at the door. At that moment its closing seemed a kind of symbolic gesture. She had thrown away something valuable. Tom still cared about her as a friend, but she felt that the closeness, the tenderness that had started to blossom between them at Christmas, was dead. She herself had killed it, tossed it aside for something false and worthless just as her mother had tossed her aside all those years ago. The feeling of sadness and regret almost overwhelmed her. She had just said that she was determined to build an independent life – to be her own person. Well, she'd made a fine mess of things so far.

243

Everything, all of it, was her own stupid fault. She'd got no more than she deserved. But at least she could try to learn from her mistakes.

The council meeting had gone well. The last item on the agenda had been Julia's proposal for the opening of a women's refuge in Victoria Gardens.

She had not been idle since the last meeting, spending the intervening time as usefully and productively as she could. On Eleanor's advice she had been careful to obtain all the information she could about opening a women's refuge. She had been to see Social Services and enquired into all the peripheral requirements: insurance, fire regulations and local by-laws. She had even been in touch with the owner of the empty property in Victoria Gardens. Communicating through the agent who was handling the house she had ascertained what the rent was likely to be. Now that the council had shelved their plan for redevelopment it could be a long-term proposition which would obviously make it more attractive to the owner.

The planning committee's site inspection team were unable to find any fault with the location and there had been no objections raised. Julia had even spoken to some of the local women's groups and persuaded them to donate furniture and help with the redecoration.

There were those on the council who were against the idea, some of them women, but when it came to a vote at the meeting she won with an easy majority, a vote that clearly had the approval of the spectators in the public gallery.

As usual the press was represented at the meeting and after the proceedings had been declared closed and the councillors had begun to leave the council chamber, a young man approached her.

'Mrs Grant, I'm Tom Markham of the *Elvemere*

244

Clarion. I was very impressed with the way you put your case this evening. Will you give me a few words for my paper?'

Julia smiled. 'There isn't much I can tell you,' she said.

'I realise that. What I'm more interested in is the personal angle. This is obviously something close to your heart. Is there perhaps some special reason?'

Julia flushed. 'I represent the people who voted for me, Mr Markham. Some of those are women who have special needs that have not been provided for in our town. I believe it is time they were.'

'Do you expect to get overall support on this one, Mrs Grant?'

'I believe it's something close to the hearts of most women.'

'And yet there were women councillors who voted against it this evening.'

'Perhaps their comfortable lifestyles mean that they are not fully aware of the problem.'

'And you obviously are, in spite of your own lifestyle. Would you say that your own experience is what makes you a champion of these women?'

Julia looked into the clear eyes of this young man and suddenly saw herself reflected. What was it that made a comfortably off middle-class housewife feel so deeply committed to abandoned and badly used women and their children? The answer to that was firmly locked up in her own past and not to be dragged out for public scrutiny.

'It's a fact that in spite of all the principles upheld by the feminist movement, women will always continue to be very vulnerable in certain circumstances,' she said carefully.

He nodded, the eyes still on her, his pencil poised. 'Would you like to elaborate on that for me?'

Eleanor had warned her about charming young journalists who smiled and noted your remarks, only to distort and quote them grotesquely and damagingly out of context in their papers next day.

'Only to say that although women have won a lot of battles on the equality front, human nature hasn't changed much since time began,' she said. 'As long as woman is the sex that gives birth she will always have a weak spot in her armour. And as long as there are unscrupulous men to exploit that vulnerability, they will continue to take advantage of the fact.'

He raised an eyebrow at her. 'That sounds rather cynical, Mrs Grant. Would you describe yourself as a feminist?'

'Good heavens, no!'

'A man hater then?'

She laughed. 'Heavens above! Is that how I sound to you? I'd like to go on record as saying that I couldn't be more happily married. I have a wonderful husband and daughter and an ideal family life. It's that very thing that makes me appreciate that not all women are as lucky as me.'

'You have first-hand knowledge of the other side of the coin, obviously.'

She met his eyes without flinching. 'Yes.'

'So you'd say that it's a case of "there but for the grace of God . . ."?'

'Of course I'd say that. Any compassionate woman would.'

Tom's pencil scribbled half a page of illegible hieroglyphics, then he looked up at her. 'Is there anything else you'd like to tell me about yourself, Mrs Grant?'

His engaging grin amused her. She found it impossible not to smile at his audacity. 'No, Mr Markham, I'm afraid there is not. I think that will have to be all for now.'

'Just one more thing. At the last council meeting you mentioned the lack of crèche facilities that would enable local young mothers, single and married, to get back to work.'

'That's right, I did.'

'I was wondering, as a member of one of Elvemere's leading business families, are you hoping that Grant Philips Construction will back you up and lead the field locally in this?'

Julia flushed. 'That is something that I haven't discussed with my family yet. But I'd very much like to think that I could persuade the board of directors to think seriously about it.'

'Good.' Tom looked up with a persuasive smile. 'I have a photographer waiting outside. Could we have one shot for the *Clarion* – please, Mrs Grant?'

She shook her head. 'Oh, I don't think so. Not now.'

'I'm sure it would go a long way to help your cause,' he said persuasively. 'The people you are trying to help – and those who voted for you – would be reassured to see how hard you are fighting on their behalf. A picture would remind them of who they're reading about.'

'Well . . .' Julia hesitated. 'All right then. Just the one.'

The photographer was a young woman. Her dark hair was cropped close to her head and she wore motorcycle leathers and a gold nose stud. She was totally professional, brisk and efficient, knowing exactly what she wanted. She took several shots of Julia alone in the council chamber, sitting in her place, pen in hand, her papers spread out before her, then, with a word of thanks and a nod to Tom she was gone. A moment later Julia heard the roar of a motorcycle from the car park outside as she sped off to her next assignment.

She had begun to pack her papers back into her

briefcase when Tom said quietly. 'Obviously you have the vision to put yourself in the position of one of these vulnerable women, Mrs Grant.'

She stopped short and gave him a startled look, her heart suddenly quickening. 'What do you mean?'

'Exactly what I say. You are clearly an intensely sympathetic person, a woman with deep emotions and a strong social conscience. And you say that you have a daughter of your own. You must have felt for these women – imagined for yourself what it must feel like to be abandoned with a small child; left to bring up a baby alone?'

'Yes. Yes, of course I have.'

'Then perhaps you could describe for our readers the way it is.'

Julia took a deep breath. The room felt suddenly much too warm. She had brought this interview to an end once so just what was this persistent young reporter trying to get her to say?

'It isn't possible for anyone truly to know what that is like without having experienced it,' she said slowly. 'But I have met a young woman who is in the unfortunate position of being a single mother, abandoned by the father of her child who has since subjected her to threats and violence. So I do have some first hand knowledge through her.'

'Really? You wouldn't like to give me her name? Would she be willing to give me an interview?'

'No, Mr Markham, I certainly will not give you her name. And if you don't mind, I really would like to go home now.'

'Of course.' Tom flipped his notebook shut and slipped it into his pocket. 'Forgive me. I shouldn't have asked, though I would have made sure that she remained completely anonymous. Thank you for your cooperation, Mrs Grant, and good luck with your project.' He smiled disarmingly and held out his hand. 'Goodnight.'

After he had gone she went to the ladies' cloakroom for her coat. As she took out her comb and ran it through her hair she was shocked to realise that she was trembling. She stood for several minutes gazing at her reflection in the mirror. Of course she knew how it felt to be abandoned with a small baby. Who better? She was sincere in her desire to do her best for these women, but she had to admit to herself that her motives were not entirely selfless. In some obscure way she hoped to make good her past shortcomings – salve her conscience. But was it all going to get out of hand? Had she the courage to follow it through? Had she bitten off more than she could chew? The young reporter's direct questions had unnerved her and for the first time the icy finger of doubt sent a shiver down her spine.

'*Buy* Victoria Gardens ourselves! Instead of the council – all thirteen houses?'

'That's what I said. Yes.'

Harry Philips stared disbelievingly at Charlie Grant across the boardroom table. This was the first he'd heard of his partner's latest scheme. He cleared his throat and surreptitiously fingered his collar For some time now he had had his doubts about Charlie's state of mind. There were times when his high-flown plans bordered on megalomania. He'd thought Meadowlands Park a touch too ambitious with its top-of-the-range executive homes complete with saunas and swimming pools, but this one went further than any of his past excesses. To take on the rebuilding of Victoria Gardens as well as Meadowlands looked dangerously like over-reaching.

'I really don't think that even with an injection of

new money from this mystery investor ...' he began. But Charlie waved both hands at him, his face almost obscured by the cloud of smoke emanating from his pipe.

'I've already looked into all that. The investor I mentioned is waiting outside at this moment and I'd like to invite her to join us at this point.' He rose from his chair and went to the door.

Harry turned an expression of outrage mingled with bafflement on Vernon and mouthed, 'What's all this about?'

He tried to look non-commital and reassuring at the same time, thankful that there was no opportunity for him to explain. His father returned with Joanna following in his wake. She wore a bottle green velvet suit and her auburn hair gleamed like a polished chestnut. She carried the gloss of confidence like an aura. Charlie indicated a chair for her and resumed his own seat.

'Mrs Hanson is here tonight for a special purpose,' he said. 'She is the person who has expressed a wish to invest some money in GPC. A very substantial sum of money. I outlined for her earlier what I have put to you at tonight's meeting and now the proposal is open for discussion.'

'Surely this is all most irregular?' Harry said boldly. 'Discussing an item on the agenda prior to the meeting with a person not even on the board? It's unheard of!'

'Mrs Hanson will automatically become a director of GPC as from today,' Charlie told him with a reproving glare. 'She will also be a full partner,' he added quickly. 'I think, Harry, that even you can hardly grudge her that when she is investing the sum of half a million pounds with us.'

'*Half a million ...*' The rest of the sentence was smothered by Harry's handkerchief as a coughing fit convulsed him. He looked at his son-in-law with watering eyes. 'Were you aware of this, Vernon?'

He fidgeted nervously. 'Well, I . . .'

'What does it matter? We all know now,' Charlie boomed. 'The important thing is how to use the cash most effectively. That is why I propose we put in an offer at once for Victoria Gardens while the opportunity is there, and put into operation ourselves what the council had in mind. That way all the profits will be ours.'

'It's a very risky project,' Harry said, shaking his head. 'Restructuring property as old as that. All kinds of problems could arise. Those houses are early-Victorian which means they'll be listed too. We wouldn't have a free hand in altering them.'

Charlie sighed. The objections were exactly what he had anticipated from Harry and they had all been brought up before. 'Nothing we can't cope with,' he said with a dismissive wave of his hand. 'I'm an experienced builder, remember, Harry. I'm prepared for things like that. As long as we leave the period facades unaltered, we can do what we want to the interiors.'

'I see. You've looked into all that too?'

'Yes. Don't worry. We'll take it all in our stride.'

'And in the meantime what about Meadowlands Park?' Harry asked. 'Do I take it that is to be shelved?'

'No. Meadowlands can go ahead using Mrs Hanson's investment,' Charlie said. 'The bank will give us a loan for the Victoria Gardens job. It's more gilt-edged than a housing estate – less of a gamble.'

'You seem to have researched all this very thoroughly,' Harry said. 'Haven't you taken a lot for granted? There's an awful lot for us to agree on and I'm not at all sure . . .'

Charlie waved an impatient arm. 'No good coming to a meeting with some half-cocked pie-in-the-sky idea, was it? I had to make sure it was workable first.'

251

'What about the bank loan?' Vernon asked. He'd been watching Joanna out of the corner of his eye. He was acutely aware that she was waiting for him to make a contribution. She'd already described him as a nodding dog. His father glared at him.

'What *about* the bank loan?'

'I take it you'd like me to get onto it at once?' He already knew that Bill Watts, their bank manager, was in his father's lodge. He assumed that Charlie had already made sure no problems were anticipated. 'Do you want me to handle it?'

'I have made some tentative inquiries,' Charlie said guardedly. 'I think I can confidently say that the loan will be forthcoming. I'll let you know when I want you to set up a meeting with them to negotiate the terms. This scheme will be of enormous benefit to the town, especially now that the council has abandoned the scheme. Victoria Gardens has been rundown for years, getting more and more of an eyesore. This way it'll be a smart, functional area instead of a near slum. We shall provide upmarket dwellings and professional premises too. We'll be doing the town a service.'

'And you feel confident that the bank will lend the money even though we still have part of a previous loan outstanding?' Harry enquired.

'Yes, it will all be taken care of in due course,' Charlie said.

'It seems to me that an awful lot has already been taken care of behind everyone's back,' Harry said, his colour rising. 'And may I ask what kind of partnership arrangement is to be made with Mrs Hanson?'

'I was coming to that. Mrs Hanson is to become a full partner,' Charlie told him, 'with the usual entitlements. She will hold the same number of shares as the rest of us and the remainder of her investment will go as uncalled capital.' He cleared his throat. 'She will also become our Company Secretary as well as acting as Vernon's personal assistant.'

Harry looked at him askance. 'Company Secretary! May I be so bold as to ask at what salary?'

'Double what she is receiving now, plus a percentage of GPC's profits.'

All the colour drained from Harry's face. He'd picked up the atmosphere and heard the gossip around the office about Vernon and this Hanson woman. He hadn't believed any of it – till now. He took a deep breath and tried in vain to keep his voice steady. 'I see. So it's all cut and dried, is it? I'm sorry but I can't seem to remember a vote being taken on this. Can you, Vernon?' He coloured and looked away. Harry nodded. 'Ah! I see that you were in on all this too. It seems that I am the only one not to have been consulted.'

'You're being consulted now, old lad,' Charlie blustered.

'Being *told*, you mean! It all smells very strongly of conspiracy to me. Well, I'm sorry but I'm not prepared to stand by and have you all ride roughshod over me. I must make a stand. I'm afraid I can't agree with any of it.'

'I don't have to ask the board when it comes to accepting an investment. I'm sure I don't need to remind you, Harry, that a limited company is structured for expansion. Anyway, you're out-voted. Three to one.'

'Of course. You've already made sure of that.' Harry rose unsteadily to his feet, the colour rushing back into his pale cheeks. 'In that case I have no alternative.' He gripped the edge of the table. 'For some time past I have had my doubts about the way this firm was being run. I respect your position as chairman, Charlie, but not when you persist in making decisions without putting them before the board in the proper way. You may be able to manipulate your son, but not me. Oh, no, not me. Not this time.' He walked stiffly to the door. 'You will receive my formal resignation first thing in the morning. Goodnight.'

As the door closed behind him Vernon turned an appalled face towards his father. 'Shall I go after him?'

But Charlie's face was unconcerned as he waved his pipe dismissively. 'Let him go,' he said scathingly. 'He's been a dead weight for years now. Time the silly old sod retired anyway.'

'Do you want me to go round to the house and talk to him?'

'No, leave it. If he crawls back tomorrow, all well and good. If not, well, so be it.'

'But what about his share of the business?' Vernon asked.

Charlie shrugged. 'We'll buy him out if that's what he wants,' he said. 'It's a damned nuisance but it can't be helped. We're better off without him, lad. Just forget it and let's get on with more important things.' He leaned forward. 'Victoria Gardens now. What I thought was that we could convert those top floors into luxury flats. They must have a glorious view over the park and the river. We'll install lifts of course. The two lower floors will be state of the art offices – maybe a couple of houses knocked into one will make a top-class health centre . . .'

'In other words, all the things the council had in mind,' Vernon put in.

Charlie grinned. 'And more, lad. Much more. For instance, I thought we could make a feature of that rubbish dump in the middle. A garden where folks could sit and enjoy the sunshine – with seats and flower beds, a fountain and maybe a statue or something tasteful in the centre.'

Vernon had a wild vision of a rotund facsimile of his father smiling benignly down on his *pièce de résistance*. He'd be after an OBE or a bloody knighthood next! For the first time he began to doubt the wisdom of the scheme.

'Yes, everything the council would've done.' Charlie went on with a satisfied smirk. 'Except that with Grant Philips Construction doing it, it'll be a hundred percent better! And the proceeds will be all ours.'

'Won't we be plain Grant Construction with Harry gone?' Vernon asked.

Joanna laid a hand on Charlie's arm and leaned forward to flash her most dazzling smile at him. 'Might I suggest Grant *Hanson* Construction?' she said innocently.

Julia had just taken off her coat in the hall when the telephone rang. She lifted the receiver.

'Hello, Julia Grant speaking.'

'Julia, it's Mum. Thank goodness you're in.' May sounded upset. 'Your father has just come home. He's in a terrible state. He's walked out – resigned.'

'*Resigned?* From GPC? You're joking!'

'Believe me, joking's the last thing on my mind. He walked out of the board meeting. Came home pale and trembling, looking like death. He frightened the life out of me. It's a wonder he didn't have an accident, driving home in that condition. I've just packed him off to bed. He won't tell me the full story, but it seems that Charlie and Vernon have taken on a new partner behind his back. He says they did it on purpose to force his resignation. He's absolutely devastated. Can you find out what's going on and let me know, Julia?'

'Vernon isn't home yet, but as soon as he comes in I'll ask him about it. Tell Daddy to try not to worry. I daresay it's all a storm in a teacup.'

'I'm afraid it's more than that. He keeps muttering something about Mrs Hanson. It seems she's putting some money into the firm. He says she's taking his place on the board, but that can't be right, can it? I thought she was Vernon's secretary.'

'Yes, she is.' Julia frowned. *Joanna?* 'Look, Mum, I haven't an idea what it's all about, and this is certainly the first I've heard about a new partner. Let me talk to Vernon and get back to you.'

'All right, dear. I'm sorry to worry you with it at this time of night, only your father is so upset. I'm just going to take him some brandy.'

'Tell Daddy to try not to worry. I'll be in touch first thing tomorrow. Try and get a good night's sleep. Things always look better in the morning. Goodnight.' Julia rang off. What on earth was going on? She knew Vernon wasn't home. His car hadn't been in the garage when she put hers away. She ran upstairs and tapped on Charlotte's door, but she wasn't home either. She sat down on the bed, suddenly aware that she had no idea where her husband or her daughter were. She remembered her words to the young reporter: *I couldn't be more happily married. I have a wonderful husband and daughter and an ideal family life.* God! It couldn't be further from the truth! Vernon and she lived virtually separate lives and as for her relationship with Charlotte, since the girl had left school it was like living with a stranger. Should she have allowed Vernon to push her into the firm when she clearly wanted a career with animals? Had she allowed him to drive a wedge between her only daughter and her? The truth was that she'd been so busy trying to get her seat on the council at the time that she hadn't given it a thought one way or the other. No one had. They hadn't asked Charlotte what she wanted – hadn't really cared whether she was happy or not. And now they were reaping the result.

Walking slowly back downstairs she lifted the telephone and dialled Kath's number. When her sister-in-law's clipped tones replied she gave a sigh of relief.

'Kath, it's me, Julia. Is Charlotte there?'

'Yes, she came over straight from work to help me bed down the horses. She stayed on for supper and to watch the show jumping on TV. Is anything wrong?'

'No. It's just that I don't like her cycling all that way home in the dark.'

'That's all right, I'll bring her home in the Land Rover,' Kath said. 'I usually do anyway.'

Julia bit her lip. She hadn't even known that!

'I can put her bike in the back,' Kath was saying. 'Are you all right, Julia? You sound a bit upset.'

'No. It's just that I've had rather a day of it. And to top everything, Mum has just rung to say that Daddy isn't well. Some trouble at a board meeting upset him.'

'I'm sorry to hear that, love. Maybe he's sickening for something. There's an awful lot of flu about. People are at a low ebb at the end of winter, aren't they? I hope he'll soon be better. I'll bring Charlotte home as soon as the programme is over. I'm sorry you were worried. She really should have left you a note or something.'

'Thanks, Kath. Goodnight.' Julia put the telephone down with a sigh. None of them ever left notes for each other. Probably because none of them cared enough. With a pang of envy she pictured her sister-in-law and daughter relaxing together companionably over supper trays in front of the TV. Maybe she had never been cut out to be a mother.

Joanna lay with her head on Vernon's chest under the duvet.

'It was wonderful, wasn't it?' she sighed.

He knew she wasn't alluding to their recent love-making, but the meeting which had ended an hour ago.

Her mind had been focused on it ever since. 'You're pleased then?' he asked superfluously.

'Delighted.' She stretched her arms luxuriously. 'In fact I'm going to give a party to show just how delighted I am.'

'Party? Isn't that a bit over the top?'

'It'll just be for all you Grants and some of the senior staff,' she said. 'I'll have it here at home. You can bring Julia.'

He stared at her. 'You can't be serious?'

'It would look a little strange if I didn't invite her, wouldn't it, darling? Anyway, she's going to have to get used to sharing her husband with me now that I'm one of his business partners.'

Vernon shifted uncomfortably. 'I'd rather keep our relationship separate.'

'I really don't see how that's going to be possible.'

'Julia is going to be pretty upset about what happened to her father tonight.'

She raised herself on one elbow to look at him. 'He was getting on anyway, wasn't he? Coming up for retirement age?'

'Yes, but all the same, to go like this . . .'

Her eyes clouded. 'Well, of course if you feel you should be at home soothing her troubled brow, you'd better go.'

'It isn't that.'

'Then what is it?'

'You don't understand, Jo. Harry Philips has been Dad's partner ever since the firm expanded, ever since . . .'

'Ever since you and Julia got married and made it all possible?' Joanna supplied. 'What are you afraid of, Vernon? I expect Harry will still want to be a sleeping partner, but if he wants his share of the business he can have it. I can even lend the firm the money to pay him

258

off if need be. When this Victoria Gardens development gets off the ground the firm will be in clover. We're right in the middle of a property boom, in case you hadn't noticed.' She looked at him. 'My God, I do believe you're afraid of Julia.'

'Of course I'm not!'

'Right then. If she doesn't like it, hard luck. What can she do about it?'

'Nothing, I suppose.'

'Then how about giving me all your attention for a change?' She cupped his face in both hands and kissed him, pushing him back against the pillows. 'I read somewhere that power was an aphrodisiac,' she murmured in his ear. 'And I'm just beginning to think there might be something in it!'

'You really should have let your mother know where you were,' Kath said as the Land Rover trundled along the bumpy drive from the stables.

'What does she care where I am?' Charlotte said truculently. 'Half the time she never even looks into my room anyway. Now that she's *Councillor* Mrs Grant she's got no time for me.'

'You don't really believe that, Charlotte,' Kath said, turning the vehicle onto the road. 'All mothers care about their daughters. You wouldn't like it if she was constantly poking her nose into what you were doing, would you?'

'I suppose not.'

'Of course you wouldn't. But you shouldn't cut yourself off from her all the same.'

'She's not interested.'

'Has it ever occurred to you that she might like it if you showed a little interest in *her* from time to time? When was the last time you asked her how her life was going?'

The girl beside her sighed. 'Okay, but it isn't as simple as you think. You should have been my mother, Aunt Kath. You and I have far more in common than Mum and me. And as for Dad . . .'

'Your dad wants the best for you.'

'He wants the best *out* of me, you mean,' Charlotte said bitterly. 'He's never forgiven me for not being a boy. And Granddad has never forgiven him and Mum for not producing one. Sometimes I wish there was no family firm. I wish I had sisters and brothers and that Mum stayed at home all day cooking lovely meals instead of rushing out to Marks and Spencer's at the last minute for something quick for tea. I wish that Dad went to work in a factory, a shop, a *coalmine* – anything so that we could live a normal family life like other people.'

Kath laughed. 'Other people's lives always look better than your own. I often wonder if there's any such thing as a normal family? Let me ask you something. When you're married, will you want to spend your entire life in the kitchen? Especially when your family hardly notice your existence.' She looked at the girl. 'Try and talk to your mother, Charlotte.'

'I would if she was ever there.'

'There must be plenty of times when you're both there. You're important to her, believe me. She's lucky to have you. You're lucky to have each other.' Kath glanced at her niece's wistful face. 'Promise me something – promise you won't ever use me to get at her?'

Charlotte looked shocked. 'I wouldn't do that!'

'Oh yes you might – without realising. You're always welcome at the stables, you know that. But come because you want to, not as some kind of rebellion.'

Charlotte grinned. Sometimes Aunt Kath could almost read her mind. 'I love working with you at the stables. I'll always want to come, you know that. But okay, I promise.'

They were driving along the Merifield Road and suddenly Kath turned left into a road of smart modern houses. 'We'll nip through here,' she said. 'It cuts off the traffic lights and the town centre. I've found you can save about ten minutes by taking this shortcut.'

The houses were neat and the road well-lit. Charlotte looked out with interest. 'This is Hazel Grove. Joanna Hanson lives down here somewhere,' she said. 'She's Dad's PA. The girls in the office call her Joanna the Hun. She's always trying to get round me, telling me how she and Mum were at school together and what fun they had. But since I've made sure she knew that I wasn't going to suck up to her, she's treated me like the other girls in the office. They all think she's an absolute *cow* with that awful put-on American accent of hers. She's unbearably bossy and she has a vile temper. Do you know, she hasn't been working for the firm for five minutes and already she's had the cheek to . . .' She broke off as she saw a familiar silver BMW parked in the drive of one of the houses. 'Hey, that looks like Dad's car.'

'Surely not? Where?' Kath slowed down and as she did so the front door of the house opened and two people came out. In the shaft of light spilling out through the open door Kath could clearly see that the woman wore a dressing gown. As they drove past she reached up to wind her arms around the man's neck, standing on tiptoe to kiss him. Kath caught her breath and pressed her foot down hard on the accelerator, hoping to speed past before Charlotte recognised Vernon.

They drove on in silence for a few minutes, then Kath stole a glance at her niece. The girl's face was white with shock.

'Did you see?' she whispered.

'There's probably a very innocent explanation,' Kath began unconvincingly.

'There's an explanation all right,' Charlotte said bitterly. 'My father is a cheat. I've suspected it for a long time and now I've seen the proof.'

Chapter 10

It was just after midnight when Vernon arrived home. Julia was waiting in the sitting room. When she heard him stealthily crossing the hall she got up and opened the door. 'Vernon.'

He stopped halfway up the stairs to look down at her. 'Julia! You startled me. You shouldn't have waited up.'

'What happened at the meeting, Vernon?'

'Happened?'

'Don't look so surprised. You must have realised that Mum would ring me. Daddy is in a terrible state. She was dreadfully worried about him. She said something about his resigning.'

He shrugged. 'Oh, it was a storm in a teacup. You know board meetings. There was a bit of a disagreement. It'll blow over.'

'I don't think so. By the sound of things it was a lot more serious than that. He's extremely upset, Vernon. Is it true that you've taken Joanna Hanson into partnership?'

'She's investing quite a lot of money with the firm. Dad's repaying her with a partnership. Nothing wrong with that, is there?'

'It must be a substantial sum.'

'It is.'

'So if she's got that kind of money to invest, why GPC?'

'Why not? She said she'd like to invest in the firm she works for. She has faith in us.'

'Evidently! So – if it's as straightforward as that, why is Daddy so upset?'

Vernon sighed. 'Look, Ju, it's late. And let's face it, company business is not exactly your strong suit, is it? Let's get some rest now and I'll try and explain it to you over breakfast.'

'No, now, Vernon.' She held the door of the sitting room open and stood back. 'I want you to explain it to me now. I need to understand what's going on. It's my father who is involved, don't forget.'

With a resigned sigh he followed her into the room and sat down. 'Your father is annoyed because he wasn't consulted at an earlier stage,' he said. 'That's all there is to it. Jo sounded me out first because she works for me. That was only natural. I spoke to Dad and he worked the whole thing out with Jo before he put it to a meeting. But only because he wanted to be sure it was workable so as not to waste everyone's time. Unfortunately Harry saw it as some kind of conspiracy. He wouldn't wait to hear an explanation.'

'And that's all it was?'

'Absolutely.' He shook his head. 'Your father has been looking very tired these last few months, Ju. Maybe you should persuade him that it's time he put everything on hold and took an extended holiday. When he's feeling more himself he'll probably see things more rationally.'

Julia paused. She had to agree that her father had been looking strained lately. Maybe there was something in what Vernon said. She decided to go round and see her parents in the morning and try to smooth things over – persuade them to take a holiday somewhere warm and sunny. She looked at Vernon. 'Right. So Joanna is to become a partner. Obviously she won't want to remain as your secretary?'

'Personal assistant,' he corrected. 'Yes, she does want to carry on, as a matter of fact. She'll be holding the position of Company Secretary as well from now on. She has a real interest in the firm and a flair for the business too. She's a definite asset.'

'I see. I'm glad,' she said dryly. She gave him a hard look. 'I take it you and she have been celebrating?'

He coloured slightly. 'No. What makes you say that?'

She glanced at her watch. 'The time for one thing. The lipstick on your collar for another.'

His hand went guiltily to his collar. 'Oh, that. I dare-say there's some on Dad's collar too. She was excited – you know, elated. It's been quite a night for her.'

'I can imagine.' Julia got up and walked into the hall, starting to go upstairs without another word. Board meetings never lasted this long, even given that this one had been out of the ordinary. It was clear from Vernon's demeanour that he had been with Joanna. He reeked of guilt – and of her perfume again. It seemed that little by little she was gradually insinuating herself into their lives and it looked as though there was little Julia could do about it.

'Charlotte in?' Vernon asked as they reached the landing.

'Yes, she's in bed. Asleep too by this time, I should hope.'

Charlotte had arrived home looking pale and pre-occupied. Kath hadn't stopped for coffee or a chat, but had driven straight off after taking Charlotte's bicycle out of the back of the Land Rover. In the hall the girl had looked at her mother, then suddenly thrown her arms around her neck and hugged her.

'Darling! Are you all right?' Julia had asked, holding her at arm's length and searching her face. Charlotte was not normally given to displays of emotion, but she just shook her head, saying that she was tired, and went straight upstairs to bed. It had been a night of unusual and inexplicable happenings, Julia told herself as she undressed. Bewildering and exhausting. Her euphoria over winning the battle for the women's refuge was almost forgotten. So far none of her family even knew – or seemingly cared – about her victory.

But their ignorance was not to last for long.

The first reaction came with a telephone call from Charlie at eight o'clock the following morning. Julia had just come down when the telephone in the hall began to ring. She picked it up immediately.

'Elvemere five-eight-four-nine-eight.'

'Julia?'

Recognising her father-in-law's voice she said, 'Oh, good morning, Charlie. I'll get Vernon.'

'No! It's *you* I want!' Charlie bellowed down the telephone. 'What the *hell* do you mean by it, eh?'

'I'm sorry. Mean by what?'

'Don't come the innocent with me, girl! All this crap in the *Clarion* this morning, that's what! All this twaddle about a women's refuge in Victoria Gardens. What the hell do you think you're playing at?'

'A refuge is badly needed, Charlie. I don't see why it need affect you.'

'Well, you bloody soon will! And what about this hare-brained notion about a crèche at GPC? First I've heard of it, but then I'm only the managing director!'

'I was speaking off the cuff. But you must admit that it is a good idea?'

'Oh, *is* it? Well, thanks for telling me. I'm supposed to start providing for unmarried mothers and their brats now, am I? You'll have me changing nappies next!

If you ask me, I think you're getting too big for your britches, madam!'

Julia winced and held the receiver away from her ear. 'I'm not deaf. There's no need to shout. There's no need to be coarse either, Charlie. I think that as one of the largest business concerns in the town, we should set an example.'

'*We?* Who's this *we* when it's at home?' Let me tell you something, girl. You didn't get the lifestyle you enjoy today by my behaving like some kind of charity! And the running of GPC is nowt to do with you anyway, so just keep your opinions to yourself!'

'Really? I was under the impression that this was a family firm . . .'

'Not *your* family. Not any more,' he interrupted. 'Your father – the Philips half – opted out as from last night. Anyway, never mind bloody crèches. It's Victoria Gardens that bothers me. How far has this refuge garbage gone? Tell me that.'

'It's under negotiation at the moment, but as the council have agreed I can't see why it shouldn't go ahead as soon as we can get up and running. And I honestly don't see why you're so upset.'

'You don't, eh? Well, perhaps you'd better ask Vernon just how it will affect me – and you too in the end! Go ahead with this and you'll be taking the bread and butter out of your own mouth, woman. Maybe even jeopardising your daughter's future too! So *think on!*'

There was a loud clatter as Charlie banged down the receiver and Julia was left staring into the receiver, her ear still singing from his vociferous assault.

In the morning room the table was laid for breakfast, but neither Charlotte nor Vernon was down yet. Tracey had already arrived and had picked up the morning papers from the front doormat and put them on the table. Julia saw that the *Clarion* was open at page two and there, staring up at her, was her own picture. The headline read,

NEW COUNCILLOR CHAMPIONS BATTERED WOMEN.

Below was an account of the council meeting and Julia's successful result. The article went onto say that plans had been passed for number six Victoria Gardens to be refurbished as a women's refuge. There then followed some of her comments as made to the young reporter. *'Although happily married with a young daughter, Councillor Mrs Grant is obviously a champion of single mothers,'* it read. *'A sympathetic and compassionate woman, she identifies strongly with their plight and in spite of some local opposition has vowed to see that Elvemere leads the field in seeing that they receive a fair deal. As the daughter-in-law of Mr Charles Grant of Grant Philips Construction she says that she intends to arrange for her family firm to set an example by opening Elvemere's first free industrial crèche so that the young single mother can get back to work without her income being eroded by the necessity of paying for child-minders.'*

'You've seen it then? Good for you. It's a really good photo, isn't it, Mrs Grant?' Tracey stood in the doorway, the vacuum cleaner in her hand. 'I hope you didn't mind me reading it.'

Julia looked up. 'No, not at all, Tracey. I told you I'd do my best and I will, but I'm afraid that even now we're going to encounter some opposition.' She smiled. 'Never mind. We expected that, didn't we? Where is Damian?'

'Asleep outside in his pram. It's quite warm this morning,' Tracey said. 'Feels like spring's on the way at last. All right if I get on with the sitting room, is it?'

'Yes, of course.' Julia sat down and poured herself a cup of coffee, reading the article through again. Would Charlie really do anything to stop her? Why was he so angry? Would he refuse to open a crèche for mothers with small children who wanted to get back to work? It was true that his workforce was predominantly male, but there were women working in the office and in the canteen too. She knew for a fact that several of them left their children with minders. It need only be a small crèche, easily staffed. She would organise it herself if only Charlie would agree.

Charlotte appeared. She still looked pale. She took a slice of toast and buttered it, still standing.

'Are you all right darling?'

'I'm fine.' Charlotte avoided her mother's eye as she took a bite of the toast.

'Why don't you take a day off? You're looking a bit peaky.'

'No, I can't.' Tracey switched off the Hoover and Vernon could be heard coming downstairs. Charlotte stopped eating. 'Look, Mum, I've got to go. I'll take this with me.' She pushed the rest of the toast into her mouth and made for the back door.

Julia called after her, 'Charlotte! Don't run off like that. You haven't even had a drink of . . .' But she was too late. Even as she spoke she heard the door slam.

'Was that Charlotte?' Vernon asked as he came into the room.

'Yes. She said she was in a hurry.'

'Who was on the phone?'

'Your father. He was annoyed – well, no furious is more like it.' She pushed the paper across the table towards him. 'Apparently because of this.'

Vernon scanned the article briefly, then, his mouth sagging with disbelief, he read it through again more slowly. When he had finished he looked up at her, his eyebrows almost meeting in a frown of horror. 'Are you completely *mad*? My God! No wonder Dad was annoyed. You realise what you've done, don't you?'

'Only that I'm hoping to provide a much-needed service,' Julia said calmly. 'I can't see what all the angst is about. I grant you that I should probably have mentioned the crèche before, but it only occurred to me when I was talking to the reporter. I . . .'

'Sod the crèche! You've only thrown a spanner into the works of Dad's latest pet scheme.'

'What scheme?'

'Now that we have Joanna's investment, he's planning to buy Victoria Gardens and refurbish it in much the same way as the council intended.'

She stared at him. 'As a speculation, you mean? But isn't that a bit of a risk? Not to mention a costly project.'

'You're right on both counts. But Dad is confident that it's just what GPC needs to put us among the most highly acclaimed in the construction business. There could even be an award for the project. Conservation and design, that kind of thing. Plus the fact that it'll send his stock soaring locally. But if you go and tie up one building out of the thirteen . . .' He peered at the article again. 'Number *six*, it says here. Christ! That's slap bang in the middle of the terrace. It would render the whole scheme a total impossibility! What respected firm of accountants or solicitors would rent an office next door to one of these women's refuge dumps? Squalling kids and shouting matches going on all day.'

Julia shook her head impatiently. 'It won't be like that. And it won't be a dump. If you ever discussed the firm's business with me I'd have known about all this before I started. As it stands now, I was in first so why should I stand down?'

Vernon buttered a piece of toast, momentarily silenced. He could hardly tell her that he had only heard of the plan himself at last night's meeting. It would make him look as weak as Harry where his father was concerned. 'You've never been interested in the firm before,' he said morosely.

'How would you know that? As it happens I would have enjoyed working with you once Charlotte started school – as your secretary, personal assistant, anything. I was never offered the opportunity.'

'Julia! Let's face it. You've neither the qualifications nor the aptitude for that kind of job,' he said scathingly. 'You married me virtually straight out of school.'

'That's not to say I couldn't have learned. I didn't leave my brain at the altar steps along with my name, you know.'

He shook his head. 'We've had all this out before. Dad doesn't believe in wives getting involved. You're just annoyed because Joanna has the job and now a stake in the firm too. She's got a fabulous head for business.' He looked at her. 'From what I can make out, you and she were always rivals as young girls.'

'Oh, she told you that, did she? You've discussed me?'

'No, of course not. It was just in passing.'

Julia got up and began to clear the table. 'Isn't it time you went to the office?' she asked dismissively.

Vernon looked at his watch and sighed. He wasn't looking forward to the coming interview with his father, knowing that he would be in the line of fire for Julia's actions. 'Look, Ju, there must be plenty of other empty houses in the town. Couldn't you find somewhere else for this refuge place?'

'No!' She looked at him, her face alight with determination and her mouth set in a firm line. 'The plans have been passed for this one. Charlie might be able to make you dance to his tune, Vernon. But after the way my father has been treated – and the way Charlie spoke to me this morning on the phone – I intend to have my way over this.'

Her election win and her council work had proved to her that she didn't always have to stand down and give way to others as she had in the past. She had already seen that people had begun to respect her for standing firm. And she was damned if she was going to give in over this, her first real victory. She wasn't prepared to take any more brow beating from Charlie either. This time he'd gone one step too far.

Speechless with surprise, Vernon stared at her back as she walked out of the room. Julia had always been so compliant. He'd never seen her in this mood. But he had to find some way to make her change her mind. If he didn't, his life at work wouldn't be worth living.

He stood up, wiping his mouth with his napkin. 'You're right. I'd better go. Maybe we can talk about this later.'

'Maybe,' she said over her shoulder. 'Not that talking will do any good.'

When Vernon arrived at Joanna's house he saw from his watch that it was already after nine. As he rang the bell and waited on the porch he wondered if she had already left for the office. But when she answered the door to him it was clear that she wasn't going in. She still wore her dressing gown and her head was swathed in a towel.

'Vernon!' She looked slightly put out. 'I can't stop now, I'm afraid. I'm in a hurry. Charlie and I are seeing the firm's solicitor this morning, then I've got an appointment with my bank manager. Later on I've got that Arden Catering woman coming to talk about the arrangements for the party.'

'This won't take long,' he said tetchily, pushing past her into the hall. 'It's a bit more important than parties.

Something's come up that I think I should warn you about.'

With ill-concealed irritation she closed the front door. 'What can possibly have come up overnight that's so important?'

'This for a start.' Vernon picked up the *Clarion* from the hall table. It was still folded and Joanna obviously hadn't looked at it. He shook it open and held it under her nose. 'Julia is planning to open a women's refuge, right in the middle of Victoria Gardens. The plans were passed at a council meeting last night. When Dad read about it this morning the proverbial hit the fan in a big way, as you can imagine.'

Joanna was staring at the headline and photograph of Julia on the front page. 'Christ! I can imagine.' She looked at him. 'But surely if you just explain she'll back down and find somewhere else?'

'I wish you were right!' He sighed. 'Unfortunately Dad got in first while his temper was still at boiling point. Tact is hardly his strong suit at the best of times. He really blew his top at her and now she's digging her heels in and refusing to back down.'

'She'll give in in the end. Shall I have a word with her?'

Vernon gave her a wry smile. 'I hardly think that would help, do you? She's pretty sore about her father's resignation and your part in it.'

'My part? I had nothing to do with his resignation.'

'You were the cause of it – indirectly.'

'Oh?' Her eyebrows rose indignantly. 'Well, in that case, maybe I should withdraw my offer!'

He sighed. 'Don't be silly. You know I didn't mean that. I'm just trying to make you see it from her point of view.'

Joanna looked at the hall clock. 'Look, Vernon, I really can't spare the time to talk about it now. I'm going to have to hurry. All this is trivial – a storm in a teacup. We'll think of something to make Julia change her mind. It shouldn't be that difficult. I'll talk to Charlie about it when I meet him.' She pecked his cheek briefly, took him by the shoulders and gave him a push towards the door. 'Off you go now, and try not to worry. Everything is going to be just fine.'

When Charlotte spotted Fleur standing at the bus stop her heart leaped with hope. Seeing her unexpectedly like this was like the answer to her prayers. She waved frantically and shouted.

'Hi, Fleur! Haven't seen you for ages. Not since that party at New Year. How are you?'

Fleur smiled. 'I'm fine. How's college?'

The other girl jumped off her bicycle and pulled the machine off the road onto the pavement. 'Crummy as ever,' she said disconsolately. 'Like work.'

'Go on, I bet you're getting the hang of it all nicely by now.'

The smile left Charlotte's face. 'As a matter of fact, life's just one big pain in the bum right now.' She paused. 'Fleur – look, I'm glad I've seen you. I was going to come round to your place later for a chat.'

'Were you?' Fleur was taken aback. 'Well, that would be nice. I've got a flat now, with my own kitchen and everything. I've decorated it since I moved in. I'd love you to come and see it.'

'A flat – where?'

'It's the same address.' Fleur looked at the girl's troubled expression. 'Was there some special reason you wanted to see me? There's nothing wrong, is there?'

'Yes, there is as a matter of fact.' Charlotte sighed. 'I haven't really got any friends, you see. Not real friends. At least none that I could talk to. Not about this. You don't belong here in Elvemere and you're not connected with my family or anything so I feel I can confide in you.' She smiled, a wry, apologetic little smile. 'I hope you don't mind? It sounds an awful cheek put like that, sort of like making a convenience of you. If you think it is, just say.'

'I don't think it's a cheek, and I'd love you to come round.' Fleur looked up as the bus arrived and pulled into the layby. 'Look, come this evening if you like – around seven. It's thirteen Victoria Gardens – flat two.' She jumped onto the bus platform and turned to wave. Charlotte waved back as she remounted her bicycle.

'Thanks, Fleur. See you.'

She found a seat, paid her fare and settled down to think about the brief conversation she had just had with Charlotte Grant. The girl had looked so worried. What on earth was it she wanted to talk to her about? The irony of her remark suddenly struck Fleur. *You don't belong here in Elvemere, and you're not connected with my family*.

Maybe she should not have encouraged the girl to visit her. Perhaps it was a mistake to get involved. What would she say if she knew that there was indeed a very strong connection between them – that Fleur was in fact her half-sister? Strangely enough the irony of their relationship had not struck Fleur until this moment. It was odd; they were related and yet they were not. A sister was someone you'd known all your life – someone who shared the same parents. In all probability Charlotte had never even heard of Dean Sylvester and certainly knew nothing of the segment of her mother's life which included him. All the same the relationship, tenuous as it was, could not be denied and it gave her a totally new view of the younger girl.

They were not at all alike. Charlotte was small and fair, the very opposite to her. Julia's second daughter took after her. No one would ever connect Fleur

Sylvester with Julia Grant – which was just as well, she told herself, because there was no way she would ever want them to. And yet, she felt a sudden protective affinity with the young girl who was her half-sister, wondering why she was so unhappy. She made a silent vow to help in whatever way she could.

Standing in the hall of Sally's house, taking off her coat, she heard her employer on the telephone. As she walked into the office Sally was just putting the receiver down.

'That was Mrs Hanson,' she said, looking up. 'You remember, the PA lady from Grant Philips? She wants to arrange a party for next week. I said you'd go along and discuss menus with her.' She scribbled the address on the pad and tore off the top sheet, handing it to Fleur with a smile. 'You can handle this one on your own. See how you get on.'

Fleur looked at the address. 'Hazel Grove. Those are the nice houses off the Merifield Road, aren't they? Is she having the party at home?'

'Yes. It's to be a fairly small affair, colleagues from work and a few friends. She hasn't decided yet whether to make it a dinner party or a buffet. You can talk to her about that. I've made an appointment for twelve-thirty. She'd like you to be on time as she has to be at the office for two.'

Fleur arrived at the house in Hazel Grove with five minutes to spare. She parked the van in the driveway and walked up to the glazed porch. As she waited for Joanna to answer her ring at the bell she looked down at herself regretfully. If she'd known that Sally was going to send her out on a preliminary visit she would have worn make-up and put on something more business like; as it was she was wearing jeans and a heavy sweater, her hair tied back in a loose knot. Sally had assured her that she looked fine, but remembering Mrs

Hanson's consistently well-groomed appearance, Fleur doubted whether she would agree.

Her doubt was confirmed when Joanna opened the door and stared at her coldly. 'Yes? What is it?'

'I'm from Arden Catering.' Fleur nodded towards the van which had the name painted on the side in large letters.

'Oh?' Joanna looked her up and down. 'I was expecting Mrs Arden herself.'

Fleur felt resentment at the woman's arrogant manner, but she forced a smile. 'I'm Fleur Sylvester, her assistant. I think you'll find me efficient,' she said briskly. 'Mrs Arden and I work very closely together.' She held up the briefcase in which she carried the file of menus, the order book and diary. 'I think you said you had limited time to spend, Mrs Hanson. Shall we get started?'

Clearly taken aback by Fleur's businesslike manner, Joanna held the door open. 'Yes – yes, of course. Come in.'

In the living room she offered Fleur a comfortable chair and seated herself opposite. 'I'll show you the other rooms in a moment,' she said. 'I'm undecided whether to have a dinner party or a buffet with cocktails.'

Fleur took out her notepad. 'What kind of party is it to be?' she asked. 'Some kind of celebration – birthday, anniversary? Or is it a business affair?'

'Both, really.' Joanna smiled and seemed to relax a little. 'Though quite informal. As a matter of fact, it's to celebrate my promotion with my firm.'

'I see. That would be Grant Philips Construction?'

Joanna's eyebrows rose. 'You know?'

'We did the catering for your Christmas lunch.'

'Ah, of course.' Light dawned on Joanna's face. 'I remember you now. I didn't recognise you in those – er – clothes.'

'So you'll be inviting your colleagues from work?'

'Fellow management,' Joanna corrected with a little smile of triumph. 'I've just been made a director.'

'I see. Congratulations. Your fellow directors then. How many would that be? And are there to be any other guests?' She reflected that if Joanna was going to need drawing out like this, she was likely to be here all afternoon.

Joanna crossed her perfect legs and smiled smugly. 'I'd like to make a magnanimous gesture and invite all the senior members of the workforce,' she said. 'Foremen, salesmen, negotiators and so on. I've been counting them up and it comes to about twenty altogether.'

'In that case I would recommend a buffet with drinks,' Fleur suggested. 'Twenty would be rather a lot round a dinner table at one time. Besides, if you're going to invite people from different levels of the firm, it might be better if you were free to circulate among them. That way no one will feel awkward and out of their depth.'

Joanna looked impressed. 'Of course. How clever. Why didn't I think of that?' She got up. 'Let me show you the conservatory. I think that might be the perfect place to lay out a buffet.'

After Fleur had approved the conservatory they sat down again and she opened her briefcase. 'I can show you the selection of menus we have for buffets,' she said. 'They are all worked out at so much per head, including wines. Spirits and other drinks are extra, the amount being up to you. Unless you want to provide your own, of course. We also hire out glasses and cutlery at a small extra charge, and extra stacking chairs. But we bring trestle tables, tablecloths, candles and table flowers as standard.'

'I see. It all sounds very suitable indeed.' Joanna

278

looked at the selection book Fleur passed her, which was illustrated with coloured photographs. She studied them all carefully and then turned back to the most expensive.

'I'll have this one,' she said. 'I want to launch my new status with the firm in the most appropriate way.'

Fleur interpreted this as making an ostentatious impression. In other words, showing off. But it was none of her business. She was just delighted that she was getting a good order. She added up the cost of Joanna's total requirements on her calculator and passed her the estimate. Joanna glanced at it briefly and nodded.

'Thank you. That will be absolutely fine.'

Fleur smiled and made a note of her client's choice on her pad.

They settled the date – a Saturday evening two weeks ahead and Fleur closed her pad and slipped everything back into her briefcase. 'I think that's all for the moment then, Mrs Hanson.' She stood up. 'We'll send you a detailed invoice through the post in the normal way and if you'd just confirm it in writing, giving us a close estimate of the number of guests?'

'Of course, naturally. And thank you very much for your advice.' Joanna looked at her watch. 'It's taken less time than I expected. Please, won't you join me for a drink before you go?'

Fleur shook her head. 'I'm driving, thank you.'

'A coffee then. I'm going to have one before I go to the office. The kettle has boiled. Please join me, Miss – er – I'm sorry but I've forgotten your name?'

'Sylvester. Fleur Sylvester.'

'Of course.' Joanna had not forgotten the name at all, she just wanted it confirming. The moment the girl had given it, it had rung a distant bell at the back of her mind. It wasn't a name one heard every day and it

brought back memories. 'Of course, *Fleur*.' She smiled.
'May I?'

'Yes – please do.'

'And you will have a quick coffee, won't you? It's
chilly outside and you must have fitted me in in your
lunch hour.'

'Well all right then. Thank you.'

During her brief absence Fleur pondered over the
woman's change of mood. She was certainly a lot less
frosty than when she'd opened the door.

When Joanna returned and put the tray down
between them on the coffee table Fleur caught her looking curiously at her. 'You're not local, are you, Fleur?'

'No. From London. I've been here since last autumn.'

Joanna handed her a cup of coffee and sat down
opposite again. 'Your name – it's quite unusual. I once
knew someone of that name. He played the guitar with
a pop group called The Sylvas.' She smiled. 'Oh, long
before your time of course. Dean Sylvester was his
name.'

Fleur's eyes widened in surprise. 'You knew him?
He was my father.' The words were out before she had
time to think.

'*Really?*' Joanna was smiling. 'How extraordinary.
How is he? What is he doing these days?'

Fleur hid her face in her cup. 'When I say that he's
my father it's true, but I never actually knew him. He
and my mother parted before I was born. He died in
America, some years ago.'

'Oh, how sad! So – your mother brought you up
alone?' Joanna's eyes glittered in an almost predatory
way and Fleur suddenly sensed that she was on thin
ice. She looked at her watch and put her cup down on
the coffee table.

'I'm afraid I'll have to go now, Mrs Hanson,' she
said, gathering up her things. 'I have another appoint-

ment in ten minutes and it's on the other side of town. Thank you for the coffee. As I said, we'll be in touch.'

'Of course. I mustn't keep you.' Joanna went to the door with Fleur and saw her out. As the van backed out of the drive and sped away she stood watching thoughtfully. There was more to that girl than met the eye. There was no doubt that she was telling the truth when she said that she was Dean Sylvester's daughter. She was the absolute image of him; the same flashing dark eyes, tumbling black hair and honey-coloured skin. But who was her mother? Why had the girl clammed up at the mention of her, and, what was much more to the point, why had she left London to come here to a backwoods town like Elvemere?

She closed the door and went upstairs to collect her coat. Standing on the landing she allowed her mind to drift back to that pop festival on the Isle of Wight. She recalled the year 1970 – remembered so clearly Julia's passionate crush on the handsome young guitarist and her uncharacteristically wild and defiant behaviour in running off with him. Fleur looked about the right age. It all fitted. Although Joanna had been jealous at the time, she'd kept her mouth shut when she came home about where Julia really was. In truth she'd rather lost interest once she began her fiery and exciting affair with Vernon. But, thinking about it, maybe it was providential that she'd remained silent at the time. A pound to a penny Vernon hadn't a clue about Julia's little escapade. She'd practically said as much on the one occasion they'd met, in the coffee house just after Christmas. If what Joanna suspected were true she might well have a powerful trump card up her sleeve. But first she must be absolutely sure of her facts.

On the way home from work that afternoon Fleur stopped off at the DIY centre on the outskirts of town and bought a tin of white paint for the balcony. She intended to make a start the coming weekend so that it would be dry long before she wanted to use it. Already she had planted pots of daffodils and tulips and was eagerly waiting for them to come into bloom. After paying for her weekend in London she had had to abandon the luxury sun lounger she had set her heart on, but she had found two little wrought-iron chairs and a tiny table in a junk shop and bought them very cheaply. The man in the shop told her they had come out of an old pub that had been demolished. They were black at the moment but she intended to paint those white to match the balcony railings.

As she carried the can of paint up the steps of number thirteen Tom passed her on his way out.

'Hi! You've decided to make a start then?'

She smiled. 'Hoping to, this weekend. If it rains I shall do my table and chairs inside.'

'Well, remember to keep the windows open for ventilation,' he warned. 'I take it you've got the correct sized brushes?'

Her face fell. 'Oh, no! What an idiot I am. I forgot all about brushes. I could have got them at the same time.'

'I'll get them for you, if you like? I'll be passing the DIY centre in the morning.' He paused. 'If you don't mind my saying so, Fleur, I think you're going to need more paint than you've got there.'

'Am I?'

'Yes. You'll need some undercoat too. It's a good while since that balcony has been painted.' He hesitated. 'Strictly speaking you should rub the railings down thoroughly and paint them with some rust inhibitor first.'

Fleur's heart sank. It was going to cost more than she had thought by the sound of it. 'Oh, should I? It's all going to take more time than I thought.'

'Worth it, though, if you want it to last.' He paused, looking at her thoughtfully. 'I could get the other stuff for you when I get the brushes, if you like?'

'No, it's all right. I'll get it all.' She could hardly explain to him why she couldn't afford the extra materials at the moment, but she saw from the look on his face that he took her refusal of help for a rebuff. 'Thanks for the advice though,' she said, too late.

'That's okay. Just as you like.' They looked at each other awkwardly for a moment, then he said, 'I'm just off to interview a local author.'

'Are you?'

'Yes. I was going to get a takeaway on my way back. Share my supper with me?'

'Oh.' She bit her lip. 'I'm sorry, Tom. I have a friend coming round.'

'I see.' His smile faded and he backed away. 'It's okay. Just a thought. Well – see you around then.'

'Yes. 'Bye, Tom.' She watched with a heavy heart as he walked up the street. They had been awkward with each other since her affair with Peter. He had kept his distance as he had promised, careful, as he put it, not to invade her space. She would have loved to have supper with him like they used to do. She longed to have back the comfortable relationship they had enjoyed before. She missed him and had often thought she should make the first move. But she worried that if she tried to re-establish their friendship he would think she was merely using him. Tonight was the first time he had offered anything more than courtesy and she had been obliged to turn him down, giving him the impression that she was still keeping him at a distance.

Charlotte arrived on time and Fleur answered the door to find the girl standing outside holding a bowl of blue and pink hyacinths.

'A house-warming pressie,' she said, holding them

283

out. 'Or I suppose I should say flat-warming.'

'Thank you. They're lovely!' Fleur unwrapped the bowl and put it on the table, bending down to inhale their fragrance. 'Oh, they smell gorgeous, don't they? Shall I take your coat?'

Charlotte took off her coat, looking around at the room. 'This is lovely, Fleur. So cosy. Did you really do all this decorating yourself? You are clever. I wouldn't know where to start.'

'It was a question of needs must,' she laughed. 'It was so dreary when I moved in. Something had to be done. I've got it almost as I want it now, though I'd like to buy some new furniture when I've saved up enough. Come and look at my balcony.' She opened one of the French windows to show the other girl. 'I got the table and chairs from a junk shop. I'm going to paint everything white and then I'll have hanging baskets and pots full of flowers. I can't wait for the summer when I can sit out here and have my meals in the sunshine.'

Charlotte looked at it all with a wistful expression. 'You are lucky, Fleur. I wish I had somewhere like this.'

'But you live in a beautiful house with a big garden,' she said. 'I bet you have a lovely bedroom with your own television and everything. You have a family, Charlotte. Nothing can make up for that.'

'Don't you believe it! Anyway it isn't a real family. I've always wished I had brothers and sisters. A house full of fun and laughter. Sharing things together, that's a real family.'

Fleur went into the tiny kitchenette to make coffee She glanced at Charlotte as she carried the tray through and put it down on the table. 'Is that what you wanted to talk about?' she asked. 'Trouble at home?'

'In a way.' Charlotte sighed. 'Having plenty of money isn't everything, you know.'

Fleur handed her a cup of coffee and sat down opposite. 'What's wrong, Charlotte? You can talk to me if you want to. As you said, we don't know any of the same people so it won't matter to me. And I promise not to gossip. It wouldn't be wise to have a loose tongue in the job I do.'

'I know.' Charlotte sipped her coffee and smiled at Fleur over the cup's rim. 'It's not just that, though. It's funny, isn't it? I hardly know you really and yet I know deep inside that I can trust you.'

Pleasantly flattered, Fleur nodded. 'It's like that with some people.'

Charlotte frowned, searching her mind for the way to begin. 'Yours was a happy home, wasn't it?' she said. 'Before your grandmother died, I mean.'

'Yes, very happy. We didn't have any of the things you have – money and luxury. Where we lived was cramped, noisy and dirty. But we did have lots of love and when Grandpa was alive there was always music and laughter.'

'Our family isn't like that,' Charlotte told her. 'Sometimes days go by and we hardly see each other, let alone sit down to eat together. I don't think my mum and dad have ever got on. I wonder sometimes if they ever really loved each other.'

'What makes you say that?'

'They're always quarrelling. Dad's always been really patronising towards Mum, as though he wanted to make her think she was really thick. I think she's been trying to prove something to him with all this council work and stuff. He has affairs though, so I don't suppose he's even noticed how hard she's trying.'

'Affairs? Other women, you mean?' Fleur remembered the two occasions on which Vernon Grant had tried to chat her up and reflected that Charlotte was probably not exaggerating.

'Yes. He always has. Funny how parents think that

kids don't notice things. I was beginning to think he'd stopped but last night I found out that he's at it again – this time with the most awful woman imaginable: his personal assistant, Mrs Hanson.'

Fleur swallowed her involuntary gasp of surprise. 'You say you found out? Are you sure? I mean, you're not just jumping to conclusions?'

'No, I'm positive. I saw them coming out of her house. She was wearing a dressing gown and they were actually *kissing*,' Charlotte said, wrinkling her nose with disgust. 'Not just a casual peck either, a real state of the art *snog*. Doesn't take much imagination to work out what had been going on. Imagine, at *their* age! The worst part is that I have to work in the same office, running errands for her – being bossed around, just as if she owned the place! I hate her *guts*, Fleur.'

Fleur said nothing. Clearly Charlotte wasn't yet aware that the woman she hated so much was now a partner in the firm.

'Poor Mum,' the girl went on. 'I'm beginning to see what it must have been like for her all these years.' She paused, her lip trembling, and Fleur could see that the girl was fighting back tears. 'The thing is . . .' She swallowed hard. 'What should I do about it?'

'What can you do?' Fleur asked, wondering if Joanna's affair with Vernon Grant was the reason she had been given a partnership in his firm. 'Does anyone else know about it?'

'My Aunt Kath was with me when we saw them,' Charlotte said. 'She was driving me home from the stables and she took a short cut down Hazel Grove. Aunt Kath is Dad's sister. They've never got on either. She saw them too, but I can't talk to her about it. At least not till I've got my head round it all. There was ever such a funny atmosphere at the office today too. Apparently Mrs Hanson has been given some kind of promotion. She was out with Granddad all morning and she's talking about throwing a party to celebrate. It all looks jolly fishy, doesn't it? And what's worse is there's a rumour flying round that Grandpa Philips has resigned because of it!' She looked appealingly at Fleur. 'I don't know what's going on, Fleur. All I do know is that I hate it. Because of that woman, everything's being torn apart! What would you do if you were in my place? Would you tell Mum or keep it to yourself?'

Fleur found her own emotions stirred by Charlotte's revelation. *What would you do if you were in my place?* Part of her insisted that if Julia was being betrayed it was no more than she deserved. It was a case of 'what goes around, comes around'. But another part of her hated seeing what it was obviously doing to Charlotte.

'You say your dad has had affairs before,' she said carefully. 'This one will probably fizzle out like the others did so surely it would be wisest to keep what you saw to yourself?'

'Fizzle out? When she's working so closely with him? Not very likely, is it?' The other girl shook her head. 'The awful part is seeing them getting away with it – cheating Mum behind her back.' Charlotte chewed her thumb nail. 'Mum knew Mrs Hanson years ago when they were both young,' she said. 'She married an American and went to live over there. I wish she'd stayed! As far as I know Mum isn't friendly with her now. I don't think they've even met since Mrs Hanson joined the firm. Do you think they could have fallen out all those years ago and now Joanna is getting even?'

'Surely not.' Fleur was silently piecing it all together. She remembered seeing Joanna Hanson and Vernon Grant together at the country club on the night she had dined there with Peter Arden. It looked as though their affair had been going on for some time, so Charlotte was right about that. And if Joanna had been Julia's girlhood friend it was quite possible that she knew about her teenage affair with Dean Sylvester. Alarm bells began to ring inside Fleur's head and she wished fervently that she hadn't blurted out the fact that Dean had been her father.

Charlotte was still talking. 'Well, why else would the wretched woman come all the way back here from America and get a job at GPC?' she said plaintively. 'Her being so high-powered, you'd have thought she'd head straight for London.'

'Without knowing all the details, I couldn't even guess, Charlotte.' Fleur refilled both coffee cups, her mind spinning. 'My advice is to leave it for a while,' she said. 'Feel free to come round and see me whenever you want to talk. That might help.'

Julia was busy in the kitchen. She was taking extra trouble preparing the evening meal in the hope that perhaps this evening they would all get to sit down together for once. First she wanted to find out what Charlotte had been so upset about last night. Then there was a lot she wanted to talk to Vernon about, but that would have to wait until Charlotte had gone to bed.

She had had a shock when she went round to her parents' house that morning and saw her father, still in bed where May had insisted he remain. His face looked an unearthly grey against the whiteness of the pillows. She had tried to reassure him that all would be well; to convince him that no one really wanted him to resign.

'You are still the same valued member of the firm you always have been, Dad,' she told him, squeezing his hand. 'I'm sure Charlie will realise that once he's had time to pause and think things through.'

But Harry had seemed too tired and dispirited even to care. All the fight seemed to have drained out of him, a fact which alarmed her even more than his appearance.

Downstairs she urged her mother to telephone the doctor. 'Better to be on the safe side,' Julia said, anxious not to worry May. 'I'm sure he's just physically and emotionally exhausted, but I think it would be wise to have him checked. Besides, he might feel better just talking things through with another man. You know how well he gets on with Doctor Frazer.'

May nodded. 'I think you're right. I'll give him a ring.' She shook her head angrily. 'That Hanson woman has a lot to answer for.'

'To be fair, I think it was more Charlie,' Julia said. 'You know how carried away he gets when he has a new idea. He was extremely rude to me on the telephone this morning when he read the report in the *Clarion* about my women's refuge. He'll probably be round later to see Daddy with an apology and some kind of peace offering.'

'Between ourselves, I hope he isn't,' May confided. 'I really don't feel I could be civil to the odious little man if he showed his face here today. The years I've put up with his appalling manners and vulgarity because he was your father's business partner! Daddy is coming up to retiring age anyway. He's been looking tired for months now. We could be having such a pleasant time together if only he'd just let go.'

Julia gave her mother a hug. 'Sometimes things work out for the best, Mum. Don't put any more pressure on him. We'll just play it all by ear, eh?'

May kissed her daughter's cheek. 'Yes. As you say, we'll wait and see what happens.'

She'd rung half an hour ago to tell Julia that Doctor Frazer had called and advised Harry to take it easy for a few days and then book the two of them on a long holiday somewhere warm and sunny. Afterwards he'd told May confidentially that Harry was suffering from severe stress and that retirement seemed a good idea.

'If only retiring had been *his* idea though,' she said with a sigh. 'It's this business of being edged out that has upset him so.'

'Tell him it isn't worth making himself ill for,' Julia told her.

'By the way, dear, Charlotte has just arrived,' May said. 'She heard about her granddad's resignation at the office today. I've asked her to stay and have dinner with us. She's upstairs with him now. She'll cheer him up so much, bless her.'

'Oh, that's nice. I'm glad she's come to see you. Look, Mum, if you get the chance, will you try and find out if there's anything worrying her? She came home looking like death last night and she was out of the house like a whirlwind this morning. I didn't get the chance to talk to her.'

'Leave it to me,' May said. 'Charlotte and I have always been good friends. I'm sure she'll tell me if there's anything wrong.'

Julia sighed as she turned back to the kitchen. It would be just the two of them then. Well, at least it would be a chance for her to talk to Vernon.

Charlotte sat beside her grandfather's bed and looked with some dismay at his ashen face.

'It's not true, is it, Granddad? You haven't really resigned?'

He turned his head and smiled at his only grand-child. 'It's good of you to come and see me, Charlotte, love, but you mustn't worry your head with my prob-lems. Your grandma thinks it's high time I retired anyway. Maybe I'll do best to take notice of her.'

'Yes, but only if it's what you want,' she said. 'I don't

see why you should go just because Mrs Hanson wants your place.'

'Is that what they're saying?'

Charlotte reddened. 'You know what offices are like. What they don't know they guess at. That's why I'm here – partly. I wanted to see you, of course, but I want to hear from you what really happened?'

He reached out and took her hand, squeezing it warmly. 'It's all very simple, my love. Mrs Hanson has been made a partner and there are some new ideas planned that I can't go along with. I was angry when I walked out of the meeting and said I was going to resign. But I haven't done so formally. Not yet.'

'Well I think you should stay on and fight them if you don't agree,' she told him. 'After all, you're a partner too, aren't you?'

'I'm afraid I'd only be out-voted,' Harry said wearily. 'It's not worth the bother.'

Charlotte edged her chair closer to the bed. 'Granddad – I've found something out. It's been worrying me and I don't know what to do. I think I should tell you.'

Harry lay back against the pillows and closed his eyes with a sigh. 'What is it, sweetheart? You know I'll help if I can.'

'It's Dad – and Mrs Hanson. They're – you know – having an affair. And it's not just talk. I know it's true because I've seen them.'

Harry's eyes were open in an instant. He pulled himself up in bed and stared at his granddaughter. '*Seen* them. My God, child, what do you mean?'

'Last night, when Aunt Kath was driving me home. We passed her house – Mrs Hanson's, I mean. Dad's car was outside and they were kissing each other. *Really* kissing, I mean, not just a friendly peck.' She paused to bite her lip nervously. It was the first time she had ever spoken to her grandfather about such intimate matters. 'And that's not all. She – she was wearing her dressing gown.'

For a moment Harry was lost for words. Fury filled his breast. He'd always known that Vernon was a philanderer. For years he'd despised him for the dance he'd led Julia. In a way he blamed himself for turning a blind eye to it because of the business, and for encouraging the marriage in the first place. But for Vernon to be so careless as to let his own child witness his depravity ... His fingers tightened round Charlotte's as he fought for control. 'I daresay there was some simple explanation for what you saw, love. Go along now and don't worry about it any more.'

'But what about Mum? You don't think I should tell her?'

'No! Don't tell anyone. Let your old granddad do the worrying for you, there's a good girl. I'll get to the bottom of it. I'm sure it wasn't what you thought.' He bent forward to kiss her forehead. 'Off you go downstairs now. It'll be nice for your grandma to have someone to eat with. I'm having mine up here tonight.'

She looked anxious. 'You're not ill, are you, Granddad? I haven't upset you and made you worse?'

'Bless you, no, my love.' He smiled at her indulgently. 'You could never make me feel anything but better.'

At the door she paused. 'Will you tell Grandma – about Dad and – and *her*?'

He smiled and shook his head at her. 'I told you not to think about it any more. Off you go now and put the whole thing out of your head. Grandma has made one of her famous chicken pies. You can tell her I've been lying here sniffing the lovely smell of it cooking and I'm feeling quite peckish after all.'

When the door closed behind her he lay back against

the pillows, feeling a sudden surge of adrenaline revitalise him. Charlotte's discovery about Vernon and Joanna Hanson had only confirmed what he'd suspected himself for some weeks. Damn that bloody little creep and his sordid affairs! Damn Charlie Grant too! The last thing he'd do was to resign now. If he did, he'd be playing right into their greedy hands. Why should he stand down and let the three of them have it all their own way? Oh, no!

A flash of inspiration brought the colour flooding back into his cheeks as an idea began to take shape in his head. There was a way that he could put a stop to all their little games and do as Angus Frazer had advised too. The plan ballooned inside his head, exploding as gloriously as a firework. He lay back with a smile of satisfaction curving his lips. He'd make Charlie Grant eat humble pie yet. For all his bombastic ways, he'd find out he wasn't as clever as he thought.

Chapter 11

When Charlotte had left, Fleur washed the coffee cups and tidied the flat. It was still only seven o'clock. She'd heard Tom come in about ten minutes ago and as she worked she kept picturing him in his room upstairs, eating his solitary Chinese takeaway. Was she being stubborn, refusing to make the first move? He had left it up to her after all, knowing that she hated to be pressured. Finally she made up her mind. Tidying her hair before the mirror and applying a dash of lipstick to give her confidence, she opened the door and walked determinedly up the stairs to knock on Tom's door.

When he opened it he looked surprised. 'Fleur! Is something wrong?'

She smiled wryly. 'No. I just wanted to see you, that's all. If you remember, you invited me to share your supper earlier.'

'You said you were entertaining a friend.'

'Not entertaining exactly. It was only Charlotte, a girl I met at the computer course I was on. I saw her this morning and she asked if she could drop in for a chat.'

His face cleared. 'Oh, I thought – oh, well, never mind that.' He held the door open. 'Come in.'

She grinned at him mischievously. 'I thought you'd never ask.'

Inside the room she saw that he had already eaten. A plate with crumbs showed that he had made do with a sandwich. 'I haven't interrupted your supper, have I?' she asked.

'No.' He whisked the plate out of sight. 'I've already eaten. I didn't bother bringing anything in. I wasn't very hungry actually.' He looked at her. 'Have you had yours? I mean, you hadn't changed your mind about the takeaway, had you?'

'I just wanted to see you, Tom. I think it's time we had a talk.'

'Oh? Yes, of course, if that's what you want.'

She came straight to the point. 'I've missed you, Tom.' She held up her hand. 'Okay – maybe I've got a nerve, saying that after well, what I did.'

'No.' He shook his head. 'It wasn't your fault. You fell in love. That can happen to anyone. I'm just sorry it didn't work out.'

'Yes, well, it's over now.' She paused, searching for words. It was harder than she'd hoped. He was doing his best to make it easier but she still didn't know what he really felt about her. She cleared her throat. 'Look, Tom, I'd really like it to be as it was before.'

'I don't think that's possible, Fleur.' He paused, his face serious. 'I wonder if you can possibly know how it makes a guy who cares for you feel, telling him you're in love with someone else?'

She saw the hurt in his eyes and realised how much it cost him to say that. 'I'm sorry, Tom. I was such a fool. If it makes you feel any better I have paid for the mistake I made.' She turned towards the door. 'Well, if you feel that it can never be the same between us, I can't say I blame you.'

As she reached the door he moved to stand in front

of her. 'Maybe it can't be the same,' he said. 'But we could try to start again. If you're really sure that's what you want?'

'Oh, Tom.' She looked at him, her eyes bright. 'I do. I really do.'

'On your terms. No strings. No obligations.'

'Right.'

For a moment they stood looking at each other, then Tom's face relaxed and they both laughed, releasing the tension between them.

'Shall I go and get that takeaway?' he asked.

'No. I'll make us an omelette. What would you like, mushroom or Spanish?'

Downstairs in her flat she made the omelettes while Tom assembled a salad and buttered bread. They chatted over the meal, sharing companionable anecdotes about their respective jobs, filling in the weeks between when they'd seen little of each other. It was after they'd washed up and were sitting with their coffee that Tom suddenly said, 'There's something I should tell you, Fleur.'

'Yes?'

'I'm moving from here shortly.'

Her heart sank. 'From Elvemere? You've got another job?'

'Oh, no. Just from this house.'

'I see.' She glanced at him uncertainly. 'Was it – because of me?'

'Partly – and partly because I had an offer I couldn't refuse. I'm going to share a house – with a colleague, someone from the paper.'

She smiled. 'Oh, that's nice. Wow! A whole house! It'll be a great improvement on this.'

'Well, not the whole house; two rooms and the use of the rest of it. Yes, it will be an improvement.'

She frowned, waiting for more. If he was happy with

the arrangement why was he so hesitant? 'So what's the problem? Is there something you haven't told me?' she prompted.

'I'm just coming to it.' He cleared his throat and looked at her. 'It's just that the colleague – the person I'll be sharing with – is, well, a girl.'

'Oh, I see.' Fleur put her cup down.

'No, you don't! Her name is Sadie Freeman and she's a photographer on the *Clarion*. She only started a couple of months ago. She's very good. In fact, I happen to think she's pretty special.'

'*Special?* Well, yes, you must think so if you're going to move in with her.'

'I'm *not* moving in with her. Not in the way you mean, anyway. And when I say she's special, I mean talented – at her work. She really wants the chance to go for photo-journalism and I'm sure it won't be long before she lands a good job with one of the national dailies. A relative died recently and left her a bit of money, that's how she's managed to put down the deposit on the house. It's only a little terraced place in Park Row. She needs someone to share to help with the mortgage. She put a notice on the board at work and I applied. That's all there is to it, Fleur.'

Only slightly reassured she asked, 'When are you planning to move in?'

'At the end of the month. My rent here is paid up till then.'

She looked at him mournfully. 'It won't be the same here without you.'

He smiled wistfully. 'I wish you really meant that.'

'But I do.'

'Well, it's only on the other side of the park. I'll be able to invite you over and make you a proper meal. Sadie got a bargain in that house. It's been nicely modernised, central heating and everything. You'll love the kitchen. Pine cupboards and blue and white tiles. I'm having the ground-floor rooms all to myself and the use of the kitchen and bathroom.'

'What's she like – this Sadie Freeman?'

'Not at all like you.' He laughed. 'I suppose she's what you'd call a feminist. Very tough and competitive. She has her hair cut in one of those spiky styles, rides a motorbike and wears leather trousers. You could describe her as formidable.'

'You make her sound like a monster!'

He laughed. 'No, she's not really, just what you'd call assertive. I guess she's had to be to get where she is. She's fantastic at her job and a good sort when you get to know her. You must meet her sometime. I'm sure you'd get along.'

'Mmm. Well, we'll have to see, won't we?' Fleur picked up her cup and drank the last of her coffee. 'Tom, can I ask you a favour?'

'Fire away.'

'Will you help me paint the balcony? After what you said I don't think I really know enough about the job.' She grinned wryly. 'How's that for assertive?'

'Don't be daft. Of course I'll help.' His face broke into a broad grin. 'This weekend?'

'Ah – no, not this. I can't afford the extra stuff you said I'd need yet.'

'It won't cost that much. I thought you were saving up.'

'I was, but I spent the money.' She looked at him from under lowered lashes. 'I sent it to Peter Arden to pay for everything he spent on me that weekend in London.'

For a moment he stared at her, then he reached out and pulled her into his arms. 'Oh, Fleur.'

She buried her face against his shoulder, grateful that she didn't have to meet his eyes. 'I wanted to be independent of him, Tom, done with him for good. But all that is over now. I don't want to talk about it any more. All right?'

He held her away from him so as to look into her eyes. 'More than all right. It's wonderful. I was afraid you might still be carrying a torch.' He kissed her softly. 'You know how I feel about you, Fleur. Nothing you could ever do would change that.'

He'd half expected her to stiffen and begin to push away, but to his surprise she stayed where she was, her body relaxed and her head against his neck, her soft black curls tickling his nose. After a moment, much to his delight, he felt her arms slide around his waist as she sighed and nestled closer. Raising her face to his, she said, 'Let's not talk about feelings, Tom. Not for a while. Just let's enjoy starting again and being together – like this.'

He looked into her eyes and gently kissed the mouth she offered, deeply grateful for the warm vitality of her body in his arms and the responsive mouth under his. He resolved that he would tread carefully this time, feel his way tentatively back into their relationship. He wanted to tell her how much he loved her; how desperately he had missed her; of the sleepless nights he had spent, wondering if he would ever stand a chance of getting her back again. But he knew that to pour out his heart to her now would be a mistake. Fleur was a girl who must *feel* sure enough, free enough, to share her emotions without obligation. Hers was an independent spirit that would only be captured when she was truly ready. The facet of her character that had once filled him with resentment now made him love her all the more.

For a while they sat silently, warm and content, hands clasped, fingers laced, cheek against cheek. For the moment words were unnecessary.

'Tell me what you've been doing.' Fleur said at last.

'I've started reporting on council meetings. It can be fascinating. Funny too, sometimes.' He reached inside his jacket and pulled the front page of the *Clarion* out of an inner pocket. 'Did you see my piece in the paper this morning?' The paper was folded into a small square but as he smoothed it out for her she found herself staring down at a photograph of Julia Grant.

'Sadie took that,' he told her. 'It's good, isn't it?'

But Fleur only nodded abstractedly. She was reading the article and marvelling at the sheer hypocrisy of the woman.

'What do you think?' Tom said. 'She's doing a good job, I reckon. A lot of councillors just sit there and never open their mouths, let alone try to actually *do* something for the community.'

'Maybe she just wants to get noticed,' Fleur said scathingly.

'Well, if she does at least she'll be doing these poor women a good turn.'

'If it comes off,' Fleur said. 'Probably only a lot of hot air.'

'No, I think she's sincere. The plans have been passed and she's done quite a bit to get the thing off to a good start. I talked to her for a long time after the council meeting and I get the impression that she's a deeply sincere woman. She certainly seems to have a strong affinity with single mothers.'

'*So she should!*' Fleur was suddenly aware that she'd spoken the heartfelt thought aloud. Tom was looking at her, his eyebrows raised in question.

'What do you mean?'

She bit her lip. 'Nothing. Just that any worthwhile councillor should be able to put themselves in the shoes of less fortunate folks.'

'True.' Tom laughed and folded the paper up again,

300

stuffing it back into his pocket. 'Hey, know what? I could murder another coffee, couldn't you?'

'Yes, okay.'

'I'll make it. You sit tight.'

As he began to get up, she reached out and took his hand, drawing him down beside her again. 'Tom . . .'

'Yes?'

'Stay here with me tonight.'

Sorely tempted, he looked into her eyes for a long breathless moment, trying to interpret what he saw there. There was so much. She was tense, maybe even a little nervous but certainly very vulnerable. Leaning forward, he kissed her gently.

'No, love. Not this time. Not yet.'

She held onto his arms, refusing to let him go. 'Why not?'

Now he saw something else in the velvet brown eyes. There was still that deep insecurity she had always tried so hard to hide. Laid bare like that for him to see, it made him slightly ashamed, though he could not have said why. And it made him even more determined to love and protect her.

'We're starting again, remember?' he told her gently. 'From day one. No strings, No obligations. That applies on both sides. Better not to rush things. I want you to be good and sure first, Fleur. When and *if* we decide to take things a step further, I don't want it to be casual. I'd like it to be a real commitment. That's important to me.' He bent to cup her face with his hands, kissing her. 'Now I'll make that coffee.'

It was some time before Fleur slept that night. Lying in bed she went over what she and Tom had said to each other. Had he thought she was throwing herself at him? Maybe she had been in a way. She was so anxious to prove something, both to herself and him. Peter had made her so insecure. Secretly she was afraid of losing

301

Tom again, especially now that he was going to live in the same house as the girl she thought of as her rival. Tom obviously admired and respected this Sadie he talked of so glowingly. Could those feelings develop into something deeper once they were living under the same roof?

She turned over and rearranged her pillow, trying hard to think of something else. The article Tom had written about Julia Grant's plans for a refuge for battered wives was interesting. What would Julia's fellow councillors think, she wondered sleepily, if they knew that their altruistic colleague had herself once been a single mother? What a flurry that would cause!

Suddenly she remembered Joanna Hanson's probing questions this morning and was wide awake in an instant. Already she was trying to steal Julia's husband. If she found out that Julia had had a daughter prior to her marriage to Vernon Grant, she could cause havoc. Joanna was a woman who would have no qualms about breaking up a family or setting people against one another. She would ride roughshod over anyone who got in her way in order to get what she wanted. It was all there in those hard green eyes.

Fleur stared into the darkness, imagining the chaos a disclosure like that could create. *But she would have to prove it before she dragged me into her tacky little plans*, she told herself. And for that she would need Fleur's co-operation. She sighed and closed her eyes again. If Mrs Hanson was hoping for that she was about to be sadly disappointed.

Fleur and Sally arrived in good time to set up the buffet in Joanna's conservatory. On occasions like this where there weren't too many guests Sally preferred to keep a low profile. She herself would remain behind the scenes to replenish plates and uncork fresh bottles of wine. Only Fleur would circulate with trays before and after the guests had helped themselves to the buffet table.

The table looked attractive with an arrangement of spring flowers and yellow candles. Joanna had chosen the deluxe menu, which included smoked salmon, caviare and oysters. Privately Fleur considered it one of the less tempting menus with its array of rich and indigestible luxuries and she wondered what the guests from the lower echelons of GPC would make of it. She guessed – rightly, as it happened – that most of them would much rather have had a selection of cold meats, ham and chicken, with perhaps a whole salmon, and simple salad accompaniments, but as she and Sally worked together in Joanna's exquisitely appointed kitchen she kept her opinion to herself. After all Joanna was paying well so who was she to argue?

Joanna was edgy. This evening was important to her. Since Harry Philips had walked out of the meeting at which she had been appointed a partner no one had seen or heard anything from him. It was the one cloud on her horizon. She would have preferred all the partners to approve of her elevation. The resignation he had threatened had not been delivered – or at least not as far as she knew. Vernon refused to talk about him and Charlie too was keeping his mouth tightly closed on the subject. Working on her own initiative, she had sent him and his wife May an invitation to the party. Now she wondered if she had done the right thing. To exclude him would have looked bad, seeing that he was still to all intents and purposes a partner in the firm, and anyway she doubted whether they would come. But if the Philipses did turn up their presence could make the most awful atmosphere and cast a shadow over the whole evening. It was something she was going to have to deal with if and when.

Looking into the kitchen she was reassured by the sight of Sally Arden, looking brisk and businesslike in her black and white striped apron as she went about the preparations. She was also glad to see Fleur, though for different reasons. The girl was to be her trump card. She could make the difference between the success of Charlie's plan and its failure. For the past few nights Joanna had lain awake, wandering what she would do if the girl went down with flu or had some kind of accident at the last minute.

Joanna could hardly wait to see Julia's face when she subtly presented her with the little surprise she had up her sleeve. The coincidence of the girl's name and those distinctive looks was too much to swallow. Fleur Sylvester was Dean's daughter and her sudden appearance in Elvemere seemed to point to the fact that she was here to contact her mother – Julia. Clearly the whole thing was being kept secret. The fascinating question was, *why*?

Joanna had rehearsed what she would say over and again, getting the innuendos just right and watching for the tell-tale signs. She had worked out that she couldn't lose. The more she thought about it, the more sure she was that Fleur was Julia's daughter, but even if her hunch was wildly off the mark Julia would hardly want to go out of her way to prove her wrong, especially when not even her closest relatives knew of her clandestine run-away affair with Dean Sylvester.

Charlie and Louise were the first to arrive and Joanna greeted them effusively, ushering them into the living room and making sure that they had a drink. It was the first time she had met Louise since she had been back in England. There had been no love lost between them all those years ago at the height of

304

Joanna's red hot relationship with Vernon that had been the talk of Elvemere. Louise had had ambitions for her beloved only son, and they did not include his being ensnared by the girl she looked upon as the town tart. Harsh words had passed between them; words which Joanna looked forward to seeing her swallow this evening. She hoped they would choke her.

As she took Louise's fur coat she could hardly conceal a smile at what it revealed. The turquoise blue evening dress Louise wore was as tight as a second skin. Joanna resisted the temptation to shield her eyes from the dazzling glitter of beads and sequins that encrusted it, struggling against the competition of dangling diamante earrings and matching necklace. She reflected wryly that the woman looked as though she had fallen off a Christmas tree.

'I'm so glad you could come, Mrs Grant,' said Joanna, smiling sweetly. 'It's so long since we last met. We must have a lovely cosy chat about old times someday.'

When she'd gone Louise jabbed Charlie in the ribs. 'She may have had two rich husbands and a haircut, but she's the same devious bitch she always was, if you ask me,' she remarked. 'Wouldn't trust her as far as I could spit!'

Charlie glowered at her. 'No one is asking you, so just keep your opinions to yourself, Lou. She's an important member of the firm now, remember? And not afraid to put her money where her mouth is. She's a talented businesswoman, not a spotty teenager any more.'

Louise took a glass of wine from Fleur's tray and turned her back on her husband, her face crimson with annoyance. 'They'll find out,' she muttered under her breath. 'Once a bitch, always a bitch.' All the same, she already knew that Joanna wasn't to be seen off with bribes and threats this time. She had power now; the power that comes with money. The kind no one, especially Charlie, could resist.

Vernon and Julia put in an appearance soon after. By contrast to her mother-in-law, Julia wore a plain black cocktail dress which Joanna instantly recognised as a Jean Muir.

The first arrivals stood on opposite sides of the room, sipping their cocktails uneasily. There was obvious tension between Charlie and his wife and Julia seemed ill at ease with her in-laws. Joanna tried hard to draw all four into conversation but she was grateful when more guests began to arrive, easing the tension. Soon she was circulating among them, making sure that glasses were full, people were mingling and conversation flowed without constraint.

'I'm sorry Charlotte couldn't come,' Julia said when Joanna appeared at her side. 'She'd promised to go to her aunt's this evening and she'll be staying over.'

'I understand. Don't worry about it,' Joanna said generously. 'This kind of affair can't seem very exciting to a sixteen-year-old.'

'She asked me to thank you for the invitation though,' Julia lied. What Charlotte had actually said was that she wouldn't go to Joanna's party if she were hung, drawn and quartered and served up as kebabs! 'It's bad enough having to see Joanna the Hun at the office all week,' she said vehemently, 'without actually spending my precious free time in her company!'

'I haven't congratulated you yet on your . . . promotion in the firm,' Julia said.

Joanna smiled. 'Thank you. You and I haven't had that little get together we promised ourselves yet either, have we? I've been hoping that we might meet and work something out regarding your women's refuge project,' she said. 'It's unfortunate, I know, but it's so

306

silly to be at loggerheads when it's all in the family, isn't it?' She lowered her voice. 'I know Charlie can let that straight-from-the-shoulder attitude of his get out of hand at times, but I'm sure his heart is in the right place.'

'Are you?' Julie said coolly. 'As far as I'm concerned it's a question of first come, first served. And it happens that I was there first.'

'Well, I'm sure we can work something out between us,' Joanna said placatingly. Out of the corner of her eye she'd just seen Fleur come back into the room with a fresh tray of drinks. She edged herself strategically into Julia's line of vision. 'Never mind business now. You're here to enjoy yourself tonight,' she said with a smile. 'I want to hear *all* about what you did after I left Elvemere. We really do have an awful lot of catching up to do.'

'There's nothing much to tell,' Julia said. 'Compared to you I've had a very uneventful life – till now.'

'Ah, that's what you say.' Joanna gave her a knowing little smile. 'But maybe it wasn't quite as uneventful as you'd have us believe.' Her timing perfect, she shifted slightly to reveal Fleur who was now moving among the other guests just a few feet away. Joanna pretended to notice her for the first time. 'Oh, by the way, have you met that girl who works for Sally Arden? Strikingly attractive, isn't she? Quite exotic. You know, looking at her reminds me of someone. Can you guess who?'

Julia glanced in Fleur's direction. 'I have met her before. As for reminding me – I don't know. She's certainly attractive but . . .'

'You don't happen to know what her name is?' Joanna asked. Julia shook her head, looking puzzled.

'Fleur. Pretty, isn't it? Though not entirely suitable for someone so tall and dark. I always think of girls named Fleur as blonde and petite. She's not local, of course. Tells me she's from London, but you can hear that from the accent.' She took a sip of her Martini, watching with narrowed eyes, noting with satisfaction the heightened colour as Julia's gaze followed the girl.

'Yes,' she went on, 'Fleur *Sylvester*, she tells me her name is. That's a clue. Now who does she remind you of, darling?'

Julia's heart seemed to freeze. She shook her head. 'I'm sorry, I can't see any likeness. I've no idea who you mean.'

'Really? You do surprise me. Sylvester? It doesn't ring any bells?' Joanna shrugged. 'Oh, well, never mind. It was just an idea. Oh!' She waved to someone on the other side of the room. 'There's Bob Jefford and his wife. Forgive me if I have a word with them. See you later . . .'

Julia watched her weave her way through the guests. She felt strange and unreal. It wasn't possible. There was no way that Joanna could know about Dean's child, let alone the fact that she had been named Fleur. So what was going on? What was she up to?

'Another glass of wine?'

Startled, Julia turned and found herself looking straight into Dean Sylvester's dark expressive eyes. She gave a little gasp of shock. It was the same likeness that had caught her attention on the night of her own New Year party. Joanna must have seen it too. But she could only be guessing at the girl's identity of course – wildly guessing. There was no way she could know. None at all.

'More wine?' the girl repeated, holding out her tray.

Julia shook her head, staring at the girl. Was it actually possible that she was . . . Suddenly the room began to spin around her and a feeling of stark panic made her heart thump dizzyingly fast against her ribs. She put her empty glass down on the tray and looked around frantically for an escape route.

'Are you all right?' The girl was looking at her now with concern. 'If you're not feeling well, I could get you a glass of water or . . .'

'It's all right,' Julia said, putting out a hand as though to hold her at bay. '*I'm all right.* I just need – need to get some air.'

'Come with me.' Fleur turned and made her way out into the hall, Julia following. At the foot of the stairs she said, 'I wouldn't go outside if I were you. It's quite a cold evening. You could catch a chill.'

'Where's the bathroom?' Julia asked, her face ashen.

'At the top of the stairs. Do you want me to find your husband – to tell someone?'

Desperate not to faint and make a scene, Julia was already halfway up the stairs. '*No!*' She looked down at the girl's upturned face. 'Please don't say anything – I don't want any fuss.'

Fleur watched her go thoughtfully then went into the kitchen and closed the door, putting her tray down on the worktop. 'Sally, one of the guests is feeling ill,' she said. 'She doesn't want anyone told. I think she's afraid of making a fuss, but I don't think she should be alone. Can you take over while I go up to her?'

'Of course.' Sally was already taking off her apron. 'Off you go. Take her a brandy. I'll see to everything here. Let me know if you need any help.'

Joanna's sumptuous green and ivory bathroom was stiflingly hot. Julia opened the window and drew in several deep draughts of the cool night air. After a moment her heartbeat began to steady and the sickly faint feeling started to subside. Surely she must be imagining it? The girl couldn't possibly have traced her here. How would she even know Julia's name, let alone where she lived? Her name probably wasn't Sylvester at all. This was just the kind of trick Joanna would play to catch her out. There was no way she could possibly know of her child's existence. There was nothing to worry about. All she had to do was take control of the situation and play it cool. A soft tap on the door made her spin round.

'Who is it?'

'Are you all right, Mrs Grant?'

Julia's heart quickened again as she recognised the girl's voice. 'I'm fine, thank you.'

'May I come in? I've brought you something.'

Julia hesitated. Something made her want to look at the girl again – just to reassure herself. Maybe she was older then she'd thought. Perhaps if she talked to her there would be some hint, some clue that would put her mind at rest. She stepped up to the door, turned the key, opened it and looked out. 'I told you, I'm quite all right. See for yourself.'

Fleur held out the glass of brandy. 'I've brought you this,' she said. 'It will help to make you feel better.'

Julia took the glass, but she was looking at the girl. Suddenly something deep inside told her that there was no mistake. This tall girl with beautiful eyes and a honey complexion was Dean's daughter – *her* daughter. She knew it with an instinctive certainty that took her breath away. And now, looking into the girl's eyes, she saw that Fleur knew it too.

Julia tossed back the brandy in one gulp. It made her gasp a little but at least it steadied her trembling. 'You're Fleur,' she said. 'You are, aren't you?'

'Yes.'

'And you know who I am. You've tracked me down. Well, what do you want now that you've found me?'

Fleur frowned. *'Want?'*

'Yes. Don't look at me like that. You must want something or you wouldn't be here. Why don't you just

310

say? Come on. How – how much?'

'How much *what*?' Fleur took a step towards her. It was a strange, almost bizarre experience, standing face to face with her natural mother at last. A thousand times, late at night when she couldn't sleep, in her secret heart of hearts, she had allowed herself to fantasise about this meeting. Now it wasn't in the least how she had imagined it would be. Never in her wildest fantasies had she imagined she would be accused of demanding money. She was shocked and hurt.

'I'm here because I'm doing my job,' she said.

'I meant, what are you doing in Elvemere?' Julia asked, her voice sharp with tension. 'I warn you, if you think you can blackmail me you're on dangerous ground. How much is your silence going to cost me?'

Anger burned Fleur's breast. She closed the bathroom door and stepped closer to Julia. She was slightly the taller of the two and Julia took an involuntary step backwards, suddenly intimidated by the angry gleam in the girl's eyes.

'I'm here because I promised Dolly, my grandmother, just before she died that I'd come and find you. That's the only reason. I found out who and where you were a long time ago. But I never intended to speak or to make myself known to you. If you want to hear the truth, I've never felt the need or the wish to know you. In my book, a woman who can walk out on her baby isn't worth the name of mother. And as for *blackmailing* you . . .'

'Please . . .' Julia winced and held out her hand. 'I'm sorry I said that. It was just that seeing you like this – finding out who you are – has been a shock. I couldn't think of any other reason, but . . .' She bit her lip. 'Look – there's an awful lot here that I don't understand. I didn't mean to insult you. I wish I could make you understand what happened all those years ago. There's

311

– oh, God, there's so much I wish you could know.'

'Don't bother!' Fleur told her bitterly, turning on her heel. 'As far as I'm concerned you're a stranger. And you always will be.' At the door she turned. 'If you're feeling better I'll go and get on with the work I'm paid for.'

Julia reached out and made a desperate grab at the hand that was about to turn the door handle. 'Please, don't go. We can't just leave it at that. We have to talk. Fleur. You must know that neither of us can walk away from this situation. Not now.' She moistened her dry lips. 'Look, can we meet somewhere?'

Fleur looked at the floor. Half of her wanted to escape, never to see or speak to this despicable woman again. Standing up in public for the rights of single mothers after the way she had behaved! But there was a small part of her that was curious to know Julia's side of the story – that needed to know that at some time in the distant past her mother had loved and wanted her. Despising herself for this weakness, she lifted her head. 'I don't really think there's anything to be gained, do you?'

'*Yes*. Yes, I do! There are things I want you to know; things I need you to tell me too. Please say you'll see me, Fleur? Even if it's just the once.'

For a long moment the two women looked at each other, then Fleur gave in. 'All right,' she said. 'Where? And when?'

Julia let out her breath in a sigh of relief. 'There's a little pub called The Millstone in a village called Eastbridge. It's about two miles the other side of Merifield on the main Newmarket road. I'll meet you there tomorrow evening – if that's convenient?'

'Yes, all right.'

'About eight?'

'Yes.'

312

'Do you have transport?'

'I can borrow some, I think.'

'Right. If you can't make it, just ring the pub. They'll give me a message.'

Joanna walked out into the hall just as Fleur was coming down the stairs. She looked up at her enquiringly.

'Everything all right?'

'Yes, thank you.'

Joanna looked past her towards the top of the stairs. 'Is Mrs Grant up there?'

Fleur hesitated. 'I don't know. I've just been to get my handkerchief.' Joanna was staring pointedly at the empty brandy glass in her hand and she added quickly, 'Oh – I found this on the landing. Someone must have put it down.'

Unconvinced, Joanna nodded. 'Well, you'd better get back to the kitchen,' she said. 'I'll be wanting to serve the buffet in about ten minutes.' As Fleur closed the kitchen door she heard the bathroom door open and saw Julia quietly step out onto the landing. Smiling smugly to herself, Joanna turned back towards the chatter of her guests. So she had been right! So far, so good.

As she went into the room Charlie hailed her. 'Ah – there you are, lass! Lovely do. I think everyone is enjoying themselves.' He slipped an over-familiar arm around her waist. 'What was that you were saying earlier about finding a way to persuade Julia to change her mind about this doss house she's planning?'

Joanna smiled at him. 'I think you can leave that to me, Charlie,' she said mysteriously. 'I don't believe in counting my chickens, but I think I can safely say it's in the bag.'

'Good girl!' Charlie, mellow with whisky, hugged

her painfully and bent to kiss her cheek. 'By heck, girl, I don't know what you're up to but you're a lass after my own heart!'

On the other side of the room Louise watched out of the corner of her eye. Was history repeating itself? Was she going to have to get rid of that woman again? Clearly this time it would be much more difficult. Joanna would not be intimidated by threats or tempted by money this time. She was also now a partner in the firm, which was regrettable, because Louise had the strongest feeling that if someone didn't do something to get rid of her, Joanna Hanson would be the ruin of them all.

Julia sat in the morning-room at Gresham House, having coffee with her parents. She'd understood and approved of their failure to put in an appearance at the party last night and after her encounter with Fleur everything else had gone out of her head. She'd got through the rest of the evening as best she could, concentrating on behaving perfectly normally, determined that Joanna should see nothing amiss. So, she'd been slightly surprised when her mother had telephoned this morning with an urgent request that she join them for coffee.

'There's something your father wants to talk to you about,' May said. 'It's quite important, dear, so we'd be grateful if you could make the time for us.'

When Julia arrived she'd been relieved to see that her father looked much better than the last time she had seen him. The doctor had put him on a mild tranquilliser and insisted that he get as much rest as possible. Already he looked more relaxed, the lines of strain around his mouth and eyes less deeply etched.

'We've booked a Caribbean cruise,' May told her

excitedly as she carried in the tray of coffee. 'We leave the first week in April. That's only a few weeks away. There's so much I have to do before then. I was wondering if you and I might go up to town on a shopping spree?'

'Is that what you wanted to ask me?' Julia smiled, pleased to see her mother looking happier.

'No.' It was Harry who spoke. 'It's something much more serious than that, Julia. Your mother and I have talked things through very carefully and I've decided not to retire.'

Julia looked at him in dismay. 'Oh, Daddy! Are you sure about this?'

'I'm not going to be an active partner,' Harry told her. 'What I have in mind will need your cooperation. That's what I wanted to speak to you about this morning. What I'd like to do is to transfer my shares in the firm to you.'

'*To me?*' Julia felt a twinge of alarm. 'But why? I've never had anything to do with the business.'

'I think it's time you did. You'd be entitled to attend board meetings and vote on my behalf.' Harry looked at her dismayed expression. 'Well, you want your own way over the women's refuge, don't you? This could be a way of getting it. I intend to exercise my right to call an extraordinary general meeting to discuss this Victoria Gardens project.'

But Julia was shaking her head. 'But I'd only be outvoted, just as you were. Surely you can see that?'

Harry leaned forward. 'But you won't only have my shares. There'll be yours and your mother's proxy vote as well.'

'Even with those, it only brings it to evens.'

'You're forgetting Charlotte.'

'Her shares are in trust.'

'But as her mother you have control – I made sure

315

that it was written into the agreement. In the matter of a decision as vital as this all shareholders have the right to vote. Charlie knows that only too well.'

'But what about Vernon's mother's shares?'

Harry smiled. 'You know what an old chauvinist Charlie is. She doesn't actually hold any shares in her own right. Theirs is a joint holding so she doesn't get a vote.'

Julia was shaking her head doubtfully. 'Wait a minute, Dad. I'm not sure I want to get into all this.'

Harry leaned forward, anxiety creasing his brow. 'Listen, Julia, Charlie Grant is going to wreck the firm with his crazy ideas. Nothing's surer than that. Think of it as saving GPC. You'll be doing it for Charlotte in the long run.'

'I'm still not sure.' For Julia the thought of sitting in at board meetings and voting against her father-in-law and Joanna – let alone Vernon – was anathema. 'They'll think I'm only doing it because of the house I've earmarked for the refuge,' she argued, looking from one to the other.

'Your motives aren't important. What is important is to stop this Victoria Gardnes madness from getting off the ground. Or at least to delay it.'

Julia sighed. 'I don't think you realise what you're asking. Vernon is my husband and you're asking me to vote against him. Can you imagine what that will do to our marriage?'

There was silence as her parents exchanged looks, then May said painfully, 'Julia, darling, there's something we feel you should know.'

'What? What is it?'

May glanced at her husband who nodded for her to continue 'Charlotte came to see us last week. The child was very upset. It seems that she had seen Vernon with that woman – that Mrs Hanson. It was clear even to her that they were having some sort of – well – close relationship.'

'An affair, you mean?'

May winced. 'Not to put too fine a point on it, yes.'

'That's no more than I'd already suspected,' Julia said bitterly.

May's colour rose. 'I can't think how you can sit there and be so apathetic about it,' she said, her eyes blazing. 'He's been doing this to you for years, yet you choose to let him get away with it. Well, now it's affecting Charlotte, Julia, and it's time he stopped. If you don't care, we do, especially when we can see what it's doing to our only granddaughter!'

'And you're offering me a way of getting even. Or am I to use my vote as a threat, to bring him into line, is that it?'

'No, *no!*' Harry leaned across the table and laid a hand on his daughter's arm. 'It might look that way, love, but Charlotte will inherit the firm one day, remember. I'd like to think it will still be there for her to inherit.' He squeezed her hand. 'Julia, it's not revenge I'm after, believe me. I'm afraid that if Charlie gets his way it will be the end for all of us; the finish of GPC. I could just let them buy me out and be done with it – escape the disaster that's coming. What I'm doing is trying to avert it.'

Julia nodded. 'All right, how?'

'The property boom has been wonderful for us. Meadowlands is the jewel in our crown. If we get on with it and sell all the properties within the next few months it could bring us in enough to sustain us over the recession that I feel is inevitable. But if Charlie goes ahead with this Victoria Gardens plan – even with the help of Mrs Hanson's cash input – it could ruin us. Someone has to stop him. I'm asking you to be the one. Will you do it, for all our sakes?'

Julia felt trapped. She tried to visualise herself sitting in at a board meeting, facing Joanna's feral eyes and the hostile faces of Charlie and Vernon as she dropped this bombshell her father was insisting on arming her with. The mere thought of it made her stomach churn. All the same, if what her father said were really true how could she refuse? 'Can I have some time to think it over?' she asked.

'Of course. But don't take too long,' Harry advised. 'Once they have my decision and my formal objection they'll have to call a meeting. That'll be your chance to exercise your voting power.'

Fleur had concocted a story in order to borrow the van for the evening. She hated lying to Sally but could hardly tell her the truth. She wanted to drive over to Eastbridge Garden Centre to buy some plants for her balcony. That was her story, and she meant to legitimise it by stopping off on the way and doing just that.

She had first tried to borrow Tom's car, but, as she had suspected he might, he was working and needed it.

'Where are you going?' he asked. 'Maybe I could drop you off and pick you up afterwards.'

Again she had been forced to fabricate a story. 'I said I'd meet Charlotte for a meal,' she said, hating to lie to him. 'I'd rather have my own transport. I don't know how long I'll be.'

'Okay.' He gave her a trusting grin and dropped a kiss on her forehead. 'Lucky you, having a slap-up nosh when I have to work. Bring me a doggy-bag, eh?'

'Sure, a doggy-bag.' She promised herself that if everything worked out he would be the first person she would tell.

She found the village without any problems. The Millstone stood at the end of the street. As she was early the car park at the side was almost empty. The

318

pub was small and thatched. Daffodils were budding in tubs and window boxes and a brightly painted pub sign swung creakily at the top of its wooden pole. The millstone that gave the place its name was depicted on the sign hanging round the neck of a dyspeptic-looking female in medieval peasant costume. Looking up at it as she went in, Fleur shuddered, wondering if it was some sort of omen.

She went in through the low doorway and found herself immediately in the bar. A round-faced woman looked up from polishing glasses.

'Evening, love. There's a nice fire in the snug. There's a lady in there, waiting for you, I reckon. She asked me to tell you to join her there. What can I get you?'

'Oh, a tomato juice, please.'

Fleur took her drink and pushed open the door the woman indicated. The snug was a small cosy room with exposed beams. It was furnished with two or three dark oak tables and wheel-back chairs whose cushions matched the chintz curtains. Julia was sitting by the open log fire, a glass of what looked like gin and tonic on the table before her. She half rose as Fleur entered.

'You came then. You managed to borrow a car?'

Fleur nodded. 'The van.' She sat down opposite and put her glass on the table. 'I had to lie to get it. I don't like lying, so I hope this is going to be worth it.'

Julia smiled wryly. 'You believe in speaking your mind, don't you?' She looked at Fleur for a long moment, searching for something of herself in the girl and failing to find it. 'There's so much you and I don't know about one another, Fleur,' she said sadly.

'Maybe we never will. Maybe it doesn't even matter any more.'

Julia took a sip of her drink. 'I was very young when you were born, you know. Much younger than you are now. Scarcely out of school.'

'I know, Grandma told me.'

'I fell desperately in love with Dean – your father.' She took a sip of her drink. 'It was the first time I'd fallen in love and sometimes I wonder if the man I thought he was ever existed or if I made him up out of my own romantic dreams. If I'd been older and more experienced I'd have seen that it was doomed to failure from the first.'

'Lots of people make mistakes,' Fleur said dispassionately.

Julia smiled. 'What you're saying is that they stick with them see them – through and take the consequences.'

'Some have no choice.'

'You're right, of course. And you're entitled to your opinion. But perhaps one day you'll meet a man who tears your heart to pieces then lets you down. I hope for your sake that you don't.'

Fleur was silent, wondering if Julia knew that her husband was cheating on her. It seemed she hadn't had much luck in her relationships. She watched as Julia took another drink from her glass then looked at her.

'I'd had a sheltered, perhaps even a pampered, upbringing. Life in that little flat in Hackney was hard for me. When Dean told me he wasn't coming back to face his responsibilities, I panicked.'

'And you ran away. I know. Maybe that was understandable.' Fleur met her eyes for the first time. 'But you could have taken me with you.'

'Yes. That must seem unforgivably cowardly to you,' Julia admitted. 'But you can see for yourself what life in a small town like Elvemere is like. It was even worse twenty years ago. I couldn't face the thought of bringing disgrace on my parents – and myself. Of being talked about, gloated over.'

'Because you'd got an illegitimate baby?' Fleur held

Julia's eyes. 'Or because of the colour of the baby's skin?'

'Both! I have to admit that it was both.' Julia leaned forward, her eyes earnest. 'We're here to be truthful with each other, Fleur. To lay our cards on the table, and I admit that to you now freely. I'm not proud of it and the guilt is something I'll carry with me for the rest of my days, though naturally I don't expect that to be any comfort to you.'

'Is that why you're campaigning for single mothers – because you feel guilty?'

'If you like. Yes, I suppose it is.' Fleur was silent and after a moment Julia went on. 'I did write and try to get you back, you know. Did Dolly ever tell you that?' Fleur's eyes swung upwards, meeting Julia's in surprise. 'Ah – I see that she didn't. She replied to my letter telling me that I was too late.'

'Too late.' Fleur frowned. 'What did she mean?'

'She said that you'd been adopted. In her letter she explained that she'd tried to manage on her own but that it was too much for her. She'd given you up for adoption and you'd gone to a childless couple who would give you a good home.'

Fleur shook her head. 'Why would she say a thing like that?'

'Maybe she'd grown too attached to you to give you up. She probably thought I didn't deserve to have you back – that I'd only leave you again. I don't know. It was months before I found out that she would have needed my permission to have you adopted. I wrote to her again, but she replied saying it had been an informal arrangement and that the couple had taken you abroad.' She took another sip of her drink. 'She said you would never know my name or anything about me. You were theirs now and it would be best for me to forget you.' She looked at Fleur, eyes dark with

321

remembered pain. 'It was terrible. Such a brutal punishment. It was as though I'd never had a child. I wonder if you can imagine how it felt? I had nothing to remember you by, not even a snapshot. Only the aching memory of your trusting little face and your arms around my neck. The thought of the way I'd betrayed you broke my heart. It haunted me.' She bit her lip. 'God help me, it still does.'

Fleur was silent, trying to digest what Julia had just told her. Her initial reaction had been disbelief, but Julia had been honest with her about everything else, so why should she lie about that, especially after all this time? Dolly had been almost desperate in extracting her promise to seek her mother out. Could this be why? Had she felt guilty all these years for the lie she'd told in order to keep her grandchild with her? Fleur looked at Julia warily, still only half believing in her anguish.

'But can you honestly say you weren't relieved when Grandma said I'd been adopted?' she challenged. 'She must have known that you could have come and taken me any time you wanted to. I was your child. It was your right. She was just throwing you a lifebelt, that's all. And you grabbed it.'

'*No!*' Julia's voice was firm. 'I'd thought it through and I was prepared to face the music. I really wanted you back, Fleur. I wish I could make you believe that. I just wish it had been possible. Life would have been so different for us all.'

'Why didn't you come back and see for yourself?'

'I believed Dolly. She'd never struck me as a liar.'

Fleur could not argue that what Dolly had done was certainly out of character. 'All Grandma told me was that you'd left a note with your address,' she said slowly. 'But she never let me forget that I'd had a mother. She always spoke kindly and sympathetically about you.'

'That's something, I suppose. Probably more than I deserved at that.' Julia sighed. 'Were they good to you? Did you have a happy childhood?'

'They were very special people,' Fleur told her. 'It's only since I grew up that I've realised the sacrifices they made for me. I loved them both very much.'

'What about Maurice? Is he still alive?'

Fleur shook her head. 'No. Grandpa was killed in an accident at work when I was twelve. I had to give school and my A levels up when Grandma got ill. But whatever happened we always had each other and we were happy.'

'I'm glad.'

Fleur's dark eyes flashed. 'Oh? Does that make you feel better?'

'Of course it does.'

'It doesn't bother you that your child grew up in near poverty while you were enjoying a luxurious life with your new husband and baby daughter?'

'You sound so bitter.'

'How would you feel? Grandpa and Grandma could have had an easier time if they hadn't had me to bring up. I could have stayed on at school and taken my A levels – maybe even gone to university. Who knows? Instead I had to leave and take a job in a fish and chip shop when Grandma's heart gave out. After she died I tried to live on alone at the flat in Brightman Lane. Perhaps you remember the place? Hardly a palace, was it? But I grew up there and it was the only home I'd ever known. But when I was left on my own I had a real struggle to afford the rent. Then, soon after that, I was attacked by a vicious thug late one night on my way home from work. That was when I decided I'd have to leave London.'

'To come and find me – as you promised Dolly?'

'Not really. It was just that I'd never been out of

London before except on a day trip. Elvemere was the only place I could think of to run to. The only place I had any kind of connection with. I told you, I never intended to have anything to do with you.' Fleur was into her stride now. The desire to hit back hard was strong, fuelled by the resentment stored up inside her. 'I suppose you could say that I ran away too. But the difference was that I had no one to run to. Although I had my mother's name and address, I couldn't expect any help from *her*. There was no comfortable home and loving welcome waiting for me!' She looked at Julia, her dark eyes defiant. 'But I survived. I got a room and a good job – eventually a nice flat. I've done without a mother for twenty years and I've coped okay. I can't see any reason why I should want or need one now. Can you?'

'Put like that, I suppose not.' Julie swallowed the last of her drink and looked long and hard at Fleur. 'I don't blame you for feeling the way you do, Fleur. And at the risk of sounding patronising, I want to say that I like the way you've grown up. You're strong and brave. You have principles and integrity.'

'If I have, I got them from my grandparents!'

'Yes.' Julia swallowed painfully. 'I deserved that. But you're right. Those things weren't inherited from me – and certainly not from your father. I've never had that kind of strength. They must have been very proud of you, the Sylvesters. What can I say, Fleur, except that I did try? I promise you that I did regret what I did and I really wanted to have you back.' She reached across the table to cover Fleur's hand with her own. 'I wish with all my heart that things could have been – could be – different. I wish I could tell everyone about you. Come out into the open.' She looked into Fleur's eyes. 'But you can see how impossible it would be now, can't you?'

Fleur withdrew her hand. 'Yes, of course.'

'It happened because I fell foolishly in love with the wrong man,' Julia went on. 'I'm not trying to shift the blame to him. I chose him. It was my judgement that was at fault. But I do know that things would have been different if he hadn't let me down.' She looked at Fleur. 'Will you let me help you – do something for you, to make up for it all? If there's anything you need ... money ...'

'*No!*' Fleur stiffened. 'You accused me of blackmail the other night.'

Julia winced. 'I know and I'm sorry. I was in a panic. I didn't know what I was saying. Please try to forget I said that, won't you?'

'Okay, if you say so. But I meant it when I said I didn't need anything – or any*body*. And it was by accident that we met in the end. I would never have approached you.'

There was a moment of silence between, then Fleur got up from the table. 'Well, I've kept my promise to Grandma. I've found you. And now I've even spoken to you, which is more than I meant to do. But I think it's best for us both that this is where it ends. Right?'

Julia rose to face her. 'Isn't there some way we can see each other? I don't want you to go out of my life again. I'd like so much to get to know you, Fleur.'

She shook her head. 'There have been too many mistakes made to risk another. Maybe I'd disappoint you. Maybe we'd disappoint each other.'

'At least think about it,' Julia said. 'You know where I am. Any time you want to see me or just ring. I hope you will.'

'Yes. Well, I'll think about it.' Fleur walked away, but as she reached the door she looked back. 'Goodbye. It was nice meeting you.'

Julia sat for some time after she had gone, thinking

about this girl who was her daughter. She had grown up with a strong character, but so bitter and full of mistrust. Had she done that to Fleur? It seemed that Julia's life was full of failures and regrets. She'd failed at being a mother, both to Fleur and to Charlotte, and it looked as though she must be a pretty unsatisfactory wife too. Was she about to lose her husband to Joanna? But would the breakdown of her marriage mean any more to her than humiliation? she asked herself. Love for Vernon had been short-lived and disappointing anyway.

She turned her mind towards what her father had asked her to do. He strongly believed it to be the right thing, and by doing it she could further her own aims too. Suddenly making up her mind, she got up from the table and walked out into the car park. She would do it. It was time she took her courage in both hands and fought for something worthwhile. Maybe it still wasn't too late to redeem herself.

Driving back to Elvemere Fleur went over the conversation she and Julia had had. One sentence had found its mark as surely as an arrow. *Perhaps one day you'll meet a man who tears your heart to pieces and then lets you down*. She thought of Peter and their ill-fated affair. Would he have deserted her in the same way if she had become pregnant? And if he had – who could know what might have happened? The thought sobered her, shaking her long-held belief in Julia's heartlessness. Everyone was vulnerable when it came to love. Could anyone really be sure of how they would behave, driven by misery and despair?

Then another, more immediate thought struck her. Maybe she should have confessed to Julia that she'd let slip to Joanna Hanson that Dean Sylvester was her father. She dismissed the thought at once. Joanna could prove nothing. There was no way she could use the information to harm anyone.

Chapter 12

'You *can't*!' Vernon stared at his father-in-law in shocked disbelief.

'I think you know perfectly well that I can.' Harry's expression was calm. 'I'm perfectly within my rights to demand an extraordinary meeting, just as I am entitled to transfer my shares to my own daughter. And I trust in her judgment in acting for me when it comes to voting. I shall be making my proposal known to your father later this morning. I'm only telling you in advance as a courtesy.'

'Very good of you, I'm sure,' Vernon said bitterly. 'And you haven't the slightest idea how she'll vote, of course! You haven't discussed it with her by any chance?'

'Of course I've discussed it with her. Julia and I are in complete agreement as regards your father's newest proposal.'

'Julia hasn't the slightest interest in, let alone any knowledge of, the business. All she wants is to gain herself some recognition as a councillor.'

'I think you underestimate Julia,' Harry said. 'You always have, Vernon, if you don't mind my saying so. It could turn out to be your downfall.'

'I'm her husband. I could forbid her to do as you

say,' Vernon blustered, his face red with alarm.

'I wouldn't try if I were you.' Harry's mild blue eyes grew cold and grey behind his spectacles. 'You see, she knows about your affair with Joanna Hanson. And what is worse, so does Charlotte. The child came to me in deep distress. She saw the two of you together – in a situation that apparently made your relationship only too obvious. The poor girl didn't know what to do, whether to tell her mother or not.'

'And you told her to tell Julia?'

'No. I told her to try and forget what she'd seen. Then *I* told Julia,' Harry said. 'This is one affair too many for my liking, Vernon. You've cheated on Julia ever since you married her. Now it seems you're not above flaunting your adultery for anyone to see, even your own daughter. This time you've gone too far and you're not going to get away with it. So unless you want the whole thing to blow up in your face, I'd go along with things quietly for a while.'

'*Charlotte* came to you?' Vernon was shaking his head. 'I don't believe it!' He was seriously taken aback by Harry's revelation. 'How could she have seen us? Where – and when?'

'Coming out of Mrs Hanson's house. It seems her aunt was driving her home, taking a short cut down Hazel Grove.'

'Kath!' Vernon muttered under his breath. 'I might have known she was at the bottom of this! So, I was coming out of her house. What does that prove?'

'Apparently your brazen behaviour said the rest,' Harry said grimly.

'All right,' Vernon challenged. 'Let Julia vote in your place. Let her try and defeat Dad's plan. She won't win. How can she?'

'With my shares and her mother's, plus her own,' Harry said. 'Then there are the shares I bought and placed in trust for Charlotte. Julia is entitled to vote on behalf of her daughter too. I think you're going to find yourself out-manoeuvred, Vernon.' Harry was unable to keep the smile off his face.

Vernon left Gresham House hurriedly, his mind in turmoil. When Harry had telephoned asking him to call and see him this morning on his way to the office he had wondered what he could possibly have to say. He'd half expected to receive his father-in-law's resignation personally. He'd almost looked forward to the interview. But never in his wildest nightmares had he envisaged anything like this.

Jumping into his car he drove straight round to Joanna's house. He arrived just in time to see her coming out of the front door. Running up the drive, he grasped her arm and propelled her back towards the house.

'Inside,' he barked. 'We have to talk.'

'Wait a minute,' she protested. 'What do you think you're doing? I wanted to be at the office early. I've got a lot to do and . . .'

'*Shut up!* It can wait. This can't!'

'Don't speak to me like that!' She shook her arm free and glared at him indignantly for a moment. Then, seeing the distraught look on his face, she took out her key and reluctantly unlocked the front door. 'This had better be worth it,' she said as she held the door open.

Inside the hall Vernon slammed the door and turned to her. 'Harry Philips rang me this morning. He asked me to go round there urgently. He's not resigning after all.'

She shrugged. 'So—?'

'So – he's transferring his shares to Julia.'

She laughed. 'And the best of British luck!'

'Not only *his* shares but May's and Charlotte's too.'

'I didn't know Charlotte was a shareholder.'

'They're in trust for her.' Vernon shook his head impatiently. 'Don't you see, that gives Julia a majority vote! And it goes without saying how she'll use it.'

'Talk her out of it,' she said abruptly. 'For heaven's sake, Vernon, you're her husband. Surely it's in her interest to vote with you?'

He raked a hand through his hair and sat down heavily on the stairs. 'She knows, Jo – about us. It seems everyone knows. My sister was driving Charlotte home from the stables and they came this way. Apparently they saw me leaving here – saw you seeing me off.' He waved one arm in the direction of the front door. 'Out there.' He groaned and lowered his head into his hands. 'Oh, Christ, what a mess! It's going to ruin everything. And I'll be the one taking the flak.'

'Oh, pull yourself together, Vernon,' Joanna snapped. 'Letting yourself go to pieces isn't going to get us anywhere.' She chewed her lip thoughtfully. 'Look, – just leave this to me. I think I can get us out of it.'

He sprang to his feet and looked hopefully into her eyes. 'How? What can you do?'

'Never mind how or what. Just trust me.'

'Whatever you're planning it's going to have to be quick,' he told her. 'Harry's getting in touch with Dad later this morning. He's demanding an extraordinary meeting and telling him about the transfer of shares to Julia. The minute Dad gets that phone call there's going to be blood all over the carpet. *My* blood!'

She grasped him by the arms and shook him gently. 'Stop panicking! Just tell him calmly that you have everything in hand. Tell him *you'll* handle Julia. Be positive for once. It'll do wonders for your image.'

He put his hands on her shoulders. 'Oh, God, Jo, are you really sure you can pull this off?'

'Ninety percent sure,' she said. 'I'd better get onto it at once though, as you say. Can you manage without me for this morning?'

'Of course.' He was relieved. If his father was going to start bawling him out he'd rather Joanna wasn't around to witness his humiliation anyway. 'Look, Jo, maybe we should let things cool off? Stop seeing each other outside office hours for a bit. Just for now, of course. Till this furore dies down. What do you say?'

She shrugged. 'Perhaps you're right. Now you'd better get moving. And remember what I said: be positive. Stand your ground with Charlie. Make him believe you're in charge for once.'

It was almost an hour later that Joanna stood on the porch awaiting Julia's answer to her ring at the bell. After Vernon had left she'd sat down to make her plan, thinking out carefully what she would say and how to approach the subject. No point in rushing into this without giving it plenty of thought, allowing for every possible eventuality. When everything was clear in her mind she'd gone upstairs and changed out of her office suit into a pair of well-cut trousers, a cashmere sweater and tweed jacket. Better to go casually dressed. It wouldn't do to appear intimidating.

To her surprise a thin young girl with blonde hair answered the door.

'Is Mrs Grant at home?' Joanna asked.

'Yes. Who shall I say wants to see her?' Tracey asked.

Joanna stepped over the threshold. 'Just tell her it's Joanna,' she said with a confident smile. 'We're old friends.'

'If you'd just like to wait . . .' The girl showed her into the sitting room. 'I'll tell her you're here.'

Joanna looked around her. The room was furnished tastefully, but in a provincial style. Pastel green walls and floral pictures; moss green carpet and matching velvet curtains. Twin settees with oatmeal linen upholstery were placed to either side of the Adam-style fireplace, and an onyx-topped coffee table stood between them. Joanna glanced at the magazines on it. Current copies of *Harper's* and *Vogue*. She smiled. She'd have taken bets on it. In one corner an antique glass-fronted cabinet displayed a collection of delicate porcelain figurines, Dresden or Meissen, Joanna wasn't sure which. She smiled to herself. It was all so predictable, restful but bland. It lacked style, like Julia herself. No wonder poor Vernon craved excitement.

When Julia came into the room she looked surprised and not altogether pleased. 'Joanna! What can I do for you?'

She came to the point at once. 'I've just heard about your father transferring his shares to you. And I thought it only fair to warn you that if you have any plans for out-voting the rest of us, you do it at your peril!'

'My peril?' Julia raised one eyebrow. 'Really? I'm surprised to hear you make a melodramatic remark like that. And what am I supposed to be in peril of?'

'Of having a small episode from your past revealed.' Joanna had the satisfaction of seeing the confidence melt from Julia's face.

'If you're talking about something that happened when I was in my teens, long before Vernon and I even met . . .'

'Oh, yes, I *am*.'

'And you think the threat of revealing that twenty years ago I had a brief affair with a pop musician is going to make headlines, do you?'

'Maybe not – if that were all.' Joanna stepped closer to her. 'I'm surprised that you seem so unconcerned. Tell me, Julia, just between ourselves, what is your daughter doing here in Elvemere?'

Julia felt her blood chill. 'Charlotte?'

'Not Charlotte. You know perfectly well who I mean, Julia. *Fleur*. She is your daughter, isn't she? Your little flower child?'

'Fleur?' Julia fought down the panic that gripped her. 'I – do you mean . . .'

'The girl from the caterer's. Sally Arden's assistant. Yes. Don't pretend you don't know who I mean, Julia. *I know!*'

'You know nothing. How could you know?'

'From her own lips. That's how!'

She couldn't. Surely she wouldn't! Julia swallowed hard and took a deep breath, trying not to show the consternation she felt. Looking up at Joanna, she asked, 'Exactly what did she say?'

'Enough. Plenty in fact. It came out in conversation that Dean Sylvester was her father; that she'd never actually met him because her parents parted before she was born. It didn't take a genius to work it out. It all fits, Julia. She's just the right age. You spun your parents some tale and ran off with him. You were away from home for long enough to make it possible. It's true, isn't it? Don't deny it. I saw your shocked reaction to her the other night at the party.'

'This is all guesswork on your part,' Julia said. 'You can't prove anything.'

'Oh, I'm sure I could if I tried. And if you do compel me to start digging into the past, Julia, I shan't do it quietly, I assure you.'

'There's a law against what you're suggesting. There is such a thing as libel.'

Joanna smiled. 'True, but do you really want to get into anything as public as that? Not going to look too good for you as a councillor, is it? Not going to give this *new philanthropic image of yours a lot of credibility.*

334

And what about your family – your parents, Charlotte and Vernon? Not to mention Charlie and Louise. Do they know?' Julia's stunned silence told Joanna that she had scored. Her guesswork had paid off.

Julia looked down at the hands that lay clenched in her lap. She was sure that Fleur would never have volunteered the information that Dean was her father. Why should she? Joanna must have tricked it out of her. She was good at that.

'All right,' she said at last. 'What is it you want me to do?'

'Not much really. Just vote with us, that's all. It's important to Charlie that he gets his way over this Victoria Gardens plan.'

'My father thinks it could ruin the firm,' Julia told her. 'His motives for wanting to sink the plan are not malicious. He's thinking about the future of the business. That's in your interest too now that you have money invested.'

'Your father lacks vision, if you don't mind my saying so,' Joanna said brutally. 'He's like a lot of old men, he's living in the past afraid to take risks, plodding along in the slow lane. Vote with us, Julia, and all will be well. Your little secret will be safe and the firm will flourish in the way it deserves to. You can trust me on that, I promise.'

A thought occurred to Julia. 'There's always the chance the council won't pass the plans. I'm only one voice there, you know.'

Joanna smiled. 'Seeing that Charlie is planning to do what the council was about to do anyway, I doubt if they'll raise any objections.'

Julia looked at her for a long moment. 'And if I do as you say, will you end your affair with Vernon?' she asked at last.

'Ah. Charlotte has been talking.' Joanna shook her

head. 'You don't really believe the highly coloured ramblings of a resentful teenager, do you?'

'You're denying it?'

Joanna sighed. 'Charlotte has always disliked me for some reason. She's just trying to make trouble.'

'You haven't answered my question. Are you denying it?'

'Vernon and I had a teenage fling years ago. Before you met him. We're old friends, that's all. I've grown up quite a lot since then, Julia, unlike some of the petty-minded people I've met since I came back. Anyway, I don't know what you're worrying about. You and he are inextricably tied together by the business.'

'But you have been seeing each other?'

Joanna shrugged. 'Of course. How could we not? We work together, don't we? And occasionally an out-of-hours meeting has been necessary.'

'You've been using him, haven't you – just to get what you want? You always were greedy and devious, Joanna. Now you're . . .'

A tap on the door prevented her from finishing the sentence and Tracey came in with a tray. 'Excuse me, Mrs Grant, but I thought you might like some coffee,' she said.

Julia stared stonily at Joanna. 'I'm afraid Mrs Hanson hasn't time,' she said pointedly. 'She has to rush off to the office. It was good of you to call, Joanna,' she said, standing up. 'I'll see you at the meeting. Goodbye'

She left Tracey to show Joanna out, sinking back into her chair with a stifled groan. What a mess. What a horrendous mess!

Tracey came back into the room and looked with concern at Julia's troubled face. 'I hope I did right, asking her in, Mrs Grant. Should I have asked you first?'

Julia shook her head. 'No, it's all right, Tracey.'

'I hope it wasn't bad news.'

Julia looked at the girl's kindly face and smiled. 'Nothing I can't handle.'

'Only you've been so good to me and Damie. If there was ever anything I could do for you, I'd be only too glad.'

'Sit down and have some coffee with me,' Julia invited. 'You've brought two cups and I'm sure you're ready for a break. There's something I need to talk to you about.' She poured two cups of coffee and handed one to the girl. 'We haven't had a chat for some time. Tell me how things are with you. Do you see anything of Rick these days?'

Tracey sipped her coffee thoughtfully. 'Now and again,' she said guardedly.

'He's not still demanding money, I hope?'

'No. He's been working. Only some casual labouring, but at least he's earning.'

'Is he still using that awful stuff?'

Tracey shook her head. 'I don't think so. I'm keeping my fingers crossed that he's off it for good.' She didn't tell Julia that Rick had found out where she was working; that he'd taken to watching until everyone had gone out, then calling round at the back door, insisting on seeing his baby son. There didn't seem any harm in it. In fact Rick had seemed almost like his old self lately. He seemed to be making the effort to pull himself together at last. Tracey looked at her employer and realised to her relief that she had only asked the question out of politeness and obviously wasn't going to press her for further information. Noticing Julia's strained look, she asked, 'Is there anything wrong, Mrs Grant? You said there was something you wanted to talk about. Was it something to do with that Mrs Hanson?'

'In a way.' Julia forced a smile. 'She's someone I knew a long time ago, but she's no friend of mine now.'

'I thought there was something. I wish I hadn't let her in now. If I'd known she was going to upset you . . .'

'I'd have had to see her anyway.' Julia looked into the girl's open face. 'Tracey, I'm afraid we're going to have to wait a bit longer for our women's refuge.'

'Oh, no! But I thought it was all set.'

'It was, but there's a hitch. We can't have the house in Victoria Gardens after all. It's only a setback though. We'll just have to look round for another empty property.' She paused. It would be such a relief to confide in someone – someone who would be on her side – totally outside her immediate circle. On a sudden impulse she said, 'Tracey – if I tell you something, will you promise to keep it to yourself?'

'Of course. You know I will.'

'Once, many years ago, when I was as young as you are now but not nearly as grown-up and sensible, I fell in love. I ran away with a young man – a pop musician. The affair was destined to end disastrously and if I hadn't been so immature I'd have seen that. But before I realised my mistake, I found I was expecting his child.'

'Oh, Mrs Grant.' Tracey's eyes were round. 'What happened? Did you have the baby?'

'Yes, a little girl. But her father wasn't interested. He only saw her the once, just after she was born, when he came home to tell me it was all over between us.'

'What did you do?'

'Something I've been ashamed of ever since. I was terribly homesick and one day I just walked out and came home. I left my baby with her grandmother who adored her. No one ever knew about it. I started again – made a new life and thought it was all over and forgotten. Till now.'

'And now – that Mrs Hanson – she knows?'

Julia nodded. 'She was a close friend at the time, the only person who knew about the relationship. Now, somehow, she's found out about the child. And she's threatening to tell my family.'

Tracey gasped. 'But that's blackmail! You could go to the police.'

Julia smiled ruefully. 'Hardly.'

'No, I suppose not. And does this have something to do with why we can't have the refuge?'

'Partly. It's too complicated for me to explain properly, but unfortunately it means letting my mother and father down very badly in order to keep my past from them.'

Tracey frowned. 'Why don't you just tell them about the baby?' she said. 'Surely that would be better? People don't bother so much about things like that nowadays.'

Julia shook her head. 'I'm afraid they'd still be dreadfully upset. But it isn't just them, you see. There's my in-laws, Charlotte and my husband. Not to mention what it would do to my present position as councillor.'

Tracey nodded. 'Yeah, I see.' She looked at Julia sympathetically. 'Oh, what a shame, Mrs Grant, after you've worked so hard and everything. You're just like us, aren't you? You know how it feels, being left with a baby. Did you keep in touch with your baby's grandma?'

'No. I tried later to get my daughter back, but I was told she'd been adopted.'

Tracey frowned. 'That must've been awful. I don't know what I'd do if I lost Damie. So – what will you do, Mrs Grant?'

Julia sighed. 'I'm afraid I don't have much choice, Tracey. I'm just going to have to do what Mrs Hanson says.'

*

Fleur sang as she worked in Sally's pleasant little office. The sun was shining and this morning she'd had a letter from Bobby to say that she was getting engaged. She'd met Jeff at college and they'd decided to marry as soon as they both qualified. Bobby had mentioned him before in her letters, but this was the first inkling she'd given that the relationship was serious. Fleur reflected that the news might once have made her sad. A few short months ago it would have felt like the end of the closeness she and Bobby had shared all their lives. When she had first arrived in Elvemere she had missed her friend so much. But now her lack of sadness and her delight in Bobby's obvious happiness made her realise how firmly she had settled here.

Sally had gone up to London that morning, intending to spend the day shopping for her coming trip to Switzerland, including choosing her wedding outfit. The date of Peter's marriage drew closer with each day, but the thought of his betrayal no longer disturbed Fleur.

During Sally's absence she planned to work in the office during the morning, catching up with the paperwork, then spend the afternoon in the kitchen checking stocks and filling the freezer up with canapes and quiches for their next function. The work was pleasant, leaving her mind free to remember the happy weekend she and Tom had spent painting the balcony. He had insisted they do it that weekend as he had a free Saturday for once. Besides, as he'd reminded her, he'd be moving out in a few days' time.

'I might need a favour from you then,' he told her. 'Packing's never been my strong point. You can have a look at my new place at the same time – advise me about furnishing and decorating.'

'You plan to make it permanent then?'

'As permanent as it can be. I'm planning to stay on at least until a better job turns up.' He grinned. 'Of course, if I'm asked to take over as editor of the *Clarion* I might stay longer.'

They worked steadily and companionably together. By Saturday evening the wrought-iron railings had been thoroughly rubbed down and a coat of rust inhibitor and undercoat had been applied. Fleur had prepared a casserole, which had been simmering away slowly all afternoon. They tucked into it ravenously after cleaning their brushes and scrubbing their hands clean of paint splashes.

'You've been in a light-hearted mood all day,' Tom remarked as he looked at her across the table. 'Has something nice happened?'

She hesitated, wondering whether or not to confide in him, then, unable to keep it to herself any longer she said, 'I do have something to tell you, as a matter of fact.'

'I thought there was something.' He laid down his knife and fork and looked at her apprehensively. 'It's nothing to do with Arden, is it?'

'Nothing at all. That's over, Tom, I told you.' She paused. 'No – it's about my mother. I've met and talked to her.'

'Hey! Good for you. How did it go?'

'It was okay. Better than I thought, Tom. I got a lot of things off my chest. We both did. It made me realise that it wasn't as simple as I've always thought.'

'There are always two sides to every question.'

'I know. I always knew that. Grandma was always making excuses for her. It's just that hearing it from her made me understand her reasons for doing what she did at the time – how she felt, and why. She told me that she did once try to get me back. I never knew about

341

that. It seems my grandmother told her I'd been adopted.'

'Well, at least you know she tried.'

'And I believe she really did suffer for what she did. She tried to make me understand how hard it was for her, especially when she couldn't tell anyone. It made quite a lot of difference to how I feel about her.'

'You've stopped being so angry with her then?'

'Well – yes.'

'And you liked her?'

Fleur nodded thoughtfully. 'Yes. More than I expected to. She was honest – didn't try to make excuses for herself. My father let her down badly and – well, I do know how that feels, don't I? But the most important thing is that now I've met her, I can think of her as a real person and not just the faceless woman who walked out on me when I was a baby.'

'That's great! So are you going to see each other again?'

'No.' Fleur shook her head regretfully. 'I don't want to make life difficult for her.'

'But surely you could still meet – see each other as friends?'

'She did suggest that, but I said no. I don't want to have some kind of hole in the corner relationship with her. I said it would be best if we just left it at that.'

'That's a pity. She won't come right out and acknowledge you then?'

'She can't. And I do see why. She's married with another daughter and a public image, I suppose you'd call it, to uphold. No one knows about me, you see, not even her parents. Admitting now that she had a child in her teens could be damaging for her.'

'Are you sure? There's a lot more tolerance and understanding about things like that nowadays.'

'I'm not so sure there would be in her case.'

'So, are you disappointed?'

'No. I've done without a mother all these years. Anyway, I've got good friends – and you.'

'What does that mean? That I'm more than a friend?' His eyes held hers for a moment, then she laughed.

'Stop fishing. Of course you're a friend. A very special one. Tell you what, when you're settled in at Park Row, I'll help you give a flat-warming party. I'll do a buffet like we do at Arden Catering. All the trimmings.'

'That'll be great.' He paused for a moment. 'Fleur . . .' He looked at her. 'Your mother – she's Julia Grant, isn't she?' He regretted his words the moment he'd said them. He saw her expression close up and her eyes cloud. She got up from the table.

'Look at the time! If we're going to get any more done to the balcony we'd better make a start. It's getting dark already.'

He rose quickly to face her. 'Fleur!' Putting his hands on her shoulders he looked down at her. 'You know there's no way we can do any more tonight. Look, I'm sorry I sprang it on you. Forget it. Put it down to journalist's curiosity.'

She looked at him. 'You knew before, didn't you?'

'I've had my suspicions for some time,' he admitted. 'But it was no more than an educated guess really. You don't have to worry. I'm not going to say a word about it to anyone.' He held her away from him to look into her eyes. 'You don't think I'd risk losing your trust now, do you, Fleur?'

'No, of course not.'

'And I'm really glad you did speak to her. It was what you needed, if only to lay a ghost.'

She relaxed, leaning against him for a moment. 'Thank you, Tom. You're the only person who's ever really cared about me. Apart from my grandparents, I mean.'

He held her close, dropping a kiss on the top of her head. 'Well, that's easy,' he said awkwardly. 'Seeing that you're you and I'm me. You do know that you're pretty special to me, don't you?'

'Yes, I know, Tom,' she said, her words muffled against his chest. When she looked up at him again he saw to his relief that her anxiety had gone. Her eyes were clear and shining again. 'So if we can't do any more work on the balcony, what shall we do with the rest of the evening – apart from the washing up, I mean?'

He grinned and pulled her close. 'Oh, I daresay we'll think of something,' he said.

Fleur sat staring at the flickering computer screen as she remembered the evening they had spent together. Tomorrow she would be helping him move out. It had been so cosy and convenient, having Tom under the same roof. She would miss him. She examined her feelings for him. He made her happy. She enjoyed his company – looked forward to being with him – being close. But was that love? Once she had thought that the heady excitement she had known with Peter was love, but that had proved to be an illusion. Was she really such a poor judge? All she knew was that if she were to lose Tom life would never be quite the same again. She sighed. If only she could be sure . . .

When Vernon got to the office he stopped by his father's secretary's desk.

'Is my father in yet, Phyllis?'

She looked up. 'No, Mr Vernon. He had some outside appointments this morning. Won't be in until this afternoon.'

He stifled a sigh of relief. 'Right. Did Mr Philips

ring?'

'Yes. He's ringing back later.'

'I see. Give me ten minutes to go through the post then send Charlotte in to me, will you? And make sure we're not disturbed until I tell you.'

In his office he hung up his coat and sat down at the desk to scan quickly through the pile of correspondence. Nothing there that couldn't wait. Just as well. He was going to have a few things to say to that daughter of his and wanted to have them quite clear in his mind before she appeared.

When she knocked and put her head round the door he was ready for her. 'Come in and close the door,' he said grimly.

She did as he said, then sat down in the chair opposite, her eyes bright and her mouth set in a defiant line. 'What am I supposed to have done now?' she asked defensively.

'I think you know very well what you've done,' he said, glowering at her. 'Going to your grandfather with mischievous tales. I hope you know the trouble you've caused.'

'I was worried,' she muttered. 'I needed to talk to someone. Would you rather I'd told Mum?'

He slapped his hand down hard on the desk, making her jump. 'You had no right to talk to anyone! Why didn't you come to me? I could have told you that you were making a mistake. But no! You interpret something you see as an illicit assignation and go running to your grandfather screaming adultery!'

Charlotte blushed and looked down at her hands. 'What was I supposed to think? Anyone would have thought the same.' She looked up at him again, her eyes accusing. 'She was wearing a dressing gown!'

'As it happened, I had to drop something off on my way home,' he said. 'Joanna was about to have a bath.

345

That's why she was wearing her dressing gown. Not that I owe you any explanations.'

'You were kissing.'

'For heaven's sake, girl, grow up! If we were really having an affair, do you think we would conduct it on the doorstep?' He leaned forward to glare at her. 'Well – *do you*?'

'How would I know?'

'Exactly! How *would* you know? You're a very silly, naive girl, yet you jump to conclusions and start spreading rumours, causing absolute mayhem. I hope you realise that because of you this firm may lose the chance to pull off its biggest deal ever!'

'I don't see how . . .'

'You don't see a lot of things!' he shouted. 'And those you do see, you get wrong. I should send you home – suspend you. But unfortunately you happen to be my daughter and I have certain obligations to you. Instead I want you to go round to your grandparents' house after work this evening and tell them you made a terrible mistake and that you're sorry for all the trouble you've caused. I'm going to insist that you apologise to Joanna too. Heaven knows what she must think of you.'

'I won't!'

'You'll bloody well do as I say, girl!' he thundered.

Charlotte stared at him, eyes blazing with bitter resentment and mouth trembling. She got up from her chair. 'Is that all? Can I go now?'

'Just one more thing, Charlotte. From now on I absolutely forbid you to go to your aunt's stables.'

Her eyes flew open in horror. '*Dad!* No, please.'

'You heard what I said. Your aunt and I have never seen eye to eye. She'd do anything to discredit me and I can see her hand at the bottom of this mess.'

'It's not like that. *Really* it isn't. She just happened to

346

be with me at the time. Look, I'll apologise to Mrs Hanson, anything you say, but . . .'

'That's *enough*, Charlotte. You heard what I said. I don't want to hear any more arguments. I won't change my mind.'

'But I can't just not turn up. I'll have to go and tell her – explain.'

'I'll do any explaining that's necessary,' Vernon said. 'I'll ring her now.' He looked up as she hovered by the door. 'That's all. You can go now, Charlotte. I've said all I have to say and I don't want to hear any more about it.'

The extraordinary meeting of GPC shareholders took place a week later and went without a hitch. Later in his office Charlie Grant closed the door and took his bottle of malt whisky out of the filing cabinet, pouring a celebratory glass for himself and another for his son.

'Got to hand it to you, lad,' he said, handing Vernon the glass. 'When Harry Philips told me what he'd done, I thought we were up the creek without a paddle. How did you pull it off, eh? How did you bring Julia into line?'

Vernon took a grateful gulp of the whisky. 'Just put my foot down, that's all. You've always known how to do it, so why not me? Chip off the old block.'

'Well, I have to admit, I didn't know you had it in you.' Charlie threw himself into a chair and took out his pipe and tobacco. 'Looked more subdued than I've seen her in years. I thought this council business was going to her head. Quite snotty with me on the phone over that stupid women's refuge business, she was.' He applied a match to the pipe and sucked thoughtfully. 'Still, you seem to have knocked all that rubbish out of her, thank God. In my opinion there's nowt worse than an arrogant, over-confident woman, 'specially when she happens to be your wife! Now ...' He leaned forward across the desk. 'The next thing is to get onto the negotiations. First off we have to find out who Victoria Gardens belongs to. I do know that one person owns all the properties, the whole shebang, which makes it easier. The question is, who?'

'There's an agent handling it, isn't there?' Vernon said. 'That seems to indicate the owner doesn't live locally, so we'll be going through him.'

Charlie drew hard on his pipe and blew out a cloud of smoke. 'Not if we can get to know who the owner is. Agents push for the last penny, lad. Now – if the owner is some old biddy, she'll likely be glad to get the responsibility off her hands for a lot less than the agent would press for. And if it means making a trip up to Scotland or somewhere then I reckon it'll be worth it.'

'But how do we find out?'

Charlie's eyes narrowed. 'Better leave it with me for now, lad,' he said. 'I've got one or two favours owed me, from several people I can think of. I'll get to know before the week's out, don't you fret.' He got up from the desk and downed the rest of his whisky. 'In fact, I think I'll make one call now – start eliminating folk.'

Eleanor was busy with her housework when the door-bell rang. Switching off the vacuum cleaner, she went to open the front door and was surprised to see who her visitor was.

'Charlie! To what do I owe this unexpected pleasure?'

He stepped inside with a grin. 'Glad you think of it like that, Lena lass. There's something I need to know and I reckon you might be able to help me.'

Eleanor turned to close the door, a wry smile on her lips. Knowing Charlie Grant she might have guessed he'd be wanting something. She smiled at him. 'I see.

It's not just the pleasure of my sparkling company you're after then. Like a coffee? I was just about to make some.'

'Why not? I've got an appointment at the bank, but I can spare half an hour.' Charlie followed her through to the living room and made himself comfortable in her armchair, watching as she went about the business of putting the kettle on and setting out cups. Eventually they sat facing one another.

'So . . .' Eleanor passed him a plate of biscuits. 'What is it you want to know this time, Charlie?'

He shook his head at her. 'Oh, come on, lass. Don't make it sound as if I'm always on the nose.'

'Well, aren't you?' she said with a husky laugh.

'Go on, you're pulling my leg again. Always were a tease.'

'So what is it?'

He took a sip of his coffee. 'Nowt much really. Look, what I'm going to tell you is strictly between ourselves, Lena.'

'Of course. That goes without saying.'

'Well, since the council gave up the idea of redeveloping Victoria Gardens, I've been thinking. I've put it to my directors and we've decided to buy the Gardens up and carry out the redevelopment ourselves.'

'Really?' Eleanor looked surprised. 'Well, the best of luck, of course, but I don't quite see where I come in.'

'I understand that the whole street is owned by one person.'

'That's right. When the council was thinking of buying it things were being handled by the agent who handles the letting. I can give you his name if that's what you want.'

'No.' Charlie shook his head. 'I know that, but I don't want to mess around with one of those fellers. I'd rather deal direct with the owner. Do you know who it is?'

349

Eleanor hesitated. 'There has to be a good reason why an agent is handling it, Charlie,' she said.

'I know all that. I'm not planning some kind of swindle if that's what you're thinking. I'll make a fair offer for the properties.'

'I daresay the owner would prefer to have an expert handling her affairs.'

Charlie leaned forward. 'Ah! So it's a woman then?'

Eleanor bridled. 'That seems to encourage you, Charlie. I wonder why? Perhaps you think a woman will be a pushover.'

'Not at all. Oh, come on, Lena, don't mess me about with all that equality claptrap. What's this woman's name? Is it someone I know? Does she live here or away somewhere?'

'She lives here. As a matter of fact, she lives in Victoria Gardens, but I'm not sure about this, Charlie. You're putting me in a very awkward position.'

'No one will know it was you who told me, Lena.' Charlie was growing impatient. 'Look, I'll be really grateful if you'll give me the name.' He glanced at her slyly. 'Tell you what, suppose I arrange a little commission for you? By way of thanks. How does that sound?'

'It sounds revolting!' Eleanor stood up, her face flushed. 'What you're suggesting is very insulting, Charlie,' she told him. 'Do you know what you're saying?'

He waved his hands at her. 'Don't get upset. I want nowt to do with what you're thinking. Corruption never entered my head. Just a little present, between friends. For old time's sake. That's all.'

'I don't want your present, Charlie, and I think you'd better leave.'

'So you won't tell me?'

'No. I won't.'

She showed Charlie out in silence and closed the

door sharply on his portly, retreating figure.

In the car he swore loudly, thumping the steering wheel with frustration. How could he have been such a fool as to try to bribe her? He might have known that Lena would come over all whiter-than-white on him. He drew a deep breath and tried to channel his thoughts in a positive direction. The conversation hadn't been entirely unproductive. He knew now that the owner was a woman and that she lived in the Gardens. That was something. And if this woman owned the whole street it meant that everyone else living there was a tenant. A triumphant smile spread across his face. Once he'd made sure of the loan it was in the bag!

After the meeting Julia drove herself home feeling chastened and depressed. She made herself a sandwich and a cup of coffee but she had no appetite for either. This morning when she'd got up she'd made up her mind to speak to Charlotte before she left the house. But the girl was still morose and uncommunicative. It was almost as though she blamed Julia for Vernon's conduct. Since the initial row she and Vernon had avoided each other as much as possible and Charlotte spent most of her time locked in her room. Over breakfast this morning the atmosphere had crackled with tension. Julia had found it impossible to concentrate on anything but the coming meeting. The three of them sat silently avoiding one another's eyes and Julia was relieved when it was over and they had each gone their separate ways. Once again there had been no opportunity to speak to Charlotte.

Now it was over. She had caved in and voted with the others. Try as she would, she could not erase the feeling of self-disgust or the memory of Joanna's triumphant smile from her mind. And now she was faced with the task she dreaded the most – that of explaining her action to her father. But at least she would not have to cross that bridge until he came back from his cruise.

The house felt empty and silent as she wandered restlessly from room to room trying to decide what she would say to her parents. They were going to see it as a betrayal whatever she said. Finally, unable to bear the menacing silence any longer, she put on her coat and went out to the car again. She had no idea where she was going, but when she reached the end of the road she decided. She turned in the direction of Eleanor Maitland's house.

The older woman was not surprised to see her. Ever since Charlie's visit she had been expecting a call from Julia.

'Come in, my dear,' she said welcomingly. 'I had your father-in-law round here earlier. This seems to be my day for entertaining members of the Grant family.' She peered closely at Julia as she took her coat. 'You look as though you could do with a stiff drink. What's wrong?'

'Everything!' Julia dropped gratefully into the chair by the fireside. 'I hardly know where to begin.'

Eleanor settled herself in the chair opposite. 'How about the beginning? That's as good a place as any.'

Julia shook her head. 'Far too long a story to bore you with. The main problem is that we're going to have to shelve the women's refuge for the time being.'

'Oh, that's a shame, but it's hardly surprising. As a matter of fact Charlie was telling me about his plans when he was here,' she said. 'I saw at once that it was going to throw a spanner in the works.'

Julia nodded. 'Yes. And I can't even protest. My father has transferred his shares in GPC to me. He wanted me to vote against the proposal, but when it came to the crunch – I couldn't.'

'Of course you couldn't,' Eleanor said sympathetically. 'It was wrong of him to ask it of you.'

Julia was silent. If only she could tell Eleanor the full story. 'It looks as though my name is going to be mud,' she said gloomily. 'With the people I'm going to have to let down as well as with my parents.'

Eleanor looked thoughtful. 'There's not much I can do about your parents,' she said. 'But I do know of another empty property we might get. It doesn't have such a central position and of course it would mean going back for planning permission again, which means a delay.'

'Oh, Eleanor!' Julia's spirits rose. 'That would be marvellous. Can we go and look at it now?'

'Of course, if you like. I'll go and get my coat.'

By the time Fleur and Tom had carried down the last of his boxes the little car was loaded to the roof.

'I'd no idea I'd accumulated so much stuff,' he said as he climbed into the driving seat. 'I just hope there'll be room for it all at Park Row.'

'You've got twice as much space,' Fleur laughed. 'So there should be.'

Sally had given Fleur the day off to help Tom. They had spent almost all of it packing and loading the car and now it was late afternoon. They made the short drive to Park Row in a matter of minutes and as they began unpacking the various boxes, suitcases and carrier bags, the front door of the little terraced house opened and Sadie came out to meet them.

'Hi, guys!' she called cheerfully. 'Want a hand with anything?'

Tom straightened up and introduced the two girls. 'Sadie, this is Fleur Sylvester. Fleur – Sadie.'

The girls smiled at each other and Fleur took in the tall, well-built girl, noting that Tom's description of her had been accurate. She wore jeans and an oversized man's shirt which reached to her knees. Her dark hair was cut very short and her face was innocent of make-up. It was clear that she was a young women well able to take care of herself; in total charge of her life.

Sadie's sharp eyes swept appraisingly over Fleur. 'I'd have known you anywhere,' she said. 'Tom talks about you *non-stop*! I've heard all about that balcony of yours and the fabulous garden you're going to create out there. If what he says is true you're going to have to open it to the public this summer!' She laughed and led the way into the house. 'Welcome to Park Row. I won't offer to help with the unpacking but feel free to bang on my door and demand a cup of coffee when you've finished.'

'Thanks, we might just do that,' Tom said over a mound of boxes as she disappeared upstairs.

The two rooms he was to occupy on the ground floor were small but comfortable. Fleur looked round admiringly at the slick new white paintwork and attractive wallpaper. She'd already peered into the smart little kitchen and looked enviously at the smooth tiled work surfaces and pine cupboards.

'You really are lucky, Tom,' she said. 'You've fallen on your feet here.' She put a hand on one of the radiators. 'Central heating too. What a luxury.'

He hung the armful of clothes he was carrying in the wardrobe and turned to look at her. 'It could be yours too, you know,' he told her. 'There's plenty of room for two here.'

She smiled and shook her head. 'When I made you a similar offer, I seem to remember being turned down.'

'That wasn't intended as a similar offer.' He put his hands on her shoulders. 'And I didn't turn you down. Far from it. What I said was that I wanted you to be absolutely sure. I don't want you making an impulsive

354

gesture you might regret. But if you wanted, you could move in here tomorrow – independently, I mean. We could have a room each. There are two. Sadie even has another small room upstairs that she wants to let.'

'I know. And I do appreciate your offer, Tom. It's just . . .'

'Just that you've realised now that I was right?' He slapped his forehead with the palm of his hand in a dramatic gesture. 'God! Why do I always have to be so damned *saintly*? Can you tell me? I must be mad!'

'That's not what I meant.' She laughed and hugged him. 'I like you just the way you are, so don't you dare change. Anyway, moving just when I'm about to get my very own balcony garden isn't on the cards, is it? Besides, if I lived here you'd have nowhere to come and have candlelit suppers, would you? Which reminds me come back to the flat when we've unpacked and I'll feed you. Call it a farewell present.'

'Not on your life.' Tom shook his head. 'I've booked us a table somewhere special. It was meant to be a surprise. Anyway I don't like the sound of *farewell* present. I hope you weren't planning to get rid of me because I warn you, it won't be that easy.'

'I should hope not!' Fleur looked round at the stacked boxes. 'Now – are we going to get this lot sorted out tonight, or aren't we?'

Charlie Grant stood at the window of Ivy Franks's basement kitchen and watched as the two young people went to and from the front door to the small car parked at the kerb, already laden with boxes.

'Looks like a mass exodus,' he remarked. 'Losing some of your tenants, are you?'

Ivy joined him at the window and craned her neck upwards. 'Oh, just one of my young fellers moving out,' she said. 'But these rooms don't stay empty for long. Soon re-let that, don't you worry.'

'No need if you were to sell,' he said.

Ivy sat down and regarded her visitor solemnly. She hadn't yet decided just what his little game was and she certainly wasn't going to be rushed. 'Which property were you thinking of, Mr Grant?' she asked cagily.

'Which *one*?' Charlie repeated. 'I thought I'd just made that clear. All of them, of course.'

'And how did you know that I owned Victoria Gardens?'

'Never mind that. Let's just say it was a process of elimination. In other words, I worked it out for myself. Come to that, why does it have to be such a well-kept secret?'

Ivy shook her head. 'My old auntie left me these houses when she died. My hubby and I rented this house from her for years and it was a big shock to me, I can tell you, suddenly finding that I owned the street. I reckon she was hoping it'd give me security, seein' I was a widow. But nowadays a woman on her own can't be too careful. Let people get the idea you're a woman of property and they think you're made of money.

'Then there's the risk of burglary. If anyone thinks I'm well off they've got another think coming. Nothing worth pinchin' here, I can tell you. The rent from these places is my only income and I'm sure I don't have to tell you, Mr Grant, what old places like these cost in upkeep and repairs. Then there's the rates – er poll-tax. Cripplin' that is.' She shook her head. 'Not worth the candle any more. Hardly break even, I don't.'

'So – if you got the chance to sell, you'd think favourably?'

Ivy paused. 'An agent handles the letting for me. Same agent who's handled it for years. He takes his cut, of course, but it's worth it to save me collectin' the rents. There's some would take advantage of a defenceless woman on her own, you know,' she told him with a knowing look. 'A while ago he did have an inquiry from the council, but that seems to have fallen through.'

Charlie swallowed his impatience. 'You were willing to sell to them then?'

'I didn't say that.' Ivy folded her arms and drew her mouth into a thin line. 'Never got round to talkin' money, so I don't know if it'd have been worth my while, do I?'

'And what would you say to a firm offer now?'

'An offer of what? And who from?'

'From me, of course. From Grant Philips Construction.'

She narrowed her eyes at him. 'Plannin' to pull 'em all down, are you? Put up one of them what-d'ya-call-'ems – shopping mawls?'

'No. Victoria Gardens would be as they were always meant to be,' he told her. 'They'd be refurbished and let as offices and flats. Maybe a couple of public buildings too.'

'Pubs, you mean?' She wrinkled her nose.

'No. A health centre and maybe a library was what we had in mind.'

'I see.' She considered it for what seemed to Charlie an eternity. 'Mmm. So – how much were you thinkin' of offering?'

'What would you say it's worth, Mrs Franks?' Charlie held his breath. In his experience old girls like this usually lived in the past. Their values bore no relation to present day prices.

'Well, now . . .' She took a cigarette from the packet that lay open on the chenille-covered table and lit it slowly, drawing thoughtfully, then shaking out the match. 'I reckon it must be worth – ooh . . .' She exhaled a stream of smoke. 'Goin' on for a couple of

357

million, I'd say. Wouldn't you?'

'*What?*' Charlie almost fell off his chair. 'You must be joking, Mrs Franks.' He waved an arm around. 'Even in good repair old places like this fetch no more than forty thousand a piece at the very most. I'd be prepared to offer you that.' He did a rapid sum in his head. 'Five hundred and twenty thousand pounds. There you are. That's a fair price. After all, I'm going to have to rip them apart, you know. It's almost a rebuilding job. God only knows what problems I'll uncover. It'll cost me a packet.'

Ivy shook her head. 'That's your problem, Mr Grant. Not mine. You must think it's worth it, mustn't you? Daresay you've worked out that you stand to make a packet. I need enough money to live on. I'd have to buy somewhere to live, remember. That'd take a sizeable sum out of it for a start, 'specially at today's prices.'

Charlie stared at her. The old crone must be getting on for seventy. How did she think she was ever going to spend that kind of money? It was sheer greed! He swallowed his irritation and considered for a moment. You had to hand it to her. She was a far tougher businesswoman than he'd given her credit for. No flies on her!

'Look. I could let you have a nice little bungalow for what it cost me to build them.' Encouraged by the gleam of interest in her eyes he went on. 'Lovely little places. Two bedrooms, central heating, fitted kitchen and coloured bathroom suite. Nice little utility room for your washing machine. Very warm and labour-saving. What do you say, Mrs Franks? You wouldn't know yourself after this draughty old place.'

She drew hard on her cigarette, shaking her head doubtfully. 'Well – I dunno.'

'Just think about it. If you invested the rest of your money you'd be set up for life. Holidays abroad. Winter in the sunshine. Live like a lady on the interest and still have your capital.'

Her fishlike gaze was unimpressed. 'Where is this bungalow then?'

'A new estate out Merifield way. There's just the one left. Clean country air – no pollution.'

But Ivy was shaking her head, mouth pulled down at the corners. 'Never could abide estates. Full o' them yuppies. All toffee-noses and hor-pair gels. Don't like the country either,' she added gloomily. 'No shops for a start. And folks can't mind their own business in the country.'

Exasperated, Charlie got to his feet. 'Well, I hope you don't live to regret it, Mrs Franks. That's my last offer: five hundred thousand pounds and the bungalow. And I think that's very handsome.'

'Twenty thousand!' she said, staring at him aghast. 'You're tryin' to tell me it costs you twenty thousand to build one of them *rabbit hutches*? You gotta be jokin'!'

Red in the face, Charlie strode to the door. 'In that case, Mrs Franks, I'll bid you good day.'

It was dark as Charlotte rode up the winding drive to the stables and parked her bicycle against the garage door. Across the yard she could see that the stables had been closed for the night, the horses obviously bedded down, but there was a light on in her aunt's kitchen window. As she stood outside the back door she shifted the heavy sports bag she had brought with her from one hand to the other. She could hear the radio playing and Kath singing along to it as she prepared her evening meal. The sound reassured her.

Things at home had been unbearably uncomfortable over the past couple of weeks. Her parents weren't speaking, either to each other or to her. It was as though they both blamed her for their trouble. Her mother seemed too distant and preoccupied to approach, and as for Dad – she knew now that he was a liar as well as a cheat. Did he really think she'd swallowed that fairy story he'd told her?

It made something inside her curl up when she remembered the humiliation of apologising to Joanna. The condescending acceptance and that smile of triumph would stay in her memory for a very long time. And the feeble explanation she'd given her grandparents had been received with obvious disbelief.

Her only consolation was the belief that after carrying out her father's wishes he would relent over his ban on her visits to the stables. But he had stuck rigidly to his decision. She was still barred from visiting the one person who cared about her – as a cruel unjust punishment because she'd caught him out. It was more than she could bear.

Kath opened the door to her knock and stood staring at her in surprise. 'Charlotte! What are you doing here?'

'Can I come in, Auntie Kath?'

'Of course, child. But you shouldn't be here, should you?'

'Dad's been in touch with you then?'

Kath sighed, remembering the vitriolic telephone call she'd had from Vernon. '*In touch* is hardly the word for it. He telephoned to tell me what a bad influence I am on you and informed me that he'd forbidden you to see me again.'

'He can't stop me coming here if I want to though, can he?' Charlotte said truculently.

'He can make life pretty unbearable for you if you persist in disobeying him,' Kath said. 'For both of us.'

'What can he do to you?'

'He can put me out of business.'

'How can he?'

'The stables are on land I lease from GPC. The lease

360

is up for renewal next September. If they decide they want to use the land for building . . .'

'Oh.' Charlotte's lower lip trembled. 'I *hate* him, Auntie Kath!' she said, her voice shaking. 'He's ruining my life! Anyway, I'm leaving home. I've made up my mind.'

Kath put her arms round the sobbing girl. 'You can't, darling. You're much too young. You must face the fact that you still need your home and your parents. I'm afraid you'll just have to do as your father says for the time being. It won't be forever.'

'It *will*! They've got me working in that rotten office, right under their noses all the time. I can't move without them knowing. I can't bear it. I *won't*! Other girls leave home and so can I.'

'Come and sit down,' Kath said kindly. 'You're all upset and you need to talk this through. I'll make you a hot drink.'

She watched her niece as she sat on the rug in front of the fire, both hands round the mug of Ovaltine. She looked so young with her fair hair loose around her pale face. But there were dark rings of strain under her eyes. She looked more stressed than any sixteen-year-old had a right to look. Her heart went out to the child.

'What happened to bring all this about?' Kath asked. 'You didn't say anything, did you – about what we saw the other night?'

Charlotte looked apprehensively at her over the rim of the mug. 'I told Granddad,' she whispered.

Kath gasped. 'Oh, Charlotte!'

'I know. I wish I hadn't now, but I had to tell someone. I could hardly tell Mum, could I?'

'No wonder there was trouble. What did he say?'

'He told me to try and forget it. But he was angry, really angry, I could see that. And next morning Granddad rang Dad. I heard them talking on the phone. Granddad must have told him what I said because Dad had me into his office later and really blew me up about it. That was when he banned me from coming here.' Her lip trembled. 'He made me apologise to that woman. Can you imagine? If you'd seen the look on her face!'

'Oh, Charlotte.' Kath reached out to pat her hand.

'Everything at home has been really horrible ever since.'

'I'm not surprised,' Kath muttered. 'I wish you'd talked this through with me first.'

'You think I should have kept quiet about it then – let him get away with it?' Charlotte's eyes were bright with righteous indignation.

'Not entirely, but the way you've handled it has only made things ten times worse, hasn't it?'

Charlotte nodded. 'For you too. I'm sorry.'

'Don't be sorry. The thing is for you not to do anything else you might regret.'

'I meant it when I said I wanted to leave home,' Charlotte told her defiantly. 'Why am I being made to feel that I'm the one in the wrong? No one's talking to anyone in our house and I feel it's all my fault when it *isn't*. It's not fair.' She looked hopefully at Kath. 'I thought I might come and live here with you. Can I – please?'

Kath sighed regretfully. 'Oh, darling, you know you can't. Your father would be furious. I'd be thrown out and then where would either of us be?'

'Are you saying that I've got to do what he says and not visit you any more?' Charlotte's eyes were brimming with tears. 'Does it mean I won't be able to see the horses or ride or – or help you?' She broke off, choked by the hiccuping sobs that shook her shoulders.

Kath slid down onto the floor and drew her close. 'Hush, darling. Don't cry. I'll have a word with your father. We'll wait a couple of weeks till things have cooled down. He'll come round.'

'He won't. He's a pig!'

'Shh. You mustn't say such things. It will all come right in the end. You see if it doesn't.' Kath rocked the sobbing girl in her arms, wishing she could believe in her own assurance. She felt powerless to help the niece she loved so much. It seemed there was nothing she could do. Vernon was the one with all the power and he had made sure she knew just what would happen if she went against his wishes. After all, the stables were her livelihood.

Fleur slipped the key quietly into the door of her flat and opened it. 'Come in,' she whispered to Tom. 'But don't make a noise We don't want Poison Ivy up here reading us the riot act, do we?'

Stifling their giggles like children they crept into the flat and closed the door. Tom's treat had been a great success. After all their hard work they had relaxed over the meal, enjoying the food and consuming a bottle of wine between them as well as liqueurs to accompany their coffee. The evening had been fun and neither of them wanted it to end, which was why Fleur had invited him up for a nightcap.

'Coffee?' she asked. 'Or there might still be some of that sherry left over from Christmas.'

Tom pulled a face. 'I think coffee would be more appropriate after what we've already drunk.' He stood behind her and slipped his arms round her waist as she plugged in the kettle. 'Thanks for this evening, Fleur,' he said, resting his cheek on the top of her head. 'I've enjoyed it so much.'

She turned in the circle of his arms to look into his eyes. 'No, thank you. It was your treat and a wonderful surprise.' She put her arms round his neck. 'And I can't think of anyone I'd rather be with.'

'Do you mean that?' His eyes searched hers. '*Really* mean it?' He kissed her and sighed deeply. 'Oh, Fleur, I love you so much. Ever since you first came here – since the day we first met – I've known. You could almost say it was love at first sight except that it's grown and grown ever since and what I feel now is . . .' He broke off to look down at her ruefully. 'You'd better listen to this. I suspect I can only say it because I'm ever so slightly pissed. I'd never have the courage otherwise. I want – want to spend the rest of my life with you, Fleur. I'm asking you to marry me.' For a moment they looked at each other, then he said, 'The trouble is that you don't feel as deeply as I do – do you?'

Fleur shook her head. 'It's not that. I do love you, Tom. I meant it when I said that there is no one I'd rather be with. It's just . . .'

'Just what?' He looked at her. 'Go on, tell me.'

'I can't tell you because I don't know.'

'If you loved me you'd know,' he said unhappily. 'If you loved me unreservedly there'd be no doubt in your mind.'

'Is it possible to love anyone that way?'

'Yes! I happen to think it is.'

The kettle boiled and she turned back to attend to it. 'So many marriages end in divorce nowadays,' she said. 'Even so-called permanent relationships seem to fizzle out after a few months. Happy-ever-after gets shorter all the time. It just makes me wonder what happens to all that love that people believed was so strong.'

'It dies because they take it for granted,' Tom said earnestly. 'They don't see that they have to work to keep it alive. People aren't prepared to make sacrifices. Anything worth having is worth working at.'

She turned and handed him the mug of coffee.

'Perhaps you're right. But who knows? Who really *knows*?'

'What you're saying is that you don't trust me,' he said exasperatedly. 'I'm not Peter Arden, you know. What do I have to do to prove it to you, for Christ's sake?'

'Nothing! I don't know. If it comes to that, what makes you so sure you can trust *me* after what happened?' She sighed. 'Oh, Tom, don't let's quarrel over it. We've had such a super evening.'

He put down his mug and pulled her into his arms again. 'No. You're right. As for trusting you, Fleur – if you ask me to, I will. It's as simple as that.'

She winced. 'You make me feel so guilty.' She took her coffee and sat down on the settee.

'Guilty! Hell, that's the last thing I want you to feel.'

'I think it's wrong to tie people down,' she said. 'Look what happens. Look what happened to me – a father who didn't want to know and a mother who walked out on me when I was a baby.'

'But they weren't married.'

She looked at him. 'If they had been, do you think it would have made any difference? I don't. The only kind of commitment that really works is the one that makes up your mind for you. When you stay with someone it must be because you can't bear to be parted from them, not just because some legal bit of paper says you've signed a contract and you're stuck with it. Feelings have to stand the test of time.'

He sat down beside her and slipped an arm around her. 'So shall we take it from here then? Take our time and see if we still feel the same, say, six months from now?'

She turned her head and kissed him gently. 'That's what I'd like, Tom. It was what I had in mind when I asked you to stay with me that night. Just as long as . . .'

'Well?' He tipped up her chin, making her look at him. 'As long as what?'

'As long as we both face the fact that it may not be real after all. One of us might still be hurt. It might be me.'

He drew her close. 'I'm willing to risk it if you are.' He kissed her. 'I want you so much, Fleur – in every way. For always.'

The eyes that looked down at her were filled with longing and as his hands caressed her Fleur suddenly knew a desire that was infinitely deeper, more passionate, than anything she had experienced with Peter. Suddenly she understood the bewildering difference between love and lust.

Neither of them heard the soft tap on the door until it was repeated, louder. Fleur's eyes opened and her muscles tensed as she looked at Tom.

'Listen! There's someone on the landing.'

He groaned. 'What's the betting it's Ivy?'

'Surely not.'

As they lay quite still and listened, the knock came again. Whoever the visitor was he or she had no intention of giving up. Fleur swung her legs to the floor and pulled on her dressing gown.

'I'd better see who it is.' She smiled at Tom ruefully. 'It might be as well to put something on before I open the door.'

He swore softly under his breath as he scrambled into his clothes.

At the door Fleur asked, 'Who is it?'

'It's me – Charlotte.'

Fleur unlocked the door and opened it, shocked to see the girl standing on the landing, looking lost and forlorn, a large sports bag clutched in her hand. 'Charlotte! What on earth's the matter? What are you doing here at this time of night?'

'I – I've left home!' The girl's teeth were chattering slightly. She looked cold and miserable.

Fleur reached out to take her arm and draw her inside. 'Come in. You're cold.'

'I'm sorry to disturb you,' Charlotte said, 'but I couldn't think of anywhere else to go. I tried the door downstairs and it was open, so I just – just came up. I've chained my bike to the railing downstairs. It'll be okay, won't it? I couldn't . . .' Suddenly she caught sight of Tom and stopped in mid-sentence. 'Oh! Oh, dear – I didn't realise. I'll go . . .'

Fleur grasped her arm. 'Don't be silly. You can't go back out there at this time of night.' She shot a look of appeal at Tom who looked at his watch and said hurriedly, 'Heavens, I didn't realise it was that late. I really must be going.'

'Are you sure?' Charlotte looked from one to the other. 'I mean, I haven't – I don't want . . .'

'You're not,' Tom said. 'Time I was leaving anyway.'

'I'll come down with you.' Fleur looked over her shoulder at Charlotte. 'Make yourself at home. I won't be a minute.'

Downstairs in the hall Tom turned to her. 'Who is she?'

'Charlotte. The girl I met on the computer course.'

'But what's she doing here? It's a bit much, isn't it, dropping in on you in the middle of the night?'

'I don't know, but I can hardly turn her out into the street, can I?' She put her arms round his neck. 'Sorry, love.'

'It's okay, I suppose.' He kissed her and tried to stifle his resentment. 'What about her parents, though? She looks pretty young to me.'

'She's sixteen.' Fleur gave him a gentle push towards the front door. 'Leave her to me, Tom. If you don't go we'll have Ivy here demanding to know what's going on.'

'All right. I'm going.'

She pulled him back and stood on tiptoe to kiss him. 'That's for being sweet. I love you, Tom.'

He hugged her briefly. 'Love you too.'

'And I'm really sorry about tonight.'

'No more than I am,' he told her wryly. 'Still, never mind. We've all the time in the world, eh?'

'Yes. All the time in the world.'

He kissed her again and was gone.

Upstairs in the flat Fleur made Charlotte a hot drink and a sandwich, then made up a makeshift bed for her on the settee.

'Is there a problem at home?' she asked as she worked. 'Have you had a row?'

'They all hate me,' Charlotte said dramatically. 'I spilled the beans about Dad and the Hanson women.'

'Oh my God!' Fleur bit her lip.

'It's caused ructions.'

'I can imagine. But your mother is bound to have missed you by now. She'll be worried about you. Shouldn't you ring her?'

Charlotte shook her head miserably. 'She won't even have noticed I'm not there,' she said bitterly.

As it happened she was right.

Chapter 13

'Isn't Charlotte up yet?'

Julia looked up from her breakfast to see Vernon looking at her over his newspaper. 'She should be. I tapped on her door about half an hour ago.'

He frowned at his watch. 'She's going to be late for work at this rate. It sets such a bad example to the other girls. Give her another shout, will you?'

'Vernon, I've been meaning to speak to you about Charlotte. She's been looking so unhappy. I think you were wrong to forbid her to go to Kath's . . .'

He rustled his paper angrily. 'I don't want to discuss it with you, Julia. You've always been far too soft with the girl. This time she's got to learn that she can't make trouble and get away with it.'

'She was upset by what she saw,' Julia said quietly. 'You're having an affair, Vernon, and you're annoyed at being caught out by your own daughter. Why bother to deny it?'

'I *do* deny it! I absolutely deny that Joanna and I are anything but working colleagues,' he said. 'If Charlotte had come to me with what she *imagined* she'd seen it might have been excusable, but to go to your father!'

Julia sighed. It was old ground. They'd been over and over it, and it was obviously an argument that was going nowhere. She rose from the table and went into the hall where Tracey was busy vacuuming.

'Tracey, go up and give Charlotte another call, would you?' she said above the roar of the machine. 'She's going to be late for work and I don't want her going off again without any breakfast.'

Tracey switched off the cleaner and looked at her employer. 'I thought she'd already gone,' she said. 'I've done her room. The bed was made and everything.'

Julia stared at her. 'Gone? Of course she hasn't gone. I've been up since seven and I haven't seen her.' Closely followed by Tracey, she ran up the stairs and pushed open the door of Charlotte's room. As Tracey had already said, the bed was neatly made and everything was unusually tidy. 'She couldn't have gone out without my seeing her,' Julia said, her heart beginning to thud with alarm. 'It looks as though she didn't sleep here at all last night. Where on earth can she be?'

'At one of her friend's perhaps,' Tracey suggested. 'Could you ring round and see?'

Julia sat down heavily on the bed. 'Most of her schoolfriends have gone off to college,' she said. 'And I don't think she's made any friends at the office.' Silently she admitted to herself that she had no idea what social life, if any, her daughter had. She'd never made friends easily. Always been rather a lonely child. Why hadn't Julia tried to find out the reason for this before?

'Is there anything I can do?' Tracey asked.

'No. I daresay there's some simple explanation,' she said without conviction. When Tracey had left to continue her work Julia got up and went to look in the wardrobe. Several items of clothing, including Charlotte's dressing gown, had gone and in the bathroom she found her toothbrush missing. Her heart sank like a stone.

Downstairs Vernon had already left for work. Going across the hall into his study Julia closed the door against the sound of the hoover and dialled Kath's number, hoping that her sister-in-law hadn't gone off on some equestrian errand or other. To her relief Kath answered almost immediately.

'Kath. It's Julia.'

'Hello. Lucky to have caught me. I was just on my way out.'

'Kath, is Charlotte with you?'

'No, why?'

'She's not here. I don't think her bed has even been slept in and some of her clothes are missing.'

'Oh, no! She did come to see me last night. She was very upset – wanted to stay here. But I sent her away.'

'But why, for heaven's sake? Where can she be, Kath? Whatever possessed you to turn her away?'

'Vernon rang me yesterday, threatening not to renew my lease if I had anything more to do with his daughter. I didn't want any more trouble for either of us. I made her a hot drink, sat her down and tried to talk some sense into her. I advised her to go home. When she left here she seemed much calmer and I thought she'd do just that. Oh, God, Julia, I'm so sorry.'

'Have you any idea at all where she might have gone?'

'Not off hand.' Kath paused, wondering whether she should say what was in her mind. 'I suppose you do realise how unhappy the child is over this business with Vernon?'

'I do *now*, of course!' Julia snapped. She was silent for a moment. She had to admit she was partly to blame. Her own problems had dimmed her awareness of others'. 'I'm sorry, Kath,' she said. 'I didn't mean to snap your head off. It's just that I'm so worried. She could be anywhere. One hears of such awful things happening to young girls who run away from home. Why couldn't she have come to *me* if she was so miserable?'

'Perhaps because she's seen you bury your head in the sand about matters like this so many times in the past,' Kath said bluntly. 'I'm sorry. I shouldn't have said that.'

'No, you're right,' Julia admitted. 'I just wish Charlotte and I were closer. Since she left school and started at the office I don't seem to have been able to get through to her. I've been meaning to do something about it – make time to sit down and talk. It's just that life has been so difficult over the past few months. Vernon has always criticised the way I've brought Charlotte up. Sometimes I feel that I can't seem to do right by one without hurting the other. But this isn't finding her. Look, Kath, could you just think? Has she mentioned any new friends to you? Is there any place you can think of where she might have spent last night? I *have* to find her.'

'Okay. Just a minute, let me think.' There was a long pause, then Kath said, 'There was the girl she met on that computer course. She's mentioned her quite a lot. She seemed to get along well with her. But she left after one term so I don't know if she still sees her.'

Julia clutched the receiver. 'Never mind. It's a start. Do you remember her name?'

'Oh, God, now what was it? It was an unusual name – Flora – Florence? No, *Fleur*! That was it, Fleur. Charlotte said she worked for a catering firm – Arden's.'

Julia's heart almost stopped beating. 'Are you sure about that?' she whispered.

'Quite sure. Look, Julia, do you want me to come over there? I was going over to Newmarket to look at a new brood mare but I could ring and postpone.'

'No, no. You go. I'll be all right. I'll try this girl first,

372

then I'll get back to you to let you know what happens.'

'Yes, please do that.'

Julia put the phone down and sat for a moment trying to put her thoughts in order. So Charlotte and Fleur actually knew each other! Had Fleur told Charlotte anything? She had to know. It could explain a lot. She opened the telephone directory and looked up the number of Arden Catering and dialled. She recognised the voice that replied instantly.

'Fleur. Is that you?'

'Speaking. Who is it?'

'This is Julia Grant. Fleur, you haven't seen anything of Charlotte, my daughter, have you?'

'Yes, I have. She came to my flat late last night. She was upset, said she'd left home. I put her up for the night. I hope that was all right. I did try to get her to ring you but she wouldn't.'

Julia felt faint with relief. 'Where is she now?'

'She went to work. I've been trying to ring you myself. I knew you'd be worried, but the number was engaged.'

'I know. It doesn't matter. Nothing matters just as long as she's safe. Look, Fleur, I think we should talk. Are you free at lunchtime?'

'Well, yes.'

'Would it be possible for you to drive out to The Millstone again and meet me?'

'I think so.'

'Good. I'll see you there then – about one?'

Charlie climbed up the area steps of thirteen Victoria Gardens and got back into the car. Damn that Franks woman! She would have to be out this morning. He looked at the street in all its decaying grandeur. If she hadn't been so stubborn it would be his by now. He could have presented his plans in time for this month's planning meeting and had things well under way by now. He could make this place look wonderful given half a chance.

Half closing his eyes he visualised the grimy Victorian façades sand-blasted to their original rose pink, the woodwork sparkling white with new paint. The rusting railings would be burnished and the road outside cobbled as it would have been when the street was first built. In the centre, replacing the railed-off patch of rubbish-strewn mud, would be manicured grass like green velvet, dotted with brilliant flower beds and maybe a fountain playing in the centre, surrounded by comfortable seats. He could almost hear the tranquil sound of birdsong and tinkling water. And somewhere in a prominent position there would be a plaque honouring the name of Charles Grant the restorer, complete with the date for all to see in perpetuity.

He seethed with frustration at the dream held just out of his reach by a greedy old woman.

When he'd told Vernon the price Ivy Franks had asked he'd laughed derisively. 'She must be off her trolley!' he'd said. 'Might as well forget it.'

But Charlie wasn't ready to forget it. He'd really set his heart on this project. Once achieved, he and the firm would be made. Of course two million was ridiculous, but he could go higher now, thanks to the security of Joanna's input. The bank would probably stretch his loan a bit further too if he played his cards right. More than half the houses on the point of completion on Meadowlands Park had been reserved so they were sure of their money there.

He lit his pipe thoughtfully, wondering what the old bat would accept. No point in offering over the odds if all she had in mind was another couple of thousand. He'd have to box a bit clever.

He saw her as soon as she rounded the corner, loaded down with supermarket carrier bags. She wore a motheaten fur coat that had seen better days and a scarf tied round her head. From the corner of her mouth dangled the inevitable cigarette whose smoke spiralled upwards into her hennaed hair. He tried to imagine her as a millionairess and failed. What the hell would a woman like that do with that kind of money? It was ludicrous!

Pocketing his pipe and composing his features into a genial smile he got out of the car. 'Mrs Franks! How nice to see you. And looking so well.'

Eyeing him suspiciously, Ivy put her bags of shopping down on the pavement while she fumbled in her handbag for her keys. 'What can I do for you then, Mr Grant?'

'Well, I was in the area and I suddenly thought about you,' he said. 'I was wondering if we might have another little chat?'

Finding her keys, Ivy picked up the assorted carrier bags and started down the area steps. 'S'pose you'd better come in then, hadn't you?'

Charlie followed her down the steps where she thrust the shopping into his arms while she unlocked the door. Inside she relieved him of the shopping and took it through to the scullery, then began to take off her coat, still eyeing her visitor balefully.

'Sit down then,' she said brusquely. 'No need to stand about. I suppose you want a cup of tea or something?'

'That won't be necessary,' he said. 'I don't want to put you to any trouble. I just wondered if you'd given any more thought to what we discussed the other day?'

'Not a lot,' Ivy said. 'Reckon I'm happy enough where I am. This old place has been good enough all these years so I can't see why I shouldn't finish my days here. Movin' house is a big upheaval at my time of life. Not sure I want to go through it.'

Ivy's friend Mrs Jennings, who 'did' for the Grants on a daily basis, had told her often enough about their opulent lifestyle. In Ivy's view Grant Philips Construction was taking a dead liberty. They could easily afford to pay her more and she'd made up her mind that if they didn't make it well worth her while she wasn't budging.

Charlie sighed. 'That's a great pity,' he said. 'Especially as I was about to make you a better offer.'

Ivy's eyes gleamed and she reached for another ciga- rette from the packet on the mantelpiece. 'How much better?' she asked without looking at him.

'Shall we say another five hundred?'

'I wouldn't bother wastin' your breath if I was you.' She threw away the match and shot him a sharp look. 'Probably cost me that to move me furniture.'

'A thousand then?'

Ivy drew the corners of her mouth down and shook her head. 'Like I said, Mr Grant, it's not worth uprootin' myself for.'

Charlie struggled to contain his irritation. 'What *would* make it worth your while, Mrs Franks?' he asked. 'And let's be realistic about this.'

She glared at him indignantly. 'You're the one not bein' realistic!' She sucked hard on the cigarette and exhaled explosively. 'I reckon if you was to double your first offer I *might* just change my mind. You know as well as I do, Mr Grant, that this street is worth that.' She leaned forward to jab the air with a nicotine-stained finger. 'An' I only said I *might* change my mind, remem- ber.'

Charlie considered for a long moment. It was more – far more – than he'd intended to pay, but he could see that she wouldn't let him have it for less. Surely

Meadowlands Park would finance the project – see them through until completion? 'I'll have to give that a lot of thought, Mrs Franks,' he said. 'But I don't want to waste time going to my fellow directors with your suggestion if you're only going to change your mind again. So am I to take that as a figure you'd definitely accept?'

Slightly taken aback by his sudden capitulation, she nodded. 'All right then. Yes.'

'Right.' Charlie stood up. 'I'll get back to you as soon as I've consulted my partners. Perhaps you could give me the name of your solicitor? It would save time when it comes to having contracts drawn up.'

'Heskith and Trowbridge, 5 Albemarle Terrace,' Ivy said briskly. She didn't add that she'd already contacted them about the likelihood of a sale.

Julia arrived at The Millstone early, bought herself a glass of white wine and went through to sit in the small snug where she and Fleur had first met. The pub was busier this time, but most of the customers were in the bar and once again she had the snug almost to herself.

These days she was becoming increasingly isolated. As well as the family rift, she had had to face the displeasure of some of her fellow councillors since she had won the vote over the women's refuge. And she'd been taken to task by the Town Clerk over the photographs that had appeared in the press too. She had been unaware that she should have asked permission to be photographed in the council chamber. And she still had to face her parents with the news that she had voted along with Vernon, his father and Joanna over the Victoria Gardens project, something she looked forward to with increasing dread.

She saw Fleur arrive in the big white Arden Catering van and watched as she got out and locked the door. It was so hard to realise that this tall, striking girl was her daughter – the little dark-eyed baby she had given birth to in such mental and physical anguish all those years ago. She looked so much like Dean. It was no wonder that Joanna had so easily put two and two together as soon as she discovered that her name was Sylvester.

A moment later Fleur put her head round the door. 'Hello. I thought you'd be in here.'

Julia stood up. 'I'm so glad you were able to come, Fleur. Can I get you a drink? Maybe something to eat? I know this is your lunch hour.'

'No, thanks. I can't stay long.' Fleur sat down in the chair opposite. 'I'm glad you rang me. I didn't know what to do when I couldn't get through to you. Charlotte begged me not to tell you she was with me, but I wouldn't promise. I wasn't comfortable with that.'

'First I want to thank you for putting her up,' Julia said. 'Heaven knows what might have happened to her if you hadn't. I didn't even miss her until this morning.' She sighed. 'I feel so guilty about that. I stopped checking on her at bedtime months ago. Anyway, she's taken to locking her door at nights.'

'I couldn't have turned her away,' Fleur said. 'She was obviously upset. What I don't understand is why you thought of ringing me.'

'I called her aunt first. She said Charlotte had talked of you quite a lot.' Julia looked at her. 'You didn't tell me that you and she knew each other.'

'No.' The unspoken question hung between them. 'We met quite by accident when we were both taking the same evening class,' Fleur said. 'And before you ask, she hasn't a clue who I really am. Obviously I knew you wouldn't want her to know about me.'

'I see. Thanks.' Julia took a sip of her drink, trying not to show the relief she felt. 'I should have spotted that she was bottling things up. She must have been very unhappy to want to run away.'

Fleur looked at her hesitantly. 'I think I should tell you that she came to me with a family problem a few weeks ago.'

'I can guess – it was to do with her father?'

'Yes. She didn't know what to do about it. I'm afraid I wasn't much help. I didn't feel I could advise her, so I told her to leave things to sort themselves out.'

'Thank you for that anyway. And you say she went to the office this morning? That's a good sign.'

'I don't think her courage quite stretched to not showing up for work. Besides, she hasn't any money and she won't get paid till the end of the month. She seems a bit scared of her father, if you don't mind my saying so,' Fleur said. 'I don't know both sides, of course, but he does seem very hard on her.'

'I know.'

Fleur waited for Julia to explain further. When she remained silent she said, 'So – if she comes back this evening, what do you want me to do?'

'I rather think it will be a question of what she wants to do. If you like, you could tell her that you've seen me and that I'd like her to come home.'

'I'll try.' Fleur had a sudden thought. 'Look, it's only an idea, but maybe it would do Charlotte good to be by herself for a while? You know – stand on her own feet and have a taste of independence. I know someone who has a room to let. It's only a house in Park Row but it's been modernised and it's a nice little room. Maybe if she had some space she'd sort herself out.'

'Do you think she'd want that?'

'I think she might. I could tell her you said it was okay. That might make it easier for her to decide.'

'I wouldn't want her to feel we didn't want her,' Julia said doubtfully. 'She's so terribly young to be on her own.'

'I was a lot younger when you left *me*!' The words were out before Fleur had time to weigh them. Seeing the stricken look on Julia's face, she said quickly, 'Sorry. I didn't mean that as a reproach.'

Julia shook her head. 'If you did, it's no more than I deserve. You really think she'd be all right on her own, do you?'

'I think she'd be fine. A friend of mine lives there and we could both keep an eye on her – see that she's okay. I could keep you posted if you'd like me to. And she'll know that if she gets homesick you're not far away.'

'Well, I suppose it's better than having her run away to heaven knows where.' She smiled at Fleur. 'Thanks. It might be an idea. Try her anyway.'

'I'll try to get her to ring you and let you know what she decides,' she said. 'But if she won't then I will.'

Julia reached out to touch her hand. 'You've been very good over this, Fleur. And I do see that letting go a little is better than laying down rules.'

'Look, I'm sorry for what I said just now.'

Julia paused, wondering if this was the right time for the question she couldn't bring herself to ask at their first meeting. 'Fleur, I've been wondering – did your – did Dean ever come back?'

'No. He died soon after Grandpa Maurice was killed, when I was about twelve. It was in America and so it was months before they traced us. A priest came to tell us.'

Julia felt numb. 'Poor Dolly,' she said quietly.

'Yes. It was awful for her so soon after losing Grandpa, 'specially when she hadn't seen Dean for so long.'

Julia looked up. 'What happened? Did they say?'

'It seems he'd been out of work for some time. Grandma never told me all the details, perhaps she didn't really know, but I think he'd taken an overdose or something.'

Julia nodded. It fitted. Like so many others Dean had always thought he was indestructible. Grab everything life had to offer, that was his motto. Nothing could harm him as long as he had his music and the golden dream of fame and fortune to sustain him. Failure would have been a bitter blow. 'That's sad,' she said. 'He was talented, you know. But so were so many other young musicians. If he'd had the right kind of luck. Maybe if he hadn't met me . . .'

'You can't blame yourself for that,' Fleur said. 'You shouldn't keep putting yourself down. You seem to take the blame for everything that goes wrong and it can't all be your fault.'

Julia smiled wryly. 'I suppose it's force of habit. I've had years of practice at getting things wrong.'

Fleur hesitated. Maybe it was time she confessed to her own indiscretion. 'Look, Julia – there's something I think you should know. When I went round to Mrs Hanson's to arrange about her party she remarked that she'd once known Dean Sylvester. I was really surprised to hear the name mentioned and without thinking I'm afraid I . . .'

'Let slip that he was your father?' Julia finished for her.

'You know?'

'Yes. I know.'

Again Julia did not clarify just how she knew and after a pause Fleur went on, 'I've been worrying about it ever since. I hope it didn't cause you any trouble?'

'No. Mrs Hanson and I were once close friends. She won't say anything.' Julia paused. Why burden the girl with her own family problems? After all, it needn't affect her in any way.

'Good. That's a relief.' Fleur realised that Julia couldn't

know that Charlotte had told her who her father's mistress was. She was silent for a moment, glancing at Julia and puzzling as to how she could feel so assured that her secret was safe with the woman her husband was having an affair with. She looked at her watch and got up from the table. 'Well, I'd better be getting back,' she said. 'Sally is off to Switzerland soon and we're trying to get as far ahead as we can in advance.'

'Thanks for coming, Fleur. And for all your help.'

Julia stood at the window, watching as she crossed the forecourt and sprang into the driving seat of the van. She looked so self-assured and full of vitality. Far more mature and adult than Julia had been at the same age. If only she had been as sound and well-balanced. With a pang of regret she thought about the prospect of having Charlotte move out of the family home. It was true of course that all children grew up and wanted their independence, but all the same she couldn't help feeling that Charlotte had been driven out. Soon she would be as distant from Charlotte as she was from Fleur. Both of them grown to womanhood and a maturity for which she could claim no credit. Was it any wonder she was haunted by guilt and regrets?

'I don't believe I'm hearing this, Dad!' Vernon raked a hand through his hair. 'I'm supposed to carry out all the financial negotiations for this firm. What on earth were you thinking of to make an offer like this without even consulting me?'

'Now you just listen to me.' Charlie glowered at his son. 'I was doing this job when you were still in rompers, so don't start getting on your high horse with me, lad!' he said. 'Believe me,' he thumped the table, 'we have to have that street! A million's nowt but peanuts to what we'd have to pay if this were one of the big cities.'

'But it isn't one of the big cities. That's just the point,' Vernon shouted. 'When it's completed we won't be able to charge big city rents, but we'll still have to pay the same price for materials and wages.'

'You don't know how tough that old bird is,' Charlie blustered. 'I defy anyone to get her down any lower.'

'Then we should have gone through the agent. And when she pressed for such a large sum, abandoned the project. Maybe we still should. After all, there's nothing in writing to commit us.' He looked at his father. 'That's why you didn't want me along, isn't it? Because you knew I'd advise you to drop it. We just can't afford it, Dad. Not even with Joanna's investment.'

'You have to have vision in this business,' Charlie insisted. 'You have to speculate to accumulate.'

'I *agree*.' Joanna, who had been silent so far, leaned forward. 'I think Charlie is right. There has never been a better time for expansion and this redevelopment project of his is so good. Have you seen the plans, Vernon?'

'Yes, I've seen them. All I know is, it's going to cost an arm and a leg.'

'And that's all you *can* see!' She turned to Charlie with a smile. 'Accountants only ever see money going out, don't they, Charlie?' She clicked her tongue maddeningly. 'They have no imagination. No creativity. No soul.'

'I am *not* an accountant!' Vernon shouted, his face red. 'I'm as creative as the next man, but I can recognise bloody lunacy when I see it.' He paused to take a deep breath. They were going to get nowhere by yelling at each other. Besides, with Joanna on Charlie's side he was outnumbered. 'Look, Dad, why don't you leave the negotiations to me? We'll start afresh. I'll get in touch with the agent handling the property and we'll deal with him as we should have done in the first place.'

Charlie glowered at him. 'I started this and I intend to finish it. I shouldn't need to remind you that this is *my* business, Vernon, so pay me the courtesy of admitting I'm right for once, will you? You young 'uns think you know the lot, but you're not always right, even if you think you are.'

Seething with impotent anger, he got up from the table and gathered his papers into his briefcase. 'Right. If that's the way you want it, Dad, on your own head be it!'

When Charlotte came home from work Fleur was waiting for her.

'I've been to see your mother,' she said at once.

Charlotte stopped in the act of taking off her coat to stare at her. 'You *haven't*! Bloody hell, Fleur, how could you? You promised!'

'No, I didn't. She had to be told you were safe, Charlotte. She'd been frantic with worry.'

Charlotte threw herself into a chair. 'You're joking,' she said moodily. 'I bet she didn't give a damn. Probably glad to be rid of me.'

'That's not true at all and you know it. Your mum cares a lot about you.'

'Is that what she told you? Huh!' Charlotte snorted and hunched her shoulders. 'So, like a good little grass, I suppose you promised to deliver me home to them then? All tied up in bows and gift-wrapped.'

'No.' Fleur sat down opposite the girl. 'Look, we talked and I suggested something. It's an option for you to think about. And your mum is prepared to let you try it.'

'Try what – *cyanide*?'

'You're behaving like a spoilt kid, Charlotte. I'm beginning to wonder why I bothered. Now – do you want to hear this idea or don't you?'

384

'Okay, go on.'

'I know where there's a very nice bed-sit. How would you like to try living on your own for a bit?'

Charlotte sat up straight and stared at Fleur. 'You're kidding! Are you saying they'd actually let me do that?' she asked incredulously.

'On certain terms, yes.'

'Ah! I knew there'd have to be a snag. What is it?'

'Only that we keep in close touch. A friend of mine has just moved into a flat in the same house. Tom. You met him here last night. We'd both keep in regular touch with you.'

'And report back?' Charlotte said suspiciously.

'Only if we thought you weren't coping. And of course you'd have to keep your promise not to see your aunt.'

Charlotte slumped again, remembering her father's veto. 'No chance of that anyway. He's threatened Auntie Kath with eviction if she lets me go round there.'

Fleur reached out to touch the girl's hand. 'I'm sorry about that, Charlotte. But maybe when your dad sees how grown up and responsible you are, he'll change his mind. What do you say? Shall we go round and have a look at the room?'

They were ringing the front door bell at ten Park Row when Sadie rode up on her motorbike. She roared to a halt and dismounted.

'Hi! What can I do for you?'

Fleur explained that she'd brought a prospective tenant to view the vacant room.

'Great! Look, I've only come to pick up some spare films,' she told them, taking off her crash helmet. 'I've just got wind of a demo on the site of the new bypass and I'm on my way to take some shots and get the full story.' She grinned. 'If I'm quick off the mark I might be able to sell to one of the nationals. But I can show you the room quickly.' She led the way inside and up the stairs, her leathers squeaking protestingly at every step. 'I only need the other two rooms for myself,' she said as they reached the landing. 'This one's a bit small and I haven't furnished it apart from the carpet and curtains so you'd have to bring your own furniture.' She opened the door. 'Most people want a furnished room which is why it hasn't been let yet, but we could adjust the rent if you like it. Kitchen and bathroom are shared, of course. Cleaning on a rota.'

Charlotte looked round the empty room. It faced south and the sun streamed in at the window. On the floor was a green carpet with matching leaf-patterned curtains at the window. She looked at Fleur with shining eyes. 'I expect Mum would let me bring the stuff from my bedroom at home,' she said excitedly. 'I'd like to take it, please.'

Fleur laughed. 'You haven't even asked what the rent is,' she said. 'And you'll be paying for it out of your wages, remember. You'll have to start budgeting if you're going to be a bachelor girl.'

Charlotte's smile slipped a little. 'Oh, yes. Er – how much is it, Miss Freeman?'

Sadie named a figure which caused Fleur to gasp. It was less than she had paid for the miserable attic room she had started out with in Victoria Gardens. She nodded her approval at Charlotte. 'That's very reasonable.'

'I'll take it.' Charlotte smiled at Sadie. 'Can I move in tomorrow?'

Sadie laughed. ' 'Course. Any time you like. Now if you don't mind, I've got to go.'

Back at thirteen Victoria Gardens half an hour later Charlotte spoke to her mother on the telephone. 'It's such a sweet little room, but it isn't furnished. So can I move my bed and things over there?'

'If you're sure this is what you really want?'

'I am, Mum. But are you sure Dad won't do something to stop me having it?'

'Leave him to me,' Julia said. 'Give me the address and I'll hire a van. We'll get your things moved tomorrow.' She paused. 'Are you coming home tonight?' Into the pause that followed she said, 'I think you should speak to Dad yourself. It would come much better from you. But I'll back you up, of course.'

Charlotte looked at Fleur and covered the mouthpiece with her hand. 'She wants me to go home tonight,' she whispered. Fleur nodded her agreement.

'You won't let him try to talk me out of it?' Charlotte asked.

'No,' Julia promised: 'But it would be nice if we could all three have a talk.'

'Okay then. See you later.'

Tracey finished wiping down the worktops in the kitchen. She loved working in Julia Grant's kitchen with its cool green-tiled work surfaces and silky wood-faced cupboards. One day, she promised herself, she would have a kitchen just like it. Damian sat in the highchair Julia had lent her, playing contentedly. The chair had been Charlotte's and it had a row of coloured balls attached to the tray, which he never grew tired of. He chuckled contentedly, watching his mother and listening as she sang along to the radio. As usual she had it tuned in to Radio 1 and Chris DeBurgh was singing her favourite, 'Diamond in the Dark'. As it came to an end a tap on the back door made her look up.

'Who can that be, Damie?' she said. Switching off the radio, she crossed the kitchen to answer it.

Outside the door Rick stood leaning against the wall.

He wore work-stained jeans and a tattered anorak. 'Hi,' he said hopefully. 'On my way home from work an' I thought I'd give you and the boy a look in.'

'I'm working,' Tracey said shortly. 'I've told you before, Rick. You can't just call here whenever the mood takes you.'

'Go on, you're entitled to a tea break,' he said. 'And Lady Muck's gone out. I saw her drive off with me own eyes.'

It was true that Julia was out. She'd gone to a committee meeting.

'Come on,' Rick wheedled. 'I got a right to see me own son, haven't I?'

'You've got no rights at all, Rick Kendle. You gave them up when you did what you did to me.'

He pulled a face. 'Oh, don't start on that again, Trace. How many times do I have to say sorry, eh? Look, I won't stop long.'

'No.' She tried to shut the door but his foot was in the way.

'I been workin' since eight this morning on that buildin' site and I've only had a bar of chocolate. I'm nearly passin' out with hunger.'

'Oh, come on in then,' Tracey sighed and held the door open for him. 'And take them filthy boots off. I've just done this floor.' She went to put the kettle on while Rick made a bee line for Damian.

'Hey, he's gettin' a big boy,' he said, lifting him out of his chair and sitting down with him on his knee.

Tracey looked round. 'He's got another tooth through. That's eight.'

'Soon be walkin', I reckon.' Rick put Damian on the floor and watched him crawl towards his mother. 'I wish I could see more of him Trace. You too. Why won't you let me move into your place?'

'It wouldn't work,' she said, her lips tight. 'I haven't

forgotten the way you treated me before. I'm not having Damie grow up with a violent man like you.' She picked the baby up and put him back into his chair. 'You threatened me. And him – a helpless little baby. Mrs Grant wanted me to go to the police.'

'What did she want to go stickin' 'er nose in for?' he said angrily. 'None of 'er bloody business!'

'Good job I had someone on my side,' she told him hotly. 'You scared the livin' daylights out of me, Rick Kendle, them things you said you'd do to Damie an' me.'

'I didn't know what I was doin'. I was clean out of my tree at the time.' He sidled up to her. 'Oh, look, that was ages ago, Trace. I'm not violent. You got to admit it was just the once. I never hit you before, did I? It was that stuff I was on, that's all. It changes you somethin' horrible. But I'm okay now. I'm off it. I got a job an' everything and I'm really tryin' hard.' He gave her a reproachful look. 'Not that I'm gettin' much encouragement from you.'

He went across to where she stood making the tea. 'You oughta see the room I'm in, Trace. A proper rat 'ole, it is, honest. An' there's you with a whole house all to yourself.'

Tracey poured the tea without comment and pushed the biscuit tin towards him. 'Knew I shouldn't have let you in,' she said. 'Look, have your tea and biscuits then go, Rick. I don't want to hear no more.'

He took a biscuit, peering at it disconsolately. 'Got any chocolate ones?'

'No.'

'There's nowhere to cook in that place I'm in,' he said. 'I get sick an' tired of fish an' chips and take-aways. You got anything you could make me a sandwich of? Bit of cold meat? Cheese?'

'No.'

He dunked the biscuit resignedly into his tea and munched. 'Just look at this place,' he said, his mouth full. 'Concealed lightin', ceramic tiles. I know what these things cost and this must've cost an arm and a leg. What you wanna work here for anyway? Givin' up your benefit money so's you can skivvy for toffee-nosed gits like them.'

'I haven't given anything up,' Tracey said.

He stopped chewing to stare at her. 'What d'you mean? You don't work for nuthin', do you?'

Instantly realising she had slipped up, Tracey tried to cover her mistake. 'I work for Mrs Grant because she's been a good friend to me,' she said.

He gave a snort. 'What you mean is, she takes advantage of you.'

'No. She pays me low, but she gives me a present now and again.'

'You mean she pays you when she remembers to? That's not a very good arrangement, is it?'

'It's none of your business, Rick Kendle.'

'Well, I hope you help yourself to the larder,' he said. 'I hope you make sure that you and the kid get well fed for your trouble.' He swigged the last of his tea and passed his cup for more. 'Anyway, how do you mean, she's been a good friend to you?' His eyes narrowed. 'Given you any money, has she?'

'No.'

He laughed. 'Thought not. Them do-gooders never do. Hands you her old cast-off clothes, I expect. Big deal! I read about her in the paper. I expect she's been generous with her advice, is that it? Warned you off nasty rough yobs like me. Her and her women's refuge. Wants to keep her nose out of other people's business, interferin' old bag.'

'Don't you talk that way about her. She isn't like that!' As he stepped up behind her and slipped his arms around her waist she tried to push him away. 'Leave off, Rick. I told you . . .'

'Oh, look, I know I've treated you a bit rough, Trace,' he murmured, pressing his lips close to her ear. 'But I always thought you liked it that way. And it don't mean I don't care about you. You were the first person I looked up when I got out of stir.'

'The first soft touch, you mean.'

'Don't be like that. I got into bad habits inside, an' when I first come out things was hard. But I've sorted meself out now. Straight up, Trace, I want us to get back together again. Set up home. Just you and me and little Damie – just like what we planned.' His voice took on a wheedling tone. 'You shouldn't be doin' a job like this, you know. You're worth somethin' better, a girl like you. You're a good hairdresser. I hate this job I'm doing. I'm not like you, see, with a trade to my name. I get all the rotten jobs to do. At everybody's beck an' call all day, I am. Now – if I moved in with you, I could look after the kid and you could go back to your proper job, full-time. What do you say, eh?'

'I couldn't do that, Rick. Mrs Grant gave me this job when I really needed it. I couldn't let her down now.'

'Not even for me?' He pulled her round to face him and fixed her with the persuasive brown eyes that had always been her undoing. He drew her towards him, kissing her hard. At first she stiffened, resisting him, but as he persisted he had the satisfaction of feeling her body begin to relax in his arms.

'Oh, Trace, I miss you,' he whispered into her hair. 'I lie awake in that dump they call a room and think of you alone in your bed, an' sometimes I feel like I'm goin' round the twist.' He pushed her back against the worktop and pressed close to her. 'I could always go an' look for some other girl, you know. There's plenty of 'em around. All of 'em willing. But you've spoilt me for anyone else, Trace. It's you I love and I want you so bad it hurts.'

Damian, feeling left out of things, chose that moment to emit a piercing shriek, drumming his little fists on the tray of his chair. Rick glanced round at him. 'Doesn't he have a sleep in the afternoons?'

'Yes.'

He pressed his mouth to hers again, parting her lips hungrily and pulling her so close she could scarcely breathe. She could feel his arousal pressing against her thigh and her heart began to beat faster. Reaching up, she tangled her fingers in his thick curly hair.

'Oh, Rick,' she murmured. But the words were lost in the moist heat of his kiss and she felt her excitement mounting, scattering her resolve like leaves in the wind.

'See to him now.' His voice was urgent and persuasive in her ear. 'Then you an' me can go upstairs.'

'No! We couldn't.'

'Yes, we could. No one'll know. Oh, come on, Trace. Please don't chuck me out again.'

'Mrs Grant – she might come back,' Tracey said breathlessly in a final, half-hearted attempt at resistance. But he was shaking his head at her, chuckling softly.

'Come off it. You know she won't, don't you? I saw her go and she had her briefcase with her. Some meetin' or other. They take hours.'

'Well . . .'

Damian was already half asleep when she put him into his pram and wheeled him out into the garden. Back in the kitchen Rick was waiting impatiently by the door, his hand held out to her invitingly.

In Charlotte's room only one single bed remained, the rest of the furniture having been removed to Park Row. Rick closed the door but Tracey opened it again.

'In case anyone comes back,' she said in a whisper. 'We wouldn't hear with the door closed.'

'You're always so scared,' Rick said as he sank onto the bed and pulled her towards him, his hands cupping her buttocks. 'You're like a little rabbit. You got rights the same as anyone else, Trace. We're not doin' any harm.'

He began to undress her, his hands roughly caressing her naked skin. Tracey began to shiver, all the promises she'd made to herself forgotten. She'd always known that if she once let Rick make love to her again she would be lost. She'd been fighting against it for weeks but now all she could think of was the clamouring need of her body for his.

He pulled her down beside him on the bed and slipped off her bra. His hand cupped one breast and he bent his head to nibble at the soft flesh, drawing the nipple deep into his mouth. She shuddered convulsively, sinking back against the pillow. His breath was warm in her ear and his lips on hers were like fire. It was too late to resist now. Much too late.

As his body pressed close to hers in the narrow confines of the single bed all thoughts of what was wise and prudent dissolved. And as he began to make love to her in the demanding, insistent way that had always thrilled her so, she felt her heart pound with feverish desire. She closed her eyes and heard the blood sing in her ears as she enclosed him with her limbs, matching her rhythm to his. It was so good, making love with Rick again. It had been so long. She wanted it to go on forever.

'So – what do you say then, Trace? Can I move in?'

Finally sated with their lovemaking she lay with her head on Rick's chest, her eyes half closed and her body bathed in a warm, rosy after-glow. 'I don't know,' she said dreamily.

He wound a strand of her hair around his fingers. 'Why not?'

' 'Cause Mrs Grant wouldn't like it.'

'What the hell has it got to do with her?' He gave her hair a tug to emphasise his resentment. 'She don't own you! Oh, come on, Trace. Just think, we could sleep together every night, all private in our own place. We could have it like this whenever we felt like it. No more snatchin' a crafty half hour in someone else's gaff. I could give up this poxy job on the buildin' site an' you could go back to your hairdressin'.'

'I'm not letting Mrs Grant down,' she said stubbornly. 'I told you, I can't leave. Not now.'

Rick shifted his position to look down at her. 'Don't kid yourself, Trace. If she decided she didn't need you no more, d'you reckon she'd keep you on out of the goodness of her heart? Would she 'ell! Why do you set so much store by her?'

'I told you, she's been a good friend. She's worked really hard to try and do something for single mums like me.'

'Well, you're not goin' to be a single mum no more, so she should be pleased for you. Anyway, what does *she* know about single mums?' he sneered.

'More'n you think,' she said enigmatically.

'How could she? A woman like her – pampered and spoilt, never been short of money in her life. How can *she* know what it's like?'

'Well, she does. Take my word for it.'

He raised himself and pinned her down, a hand on each shoulder. 'You believe anything anyone tells you, don't you? You'd believe the devil 'imself if he smiled at you. Time I was lookin' after you again, if you ask me.'

'It's true. I'm not stupid,' she protested. 'It's not just some story she made up. No one'd make up a thing like that.'

394

'A thing like what?'

'I can't tell you.'

'No, because there's nothing to tell. You're makin' it up just to let her off the hook.'

'No, I'm not!'

'Tell me then.'

She paused. Suddenly he seized her face in both hands and kissed her long and hard. Then he began to stroke her again in the way she always found irresistible, his fingers teasing the velvet soft skin of her inner thigh, breathing softly in her ear as his hand moved higher.

'Rick! Leave off,' she protested, trying to push his hand away. 'Time must be getting on. We can't risk gettin' caught.'

'Tell me then.'

'I told you, I can't.'

'Right.' He moved on top of her, pinning her down with his weight. 'Once more then. And afterwards I'm gonna have a bath in that ritzy bathroom next door.'

'*No!*' She struggled frantically. 'We've been up here for hours. Damie'll be awake by now and Mrs Grant must be due home any minute.'

But he held her fast, his knee holding her thighs apart, one hand grasping her breast, squeezing till he heard her gasp with pain. 'Tell me then! How come Lady Muck knows so much about bein' a single mum?'

'Because she had a baby herself before she married Mr Grant.' She twisted her head this way and that. 'You're hurting, Rick. Stop it and let me get up, can't you?'

He stopped his rough caressing and raised himself up to stare down at her, his eyes wide and incredulous. 'No *kidding*? Well, who'd have thought it? Just shows you, don't it? No better than anyone else for all their airs and graces. To some other guy, you mean?'

395

'Yes. And no one else knows. She told me in confidence, so don't you go shootin' your mouth off about it, Rick Kendle.'

' 'Course not.' He rolled over, releasing her abruptly. 'Go on then, *chicken*. I'll let you off – this time. Get up if you must.' As she got off the bed he gave her bottom a resounding slap. 'What do you say then, Trace? Can I move in or not?'

'No! Not after what you just did,' she said, close to tears as she pulled on her clothes. 'You always have to spoil things, Rick. You always did.' She looked down resentfully at him, lying on the bed with his hands behind his head, grinning impudently up at her. 'Are you gonna get up then, or what?'

'Okay, in a minute. But I'm still havin' that bath, no danger!' He grinned at her wickedly. 'An' if Lady Muck comes home you can just send her up to scrub my back! Give the poor cow a treat for once in her life.'

'So, I've been volunteered as baby-sitter in general, have I?'

Tom took the last of the planted hanging baskets from Fleur and hung it on its hook. 'There – what do you think then?'

Fleur beamed with pleasure. 'Trailing fuchsias, petunias and lobelia. It's all going to look wonderful when the flowers come into bloom. Thanks for helping, Tom.' She threw her arms around his neck and gave him a resounding kiss. 'What was that you said about baby-sitting?'

'This little Charlotte what's-her-name? I'm supposed to keep an eye on her, am I?'

'Only from a distance. I feel a bit responsible for her. You see, it was my suggestion that she should leave home and try living on her own.'

'What did you say her name is again?'

'I didn't.' She gave him a rueful look. 'But it happens to be Grant.'

He stared at her. 'Oh my God! She's not one of *those* Grants, is she?'

'Afraid so.'

'Does she know – about you?'

'No.'

'Why get involved then? Are you mad? Isn't life complicated enough for you? I thought you were keeping your distance.'

'I was. But you saw what happened the other night. I couldn't just turf her out into the night, could I? Look, when I first met Charlotte at night school I had no idea who she was. She doesn't seem to have any real friends and she's been having a rough time at home. Problems with her parents.'

'She's confiding all that to you?' He groaned. 'It gets worse!'

She took his hand and drew him back inside the flat. 'Never mind all that. Let's eat now.' She laughed. 'You know, you spend more time here now than when you lived here.'

'Don't change the subject, Fleur. You're playing with fire, do you know that? Next thing you know you'll be expected to take sides. Fancy letting yourself get sucked into the Grants' family problems.'

'I don't see what else I could have done. Once Charlotte's had a taste of coping alone, and when things have had time to cool down, she'll probably go home again anyway.'

'Well, I hope you're right.'

They prepared their meal together in companionable silence. Outside spring was beginning to bloom in earnest. The sun still shone and a solitary blackbird was singing in the dusty branches of the fir tree at the bottom of the garden. They left the doors to the balcony open, enjoying the balmy air and the last of the evening sunshine.

'When does Sally leave for Switzerland?' Tom asked.

'In a couple of weeks' time.'

He ate in silence for a moment, glancing across at her surreptitiously. 'Does it bother you?'

'No. I'm looking forward to managing on my own. There's an eighteenth birthday party booked for the Tuesday of that week and Beardsley Engineering is having a social evening on the Friday.'

'That's not what I meant, and I think you know it.'

'Oh. The wedding, you mean. I've told you, Tom. Whatever I felt for Peter is over and done with.'

'And the thought of him marrying someone else doesn't hurt?'

'Why should it?'

He nodded. 'Just wanted to know.' He got up and began to clear the table, but Fleur stood up and took the dishes from him, putting them back on the table.

'Leave that for now.' She took his hand and drew him towards the settee. 'Tom, what do I have to do to convince you?' She sat and pulled him down beside her. 'I allowed myself to be taken in. I was made a fool of and I want to forget it. I wish you'd let me.'

'Sorry.' He sighed and leaned back, his arm around her shoulders. 'Call it vanity if you like but I hate the thought of being second best.'

She turned her head to look up at him. 'You could never be that, Tom,' she said softly, 'especially to someone like Peter Arden.'

For a moment her eyes held his, then he said, 'It's just that I love you, Fleur. Okay, I know I'm not supposed to say it and I don't expect you to respond, but it's nice to get it off my chest.'

She reached up to kiss him. 'You're the nicest person in the world.' Her dark eyes twinkled at him. 'By the way, did you remember to bring your toothbrush?'

He smiled. 'Funny you should ask.' He kissed her and for a while they sat wrapped in each other's arms, contentedly silent. Then he asked, 'You don't regret not being able to be a part of your mother's life, do you, Fleur?'

'No. I always knew she'd have a new life and family,' she said. 'I never really expected her to want to acknowledge me.' She rubbed her cheek against his. 'Besides, look at all I've got. I've got the flat almost the way I want it. I've got a super job that I enjoy. And best of all I've got you. Sometimes I wonder what I've done to be so lucky. I think that coming to Elvemere was the best thing I ever did.'

Fleur wakened during the night. The moon was full. Shining in through the windows, it bathed the room in silver light and made everything, even the threadbare carpet, look brand new. That was how she felt. Last night, her first with Tom, had been like a revelation. He had made love to her so reverently and gently. Yet his lovemaking had been no less exciting for that.

Now I know, she told herself with a little shiver of satisfaction. Now I know what love really is. And now that I know everything suddenly makes sense, like the last piece of a puzzle falling into place. She raised herself on one elbow to look down at Tom's sleeping face. In repose he looked so young and defenceless and a surge of love swept through her as she bent to kiss him. He stirred and opened his eyes.

'Hello,' he mumbled drowsily.

'Hi. Can I tell you something?' She snuggled down close beside him, her eyes intent on his face.

He yawned. 'Can it wait till morning?'

'No. It can't. It can't wait a second longer.'

'Okay then, what?'

'It's just that I love you,' she whispered, her lips close to his. 'Really love you, I mean. In other words, I think we've passed the test.'

His arms closed around her and he smiled in blissful content. 'That's wonderful,' he murmured sleepily. 'Now, can we get some sleep? I'll give you your certificate in the morning.'

Chapter 14

Sally was packed and ready to go. Her suitcases were in the car and she stood giving final instructions to Fleur on the front doorstep.

'I think you'll manage all right with two helpers for the birthday party, but for the social at Beardsley's you might need four,' she said.

Fleur laughed. 'It's all laid on, Sally. I did it yesterday. Betty and Paula are helping me with the party and I've booked Mrs Thompson and her daughter Doris to team up with them on Friday.'

'Of course.' Sally smiled apologetically, but halfway through the door she stopped again. 'The birthday cake. They asked for it to have a floral decoration. You'll have to get onto Harvey's the florist's. Freesias, I think. Ask them to make you a spray with . . .'

'Ordered yesterday,' Fleur told her. 'Stop worrying, Sally. Go and enjoy yourself.'

Sally sighed. 'I know I shouldn't keep reminding you. It's natural, I suppose. This is the first time I've ever left the business in anyone else's hands.'

'I know. You told me – several times.'

'Am I being a frightful fuss-pot?' Sally took both of Fleur's hands in hers. 'Thank you, Fleur. Without you I might not have been able to go to Peter's wedding.

These two functions were booked months ago. I couldn't have cancelled them.'

'Of course not. Don't worry, everything will be fine.'

'Of course. I know it will. Now – have you any messages for Peter?'

'Messages?' Fleur was startled for a moment.

'Yes. You two did become quite good friends when he was here last, didn't you?'

'Oh.' Fleur made herself laugh. 'Of course. Just wish him every happiness from me.'

Sally kissed her cheek. 'I will, my dear.' She began to pull on her gloves. 'And I'll ring, of course, the minute I get there.'

'If you ever do get there!' Fleur gave her a little push. 'Go *on*. You'll miss the plane.'

She followed Sally, still fussing, out onto the drive. 'Maybe I should have gone up last night,' she said as she seated herself behind the wheel. 'By train – stayed in one of the airport hotels overnight. That would have meant taking another day though. I just hope the traffic isn't too heavy on the motorway.' She started the engine and slipped the car into gear. 'Well, here I go. 'Bye then!' She waved as the car moved forward. 'See you in a week's time.'

'See you. Have a lovely time! And don't worry!' Fleur waved until the car was out of sight, then went back indoors and closed the door with a sigh of relief.

Sally had done nothing but worry and fret for the past week. She had even suggested that Fleur should move into the house while she was away, but Fleur had managed to talk her out of that idea. Now that the days were getting warmer she had been able to have the balcony windows open so she could see her plants growing. It was so exciting watching the buds grow fatter and burst into bloom. Not long now before she'd be able to have breakfast outside in the morning sunshine. She planned to share the experience for the first time with Tom, on the very first warm morning. It was something special to look forward to.

As she went through the morning routine, dealing with the mail and attending to orders and accounts, she thought of Charlotte. The girl seemed to have settled in well at Park Row. Sadie reported that she took her turn diligently along with herself and Tom when it came to the chores. She was quiet and clean. 'In fact, I'd hardly know she was there,' she said. Fleur worried slightly about this. Charlotte had been a bright, outgoing girl when she first met her. Now she seemed to have lost touch with most of her schoolfriends and become withdrawn and solitary.

Fleur had left the younger girl to settle for a week before popping round to Park Row to see her one evening. She found her in the kitchen, happily preparing her evening meal, a businesslike apron over the skirt and blouse she wore for the office, and Fleur was pleased to see her looking happy and relaxed.

'I never knew that cooking could be such fun,' Charlotte said, looking up from the pan she was stirring. 'I got fed up with those supermarket ready-meals so I bought myself this little book. It's got recipes for meals for one person. It's really good.'

'Why don't you ask a friend round?' Fleur suggested. 'To show off your cooking.'

Charlotte looked doubtful. 'I don't think anyone I knew at school would be interested,' she said.

'Don't you see them any more?' Fleur asked. 'Don't you go out – to discos or the cinema?'

Charlotte shook her head. 'Not really. Most of the people I used to be friendly with have gone to college.'

'Surely they aren't all away at college? Why not look up some of them now that you're here?' Fleur suggested. 'I bet they'd be impressed no end to know you had your own pad.'

The younger girl shrugged. 'I'm happy on my own.'

'My best friend has gone to college but I haven't lost touch with her,' Fleur said. 'We write to each other. I'd hate to think of us drifting apart after all the years we've been friends.'

'Maybe you've still got things in common,' Charlotte said. 'Anyway I never really had a best friend.'

'Well then, why not ask your mum?' Fleur suggested. 'I know she must be dying to see your room and she won't come unless you invite her, you know.'

'I don't know that I'm ready for that yet.' Charlotte stirred her pan, eyes downcast. 'She'd probably just say she was too busy anyway.'

'Not for you. I'm sure she'd love to come.'

'If I did ask her, would you come too? It would help to have you here.'

Fleur hesitated. 'I'm sure she'd rather it was just the two of you,' she said. 'But whatever you decide, you don't have to be lonely.'

'I know.'

'Tom and I aren't far away.'

'I *know*. You don't have to baby me.' Charlotte looked up. 'If you've come to see him, he's not in yet.'

'It was you I came to see, not Tom.' Fleur looked at her. 'Charlotte – you are happy here, aren't you? I mean, you're not just sticking it out to prove a point?'

'No! This is the best thing I ever did. Even work doesn't seem so bad now that I have my own place to come home to.'

'Have you been back to see them?'

'Mum and Dad?' Charlotte shook her head. 'If I went there'd only be a row. Anyway I see enough of Dad at the office and he's in a rotten mood most of the time.'

'Look, it's just a suggestion, but if you're at a loose end you could always come and give us a hand at

Arden's if you felt like it? Earn yourself a bit of extra pocket money.'

Charlotte's face brightened. 'Could I really? That might be good fun.'

'Come and help me while Sally's away,' Fleur suggested. 'There's a birthday party on the Wednesday. I'll come and pick you up – around six okay?'

'Yes, fine.' Charlotte hesitated, then said confidentially, 'To tell the truth, Fleur, I've been out to the stables a couple of times on the quiet to see Auntie Kath. I hate doing it behind Dad's back and I'm scared that if he found out she would get into trouble.' Charlotte sighed. 'But when he plays the heavy father the way he does, he leaves me no alternative.' She turned back to her cooking. 'Sometimes I think that Dad doesn't really know me at all. He just knows what he wants me to be like. I hate lies and deception,' she said unhappily. 'There have been too many lies in our family already.'

Too many lies. Fleur was silent. Charlotte was unaware of just how many lies and secrets there really were. Or the enormity of them. Maybe it was just as well. She watched as the younger girl began to dish up her meal, tipping the drained spaghetti onto her plate and heaping the Bolognese sauce she had prepared on top. She turned to look at Fleur, her eyes shining.

'Can you keep another secret, Fleur?'

'Of course. If you're sure you want to tell me.'

'I do. Auntie Kath has taken this boy on. Well, he's a man really. He's nineteen! His name's James Parker and he's hoping to become a show jumper. He's a terrific rider and absolutely marvellous with the horses. His dad is an ophthalmic surgeon and James works in an accountant's office in the daytime and helps out at the stables in the evenings and weekends.'

Fleur smiled. 'I see. Is he good-looking?'

'Not bad,' Charlotte said, blushing.

'And you and he get along well, do you?'

Charlotte smiled as she put her plate on a tray along with a knife and fork. 'Yes. It's amazing how much we've got in common. His dad wants him to drop the horses and concentrate on exams, but James is determined to have a career with horses if he possibly can – like me.' She picked up her tray and looked at Fleur enquiringly. 'Are you coming up with me?'

'No. I'd better go now – let you eat your meal in peace. Don't forget where I live, will you? Come and see my balcony soon. The spring flowers are coming out and it's going to look lovely.'

As she went about the morning routine Fleur thought about Charlotte. She seemed to be much more like her old self since she'd moved into her little bed-sit and met this James of hers. And she really didn't seem to mind being on her own.

As for her own life, she could hardly believe how much things had changed in one short year. Tom still wanted her to move in with him, but Fleur was adamant. Spending their free time together, having him stay for the occasional night, was as much as she wanted for the moment. She was so afraid that their relationship might burn out if they took things too hurriedly. She knew now that she loved and trusted him. She looked forward to being with him whenever they were both free. But although she couldn't tell him as much, she still wasn't completely convinced that she wanted to devote her whole life to him, or to any one person if it came to that. Her new independence was valuable to her and for the moment what she and Tom had was enough. Sometimes he grew frustrated and impatient when she refused to budge, but she stood her ground, believing that if their feelings were strong enough they would stand the test of time.

When she had finished dealing with the mail she rang the client whose party was next on her list and discussed details and checked times. Then she rang Beardsley Engineering and asked to be put through to Anne Roberts, the personnel manager, who was arranging the social evening. There was quite a lengthy wait before she came to the phone. When she did she sounded harassed and put out.

'I'm sorry to keep you waiting,' she said. 'We've had rather a traumatic morning here.'

'Really? Is anything wrong?'

'You could say that.'

'Anything I should know about?'

'Not really but the news will be public pretty soon so I might as well tell you. I've just been informed that the firm is going into liquidation.'

'Oh, no!'

'Afraid it's true. And I've got the thankless job of handing out all the redundancy notices. You can guess how I feel.'

Fleur's heart sank. 'Oh, dear. So are you saying that you want to cancel the social evening on Friday?'

'Looks like it. I'd have got round to ringing you later in the day.'

'Well, I understand of course, under the circumstances.'

'I can't see anyone enjoying themselves, even if they turn up. I'm sorry about that.'

'I'm sorry too,' Fleur said. 'But it can't be helped.'

'Thanks. It's good of you to be so understanding. I'm afraid we won't be the last firm in Elvemere to feel the pinch,' Anne said. 'From what I hear everyone's orders seem to have been dropping off over the past months.'

Back in the kitchen, as Fleur sliced wafer thin bread for sandwiches, she wondered how the closing of

Beardsley's would affect the town. It was the largest factory in Elvemere and employed a lot of people. It would certainly swell the number of unemployed in the area and was bound to have a knock-on affect on all other businesses in the town too, including Arden Catering. She wondered if Tom had heard the news.

Wiping her hands, she went to the telephone and dialled the number of the *Clarion*. She asked for the news desk in the hope that he was in. Luckily he was.

'Fleur? Is something wrong?'

'No, I'm fine. I wouldn't have rung you at work but I wondered if you'd heard that Beardsley's is going out of business.'

'No! Are you sure?'

'Positive. I've just been talking to Mrs Roberts, the personnel manager. She was pretty choked about it. They've cancelled their social evening on Friday.'

'Well, thanks for tipping me off. I'll get round there right away.'

'You won't say Mrs Roberts told me, will you?' she asked. 'She probably wishes by now that she'd kept quiet about it.'

'A journalist never reveals his sources, don't you know that?' Tom told her. 'Have to go now, love. See you.'

Fleur hung up and paused to think about Sally. It was a good thing she had already left for Switzerland. She'd worried enough about leaving as it was. If she'd heard this news before she went she'd have worried even more.

Louise paid off the taxi and walked up the drive of the house in Hazel Grove. Joanna's little red sports car stood on the drive so Louise knew she was home. She hoped Joanna was alone. She'd thought carefully about what she'd come to say and it was for Joanna's ears only.

Louise had dressed very carefully for her visit, putting on the one classic navy blue suit in her wardrobe. Some instinct told her that she was going to need every shred of dignity she could summon for the coming interview. Nevertheless, when she stood looking at herself in the full-length mirror in her bedroom she couldn't help feeling how stark and plain she looked in the dark suit and white blouse. Opening her jewel case she put on her anniversary pearls and matching earrings, and, after a moment's consideration, added the large diamond and ruby brooch Charlie had given her last Christmas. Jewellery always gave her confidence. Without it she felt naked and vulnerable. The opulent pieces in place, she smiled at her reflection with satisfaction. Yes. That was better.

She paused outside the front door of Joanna's house, then extended one gloved finger and rang the bell.

When Joanna opened the door, her eyebrows rose in surprise. 'Oh! It's Mrs Grant, isn't it?'

'I think you know very well it is,' Louise said between gritted teeth. 'Unless my memory is better than yours.'

'What can I do for you?'

'You can ask me in for a start,' Louise told her bluntly. 'Unless you want your neighbours to hear every word I say.'

'Of course.' Joanna held the door open. 'Do come in, Mrs Grant. Can I get you something? A cup of tea perhaps?'

'No, thanks.'

'Well, come through anyway.' Joanna led the way to her sitting room and invited her to take a chair. She looked at Louise enquiringly. 'Now – is there something I can help you with?' she asked pleasantly.

'There certainly is! I want you to withdraw your

409

investment from GPC and go back to where you came from,' Louise said bluntly.

Joanna's smile remained though her eyebrows rose a fraction. 'I'm sure you know that isn't possible, Mrs Grant,' she said patronisingly. 'I'm a partner now. And I think the money I put into the firm is already committed.'

'That's just the point. My husband is overstretching the firm. You've given him big ideas with all your talk about your big business in American – what-d'you-call-it? – *real* estate! Vernon and I are right worried about it, I can tell you. But we'd just about manage if you were to pull out now . . .'

'But I'm not *going* to pull out.' Joanna's smile turned frosty. 'Did Vernon send you?'

'Of course he didn't! No one knows I'm here. I'm asking you to leave. Your influence is going to wreck everything my husband and son have worked for, so if you've got any kind of a conscience at all you'll do as I say.'

Joanna reached into the box on the coffee table for a cigarette and lit it slowly. 'Why is it I'm getting such a strong feeling of déjà vu?' she asked, exhaling smoke. 'I seem to remember our having a very similar conversation once before. In fact, when I come to think of it, you used the very same words that time.'

'Oh, so your memory's come back, has it?' Louise folded her arms and met Joanna's gaze levelly. 'That time you saw the sense of what I was asking,' she said. 'I'm asking you to see sense again now, before it's too late.'

'It rather depends on your idea of what good sense is, doesn't it? Last time you bribed me to leave your son alone. If I remember correctly I don't think you saw me as quite suitable. I was young and as it happened I needed the money you tempted me with.' She shook

410

her head mockingly. 'Oh, you were *seriously* interested in getting rid of me that time, weren't you, Mrs Grant? But this time the situation is rather different. We've all moved on in life. I don't know what incentive you were thinking of offering this time, but I can tell you that whatever you have in mind, it won't work. I'm here to stay because it suits me, and there's nothing you can do about it, I'm afraid.'

'I've got money invested in the firm too, you know.'

'Ah, but only in a joint holding with Charlie,' Joanna said. 'You have no vote, have you? No actual say in what happens. That rather surprises me, Mrs Grant, for a strong-minded woman like you, if you don't mind my saying so.'

Louise seethed inwardly. 'That's none of your damned business.' Her eyes narrowed. 'Come to that, why have you come back here anyway? Vernon tells me you did pretty well in America. You got a good divorce settlement. Why come back when you could spend your life enjoying yourself – do anything you wanted?'

'Because I want to do this,' Joanna said simply. 'This is what I enjoy.'

Louise was silent for a moment, wishing she could see into the mind of this complex woman; figure out what was really going on in that devious mind of hers. 'Is it *him* – Vernon – you want?' she said at last. 'Because you won't get him. If you insist on staying I might find it necessary to tell him how readily you dropped him before, for cash in hand. I don't think he'd find it very flattering, do you?'

'Maybe not.' Joanna shrugged. 'But if that's what you feel you must do, then tell him by all means,' she said. 'I think Vernon is mature enough now to appreciate his mother's motives for getting rid of girls she disapproved of. How many more were there, Mrs

411

Grant, before you found a girl who was stupid and gullible enough to be manipulated into fuelling your greed?'

'How dare you! It was nothing of the sort!' Louise's self-control was running out fast. She got to her feet, her colour heightening. 'How could I let him ruin his life with a little trollop like you?' she said. 'Everyone in town knew you'd sleep with anything in trousers – married or single. You even squeezed extra money out of me by conning me into thinking you were pregnant. You weren't having our Vernie's child at all, were you? It was just a trick to get more cash out of me.'

Joanna smiled. 'How perceptive of you, Mrs Grant. How could I *ever* have hoped to pull the wool over your eyes? But you seem to forget that this was all a very long time ago. Even money loses its potency in the end. I'm sure we've all learned the cruel lessons nature teaches us by now.' She stubbed out her cigarette. 'I'm afraid that, whether you like it or not, I am part of GPC now and there isn't one single thing you can do to alter the fact.' She walked to the door and held it open. 'I'm afraid I'll have to ask you to leave now. Shall I ring for a taxi for you?'

'*No!*' Louise pushed past her into the hall. 'I'll walk down to the phone box and ring for one myself. I'm not stopping in this house a minute longer than I have to.'

'Just as you wish.' Joanna opened the front door and saw with some satisfaction that it was beginning to rain. 'In that case, I'll say goodbye. Thank you so much for calling, Mrs Grant,' she called to Louise's broad, indignant back. 'Please feel free to call again – any time you're passing.'

She closed the door and leaned against it, a smile of triumph on her face. The telephone kiosk was about half a mile away. By the time Louise had trekked down

412

to it she'd be soaked through. Joanne began to laugh. She'd dreamed of such a scene for years. It had been well worth waiting for.

Charlie had just finished dictating the last of his letters when Vernon burst into his office.

'Have you heard the news?'

Charlie nodded to his secretary. 'Thanks, Phyllis. I'd like those to go off as soon as possible.' He looked up at Vernon as the door closed behind her. 'I wish you wouldn't come bursting in like that,' he said. 'I could have had anyone with me; might have had old Phyllis on my knee – been at what you might call a delicate state of negotiations.' He chuckled up into Vernon's anxious face.

'This is a delicate state all right,' he said. 'I've just heard the local news on the car radio. Beardsley's is going into receivership.'

The grin vanished from Charlie's face and he stared at his son in disbelief. 'Can't be. That can't be right! I saw Jim Beardsley only the other night at the Lodge meeting. He never dropped s' much as a hint.'

'Well, he wouldn't, would he? But it's true! They'd hardly have put it out over the radio if it wasn't.' Vernon dropped into the chair that Phyllis had vacated. 'You know what this means, don't you? Nearly all the houses that have been completed on the Meadowlands Park Estate have been reserved by executives and senior employees of Beardsley's.'

Charlie waved a dismissive hand at him. 'So what? We'll soon resell them. Houses like those are always in demand.'

'At the price we're asking? When there's such insecurity about? What we have to ask ourselves is, if Beardsley's have gone bust, who's going to be next? You know as well as I do that they were the key industry

413

in Elvemere. Dad, look, I'm serious . . .' Vernon leaned forward earnestly. 'I think we should drop the Victoria Gardens project – now, before it's too late.'

'It's already too late. I signed the contract with old mother Franks yesterday. The plans have been passed. We've got the go-ahead. We can't pull out now.'

Vernon's colour drained. 'It's sheer madness. Did you get a survey done?'

'What for? We're going to have to gut the places anyway. Oh, don't be such an old woman, Vern. You're getting as bad as Harry. Look, if Meadowlands is going to take a bit longer to get off the ground, all the more reason for us to have another iron on the fire. We'll drop the price of the Meadowlands houses if necessary. Get them off our hands.'

'We're working on a low profit margin now,' Vernon argued.

'Well, we'll put cheaper fittings in those we haven't finished.'

'The fittings have already been bought. They're sitting in the store now, waiting.'

'Leave out the jacuzzis and the swimming pools then. Oh, don't worry about it, Vern. Everything's going to be fine. I'm seeing Bill Watts at the bank this afternoon. I'll ask him to extend our overdraft. He'll understand.'

Vernon sighed. 'I hope to God you're right.'

Charlie looked at his watch and began to get up from the desk. 'Damn you, Vern. Look at the time! I'll be hard pressed to be on time for my appointment now. You and your mitherin'.'

'Look, maybe I'd better come with you?'

'*No!*' Charlie was pulling on his coat. 'Bill and I go back a long way. We understand each other. You go sticking your panicky four penn'orth in and you'll only go and mess things up.'

Fleur was halfway up the stairs to her flat that evening when the telephone began to ring in the hall. She paused. It was probably for Ivy or one of the other tenants. But when no one else answered it she retraced her steps and walked down the hall to pick it up.

'Hello. Thirteen Victoria Gardens. Who are you calling?'

'Can I speak to a Miss Sylvester, please? Miss Fleur Sylvester?'

'Yes – speaking.' Fleur was surprised. She didn't recognise the voice. 'Who is it?'

'Sergeant Stanbridge of Hertfordshire Constabulary. I'm speaking from the police station, Miss Sylvester. Are you a friend of a Mrs Sarah Arden of twenty-two Fairfield Drive, Elvemere?'

'Yes, I work for her. I'm her assistant. Why – is something wrong?'

'I'm sorry to have to tell you that Mrs Arden was involved in an accident on the M1 several hours ago. We've only just recovered her handbag from the wreckage of her car. We found your name and number in it.'

The wreckage of her car! Fleur's heart froze. Out of the corner of her eye she was aware of Ivy's presence. She was standing at the top of the basement stairs, watching and listening, but Fleur was too preoccupied to be irritated.

'Where is she now?' she asked.

'She's in the intensive care unit at St Elspeth's Hospital, Miss Sylvester. I'm ringing to ask if you know who her next-of-kin would be?'

'Her son. But he's in Switzerland. She was on her way to his – his wedding!' Her throat constricted. Oh, God, poor Sally! All afternoon Fleur had been picturing her happy excitement at landing in Switzerland and meeting

Peter, when all the time she had been lying in hospital. 'I'll ring him at once,' she said. 'I've got his number, but I've no idea how long it will take him to get here. How is Sally? Can I drive down there and see her?'

'She's unconscious, I'm afraid.'

Fleur's blood ran cold. 'How – how bad?'

At the other end of the line the policeman cleared his throat. 'I can only tell you that she has severe injuries, miss. They'll be able to tell you more at the hospital.'

Fleur's hand clutched at the receiver convulsively. It sounded so ominous. 'But – she'll get better, won't she?'

'I'm very sorry, miss, but I can't tell you any more.' Again he cleared his throat. 'If you could let her son know as soon as possible? We can notify him if you wish but I think if you know him . . .'

'Yes, of course. I'll do it now.'

'Not bad news, I hope?' Ivy was standing at her side now, her eyes bright with morbid curiosity.

'Yes. Yes it was. I have to make a call.' Fleur's hands shook as she rummaged in her bag for coins then leafed through her diary for the number of Peter's future father-in-law's hotel, the contact number that Sally had given her only this morning. She found it and turned to Ivy who was still standing there. 'Please – if you don't mind, it's private.'

Ivy bridled. 'Well, pardon me I'm sure! I was only trying to help. The last thing I ever do is pry into other folks' business!' She began to turn, then paused. 'While I think of it, I've been meaning to speak to you. P'raps you'll come down when you've got a minute?'

'Yes, all right,' Fleur said abstractedly as she began to dial.

Snorting indignantly, Ivy turned and stumped down the basement stairs, closing the door with a bang at the bottom.

Fleur finished dialling the number, then stood biting her lip anxiously as she waited. To her relief it was Peter's voice that answered. She could not have coped with someone who didn't speak English.

'Peter, it's Fleur. I'm afraid I've got some very bad news for you.'

'Mother? Something's wrong? I've been waiting for hours at the airport and there are no more flights today. I've only just got in.'

She told him as gently as she could, trying hard to keep her voice from breaking. 'I'm going to drive down there now to be with her,' she told him. 'Can you get a flight, do you think?'

'Of course. It may not be until tomorrow, but I'll be there.' He paused, then added, 'Fleur – how bad is she? Have they said?'

'I only spoke to the policeman. All he said was that she had severe injuries. I don't know any more than that. Shall I ring you again from the hospital when I've seen her?'

'No, I'll get onto the airport at once and see if I can get a night flight.'

Fleur was halfway up the stairs again when she remembered that Ivy had asked to see her. It was probably just an excuse to pump her for information about Sally, but if she was going to have to drive down to Hertfordshire this evening she had better get it over with. She turned and made her way down to the basement. Ivy was in her small scullery, frying fish for her tea. Fleur tapped on the door.

'You said you wanted to see me.'

Ivy removed the cigarette from the corner of her mouth. 'After tea would have done,' she said tetchily.

'I have to go out right away,' Fleur said. 'I have to drive down to Hertfordshire this evening.'

With a resigned sigh Ivy put her half-smoked

cigarette down on the corner of the draining board and turned off the gas under the frying pan. 'Well, since you ask, I'm afraid I've got to give you notice to quit,' she said abruptly.

Fleur stared at her. '*Notice?* But why?'

Ivy folded her arms. 'I told you when you first come that I wasn't keen on girl tenants and now you've proved me right.'

'I – don't know what you mean. How have I proved you right?'

'You been havin' men up in your room,' Ivy said accusingly. '*All night!*'

'Men. Do you mean Tom?'

'He's a man, isn't he?'

'Yes, but it isn't the way you make it sound,' Fleur argued. 'Tom and I, we're . . .'

'You're not *married*, are you? Nor yet engaged either – not as far as I know. In my book that amounts to loose morals and I don't allow it. Not under my roof.'

Fleur bit her lip. She was going to lose the flat that she'd worked so hard on. Her beloved home. And her balcony garden. Just when it was coming into bloom. A lump thickened her throat. 'Please, Ivy, I'm sure we can work this one out,' she said. 'If you don't want Tom to stay then he won't, but don't make me leave. I've worked so hard to make the flat nice.' It felt like grovelling but she didn't care. Coming on top of the news about Sally it was too much to handle.

'I'm sorry but I got me principles,' Ivy said self-righteously. 'And even if I hadn't, I'd still have to ask you to leave. I've sold this place, y' see.'

Fleur stared at her. 'Sold it? Who to?' Her shattered hopes rose. 'What about the new people – will they let the rooms?'

'Gonna pull it to bits,' Ivy said, her eyes glinting with vindictive triumph. 'Turn it into a block of offices.'

418

Fleur's heart sank. 'How long?' she asked resignedly. 'When do you need me to get out?'

'A month's notice is what I have to give,' she said. 'But if you take my advice you'll go as soon as you can find somewhere else. If you find a place before your time is up, we'll come to some arrangement about the rent.'

Fleur was stunned into silence. It was as though history was repeating itself. Last time she'd been given notice it came at a traumatic time. 'I can't do anything right now,' she said. 'I have to go out. I may not be back at all tonight.'

'Oh? Goin' off on some jaunt with 'im then, are you?' Ivy said nastily.

Fleur turned, her dark eyes flashing dangerously. 'As a matter of fact, Mrs Arden, my employer, has been seriously injured in a car accident. I'm on my way to the hospital in Hertfordshire to see her!' Banging the door on Ivy's indignant expression she ran up the stairs, her eyes stinging with tears. In the hall she picked up the telephone and dialled. Charlotte answered.

'Hello?'

'Charlotte, it's me, Fleur. Is Tom there?'

'No. He rushed in and grabbed something to eat about half an hour ago – said he had to go out on some assignment or other.'

'Oh, no!' Fleur bit her lip. Just when she needed him so badly.

'Can I give him a message? Can he ring you back?'

'No. Look, Charlotte, will you tell him that I have to go down to Hertfordshire tonight? Mrs Arden has been involved in a serious road accident.'

'Oh, Fleur, how awful! Can I do anything to help?'

'No. Just tell Tom.'

'I'll leave a note for him on the board in the kitchen,'

Charlotte said. 'That's what we do. He'll be sure to see it there.'

'Are you all right, Charlotte?'

'I'm fine. Mum was going to come round this evening but she rang to say there was some kind of crisis. I think she and Dad have had another row.'

'I'll call you when I get back. 'Bye for now.'

Upstairs Fleur pushed a change of underclothes and her toothbrush into a bag and checked to see that she had enough money for food and perhaps an overnight room. The fact that she was about to lose her flat was only just sinking in. She stood in the middle of the room and looked around her. Everything she had was between these four walls. Her space and privacy, her independence. It was her achievement, the vital proof to herself that she could stand alone. She'd had it for such a short time and now she was about to lose it again. She went to the window and looked out onto the sunlit balcony. The tubs of daffodils, crocuses and grape hyacinths were in flower now and the bulging green tulip buds were magically changing colour, a little each day, scarlet and pink and gold. Soon the little balcony would be a riot of sumptuous colour. But before that happened she'd be gone – who knew where? She swallowed hard at the lump in her throat and turned quickly away, ashamed of her selfishness. How could she stand here feeling sorry for herself when Sally lay unconscious and gravely hurt?

Since the afternoon of reckless abandonment Tracey had enjoyed with Rick at the Grants' house she had been filled with fear and trepidation. Remembering that afternoon still made her go hot and cold at the thought of what might have happened. It was a miracle they'd got away with it.

After she came downstairs that afternoon she'd gone

through torture, knowing that Rick was still upstairs taking a leisurely bath in the Grants' en-suite bathroom when Julia might walk in at any minute.

She had remained in the hall, eyes glancing anxiously upwards as she strained her ears for the sound of Julia's car on the drive outside. Every muscle in her body was tense until at last Rick had come swaggering downstairs trailing a cloud of Vernon's aftershave in which he had obviously drenched himself. He wore a smile of smug defiance on his face.

'That was ace!' he announced. 'I could get used to living in a place like this.'

With a shrill admonishment she had grasped him by the arm and bundled him hastily out through the back door, telling him not to come back if he knew what was good for him. Locking the door firmly, she had rushed upstairs to eradicate every trace of him. Flinging the window open to let out the tell-tale steam, she had cleaned the tidemark off the bath and picked up the sodden towels from the floor where he had dropped them. Fetching the hoover, she had swept up the spilled talcum from the carpet and put the top back on the big bottle of Givenchy bath essence. As she worked she cursed herself for the fool she had been. She had known all the time they were making love that she was storing up trouble for herself. Why was she so weak when it came to sex? Why couldn't she have just said no and told him to sling his hook?

For a couple of weeks she thought she had got away with it. But now to her horror it was catching up with her in more ways than one. Rick had obviously taken more than just a bath that afternoon.

Two days ago she had frozen with dismay when she overheard Vernon asking his wife if she had seen his gold cufflinks. Then this morning he had missed the Rolex watch he'd been given for his twenty-first birthday. As she lingered over dusting the stairs this morning she had heard herself accused of theft as Vernon ranted at Julia over breakfast.

'It must be her. Who else could it possibly be? I told you at the time it was madness to employ someone with no references when we're both out so much. Why are you so easily taken in when it comes to these people? You're incredibly naive and stupid! You're so obsessed by all your do-gooding that you can't see that you're being taken for a ride. Soon we'll have every villain in the county round here, robbing us blind!'

'You don't know that you've been robbed,' Julia protested weakly.

'Can't you see that these wretched inadequate so-called battered women of yours probably deserve all they get?' he said. 'Well, you do what you like, but I'm not having them in this house, helping themselves to whatever takes their fancy. Get rid of her, Julia. Do it today.'

'I know Tracey wouldn't do a thing like that,' Julia insisted. 'She's honest, I'd stake my life on it. I once offered to pay her electricity bill when she'd been cut off and she wouldn't take the money.'

'You did *what*? You fool, Julia. Can't you see what kind of message that sent out? It was worth her while to refuse the money then, wasn't it? A sprat to catch a mackerel! The girl obviously thinks you're a soft touch.'

'I don't believe for one minute that your watch has been stolen,' Julia said firmly. 'You can't have looked properly. 'You're always putting things down somewhere and mislaying them.'

'It's gone, I tell you. The watch *and* the cufflinks. They were both in the top drawer of my bedside table. For heaven's sake, Julia! As if I hadn't enough to worry about, what with my only daughter cast out to live among drop-outs and getting up to God knows what.'

'Charlotte is *not* living among drop-outs, and if you took the trouble to go round to see the house where she's living, you'd know that. Anyway, it was you who drove her out with your bullying and lies.'

Vernon snorted impatiently. 'As if I've got time to worry about things like that when Dad's doing his level best to ruin the business. You're the girl's mother. That kind of thing is down to you – along with the domestic arrangements. Surely you can do that! I want you to sack that thieving girl! Do you hear what I'm saying? That's one worry I *can* eliminate. I don't want her in the house any more after today. And if she's here when I get home, I'll kick her out myself!'

'Before you ask me to start accusing innocent people of stealing, perhaps you should ask Joanna if you left your watch and cufflinks there last time you slept with her!' Julia said.

'Listen to you!' Vernon's voice was scathing. 'You're even beginning to think and talk like them!' From where she stood on the stairs, Tracey heard his exasperated snort and the scraping sound his chair made on the ceramic floor tiles in the kitchen. She hurried to the landing and kept out of sight behind the banisters until she heard the front door slam, then she crept down to the kitchen and put her head round the door.

'Mrs Grant.'

'Oh, Tracey, have you finished upstairs?' As Julia turned with a start from the sink where she was washing up the breakfast things, Tracey was dismayed to see tears on her cheeks.

'Not quite. I came down because I couldn't help overhearing Mr Grant just now. There's something I think you ought to know.'

Julia dried her hands and indicated a chair. 'Sit down, Tracey. I'll make us some coffee.'

'No, I'll make it in a minute. I want to tell you first –

get it off my chest.' She sat down opposite Julia. 'Rick's been coming round here. I never asked him to and I tried not to let him in but there was one afternoon a few weeks' ago when he wouldn't take no for an answer.' She took a deep breath. 'He talked me round. Said he was sorry about that other time – that he'd turned over a new leaf. He said . . .' She glanced anxiously at Julia. 'Said he still loved me. I know it was wrong and – and silly of me, but I let him . . .' Unable to find the words to confess her weakness, she raised her eyes to Julia in mute appeal.

'Are you saying you let him make love to you? Here, in this house?' Julia saw beyond the audacity of the situation to the implications of what Tracey was trying to tell her. Suddenly her confidence evaporated. Had Vernon been right when he said she was a soft touch, to be taken for a ride by every villain in the county?

'Did you leave him alone upstairs at any time?'

Tracey nodded unhappily. 'But I can't believe he'd do a thing like this to me, Mrs Grant,' she said tearfully. 'He made me believe he meant it when he said he'd turned over a new leaf. He promised me all sorts that afternoon, he did. For a little while I was so . . .' She swallowed. 'So *happy*.' She fumbled in her apron pocket for a handkerchief. 'I thought everything was going to be all right again.'

Julia sighed. Why were women so easily taken in by a few flattering words and easily made promises? She remembered Dean suddenly: the soft husky voice, the lips and the hands that could lift her to the skies and beyond. She remembered too the misery that had resulted. The repercussions that were still resounding – even yet.

'Are you still seeing him?' she asked.

Tracey blew her nose. 'He's been round a few times but I sent him packin',' she said. 'I think he's been to the house too. He wants to move back in with us, you see. But I never open the door after dark these days.' She sighed. 'I should have known he'd take advantage as soon as he got what he wanted. That afternoon – soon as I said I wouldn't have him back to live with me and Damie, he got nasty.'

'He didn't hit you again?'

'Oh, no, nothing like that.' With a sudden cold feeling Tracey remembered what Rick had forced her into telling him that afternoon in bed. That was one thing she couldn't confess to. 'He got a bit rough,' she said. 'And just – just sort of turned off. You know how they do.'

'Oh, yes.' Julia nodded ruefully. 'I know.'

'Now it looks like he found another way to get even too.'

'The watch and cuffflinks, you mean?'

Tracey nodded unhappily. 'Mr Grant wants you to sack me, doesn't he?'

'I'm sorry, Tracey. I know you didn't take the things. You wouldn't do a thing like that, but I can't convince him unless the things can be found.'

'If I can get Rick to give them back, I will. But I reckon if he did take them they'll have been sold on by now. Oh, I could *kill* him for muckin' things up for me! I've loved working here for you.'

'Maybe I could get you another job if I asked around.'

'No, you won't be able to. It's like Mr Grant said, I've got no references.'

'I'll give you a reference.'

'It won't be any good. No one'll want me with Damie, will they? He's getting bigger now. Soon he'll be walking and then what? Get into everything, don't they, at that age? No. I'll just have to manage on the benefit money.'

425

'Can't Rick give you anything? You said he was working.'

'That labouring job won't last long. He hates it. That's why he wants to move in with us. So that he can give up his job and I can go back to the hairdressing,' Tracey said. 'Maybe it's something I should look at.'

'You can't really want that? Not after the threats he made.'

'He swears he never meant them – that he's off that stuff now. And he is Damie's dad,' she said. 'Anyway, I might not have much choice.' She looked up at Julia despairingly. 'You see, I think I might be pregnant again.'

'Oh, Tracey, no!'

The girl gave her a wistful look. 'Well, I'm only a few days late so I'm keeping my fingers crossed, but I got this feeling. You know how you do?'

Julia sighed. She was far from happy about the girl's decision but, like Tracey, she had little choice in the matter.

It was dark by the time Fleur arrived at the hospital but she was infinitely relieved to get there. She'd never driven on the motorway before. It had seemed so long and so monotonous. Even then she'd missed the turn off and had to drive onto the next roundabout and find her way back. Then she'd had difficulty in finding the hospital. But at last she saw it looming ahead of her, lit up like a huge ship sailing through the night. With a grateful sigh she drove into the car park and found a space.

Inside the entrance hall the reception desk was closed for the night, but looking on the direction board she saw that the intensive care unit was on the fourth floor. She made her way to the lift.

The unit was dim and hushed but the sound of

bleeping monitors reached her ears as soon as she slipped inside the doors. At the nurses' station the night sister sat quietly working on some charts by the light of a desk lamp. She looked up.

'Can I help you?'

'I've come to see Sally – er – Mrs Sarah Arden.'

'Are you her next-of-kin?'

'No. That's her son. He's on his way over from Switzerland. He might not be able to get here till morning so I said I'd come. I'm Fleur Sylvester, her assistant.'

'Oh, yes, the policeman said he'd contacted you.'

'How is she?'

The sister glanced towards the drawn curtains of a cubicle. 'The doctor is with her now. Perhaps he'll have a word with you before he goes.'

Fleur waited until the curtains parted and a grey-haired doctor emerged. The sister looked up and said, 'This is Miss Sylvester, Mr Farrar. She's a close friend of Mrs Arden's.'

Fleur looked at the doctor. 'How is she?' she asked, holding her breath. 'Is she badly injured?'

His face was grave. 'I'm afraid so. She suffered multiple injuries in the accident. She has a fractured skull and there's some internal bleeding too.'

'Is there anything . . . can't you operate?'

He shook his head. 'We've done what we can for the moment. We'll see how things go.' He glanced at the sister. 'Her next-of-kin?'

'On his way,' Sister said briefly.

'Can I see her?' Fleur asked.

'She's unconscious.' The doctor hesitated then nodded. 'All right then, just for a few minutes.'

Fleur was appalled and frightened by the sight of so many tubes and the array of bleeping monitors surrounding the bed. Sally's head and one arm was swathed in bandages and her face was bruised almost beyond recognition, but one hand lay on top of the covers. Fleur touched it gently. She'd read somewhere that unconscious people could sometimes hear if you spoke to them or played music. She bent closer.

'Sally,' she said quietly, 'it's me, Fleur. Peter is coming. He's on his way and you're not to worry. You're going to be fine.'

For several minutes she sat there talking to Sally, urging her to recover, telling her that everything was going to be all right, until the curtains parted and the sister touched her on the shoulder.

'I must ask you to leave now, Miss Sylvester,' she said. As they moved away from the bed she asked, 'Have you made any arrangements for the night?'

Fleur shook her head. Finding somewhere to sleep had completely slipped her mind. 'No. Do you know of any place I could get a room?'

'You won't find anything now, dear. It's after midnight. But I'm sure we can find you a room here in the hospital under the circumstances. There's usually one vacant in the private wing.'

In the small impersonal room Fleur sat on the high bed and stared numbly at the wall. A kindly nurse had brought her a tray of tea and a sandwich. She'd drunk the tea but the sandwich seemed to turn to ashes in her mouth and in the end she had to abandon it.

She couldn't get the sight of Sally out of her mind. She had looked so dreadful. Was it a bad sign that they weren't going to operate? And if the unthinkable happened and Sally were to die – what then? At last, out of sheer exhaustion, she lay down on top of the bed and closed her eyes. But behind her closed lids she could still see the swollen, bruised face and the body that lay there, so still and lifeless, and although she was exhausted, sleep seemed out of the question. At last, just as the sky was beginning to lighten, she fell into a fitful, restless sleep, but it was full of haunting images and deep, dark fears.

She was awakened by a nurse coming into the room. 'Good morning,' she said breezily. 'It's eight o'clock and I've brought you some tea. If you'd like some breakfast you can get some in the staff canteen.'

'Oh – thank you.' Fleur sat up, rubbing her eyes. Her mouth was dry and her head ached as she stared bemusedly round the strange room. Then the events of the previous day slowly filtered back into her mind and she remembered where she was – and why. 'Can you tell me how Mrs Arden is?' she asked anxiously.

The nurse shook her head. 'I'm sorry, I don't know, but I do know that her son arrived about half an hour ago. He's up in ICU. Sister rang down to ask me to let you know.'

As Fleur turned the corner of the corridor she saw Peter come out through the swing doors of the intensive care unit with the doctor she had seen the previous night. They stood together for a moment outside the doors, heads bowed, faces grave. Fleur stopped. Something about the way Peter stood, the set of his shoulders, filled her with a cold feeling of dread. After a moment the doctor touched him on the shoulder in a gesture of sympathy, then walked away in the opposite direction.

Peter turned slowly and their eyes met. In that instant she knew that Sally had lost her battle for life.

Chapter 15

Peter drove the van back to Elvemere. Both of them were in such a state of shock that afterwards Fleur hardly remembered the journey at all. They spoke of immediate mundane things, blocking out the suddenness and horror of their loss. Peter asked if Fleur would carry out the catering engagements already booked and she agreed, knowing that Sally would have wanted that.

At the house he parked the van in the drive and they went indoors together. In the office Fleur attended to the answering machine, relieved when there were no pressing messages needing attention. So far she was in no fit state to break the news to people.

In the kitchen she made a snack meal for them both while Peter took his case upstairs to his old room. When he reappeared he had showered and shaved and looked refreshed. Sitting opposite each other at the kitchen table, they tried to eat.

'She was looking forward to the wedding so much,' Fleur said. 'When she left here she was so excited. It's hard to believe it was only yesterday morning.'

Peter laid down his knife and fork. 'We should have had the wedding here,' he said. 'It was what she wanted. She wanted to do the catering herself, but I . . .'

He broke off. 'Oh, my God. If only . . .'

'Don't.' She reached out to touch his hand. 'Nothing can make any difference now.' She looked at him. 'Have you telephoned your fiancée yet?'

'Lorraine?' He shook his head. 'No. I'll have to tell her to postpone the wedding. There'll be an inquest, of course. God, I'm not looking forward to it.'

Fleur glanced at his ravaged face. He looked terrible; his eyes were bloodshot and his skin had a greenish pallor. She imagined she must look as bad. Both of them were still reeling from shock and lack of sleep. 'You'll stay on then?' she said. 'Till it's all over?'

'Of course. I must. There'll be so much to arrange. Even after the funeral. There's the business, the house – all her things. I can't begin to think.'

'Yes, I know.' She glanced at him. 'What can I do to help?'

'I'll need a hand with her personal belongings, if you wouldn't mind?' He took a deep breath and straightened his shoulders. 'I know she made a will, but I don't know what her wishes were. I always thought it would be years and years before . . .' He looked at her. 'For the time being, will you carry on with the business?'

'Of course. I said I would, didn't I?'

'I don't mean just this week. I'd like you to take over Arden Catering for me permanently. I'd like to keep it going if possible, but being abroad I'll need someone I can trust. What do you think?'

'Well . . .' Fleur swallowed hard. 'I might need some help, part-time perhaps, but I can do most of it myself. Luckily we were well stocked up.'

'Good. Get in anyone you think you need, of course. We'll work out the financial details later. I expect we'll need some kind of contract drawing up.' He looked up at her. 'Do you think you could move into the house

431

too? This is the business premises in a manner of speaking and I think it might be a good idea for security reasons. After I've gone back, of course,' he added quickly.

'I'll move my things over. I was going to have to leave my flat anyway.' She looked at him. 'How long do you think you'll be staying?'

'As long as it takes.' He pushed his plate away, barely touched. 'Sorry, Fleur. I'm not hungry. You've been marvellous over all this, but . . .' He looked at her. 'Look, I think we should clear the air. There's something that has to be said.'

'No. There's no need.'

'Yes, there is. I'm sorry about the way I treated you – really sorry. It was unforgivable. I suppose you . . .' He looked at her sheepishly. 'Did Mother know?'

'Of course she didn't.' Acutely embarrassed, she got up from the table and began to clear the used dishes, scraping the uneaten food into the waste bin. 'Your mother thought the world of you. I could never have done anything to hurt her.'

'I'm grateful to you for that. But . . .'

'Please, Peter. It's all in the past. I'd rather forget all that if you don't mind, especially now.'

'Yes, of course. But thanks anyway.'

She stacked the dishes into the dishwasher and switched it on. 'I'd better go home,' she said. 'My number is in your mother's desk diary if you need me. I'll come in tomorrow and work in the office – deal with anything that crops up. And there's an engagement tomorrow evening. A birthday party. I was going to do that on my own anyway.'

He smiled. 'Looks as though you've got everything buttoned up.'

'If you need my help with anything, just ring.'

'I'll remember.'

'There's plenty of food in the fridge. And your room is ready. Your mother always kept the bed aired in case you . . .' Her voice trembled. 'I'd better go.'

'*Fleur*. Oh, damn it, come here.' He reached out and grasped her shoulders, drawing him towards him, and for a moment they clung to each other, drawing comfort from the closeness of their shared grief.

'Thanks for all you've done,' Peter said huskily. 'She was very fond of you, you know.'

'And I thought a lot of her too,' Fleur said. 'I owed her so much. It seems so cruel. I still can't . . .' She swallowed painfully. 'I can't believe . . .'

'Neither can I. It's going to take a hell of a lot of getting used to.' He looked down at her and wiped the tears from her cheeks with his thumbs. Then he bent and kissed her lightly. 'Come on, I'll drive you home.'

'There's no need, really. I can get the bus.'

'I wouldn't hear of it. You look tired out. You should try and get some sleep.'

In the flat that had become so dear and familiar Fleur opened the windows and stood for a moment on the balcony, breathing in the fresh spring air. Since this time yesterday her whole world had been turned upside down. She looked around her at the tubs and baskets she had planted, inhaling the honeyed scent of the spring flowers, her heart heavy with the knowledge that she must soon leave before she had enjoyed even one summer. It was cruelly ironic that she would be moving into Sally's house just now when she most needed somewhere to live. Sally would have offered her a home anyway. She'd been a kind friend as well as employer. It was impossible to believe Fleur would see her no more. It was hard to believe that so much could have happened in just twenty-four hours. She went inside and closed the windows, then, too weary even to

433

undress, she lay down on the bed and was almost instantly asleep.

Tom had been turning his car into Victoria Gardens when he saw the distinctive white Arden Catering van drawing up outside number thirteen. He'd got in very late the previous evening and gone straight to bed. He'd decided to drive round to the gardens on his way to work on the off-chance of catching Fleur before she left, but she must have been out before him.

But before he could drive up behind her he was surprised and puzzled to see Fleur getting out of the passenger side. She seemed to be talking to someone in the van and did not glance in his direction. He pulled into the kerb as a man got out of the driver's side of the van and escorted her to the front door. Tom watched as they exchanged a few words, then the man bent and kissed her cheek, pressing one of her hands in both of his.

Tom sat in the car, trying to control the surge of jealousy and resentment that overwhelmed him. As he sat there trying to decide what to do the white van turned and drove past him, giving him a glimpse of the man at the wheel. Dark and smooth-looking. He'd seen him once before – passed him on the stairs when he lived at Victoria Gardens. It was that bastard Peter Arden! What the hell was going on? He was supposed to be in Switzerland, getting married but now it seemed he was back in England instead. Back in Fleur's life again, after all she had said and in spite of what he had done to her.

The first thing May Philips did on the morning after she and Harry returned from their cruise was to telephone her daughter.

'Darling, we're home. Our plane was late getting in, but we drove straight back – didn't get in till about eleven o'clock last night. I can't tell you what a wonderful time we've had! Your father looks so much better – tanned and relaxed. I wish I'd been able to persuade him to take a holiday like that years ago. Now, when are you coming round to see us? I've bought presents for you and Charlotte, and of course Daddy is longing to hear all the news from GPC.'

Julia's heart sank. She had been dreading the coming interview. 'You must both be dreadfully jet-lagged. Why don't I leave it until tomorrow?' she offered hopefully.

'No. We've had a good night's sleep and we both feel fine. Do come, darling. We're both longing to see you.'

Julia sighed resignedly. There was obviously no hope of postponing the interview. 'Well, I've got two meetings this afternoon,' she said. 'But I could come this morning if you're not too busy unpacking?'

'Of course. Come for coffee. And if I'm busy with all my little chores, I can leave you and Daddy talking. I'm sure you two will have a lot to talk about.'

Julia sighed. She doubted it. Once she'd told him she'd let him down he probably wouldn't want to speak to her again. 'Right. See you about half-past ten then,' she said with an enthusiasm she didn't feel. She had planned to visit the women's refuge this morning. Now that things were well and truly under way she made regular trips round to Alexandra House and enjoyed watching her project taking shape.

The empty property that Eleanor had found was a rambling Edwardian house in the maze of rather rundown streets between the park and the railway. The owner had died eight years before, leaving the house to a nephew who lived in Yorkshire. But it was in such a sad state of repair and so lacking in mod-cons that he had little hope of selling it. In the end, thanks to Eleanor, he'd been happy to agree to rent it to the local council for use as a women's refuge. There were three storeys to Alexandra House and eight bedrooms. The ones on the first floor were large enough for four beds with space for cots too. On the ground floor there were four reception rooms and a kitchen large enough to be used as a communal dining room. Two of the ground-floor rooms were to be turned into a small flat for a caretaker, yet to be appointed.

The structural repair work was being carried out by a local builder and the decorating by a team of volunteers whose lack of skill was made up for by their enthusiasm. Furniture, carpets and curtains had been generously provided by donations and charity shops and the house was beginning to look bright and welcoming already. The opening, which was now only weeks away, was to be covered by the press and, some-what to her surprise, Julia had been asked to perform the opening ceremony.

She tried to visit the refuge at least twice a week to encourage the volunteers and supervise the progress. It gave her battered self-esteem encouragement to know that at least one thing she was doing was promising to be successful.

As she parked the car on the drive of Gresham House her stomach began to churn with apprehension. May, who had seen her arrival from the window, came out onto the front porch to greet her, arms outstretched in welcome.

'Darling! I've missed you all so much.' She kissed her daughter warmly then held her at arm's length to look at her critically. 'Oh, you're looking very tired, darling. I hope you're not overdoing things, what with your council work and everything?'

'I'm fine, Mum, honestly.'

'How is the refuge coming along?'

'Wonderfully well. Everyone is working really hard, though it's a bit nerve-racking, wondering if everything will be done in time for the opening.'

May looked at her searchingly. 'And Vernon?'

'As far as I know he is fine,' Julia said, fielding her mother's unasked question about his relationship with Joanna. 'Preoccupied with work, of course, but that's par for the course.'

May looked at her daughter's closed expression and knew better than to pursue the subject. Sometimes she wished Julia would confide in her more. She had always been the same. Could she have gone wrong somewhere? She made herself smile. 'I see. Well, shall we go through? Daddy's in the garden. Everything out there has just gone mad since we left. There's always a lot of work to do in the spring but what with having been away for so long . . .' She smiled. 'Still, now that he has more time, I'm sure he'll enjoy it.' She led the way through to the sunny little morning room at the back of the house. Opening the window, she called to Harry whom Julia could see pottering away with his secateurs in the rose beds, battered old gardening hat perched on his head.

'Harry! Julia's here. Come in now and have some coffee.' May picked up two brightly wrapped parcels from the coffee table. 'These are for you and Charlotte. I do hope you like them. There's a carved fruit bowl for you and a silk shawl for Charlotte.' She turned as Harry came in at the door. 'Are, there you are, dear. I'll go and make the coffee now and you two can have a chat.'

He kissed his daughter's cheek. 'Good to see you, love.'

'And you, Dad. You look so well. I hear you had a wonderful time.'

'We certainly did.' Harry nodded and sat down in the wing chair near the window. 'Pity about the garden, though. Going to take me weeks to get it round again in time for planting.' He looked at her. 'Sit down, love, and tell me how things are going. How did the meeting go? I must admit I thought you might have cabled to let me know the outcome.'

'Well, I would have but . . .' Julia sat down and took a deep breath. 'I might as well come clean right away, Dad. I couldn't do as you wanted. I had to vote along with the others when it came to the crunch.'

Harry's jaw dropped. 'My God, you're not serious?'

'I'm afraid I am.'

'Oh, Julia.' He shook his head in disappointment. 'But why?'

She had given a lot of thought to what she would say in reply to the inevitable question. Obviously she couldn't tell him the truth. 'Try to see it my way, Dad. It would have meant ending my marriage right there and then in the boardroom.'

'But what about Vernon's affair with that Hanson woman? Do I take it you've forgiven him for that?'

'He swears there was nothing in it.' She avoided her father's reproachful eyes. 'Don't you see, Dad? Having me wield power over him and his father would only have inflamed the situation. It would have made things so difficult. And if we had separated, it would have been impossible for me to remain as a director anyway.'

'Ah – I suppose you're right.' Harry slumped in his chair. 'If I'd known you were determined to remain loyal to Vernon, no matter what, I would never have put you in such an impossible position.' He sighed. 'You've been looking so unhappy, Julia. I have to admit that your mother and I hoped . . .'

'Leave it, Dad.' She shook her head. 'Let's just leave it, shall we?'

'Of course. If you say so.' Harry paused and cleared his throat. 'So – Charlie is getting his own way after all, then? He's going ahead with this crazy Victoria

438

Gardens scheme in spite of everything?'

'Yes, I'm afraid so. But it isn't all plain sailing. To begin with I think he had to pay over the odds for the Gardens and now there are other complications too. Things have moved fast since you left. Beardsley's has gone into liquidation, which means most of the prospective buyers of the Meadowlands houses have pulled out. Vernon doesn't say much but I think he's very worried.'

Harry looked startled. 'Beardsley's? My God, that's a blow!' He was quiet for a moment. 'This looks extremely serious, Julia,' he said. 'With Beardsley's gone it's inevitable that others will follow. Under the circumstances, I feel I should resign formally. Sell out.'

She looked at him. 'GPC is stretched to the limit, Dad. I doubt if they can afford to buy you out. If you insist it could be the last straw.'

'Not necessarily. Perhaps there are too many eggs in the family basket. Selling my shares would spread the load.'

'Another new partner, you mean. Who, though?'

'Would you be prepared to sell your shares too?' he asked.

'Yes. Vernon has never liked my taking any part in the business anyway.'

'Never mind what Vernon wants for a moment. Is it what you want? In fact, I think it's high time you started asking yourself that question about a good many things.'

'Yes, Dad. It is what I want. I'd be only too happy to sell my shares.'

'Right.' Harry fell silent as he gave the idea some consideration.

Julia watched him for a moment, unsure what was in his mind. At last she asked, 'Who would buy them under the present circumstances, Dad? Things are beginning to look bad for a lot of the town's business people already. I really can't see anyone taking on new commitments.' She sighed. 'I'm really sorry. I feel I've let you down badly after you trusted me enough to transfer your shares to me.'

'Don't be sorry,' he said. 'We might come out of this better off in the long run, as you say.'

May came in with the coffee tray, but the bright smile on her face faded as she looked from one to the other. 'Oh, dear, you do look serious. Don't tell me you two have been falling out?' she said as she put the tray down.

'We've been talking about the possibility of selling our shares in GPC,' Julia told her.

May looked relieved. 'Well, if you ask me, I think that's an excellent idea,' she said. 'Charlie Grant has always wanted to prove to everyone how clever he is. Always wanted to be the local rags-to-riches success story and cock a snook at everyone. He's let it run away with him and this time he's gone too far.' She shook her head. 'You know, there's a lot of truth in the old saying: "Pride goeth before a fall." '

Julia glanced at her father as he sat there in his chair, eyes glinting. She knew that look of old. Harry Philips was a mild man but once he had the bit between his teeth there was no stopping him. 'Have you got an idea, Dad?' she asked.

He nodded. 'I might have, but I don't want to say anything at the moment. Just bear with me for the time being.'

May smiled confidently as she poured the coffee and handed them each a cup. 'Now,' she said, sitting down, 'tell us how Charlotte is? What's she been up to? I want to hear all about her.'

Julia took a long drink of her coffee. She had successfully negotiated one hurdle. Now she had to tell her

440

parents that their only granddaughter had left home to live in a bed-sit!

When Fleur went round to Park Row to pick Charlotte up on her way to the birthday party the following evening, she found Tom's door firmly closed. When she knocked there was no reply.

As they drove to the party venue she asked Charlotte if she'd seen him. The younger girl shook her head.

'I left a message on the board in the kitchen when you called and it wasn't there next morning so he must have found it,' she said. She looked at Fleur. 'It's terrible about Mrs Arden. What will you do now?'

'I'm going to run Arden Catering for her son Peter,' Fleur told her. 'He's going to get everything legally worked out. I'm going to move into the house.'

'Will you like that?' Charlotte glanced at her doubtfully. 'What about your lovely little flat?'

Fleur sighed. 'I had notice to leave anyway. Mrs Franks has sold the house.'

'Sold it? Oh!' Charlotte's face cleared. 'Of course! Victoria Gardens. GPC has bought the whole street. It's going to be redeveloped. Granddad is really excited about it.' She looked sympathetically at Fleur. 'I'm sorry, Fleur. It's rotten for you when you like the place so much.'

'I might have been homeless for all Ivy cared,' she said. 'And she had the cheek to pretend that she was giving me notice because I've had Tom there once or twice.'

'Did you know she owned the whole street?' Charlotte asked.

'All of it?' Fleur stared at her in amazement. '*Every house?*'

441

'That's right. I don't know for sure, but they're saying that Granddad has paid her a cool million for the deal.'

Fleur gasped. 'Ivy – a millionairess? I can't believe it!'

The party went well. The news about Sally Arden's death wasn't public yet and few people knew though the hostess had heard. She took Fleur aside halfway through the evening.

'My dear, I just wanted to say how grateful I am to you for carrying on as though nothing had happened,' she said. 'I only heard the news this afternoon.'

Fleur shook her head. 'Sally would have wanted everything to go on as normal,' she said. 'I'd have felt it was letting her down to cancel a booking.'

It was late when she dropped Charlotte off at Park Row. As they drew up outside the house the girl looked at her.

'Thanks for asking me along this evening, Fleur. I've really enjoyed it. Are you coming in for a last coffee?'

Fleur was about to refuse. In spite of what she had said to the party hostess earlier, putting on a brave face all evening had been a strain and she was tired. Then she noticed a light in Tom's window at the front of the house. 'All right then. Just a quick one. I can say hello to Tom as well. I haven't seen him for days.'

She tapped on his door while Charlotte went through to the kitchen. He opened it at once.

'Hi! I thought I'd drop in and see you as you haven't been in touch,' Fleur said. Then, seeing his grim expression, she asked, 'What is it? What's wrong?'

'I'm surprised you have to ask!'

'*Tom!* What is it?'

'I came round to see you on my way to work yesterday morning.'

'Did you?'

'Yes, I did,' he said angrily. 'But you were too busy to notice me.'

'Busy?' She shook her head at him, bemused.

'Yes, busy. As a matter of interest, it *was* Peter Arden who was kissing you, wasn't it?' Without waiting for her reply he went on, 'How could you, Fleur, after the way he treated you? After all the things you said! Anyway, I thought he was supposed to be in Switzerland, getting married.'

'He was. You obviously don't know. He came over because . . .'

'I don't want to *hear* any more. It seems to me there's a hell of a lot I don't know about you, Fleur. And if you ask me, I think I'm better off *not* knowing!'

As the door was closed in her face, she stood there, too stunned to react. She raised her hand to knock again. Obviously he didn't know what had happened to Sally – hadn't received the message she had left for him. It was all a misunderstanding. Then suddenly angry resentment flared up inside her. She didn't deserve – didn't *need* – this. Why should she beg him to listen to her explanation? He didn't trust her, thought her a liar. Seeing Peter and her together, he'd jumped to the first conclusion that came into his head. Turning away towards the front door, she blinked hard at the stinging tears that sprang to her eyes. She had no reason to apologise or to beg him to listen to her. And she'd be damned if she'd give him the satisfaction of seeing her cry!

'I won't stay for coffee after all, Charlotte,' she called. 'Goodnight! Thanks for your help.'

After he had heard the van drive away Tom went through to the kitchen and found Charlotte there making coffee. 'Hi,' he said moodily.

'Why didn't Fleur stay?' she asked him. 'You haven't had a row, have you?'

'Nothing you need concern yourself with,' he said rudely.

She looked at him. 'You did get the message Fleur asked me to give you, didn't you? The one I left for you the day before yesterday?'

He turned a blank face towards her. 'Message?'

'She rang to speak to you but you were out. She wanted you to know that she had to drive down to Hertfordshire. The police had rung to say that Mrs Arden had been injured in a car crash on the motorway.'

Tom's jaw dropped. 'Oh, bloody hell! No, I didn't get any message. Where did you leave it?'

'On the board – I couldn't find a pin so I stuck it behind . . .' Charlotte reached out and moved the row of storage canisters on the worktop. The slip of paper was behind them. 'Oh! It must have fallen down. The draught from the front door is . . .'

'Let me see that.' Tom snatched it from her hand and read it. 'Oh, God! Is Mrs Arden badly hurt?'

Charlotte stared at him. 'You mean you haven't heard? I'd have thought – with you working on the *Clarion* and everything . . .'

'Heard what?'

'She died, Tom. Mrs Arden died in hospital later the same night – of her injuries. It was awful.'

'I see.' He stood there, crumpling the note in his clenched fist as he tried to decide what he could do to repair the damage he had caused, then he turned on his heel and flung out of the kitchen, slamming the door behind him.

'I've missed you,' Vernon sat in the conservatory at Joanna's house. It was warm from the day's sunshine and the scent of flowers drifted in through the open French doors. He felt pleasantly relaxed from the double brandy she had poured him.

'How can you have missed me when we've seen each other every day?' She said as she tucked her feet under her in the chair opposite.

'You know damned well what I mean.'

She raised an eyebrow as she took a sip of her Campari and soda. 'As I remember, it was you who said we should cool it.'

'Haven't you missed me at all?'

'Have I missed sleeping with you, you mean?' she said bluntly. 'The answer to that is yes. But why should you care about my feelings?'

'I do care, Jo. And it isn't just the sex. You know how I feel about you – how I've always felt. It was just that things were beginning to get out of hand.'

'So why are you here now, Vernon?'

'Because I couldn't stand it any longer. I need you, Jo. I want to be with you.'

'Then ask Julia for a divorce and marry me.'

He stared at her. '*Marry . . . ?*'

'Why look so shocked? Am I not the sort of woman a man marries?' she said. 'Am I just the eternal *bit on the side*?' She stood up, her green eyes flashing. 'Well, if you think you can just walk in here whenever you feel like it, Vernon, you'd better think again.' She took a cigarette from the box on the table and lit it. 'Maybe I made a mistake when I put money into the firm. Maybe I should get the hell out of Elvemere and away from you.'

He was on his feet, his hands on her shoulders. 'Jo! Don't talk like that. You know I love you. It's just – well, not that easy.'

She stood very still and looked into his eyes. 'Nothing worth having is ever easy, Vernon. I know that. But if you really want it, you'll find a way. I did.'

'Are you saying that you came back to Elvemere just – just for me?'

'What do you think?' She pushed him away. 'But I can just as easily go away and start over. I'm tough, Vernon. I've had to be, the kind of life I've had. But if I go I take my money with me. Business partners don't make good mistresses. So it's up to you.'

He paused, moistening his lips as he tried to think. 'It might take time. It's not the kind of thing you can fix overnight. There's more than just the three of us to consider.'

She shrugged. 'Who else? You don't have old man Philips to consider any more, do you? I'd have thought it'd be fairly straightforward.'

Vernon frowned. 'Julia has her parents' shares, remember, as well as her own, and voting power on Charlotte's.'

'That's something you're going to have to resolve yourself,' Joanna said. 'But knowing Julia I'd say she'd probably be happy to take the house in place of the shares as settlement. She's never seemed quite comfortable in the boardroom, has she?' She crushed out her half-smoked cigarette. 'Can I leave it to you then, darling? Can we trust each other?'

'Of course we can. Oh, Joanna, you know I'd do anything for you.' He moved towards her and drew her into his arms, kissing her hungrily. 'I'll talk to Julia tonight, or at least as soon as I can. Our marriage has been dead for years and, as you said, Harry Philips is out of the frame. Even Charlotte has left home now, so there's nothing to stay for.'

'Nothing to lose and everything to gain.' As she hid her face against his shoulder Joanna was smiling.

There was a strong smell of frying bacon coming from the basement kitchen of thirteen Victoria Gardens as Tom stood waiting for Ivy to answer the door. Finally

446

she opened it a couple of inches and squinted out at him suspiciously.

'Oh, it's you!'

'I'm sorry to bother you, Ivy but I've been up to Fleur's flat and she doesn't seem to be in.'

'No and she won't be neither,' Ivy interrupted with some satisfaction. 'She's left – *gorn*.'

'Gone?' Tom's eyes opened wide. 'Where to?'

'Well now, I'm surprised *you* don't know.' Ivy smirked at him mockingly. 'You two had a row then, 'ave you?'

Tom wanted to tell the old witch to mind her own business but he swallowed his irritation and forced himself to smile. 'I've been away,' he said lamely. 'So if you can tell me if she left a forwarding address.'

Ivy cackled derisively. 'Oh, she done that all right. It's twenty-two Fairfield Drive. Very posh. Moved in with her *other* fancy man, 'asn't she?' She clicked her tongue disapprovingly. 'And 'is poor mum hardly cold. Disgustin', I call it! I expect he stands to inherit a few bob and that's what the attraction is.' She looked him up and down. 'But there. That's 'ow you young people carry on nowadays, isn't it? You've 'ad your chance. Now it's 'is turn. But there, you can 'ardly complain, can you? No more 'n you deserve if you ask me!' And with that final parting shot she shut the door in his face.

As he climbed up the area steps Tom's head spun with angry bewilderment. How could Fleur coolly move out of the flat she loved so much and into her late employer's house the minute Peter Arden invited her to? By the time he reached the car he was shaking with hurt and rage. She might at least have had the decency to tell him. If that was all he meant to her – if she was really that shallow, he was well rid of her!

*

447

Charlie sat in his study at Queen's Lodge, the desk before him covered in papers. He'd had a heavy afternoon with the firm's accountant. At tomorrow's board meeting he would have the uncomfortable task of presenting the surveyor's report on Victoria Gardens and telling Vernon and Joanna that the bank had refused to extend their loan. He was still reeling from the shock.

The survey had come as a blow. Charlie hadn't expected any problems apart from the odd bit of dry rot or perhaps a little rising damp. In his experience the Victorians had built houses to last. How could he or anyone else living possibly have known that this particular development had been built directly over an ancient chalk pit, as the searches had proved?

When he'd received the report he'd gone straight round to the firm of surveyors he'd employed and demanded an immediate interview. The houses had stood for a hundred and twenty years, he'd argued. So why not another hundred and twenty? But the surveyor had pointed out that as long as the houses remained as they were there wasn't much to worry about. It was only when structural work was begun that things could go badly wrong.

'But if we find ways of doing it?' Charlie had said. 'Locating this old chalkpit and filling it in, for instance.'

The surveyor shook his head. 'That could prove to be a very costly business, Mr Grant,' he said. 'Extremely costly and there's no guarantee it would be effective either.'

'But damn it all, the council itself was prepared to do this work,' Charlie blustered, his fist hitting the desk. 'Surely they must have looked into it.'

The surveyor smiled wryly. 'Has it ever occurred to you that maybe they knew what they were doing when they abandoned the idea?' As Charlie digested this unpalatable thought the man leaned forward. 'What I would suggest, Mr Grant, is that you change your plan for something that requires less structural alteration. A tasteful restoration of the properties perhaps, with sympathetic modernisation. It could be very attractive. Victoriana is coming into vogue.'

Just remembering the interview made Charlie groan. All that cash! And all his plans for civic eminence, gone out of the window in a puff of smoke – or chalk! He dropped his head into his hands. Surely if the council was already in possession of this devastating knowledge someone could have told him. When he thought of all the favours he'd done for that bunch in the past! He'd have no alternative but to cut his losses by doing as the surveyor had suggested.

There was a tap on the door and Louise came in with a glass in her hand. 'I've brought you a whisky,' she said. 'And I think it's about time you stopped poring over those old papers and came and had something to eat.'

Charlie took the glass from her and downed the contents in one gulp. His wife looked at him.

'What's up, Charlie?'

'Oh, just a snag we've hit.' He sighed deeply. 'I've rung Vernon and asked him to drop round after supper. I need to talk to him.'

'I wish you'd said. You could have asked him to supper. I daresay Julia is out again, or too busy to cook a proper meal for him – as per usual!'

'As a matter of fact he wasn't at home.'

She frowned. 'How could you speak to him then?'

He hesitated. 'I took a chance and rang Joanna's. He was there.'

'*Was* he now?' Louise's cheeks coloured. 'Does he spend a lot of time round at her place?'

'I don't think so. But if he does you can hardly blame him, Julia being out so much.'

449

Louise's lips tightened. *Damn* the woman. She was probably trying to get her claws into Vernie just to get back at her. Well, she'd see about that. She looked at her husband's worried face. 'What's wrong, chuck? Is it anything I can help with?'

He shook his head. 'No. Like I said, just a hitch with the surveyor's report. Nothing for you to worry about.'

'Well, I'll get back to the kitchen. Supper in about ten minutes, right? And don't go shutting yourself in the lav the minute it's on the table!'

Vernon had been extremely irritated by his father's phone call. He and Joanna had been in bed when the telephone rang. It had taken him an hour to convince her that what he felt for her was all-consuming passion and not just sexual attraction. By the time they reached the bedroom his need had become desperate and they'd undressed frenziedly – only to have the phone ring the moment they fell onto the bed together.

He'd tried to persuade Joanna to ignore it, but by the time it had shrilled persistently in their ears for several minutes their passion had evaporated somewhat. At last Joanna had rolled over and reached for the receiver with a resigned sigh.

'Hello. Joanna Hanson.'

'It's me, Joanna – Charlie Grant. Vernon wouldn't happen to be there, would he?'

She hesitated. 'As a matter of fact he is. He dropped in on his way home. Hold on.' Her hand over the mouthpiece she whispered, 'It's your father.'

Vernon swore softly and took the phone from her. 'Hello, Dad. What is it?'

'I need to see you, Vern.'

'You will see me, Dad. First thing in the morning.'

'No, I mean now. I wouldn't ask if it wasn't important.'

Vernon sighed. 'What on earth can be so urgent that it can't wait till morning?'

'Can't talk about it over the phone. Get yourself round here as soon as you can.'

And to Vernon's extreme annoyance he hung up.

Charlie opened the door to his ring and ushered him into the study straight away. 'I'll come straight to the point,' he said. 'I couldn't get the bank to extend our loan.'

'Why?'

'Mainly because of this.' Charlie pushed the surveyor's report across the desk. 'Though the fact that several local businesses are going bust didn't exactly help.'

'You'd think the banks would be keen to look after the ones that are solvent, wouldn't y . . .' Vernon broke off as he got to the crucial paragraph. '*Christ!* I see what you mean.' He looked up at his father, his face flushed. 'I told you not to touch Victoria Gardens. Why in God's name wouldn't you listen to me?'

Charlie waved the pipe he was in the process of lighting. 'Don't get on your high horse with me. You couldn't have foreseen this any more than I did.'

'That doesn't make it any better. It's still a disaster! We've got most of the Meadowlands houses back on our hands now too. What the bloody hell are we going to do?'

'Well, all I can say is, thank God for Joanna.'

'You're *joking*!' Vernon stared at him. 'You can't ask her to throw good money after bad. What do you propose to do with this white elephant you've landed us with?'

'The surveyor suggested a tasteful restoration,' Charlie said, carefully employing the man's exact phrase. 'With sympathetic modernisations. That would

451

mean we wouldn't have to hack them about too much. And Victoriana is coming into vogue, or so I'm told.'

'And then what?'

'We'll sell them.'

'Oh, we'll sell them will we – just like that? More houses on the market that no one wants to buy. Another lot of plans to have drawn up at enormous expense! Besides, anyone intending to buy will have a survey done the same as you did. Once they know about this bloody chalkpit you won't see their heels for dust. What's more the word will spread.'

'Stop panicking. If we can't sell we can turn the places into luxury flats and rent them out lucratively.' Charlie leaned back in his chair. 'Suppose we ask Joanna what she thinks?'

Vernon gave a derisive snort. 'Ask her if you like – as long as you don't mind her telling you! I dread to imagine what she'll say when she knows how you've wasted her investment. She'll probably demand her money back and book herself on the first flight to the States!'

'It's not wasted.' Charlie looked at his son speculatively. 'Look, there is another alternative.'

'Yes? Come on then, let's hear it.'

Charlie lit his pipe with a painstaking precision that made Vernon want to scream. At last he looked up through a cloud of exhaled smoke. 'We could mortgage the houses.'

Vernon stared at him. 'What houses?'

'Yours and mine of course. Charlie puffed on his pipe with an attempt at nonchalant bravado. 'We'd get a tidy sum for the both of them. Enough to tide us over.'

Vernon's expression was one of incredulity. 'You *are* joking, I take it?'

' 'Course I'm not joking. That what property's for – investment. If we can't realise a bit of ready cash on our own bricks and mortar it's a poor do. For God's sake, Vern, don't look at me like that. We'll get our money back in the end. This is just a bit of a cash flow problem. Luckily we've got the means to deal with it.'

'I only wish I had your confidence, Dad.' Vernon's head was reeling. He was thinking about Joanna's remark earlier, that Julia would probably be happy to take the house as a settlement in a divorce. It looked as though that would be out of the question now. At least for the time being.

Louise tapped on the door and put her head round it. 'Come and have some coffee, you two,' she said. 'You've been shut away in here too long. Vernie, come out into the kitchen and talk to me while I make it. It's weeks since I saw you to talk to properly.'

Glad to remove himself from his father's presence for a while, Vernon followed his mother through to the kitchen and sat on one of the breakfast bar stools while she spooned coffee into the filter machine. She glanced at him sideways.

'I hear your father caught you round at Joanna Hanson's.'

He looked up, suddenly defensive. 'How do you mean, *caught me*?'

'Just that. You want to stay away from her out of office hours, Vernie. She might have money but as a woman she's bad news.'

'Don't be ridiculous, Ma. I've known Joanna ever since we were kids.'

'You knew her when you were kids. That's not quite the same thing,' she said meaningfully. 'You and her had a red hot affair when you were very young.' She shook her head at him. 'Oh, I knew what was going on, don't worry. I wasn't born yesterday and I could see the way things were going. I can read her sort like a book.'

'A teenage fling. That's all it was.'

'Mmm, to you, maybe,' Louise said. 'Take it from me, that one had other ideas.'

'How do you mean?'

'Oh, Vernie, how can you be so naive? She knew your dad's firm was doing well. She was after a lady's life. An easy time with plenty of money. She was a slut and she'd have led you a right merry dance if you'd married her.'

'Rubbish!'

Louise swung round, stung by his abrupt dismissal of the truth. 'Rubbish, is it? If that's so, why did she accept money to leave you alone then?'

For a moment he stared at her, his mouth agape in astonishment. '*Money!* Who from?'

'From me.'

'You – you paid her to – to . . .'

'To go as far away as she could and leave you alone. And it didn't take her long to find a Yank with plenty of cash to chuck about, did it?' Louise retorted. 'I dangled the bait and she swallowed it without a single qualm. No, I tell a lie. She pushed my offer up by pretending she was pregnant.'

'She what?'

'You heard. She said she was expecting. I couldn't prove otherwise so I had to take her word for it and give her the money for an abortion. I told you she was a scheming slut.'

Vernon was on his feet now, his face dark with anger. 'You gave her money to get rid of my child?'

'There was no child,' Louise said scathingly. 'She more or less admitted as much later. But I couldn't risk calling her bluff, could I? She threatened to make it all public if I didn't pay her.' She slapped her hand down on the worktop. 'That's the kind of woman she was then. And she still is, Vern, only twice as cunning. Take my advice and drop her before she ruins your life again!'

Fleur had moved all her belongings over from Victoria Gardens single handed, using the van. When the flat was empty she'd stood for a long time at the open French windows, looking out at the now bare balcony. All her pots, tubs and hanging baskets had been removed to Sally's house. There was a large patio there which easily accommodated them. But it wasn't the same. The house was lovely, but it didn't feel like home. Everywhere she looked there were reminders of Sally. It was too large for her too. She had never been used to so much space and felt more lonely than when she had first arrived in Elvemere.

She'd kept busy since Peter's departure for Switzerland after the sad business of tying up Sally's affairs. She had helped all she could and Peter had promised to return after his honeymoon to attend to the legalities of her new job as manager of Arden Catering.

Meantime there was plenty to do. There were scores of letters to reply to in Peter's absence. Over the years Sally had made a good many friends among her clientele. At first Fleur had worried about whether Sally's clients would trust her with their future business, but to her relief, once people knew that she was to stay and carry on, the bookings began to resume as briskly as ever. Bookings for summer barbecues, weddings and garden parties were being made now and Fleur could see that it was about to be a busy season in spite of the recession that was beginning to stamp its mark on the town.

In the daytime she was too busy to think much about her own emotions, but when she was alone in bed at night they would rush in on her like an overwhelming tide, almost suffocating in their intensity. Why had Tom been so unyielding in his accusations? He must know by now about her reasons for meeting Peter. He would have heard from Charlotte about her move from Victoria Gardens too. Yet she'd had no word from him. Why was it that everyone in her life – apart from her grandparents – eventually rejected her? Sometimes she wondered whether it could be the old racist thing that she had seen so many people fight. Her skin was pale it was true, but she was and always had been aware that she looked different. Perhaps if she were truly black like Bobby she would be more acceptable. And perhaps it was nothing to do with any of that. Perhaps it was she herself who was somehow lacking.

It was about a week after her move that she received an unexpected telephone call in the office one morning.

'Arden Catering. Fleur Sylvester speaking. Can I help you?'

'Fleur, hello. It's Julia Grant.'

'Oh! – Hello.'

'I had to ring you to say how sorry I was to hear about Sally Arden,' Julia said. 'I was at the funeral service but I – didn't get a chance to speak to you.'

Fleur didn't reply for a moment, guessing that what Julia really meant was that she was afraid to be seen speaking to her, foolishly and guiltily terrified in case someone should speculate about their relationship. 'No,' she said. 'I did see you in the distance. The church was full.'

'Yes. Sally was a well liked woman.'

'She was very good to me,' Fleur said. 'I'm so proud to be taking over the business. A mother couldn't have done more for me than Sally did.' She bit her lip, wincing at her unintentional gaffe.

'Quite.'

Into the awkward silence that followed Julia said, 'I'd like to thank you for keeping an eye on Charlotte for me.'

'Oh, there's no need really. She's coping fine. Have you been round to see her room?'

'No. She rings occasionally, but I haven't been invited yet.'

'Maybe she's hoping you'll ask, or just turn up,' Fleur said. 'She's quite stubborn when it comes to making the first move, isn't she?'

'Don't I know it!' Julia said.

'I've moved myself. I'm living here at Sally's house now. It made sense from a security point of view, but I would have had to move anyway with Victoria Gardens being redeveloped.'

'Oh, of course. I'd forgotten you lived there.'

'There's no reason why you should remember, is there?' Fleur said with a hint of sharpness. 'By the way, I see from the *Clarion* that your women's refuge is coming along well.'

'Yes, everyone has worked really hard.' Julia paused. 'As a matter of fact, Fleur, I was planning to give a little luncheon, just for the press and councillors on the day of the opening. Would you be free to do it for me?'

'What date would that be?'

'The fifteenth of next month. There'll be room in the dining room at Alexandra House. I heard just this week that the local television and radio people will be there too, so better cater for about forty. Just a simple finger buffet will do nicely.'

As Fleur replaced the receiver she couldn't help feeling that Julia might easily have thought up the idea on the spur of the moment; or offered her the job as some kind of compensation. She wished now that she'd invented some prior booking. The last thing she wanted was Julia's patronage.

Charlotte hated the Saturday afternoons when she didn't go to the stables. She spent the mornings doing her washing and cleaning her room – doing the other household jobs on the rota when it was her turn. But the afternoons were a drag. Usually the house was empty. Both Sadie and Tom were usually busy with sports events for the paper, and Saturday was Fleur's busiest day too. Everyone seemed to have something to do, except her. So when she heard the front doorbell ring soon after lunch that Saturday she went down to answer it with a sense of anticipation. Perhaps one of the friends who had deserted her had found out where she lived and come round to visit, though she didn't hold out much hope of that.

'Hello darling.' Julia stood on the doorstep, an overflowing shopping basket in one hand.

Charlotte stared in surprise at her mother. 'Mum!'

'Well, I got tired of waiting for an invitation,' Julia said. 'So I thought, if the mountain won't come to Mohammed . . .' She peered past Charlotte into the hall. 'It all looks very nice. Am I going to be asked in?'

'Oh! Yes, of course. I'm sorry.' Charlotte held the door open to admit her mother and led the way upstairs, feeling glad that she'd given the little bed-sit a good turn-out this morning. She opened the door with a flourish.

'Ta-raa! This is it,' she announced. 'My very own home.'

Julia looked round with a smile. 'Darling, it's charming. And you're keeping it so nice.'

Charlotte flushed with pride. 'There's no one else in at the moment. I'll show you the rest of the house if you like?'

Julia shook her head. 'No. It's you I've come to see.' She put the basket down. 'I brought you a few goodies. Some of those chocolate chip cookies you like and some of your other favourites. Grandma and Granddad are home from their cruise and they sent you a present.'

458

She unpacked the basket including May's brightly wrapped parcel. 'It gave me a good excuse to come and see you.' She looked at her daughter. 'I've missed you so much darling. You are all right, aren't you? You're happy?'

'Yes, Mum.'

'And eating properly?'

'Fine. I've discovered I like cooking.' Charlotte grinned cheekily. 'As a matter of fact I think I eat better than I did at home.'

Julia smiled apologetically. 'I was getting a bit slack about meals, wasn't I? I got fed up with neither you nor Daddy ever being there to eat what I'd cooked.'

'I know. I see that now. Look, Mum, I would have asked you before but I didn't feel . . . I didn't know how I'd feel when I saw you again. It was important that I – gave it enough time. Do you see?'

'Of course.' Julia knew exactly what Charlotte meant. She'd suffered the pangs of home sickness herself. The difference was, she'd given in to it – hadn't given herself enough time to adapt.

The two of them looked at each other for a long moment, then Julia reached out and drew her daughter into her arms. 'Oh, come here. It's lovely to see you,' she said.

'And you, Mum.' Charlotte hugged her mother tightly, then said. 'Come down to the kitchen with me and we'll make some tea.'

Julia was impressed with the bright little kitchen, and with the new competent young woman her daughter had become. Fleur had been right to say she would benefit from being allowed to stand on her own feet.

'How are things going?' Charlotte asked as she set a tray with cups and saucers. 'The refuge must be almost ready for opening.'

459

'It is. You must come along to the opening on the fifteenth. Fleur is doing a buffet lunch for me.'

'Is she? Sounds great, but I doubt if I could get the time off.'

'It's going to be quite an occasion, photographs for the paper and there's a chance that the local television and radio people will be there too.'

'Wow! My mum on the telly! I can't wait to see you!'

Upstairs Charlotte opened her grandmother's present and shook out the brightly embroidered shawl with an expression of dismay. 'Oh God! When on earth would I wear a thing like this?'

Julia smiled. 'I have to admit that it wouldn't look quite right with jeans or a mini skirt, but it's very pretty. You could always drape it over the bed or perhaps here . . .' She draped the heavily fringed shawl over the headboard, bringing a splash of colour to the corner of the room. 'There. How's that?'

'Brilliant! Just the thing. Thank Grandma for me when you see her.'

'Why not go round and thank her yourself? You're still part of the family, you know.'

'Am I?' The girl sighed. 'What about Dad?'

'You see him at the office every day. You tell me.'

'He treats me like any other member of the staff. And I still have to work under *her* of course. I just wish I could leave and do something else, but I have to eat.'

'Of course.'

'And whatever he says, Mum, I wasn't just trying to make trouble. I *did* see them that night. And it wasn't innocent like he said.'

'I know.'

'You do? Then why . . .' Charlotte paused, looking at her mother. 'Oh, Mum. It wasn't because of you that I ran away from home, you know. At least . . .'

'Tell me the truth,' Julia said quietly. 'It's time we

talked to each other woman to woman. You're grown up now.'

'Well – it was the way you've always let Dad walk all over you,' Charlotte said. 'Ever since I was old enough to see what was going on I've wanted to yell at you to stand up for yourself. He's always been so patronising – treated you as though you were half-witted when I knew all the time that you were a damn sight more intelligent than he was. I've known since I was little that he was seeing other women, but you seemed to prefer to look the other way. It made me . . .'

'It made you despise me?'

'Not exactly, but . . .'

'I wouldn't have blamed you,' Julia said. 'I know now what a fool I've been all these years.'

'I was a selfish little kid though. When you did start to be your own person; when you got your seat on the council I should have been pleased – proud of you. Instead I felt resentful because I thought I was being neglected.' Charlotte smiled ruefully. 'I could easily have done what I do here; just got on with things and helped instead of moaning.'

Julia smiled gently. 'We all have to learn.' She reached for Charlotte's hand. 'So – what do you do in your free time these days?' she asked.

'I still go to Auntie Kath's occasionally,' she admitted. 'Mostly in the evenings when there's no chance of Dad driving by and catching me. I've been helping Fleur too, occasionally – for a bit of extra money.' She looked at her mother. 'Poor Fleur. Wasn't it awful about Mrs Arden?'

'Yes, terrible. You and she are good friends, aren't you?'

Charlotte nodded. 'I like her so much. She's been a good friend. She doesn't hassle me, that's what I like. She's there for me when I need her. She even tells me

461

off if she thinks I'm being a prat, but she doesn't preach or push.' She looked at her mother with a wistful smile. 'She's almost like an older sister might be, though that's something I wouldn't know about.'

Julia was silent. If only she could tell Charlotte that Fleur was the closest she'd ever have to a real sister. If she just had the courage to stand up and tell the world about her. This new adult Charlotte would understand. She might even be pleased. For a moment she had a crazy impulse to tell her. She opened her mouth. 'Charlotte . . .'

'Yes?'

'Oh – nothing.' The urge – and the sudden burst of courage faded. 'I just wondered if there was any more tea in the pot.'

'I think so.' Charlotte refilled her mother's cup. 'There's something else, Mum,' she said. 'I've met this boy. He helps out at the stables in his free time and his name is James. He's really nice. I know you'd like him.'

Julia smiled, though deep inside she felt a pang of anxiety. Charlotte was so young and inexperienced. If she were to be hurt as Julia herself had been hurt. If she were to run off as she herself had done . . . Yet what could she do to prevent it? What could any mother do?

'I'd like to meet him,' she said, forcing down her rising dread.

'I'm not bringing him home!' Charlotte said at once.

'Well, perhaps I could drop round sometime when he's here.' Julia looked at her daughter. 'He does come here, I take it?'

'He hasn't so far,' Charlotte said, her colour rising. 'And if you want to know if I'm sleeping with him, I'm not!'

In spite of herself Julia felt immense relief. She laughed to cover it. 'Darling! There's no need to be touchy. I remember what it was like being your age.'

'We're just friends,' Charlotte said defensively. 'We have a lot of things in common.' She glanced at her mother. 'Would you really like to meet him?'

'Of course I would.'

'Maybe I'll have a party,' Charlotte said with a sudden flash of inspiration. 'A flat warming.'

Julia smiled. 'That sounds fun. I'll look forward to it.'

'I'm really glad you came today, Mum,' Charlotte said. 'It was horrible feeling cut off from you.'

'You were never cut off, darling. Not as far as I was concerned.' Julia looked at her watch and stood up. 'Time I was going. Can I come again?'

'Of course.'

'And will you at least think about coming home? Maybe for lunch next Sunday.'

Charlotte chewed her lip. 'Well . . .'

Julia hugged her. 'At least give the idea some thought. Ring me and tell me what you think.'

'Okay. I'll think about it.'

Rick turned up the volume on his radio as he slapped mortar onto the brickwork of the porch at Alexandra House. At least a bit of music drowned out the churning of his tortured mind. The job of pointing the brickwork was boring and he was already fed up.

When Tracey had first agreed to his moving in with her and the kid he was over the moon – a feeling that was to be short-lived once he discovered her reasons for giving in. It had been a bitter blow to learn that she was pregnant again. He really would have thought that the stupid little bitch would have taken care not to let it happen. To make matters worse, she'd lost her job at the Grants. Something for which she blamed him. He'd never have believed that people with all that money would be so mean over a pair of poxy cufflinks and a watch. If they left them lying around in unlocked drawers they deserved to have them nicked. What did they expect? To add insult to injury he'd had to get rid of them quick and he'd got nothing like what they were worth. Barely enough to pay off what he owed at the bookie's. Talk about out of the frying pan into the fire! Instead of being able to give up his job, have an easier time with Trace as the breadwinner and a roof over his head, it now looked as if he was going to have a council rent to pay and three mouths to feed. He felt well and truly lumbered.

'Do you think you could get out of the way, please?'

Rick looked round to see an elegant high-heeled shoe hovering delicately above the board that held his mortar. The shoe was on the end of a well-shaped leg in a sheer black stocking and, glancing up from where he crouched on the ground he glimpsed a pleasantly dimpled knee and the thigh above it, tantalisingly concealed under a skim skirt.

'Sorry darlin'.' He grinned cheekily, pushing his baseball cap onto the back of his head. 'Can't have you stepping in anything nasty, can we? Not with them sexy shoes on.'

She gave him a withering look and stepped over him to disappear into the house. He stared after her. Councillor Mrs Julia bloody Grant. Snotty cow! Looking down on him like he was dirt. All dressed to kill in her sharp suit, blonde hair all done up and nails varnished. He wouldn't mind betting she'd spent more money just on her hairdo than he earned in a week. And from what he'd heard about her from Trace she was no better than any of those women who'd be moving into this place when it was finished. That was well-off folks for you. Underneath they were no better than anyone else. But give them some cash, a posh house and fancy car and they treated everyone else like they was muck!

Swallowing his resentment, he carried on with his work only to be interrupted a few minutes later by another female voice.

'This is Alexandra House, isn't it?'

Looking up, he saw that the woman addressing him this time was very different. She wore motorbike leathers and sported a nose stud. And if he wasn't mistaken the classy machine parked by the gate was the one he'd heard roar up the road just now. He got to his feet and looked at her respectfully.

'That's right miss. There is a sign but I took it down in case it got splashed with the mortar.'

'Right. Thanks.' She swung off the heavy bag she carried on her shoulder and he saw that it was in fact a camera.

'Oh – you the press then, are you?' As a mark of respect, he pulled off his baseball cap to reveal his mass of curly hair.

Sadie nodded. '*Clarion*. I want to get some pictures of the final stages of the work, as a lead in to next week's big opening story.' She took out her camera, peered at him through the lens. 'How about a shot of one of the handsome building workers in action?' she asked with a lift of one eyebrow.

'Okay then. Anything to oblige a lady.' Rick grinned, his eyes glinting mischievously. 'Want me with the shirt on or off? How about a touch of the old Chippendales, eh?'

Sadie laughed. 'What's your name?'

'Rick,' he told her. 'Rick Kendle.'

'Go on then, Rick. The sun's shining, why not?' She took several shots of him from various angles, then thanked him and disappeared into the house.

Rick pulled on his shirt thoughtfully and prodded the hardening mortar with his trowel. Photos in the paper, eh? No telling what a thing like that could lead to. He was a good looking guy – that photographer bird had seen that all right. He might be seen by some big London photographer and taken up by a modelling agent. He dabbed abstractedly at the brickwork, his eyes far away as he dreamed of seeing himself in telly commercials and up there on the hoardings, his well muscled torso tanned and oiled and ten times as big as lifesize, advertising sports gear or hair gel. He thought of what he could do with the cash he'd earn, holidays in the Bahamas and Acapulco, the classy birds he'd pull and the cars he'd buy, and sighed with longing. Maybe it needn't just be dreams though. What if he were to chat up that photographer bird a bit? Not that she looked the kind to fall for his kind of line. Not exactly what you'd call a pushover. Not even his type, come to that. Nose studs were a dead turn off as far as he was concerned. But what was important was that she worked for a newspaper and looked as if she might have some clout behind her. If he could get some cash together he could get out before things got too heavy with Trace. The way things were heading he'd be in up to his neck before he was much older.

Julia came out of the house to find him sitting on the front step smoking a roll-up and leaning against the wall.

'Have you finished?' she asked briskly.

He squinted up at her. 'No.'

'Then don't you think you should get on? At this rate we'll never be ready for the opening next week. You're not paid to sit there listening to the radio.'

'All right, missis. No need to get your knickers in a knot,' he said. 'I'm entitled to me break, same as anyone!'

He had the satisfaction of seeing her blush as she turned away. Serve her right, cheeky cow. He could make her sneer on the other side of her snooty face, he

466

comforted himself, if he were to let slip what he knew about her!

He was working again when Sadie came out of the house. She grinned at him. 'Still hard at it?'

'You bet.' He dropped his cigarette stub on the ground and trod on it. 'You doin' anything tonight then?'

She looked surprised. 'Depends. What did you have in mind?'

Rick winked. 'You can show me your etchin's if you like. Or how about bringing them shots you took of me? Maybe they could make the two of us some cash.'

She laughed. 'How would they do that?'

He flexed his muscles. 'Always fancied a bit of modellin'. Reckon I got the body an' the looks for it. Don't you?'

Sadie laughed in a way that brought angry colour to his cheeks. 'Modesty isn't exactly one of your failings, is it? Modelling is more than just strutting about with your shirt off, you know.'

He gave her what he thought of as his Mel Gibson look. 'You think I don't know nothing, don't you? Well, you might learn a thing or two if you got to know me better. Right, are we on? The King's Head – eight o'clock. Okay?'

Sadie looked him in the eye. 'You've got to be joking! Give me one good reason why I should want to have a drink with you.'

Rick burned with indignation. Who the hell did she think she was? Her and her spiky hair! Wouldn't normally touch her with a barge pole! He glanced from side to side and pushed his face close to hers. 'I reckon we've both got something the other one could use.'

'No kidding! What would that be then?'

'How about if I've got a juicy bit of gossip?'

'So – how about it?'

'Real gossip, I mean. I know something that'd make your hair curl,' he said. 'Something about a certain woman on the town council.' He jerked his head in the direction of the house. 'Mentionin' no names, but not a million miles from here.' He watched her face carefully. 'It'd make a story any newspaper reporter would kill for. Topical too. Still – if you're not interested . . .' He shrugged and turned back to his pointing.

'Is this some kind of wind-up or are you on the level?'

He looked at her. 'Oh, I'm on the level all right. Not that I'm givin' it away, mind.'

'If it's as hot as you say, I'd pay.'

'How much?'

'Come on, Rick. I can't make wild promises until I know what it's worth.'

'I'll think about it,' he told her. 'Be in the pub at eight. If you're not there by ten past I'll ring up another paper.'

Chapter 16

When Joanna answered the door on Sunday evening she was surprised to find Vernon standing on the doorstep. But any pleasure she might have felt was to be short-lived.

'I can't stay,' he told her breathlessly. 'I've slipped out on the pretext of driving round to the office for something I left behind.'

'So why are you here?' she asked.

'I had to see you. Something has come up. I thought it only fair to put you in the picture as soon as I could.'

'In that case you'd better come in.' Joanna held the door open. Inside the hall she looked at him. ' "Only fair to put you in the picture as soon as I could" sounds ominous,' she said. 'Is something wrong?'

'Dad had the result of the survey on the Victoria Gardens properties.'

'Right. But I don't see . . .'

'Apparently there are old chalkpit workings running underneath. It looks as if we won't get the planning permission to re-structure after all. We're going to have to rethink the whole thing and it's likely to take longer, not to mention being considerably more expensive than we'd allowed for.'

'I see. That's bad news.'

Vernon ran a hand through his hair. 'I *told* him to leave it alone. If only he'd listened to me.'

'Vernon – have you come here just to tell me you were right all along?'

'Of course not.'

'Then why—'

'Because it affects us, that's why. You and me. Our future.'

'How?'

'Dad has come up with the idea of mortgaging both our homes. If I have to do that, there's no way I can afford to divorce Julia. At least, not for some time.'

'Then tell him you won't do it.'

'I can't.' He shook his head helplessly. 'You know Dad.'

Swallowing her exasperation, Joanna said, 'I thought I was supposed to be a partner in this firm. Why wasn't I consulted about this?'

'You mean, you'll help?' Vernon looked at her hopefully. 'You'll put more money into the firm – to tide us over?'

'I'm not made of money, Vernon. And if I'm not considered trustworthy enough to be consulted, why should I offer to bale the firm out?'

'But I thought . . .' he swallowed nervously. 'Look, I expect Dad felt he couldn't talk to you about any of this because it was more a family matter than business,' he offered.

'Oh, I see,' Joanna said icily. 'Well, until he treats me like a business partner and not just an endless source of cash handouts, until he takes me into his confidence in the way I deserve, there'll be no more money available.' She looked at him. 'Just as a matter of interest, Vernon, why did you really come round? Is it to tell me we should cool it again?'

He winced at her cold directness. 'Well – until we get

over this blip I do think it might be best.' He reached out to touch her shoulder. 'Don't take it like this, Jo. We can still be together occasionally, can't we? We'll still be working together and there's no reason why we shouldn't stay – well, more or less as we are now. Just for the time being, of course,' he added with an attempt at a reassuring smile.

'*Just for the time being?* It seems to me that investing with GPC was the worst thing I could have done – for all concerned!' Joanna was seething. No one – no one – got away with treating her like this! Vernon had always been weak. There could never be any kind of future for her with a man this spineless. She must have been mad ever to think there could be. In that moment her mind was made up. She walked to the door and opened it.

'Goodnight, Vernon,' she said. 'Thank you for "putting me in the picture", as you put it. I think this might well be crunch time, don't you?'

He stared at her. 'Oh, come on, Joanna. It's only for a . . .'

'I mean it. *Goodbye*, Vernon!'

The look she gave him almost froze him to the spot. He opened his mouth to remonstrate, then closed it again. As he passed her he said, 'Don't do anything hasty that you might regret, Jo. What we have is worth waiting a little longer for, surely?'

'I think it's you who might be the one with regrets, Vernon,' she told him. 'I never regret anything. I've tried to overlook your weakness and your shortcomings, but this is the final straw.'

She stood in the hall and listened to his car backing out of the drive, her blood racing with anger. Just for a while she'd allowed her guard to slip with Vernon. She'd actually imagined that their relationship would make a real man of him. She'd even, God help her, been prepared to take on that vulgar old hag of a mother of

471

his. She'd nurtured dreams of herself and Vernon running the firm in double harness – raising the name of Grant Hanson to national greatness like Wimpy or Barratt. She shook her head as if to rid herself of the ridiculous, fanciful notion. It would never have worked with a man as feeble as Vernon at its head. She would have had to push him every inch of the way; wring every decision out of him. Thank God she'd come to her senses in time. But she'd have the last laugh yet. She'd see the Grants grovelling at her feet before she'd done. Including Julia! The trump card was right there within a telephone call of her grasp. For the past few days, ever since she'd had the surprising and unexpected offer from Harry Philips, she had been tortured with indecision, but tonight Vernon had unwittingly pointed the way to her.

Lifting the receiver, she dialled carefully then sat down to wait. At the other end of the line a woman's voice answered: 'Elvemere nine-eight-seven-three-six.'

'Good evening, Mrs Philips. It's Joanna Hanson speaking. Can I have a word with your husband, please? I think he'll be expecting my call.'

Among the letters on the mat when Fleur went downstairs on Monday morning she saw that two were addressed to her personally. The first was addressed in Bobby's round handwriting and the other was typewritten and had a Swiss postmark.

Sitting at the table in the kitchen as she waited for the kettle to boil, she eagerly tore open Bobby's letter. It contained an invitation to her engagement party, to be held at her mother's flat in Hackney the Saturday of the coming weekend. With it was a short letter from Bobby, who sounded happy and excited.

Bring this Tom of yours I've heard so much about. I wouldn't want you to go falling for any guy who didn't have my personal seal of approval!

P.S. Mum says to tell you she'll find room for you both if you want to stay over. Please, please, please come! It won't be the same without you.

Take Tom with her? Fleur sighed. Bobby knew nothing about the rift that had opened between them, of course. Tom had been constantly in her thoughts since their angry exchange at Park Row. Determined not to be the one to make the first move, she had waited for him to get in touch with her again. After all, he had been the one in the wrong. He had hurt her deeply with his wild assumptions, and at a time when she was already upset and needing him.

Eventually there had been a note from him. It arrived on the day before Sally's funeral, short and to the point. In it he said he was sorry about the misunderstanding – that he'd be covering the funeral for the *Clarion* and would be at the church if she wanted to speak to him afterwards. But in the absence of family or relatives she had been at Peter's side throughout the service and had been required to play hostess to the handful of guests at the house afterwards. Although she had seen Tom in the distance, exchanged glances with him across the churchyard as she and Peter were getting into the car, there had been no opportunity for her to speak to him. She hadn't heard from him since that day. As for asking him to go to Bobby's party with her . . .

She looked again at the invitation. It was to take place on the Saturday after the opening of the women's refuge and she knew that so far there were no bookings for that weekend. She made up her mind to keep it clear. Her best friend's engagement party was something she was determined not to miss, though she was pretty sure that she'd be going alone.

The kettle boiled and she made a pot of tea, then sat down again and opened the other letter. As she'd guessed, it was from Peter. She read it through once. Then, with a cold feeling in the pit of her stomach, she went back to the beginning and read it again, her heart sinking like a stone.

Dear Fleur,

After careful consideration and a long discussion with Lorraine, my wife, I have come to the reluctant decision to put Arden Catering on the market. This of course will include the house and other effects integral to the business We – that is Lorraine and myself – are eager to buy a hotel of our own over here in Geneva and for this we will need all the resources available to us.

The agent handling the sale is R.J. Matthews and Co. of 128 High Street, Elvemere. I shall not be coming back to England until an acceptable figure is negotiated, at which time I shall be required to sign the contract. I shall understand if you wish to leave to take up alternative employment, but I would be grateful if you would remain to honour any existing bookings. Also it would be helpful if you were on hand to show prospective buyers round and answer any queries regarding the books, etc.

With thanks in advance for your help.

Yours sincerely,

Peter

She laid the letter down on the table, her heart racing with anger and hurt. She'd been conned! Once again Peter Arden had used her. He had accepted her support; taken advantage of her fondness for his mother and her willingness to help. And now that she had fulfilled her purpose she was to be tossed aside without consideration or regard. But apparently not before she had carried out Peter Arden's wishes to the letter.

Her first impulse was to pack and get out right away; to write him a letter telling him what she thought of him, advising him to get over here and attend to the sale himself. He clearly had not the slightest qualm about depriving her of her job and her home. He even expected her to help sell the business! Not one word was mentioned about a reference for a future employer. With Sally gone she had nothing to show for all her hard work.

All that morning as she worked, the words of Peter's stiff, formal letter swam before her eyes, mocking her for the fool she had been. As she planned the week's work, the pleasure and enthusiasm she normally felt were gone. Luckily there was little preparation to be done for the two functions booked for that week. She had already seen to it that all the freezers were full which was just as well. She would have had little heart for the creative cooking she normally enjoyed so much.

If she were to walk away today, no one in Elvemere would miss her, she told herself bleakly. She had never been anything but an embarrassment to Julia. Only Charlotte had been anything like a friend.

By lunchtime she had decided. She would pocket her pride and go round to see Tom, show him Bobby's invitation and let him decide whether he wanted to go with her or not. After she had closed the office for the day she took the van and drove into Elvemere.

At Park Row Charlotte was just arriving home from work. She was delighted to see Fleur and invited her in.

'You'll never guess. Mum came to see me last Saturday,' she said as she dumped her bag on the hall table. 'She brought me this silk shawl that Grandma

475

lugged back from some Caribbean island or other.' She laughed. 'Wait till you see it. It's *ghastly*! Are you coming upstairs for a minute? I'll make us a coffee.'

'That'd be lovely,' Fleur said, glancing towards Tom's door. 'I'd like a word with Tom first though. You go on up. I'll join you in a few minutes.'

'Tom? Oh, he's not there,' Charlotte said.

'Not in yet, you mean?'

'No. He's away. The paper has sent him on an assignment somewhere in the Midlands. I think it's to do with the local football team. Some hunk they're buying – I don't know the details but he seemed quite chuffed about it. It's to be a two-page spread, whatever that is. With a by-line. Then he's got this interview.'

Fleur looked at her. 'What interview?'

'I'm not sure. Didn't he tell you? A job interview. Sports editor, I think. On some Northern paper.' Charlotte looked at Fleur's crestfallen face. 'Oh, I'm sorry. I thought you'd have heard.' She paused. 'You and Tom haven't been hitting it off too well lately, have you?'

Fleur lifted her shoulders in an effort to disguise the pain and disappointment that threatened to overwhelm her. It was such an anticlimax after she'd plucked up all her courage. 'He did write me a note on the day before the funeral, but I haven't had a chance to reply.' She opened her bag. 'This morning I had an invitation for both of us to go to an engagement party and I wanted to see if he'd like to go.'

Charlotte smiled. 'That's great! It might break the ice, get you two back together again.'

'I know but it's this coming Saturday, in London. I'll have to go up on Friday evening. Will he be back?'

'Oh! Probably not. I couldn't say.' Seeing Fleur's disappointment, Charlotte held out her hand. 'Look, give it to me. If he does get back before the weekend I'll

476

make sure he gets it this time. I'll pin it to that board with a six-inch nail if I can find one.' She looked at Fleur sympathetically. 'You've had a really rough time lately, haven't you?' She reached out her arms shyly. 'Can I give you a hug?'

Touched, Fleur nodded and Charlotte hugged her warmly. 'There,' she said. 'I know a hug always helps me when I'm fed up. Come up and have that coffee. Stay for supper, if you like? I'm making lasagne and there's always too much for one.'

Over the meal Fleur showed Charlotte Peter's letter about the sale of Arden Catering. The girl was indignant.

'Of all the nerve! After all you've done too. What'll you do, Fleur?'

'I've more or less decided to leave Elvemere,' she said. 'I might even stay on in London, not just for the weekend but for good. Bobby's mother will put me up until I find a job and somewhere to live. There isn't anything here for me any more.'

Charlotte looked dismayed. 'Don't make any quick decisions, Fleur,' she said. 'Things will work out somehow. You could even move in here, especially if Tom's leaving. I'd really miss you if you left now.'

Fleur smiled at the younger girl. It was a comfort to know that at least there was one person who would miss her. 'Well, I'll see,' she said.

Sadie's meeting with Rick at The King's Head had been well worthwhile. At first she had been sceptical about the 'juicy piece of gossip' he had dangled in front of her, suspecting it was an elaborate chat-up line. But he'd turned up at the pub looking as if he meant business, his curly hair shampooed and brushed and his cheeks shaved smooth. He'd tried hard with his appearance, wearing a rather flashy shell suit. She guessed he was still under the false impression that she could help him onto the first rung of the ladder to a modelling career, and until she had some inkling as to whether he was on the level about this story she was content to let him go on nursing it.

'Well,' she challenged as they sat over tall glasses of lager in the bar. 'Do I get to hear this amazing story of yours then?'

He grinned at her. 'Tell me what it's worth first.'

'You know I can't, Rick. Can you at least give me a clue?'

He sipped his beer thoughtfully. 'I told you already, it's about a woman councillor,' he said.

'Yes. And that she has something to do with the new women's refuge. I'd have to be a complete idiot not to realise who it is we're talking about, but that still isn't to say it's a story I could use.'

Rick stared into his glass for a moment. 'Ever asked yourself why she's so keen on this refuge place?'

'She's sympathetic? A bit of a feminist? Feels that in spite of the advances that have been made, women – especially single mothers – still get a raw deal?' Sadie shrugged. 'All that has already been in the *Clarion*.'

'All that crap, yes.' He looked up and his eyes met hers. 'But not the *real* reason,' he said softly. 'Not many people know that she was once a single mum herself.'

Sadie looked up, her attention focused. 'You mean her daughter was born out of wedlock? That's hardly hot news nowadays, Rick.'

'Yeah. But I'm not talking about the daughter everyone here knows. This was another one, born and hushed up when she was a teenager. And only me and one other person knows about it.' He paused for effect. 'Not even her old man.'

Sadie's mouth dropped open for a second. 'I couldn't print that.'

'Why not?'

'My editor would never agree, not even if it were true,' she said. 'This is Elvemere, not London. The Grants have a lot of clout in the town. They'd probably sue the *Clarion* for every penny it owns for printing a story like that. Anyway, how would I ever prove it if no one else knows?'

'It *is* true,' Rick insisted. 'The person who told me got it from the lady in question. Straight from the horse's mouth.'

Sadie was silent. If it was true there could be a whale of a story here. She could see the headlines already. *Secret Love Child of Local Councillor. Champion of battered mums and wife of local businessman makes startling confession.* Not that Councillor Mrs Grant *would* confess, of course. The child would presumably have been adopted and proof of a thing like that would take some digging up after all these years. She sucked in her cheeks thoughtfully. Although there might be ways . . .

'Come on then.' Rick was looking at her. 'You gonna buy it or ain't you?'

'I don't know. I mean, that fact on its own isn't madly exciting, is it? How much more do you know?'

'Quite a lot. It's hot stuff too.' He rolled a cigarette deftly with one hand, peering at her as he flicked his tongue along the edge of the paper. 'You don't get no more though, not till you've made me a proper offer. I told you too much already.'

Earlier that day, after Damian was in bed and Tracey was too tired to withstand his determination, he'd wheedled the rest of the story from her. Using his not inconsiderable cajoling skills, he'd extracted from her the rest of what Julia had told her.

Sadie was eyeing him suspiciously. 'If you're winding me up, Rick . . .'

'I'm not. There's stacks more. Straight up.'

Sadie made up her mind. 'Okay then, providing it's worth it . . .' She named a figure that disappointed him.

'No deal,' he said, getting up. 'I thought you news hounds paid good money for stuff like this. Maybe some other paper – the *Eastern Chronicle*.'

'No, *wait*!' Sadie's appetite for the story was well and truly whetted now. If she had to pay him the rest out of her own pocket she was determined to have exclusive rights. 'You'll have to promise me not to sell it anywhere else though.'

'Okay, you're on. What do you reckon?'

She named a new sum and Rick sat down again. It wasn't a fortune but it would be enough to get him out of Elvemere. Going straight had got him nowhere, had it? If he didn't get out of here soon he could see himself being well and truly trapped. He'd made a couple of good contacts when he was inside – up in London. If he could get up there with enough over to keep him in food and a cheap room for a few days . . . Freedom beckoned seductively. 'Okay,' he said eagerly. 'You're on!' He leaned forward confidentially. 'It was in nineteen-seventy. At a pop festival . . .'

Julia knocked on the door of Eleanor's little house and waited. She'd been intrigued by the mysterious phone call she'd received this morning. Eleanor had refused to tell her over the telephone why she wanted to see her, insisting that she call round at the house as soon as possible. And when the older woman opened the door Julia could see at once that she was pleased about something and eager to tell her about it.

'Julia! Come in, my dear.' Eleanor led the way through to her sunny little living room where coffee was already brewing. 'Forgive me for dragging you round here but as I have no transport of my own . . .'

'That's all right. I don't mind in the least. What is it,

Eleanor? Has something exciting happened?'

'Well, yes, it has rather.' The other woman poured the coffee and sat down. 'I had a telephone call from the Town Clerk yesterday afternoon,' she said. 'It's off the record for the moment, but Philip Forsyth, the Deputy Mayor, is about to resign. It's something to do with his wife's health. He doesn't think she could stand the taxing round of engagements entailed in his being Mayor.'

'I see.' Julia was still wondering in what way the news could affect her when Eleanor said, 'So it seems they're about to ask me officially to take over from him.'

'Eleanor!' Julia smiled. 'Congratulations. No one deserves the honour more than you do.'

'I must admit that I am thrilled,' she said. 'Though I have a sneaking suspicion that as the longest standing member of the council I'm the only one who knows the drill well enough to take it on at short notice.' She paused to sip her coffee. 'Because, you see, it'll mean taking over as Mayor very soon. Next month, in fact, and the only snag is that as I no longer have a husband, I'm going to be short of a Mayoress.'

'Well, yes, but that shouldn't be a problem, should it? You must know plenty of nice men who would be only too happy to be your consort.'

'Yes, but I don't want any of them, Julia. I want you.'

Julia's eyes widened with surprise as she stared speechlessly at her friend and fellow councillor. '*Me?*'

'Who better? You have the necessary charm and grace. I don't want some old bald-headed deadbeat trailing round after me. I'll be needing all the glamour I can get.' She chuckled good-naturedly. 'After all, who's going to turn out to see what an old bag like me is wearing? Besides, you've already proved yourself a damned good councillor. You've tackled a controversial

481

social issue many would have baulked at, and won.' She peered at Julia's stunned expression. 'Well, my dear, what do you say? Will you do it for me?'

'Well – I'd be honoured, of course.'

'Naturally you'll want to speak to Vernon about it before you commit yourself. It'll mean a bit of disruption to your domestic arrangements, so it'll be as well to have his cooperation and support.'

'Yes. I'll tell him what you've proposed tonight. I won't keep you in suspense, Eleanor. I'll get back to you as soon as I can.'

It wasn't difficult for Sadie to find out where Julia went to school. She only had to look in back numbers of the *Clarion* for her election details. The records showed that the headmistress at that time had been a Miss Treadgold, now retired and living in a cottage down at Ormsborgh on the Norfolk coast. On being told on the telephone that Sadie was researching the history of the school for a newspaper article the old lady had readily agreed to see her the following Sunday.

It turned out that Miss Treadgold had kept every copy of the school magazine between the years 1958 and 1980 when she had retired, and from them Sadie obtained a list of teachers and pupils, including Julia Philips, as she had been then.

Mrs Mary Griggs, who taught Form 5A at St Hilda's, had been a young newly qualified teacher in 1969 and Sadie discovered to her delight that she was still teaching at the school. On the same pretext she had used to see Miss Treadgold, Sadie got her to agree to see her in the lunch break.

'I married an Elvemere man soon after I came here,' Mrs Griggs told her. 'We made our home and brought up our family here, which is why I never moved on. I love the town and the school, and I'm so pleased you're going to write an article about the history of it.'

Sadie listened politely to what seemed an endless stream of reminiscences and anecdotes, wondering how she could lead the conversation around to what she really wanted to know. At last she said, 'Quite a lot of your girls have done well, haven't they, Mrs Griggs?'

'Oh, yes. There are several doctors and a barrister whom I remember well,' the teacher said proudly. 'One girl became an opera singer and . . .'

'And there's Councillor Mrs Grant, of course,' Sadie broke in. 'The councillor responsible for the new women's refuge that's about to be opened.'

'Yes.' Mrs Griggs looked doubtful. 'Yes, I remember Julia very well. Not academic, of course, but a pleasant enough girl – if only she hadn't been so easily influenced by the unsuitable friendship she formed.'

'Friendship? Who with?' Sadie was intrigued. Maybe at last she might be getting somewhere.

'A girl called Joanna Bloom,' Mrs Griggs said, drawing down the corners of her mouth. 'They were inseparable, unfortunately. I always wondered what they could possibly have in common. They seemed such opposites. Joanna's family was – not to put too fine a point on it – rather bohemian in outlook, whereas Julia came from a very nice family, highly respected. Her grandfather was the most popular doctor in the town in those days.' She sighed. 'I did my best to part them when they were in my form, but that just seemed to make matters worse.'

'What became of her?' Sadie asked.

'Joanna? She married an American serviceman at quite an early age and left the country.'

An American! Sadie's heart sank. Obviously if she'd been able to talk to this Bloom girl she might have uncovered a lot of useful information. 'I see. So she –

this Joanna Bloom – lives in America? You don't happen to know . . .'

'Oh, she's not there any more,' Mrs Griggs interrupted. 'She must have come back here after her divorce. A few months ago I saw a photograph of her in your paper. There was a small article saying that she'd just become a partner in the building firm of Grant Philips. Her name is different now, of course. I can't remember what it is, but I would have recognised her anywhere. Obviously she and Julia must have remained in contact which is why she joined the firm. I daresay she has grown out of her wild ways by now. I certainly hope so!'

Back at the office Sadie returned to the *Clarion*'s back numbers and found the article in question. It was quite a small piece with a photograph, just as Mrs Griggs had said, and reported that Joanna Hanson, ex-wife of an American real-estate tycoon, had become a partner in Grant Philips Construction last November. Sadie realised that it must have been just before she had joined the staff of the *Clarion*.

She sat back to think. If Joanna was a partner in Julia's family firm – if the two women had been close friends and, presumably, still were – it was hardly likely that Joanna would want to spill the beans on her pal's secret past. All the same, it was her only lead, and as such she couldn't afford to pass it up. Thumbing through the telephone book she found Joanna's address and made a note of it. She wouldn't ring first. She'd pay her a surprise visit later this evening. Taken off guard, she might open up. You never knew your luck!

Julia had waited until they'd finished eating that evening to break the news to Vernon. She wasn't sure how he'd take it. He'd never been keen on her being on the council and as for her being Mayoress . . . He'd been preoccupied over the past few days. Several times she thought he was about to tell her something, but so far he had held back on whatever it was. She looked up at him over her coffee cup.

'Eleanor asked me to go round and see her this morning.'

'Oh, yes?'

'I thought I might ask her to come and have a meal with us. I thought perhaps next Sunday. Charlotte is coming too.'

Vernon grunted a reply which could have been yes or no. Julia cleared her throat. 'Vernon, Eleanor . . .'

'Look, Julia,' he interrupted. He put down his cup and met her eyes across the table. 'There's something I think you'd better know.'

'What?'

'Dad has got himself into a bit of a bind about the Victoria Gardens project. There's a problem with the survey and he thought – *we* thought – it might be a good idea to mortgage both houses.'

She stared at him. 'You mean, hand them over – to the bank?'

He groaned. 'It's merely a business arrangement, Julia. It won't affect you at all. This will still be your home. It's just to tide us over for a few months – as security.'

'I can't see anything secure about living in a house that belongs to the bank,' she said. 'What if the Victoria Gardens thing falls through? We could be homeless just like that.'

'Trust you to overdramatise it! Thousands of people have mortgages. It's perfectly normal.' He shook his head. 'This is the kind of reaction that stops me from telling you things about the business!'

'I'm not a fool, Vernon. With Beardsley's going

485

under, the Meadowlands Estate is in jeopardy. Things look bad, don't they?'

He shook his head. 'You know nothing about it, Julia. Why don't you leave these things to people who do?'

'The people who *do* don't seem to be making much of a job of it, do they?' she said hotly. 'I think your father is playing with fire. He's contemplating taking our home from us without any guarantee we'll ever get it back.'

'I know that!' Vernon snapped. 'But as he bought it in the first place there isn't a lot I can say, is there?'

'It is in your name though,' she pointed out. 'You could refuse. You've always been against the buying of Victoria Gardens anyway.'

'He's my father. How can I leave him out on a limb, for God's sake? Besides I do have a pretty big interest in what happens to GPC.'

'Then why didn't you block his buying Victoria Gardens in the first place?'

Vernon shrugged impatiently. 'Joanna seemed to agree with Dad and I trust her judgement.' He glared at her. 'Damn it all, Julia, even *you* voted for it!'

She fell silent, unable to argue. 'Well, there's obviously nothing to be done about it, is there? All we can do is hope for the best.' She cleared her throat and made another attempt at breaking her own news. 'Vernon – I've been trying to tell you,' she said, 'Eleanor Maitland has been asked to be Mayor.'

He frowned. 'I thought Philip Forsyth was Deputy.'

'He's resigned because of his wife's health. The thing is, Vernon . . .' She glanced at him. 'Eleanor has asked me to be her Mayoress.'

For a moment he stared at her, then he threw back his head and began to laugh. 'You? *Mayoress!* Oh, my God! I can just see the two of you. Talk about

Morecambe and Wise! I sincerely hope you told her where to go.'

'As a matter of fact, I said I'd be delighted,' Julia said coolly. 'I'm glad you see it as amusing. I take it you have no objections then?'

He stopped laughing to glare at her. 'If you think I'm going to come home to an empty house night after night, no meal waiting, no shirts ironed, you can bloody well think again, Julia! I think it's high time you came down to earth. This council business has gone to your head.'

She sprang to her feet. 'When are you ever here to eat a meal I've prepared?' she demanded. 'And if it's clean shirts you want, why don't you ask Joanna to wash and iron them for you? Most of your spare time seems to be spent with her anyway!'

He stood very still, looking at her with an expression of near loathing. 'As a matter of fact up till now it's only been my sympathy – my *pity* for you – that has prevented me from asking you for a divorce.'

'Your *pity*? Well, you can stop feeling sorry for me, Vernon. You can have your divorce any time you like.'

'Don't be ridiculous!' He looked at her incredulously. 'You couldn't possibly manage on your own. What do you think you'd do for money? You haven't a clue. You need my support, Julia. Without me you'd fall apart.'

'I don't think so.' She stood up very straight and took a deep breath. She felt like a swimmer coming to the surface after being submerged for a long time; filling her lungs with the clean, sweet breath of life. 'I've got news for you, Vernon,' she told him. 'Dad sold our shares in GPC a few days ago. Mine and Charlotte's as well as his own and Mum's.'

'Sold . . .' The colour left Vernon's face and he turned a sickly white. 'Who – who to?' he whispered.

'To Joanna. I'm sure your father will be immensely relieved. And you will soon have a taste of what it's like to be in Joanna's pocket!' She pushed past him on her way to the door. 'That's what you wanted, isn't it? Well, I hope you find it cosy there, Vernon, because you'll never get out.' At the door she turned. 'And you can start divorce proceedings as soon as you like!'

Joanna opened the door and looked at the young woman standing on her doorstep with distaste. She loathed women who dressed like men. And as for the nose stud . . . 'Yes?' she said sharply.

'Mrs Hanson?'

'That's right. Who would you be?'

'My name is Sadie Freeman. I work for the *Clarion*.'

'I see. What do you want with me?'

'I wondered – could I have a word with you, Mrs Hanson?' Sadie paused. This woman was clearly a tough cookie. It wasn't going to be easy. If she really was a friend of Julia Grant's there was no way a woman like this would dish any dirt on her.

Sadie smiled and took a deep breath. 'I've been doing some research on St Hilda's School,' she said, 'and one or two of its more notable ex-pupils. Some rather interesting stories have emerged that I'd like verified. You know how things get twisted and exaggerated over the years. Someone said that you and Councillor Mrs Grant were once close friends and I thought . . .'

The expression on Joanna's face changed from hostility to one of delight. 'Julia?' Her green eyes shone. 'Oh, yes, we were as close as two peas in a pod at school. But that's going back a long time. What have you heard?'

'May I come in?' Sadie asked. 'It's a little confidential. I don't want to talk about it on the doorstep.'

'Of course. What must you think of me?' Joanna opened the door wide. 'Do come in and have a drink. I'll tell you anything I can.'

Half an hour later Sadie left the house in Hazel Grove almost punch drunk with what she had learned. Without the slightest hesitation Joanna Hanson had told her more then she could ever have dreamed about Julia Grant. It was an incredible story and she told it as though it was common knowledge. At seventeen Julia Philips had run away to live with a pop musician she'd met at a festival on the Isle of Wight. That much she'd already heard from Rick, though not that he was half-West Indian. Or that the daughter Julia had abandoned as a small baby was right here in Elvemere running a local catering firm. But the most stunning revelation of all was that the daughter in question was – had to be – Tom Markham's girlfriend. Yes, *Fleur*! There could be little doubt. It all fitted, her age, her looks, all of it.

But why had she come here? Sadie mused. That seemed to be something Joanna would like to know too. Was it merely a daughter's curiosity about her real mother, or did she have a deeper, darker motive? Revenge, perhaps. But one glaringly hard fact had emerged from her interview with Joanna Hanson. She was no friend of Julia Grant's! For some reason she wanted – intended – to do her as much harm as possible. And that intrigued Sadie most of all. One thing was for sure: there was more – far more – to be extracted from all this than a mere piece of small-town gossip!

On the morning of the opening of the women's refuge Julia was up early. Since their row Vernon had removed himself to the spare room. Each morning he rose early and left the house without breakfast. They had hardly made contact since that night. It was a miserable existence. She had thought he would move out to join

Joanna but as he hadn't it looked as though it was up to Julia to find somewhere else to live.

In the silent kitchen she made herself some toast and coffee and tried to prepare herself for the coming day. Fleur had promised to be at Alexandra House early to lay out the buffet lunch and Julia had booked a nine o'clock hair appointment so that she could be there to help. Everything seemed to be satisfactorily organised. She was just about to go upstairs to get dressed when the back door bell rang.

With a small exclamation of annoyance, Julia went to answer it and found a distraught Tracey standing outside with Damian in his buggy.

'Oh, Mrs Grant, I'm sorry to trouble you. I know you must be busy but I had to come.'

'What on earth is wrong, Tracey?' Julia held the door open. 'Look, you'd better come in.'

'It's Rick,' she said as she manoeuvred the buggy through the door. 'He's gone. When I woke up this morning he'd just – just left.'

'Are you sure?'

'Yes. He left a note. He isn't coming back.'

'But where has he gone?'

'He didn't say.' The girl fumbled in her bag. 'Look . . .' She held out a crumpled scrap of paper that looked like part of an old envelope. Julia took it.

Deer Trace, Sory I got to go. Being a dad is no good for me. You are beter of without me. Love Rick.

Tracey burst into tears. 'What am I going to do, Mrs Grant?' she sobbed. 'I thought we were gonna be okay. I thought he was as happy as me. Now this!'

Julia put down the letter and put her arms round the girl. 'Oh, Tracey, I'm sorry. I know it isn't helping you right now, but I do think Rick has a point. He wasn't

490

very good father material, was he? He would have broken your heart in the end – may have even turned violent again. You really are better off without him. Maybe some day you'll meet someone else – someone kind and hard-working who'll take care of you.' She knew the words were banal and unlikely and wished there was something more constructive she could do for the girl.

'There's no way I'm going to be able to manage,' Tracey said desperately. 'Not with two kids. Rick took all the rent money with him too. I save it, see, in a jam jar on the top shelf of the kitchen cabinet. I looked before I came out. It's gone – every penny of it. They'll chuck me out if I can't pay again this month.'

'Well, that's one thing we can do something about.' Julia went to her bag and opened it but Tracey held up her hand. 'No! Rick took them things from Mr Grant. I still owe you for them. I couldn't take any more from you. No, *really*.' She took a handkerchief from her sleeve and blew her nose. 'If I could just get a job. Maybe a housekeeper's job where I could live in. But with one kid and another on the way, who'd take me on?'

'I do see what you mean . . .' Suddenly the idea hit Julia. 'Of course! Why didn't I think of it before?' she muttered. 'Tracey – how would you like to be caretaker of the women's refuge?'

Tracey's brimming eyes opened wide with hope. 'Oh! Oh, Mrs Grant, do you really think I could do it?'

'I don't see why you shouldn't apply. I can vouch for the fact that you're honest and a good worker. There's a little flat with the job. Only two small rooms but it's on the ground floor so it would be handy for you with the children. And the rule at the refuge is to be that the women will be responsible for their own rooms, so you wouldn't be expected to keep the whole place clean.

Just supervise and be there to take charge. What do you think?'

The relief on the girl's face was touching. 'I'd be ever so grateful, if you'd put in a word for me Mrs Grant. It's like the answer to a prayer.'

'Look, Tracey, I've got to go to the hairdresser's now but why don't you come along to the opening?' Julia suggested. 'I can introduce you to the social worker who'll be in charge of Alexandra House and you can have a chat with her.'

Sadie arrived at Alexandra House just as Fleur was putting the finishing touches to the buffet table. She unstrapped her camera and equipment from the bike and dumped them in a corner of the kitchen, eyeing Fleur as she did so.

'You're early,' Fleur remarked.

'Yes. As a matter of fact, I was hoping to have a quiet word with you.'

Fleur smiled. 'Well, here I am. What can I do for you?'

'It's awkward. Look, there's a rumour that you are Julia Grant's daughter. Is it true?'

Fleur was stunned. 'I've heard no such rumour. Where did you hear it?'

'I can't tell you that. I just want to know if there's any truth in it?'

'Why?' Fleur asked suspiciously.

Sadie shrugged. 'I hate uncertainties. Besides, you have to admit that it's a damned good story.'

Fleur turned away to hide the flush that she could feel warming her cheeks. 'I've heard no rumours,' she said non-commitally. 'I can't think who could be spreading a story like that.'

'So – there's nothing in it?'

'Do you think I wouldn't know if there was?' she stalled.

'It's possible you wouldn't.' Sadie looked at her. 'Tell me – were you an adopted child?'

'No,' Fleur said firmly. 'And now, if you'll excuse me, I have to get on.'

She escaped to the dining room and stood for a long moment looking out over the back garden, her mind in a whirl. Where had Sadie's information come from? As far as she knew Tom was the only other person who knew. Was it possible he had told Sadie? She shrank from the thought. Surely he would never betray her confidence, however angry he was with her. Would Sadie publish the story in the paper? Not without solid proof, surely? It could do untold harm to Julia. Somehow she must warn her before Sadie sprang her startling accusation. It could ruin the whole day.

She saw Julia arrive, but she was accompanied by a social worker. Then a girl with a baby in a pushchair claimed her attention and the three of them were engaged in earnest conversation. Soon a party of councillors arrived, then the TV and local radio people began milling around, setting up their equipment. Finally it was almost twelve o'clock and time for the Mayor to arrive and perform the opening ceremony. If she didn't get Julia's attention now it might be too late. Fleur seized the opportunity of a small lull to edge through the crowd to Julia's side.

'Can I have a quick word?'

'Of course. Is there a problem with the buffet?'

'No. It's a bit more worrying than that,' Fleur said, taking her arm and drawing her to one side. 'One of the journalists – the girl in the motorbike gear – has been asking me if, well, if there's any truth in the rumour that I'm your daughter.'

493

The colour drained from Julia's face. 'Oh, God! Where did she get hold of that?'

'I've no idea. It wasn't from me.'

'What did you tell her?'

'That I'd heard no rumours myself. She asked me if I was an adopted child. I said no, but I don't think she was convinced.'

One name was in Julia's mind. *Joanna*. She glanced anxiously at her watch. 'I've a pretty good idea who's responsible for this,' she said. 'But I haven't time to worry about it now. Thank you for warning me, Fleur. Don't worry, I'll think of something.'

There was a sudden flurry of activity as a limousine pulled up in the street outside. Julia said, 'I think that will be the Mayor arriving. It will have to wait for the time being.'

Fleur watched as the Mayor, resplendent in his scarlet robes and chain, cut the ribbon strung symbolically across the doorway and declared the refuge open. Cameras flashed and for the half-hour that followed Julia was surrounded by reporters, either wanting to record statements for the radio, TV or for the papers. Sadie waited, biding her time until last. Fleur watched her but, frustratingly, the other girl had still made no move towards Julia when she received the signal to begin serving the buffet.

'Mrs Grant, can I have a few words from you for the paper?' Sadie placed herself squarely in front of Julia, her pencil poised. 'I know you've made statements for the other papers, radio and so on, but I thought there might be something more personal you could say. Your own intimate view of all this as a local woman and – er – mother?' She was watching Julia's face intently. 'For instance, there's a rumour going round that you yourself might have had occasion to use a refuge like this some years ago.'

'I can truthfully say that I have never experienced domestic violence, I'm glad to say,' Julia said carefully. 'But that doesn't mean that I can't empathise with the plight of women who have.'

'I was talking about being a single mother,' Sadie said daringly. 'Rumour has it that you had a child prior to your present marriage. A daughter. And that she actually lives and works here in Elvemere.'

Julia's expression did not change. 'Really? Is that how rumour has it? How interesting.'

'So – will you deny that?'

'I really don't see why I should deny or confirm anything. I'm not on trial, am I? I think my personal life, especially something that allegedly happened so long ago, is entirely my own business.'

'Some people might not think so, Mrs Grant,' Sadie said. 'I'm sorry, *Councillor* Mrs Grant, I mean,' she added pointedly. 'There is also a rumour that you're being tipped as the town's next Mayoress.'

'So many rumours. And all in one day!' For a long moment Julia stared at the reporter, suddenly aware that she was fighting a losing battle. She was facing a turning point in her life. In the next few minutes her life – her whole future – would be in jeopardy. Now it was all down to her. The next hour was make or break time. She could give in and watch her life crumble round her, or she could stand with her back to the wall and fight. Gathering every ounce of her courage, she said firmly, 'After lunch I shall be making a speech. If you'd like to stay until then you can print everything I have to say. In fact . . .' She took a deep breath. 'In fact, I'm relying on you to do just that!'

During lunch, trying not to think of her coming or-deal, Julia made sure she spoke personally to everyone

495

and thanked them for coming. Afterwards, the guests mellowed by wine and good food and the atmosphere more relaxed, Julia decided that the time had come. Her heart drumming with apprehension, she clapped her hands for silence.

'If I could just have your attention for a moment or two, ladies and gentlemen, I'd like to say a few words,' she said. 'As many of you know, this refuge has been the dream of local underprivileged and abused women for some time and I am very proud to be able to say that it was I who finally managed to bring the scheme to fruition. I hope that it will prove to be a haven for all the women and children who need respite and sanctuary, either for a few days or for longer. My hope is that it will prove to be a quiet place where they can pick up the threads of a broken life, heal their damaged self-esteem and make a new start.' She paused, trying to calm her nervousness. 'I would also like to take this opportunity of telling you my own story so that you will understand why this place is so close to my heart.'

She saw that she had the attention of everyone in the room and had to pause again to gather all her strength and wait for her heartbeat to steady. 'Most of the women who will take shelter in this refuge will do so because they have made a very basic but devastating mistake,' she began. 'I have good reason to know that no one, however clever or wise, from whatever walk of life, is ever immune from that folly. My own mistake was a familiar one. I fell in love too young, and with the wrong man. Too naive to realise the heartache I was causing, I ran away with him. But that wasn't my worst mistake. I'm ashamed to say that I later followed it with an even worse one: that of not facing up to the havoc I had caused, of failing to see it through.'

Suddenly aware of the deep silence that had fallen

on the room, she looked at the faces turned towards her. All eyes were upon her – waiting intently. She had passed the point of no return. There was no going back. She cleared her throat and went on.

'I was seventeen when my first child was born, and by that time her father had already left me. But I was too unhappy, too homesick, to see how lovely my baby daughter was; too immature to realise how trusting, how totally dependent on me she was. When she was a few months old I could bear it no longer. I took the easy way out – left her behind with her grandmother and ran away again. I ran away from my responsibilities, but I couldn't run away from the consequences. I didn't see that because of my cowardice I was sacrificing the love of my child. I didn't foresee the pain of not being there to see her take her first steps or hear her first words. And because no one knew my secret, I had to suffer the heartbreak alone. The fact that I never saw my child grow up and blossom into the beautiful young woman she is today is something I shall regret for the rest of my life.'

Julia suddenly caught sight of Eleanor, standing on the fringes of the crowd. The older woman was watching her, eyes misty with compassion. Strengthened by her sympathetic support, Julia turned towards the back of the room where Fleur stood.

'This afternoon, for the first time, I would like to introduce you publicly to my elder daughter,' she said boldly. 'Although she has not been in Elvemere long, many of you already know her. In the few months that she has been here she has made her mark as the late Sally Arden's very capable assistant: Fleur Sylvester.' She held out her hand. 'Fleur – will you come and join me, please?'

All eyes turned to look at her, and after a moment's hesitation Fleur moved forward to stand beside Julia as cameras flashed from all sides of the room.

'May I introduce you to my daughter?' Julia said. She reached for her glass and held it up. 'Please will you join me in drinking to the future of Alexandra House Women's Refuge, coupled with a toast to my daughter, Fleur!'

There was a pause as everyone drank. Then a burst of enthusiastic applause.

'I wish you'd warned me, Julia,' Fleur whispered. 'It was very brave, but if I'd known what you were going to do . . .'

'I should have done it years ago.' Julia reached out and squeezed her hand. 'Don't worry, neither of us has anything to be ashamed of,' she said. 'Later we must talk, but first there's something I have to do. You won't go away, will you?'

'No, of course not.'

Julia smiled. 'Right. I'll see you later.'

She walked across to where Eleanor was waiting. 'I'm sorry, Eleanor,' she said. 'All that happened on the spur of the moment. If I'd planned it I would have prepared you. It's a long story. I'll explain everything to you in detail some time. I'll be resigning my seat on the council, of course. And naturally I won't hold you to your offer to appoint me your Mayoress.'

'Stuff and rubbish! If you won't be Mayoress, I won't be Mayor!' Eleanor said stoutly.

Julia laughed and bent to kiss the older woman's cheek. 'Bless you for that, but you must accept. You know that.'

'And so must you, whether you're on the council or not. I mean it!'

'Well, we'll see.'

Sadie paused at Julia's elbow. 'Excuse me. Did you mean what you said about going public, Mrs Grant?'

'Of course. I want you to print every word,' Julia

said firmly. 'Just make sure you spell the names right, that's all.'

Sadie laughed. 'I'll do my best!'

The media people moved in after that. Julia gave a brief interview to both radio and TV reporters and more photographs were taken. The rest of the guests drifted away in groups until at last Fleur and Julia were left alone.

'It's been quite a day,' Julia said.

Fleur nodded. 'Tomorrow will be difficult for you.'

'When the papers come out?' Julia sighed. 'Maybe radio and TV will be even quicker with the story.' She gathered her coat and handbag together. 'I think my first priority is to get round to my parents' house. It's vital that I break this news to them before they see or hear it from some other source. I'll go round and see Charlotte when she gets home from the office. She must be told too.' She looked at Fleur. 'Will you come with me?'

Fleur shook her head. 'I think it's probably a bit too late for that, don't you?' she said. 'There isn't much point anyway. I shan't be around for much longer.'

'You're surely not leaving?'

'I'm afraid I'll have to. Sally's son is selling Arden Catering, complete with the house and everything that goes with it. When it's sold I'll be out of a job and a home. I'm going up to London tomorrow for a friend's engagement party. I'm thinking seriously of moving back there once everything is tied up here. After all, it's where my roots are.'

'I suppose it is.' Julia smiled wistfully. 'So – unlike me, you won't be around to catch the fall-out when the local paper hits the street!'

'No.' Fleur opened her handbag and took out a tattered brown envelope. 'You might like to have these,' she said. 'It's just a few old photographs. There are some of me as a baby and a couple of Dean – all I ever knew of him.'

Tears sprang to Julia's eyes as she took out the snapshots and looked at them. Her heart contracted painfully as she looked at the fading images she had carried in her memory. 'But they're yours,' she said.

Fleur shook her head. 'Take them. I know them by heart. Maybe your parents might like to see them.' She looked at Julia. 'I don't need reminding of the past any more now. You laid all those ghosts for me when you made your speech. I have to concentrate on the future now.'

Julia put them into her bag, looking at Fleur with regret. 'I'd have liked that future to have included me. It's such a shame you're leaving just when we've found each other.'

Fleur wanted to correct her, to say, 'Just when I've finally been forced to acknowledge you, you mean.' But she reminded herself that what Julia had done that afternoon had taken courage and instead she shook her head and said, 'Let's face it, I daresay I'd only be an embarrassment to you if I stayed. After all, there's your husband to think of, isn't there? I don't suppose the prospect of running into me round every corner would please him much.'

'None of this will concern Vernon,' Julia said. 'It isn't public knowledge yet but we're about to start divorce proceedings.'

'Oh. I'm sorry.'

'Don't be. It's for the best.' Julia looked at her. 'I wish things had been different, Fleur. I meant everything I said, you know. I wasn't just looking for cheap publicity when I made that speech this afternoon. Leaving you the way I did was the worst thing I ever did. It has been the greatest regret of my life and if I could turn back the clock and do it differently, I would. All this means that I'm going to have to resign my seat on the council, but I know now that it isn't important. For the first time in my life I feel like a complete person. I feel strong enough to face the future.'

Chapter 17

Julia was packing. The past few hours had been traumatic and once tomorrow's paper came out she would be obliged to move out. She decided that she might as well go now, before Vernon came home from work. *If* he came home, that was.

After the opening of the refuge the previous day she had gone straight round to Gresham House, anxious to get the ordeal of telling her parents over as soon as possible. A surprised May had opened the door to her.

'Julia! What a nice surprise, dear. I thought you were going to be tied up all day and too busy to . . .' The look of pleasure on her face faded when she saw Julia's expression. 'Darling, whatever is the matter? You look as if you've seen a ghost.'

'I need to talk to you and Daddy right away,' she said.

'Of course. Come into the morning room. We've just come in from the garden and I've made some tea.'

Harry looked up with a smile as his daughter came into the room. 'Hello, Julia. Just in time for tea. I always . . .'

'Julia has something she wants to talk to us about,' May interrupted him. She pulled out a chair. 'Sit down, darling, and take your time. I'm sure that whatever it is, it can't be as bad as you think. And Daddy and I will be able to help.'

'To begin with, Vernon and I have agreed to divorce,' Julia said. 'That will come as no surprise to you. He told me that Charlie wants to mortgage both houses to tide the business over financially. It seems he's had some kind of setback over the houses in Victoria Gardens. That brought things to a head but . . .' She paused to take a deep breath. 'But when tomorrow's *Clarion* comes out, I think he'll probably feel that he has good grounds for divorcing me.'

'Julia!' May looked alarmed. 'Whatever do you mean?'

'Someone – Joanna, I suspect – told a reporter from the *Clarion* about something that happened a long time ago; something I did.'

Harry glanced at his wife's distressed face and cleared his throat. 'I think you'd better come to the point, Julia. What has Joanna said?'

'You remember the time when I lived in London – before Vernon and I met?'

May frowned. 'When you had that secretarial job and shared a flat with that girl – what was her name?'

'There was no job, Mum. No flat either. I went to a pop festival with Joanna on the Isle of Wight that weekend, not on a school trip as I led you believe. I met someone there – a musician called Dean Sylvester. I fell wildly in love with him and when he asked me to stay with him, I couldn't resist.'

A little cry of dismay escaped May's lips. 'Oh, Julia!'

Harry frowned at his wife. 'Let Julia finish the story,' he said. 'What happened?'

'It didn't work. If I'd been older, more mature, I'd have known it was destined for failure. When I became pregnant he took me to his parents' home in East London and left me there. I saw him a few times after that, but eventually he told me it was over between us.'

'So you had an – an abortion. Is that what you're trying to tell us?'

'No, Mum.' Julia looked at her mother. 'I had a baby daughter. I called her Fleur. Dean's parents were very kind to me. They were disappointed in their son but they adored the baby. They were quite happy for me to stay there with them. But I couldn't settle. As time went by it grew worse. I was so unhappy and homesick that I couldn't see things straight. In the end, when Fleur was just a few months old, I left her with them and I – came home.' She looked at the faces of her mother and father.

'I knew it. I knew there was something wrong.' May's eyes were brimming with tears. She was remembering all the little things that had puzzled her at the time; the muffled sounds of sobbing, heard through the bedroom wall late at night, the wraith-like thinness and the haunted look in the girl's eyes.

Harry looked hurt and angry. 'How could you do that to us, Julia?' he said. 'Didn't you trust us enough to know that we would have forgiven you? We would have been hurt, of course; disappointed maybe. But to leave your child – to keep this secret from us all these years.' He shook his head, trying to come to terms with this new facet of the daughter he thought he knew so well. 'What did you think we were – monsters?'

'I can't help feeling that we must have failed you somewhere,' May said sadly. 'But I think I can understand how you must have felt.'

'I did try to get Fleur back,' Julia told them. 'I hadn't realised how much I'd miss her. I wanted her so desperately that I thought my heart would break. I wrote to Dean's mother, but she wrote back saying that Fleur had been adopted and that it wouldn't be possible to get her back.'

'And all through this you never said a word,' May said, shaking her head. 'You suffered all of it alone.'

'Soon after that I met Vernon,' Julia went on. 'It seemed to please you both so much when we were married. Then Charlotte was born and having another baby in my arms helped take away the pain.'

'Vernon – does he know about this?' Harry asked. 'Did you tell him?'

'No.' Julia turned to look at her father. 'That's what I meant when I said he'd have grounds to divorce me. You see, all this came out at the opening of the refuge today. One of the journalists asked me about it point blank. It was obvious that it was going to be exposed so I decided my only course was to spike their guns. I stood up and told them about it. The story is bound to be in tomorrow's paper.' May began to weep quietly into her handkerchief and Julia reached out to touch her shoulder.

'Oh, Mum, I'm so sorry. I thought after all these years I'd saved you the pain of this.'

'It's not for me I'm upset,' May said. 'It's for you. All this time without seeing your child and now you're to be made to suffer for it all over again.'

'You never found out what became of her?' Harry asked.

'Yes, I did. You haven't heard everything yet. Fleur came to find me,' Julia told them. 'She was never adopted at all. Dean's mother must have felt guilty about lying to me about it. She made Fleur promise to come and find me, and last year, after her grandmother died, Fleur kept her promise and came to Elvemere to look for me.'

'So you've met her?'

'Yes, we've met. At first she was bitter. She didn't know I'd tried to get her back, and somehow we never managed to find any common ground. There was no

505

way we could make our relationship public so there seemed to be no future for us. I'd have liked us to be friends and remain in touch, but she wouldn't agree to that and now I'm afraid she's going back to London. Perhaps she could never quite bring herself to forgive or trust me. And who can blame her?'

'You mean she's going away again without our having had a chance to meet her?' May said. 'Our own granddaughter?'

'I'm afraid so.' Julia opened her handbag and took the envelope out. 'I've got some photographs though. Fleur herself gave me these today.' She passed the faded snapshots to her mother. 'The young man is Dean, Fleur's father. She never actually knew him. He died in America when she was a little girl. The others are of her when she was little.'

May looked for a long time at the photographs, then at her daughter. 'Dean – he was black?'

'Yes. Half-West Indian on his father's side. I loved him very much, Mum,' Julia told her. 'He was very talented and so – so beautiful. For a little while we were very happy. It was entirely my fault that things fell apart. I was too immature. I thought life was going to be some wonderful idyllic dream and when it wasn't I complained – all the time. I must have been a real pain.'

May studied the photographs carefully, then passed them to Harry. 'This was the real reason you didn't bring the baby home, wasn't it?' she said quietly. 'Little Fleur looks so sweet. Oh, Julia, if only you'd brought her home with you all those years ago.'

'How could I, Mum?'

May frowned. 'Are you trying to tell us that you were ashamed of her?'

'No!' Julia said hotly. 'Not of Fleur – of the fact that I hadn't married her father, perhaps; ashamed that he'd abandoned me. I thought you might be embarrassed;

506

that you'd think I'd let you down. I was thinking of your friends and your social life. Elvemere always was a narrow little place. In many ways it still is.'

'What would any of that have mattered?' May said angrily. 'We would have stood by you and your child, Julia. We would have made sure she had everything she deserved – a good upbringing and education. None of this was her fault, bless her. If you'd brought her home with you, you might never have married Vernon. It hasn't been a happy marriage for you, has it? And now, to know that we have a granddaughter of – what? – twenty years old, that we will never know . . . might never see!'

'You have seen her actually,' Julia told them. 'Her name is Fleur Sylvester and she is – rather was – Sally Arden's assistant.'

May frowned, biting her lip as she tried to remember. 'At your New Year party? The tall attractive girl with the long dark hair? Do you mean you knew then?'

'No, not then. It was later.'

'Julia.' Harry was looking thoughtful. 'You say Joanna knew all this. Is that why you voted with her and the others?'

'Yes, Dad.'

'So she's been blackmailing you? Of course, so much is clear now.' He shook his head. 'If only you'd told us.'

Julia left Gresham House feeling chastened. Her parents' reaction was not what she had expected. She should have known them better than to think they would have set more store by public opinion and their social life than the future of their daughter and granddaughter. If only she had confided in them back in those far-off days, so much misery might have been avoided.

The house was empty when she arrived home. She worked quickly, packing as many of her belongings as

507

she could into a large suitcase. Eleanor would put her up for a few nights until she could begin to sort out something more permanent for herself. She wrote Vernon a letter, explaining as much as she could, preparing him for tomorrow's revelation in the *Clarion* and agreeing to a no fault divorce.

It was a bitter irony that after all the years of infidelity it would finally be Vernon who could claim to be the injured party.

As an afterthought, she added Eleanor's telephone number to the letter so that he could contact her if he needed to, sealed the envelope and propped it up on the hall table, where he would see it as soon as he came in.

Outside she pulled the front door firmly behind her and stood looking up at the house. It had been her home for the past eighteen years and although she had never liked the house, she felt oddly bereft at leaving it. Now she must go and see Charlotte. The sooner she told her about Fleur, the better.

Fleur did not open her copy of the *Clarion* until she was on the train the following afternoon. It was all there – a centre-page spread complete with photographs. Sadie had really gone to town. There was a picture of the Mayor performing the opening ceremony; one of Julia and Councillor Eleanor Maitland; even one of the waif-like Tracey Brownlow, in line for appointment as the refuge's resident caretaker, pictured with her small son, Damian. Fleur read it through very carefully but there was no word of Julia's personal revelation until right at the end when the reader was instructed to: *Turn to page eight for the heart-tugging personal secret of one of Elvemere's women councillors – as told to our reporter, Sadie Freeman.*

Fleur quickly turned to page eight and there it all

508

was – Julia's speech almost verbatim, along with another photograph, this time of Julia and herself together. She'd never forget the way she had felt when Julia made that speech. In front of everyone, including the press, she had revealed the secret she had kept all these years. It had taken courage, Fleur had to admit that. But Julia seemed to have no understanding of what the revelation would do to her daughter. It would have been nice to have had some kind of warning. Julia's speech had made Fleur feel so vulnerable; the fact of her illegitimacy and rejection laid bare for all to see had been humiliating. Julia clearly had not given a thought to her feelings on the matter.

But her mother had still to face the hardest part – telling those closest to her how she had deceived them. That would not be easy, and it was something she must do alone. Their situation was reversed. Ironically, this time it was Fleur who was running out on Julia at a time when she needed her most. She supposed she should be feeling that justice had been done. But strangely, she could feel no triumph, only a sad nostalgia.

When it came to leaving Elvemere she had felt surprisingly emotional. She would have to return after her weekend visit. During the next two weeks there were functions booked that she would have to fulfil and there would be the rest of her packing to do. But it was today that she felt she was symbolically saying goodbye to the town that had been her home for the past ten months.

She had wanted to go round to Park Row and say goodbye to Charlotte, but in the end she couldn't face the girl. Would Julia have told her by now of their blood relationship? And how would she have taken the news? Perhaps Charlotte would resent her. Fleur shrank from the thought, preferring to remember their friendship as it had been.

Tom had not been in touch. Each time the telephone rang, right up till the moment she had left the house, her heart had leaped in the hope that it might be him. In her mind she had worked out what she would say to him. But now she had to face the fact that he did not intend to see her again; had no wish to hear her explanations. And certainly had no intention of accepting her invitation to join her at Bobby's engagement party. Their relationship, it seemed, was at an end.

Till now she had been too busy to make any firm plans for her future. There had been a lot of work to do in the office. She had suspended all future bookings for Arden Catering, explaining to potential clients that the business was to be sold. She had written to Peter, saying that she intended to move back to London as soon as she could and that he should make other arrangements for showing prospective buyers round. Finally she had notified the estate agents that she would be away for a few days, recorded a new message for the answerphone and given the house a thorough clean in case any prospective buyers came while she was away.

Folding the newspaper and pushing it into her bag, she leaned back in her corner seat and looked out of the window. As the train gathered speed the outskirts of Elvemere gave way to the suburbs, the sports field with its football and cricket pitches flashing past; she could catch a glimpse of the roof of the Fairwoods Country Club, and the serried rows of cars in the car park. But dominating everything still were the great twin towers of the medieval cathedral, grey and majestic in the spring sunshine. Fleur swallowed hard, caught by a sudden and unexpected pang of nostalgia. Elvemere was a beautiful town. It had come to mean so much to her. There had been a time when it had felt like home, the place that held her future. But now there was nothing left for her here. She blinked back the tears that blurred her vision and turned her face away from the fast receding town. Her roots were in London. She should never have left it. Now she must forget the past months and look determinedly towards a new start.

Bobby was waiting to meet her train at King's Cross. Fleur saw her waiting at the barrier almost as soon as she stepped down from the train, her scarlet jacket making a splash of colour against the grey surroundings. Her eyes were bright with excitement as she scanned the faces of the disembarking passengers and Fleur felt her heart lift in anticipation as she waved. Bobby's face lit up in a broad smile of recognition as she caught sight of her and waved frantically back.

'*Fleur!* It seems like years since I saw you. You look marvellous! Here give me your case. Shall we go and have a coffee before we catch the tube?'

'Where's this Jeff I've heard so much about?' she asked, looking round.

'I left him at home,' Bobby told her. 'I wanted to come and meet you on my own.' She linked her arm through Fleur's. 'I want to tell you all about him and I can't do that with him listening, can I?' she laughed. 'Can't have him getting big-headed! Now, I want to hear all about you – *everything*. Wasn't it exciting, finding your mother like that?'

Fleur smiled wryly. 'It wasn't difficult. I knew where she was.'

'And how did you two get along together?'

Fleur shook her head. 'We got along all right. But it's far too late to form any kind of relationship, Bobby. I should never have tracked her down really.'

Bobby looked crestfallen. 'Oh, that's a shame. But going to Elvemere has obviously worked out. Tell me all about this balcony garden of yours and the flat, your

511

job – and Tom, of course. All about Tom. He is coming to the party, isn't he? If he is he can share the spare room with Jeff.' She giggled. 'Mum has put you and me in together. I think it's to avoid what she calls hanky-panky. You know Mum!'

Fleur sighed. She hadn't written Bobby a proper letter since her world had started to fall apart. She was going to have a lot to tell her. Most of it difficult and painful.

To Fleur's surprise, Hackney looked exactly the same as when she had left it. Somehow, although she had been away only a few months, she had imagined that there would be changes, but apart from the fact that Bobby's mother had moved into a small modern flat in one of the high-rise blocks since Fleur left, everything was much the same. As they passed Wallace's Fish Bar Bobby nudged her.

'Remember when you hit that skinhead with the fish slice?' she said. 'I laughed so much when you wrote and told me about it. I'd have given anything to have been here and seen it.'

Fleur nodded with a smile. Maybe some day she'd tell Bobby about the savage revenge that skinhead had subjected her to. Or maybe not. It was something she preferred not to dwell on. There was a time when neither of them held anything back. In childhood and their early-teens the two girls had known everything about each other. Already that had changed. Bobby chattered happily about her life at college and friends whose names were unfamiliar to Fleur. Although they were still close friends their lives had taken separate courses. A small but unmistakable gulf had opened between them that would inevitably widen as the years went by. Nothing would ever be quite the same again.

As they walked down Brightman Lane, past the

Smiths' shop, Fleur noticed that Ethel's daughter had acquired an off-licence and had opened a video library, advertised in the window by a lurid poster. There were different curtains at the windows of the flat too, but apart from that the building looked the same. She tried to summon up a feeling of homecoming, but somehow the sense of belonging she had once known was missing.

Auntie Ada's iron grey hair was newly permed ready for the party and Fleur was comforted to find her the same as ever. She stood at the cooker in the neat little kitchen, her plump figure enveloped in a brightly coloured print overall as she prepared supper for them all. When she saw Fleur she held out her arms to her, enfolding her in a characteristic bear-like hug.

'Welcome home, love,' she said, kissing her soundly. 'We're so glad you could come. Now, off you go and freshen up. Supper in about ten minutes.'

Bobby took Fleur by the hand and led her into the living room. 'Come and meet Jeff first,' she said.

A young man sat watching the television. 'Jeff, this is my best friend Fleur,' Bobby said.

He stood up and held out his hand to her. 'Hi Fleur. I've heard a lot about you.'

Fleur saw a tall serious boy with gentle dark eyes. Bobby had already told her he was of mixed parentage. His skin was dark like hers and they looked so perfect together that the sight of them brought a lump to Fleur's throat. She shook the hand Jeff offered and smiled up at him. 'You're lucky. She's the best,' she told him. 'Even if she is a bit mad.'

Jeff slipped an arm round Bobby and grinned. 'Right,' he said. 'On both counts!'

Later, when the light was out in the room the two girls shared Bobby asked the inevitable question.

'You haven't said much about Tom. When are we going to meet him?'

'I'm afraid you aren't.' Fleur poured out the whole sorry tale, from the sale of Victoria Gardens and the loss of her flat to Sally's tragic death and the subsequent failure in communication between Tom and herself.

'Just when everything seemed to be going so well,' she said. 'Now it's all in ruins. There isn't a single thing that's worked out for me. I even feel guilty now about Julia's having to tell her story to the press. If I hadn't been in Elvemere I doubt if it would ever have happened. It's all my fault and it's going to make so much trouble for her.'

'I don't think I'd waste too many tears on her,' Bobby said. 'After all, she didn't give you too much consideration when she walked out on you, did she?'

'I don't know. She says she did – that she tried to get me back.' Fleur sighed. 'I'm so mixed up about it all. Now that I've met Julia, got to know her, I can see that things weren't as simple as I'd thought.'

'And Tom?' Bobby asked.

'I think I've lost him,' Fleur said in a small voice. 'If he wanted to make it up he'd have done it by now. Anyway, he's been interviewed for a new job up North. I bet he'll get it. I'll probably never see him again.'

'I'm so sorry about it all, love,' Bobby said. 'I know from the letters you wrote how much it all meant to you, finding your feet – making a new life. And your garden. You sounded so excited about it. You always did like growing things. Remember Dolly and her geraniums? The window sills were always full of them . . .' Bobby broke off. In the darkness she could hear Fleur quietly crying. 'Oh, Fleur, don't cry, love. Everything will be all right, you'll see. I bet when you go home . . .'

'I haven't got a home,' she said brokenly. 'Definitely not in Elvemere. I'm coming back to London as soon as I've got all the loose ends tied up. It didn't work, Bobby.

I'm going to have to start all over again.'

Bobby threw back the covers and crossed the room to the other bed. Putting her arms round Fleur in the darkness, she held her close. 'Maybe it's for the best,' she whispered. 'At least you have friends here. No one here will let you down.'

Tom arrived back at Park Row soon after nine o'clock on Friday evening. As he let himself into the house the first person he saw was Sadie, on her way upstairs with a mug of coffee. She looked him over dispassionately.

'God! You look shattered.'

'I feel it. Had a terrible drive down from York. I've been on the road for hours and I feel filthy. First the fan belt went and then I had a puncture.' He pulled a face. 'Wouldn't you know it, the spare was knackered too. Been meaning to get it fixed for weeks. You know how it is.'

Sadie grinned. 'You should get yourself a good bike. A BMW or a Harley maybe.'

Tom groaned. 'You're joking!'

'So – was it all worth it?' she asked.

'Depends what you mean by worth it. I managed to interview this footballer, Graham Moxton, but he turned out to be an insufferable moron, arrogant and ignorant at the same time. More interested in boasting about how many birds he could pull than anything else.'

Sadie laughed. 'Tell me about it! I know the type all too well.'

'I did what I could with it. Tried to make him sound like a member of the human race, but it read like pretty routine stuff. I faxed the article last night, but it's hardly likely to win me Journalist of the Year.'

'Poor old you. You do sound depressed. And the job interview?'

515

He shrugged non-committally. 'You know the drill – don't ring us, we'll ring you. I'm not sure I'm bothered one way or the other.' He looked at her. 'Any messages for me?'

'No. Look, if you want to make yourself a coffee the kettle has boiled.' Halfway up the stairs she paused. 'Oh, by the way, there's a copy of the *Clarion* in the kitchen. Have a look at it when you've got a minute. I'm rather chuffed with myself. I think I might have pulled off quite a coup.'

Tom made himself a coffee and dithered over whether to cook some bacon and eggs. He decided against it. Maybe when he'd had his coffee and a look at the paper he'd pop out for a Chinese or some fish and chips.

When he opened the door of his sitting room he groaned. It looked as though a bomb had hit it. There had been no time to tidy up, and now he remembered that he hadn't even had time to make the bed before he left for York. He sighed and decided to forget it. Sitting down, he opened the paper and saw the article about the opening of the women's refuge. It had Sadie's by-line and he assumed that this must have been what she meant him to see. There were some nice photographs, including one of Fleur who, apparently, had done the buffet lunch. His thoughts lingered painfully on her. Obviously she hadn't tried to get in touch with him – probably didn't even know he was out of town. He still smarted when he remembered the way she'd clung to Peter Arden's side on the day of the funeral. It was almost as though she was flaunting her closeness to the creep, wanting Tom to see that she had no further interest in *him*. He read through the article, wondering why Sadie had thought it so special. Then he spotted the footnote and quickly turned to page eight.

Five minutes later he was taking the stairs two at a

time and hammering furiously on her door.

'What the *hell* did you think you were playing at?' he demanded angrily when she opened the door. 'Do you have any idea what you've done?' He waved the paper under her nose.

Sadie's eyebrows rose. 'Keep your hair on. What's eating you, Tom? It's a damned good story.'

'Where did you get it?'

'A tip off, but I did a lot of work researching it thoroughly. There's nothing in there they can sue us for. It's all true. If you read it you'll see that she admitted everything.'

'Obviously she knew bloody well you'd blow the lid off if she didn't.'

Sadie shrugged. 'All's fair in love and journalism.'

'That's not the point! It's Fleur I'm thinking of. How do you think this made her feel? How did she react?'

'She didn't seem all that upset to me. What did you expect – hysterics?' Sadie shook her head at him. 'Look, Tom, I'm a journalist. I thought you were too. I know you and Fleur were an item and that you've had some kind of bust up, but if you're going to get emotionally involved with every story you write, you're going to get nowhere fast.'

'Don't tell me how to do my job!' he shouted. 'My relationship with Fleur has nothing to do with this. It's none of your business either! I might not be the greatest journalist in the world – as you obviously think *you* are! – but at least I don't grind people's faces into the dirt, screw up their lives.'

'Sometimes it's unavoidable, Tom,' she told him calmly. 'And what's more, you know it. You have to hold yourself back from all that angst, keep your personal feelings in check. If you can't do that then I'm afraid you're in the wrong job.'

'*Really?* Is that a fact? You'd know all about that, of

course, wouldn't you? Well, for your information I've been offered the job of deputy editor of the *Clarion*, so not everyone can have your low opinion of my work, can they?' Fuming, he turned on his heel and ran back down the stairs.

His coffee was cold and suddenly he'd lost interest in food. He was too angry to relax now. What in God's name had made him blurt out the offer he'd had when it was supposed to be hush-hush? He'd probably blown his chance of that too now! Was everything he touched doomed to explode in his face? Maybe he'd go to the pub. If ever there was a night for getting drunk, this was it! He took his mug into the kitchen and poured the cold coffee down the sink, swilling the mug under the tap. It was as he turned to put it back on the worktop that he noticed the card on the notice board with Charlotte's message attached.

She called out 'Come in' to his tap on her door and he found her sitting on the bed with her feet tucked under her, wearing a blue wool dressing-gown that made her look about twelve. She was watching a play on her portable television.

'Sorry to disturb you,' Tom said, 'but I've just seen this card and the message you left for me on the board. When did you see Fleur?'

'A few days ago. She came round to see you but you'd already left. You saw the invitation for you both to her friend's engagement party in London?' She looked at him. 'I suppose it's too late now?'

'She's already gone?'

'Yes, this afternoon. The party's not till tomorrow though.'

Tom closed the door and sat down beside her on the bed. 'Charlotte, I've only just seen the paper – all this drama at the opening of the refuge.'

She nodded. 'I wasn't there but Mum came round

and explained it all to me afterwards. It was a big surprise, I can tell you – took me a while to get my head round it, this business of Fleur's being my half-sister.'

'But you're pleased?'

'I would be if I thought we were going to be a family, but she's going back to London to live. We'll probably never see her again.'

'Back to London? Because of this, you mean?'

'Oh, no. She'd already decided before that.' She looked at him. 'She's been having a pretty rough time lately, Tom.'

'Has she?' He sighed. 'Yes, I suppose she has.'

'She showed me a letter she'd had from Peter Arden to say he was selling his mother's catering business. I think that was the last straw for her. I think he's a real rat after all that Fleur did for him. She really put herself out to support him when his mother was killed, you know. He just wrote her this really stuffy letter saying that he needed the money so that he and his new wife could buy a hotel. He even expected her to stick around and help sell the place for him. Cheek!'

Tom felt his heart sink. 'And you say she's decided to leave?'

'She says there's nothing to stay for so she might as well.' Charlotte sighed. 'You can't blame her, I suppose. I know I'm going to miss her though.' She glanced at him hesitantly. 'Maybe I shouldn't say this, Tom, but you haven't helped her much, have you?'

He was silent. It looked as though he'd made a prize fool of himself. 'Was it losing her job that upset her – or was it because Arden let her down?' he asked.

'Well, it's the same thing, isn't it? She was losing everything. She'd already lost her flat in Victoria Gardens.'

'*Lost* it? Moved out to be with him, you mean?'

'Mrs Franks had given her notice, didn't you know?

She said it was because Fleur let you stay overnight but really it was because my grandfather had bought the place from her. Poor Fleur. It hit her very hard and . . .' Charlotte stopped as his words sank in. 'To be with him? What, you mean you thought she – like *that*? Oh, Tom! How could you think she'd do that?'

To his embarrassment he felt himself colouring. 'Well, I don't own her! It's up to her who she . . . I just thought . . .' He looked at his watch. 'Oh, hell! Look, what time did you say she left? Would she be there by now?'

Charlotte looked doubtful. 'She might be.'

'I could ring her then.'

'You could, but I haven't got a phone number for her. I don't know her friend's surname either. There's just her Christian name and the address on the card.'

Tom grimaced. 'Oh, shit!'

When Joanna opened the door she was wearing her outdoor clothes and, seeing Vernon standing there, looked less than pleased.

'Oh, it's you!'

'Have you seen today's *Clarion*?' He held out his own copy of the paper. 'God what a shock! When I got home last night Julia had already moved out. It wasn't too much of a surprise. We've hardly spoken for days. But when I read the letter she'd left, explaining that all this would be in today's paper and offering not to contest a divorce, I had to come round at once.'

Joanna looked faintly irritated. 'Vernon, what does any of this have to do with me?'

'What does it have to do with you! It's what you wanted, isn't it?' Realising he had raised his voice he leaned forward. 'Look, can't we go inside, Jo? We can't talk about this on the doorstep.'

'I don't really think we need to talk about it at all.'
She turned and picked up her car keys from the hall
table. 'I'm sorry but I have to go, Vernon. My case is
already in the car. I'm booked on the eleven-fifteen
flight out of Heathrow tonight.' She looked at her
watch. 'I'll have to go right now if I'm going to check in
in time.'

He stared at her open-mouthèd. 'Flight? Where to?
Where are you going?'

'To the States,' she told him calmly. 'I've got some
business to attend to.'

'How long will you be gone?'

'I don't know. Not more than a week or ten days at
the most. I've told Charlie about it.'

'You've told *Dad*? Didn't it occur to you to tell me?
We have to talk, Jo. It's important. Look, let me drive
you to the airport then we can talk on the way.'

'There's no need, really.'

'Yes, there is.'

With a sigh she gave in. 'Oh, all right then, if you
must. My case is in the boot. You'd better get it.'

After Vernon had negotiated the town traffic and
they were on the motorway he looked at her. 'You
haven't reacted to my news yet. Have you seen the
Clarion? Julia actually stood up in front of everyone at
the opening of that refuge place and confessed that she
gave birth to a child after some mad teenage affair. It's
bizarre but it solves everything, doesn't it? I mean, I can
divorce her now without involving you! She hasn't got
a leg to stand on. We can be married, Jo. It's good, isn't
it?'

Joanna seemed unimpressed. 'I think you should
make up your mind, Vernon. First you come and tell
me we have to cool things because you can't afford to
divorce Julia. Now, you're back with a different story.
As far as I'm concerned nothing has changed. As I told

you, I don't think marriage is on the cards for us.'

Vernon felt his blood chill. Ever since he had discovered that Joanna was now the major shareholder in GPC he'd felt as though he was walking a tightrope. 'Well, maybe not – not yet. But we certainly don't have to hide our feelings for each other any more. We can be together as much as we like from now on. It's what we've always wanted, isn't it?'

'I think that for the time being we should do as you said before and put our relationship on hold.'

'Jo . . .' He glanced at her. 'Ma said something when we were talking one evening recently. She said . . .' he cleared his throat nervously, 'said that she'd paid you to get out of Elvemere. You know, all those years ago.'

She looked at him coolly. 'Really? She said that, did she?'

'Yes. She also said that you told her at the time you were pregnant with my child. Was it true, Jo?'

'Give me *some* credit, Vernon. I was never that kind of a fool, even then.'

'That's what I thought.'

'Your mother assumed that I was pregnant. She even offered me the money for an abortion, she was that keen to be rid of me.' Joanna shrugged. 'Having been grossly insulted, I figured I might as well let her pay for the privilege.'

'So there was no truth in it?'

'What do you think?'

He nodded. 'Jo, look, just one more thing. I've been wondering – about that article: where did the press get all this stuff about Julia's past from?'

'I suppose it was from me – partly,' she said casually.

'But how was it that you knew and no one else did?'

'Simple. We were schoolfriends, remember? I didn't know the whole story though, not until recently when I found out some things about the Sylvester girl and began to put two and two together.' She looked at him. 'How did you think I was able to get Julia to vote with us over Victoria Gardens? Didn't you ever wonder?'

'No. I just thought that as you'd been friends . . . You mean you threatened to spill the beans if she didn't toe the line?' Vernon fell silent as he digested this. He was beginning to see just how ruthless Joanna could be and reflected that it was going to be infinitely safer to have her with him than against him.

'But what made you decide to tell them now?' he asked. 'It came as a shock to me, I can tell you.'

'I daresay it did.' She looked faintly amused. 'On the other hand I daresay there are things about you that would probably come as a shock to Julia.'

He ignored the remark. 'I must say, you might have warned me before running to the press. It would have made me look pretty foolish if they had come asking me questions about it.'

'How was I to know that Julia had kept you in the dark about her past? After all, you are her husband. Anyway, I didn't run to the press. They already knew. Don't ask me how. Some reporter girl came round asking questions. She was remarkably knowledgeable about most of it, so someone else is obviously in the know. I figured that if she already knew that much I might as well fill in the blanks.'

'Why are you going to the States?' he asked. 'It's a pity you have to leave right now. If you'd asked me to go with you, I would have.'

'No need. It's just some loose ends I need to tie up. Besides, someone should be here to keep an eye on Charlie. He seems to be getting more and more manic these days. God knows what he might do if he were left to his own devices.'

Vernon opened his mouth to point out that up until now she had positively encouraged him in his excesses, but he thought better of it and bit back the retort.

At Heathrow Joanna wouldn't let him wait and see her off, insisting that he'd only have to hang around and that she'd rather be alone. It seemed to Vernon that there was an air of intrigue about this flying visit to the States. Did it have something to do with the business, and if so why hadn't she told him? He drove back to Elvemere feeling resentful and distinctly uneasy.

All Saturday afternoon Fleur and Bobby helped Ada with the preparations for the party. It was to be held in the large community room on the ground floor of the block and Jeff and two of Bobby's brothers were busy decorating it with streamers and balloons. All her family would be at the party as well as some of the girls' old schoolfriends. Jeff was from Notting Hill but his family and some of his friends would be there too. Bobby prattled away happily as they worked.

'Jeff is very talented,' she told Fleur. 'He's a year ahead of me at college and last year he won the Student of the Year award. He's hoping for a career in advertising.' She smiled proudly. 'His mother is American. Her family came from New Orleans, but she's been here for a long time, ever since she was a baby. Both her parents were musicians and she's a singer. She has the most beautiful voice. I'm hoping maybe she'll sing for us tonight.'

'And his father?' Fleur asked.

'His dad is a sergeant in the Metropolitan Police. He's from Yorkshire.' Bobby laughed. 'One of the biggest men I've ever seen and with a Yorkshire accent you could cut with a knife! Jeff says he couldn't be more of a mixture if he'd been born in a cement mixer.'

'Well, it must have worked well. He's gorgeous,' Fleur said.

Bobby smiled happily. 'Well, I think so, but then I just might be a little bit prejudiced.'

For most of the evening Fleur occupied herself with serving drinks and food. She was dismayed to find that she felt like a stranger. Most of her old acquaintances were engaged or married and all of them came with partners. They had other topics to discuss. When they weren't dancing they sat around in huddles discussing babies, husbands and their homes. Although they didn't mean to exclude her she felt left out, and without a partner of her own, awkward and out of place.

Jeff asked her to dance, but she suspected that he had been prompted by Bobby.

'I like your dress,' he said.

'Thank you.' Fleur looked down at the flame red dress she'd bought 'specially. There was a defiant quality about the colour she had chosen, but now that the evening had come she found that its gaiety didn't match her mood. She smiled up at Jeff in an effort to be light-hearted and vivacious. The last thing she wanted to do was to spoil Bobby's engagement party with a gloomy expression.

Jeff's mother was persuaded to sing. She was an attractive woman with a beautiful soprano voice. She sang Gershwin's 'Summertime' with a haunting poignancy that enchanted everyone. Fleur sat at the back of the room, grateful for the excuse not to have to talk and appear sociable.

At midnight Bobby and Jeff stood up and formally announced their engagement. As they stood side by side he put the ring on her finger and they kissed to delighted cheers and applause. The DJ had put on a romantic waltz and Fleur watched wistfully as they led the dancing. They looked so happy that she felt her eyes fill with tears. Soon Bobby will be married to Jeff, she reflected. She'll have a whole new life ahead of her and that will be the end of one more chapter of my life. Why are there only ends and no beginnings for me? she asked herself unhappily.

She busied herself clearing the remains of the food away and washing up in the kitchen until Ada came to find her.

'Fleur, love, why don't you go and have a dance before the party's over?' she said. 'You've done nothing but work all evening. Haven't you enjoyed yourself?'

Fleur smiled and hugged her. 'Of course I have, Auntie Ada. It's been a lovely party, something I wouldn't have missed for the world. I'm so happy for Bobby.'

'And what about you?' Ada asked, searching her face. 'I've been too busy to chat to you since you arrived.' She pulled out a chair. 'Come on, sit down. We'll have a glass of that wine and a chat.'

'But there's so much to do,' Fleur began weakly. Ada waved her protests away.

'You're supposed to be a guest. Besides, we've got all day tomorrow to finish what don't get done tonight,' she said. 'Bobby tells me things haven't worked out quite as you hoped and that you want to come back to Hackney?'

'That's right.'

'Are you sure it's a good idea?' Ada's kindly face was serious. 'This is no place for a young girl livin' on her own any more.' She peered into Fleur's eyes. 'You're not running away from something, are you?'

'No. There just doesn't seem to be anything for me in Elvemere any more.'

'Bobby says you found your real mother.'

Fleur looked down at her hands. 'Yes, I found her. I never really meant to, and none of it was as I imagined it would be. She isn't the selfish bitch I'd always imagined. She's quite nice actually. But even though she's acknowledged that I'm her daughter she still doesn't really want me around.'

'But do you really need her?' Ada asked. 'You're a person in your own right, love. Some day soon you'll have your own family. Wouldn't it be better to forget about Julia and get on with your own life?'

'She told me that she tried to get me back once but that Grandma told her I'd been adopted.'

'I know.' Ada nodded gravely. 'Poor Dolly always regretted telling that lie.'

'It's true then?'

'Oh, yes, it's true. She loved you so much, you see. She couldn't bear to part with you. But not only that, she didn't trust Julia not to leave you again. She never even told your grandpa what she'd done and that troubled her conscience, bless her. That was why she was so anxious for you to go and find Julia for yourself after she'd gone.'

'Julia never told anyone that she'd had me,' Fleur said. 'I knew that the chances were she'd have married and had a family by this time, but I thought at least someone would know about me.'

'You must have come as a bit of a shock to her then,' Ada said, 'turning up out of the blue after all those years.'

'I know, and I never expected a big welcome. But I wasn't prepared to be swept under the carpet like some shameful secret.'

'Maybe her worst mistake was making a secret of it in the first place. I daresay none of us gets through life without doing something we're ashamed of,' Ada said wisely. 'We have to learn to make the best of it. Try and turn the mistakes into blessings and hope that others can understand. But it's not always easy.' She was silent for a moment then asked, 'What about this young man of yours? Have you fallen out? Is that why he didn't come with you?' Fleur nodded. 'Not a race thing, is it, love?' Ada asked with a sigh. 'I know it's not easy for you kids from mixed marriages. That's why I'm so grateful my Bobby's found someone who has that in common with her.'

Fleur shook her head. 'No, it's nothing to do with that. Tom just . . . It just went wrong between us.'

'And that's why you've been looking so unhappy all evening.' Ada reached out to touch Fleur's hand. 'Poor baby. It's hard to be young. But it'll all come right in the end, you just see if it don't. That Tom of yours will be sure to make it up. And if he don't then he's a fool. He don't know what a good girl he's letting slip through his fingers.'

Fleur looked up at Ada and smiled. 'Oh, Auntie Ada, I do love you. You always make everything seem so simple.'

'Most things are, love,' Ada said with a smile. 'It's people make the complications.' She patted Fleur's hand. 'Now listen, if you're set on comin' back to Hackney you can come and stay with me for as long as you like. That goes without saying. I'd love to have you. I get lonely now they've all gone. But if you take my advice you'll go back to that Elvemere place and face all these problems. Kick 'em all into touch and stand on your own feet just to show folks you can do it, 'cause you can, you know. And if you're honest with yourself it's what you really want, deep in your heart.'

It was very late when they all got to bed and Ada let the girls sleep late the following morning. It was almost midday when they eventually sat round the kitchen table for breakfast. Ada put bacon and eggs in front of them and returned to the stove to make toast.

'Where's Jeff?' Bobby asked.

'Gone down the shop for a paper,' Ada told her. 'He should be back in a minute. I hope he is. His bacon's gonna get cold.'

Jeff came in a moment later and dropped an assortment of Sunday papers on the table. 'I found some guy wandering about downstairs,' he said.

'I hope you didn't try and talk to him,' Ada said. 'Sometimes we get some queer types hanging around down there, 'specially at weekends. Dropouts and winos, most of 'em. It's best to leave 'em be.'

'He wasn't like that,' Jeff said. 'He asked where this flat was. Said he was looking for a Miss Fleur Sylvester.'

Fleur looked up in surprise. 'For me?'

'That's right.'

'Well – where is he?' Bobby asked, looking from one to the other.

'Outside. He wouldn't come in.' Jeff was trying hard not to smile. 'I think he said his name was Markham or something. Tom Markham. Does that ring a bell?'

Bobby nudged Fleur excitedly. 'Hey, it's your Tom, isn't it? Well – what are you waiting for? He's come all this way to find you. Least you can do is ask him in for some breakfast.'

He was standing at the open front door, his back towards her, and Fleur felt her heart quicken. Closing the kitchen door carefully, she walked down the hall towards him.

'Tom. What are you doing here?'

He turned. 'I didn't get back till late Friday evening. I'd have telephoned you but Charlotte didn't have a number. I thought at least I could come and take you home.'

'You needn't have bothered. I've got a return ticket.'

He looked wounded. 'Oh, well, I'm sorry I bothered. Do you want me to go away again?'

529

'No.' She bit her lip. 'I didn't mean to sound ungrateful. I . . .'

'I don't want your *gratitude*, Fleur. I thought you might be pleased to see me.'

'You missed the party,' she said lamely.

'I know.'

'It was a good party.'

'Good. I'm glad you enjoyed it.'

'I didn't enjoy it,' she told him angrily. 'I didn't enjoy it one bit without – on my own when everyone else was there with a partner.'

'Well, I'm sorry I couldn't have been there to provide you with one.'

Suddenly her eyes filled with tears. Here he was. Here they both were, speaking to each other again, yet it wasn't working. He was spiky and defensive, spoiling for an argument, and it was making her nervous.

'Oh, why did you come, Tom?' she said. 'Was it just to taunt me – to make me feel worse? If it was you won't succeed because I couldn't feel any more miserable than I already do!'

His hands shot out and grasped her shoulders. 'God, Fleur, you make me want to shake you!' he said. 'I'm trying to say I'm sorry, but you don't make it easy, do you? I know I've made a fool of myself but if it's any comfort to you, I've been miserable too. It was seeing you with Arden again.'

She shook him off impatiently. 'He was here for his mother's funeral, Tom,' she said. 'What was I supposed to do?'

'I know.' He ran a hand through his hair. 'I know, I'm sorry. Look, Charlotte told me about the letter he wrote you, saying that he was going to sell the business.'

'Did she? That must have given you a good laugh,' she said bitterly.

'*Fleur!* Of course it didn't!' He pulled her towards

530

him. 'Look, I love you,' he said raggedly. 'If I didn't love you I wouldn't give a damn what you did or who you saw when you weren't with me. I thought we had something good going for us.'

'*So did I!*' She was close to tears now and blinked hard, not wanting him to see. 'So did I, Tom. That's why it hurt so much when you didn't trust me. I was only doing my job – and what I felt I owed to Sally.'

'I know. I know!' He pulled her close and kissed her. At first she resisted, trying to push him away, unwilling to give in, in spite of the fact that she knew they were both to blame. But at last the pressure of his lips and his arms holding her close in the way she had missed so much were too much for her. She relaxed and responded. When they drew apart he looked down at her.

'Am I forgiven?'

She nodded.

'And can I take you home or are you going to insist on using that return ticket?'

She managed a smile. 'No. I'm glad you're here. I'll come with you.'

'We've got some talking to do on the way. Shall we make a start now?'

Before she could reply the kitchen door was flung open and Ada's voice rang out. 'Fleur Sylvester! Are you gonna keep that feller standin' on the doorstep all mornin', or are you gonna bring him in where we can all get a dekko at 'im?'

Fleur laughed. 'I think you'd better come and be introduced to Auntie Ada, Bobby and Jeff. If not I'm going to be in big trouble!'

An hour later they were on their way. It was a glorious morning and Fleur felt happiness and relief lighten her heart as they left London behind and headed northeast for Cambridgeshire and Elvemere.

'You're not seriously thinking of going back to London to live, are you?' Tom asked.

'Why not?'

He glanced at her. 'I don't think you really belong there any more.'

She sighed. 'The thing is, do I belong anywhere?'

'I think you do.'

She looked at him. 'Where, Tom?'

'Do I have to spell it out for you? Elvemere, of course – with me.'

'But you're leaving Elvemere too, aren't you?' she said accusingly. 'I hear you've applied for a job up North.'

'I only applied when I thought you and I were finished,' he said. 'I had an interview last week, but in the meantime my editor on the *Clarion* has offered me the job of deputy editor.'

'And—?'

'And I'd say that was largely up to you. If you stay then so will I.'

'I'll have to look for another job – and a home too. It'll mean starting over again. Back to square one.'

'There are worse places to start.' He looked at her. 'Look, you say that Arden Catering is for sale. Why don't you buy it? That way you'd be killing two birds with one stone and you'd be your own boss into the bargain.'

'*Buy* it!' She stared at him. 'Would you mind telling me with what?'

'Money. You get a loan – go and talk to the bank manager.'

Fleur shook her head. 'With the house and the van and all the other equipment it's going to cost a fortune. No one in their right mind would ever lend *me* that kind of money.'

'Why not? 'Course they would. That's what banks

are for. I'd say you were a pretty good risk. You're young and healthy and you're good at the job.'

'But what would I do with a house that size?'

He shrugged. 'Take in lodgers. Or you could always marry me? It might come in handy if we ever got around to raising a family.'

'It wouldn't work, Tom.'

He pulled the car into a lay-by and stopped, turning to look at her. 'What wouldn't work? Marrying me or buying the business?'

'I meant buying the business, but since you ask . . .' She laughed but the expression on his face stopped the laughter in her throat. 'Tom? Oh, Tom – you're serious!'

'Of course I'm serious. Would I joke about a thing like that? I've never been more serious about anything in my life.'

For a long moment she was silent then she looked up and met his eyes. 'Auntie Ada was talking to me last night,' she said. 'She knew I was unhappy and asked me if it was the *race thing*, as she put it. If we were to marry, Tom, if we were to have that family you mentioned, our children might be – might take after their great-grandfather.'

His eyes held hers. 'They might be black, you mean?'

'Yes. We have to think about that, Tom. You're going to have to ask yourself how you feel about it.'

He reached out to touch her cheek. 'I want you, Fleur. No other girl – ever. I think I've known that since the first moment I set eyes on you. And anything you ever give me of yourself can only be wonderful as far as I'm concerned. Our children could never be anything but perfect.'

She swallowed hard at the lump in her throat. 'Oh, Tom,' she whispered.

'These last weeks without you have been hell. I felt I had no purpose, no direction any more. I don't intend

533

to lose you again whatever happens.' He cupped her chin and looked into her eyes. 'So I think you'd better tell me right now how you feel about marrying me, because if the answer's no I'm going to take that job in York and get the hell out of it.'

Stunned, she looked into his eyes for a long moment. 'Tom! Oh, Tom, I don't know what to say. It's . . .'

He put his fingers across her lips. 'If you dare say, This is so sudden, I'll tip you out and drive off without you!' He pulled her close and kissed her hard. 'Tell you what,' he whispered, stroking her hair, 'come back to Park Row with me tonight and let me show you how much I need you.'

'Yes – yes, please.'

'I love you, Fleur.'

'I love you too.'

He kissed her again.

Julia's time was fully occupied. She was glad. Having no time to dwell on the happenings of the past few days was a distinct advantage. Since leaving Vernon and the home she had known for the past eighteen years she had felt disorientated. Eleanor had made her welcome, but her home was small and Julia felt it would be unfair to impose on her hospitality for too long. Besides, she felt the need to put down new roots. She had been married for so long that making major decisions and taking charge of her own life was uncharted territory and the business of finding herself a flat or a small house somewhere, furnishing it and making it her home was slightly daunting. She would need a job too – something to help augment her income. For although the money from her GPC shares would be adequate for her to live on, buying a house and furnishing it would take up a large chunk of it.

But quite apart from that she needed some kind of rewarding work with which to fill her time and occupy her mind. She already had a vague idea at the back of her mind. She had tried to telephone Fleur over the weekend and ask her advice. After all, it wasn't so long ago that she had started out on a totally new life herself. Julia had meant to talk to her after the opening of the refuge. They had had little time together and there was so much she wanted to say to her. It was only when she tried to reach her and heard the recorded message on the Arden Catering answerphone that she remembered Fleur's saying she would be away for a few days.

Having written and posted her letter of resignation to the Mayor via the Town Clerk Julia prepared herself for the coming council meeting with some trepidation. Everyone would have read about her public confession in the *Clarion* by now and although she was quite prepared to be ostracised by her fellow councillors, she dreaded the ordeal. Only Eleanor remained firm and positive.

'I'm sure you underestimate them,' she said. 'Remember the old adage, "Let him who is without sin cast the first stone." There are very few on the council without sin, believe me, my dear! What happened to you was no crime, it was human error. One that is all too common. Besides, it happened so long ago. It would be a pretty bigoted person who would judge you by it after all these years.'

There was a meeting of the planning committee to follow the main council meeting scheduled for the same evening, and Julia saw from the agenda that Charlie's plans for Victoria Gardens were down for consideration. As she was no longer anything to do with the business, she wondered whether she should declare an interest or not. In the end she decided that she must. She had no wish to risk taking the blame should the plans be turned down.

As the council chamber filled she took her seat beside Eleanor, her heart quickening with nervousness. The Mayor arrived and took his seat as chairman and the Town Clerk tapped his gavel for silence.

The agenda that evening was not too lengthy. Julia calculated that her resignation would come up under the category of Any Other Business, right at the end of the meeting. Before that came the proposal that Councillor Mrs Eleanor Maitland should be next Town Mayor in place of Councillor Philip Forsyth. On a show of hands the motion was unanimously carried. Eleanor rose to her feet.

'I am honoured to be asked to be Town Mayor,' she said,'and I would like to say thank you to all who voted for me. However, as you all know, as a widow I have no natural consort and shall need to appoint someone to support me in office.' She turned to glance at Julia. 'I have decided that there is no better person for the job than Councillor Mrs Grant. I know that Mrs Grant will only agree to do this with your approval, so I am asking you to support me in my choice.'

The Town Clerk asked for a show of hands from all in favour of the proposal and Julia held her breath, hardly daring to look as, one after another, all the hands in the council chamber rose. Then the Mayor himself got to his feet.

'In view of what Councillor Mrs Maitland has just proposed, I must tell you that I have received a letter from Councillor Mrs Grant offering her resignation from the council.' He glanced briefly across at Julia over the top of his spectacles and cleared his throat. 'I'm sure she will have no objection to my telling you that she gives her reason for resignation as the personal disclosure she recently made on the opening of the Alexandra House Women's Refuge and its subsequent coverage in the press.' He removed his glasses and looked round at them. 'As this is a personal matter I have taken the liberty of speaking informally to my fellow councillors and everyone agrees with me that events that happened in the distant past can have no bearing at all on the good character of Councillor Mrs Grant as she is today. Therefore, I think I can safely say on behalf of all present that it is not the wish of this council to accept Councillor Grant's resignation on these grounds.' Smiling directly at Julia he concluded, 'So, Councillor Grant, we would ask you to reconsider your resignation and remain as the very valuable and hardworking councillor we have come to appreciate.' His eyes swept round the room. 'Can I please have your endorsement of that point?'

There was a unanimous show of hands, followed, to Julia's surprise and embarrassment, by applause.

Eleanor leaned over and patted her arm. 'What did I tell you?' she whispered. 'They're all on your side.'

When Charlie's plan came up for consideration at the planning meeting later, Julia declared an interest and left the council chamber. It was only after the meeting was over that she learned that the plan had been turned down. Philip Forsyth explained why to her when they were putting on their coats after the meeting.

'The whole place is likely to collapse. We discovered that for ourselves some months ago when the council had the idea of putting a compulsory purchase order on the street. Under the circumstances it's amazing the old places have stood up for so long. If Charlie Grant hadn't bought them the council would have had the job of demolishing them eventually.' He smiled wryly. 'Now he can have the pleasure himself.'

Julia's heart sank when she remembered the amount of money her father-in-law had invested in the property. 'Is there nothing that can be done with them?' she asked. 'Not even renovation?'

Philip shook his head. 'Afraid not. It'd be risky even replacing the windows. Looks like poor old Charlie has caught his toe badly this time!'

Chapter 18

Sadie paused in the hall outside the kitchen door. She knew that Fleur had spent the previous night with Tom and that they were washing up their breakfast dishes together. Normally she would have kept a discreet distance. Ever since the row she and Tom had had they'd been wary of each other, each of them maintaining an excruciating politeness whenever they happened to meet. But this morning she needed to speak to him urgently and was glad that Fleur was there too. She opened the door and put her head round it.

'Hi, you two. I'd like a word, if you're not too rushed?'

Tom looked round. 'If you're about to give me notice . . .' he began defensively. Sadie held up her hand.

'No. Relax, it's nothing like that. Look, Tom, how about burying the hatchet – declaring a truce?'

'Okay with me if you say so.'

'I do. What I wanted to tell you was that I'll be moving on very shortly. I've just heard this morning, I've been offered a job on *Good Morning* magazine.'

'*Good Morning*, eh?' Tom whistled softly. 'Wow! Well done,' he said admiringly. 'How did you pull that off?'

Sadie had got the job on the strength of the piece

she'd done about Julia Grant for the *Clarion*, but with Fleur there she could hardly say so. Instead she shrugged. 'Oh, you know, just my natural talent.'

Tom grinned. 'Plus all that reticence and modesty, I expect! From now on you'll be chasing the cream of society round Europe, looking for the latest scandal, eh? I hope they're paying you well for the privilege.'

Sadie grinned. 'Well enough, I'm happy to say.'

'Great! So – when do you start?'

'Next month, which brings me to what I wanted to speak to you about. It means I'll be putting the house on the market straight away, and in view of the fact that you two seem to be a fixture, I'd like to offer you first refusal. If I could count on a quick sale I'd let it go at below the market price.' She looked from one to the other with a grin. 'Well? I take it you two are together again on a permanent basis? I thought you might just be looking for something.'

Tom looked at Fleur. 'Well, we'll need a bit of time to think about it, Sadie, but thanks for the offer.'

'That's okay. I had a survey done before I bought it so you'd save money there too. It's the least I can do under the circumstances.' She glanced at Fleur. 'Maybe it'll go some way to making amends for – well, for what we fell out over, Tom.'

'Fell out? What's all this about?' Fleur asked.

Sadie smiled wryly. 'Oh, he hasn't told you then? Tom gave me one hell of a rocket over the article I wrote about your – er – about Mrs Grant.'

'But you're a journalist. You had every right to report the story.'

'That's not exactly how Tom saw it. At least, not at the time.'

'Let's forget about it,' he said quickly.

'Well, think about my offer and let me know by the weekend,' Sadie said. 'I don't want to rush you but

540

time is short and I'll have to put the house on the market soon.'

As the door closed behind her Fleur said, 'You never told me you'd had a row with Sadie?'

Tom shrugged. 'It's water under the bridge. It made me angry, that's all, to think of her walking all over your life without even asking.'

'How did you know she didn't ask?'

He stared at her. 'You mean – she did?'

'She did try to confirm that what she'd found out was true. I suppose you could count that as a tip off. At least it enabled me to warn Julia and give her time to think what to do about it. If the whole thing had been sprung on her suddenly it could have been much worse.'

He sighed. 'And it did get us back together again, so it did some good. Put it down to my jumping in with both feet again.' He looked at her. 'So – what do you think? About buying the house, I mean?' He put his arms around her and drew her close. 'We were going to get married anyway. And you've already moved in – almost.'

'I know, but I think you're forgetting something.'

'What?'

'Suppose – just *suppose* – I were to get a loan to buy Arden Catering? Sally's house goes with it, remember?'

'Ah, I'd forgotten that.' Tom looked down at her. 'That means we can't take the next step until we know one way or the other.' He looked at her. 'It's make-up-your-mind time, Fleur. I think you should get along to the agent's right away and see what the asking price is.'

They went together, Fleur making a detour down the High Street on her way to catch the bus. They stood hand in hand in front of the window of Matthew's Estate Agents and looked at the properties for sale. Arden Catering was in the business section. There was a photograph of the house, but to Fleur's surprise and dismay there was a SOLD strip pasted across it. She looked at Tom.

'How can it be sold without my knowing?' she said. 'No one has been to view, or asked to see the books or anything.'

Tom shrugged. 'Maybe just an estate agent's trick to make people keener.'

'Why would they do a thing like that?'

Seeing her disappointment, he slipped an arm round her and hugged her close. 'Oh, I'm sorry, love. I know how much it meant to you. But you'll soon find another job.'

'Oh, yes? In a factory canteen maybe, or as a school dinner lady,' she said bitterly. 'Arden's is the only catering firm for miles around.' She was dismayed to discover that she was much more upset at losing the chance than she'd envisaged.

'At least we still have the option on Sadie's house,' he said, giving her a reassuring squeeze. 'Look, darling, I'll have to go now or I'll be late for work. Give me a ring at lunchtime and we'll talk, yes?'

'Yes. Yes, okay,' she said absently. After he'd gone she stood for a long time staring at the photograph with its SOLD sign, wondering how on earth it could have been sold without her knowledge. At last she made up her mind. Walking into the shop, she asked to see one of the sales staff.

'I was interested in making an offer for Arden Catering,' she said boldly. 'As a matter of fact I'm managing it at the moment for the owner. I see from the window that it seems to be sold, but as I'm the one in charge at the moment I thought there might be some mistake?'

'I see. No, there's no mistake,' the young man told her. 'It's a pity you didn't make an offer sooner. I had acceptance of the offer from the owner just before closing yesterday afternoon.'

'From Mr Peter Arden, you mean?'

'That's right. The buyer is eager to exchange contracts as soon as possible and that suits Mr Arden too. We hope to close the deal very quickly, all things being equal.'

Fleur was silent. Peter hadn't even contacted her to say he'd had an offer, let alone that he was going ahead with the sale. 'Who – who has bought it?' asked Fleur.

He shook his head, smiling apologetically. 'I'm sorry. I'm afraid I can't tell you that. We have to observe discretion about these things.'

'Yes, of course. I only thought . . .' Embarrassed, she backed towards the door. 'Well, if the sale should fall through for any reason, I'd be glad if you'd let me know.'

'It's very doubtful, but I will of course. And your name?'

'Sylvester. Fleur Sylvester. And for the moment you can contact me at Arden Catering.'

'Certainly, Miss Sylvester. Good morning.'

Fleur's shoulders drooped as she walked down the street. It had all been a crazy dream anyway. Tom had almost persuaded her to believe that she might have been granted a loan to buy the business. Now she'd never know.

The telephone was ringing when she let herself in. Without pausing to take off her coat she snatched up the receiver. 'Good morning, Arden Catering,' she said breathlessly. 'Can I help you?'

'Good morning, Miss Sylvester, this is Eleanor Maitland. Councillor Maitland. I'm ringing to ask if you're booked for Friday, May the twenty-eighth.'

'Just a moment.' Fleur quickly found the appointments diary and thumbed through to the relevant week. 'Yes, that date seems to be vacant at the moment, Mrs Maitland,' she said.

'Oh, good. I'm so glad. I'd like to book a buffet luncheon for my Mayor-Making reception,' Eleanor said. 'I thought that the lunch you provided for the opening of the women's refuge was excellent and I'd like something similar. It will be at the Town Hall, of course. Catering for about two hundred guests. What can you suggest?'

'We have several menus,' Fleur said. 'I think the best thing would be for me to come round and show them to you.'

'Well, if you could do that I'd appreciate it.' Eleanor gave her the address and Fleur arranged to go round that evening.

She replaced the receiver with a sigh. A lunch for the Mayor's reception at the Town Hall would be a feather in her cap. But, ironically, it looked as though it would most probably be the last job she ever did for Arden Catering.

Vernon was already tired of living alone. The house seemed so dreary and empty and he hated coming home to the prospect of making his own dinner and spending the evening alone. His mother, appalled and indignant that Julia should have walked out and left him, insisted on sending her own cleaning woman round for an hour each day to tidy up and make his bed. Vernon hated the thought of a strange woman invading his private space, poking her nose into his cupboards and drawers when he wasn't there, touching his clothes.

Once Julia had left he'd envisaged Joanna sharing his home with him but he hadn't heard from her since she had left for the States. She must be due back any day now but she hadn't been in touch. Not even so much as a postcard from her. He missed her. As far as he was concerned she couldn't come back soon enough.

Most evenings after work he either ate out or went round to Queen's Lodge to eat with his parents, but his mother's constant carping about Julia's deceitfulness and the shocking transgression she had recently disclosed was beginning to grate on his already raw nerves.

This evening was to be no exception. Vernon had arrived early, going on ahead of his father who had driven into town to see if he could gather any information about the result of that evening's planning meeting. Louise began almost before Vernon had time to take off his coat.

'There was always something about her I couldn't fathom, you know,' she said as she poured him a sherry. 'A slyness. Never could get to the bottom of her.'

'You mean, she wouldn't tell you all her business?' Vernon said, irritably.

Louise went on as though she hadn't heard him. 'And of course she always acted as though she thought herself a cut above us Grants. It just shows, doesn't it? No one in *my* family, or your father's either, ever went off the rails like that. Or lived a lie about it like she has. Just fancy – she had that child and never told a soul about it. Not even her poor mother. The deceit of it! If you ask me a woman who can do that is capable of anything!'

Vernon was relieved to hear the front door slam, heralding his father's arrival. A moment later Charlie came into the room and went straight to the drinks cabinet, pouring himself an enormous whisky.

'Oh, Charlie, really!' Louise admonished. 'You won't want your dinner, drinking all that whisky. I've made your favourite too. I've been . . .'

'Don't *start*!' Charlie shouted, his face red. 'I can't

cope with any more tonight.' He looked up at Vernon with bloodshot eyes as he slumped into a chair. 'The bastards have scuppered us!'

Louise and Vernon both stared at him. 'The plans?' Vernon ventured. 'They've turned them down?'

'I can't understand it. They were going to buy Victoria Gardens and do what I planned to do. They must have known about the chalkpit workings all along. Why couldn't one of the devious buggers have had the decency to warn me?'

'Maybe if you'd asked . . .' Vernon ventured, but Charlie wasn't listening.

'They won't even let us restore the properties and recoup our money.' He looked up at his son despairingly. 'What the bloody hell are we going to do?'

'Well, I always said Victoria Gardens was a white elephant,' Vernon said. 'It's a good job we're mortgaging both houses. At least we can keep our heads above water for the time being. There will have to be some cut-backs. First we'll have to lay off some of our workforce, then tough it out and hope we can shift the Meadowlands houses.'

Louise spun round, her face colouring as she looked from one to the other. 'Mortgaging the houses! What houses?'

Charlie shot Vernon a savage look. 'Ours, love, Vernon's and Queen's Lodge,' he said, trying to sound nonchalant. 'We've had to, Lou. There was nothing else for it. I was going to tell you . . .'

'Going to tell me!' Louise's face was red. 'I think you must mean ask me! It was my money bought this house, Charlie Grant, even if it is in both our names. I think I was due a bit of consideration. This is *my* home, remember?'

'It can't be helped,' Charlie said. 'It's not a decision I took lightly. We've hit a rough patch and we're strapped for cash. These things happen in the best of businesses. It's only a bit of a blip.'

'*Bit of a blip!* I've heard that one before somewhere!' Louise stood looking at her husband and son, her arms folded. 'It's all that woman's doing,' she announced.

Vernon looked up. 'Julia?'

'No! Not Julia – Joanna Hanson,' she said. 'Ever since she joined the firm things have started to go down the pan. And where is she now, I ask you?' She shook her head as both men looked blank. 'She's gone, that's what. Buggered off. Left the sinking ship like the rat she is! You'll be lucky to see her again! She's taken both of you for the ride of your lives and you still can't see it!' She turned on Vernon. 'I told you to watch your step with her, didn't I? It was only down to me that she didn't land you in a right old stew years ago. Now what are you left with? A wife and daughter who've both left you and a mortgaged house!' She blew out her breath in an explosive snort. '*Sex!*' she said scathingly. 'That's what it all comes down to in the end. You men are as weak as kittens when it comes to sex. One flash of a stocking top or a bit of cleavage and you're putty in any tart's hands. You make me bloody *sick*, the lot of you!'

She stormed out of the room, banging the door so hard behind her that the silver on the sideboard tinkled.

Charlie looked at his son. 'She'll calm down,' he said unconvincingly. 'I suppose I should've told her about the mortgage. Didn't want to worry her. You know how it is.'

Vernon sighed. 'Joanna – you don't happen to know when she's coming back?'

Charlie shrugged. 'Soon, I suppose. No reason to think different. Nothing in what your mother said. I mean, why would she clear out when she's got money tied up in the firm?'

'No. Of course not. Jo wouldn't do a thing like that.'
Vernon looked at his father. 'I haven't heard from her
since she left. Have you?'

'No.' Charlie cleared his throat. 'What did your
mother mean about it was down to her that Joanna
didn't land you in a right old stew years ago?'

'Nothing.' Vernon avoided his father's eyes. 'You
know Ma. It was when Jo and I were in our teens. She
didn't approve of our going out together.'

Charlie nodded. Heaving himself out of his chair, he
said with a resigned sigh, 'Oh, well, I suppose I'd better
try and make my peace with her or we'll get no dinner
this side of breakfast!'

Fleur hadn't been able to get Tom on the phone at
lunchtime. He'd been out on an assignment. She went
round to Park Row after work, but arrived before him.
She was just scribbling a note to leave for him when
Charlotte appeared.

'Hi, Fleur. I saw you arrive and thought we might
have a word.'

'Of course. Come in.'

'I take it you and Tom have made it up? I mean –
well, I know you've been spending quite a lot of time
here.'

Fleur smiled. 'You could say that.'

'I'm glad. I know how fed up you were. I've been
hoping to see you.' She paused, tucking a stray strand
of hair behind her ear. 'Look, Fleur, I've been trying to
pluck up the courage to come and see you,' she said.
'You can probably guess how I felt when I found out
that you and I were actually half-sisters.'

'I was afraid it might have been a shock. That's why
I haven't been in touch. I wanted to leave it up to you.'

Charlotte looked surprised. 'It wasn't a shock. A
surprise. A nice one. I thought you hadn't been to see

548

me because you were mad at us all.' She smiled shyly. 'I've always wanted a sister and if I'd been able to choose, I'd have chosen someone just like you.'

'That's sweet, Charlotte. Thanks.'

'I mean it.' The younger girl bit her lip. 'I take it you already knew?'

'Yes. Before my grandmother died she gave me your grandparents' address and asked me to promise to come and find Julia. I kept my promise but I never meant to do anything to disrupt your lives.'

'You haven't.' Charlotte shook her head. 'To think you knew all along and never let on. I'm sure if it had been me I wouldn't have been able to keep quiet about it.' She bit her lip. 'Look, you probably haven't heard – Mum and Dad aren't living together any more. They're getting a divorce.'

Fleur nodded. 'I knew it was on the cards, but I didn't know Julia had actually left. Where is she? I feel I should go and see her.'

'She's staying with Mrs Maitland at the moment. I daresay she'd like to see you if you felt like it. She's looking for somewhere to live and says she's going to try and find a job,' Charlotte told her. 'It's not going to be easy for her after all these years. An enormous change. As far as I know she's never actually been out to work.'

'You'll have to try and support her as much as you can,' Fleur said. 'I'd like to help too – if that's what she wants, of course.'

'I thought I might go and live with her when she gets a new place,' Charlotte said. 'It might be nice, just Mum and me.' She looked at Fleur tentatively. 'I daresay you could come too if – well, you know.'

Fleur smiled. 'As a matter of fact, Tom and I are thinking of getting married.'

'Oh, Fleur! That's wonderful!' Charlotte hugged her

549

warmly. 'If you want a bridesmaid, can I put my name down?'

'I daresay we'll be having something very simple,' she said. 'We're going to need all our money. Sadie's leaving, you see, and we might be buying this house from her. I've got to start looking for another job too. Tom wanted me to try and get a bank loan and buy Arden Catering but someone has beaten me to it.'

'Oh. That's a shame.'

'Yes, it is,' Fleur sighed. 'Arden Catering is a good business. Councillor Mrs Maitland rang today and booked me to do the lunch for the Mayor's reception.'

'That's great!' Charlotte's face lit up. 'Did you know that Mum is going to be Mayoress to her Mayor? I'll be taking time off to go along,' she said. 'Wouldn't miss that for anything. Auntie Kath and James are invited too. If Dad doesn't like it he can sack me. In fact, I hope he does!' She looked at Fleur. 'I'm sorry you didn't get the business, though.'

'Oh, well, it was probably a mad idea. I don't suppose anyone would have lent me the money anyway.'

When Tom arrived home he found Fleur in the kitchen preparing a meal.

'Sorry I couldn't ring you back, darling,' he said. 'I've been out all day. Any more news?'

'I went into the agent's after you'd gone. Sounds as though the sale is going through quite quickly. I've definitely lost it, Tom.'

'Poor love.' He kissed her. 'Never mind. Something else will turn up. You'll see.'

'I could have made a success of it, I know I could,' she told him. 'I was even booked today to do the lunch for the Mayor's reception. Why couldn't Peter at least have let me know?'

'Consideration is hardly his strong suit, is it? But having said that, he couldn't have known you wanted to make an offer yourself, could he?' He put his arms round her. 'Listen, I went to see the editor today. I accepted the job of deputy editor and start next month. It means a rise in salary. I saw Sadie at lunchtime and asked her what her lowest figure for the house was. And – guess what? I've worked it out and we could just about afford it.' He kissed her. 'So what do you say? Are we on?'

'Oh, Tom!' She slipped her arms around his neck. 'I want it to be something we do together. I want to make my contribution too. And I will too – when I get another job . . .'

'To begin with, what about accepting the job of being Mrs Markham?'

'Are you sure? We don't really have to rush. We're fine as we are.'

'Speak for yourself,' he said, giving her a little shake. 'I want to put a ring on your finger so that everyone can see you're mine. Besides . . .'

'Go on, besides what?' A wicked glint had come into his eyes and Fleur half guessed what was coming.

'Besides, you're not a bad cook. And you are quite good at keeping the place nice and clean. I never was much of a hand with a duster.'

'*Tom Markham!* For that you can get the rest of the meal by yourself!'

He grasped both her flailing arms and held her quite still. 'Who cares about the meal?' he said, looking deep into her eyes. 'I can think of much more interesting things we can do to celebrate.'

'*Joanna!*' Vernon stopped short as he walked into the office and saw her sitting at her desk. 'I'd no idea you were back. Why didn't you let me know?'

'It was very late last night when I got in,' she told him coolly. 'The small hours of this morning actually.'

'You must be jet-lagged. You should have stayed in bed this morning. Can I get you some coffee?' He fussed around her like a mother hen and Joanna shook her head impatiently.

'I'm fine, thank you, Vernon. I don't need anything and I don't feel sleepy at all. I daresay it'll hit me later. If it does I'll go home.'

'Dad is going to be pleased to see you,' he said, perching on a corner of her desk. 'Though the news isn't good. I'm afraid the plans for Victoria Gardens were turned down at the planning meeting last week.'

'Really? That's too bad.'

'Too bad? It's disastrous! I think we should have a meeting as soon as possible so we can work out a plan of action.'

'I agree. Suppose we schedule it for tomorrow morning?'

Vernon was slightly taken aback by her eagerness. 'Oh – well, of course. If you're sure you're going to be up to it that soon?'

'I'll be up to it. The sooner the better.'

'Right – if you say so.' He glanced over his shoulder to make sure they weren't overheard. 'Julia has finally left,' he said. 'If you wanted to you could move in with me – right away.'

'I don't think so, Vernon,' she said. 'Not right now.'

'Well, no. Maybe it wouldn't look too good at this particular moment in time,' he said. 'Would you like me to move in with you?'

'No, Vernon.'

'I've missed you, Jo,' he said, covering her hand with his. 'Shall we have lunch together? I could book us a table at the Fairwoods – and a room for afterwards if you . . .'

552

'*No, Vernon!*' She looked up at him, eyes glinting with something he hadn't seen before. The shock caused him to take an involuntary step backwards.

'Oh. Right then. I expect you'll need a couple of days to catch up. Well – I'll leave you to get on with it then.'

All morning he sat in his office unable to keep his mind on work. Through the glass panel of his door he could see Joanna, her head bent in concentration. She made several telephone calls, her voice lowered and face earnest. He had the distinctly uncomfortable feeling that she was planning something. And that, whatever it was, he did not figure in it.

When Louise heard that there was to be a directors' meeting the following morning she insisted on attending.

'It's my right,' she told her husband and son. 'And if you ask me, this is something I should have done a long time ago. Maybe we wouldn't be in the mess we're in now if I'd been allowed to have my say.'

The meeting had been arranged for ten-thirty and she arrived at twenty past, wearing her dark suit and hardly any jewellery. Today she was determined to be taken seriously. After all, it had been her money that had started the company. She was responsible for the birth of GPC, and no mother gave up her child without a fight – with the possible exception of Julia, she reminded herself wryly.

Charlie's middle-aged secretary, Phyllis, greeted her warmly. 'Good morning, Mrs Grant. They're almost ready. Can I get you a coffee while you're waiting?'

'No, thank you.' Louise's face was a mask of determination as she settled herself stolidly on a chair by the door.

Ten minutes later, after a buzz on the office intercom, Phyllis ushered her into the boardroom where she took a seat beside Charlie. Her eyes were steely with the light of battle as she eyed Joanna across the table. Joanna herself looked calm and in control.

Examining the current situation they all agreed that at present things looked bleak for the firm. The Meadowlands Estate remained unfinished, with two houses still incomplete, and insufficient funds to continue building to the required specifications. Many of the buyers who had reserved houses had now withdrawn and the only two who had not were still trying to sell their present properties in a failing market.

'Then there is the problem with the Victoria Gardens project,' Charlie said reluctantly. 'Of course it's not the end of the road. We could always re-think our plans and present them again.'

'What could possibly be done with the place when there are chalkpit workings running underneath?' Joanna asked. 'Even if we demolished the houses there is no way we could ever rebuild on the site.'

'No. Well, um . . .' Charlie cleared his throat noisily. 'I thought perhaps an ornamental garden?' he suggested. 'For the public. We'd build it and get the council to take it over – maintain it and so on. You know, children's corner with animals and birds, a paddling pool . . .'

'And have the kiddies vanish down a gaping hole some sunny afternoon?' Joanna challenged. 'Realistically, I can't see us even getting planning permission for that, can you? And I wouldn't put money on the prospect of persuading the council to take it over even if they sanctioned it.'

'So what would *your* proposal be, Mrs Hanson?' Louise put in. 'You're quick enough to pour cold water on everything. How about letting us hear your ideas.'

'My suggestion is that we write it off. Chalk it up to experience, if you'll forgive the pun.'

Vernon gave a nervous laugh which his mother silenced with a searing look.

'A million quid's worth of experience?' she cried. 'Hardly a matter to joke about!'

Joanna shrugged. 'Sometimes we have to pay a high price for our little mistakes.'

Louise puffed herself up like a balloon, her face turning puce. 'A high-priced little mistake, was it? More like a ruinous flaming *catastrophe*, if you ask me! Do you realise that us Grants – Charlie, Vernie and me – are in danger of losing our homes over this *little mistake*, as you call it?'

'I realise that and I'm sorry,' Joanna said, unmoved. 'However, I do have a suggestion to make, if you'll allow me?'

The other three waited with bated breath, watching as she scribbled some notes on her pad. At last she looked up at them. 'I have to admit to you that I did see this blow coming, which is why I went over to the States. I have brought someone back with me who would be interested in a joint takeover of GPC. If you are all in agreement I will personally underwrite the outstanding debts.' She looked at Louise. 'That would mean, of course, that you would not lose your home, Mrs Grant, and I would like to suggest that Charlie take this opportunity to retire so that you can enjoy it together.'

She paused while they all digested her recommendation. 'My partner and I would take over as joint managing directors.'

'In other words, you're offering to buy us out?' Vernon said.

Joanna turned to look at him. 'In effect, yes, although of course as I am already the major shareholder – and the only solvent one – no money will actually change hands.'

Three stunned faces stared speechlessly at her. Then Louise said, 'Would this mean that Queen's Lodge will belong to you?'

'If you want to look at it that way, yes,' Joanna said. 'But you'll be paying me back instead of the bank. I'll charge you a lower rate of interest, which has to be of benefit to you. Don't you agree?'

Vernon said, 'May I ask where I stand in all of this? Do I still have a job?'

She turned to him. 'If you want to stay on, of course, Vernon.'

'In what capacity?'

'I think we could offer you the position of sales manager or something of that kind.'

'Sales manager?' He stared at her. '*Sales manager* when I was joint MD with Dad?'

Joanna shrugged. 'Things alter, Vernon,' she told him coolly. 'As I said before, there is often a high price to pay for mistakes.'

'But it was you who egged Dad on to buy Victoria Gardens!' he said, his colour deepening.

'You voted for it too,' she reminded him. 'As I remember, you even asked me to go along and persuade your wife to vote with us when she had voiced her dissent. I agree that we all made the same mistake. All I'm doing is offering to get you out of the difficult situation you find yourselves in.'

Charlie, who had been sitting slumped dejectedly in his chair, suddenly sat up and asked, 'Who might this new partner of yours be when he's at home? Are we allowed to know?'

'Of course you are.' Joanna rose from her seat. 'His name is Vince Kendrick and, unless I'm very much mistaken, he'll have arrived in the building by now. With your permission I'd like to ask him to come in and meet you all.'

In response to their dazed affirmation she went to the door and slipped out. A moment later she reappeared accompanied by a tall young man with dark hair and horn-rimmed glasses, whom she led forward.

'I would like to introduce you all to Mr Vince Kendrick. Vince – Mr and Mrs Grant – Louise and Charlie. And this is Vernon, their son.' The young man shook hands gravely with each of them in turn.

'Happy to meet you all,' he said pleasantly. 'Mom has told me a lot about the company and all of you.'

Three pairs of shocked eyes opened wide as Joanna smiled coolly at them. 'Yes, it's true. Vince is my son,' she announced triumphantly. 'And I need hardly tell you that this is a very proud day for me. Having my son as my business partner is something of a dream come true, as I'm sure you will all understand.'

She pulled out a chair at the boardroom table for Vince. 'Sit down, darling. We have a lot to discuss.'

Joanna was in the cloakroom freshening up after the meeting when the door opened and Louise came in. She stood with her back against the door, face pink with suppressed fury and eyes glinting stonily.

'You *knew*, didn't you?' she demanded.

Joanna did not turn round. Putting the top back on her lipstick she glanced up at Louise through the mirror. 'I'm sorry – knew what?'

'You know what I'm talking about. Victoria Gardens. You knew it would finish us. I bet you even had your own searches done on the quiet, you devious bitch. You knew about the chalkpit and everything. You set this whole thing up. Admit it!'

Joanna's eyes narrowed. 'I don't think you'd better say any more in your present frame of mind, Mrs Grant,' she warned. 'You're on dangerous ground and unless you have positive proof of your allegations ...'

'And another thing: that Vince of yours – he's our Vernon's boy, isn't he?'

The silence that hung in the air between them was almost tangible. Joanna broke it. 'That's nonsense,' she said, turning to face Louise. 'And you know it.'

'I know nothing of the sort,' she said. 'He's the living spit of our Vernie at that age – same build, same colouring. He's the right age too. You said you were pregnant before you went off and wed that Yank.'

'But you always knew I was lying, didn't you?' Joanna said carefully. 'You left me in no doubt about that. And even if I wasn't lying, don't you remember making me promise to have an abortion? Why, you even gave me the money for it. So how can you possibly claim that Vince is your grandson?'

At the word 'grandson' Louise blanched. 'He is. I know he is,' she insisted. 'There has to be some way of proving it. His birth certificate . . .'

'It has his father's name on it,' Joanna said. 'Jim Kendrick. My first husband.'

'The date . . . a blood test . . .' Louise blustered.

'Don't be ridiculous!' Joanna laughed. 'On what grounds could you possibly demand a blood test? Vince is nineteen. He's a man in his own right. You'd have to get him to agree and I can tell you now that he wouldn't. What you're suggesting is bizarre in the extreme. You're clutching at straws, Mrs Grant.' She took a step towards Louise. 'You wanted me out of your lives all those years ago. Well, I got out. And now I'm getting out again. You should be thanking me for saving your husband's face; for saving your home for you. I could always change my mind, you know. Do you want the disgrace of bankruptcy? Do you want to move out of Queen's Lodge and into a council flat?' she added brutally.

Louise flinched, her plump face sagging in defeat.

She was beaten and she knew it. Charlie and she had always wanted a grandson to inherit the business he had worked so hard to build. She had never been more convinced of anything than that Joanna's son was that grandson. But there was no business any more. It was all gone. Even their home wasn't truly theirs now. And there wasn't a single thing she could do about it.

Julia was preparing a meal for herself and Eleanor when the front doorbell rang. She dried her hands and went to answer it. To her surprise Vernon stood on the doorstep.

'Julia, I wondered – could we have a word?'

She held the door open reluctantly. 'You'd better come in. Eleanor is out at a committee meeting and I'm preparing a meal so if you don't mind coming through to the kitchen?'

'No, of course not. Anywhere.' He followed her through to the tiny kitchen at the back of the house and she pulled out a chair for him. 'I'd offer you a drink, but . . .'

'No.' He shook his head. 'No, it's all right.' He ignored the chair and stood awkwardly in the middle of the floor, looking at her.

'So – what can I do for you, Vernon?' she asked. 'Is it about the divorce? I told you, I won't contest . . .'

'No. Nothing to do with that. I wanted you to hear the news firsthand – before it has the chance to be garbled and exaggerated.'

'What news?'

'GPC has been taken over,' he said. 'It was either that or voluntary liquidation.'

She nodded, unsurprised. 'I see.'

'It's a bit worse than you might have thought. Dad had already mortgaged both our homes, so the house isn't mine any more. It will obviously affect any settlement I might be required to pay you.'

'That doesn't matter.'

'Both houses now belong to the new owner.'

'And that is?'

He swallowed painfully. 'Joanna Hanson.'

'I see.'

'Joanna – and her son.'

Julia's eyes widened. 'Her *son*?'

'Yes. He came back with her from the States. It was a surprise to us too. His name is Vince Kendrick, her first husband's child. Apparently his father left him pretty well provided for, so with that and Joanna's share of her second husband's real-estate business, they're well able to pick up GPC's debts.' He cleared his throat. 'I don't figure in the new scheme of things at all. At least not in any kind of executive capacity.'

'I'm sorry to hear this, Vernon,' she said. 'I feel partly responsible. If Dad hadn't sold her our shares . . .'

He shook his head. 'It would have happened anyway. Looking back, I think this was always in her mind.' He smiled wryly. 'It might amuse you to know that she's offered me the job of sales manager.'

Julia tried to hide her shock. 'But I thought – thought that you and she were . . .'

'Apparently not. Not now that she's got what she wanted. I have the uncomfortable feeling that we've all been taken for a ride, but that's something none of us wants to face. I've decided to get out, Julia. I'll find a job down south somewhere.' He took a step towards her and reached out to touch her shoulder. 'I suppose you wouldn't consider – coming with me? We could forget about divorce – put the past behind us and start again. I wouldn't hold what you did, this public scandal thing, against you. We could forget it all and . . .'

'No, Vernon!' She heard her own voice, firm and strong. 'My big mistake was to try and forget it. I regret

560

that more than anything I've ever done. Now I mean to acknowledge Fleur and try to make up for what I did.'

'Well, all right. You can still do that.'

'No, I can't. Even if I wanted to come back to you, I have commitments here, people I can't let down. For one thing I've promised to support Eleanor for the coming year; then there's Charlotte to consider. But in any case you know as well as I do that our marriage has been over for a long time. We really should have parted years ago. Now I think we should make a new start, each of us, while there's still time.'

He nodded his agreement. 'I thought you'd probably say that.' He shrugged. 'It was worth a try, though. You can't blame me for trying.' He gave her a crooked smile. 'It was good once though, wasn't it? At the beginning.'

Julia was silent, remembering only the numberless affairs she had turned a blind eye to, the hurt and the feeling of rejection that had lowered her self-esteem. The put-downs and humiliations he had subjected her to in order to boost his own ego. The past few weeks had been an eye-opener. She was a whole, complete person now; someone who counted. She was discovering more about herself every day. It was like being reborn. But even now it wasn't in her to kick him when he was down.

'Yes,' she said quietly. 'It was good once – for a little while. Now it's over.'

'I'll be moving out of the house,' he said. 'I daresay Joanna and her son might move in. But in any event I'll try to get the furniture for you. You'd like it, I expect.'

'Thank you. Yes, I would.' She went with him to the door and watched him drive away, slightly surprised at the lack of regret she felt; the utter absence of remorse or pity. A chapter of her life was officially closed and new and exciting horizons were opening up for her.

On the morning of the Mayor-Making ceremony Fleur was up bright and early. She had arranged to pick up her regular band of helpers on her way to the Town Hall. The waiters she had hired from the agency would be arriving later. Charlotte was going along with her too at her own suggestion.

'If I come and help you, you'll be able to finish in time to watch the ceremony,' she said. 'It would be a pity for you to miss all the excitement.'

Cleaners were still busy when they arrived. As they carried in their boxes they could hear the sound of hoovering coming from the council chamber and the Mayor's parlour.

'Is Julia nervous?' Fleur asked.

Charlotte nodded. 'As the proverbial kitten! Wait till you see her outfit though. If that doesn't give her confidence, nothing will.'

They worked hard for the two hours that followed, spreading the long buffet tables with snowy cloths, then setting out the array of tempting dishes. The florist arrived with the table arrangements: blooms in delicate pastel shades, iris and delicate freesias, arranged simply in gilded baskets, their sweet perfume filling the air. The wine merchant came next and Fleur set Charlotte to work uncorking the red wine to allow it to 'breathe' while she packed the champagne and white wine in ice buckets to chill.

At half-past eleven the main protagonists began to arrive. First the Town Constable who was responsible for seeing that all procedures were carried out correctly. He bustled round making sure that the cleaners had done their work efficiently and that programmes were placed on every seat then disappeared into the Mayor's parlour to attend to the civic wardrobe which was also his responsibility. Then the Town Clerk arrived, closely followed by the outgoing Mayor and Mayoress, who would begin the ceremony robed and wearing their chains of office. They went straight through to the Mayor's parlour to change.

'Isn't it exciting?' Fleur whispered to Charlotte. The other girl nodded.

'Yes, but not half as exciting as my news. I leave GPC at the end of this week! Joanna the Hun has taken over the firm so I don't have to stay any more. I'm working full-time for Auntie Kath as from a week next Monday!'

'That's good news for you, Charlotte. But I imagine it isn't so good for your family.'

She shrugged. 'Looks like it lets them off the hook,' she said. 'No one ever tells me anything though from what I gather Granddad made a bad mistake money-wise and Joanna's buying him out, debts and all. She's even brought her son over from America to go in with her.' She pulled a face. 'Vince, his name is. *Vince!* I ask you! He looks a bit of a wally to me, but what do I care? I'm well out of it.'

Fleur laughed. 'Well, I'm glad it's worked out for you.'

When Fleur was satisfied that the tables were perfect and everything was ready she and Charlotte went along to the council chamber where guests were already beginning to take their seats. Standing by the door Charlotte pointed out her grandparents, May and Harry Philips, who had already taken their places. Next to them sat Kathleen Grant. 'They're all dying to meet you,' she said. 'Mrs Maitland asked me to tell you that she's had this seat reserved for you,' she said, pointing to a chair close to the door, 'so that you can slip out before everyone else at the end of the ceremony. My seat is over there with James, next to Auntie Kath. I'd better go down to the front entrance now. I said I'd wait for him there.'

When Charlotte had gone Fleur sat looking around her with interest. She had never been inside the council chamber before and she was impressed by the huge oak-panelled room with its circular benches of polished wood and leather. The walls were hung with portraits of past Mayors looking suitably dignified in their official scarlet robes. Charlotte reappeared after a few minutes with a young man Fleur assumed was James, but there was no time for introductions. As they took their seats the ancient clock in the tower above them struck twelve.

A hush settled over the assembly and a moment later the doors to the Mayor's parlour opened and everyone stood as the procession entered. First the Town Constable, resplendent in his dark blue livery, carrying the mace, then the Mayor and his Mayoress, followed by the black-gowned Town Clerk. The councillors and aldermen followed, walking in pairs to take their seats on the council benches.

The Mayor made his outgoing speech after which the incoming Mayor was proposed and seconded and officially adopted by the council. Fleur listened as Councillor Eleanor Maitland's qualifications and achievements were read out by a senior alderman, followed by an appreciation of her character as a worthy citizen of Elvemere. Then the Mayor and his Mayoress were escorted back to the Mayor's parlour to pass over their robes and chains of office to the incoming Mayor and Mayoress. Fleur knew that Sadie would already be there with her camera to photograph this unseen part of the ceremony for the *Clarion*.

When they re-emerged it was Eleanor who wore the scarlet robe, white frothy jabot and heavy gold chain. It suited her. Her stout figure carried it with dignity. Fleur

564

watched as she stepped proudly up onto the dias followed by Julia who looked beautiful in a cream wool suit, the slender chain of office gleaming against the pale material. To complete her outfit she wore a pale lemon straw hat trimmed with a single cream rose.

Eleanor made a good maiden speech, spiced with her characteristic pithy wit. It was clear that she was enjoying every minute, her eyes twinkling with delight as she looked around at the distinguished assembly.

Fleur seized the opportunity of the applause at the end to slip from her seat and cross the hall into the room where the reception was being held. Swiftly she checked everything, satisfying herself that nothing had been left undone. The wines were at the perfect temperature, the bread rolls were warm and fragrant and her helpers stood by, ready to serve and replenish the tables. The hired waiters looked immaculate as they waited with trays of wine to welcome the guests. The pianist was seated at the grand piano by the fireplace softly running through the music Eleanor had chosen. The doors were opened and guests began to crowd into the room. The social part of the morning had begun.

During lunch Fleur circulated among the guests, keeping her eye open for empty glasses and plates. She had seen Tom arrive, wearing his best suit, to report on the reception, but she had been too busy to speak to him.

Eventually Julia tracked her down. 'Eleanor wanted me to tell you how pleased she is with everything,' she said. 'It's all been so well organised, Fleur. And the food is delicious.'

'Thank you. I'm glad she's pleased,' Fleur said. 'I enjoyed watching the ceremony very much. It was fascinating. And you look lovely,' she added shyly.

Julia smiled. 'Thank you, Fleur. I can't tell you how glad I am that you decided not to leave Elvemere after all. Charlotte tells me you're engaged to the young man from the local paper?'

'Yes. I don't know when we'll be getting married though. I'll have to find a job first. I'd been hoping to get a loan and make an offer for Arden Catering but someone got there before me.'

Julia took her arm and drew her to one side. 'I've been meaning to speak to you about that, Fleur. I've bought Arden Catering.'

Fleur stared at her. '*You* have?'

'Yes. No one else knows yet. I wanted you to be the first. I needed a home now that Vernon and I have parted. I wanted somewhere large enough to have Charlotte with me, if she wants to come, and I'll also need to earn a living of course. I'd always liked Sally's house and when I saw that it was for sale along with the business it seemed the ideal solution. I'm sure I shall be very happy there.'

'Oh – yes. I'm sure you will,' Fleur said faintly.

'But I haven't a clue about the catering business,' Julia went on. 'And with this coming year promising to be so hectic with my work as Eleanor's Mayoress, I can't see that I'll have much chance of getting to learn it. Which is why I was hoping to persuade you to run the business for me.'

'*Me?*'

Julia laughed. 'Well, who better? After all, Sally herself taught you. I know you're popular with the clientele and you've certainly proved today that you're more than equal to the job.'

'Oh!' Fleur's heart was beating fast. 'I – I don't know what to say.'

'Do you want to think about it before deciding?' Julia asked.

Fleur shook her head. 'Oh, no! I'd love to stay on and run the business for you!'

'It will be permanent, of course,' Julia said. 'We'll talk about salary later but the fact that you'll be taking full responsibility will mean you will be paid more than you were as an assistant.' She smiled. 'And of course you're going to have to teach me a bit about the business eventually too. I'll ring you tomorrow and we'll have a long talk – think about drawing up some kind of working plan.'

Fleur's head was still reeling as Eleanor joined them. 'My dear, the lunch is perfect,' she said with a smile. 'Everyone is delighted. I'm having a few close friends round to my house this evening for a celebratory drink. I'd like you to come – around eight. It's quite informal. And bring that young man of yours along too, of course.' She smiled. 'All your family will be there, so you'll be in good company.'

'Thank you, Mrs Maitland. I'd like that very much.' Fleur looked at Julia. The significance of Eleanor's phrase 'all your family' had escaped neither of them. Julia smiled.

'It's time you met your other grandparents,' she said. 'I know they're looking forward to getting to know you.'

Julia and Eleanor were just getting into the Mayoral car at the rear of the Town Hall when a raucous shout made them look up. A portly, red-faced figure was weaving its way towards them across the car park.

'Hey there, *Madam Mayor*! I want a word with you.'

Julia recognised Charlie Grant and her heart sank. He was clearly very drunk and obviously spoiling for a fight. 'Eleanor, I think you'd better get into the car quickly,' she said. 'He'll only make a scene.'

But Eleanor stood her ground. 'No,' she said. 'I've an idea what it is he wants to say. Let him get it off his chest.'

With great reluctance Julia waited until Charlie reeled up to them. He stood swaying in front of Eleanor.

'Fine friend you turned out to be, *Councillor*,' he said, his words slightly slurred and his eyes bloodshot. 'You could have told me what I was letting myself in for,' he said accusingly. 'You could've warned me off paying that greedy old cow good money for a crumbling heap of old crap. But *did* you? No, you bloody didn't!' He took a step towards her, standing close enough for her to get the full force of his whisky-laden breath. 'You stood by and let me walk right into it. And all the time . . .' he shook his finger at her '. . . all the time you knew that Victoria Gardens were falling down a sodding great hole in the ground. And I – I was going to lose – lose my shirt!'

To Julia's horror the bleary eyes filled with tears which began to roll down his cheeks and drip onto his crumpled shirt-front. 'We were mates as kids, Lena,' he mumbled. '*Mates!* And you stood by and watched me slide down the pan without lifting a finger!'

Her face compassionate, Eleanor put out a hand to steady him. 'I told you to forget it, Charlie,' she said softly. 'I'm sorry about what's happened but I really did try to warn you. There wasn't any more I could say without breaking a confidence. Look, let us take you home. You're in no fit state to drive.'

But he shook off her hand angrily, almost losing his balance in the effort to regain his bruised dignity. 'Get off me! I might be ruined but I've still got my pride. I'm having no woman drive me home. I'll get a bloody taxi.' He drew himself up, turned and began to make his unsteady way across the car park. The two women looked at each other helplessly.

'Poor Charlie,' Eleanor said, shaking her head. 'Poor old devil.'

Fleur found Tom in the kitchen at Park Row. He was slicing onions for the spaghetti Bolognese he was making for supper. Without a word she went to him and threw her arms around him, hugging him tightly.

'*Hey!*' Taken off-guard, he stood with both his hands sticking out straight. 'I'd like to have warning of this kind of thing, if you don't mind,' he said. 'You never know what a shock like that might do to a fragile person like me. Besides, my hands are all oniony and I can't . . .' She stopped the rest of the sentence with a kiss.

'You'll never *guess!*' she told him excitedly. 'Oh, Tom, it's been the most wonderful day!'

He grinned at her. 'Well, whatever it is, I'm already in favour of it. Look, let me wash my hands, then I can respond properly.'

'Guess who's bought Arden Catering?' she demanded.

'Mickey Mouse.'

'Come on, don't be silly.'

'Okay then, Margaret Thatcher? Terry Wogan?'

She grasped his shoulders and looked into his eyes. '*Julia Grant*, that's who! She and Charlotte are going to live in the house. And she wants me to run the business for her. Take sole responsibility – at an increased salary!'

'Well, why shouldn't she?' Tom's eyebrows rose. 'She knows when she's onto a good thing if you ask me!'

'Yes, but don't you see? That's just the point,' she told him. 'I never wanted Julia to do me any favours – to give me anything. I'd have hated the idea that she was trying to ease her conscience. This way we'll be helping each other, on an equal footing – a proper business footing. And I really believe she needs me. I wonder if you know what that means to me, Tom.' She hugged him again. 'And not only that: I'll be able to pay my share of the mortgage here. Oh, darling, I'm so happy, and so *excited*!'

He looked into her shining eyes and his face softened. 'You really are an independent lady, aren't you?'

She nodded. 'Independence means everything to me. Being my own person is so important after the way I began life.'

'I know it does, darling.' He kissed her. 'And I'll always respect that.'

'We have an invitation for tonight,' she told him. 'We are invited to the Mayor's house to have a celebratory drink with her and some friends.' She drew back her head to look at him. 'Do you know what she said to me, Tom? She said, "All your family will be there." Can you imagine that? All my life I've dreamed of what it would be like to be recognised as part of Julia's family. But the funny thing – the magic thing – was that quite suddenly when I heard Mrs Maitland say that I realised that it didn't really matter any more.' She hugged him close, her cheek pressed against his. 'And do you know why?'

'No, tell me.'

'Because *you're* the only person that matters to me now, Tom. You're the only family I'll ever want. You and the children we'll have some day, here in this house – our home.' She kissed him. 'Oh, Tom. I love you so much!'

He held her close. Now he knew she'd come home at last. She'd found herself and her own special place in the world. And his heart was filled with gratitude that that special place was with him.